Ernestine Hill was born in 1899 in Rockhampton, Queensland. Travel was always in her blood and after the death of her husband in 1933 she embarked on a life of almost continuous travel and writing. Her first publication was *The Great Australian Loneliness* (1937), followed by *Water into Gold*. Her only novel, *My Love Must Wait*, the story of Matthew Flinders, appeared in 1941. Apart from *Flying Doctor Calling* (1947), her best-known book is *The Territory* (1951), a book many have thought should 'be in the swag of every Australian'.

Ernestine Hill died in 1972.

The Territory

The classic saga of Australia's far north

ERNESTINE HILL

Angus&Robertson
An imprint of HarperCollins*Publishers*

Angus&Robertson
An imprint of the HarperCollins*Publishers,* Australia

First published in Australia by Angus & Robertson Publishers in 1951
Outback Classics edition 1981
Imprint Travel edition 1991, reprinted in 1993
This edition published in 1995
Reprinted in 1997
by HarperCollins*Publishers* Pty Limited
ACN 009 913 517
A member of the HarperCollins*Publishers* (Australia) Pty Limited Group

HarperCollins*Publishers*
25 Ryde Road, Pymble, Sydney, NSW 2073, Australia
31 View Road, Glenfield, Auckland 10, New Zealand
77-85 Fulham Palace Road, London W6 8JB, United Kingdom
Hazelton Lanes, 55 Avenue Road, Suite 2900, Toronto, Ontario M5R 3L2
and 1995 Markham Road, Scarborough, Ontario M1B 5M8, Canada
10 East 53rd Street, New York NY 10032, USA

National Library of Australia Cataloguing-in-Publication data:

Hill, Ernestine, 1899–1972.
The Territory: the classic saga of Australia's far north.
ISBN 0 207 18821 1.
1. Frontier and pioneer life – Northern Territory.
2. Pioneers – Northern Territory – Biography.
3. Cattle drives – Northern Territory.
4. Northern Territory – History – 20th century.
5. Northern Territory – Description and travel – 1901-1950. I. Title.
994.2904

Cover photograph courtesy of Lutheran Archives, Adelaide.
Cover design by Penny Maxwell.
Printed in Australia by Griffin Paperbacks, Adelaide.

9 8 7 6 5 4 3 2 97 98 99

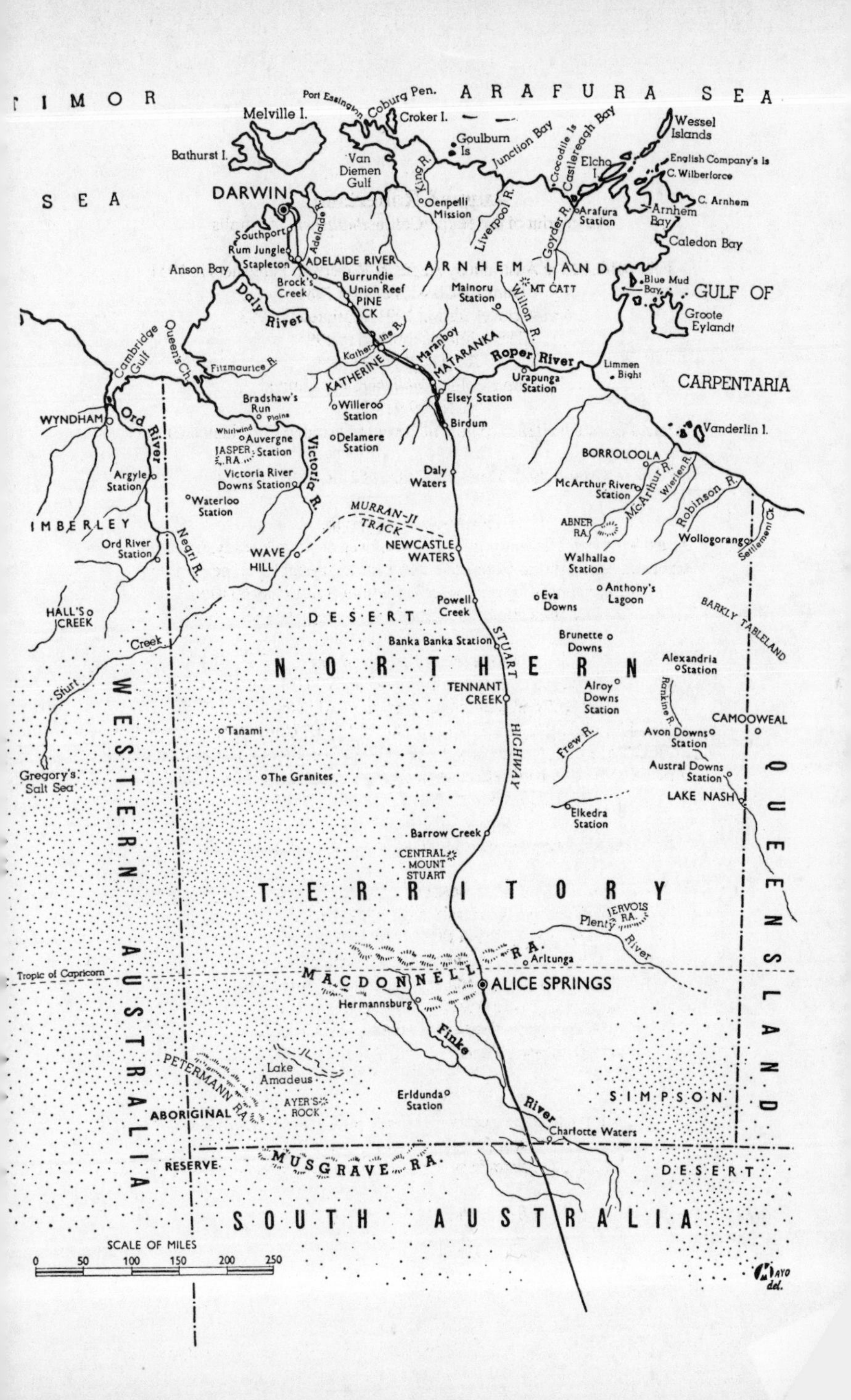

TIMOR SEA
ARAFURA SEA
Melville I.
Bathurst I.
Port Essington
Coburg Pen.
Croker I.
Goulburn Is
Wessel Islands
English Company's Is
C. Wilberforce
Elcho I.
Crocodile Is
Castlereagh Bay
Junction Bay
Van Diemen Gulf
DARWIN
Oenpelli Mission
King R.
Liverpool R.
Goyder R.
Arafura Station
C. Arnhem
Arnhem Bay
Caledon Bay
Southport
Rum Jungle
Stapleton
ADELAIDE RIVER
Adelaide R.
Anson Bay
Brock's Creek
Burrundie
Union Reef
PINE CK
ARNHEM LAND
Mainoru Station
MT CATT
Wilton R.
Blue Mud Bay
GULF OF CARPENTARIA
Groote Eylandt
Daly River
Cambridge Gulf
Queen's Ch.
Fitzmaurice R.
Katherine R.
KATHERINE
Maranboy
MATARANKA
Roper River
Urapunga Station
Limmen Bight
Elsey Station
Birdum
WYNDHAM
Ord River
Bradshaw's Run
Plains
Whirlwind
Auvergne Station
JASPER RA.
Victoria River Downs Station
Victoria R.
Willeroo Station
Delamere Station
Vanderlin I.
BORROLOOLA
Argyle Station
Waterloo Station
Daly Waters
McArthur River Station
McArthur R.
Wierien R.
Robinson R.
KIMBERLEY
MURRAN-JI TRACK
ABNER RA.
Settlement Ck
Wollogorang
Ord River Station
Negri R.
WAVE HILL
NEWCASTLE WATERS
Walhalla Station
HALL'S CREEK
Powell Creek
Eva Downs
Anthony's Lagoon
BARKLY TABLELAND
DESERT
Banka Banka Station
Brunette Downs
Creek
Sturt
NORTHERN
STUART HIGHWAY
Alexandria Station
TENNANT CREEK
Alroy Downs Station
Rankine R.
CAMOOWEAL
Tanami
Frew R.
Avon Downs Station
Gregory's Salt Sea
The Granites
Austral Downs Station
LAKE NASH
Elkedra Station
WESTERN AUSTRALIA
Barrow Creek
CENTRAL MOUNT STUART
TERRITORY
QUEENSLAND
Plenty River
JERVOIS RA.
MACDONNELL RA.
Arltunga
Tropic of Capricorn
ALICE SPRINGS
Hermannsburg
Finke River
PETERMANN RA.
Lake Amadeus
AYER'S ROCK
Erldunda Station
SIMPSON DESERT
ABORIGINAL RESERVE
Charlotte Waters
MUSGRAVE RA.
SOUTH AUSTRALIA
SCALE OF MILES
0 50 100 150 200 250
MAYO del.

Acknowledgments

My thanks are due to *Walkabout*, the Geographical Magazine of Australia, for permission to include the history of the Murran-ji Track, first section of "Gold Mine in the Sky", McKinlay's horse-boat journey, and for extracts from two articles on cattle-droving and one on the Darwin Chinese.

My thanks are also due to *Man* magazine, Sydney, in which the story of "Chokey" (Rodney Spencer) first appeared, and to the *Cornhill Magazine* for permission to include an extract now in Chapter XXVIII.

ERNESTINE HILL.

Australian history is always picturesque. Indeed, it is so curious and strange that it is itself the chiefest novelty the country has to offer, and so it pushes the other novelties into second or third place. It does not read like history, but like the most beautiful lies, and all of a fresh new sort, not the mouldy old stale ones. It is full of surprises, and adventures, and incongruities, and contradictions, and incredibilities, and they are all true.

MARK TWAIN.

Contents

Chapter I

Winged Victory

HERE I give you history galloping wild for a century over half a million square miles, the life-story of a colony in quicksand. . . .

A nameless land, a land without a flag, a vague earth bordered by the meridians of God. . . .

Black men wandering and white men riding in a world without time where sons do not inherit, and money goes mouldy in the pocket, where ambition is wax melted in the sun, and those who sow may not reap.

I write of the Northern Territory of Australia, problem child of empire, land of an ever-shadowed past and an ever-shining future, of eternal promise that never comes true. . . .

From tropic seas a thousand miles south to the salt lakes, between desert and desert five hundred and sixty miles wide, here is the strangest country of white men in the world, where they rode for a lifetime without a home, without a wife, safe from yesterday and tomorrow, drifting from tree to tree like the blacks. They bought a kingdom for a billy of sweet tea and a stick of tobacco, found millions in reefs of gold and precious metals. Finest nation-building fibre the world has known, swept away in high tides of emotional nature with none to care or follow, too many of them died unburied.

Here is a passionate and prolific earth never yet tamed and trimmed to the small designs of man; its human interest and natural history are superhuman interest and unnatural history. Now most of its own people are scattered and gone. They laboured for three generations, knowing nothing but failure, to be whipped out in a scourge of war. Faithful for seventy years to its sun, sweat and sorrow, even when the bombs of destruction were falling they wanted to stay, and when they were forced to leave it, with what they could carry in their hands, those that are living lived on to go back—to their looted homes in ruin, to the spectre of their poor little city by the sea, to their free-hold in illusion.

A sixth of Australia . . . a State, and one of the greatest in its own geographical right—523,620 square miles from under Capricorn to the Timor Sea—there is never a ray of light to its honour in the Seven-pointed Star that waves above the five mainland States, the island of Tasmania and British New Guinea.

Nameless, it is still a Northern Territory, as once it was of South Australia, though it has been separated from South Australia for forty years. Never yet has it been fully surveyed or explored. You can draw a map of England to scale in the map of the Territory without a single name in it, not even a native well—which means a sump of mud.

Borders are imaginary, slant of the sun by a cairn, the 129th meridian to the 138th meridian of east longitude, the 26th parallel of south latitude between them—immeasurable planes of vacant earth silent by day, at night a blur of darkness under a myriad bright stars. A few noble surveyors began their desert ordeal of pacing out infinity, but what was the use where time and space run into the red sand? The netting fence that once divided it from Queensland has many times fallen. There never was a frontier to south or west.

The bad and beautiful Territory is not the youngest of the Australian family, as many believe, but the third eldest. It was founded in 1824, following New South Wales and Tasmania. The black sheep never celebrated a centenary parade of its pioneers for the congratulations of empire. In September 1939, on the eve of the hundredth anniversary of the discovery of Darwin Harbour, came declaration of war in Europe, a threat from Asia, swift apparition of armies, a lightning colonization in chaos of armed camps —that insubstantial pageant soon faded back into the long grasses.

The graph of all its history is the same mad zigzag up and down, from the crest of the wave to the hollow, from false glory to dejection, from the bright spotlight of sensational interest to oblivion and neglect.

Someone is always discovering the Territory, its colour and its beauty, infinite resources, boundless wealth, "forever piping songs forever new".

What is the truth of this changeling child of ours? Is it paradise or hell, milk and honey or Dead Sea fruit? Has it a transcendent future or only a pitiful past? Is it true, as the American servicemen said, that in colonizing Australia we "began the wrong end" or, to use the cynical old phrase you hear so often up there, shall we "hand it back to the blacks with apologies"?

"If this country is settled," said John McDouall Stuart, who grew old and blind to find it, "it will be one of the brightest under the Crown, suitable for the growth of anything and everything . . . a splendid country for cotton." That was in 1862.

"Rich to rottenness!" cried Boyle Travers Finniss, first Administrator, in 1864, yet few save the cattle-men, remote in so many thousand miles of wilderness, have wrested from it even a poor living. Its gold-mines and its gardens all are graveyards. Until twenty years ago it was so far away from the rest of Australia that it was a land of legend—two thousand miles of desert tracks, two thousand miles by sea. Only a pilgrim could reach it.

After a century of endeavour, wilderness still. In 1942 Professor C. J. Hart of Toronto University, in an article in *Asia*, advised the world in general that it was not worth owning: ". . . a land of vast empty spaces marked on the map with rivers that contain no water and towns that contain no people . . . an empty barren country, one of the most hopeless in the world to live in, one of the most difficult to get away from."

Yet in 1943 Nelson T. Johnson, ambassador to Australia from the United States, of his own knowledge in thousands of miles of travel by aeroplane and car, announced in emphatic terms: "The Northern Territory can be built into an empire. . . . If the government provides chances for young men and women, great cities will grow up there within forty years. No country in the world offers greater opportunities for young people."

The bagmen of today, the "old death-adders Major Mitchelling around", they were the young men of yesterday, with all the energy and dreams of youth. Forgotten men, they failed—but they believe. So hope withers away and springs eternal in a pattern of nature too vast for human vision, a power insensitive to human hands.

There is a school of thought among the nation-builders of 1945 that before they shed the light of their countenances on the notorious north its people were a pack of old reprobates living with the blacks, derelicts, do-nothings, scallawags running away from the law. This is not true.

Too little is known of a long-drawn tragedy of living, and of dying, in the land without a memory, of a *danse macabre* of destiny incredible in any country in the world.

I write a saga of the silent pioneers, and even as a Government is building a fifth New Darwin, I shall try to tell the story of the old.

The stars danced when Darwin was born. "Exhalations whizzing in the air" portended a curious future. While the sails of discovery were wan in the blue, the drama of its first hundred years began with a rain of fire from the skies—and so it ended.

From H.M.S. *Beagle* in that hazy harbour in September 1839, John Lort Stokes has written: "Brilliant meteors fell in the evening of the 20th, a long train of light visible for ten seconds, while others of less brilliance fell from the same place within the hour. Again on the 23rd the dark vault of heaven was illumined, and again on the 28th."

Before dawn on 9th September Lieutenants Stokes and Forsyth by chance discovered the harbour, out in a boat from the *Beagle* at anchor in Shoal Bay when Van Diemen's Gulf was reddened by bale-fires on Melville Island. They scaled the cliffs with lanterns, a weird apparition had the native Larrakia been abroad. With the blue smoke of a breakfast fire curling below on the beach, they looked upon a far and dazzling haven. The snow-white headland on which they stood was of talc embedded in quartz—Talc Head—the rocks near it of fine-grained sandstone, "a new feature of the geology which afforded us an opportunity of convincing an old ship-mate and friend that he still lived in our memory. We accordingly named this sheet of water Port Darwin". Darwin had sailed with Stokes in the famous voyage of the *Beagle*, five years round the world.

It is improbable that the Darwins ever considered each other. Both were unknown for thirty years after the discovery. It is doubtful whether Darwin (Charles) would have been gratified had he ever beheld his namesake, and it is quite certain that Darwin (Port) was not honoured in the name of the man who "made hell a laughing-stock and heaven a dream". Its career began just at the time he scouted Adam and Eve from the front page of creation, to be denounced from every pulpit and belittled by every newspaper in the Christian world. In righteous indignation the newborn settlement renounced its immortal godfather, and officially changed its name to Palmerston, taking refuge under the robes of office of a Prime Minister of England. But to its own people it was always Port Darwin.

Stokes, a poetic writer, has left us a tranquil picture of civilization's dawn. Threading silver mangrove creeks they were eaten alive by sandflies and mosquitoes and dodged swarms of crocodiles to temper their joy of a keel in uncharted waters as they rowed ten miles south and east. Ashore, "the brittle brushwood cracked and snapped as we walked through it, a spark would have wrapped the whole country in a sea of fire. Blasts of heated withering air, as though from an oven, would strike the face with peculiar and agreeable odours from the white eucalypts and the palms". Brilliant fish were caught in the seine and brilliant birds flew up from the lagoons.

Not a smudge of native smoke in the sky—but back at the ship in Shoal Bay they learned that the friendly Larrakia had made a tour of inspection, twenty-seven tall laughing huskies, splits of bamboo fourteen inches long through their flat noses, dentally perfect smiles—not a tooth missing. The Larrakia of Darwin is the only tribe north of the Tropic that has never practised circumcision in the initiation rites, a mystery for the anthropologist here. Generously at the end of the dry season they shared their brackish wells with the sailors, and showed them the water-mallee tree, standing the roots in a coolamon to drain till it was full to the brim.

H.M.S. *Beagle* tacked down-harbour, first sail in, and anchored under Point Emery, for there Lieutenant Emery dug a red-white-and-blue well, twenty-five feet deep in ironstone, marl and clay, plenty of fresh water for the ship and the Larrakia, who drank two quarts each with *yacki* of amazement and delight, and noted the art of deep-sinking. But one of the gentlemen lit a cigar and with a puff of perfumed smoke frightened them all away—an intuition, perhaps, that tobacco would be the downfall of their race. Tranquillity was gone in a night. *Beagle*, her survey completed, set sail in a squall.

A hundred years is not so long ago. In Sydney in 1939 I met Captain H. M. Green, marine superintendent of Burns Philp and Company, that day celebrating his birthday with a cake of eighty-seven candles, and well he remembered John Lort Stokes. As a cadet on leave at Scotchwell, Haverford, Pembrokeshire, he raided an apple orchard, to be caught red-handed by the admiral himself. He was saved by his family tree. Hearing, in cross-examination, that he was one of the old Navy Greens who served with Nelson, and destined for the sea, the admiral called off the dogs and regaled the robber with tales of his own eighteen years in the *Beagle*, of the wonders of New Zealand and Australia, and of how he discovered most of the big rivers of the north from the western Fitzroy over to the Flinders. Within a few years young Green was away with Eastern and Australian steamships to travel a lifetime in the wake of H.M.S. *Beagle*, to carry ingots of gold from Admiral Stokes's Port Darwin, to bring flour for its daily bread two thousand miles from the south on the monthly Singapore ship, and to watch its tangled weave of fate for more than sixty years.

The place has nine lives. The last twenty years have seen the passing of three.

When I first came to Darwin in 1930 it was visibly, painfully, and for the third time, dying. As J. T. Mackenzie, a pearler friend, of Broome, observed to me, there was "only one thing to do, drop a bomb on it and begin again". Little did we dream that a grim prophecy had been spoken in jest.

Shabbiest seaport of the Australian coast, far out in isolation, with the monthly ship to Singapore calling for subsidy, not trade, it existed on Government pension with not a single industry to keep it alive. Public works and private works were conspicuous by their absence. A million-pound meatworks was a hollow shell, one of the local proverbs of inevitable failure. There was no shipping of cattle. The crazy little capital of the land of lost endeavour, with its few half-built streets and ragged palms, was like one of the small banana ports of *dolce far niente* we read of in South America, but without the *dolce* and with very few bananas. Peanuts were the only harvest from that vasty hinterland, a few tons with no markets, and most years the rivers in flood swept them away. A twenty-five-ton boat, on three thousand miles of uninhabited coast, travelled as the wind listeth. A straggle of railway meandered three hundred miles into bush. There was only a monthly mail and very little water except while it rained seventy inches. A gang of black prisoners guarded by a warder with a rifle worked on the roads by day—at night their plaintive corroboree cried to the stars from the jail of white and black at Fannie Bay.

In its glorious setting Darwin was unloved and unlovely. Apart from a few old faithfuls, there were only two classes—those paid to stay there and those with no money to go.

A thousand white people included three hundred Government officials and three hundred unemployed men who camped in the greenwood and, except for two days' wharf-labouring in the month, lived on a dole. They staged an occasional harmless riot in the humidity, wearing red poinciana blossoms a foot wide, waving nulla-nullas, and insisted on unloading the ship themselves if they were not on strike. If they were, stores were carried to Singapore and back while the Territory went hungry. Nabobs from Malaya, on the top deck, laughed at a White Australia, seeing them stagger all day in the heat with bags and barrels on their shoulders while the blacks lay around on the jetty in lazy grace to watch them, and Chinese in taxis wafted passengers off to see the sights.

Of a thousand coloured people six hundred were Chinese and the only real street was Chinatown, a crowded Asiatic quarter of stores, cafés, laundries, peanuts and *pak a pu*. Of all our Chinatowns, from Ballarat to Broome, Darwin's was most faithful to the Flowery Land and most picturesque to see. Its roots were deep in Territory history.

Sixty to a family, from kippered ancients to bevies of babies, swarmed in those patriarchal shacks and shops that with all their sins in sanitation and ventilation for seventy years were a public scandal, right in the heart of the City that Hoped to Be. For ever threatened with the flaming sword of Government eviction, its smiling dark-eyed people survived the storms of indignation to the bitter end. Then it was not the march of progress but the common enemy, the Japanese, that routed them out to shiver in southern cities of winter cold, to look for work in an unfamiliar world.

Gone, now, are the spry little tailors who could make the sweating tourist a set of six immaculate white drill suits of exquisite stitching and excellent cut while the ship was in port between morning and midnight; the fat jolly laundrymen, spitting on their red-hot irons by a red-hot fire in the heat; the god-shrines lit in the evening in the dim shops that sold nothing but dusty nuts; old men, with faces of yellowed ivory, squatting to smoke their water-pipes on the doorsteps, and grave young clerks, with fantastic flourish of brush, bent to their bookkeeping in naked acetylene light.

Gone are the laughing daughters of Fang Cheong Loong, steps and stairs, selling you coloured silks, carved ivories, fragrant trifles of the East, the prettiest girls in Darwin in their shiny tunics and trousers, bare ankles, magnolia faces and ravens' wing hair—the pantalooned children running in droves through all the devious laneways, and solemn little sons in proud mothers' arms, their pates shaven blue, padlocked to life.

Chinese New Year—who could forget it?—last stronghold of the dragon in Australia. Thirty years after he had been banished from the south he capered down that shoddy street a fiery blaze of colour, two hundred legs and a tail half a mile long, gongs crashing, flutes shrieking, masques dancing, devils prancing, Roast Pig on a canopied joss throne in a cannonade of crackers, a painted beauty on a white horse in silken trappings, painted warriors fighting with swords round a bonfire on a vacant lot—it was a scene typical of the East, poverty in splendour. The town had to put up with the racket and reek of gunpowder all night for a week—but what goodwill and hospitality went with it! Many a hungry bushman in from the drovers' camp or the buffalo-hunter's beat, many a white-clad Government clerk, has eaten his fill of *soo kai* with ginger sauce and bamboo pickles to the strains of a tortured bagpipe under yellow lanterns at the back of a tailor's shop.

Buried in the bomb raids were the beautiful fretwork teakwood doors of the old Joss House, brought at a cost of £1000 from Hong Kong. They had seen five generations of sandalled men and trousered women coming to toss the sacred bean in that dark iron temple—and the bearded josses, gilded faces and twisted eyes under their peacock feathers, watching them come and go. Mah Buk, the white-headed shuffling old priest who guarded them night and day, has long crossed the Bridge of Magpies to the Inn of Ten Thousand Flowers. From Cavenagh Street the glory and the squalor have departed . . . but under the Tree of Knowledge still hover scents of sandalwood and *soy*, where ghosts of coolies of the past go shuffling by with their shoulder-poles, seeking some scrolled doorway where a sloe-eyed woman is waving a palm-leaf fan.

Multum in parvo was the electoral roll, thirty or forty races in five or six hundred names that began with Abala, Ah Chin Fook, Amat, Banaquiotis, Berghoefer, Beurteau, ran the whole gamut through Innocencio and Ivanitch McSweeney and MacTaggart, to Xuereb from Malta, Yamamoto from Yokohama, Zuazo from Chile. Vital statistics never included three or four hundred pariah half-castes and all the Territory coastal tribes, still tribal, that wandered in and out, worked anywhere for 5s. a week, camped in Kahlin compound—each in its own tribal area with backs turned to black magic of the others—went yachting in canoes with bag sails and danced corroboree for the white folk on Sundays. Malays and motley of the pearling fleet lived on the ships or down in the mangroves below high-water mark to conform with indentured labour laws. Dapper Jap divers at £1000 a year were lords of the lugger at sea.

In a mandated territory of Australians within Australia, Colonel Robert Weddell was Administrator under direct control of a Government department in Canberra, with a North Australia Advisory Commission of three. They were J. Horsburgh, G. A. Hobler and W. R. Easton, men of proved ability in development of mining, railway construction and lands—but there was no development of mining, railways or lands.

The step-child of the Commonwealth was governed—as it still is and ever has been—from departmental pigeonholes two thousand miles away, with tons' weight of ordinances appended to the laws to meet, in an uncolonized country, its own peculiar case. Those who framed the ordinances knew little of the north. The people had no share in Australian democracy. There was one Member of Parliament for the half million square miles, with no voice in the House of Representatives, being odd man out. A knowledgeable surveyor who had travelled far in the country and served its interests well, he was Mr A. M. Blain. He was elected mainly from Darwin and Alice Springs. Remote pioneers of river and range, five hundred bush miles from a ballot box, had never voted in their lives.

Most of the northern Administrations had deteriorated into a sort of departmental one-man band. Chief Secretary was L. H. A. Giles. Mr Justice R. I. D. Mallam comprised the Supreme Court, with Crown Prosecutor Eric Asche, and F. T. Macartney—later G. A. Nicholls—acting in twenty-eight capacities as Registrar of all things and Clerk of picturesque Courts. V. L. Lampe was Director of a limited Education—a public school of polyglot, a convent full of half-castes, and Mrs Carruth with the first little school of half-caste black and white. The only other school was at Alice Springs, a thousand miles away. Norman Bell was Director of vanished Mines.

At the hospital out on the cliff for the first time in history four doctors were in attendance, Kirkland, Brown, Fothergill, under the superintendence of Dr Cecil Cook, in a Northern Territory Medical Commission to relieve all woes from malaria to mauling by crocodiles, and those of the leper station across the bay.

First to establish a Government clinic for aboriginal and half-caste children was Sister E. M. Stone, visiting wurleys in the bush and tumbledown huts in the compound, teaching mothercraft to the Stone Age, a heavyweight black baby on the scales. For her fine work she was awarded the M.B.E.

All of these patient people had given at least ten years to hold the fort of the rapidly fading north.

Far from civilization were several missions to redeem the natives to Christianity, the largest and most noted being the Lutheran mission at Hermannsburg, near Alice Springs, in charge of Pastor Albrecht; the Anglican missions at Roper River and Groote Eylandt, under Rev. J. Warren; Father Gsell's little Roman Catholic colony of the stalwarts of Melville and Bathurst Island, and the Methodist mission, in charge of Rev. Mr Webb, at Milingimbi in the Crocodile Islands, of which Charles Barrett has given us a vivid description in his book of the north, *The Coast of Adventure.*

A quaint and interesting company was scattered around the headland in houses shaded by tamarind-trees and shuttered with bamboo. A few hardy old first-footer families—Stretton, Giles, Brown, Killian, Finniss, Bell, Stiles—had weathered three generations, seeing thousands come and go. There was even a centenarian, Grannie Susannah Mansfield, who lived through Eureka Stockade as a child and survived these torrid summers till she was a hundred and three years old. Cable men were transferred to Darwin from all over the world. The police included a "mountie" or two from the Canadian North-west, with stalwart young Australians such as Eric McNab, Ted Morey, Tas Fitzer—a New Zealander—and Tony Lynch down in the Centre, sailing native canoes and riding packhorses on the trail of tribal murderers—they gave Ion Idriess some of his best adventure stories. Among the master pearlers were V. J. Clarke, Captain Ancell Gregory, Roy Edwards—later a Flying Doctor pilot—Connor, Kepert, Lepoigneur, and Muramatts, a Japanese, their pearl-fleets sailing uncharted seas.

Billiard-marking at the Club Hotel was old Joel Cooper, who conquered Melville Island when it was a savage strand; and when the white-winged mission lugger *St Francis* from Bathurst Island came into harbour, you might meet aboard her—once in three years—a second St Francis, a gentle-mannered priest from Alsace-Lorraine, blue-eyed, square-cut, with a square-cut beard like a medieval saint, the now famous Bishop Gsell.

Old Darwin told a story in every shack. Jack Buscall, the cripple of Curio Cottage, stored in his mind and his miniature museum the chronicles and relics of outlandish years. That fine old gentleman, Florenz Bleeser, in a lifetime of telegraph service, was the Territory's only naturalist, with invaluable collections of specimens and data, mainly botanical, which he generously shared with scientists, to their benefit and never his own. Rodier, the French-Canadian photographer, had won a Grand Prix in Paris long ago. "Singapore Joe" Marlowe, who spoke five languages, had gone bush from the cable company to live in a bough shade, and Charles Harford Richard Octavian William Woodleigh Goodwin, scion of an English family, had cruised through adventure via India and the Indies—he was known as "the Deep-sea Stockman" for his prowess on the saddle and the wave. Dolly Bonson was there, half-caste original of *The Little Black Princess*, by Mrs Aeneas Gunn, and driving the town ambulance Barney McGuinness, whose dark mother, Lucy, out in the Pine Creek ranges, had led his father to a fabulous mine of tin. They whispered of a pirate, of men of the secret service, a lady who smoked opium, a smuggler and a Russian spy. Many a strange character found a home in a queer corner. At least two authors well-known beyond

Australia, Xavier Herbert of *Capricornia*, W. E. Harney of *North of 23°*, found treasure in the flotsam that drifted to Ultima Thule in every tide. And from away back in the twilight of time came white-haired and genial Burbar, who had roamed the beaches of Darwin before the white man came, and arranged choreography for corroborees of the dreaming for the last of the Larrakia.

Let them sing anthems to that mythical new Darwin, model tropic bungalows, air-conditioned suburbs, poinciana parks and palatial hotels, a garden city cut and dried, Front Gate of Australia that never yet came true. We who knew it like the old one best. It was poor, it was abject, its crest a white ant rampant, its motto *Laisser faire*, but it was jerry-built of the hearts of men.

Below Katherine the Territory was outside religion, politics, the world, the flesh and the devil and clothes that make the man. Five hundred people might have been scattered down there. Nine mail services, often enough by packhorses, tried to cover four hundred thousand square miles—the rest was out of ken. Blacks still carried letters in a split stick, addressed with a cattle brand. Transport, in some regions, was a donkey team a year. Milk and butter had never been seen. To borrow a bag of flour to live on for a month a settler would ride two hundred miles—you might travel a thousand and never see a cup, a sheet or a chair. White children were a novelty and white women were rare.

Two ruts through the spinifex from Birdum to Alice Springs, scrambling through rivers and bogged on the plains under the telegraph line for seven hundred miles, they called the Great North Road. Little Jack McCarthy with Bohning of Helen Springs had "punched" that road through with a fire-plough, horses and donkeys hauling beams with a phalanx of steel to mow down the ant-hills and grub up the trees. Roads to the Barkly Tablelands, to Victoria River and Wyndham, were all made in this way, following the bridle track and the dray. Yet such a remarkable network ran for so many thousand miles in all directions that when the Army came, like the Romans, to build the highroads of war, they opened not one new by-way, but surveyed and graded the well-worn pads of the pioneers.

A million square miles of Australia was "The Great Unfenced". There were no station boundaries, no State borders. The eastern border had been a Herculean job for many noted surveyor explorers for over fifty years, the endless building of a legendary fence, the notorious "Queensland netting", here today and gone tomorrow, finally buried three fences deep under the Dead Heart sand.

The western border had no place in the minds of men until 1921, when Messrs G. F. Dodwell, H. B. Curlewis, C. M. Hambidge and C. A. Maddern, government astronomers and surveyors of South Australia and Western Australia, drew an imaginary line for fifteen hundred miles across stark wilderness. On Argyle Station in Kimberley, with M. P. Durack, their host, they carried their radio sets from the homestead sixteen miles east, and there listened to signals from Annapolis, U.S.A., from Lyons, France, and Bordeaux's Lafayette, then the most powerful transmitting station in the world. They marked the 129th meridian from a point nearly one and a half miles east. General Ferrie, Admiral Hoogewerff, Mr Dodwell and Mr Curlewis worked in the bond that unites men of science across many thousands of miles while Boxer, Ulysses and Billy-Joe, natives of Argyle, listened to music of the spheres and at the right moment registered delight. The border was marked by the concrete pedestal on which the portable transit and almacanter instruments were fixed that night. It bisects the desert from sea to sea, but a cairn at Deakin, on the trans-continental railway line a thousand miles south, was the only outward and visible sign. Between Deakin and Hall's Creek it was a border that only the wind and the wild dogs would cross.

Central Australia, after 1927, with a fortnightly train from Adelaide to its red-crowned mountains and high valleys of promise, was making progress, slow but sure. For a few years it was declared—as it should be—a colony self-contained, with a new little capital, Alice Springs, growing brighter in the map. But Darwin was still far away, idle, and bitter and old. Nothing but a miracle could save it.

The miracle happened—the British airmail, laurels to the memory of Ross Smith.

In 1919, when the phœnix of science was rising from ashes of war, the world was thrilled with Atlantic Ocean crossings by air. The Commonwealth Government, with W. M. Hughes as Prime Minister, offered £10,000 for a path-finder flight from England to Australia.

Into his place in history stepped a young Anzac from South Australia who had flown with the R.A.F.—Ross Smith. With his brother Keith and two mechanics, J. M. Bennett and W. H. Shiers, in a big wooden Vickers-Vimy like a chicken-house, few controls, no radio, no weather reports, no diplomatic protection, he set out southward-bound. Batavia was the only aerodrome south of the Equator. Over snows of Europe and sands of Asia, with a thermos of coffee and a packet of sandwiches to cheer them through each day, they flew a roundabout. GEAOU was their identification register—"God 'Elp All of Us". Lyons, Pisa, Rome, Taranto, Suda in Crete, Heliopolis, Damascus, Ramadi near Baghdad, Basra, Bandar Abbas, Karachi, Delhi, Calcutta, Akyab, Bangkok, Singapore, Kalidjati in Java to Surabaya, they found a way through the clouds. Over the Timor Sea on the twenty-seventh day they came to Darwin and landed near the jail at Fannie Bay. Two days later Captain H. N. Wrigley and Lieutenant A. W. Murphy, in a little single-engined bi-plane, completed the trans-Australian flight from Melbourne to Darwin to meet them.

Famous free-lance aviators followed in Parer and McIntosh in 1920, Sir Alan Cobham and his mechanic Ward in 1926, Bert Hinkler flying solo in 1928, also Lancaster and Mrs Keith Miller. Chichester followed in 1929.

Moir and Owen landed at nightfall in crocodile seas off a reef at Cape Don, Piper and Kay, Amy Johnson, Matthews, Hill, touched down in 1930, and Kingsford Smith with the England-Australia record.

These were the first of many—two lone young women among them, Jean Batten and Eily Beinhorn—anxiously watching through an oil-spattered wind-screen for that horizon of green where the terrors of the Timor ended and Australia began. They were glad to see Darwin and quick to leave it. For fifteen years it was no more than a whistling station, hail and farewell to heroes of the sky. In time it was bored with the supermen.

"What's the good of these aces to us?" a mayor of the town asked me. "They stay only a night, they get free beer and board at the pub, and they never spend sixpence in my bicycle shop!"

Kingsford Smith, in 1931, made an urgent flight to meet a British air mail at Karachi. In 1934 an excited flock of planes passed by in the London-Melbourne centenary air race, won by C. W. A. Scott and Major Campbell Black. A few weeks later the first British air mail to Australia came in with pennants flying, pilot, Captain R. Taylor.

For a while the service was operated by land planes, Captain L. Brain of Qantas first to meet Imperial Airways at Darwin, but by 1938 the flying-boats with passengers and mail anchored for the night under Fort Hill, ten thousand miles twice a week from Southampton to Rose Bay, Sydney. Completing the circle of the continent, MacRobertson Miller Airways from Perth linked up with the English mail at Darwin.

Australia opened the Front Gate.

Up went the swing of the graph in progress and population. A Government shamed before thousands of international visitors began to plan the fourth New Darwin, residential area to cover eleven miles. Million-gallon oil tanks loomed up on the pearling beach and bond stores in the horehound scrub. Where the Territory's only aeroplane had been Larkin's humble Moth from Cloncurry to Daly Waters, sheltered there in a bough shed when it could make the journey, soon Darwin had three aerodromes to accommodate twenty-eight planes a week. Where a blackfellow sat on a post behind Fannie Bay jail to watch for a black spot in heaven, a radio beam and a powerful beacon guided in the aero-expresses across four hundred and fifty miles of Timor Sea to our first national airport—a hot-house flower of such rapid growth that Rip Van Winkles of the old régime were lost there.

Fort Hill and Stokes Hill, enclosing the jetty, were to be levelled for a fine new wharf, warehouses, promenades, yacht clubs—excavations night and day. A garrison to guard the oil tanks moved in to the meatworks, with a few old guns from Thursday Island set up on the headlands to warn trespassers away in a world, even then, of war's alarms. Casual Australian boys in khaki, they married Darwin's daughters and increased the prosperity with their pay. Tin shacks on the headland faded up to offices, banks, public buildings, Government and aviation hostels at a cost of thousands, blocks of shops and flats. Ramshackle pubs played second fiddle to a Hotel Darwin that cost £65,000, to be a Grand Babylon of tropic elegance—in time. Chinese, Malays and what-not received notice to quit the metropolitan area and the native Larrakia were to be moved miles out to the new aboriginal compound built on anthropological lines, each tribe to its own self-contained flat with electric light, sewerage, h. and c., walled in from tribal vendettas, garden city with two picture shows, laundries, churches, schools, sports oval and/or corroboree ground.

With the foundation of Tennant's Creek as a permanent town of gold, roads from the south—with the efforts of D. D. Smith, the one resident engineer—now steadily improved. The motor-trucks brought mining agents, insurance agents, real estate agents, book agents, commercial travellers, newspaper representatives to meet celebrities from overseas, anthropologists studying the blacks and missioners redeeming them, scientists and museum collectors after bones, stones, fossils, fronds, moths, meteorites and marsupial mice; gold-seekers and bore-sinkers with their wives and children, union officials, mechanics, cooks, authors and lunatics at large. They travelled the long trails putting up at the stations on the way or camped on the creek with "the Spotted Wonder" and "Tommie the Nut". A credulous crowd of optimists camped on Mindil Beach with all their tins and tatterdemalion among the pookaminny graveyard posts of the Melville islanders under the coconut palms. Houses sprang up in the green like toadstools and white-anted verandas were crammed with beds twelve deep.

By 1938 the population had risen to six thousand. There was still not so much to eat, but, with transport a little more lively, the *élite* rejoiced in refrigerators and electric fans. Where home beautiful had been limited through seventy years to rattan lounges or packing-cases frilled with cretonne, there was even a furniture shop. There was a new hospital, a new school with a few scholarships awarded to clever children. A Country Women's Association induced the Government to reduce steamer fares that white women might refresh themselves for the battle with cruel summer, especially in ill-health, with an occasional change to the south. One Flying Doctor, Dr C. Fenton, of whose epic and remarkable work I have written in *Flying Doctor Calling*, had appeared in the infinite, alone in his own plane. Flying a thousand miles to save a life, and risking his own to give relief from pain, throughout the whole Territory, for his never-failing help and dauntless spirit, Dr Fenton was respected and beloved. These benefits to women and children of the north, for the first time in history, were colonization's brightest hope.

The aeroplane was Darwin's triumph and, with triumph in sight, its doom.

In 1939 the world plunged headlong into the horrors of war. The rest is military history. On Friday, 19th February 1942, came a rain of fire from the skies in the malevolence of man. Ninety-two bombers from Japan wheeled in from the sea on a bright morning, leaving a massacre and a shambles, a harbour of death and a port of wrecks. As a settlement of peaceful living it was blotted out of the map. It became a front line of battle, for three years its very name a secret.

Except for the men drafted into the Army, its people were rushed to the south on darkened ships and down across the continent, many in open trucks and thinly clad through heat and heavy rain, with a few poor belongings, a thousand miles by the rough road to Alice Springs and a thousand miles in four days by railway. The train crept in to Adelaide in black-out at one o'clock in the morning with a pitiful little huddle of two or three hundred of the first refugees in Australia's history—nuns, half-castes, Chinese, over two hundred white people including a few old bushmen. Among them was a hospital nurse—in shorts—doing her best to care for the sick; they had all left while Darwin was still smoking. Mrs Herbert was there, of Koolpinya Station, eighty-four years old, wife of a former Administrator of the Territory. She was valiant and bright, but very tired—she died soon after.

Most were strangers in the southern city, but in morning light they found a place to live. Everything they owned, whether worth a few shillings or hundreds of pounds, had been left for the looting and the bombs. Some were welcomed by friends and later made pleasant homes, some went to rooms, and camps and institutions. It was a cold and difficult winter in the south—many died, among them Florenz Bleeser. Though surrounded by comfort and cared for by his wife and daughter, when he learned that his botanical and zoological books, with their carefully annotated specimens in tissue and their indexed photographic plates—a fifty years' labour of love and patience for knowledge of the north—had been thrown out of his home in the wet season to be trampled and destroyed, he sat by the fire through that long winter, failing every day, not caring to live on.

Other little bands of refugees were scattered round the five States of Australia, waiting till the war was over. In a land where roots are in shallow ground, and great trees easily fall, the hearts of its own people were rooted deep.

In 1945 I was away on the long roads to Darwin for the third time in an eventful twenty years, this time across the Barkly Tablelands and northward bound. The war had just ended. I travelled as a pilgrim in a dream of khaki thousands—soldiers' ghosts.

In the bewildering and terrible sequence of war, all had changed. The bridle track of the bushmen from Camooweal to Tennant's Creek, the two ruts through spinifex from Alice Springs to Darwin, were great arterial highways of perpetual military motion and the big convoys' ceaseless roar. The quiet bush had been the stronghold of over a hundred thousand regimented men in a myriad armed camps that were virtually towns, far more populous and prosperous than the Territory had ever known. To each were metalled roads, wealth of water from a bore, electric light and power, freezing chambers, sewerage, Army stores, recreation halls, picture shows, garages and bowsers, streets and streets of huts, all with cemented paths and floors, many thousands of beds, tables and chairs, hundreds of miles of plumbing and acres of insect-proof gauze. Within a month of evacuation they were white ant ruins, bower birds' playgrounds, mounds of decay, banging shutters and falling walls.

The Territory had been colonized in three brief years, and now it was swiftly fading back to bush. Civilization had passed that way and—overnight—was gone, with the multitudes that made, and marched, and thronged those miracles of road, those splendid roads through nothing.

The Stuart Highway, an endless stream of bitumen blue bisected by an endless yellow line, flowed rapidly north for a thousand miles. Weird as the race of Alice's Red Queen, it ran backwards through the alphabet in mysterious Army letters, symbols, figures, fractions, signs, with hidden tributary roads to airstrips of vanished aeroplanes, haunts of vanished men—sometimes with never a soul nor a sound for over a hundred miles.

All that the Territory needed in the pitiful old times had rushed to it by that benediction of a road, built in the frenzy of a year but, sadly enough, in our insane cycle of world history, dedicated to the science of death and not to the science of life. Here was one of the great handiworks of man, a crown of achievement to Australia, yet its name not spoken nor its story told, for fear of the ferocity of man. Now it threaded a land bewitched, the endless mazes of those silent camps.

Hostels and hospitals of the valleys and the heights, equipped on a lavish scale in desperate haste, each at a cost of many thousands of pounds, had been forsaken in haste to moth and rust, and in all the camps rubbish dumps were hills high—ten thousand rusted beds, elaborate wrought-iron furnishings, hillocks of hardware, laundry boilers, lacquered tables, hundreds of chairs and dozens of porcelain baths, every amenity and luxury that had never been known under the Territory sun . . . where men had died alone there in their swags. In the vast Army car-parks were vehicles in thousands, the movement and the might of war, mountains of petrol in forty-gallon drums and in caverns under the earth, valleys filled with perishing rubber tyres . . . in a land where a woman has walked forty miles with a dying child in her arms. There was timber to build a score of towns, square miles of iron for roofs, a hundred towns built and established—the Territory might have been fully colonized, and lived for fifty years, on all that the war had thrown away. Army disposals, Lend-lease, it vanished from the earth. Down came the monsoon and covered a million pounds, creeks singing and water-lilies blowing over a million pounds' worth of rust and decay, and food for a multitude covered in mould. In the bush-fires even the memory withered away.

While the last of the Army in Darwin was packing its kitbag to go, the vanguard of Darwin's returning people waited at Pine Creek.

It was a sad homecoming to ruined and looted homes, skeleton houses and scarecrow streets—and even these no longer their own. In another false dawn for a fifth New Darwin, this time to cover thirteen square miles of elegance and glory, a Rio of the south, they were denied the freehold of those homes.

Six years of golden dreams have gone since then. Patchwork of Government affluence and striving pioneers, with more humour than hope, Darwin, as one of the old hands quaintly told me, is still "a steak and egg town". Even as I write, I hear from the radio that the first national airport is to be transferred to Perth, once again closing the Front Gate of Australia.

But of the rising generation of Australians who came to the Territory in the war years, ten thousand adventurous men and women have made that lovely, luckless land their own. Their path is no longer the tragedy of the old pioneers, and they will not easily be cast down, with much in this age to help them.

There remains the Stuart Highway, and on either side for a thousand miles their heritage the Australian bush, pathless and splendid in the yellow sundown.

Chapter II

Land of The Moon-Bow

Where the Portingales see popingayes commonly of a wonderfull greatnesse. . . .

FROBISHER.

THIS IS the fabled land of old Spanish maps, *Terra psittacorum*, Land of Parrots, its fan-palm jungles and forest creeks a wheel of colour and light, pools of stippled silver where piccaninnies go swimming and little Johnson crocodiles smile . . . where the "bue flamingo" dances and the white heron wears her egret plumes unseen, and where the lunar rainbow plays all summer through, delicate as soap-bubble above the rain-wet forests, cycles of Zoroastrian light around a watery moon.

Green spears of pandanus guard the ferned waterfalls and secret springs of eerie worship slowly bubbling from mysterious earthy deeps where drowned lilies and toad-growths waver and wave. Scarlet dragon-flies hang above the aspic stillness, translucent fish dart in the water-sunlights in wishing wells of optical delusion where concave brilliance of waters lensed in electric blue sand turns the bodies of the bathers into dwarfs. Well I remember the pure cool pleasure of these springs in the tangled ranges of Macarthur River, on the headwaters of Mainoru River in Arnhem Land, and at Nedjik and Jindik of the Elsey near Mataranka.

Walt Disney with his flying crayons never conjured a gayer fantasia in natural history than those evanishing jungles that fade from arsenic green to sulphur yellow and crackle away in fire. From January to April the world is drowned. By July an Amazonian undergrowth has withered from the bald red earth, leaving the screwy screw-palms, burnt black, like warriors on walkabout in the scrub.

Nature figures the trunks of trees and rocks of the sea in Egyptian colour-design of aboriginal art so rich in pigment that from flowers, birds' feathers and bark the paint comes off on your hands. Tides of coloured grasses, wild lupins in a spill of sun, staghorns with ferny antlers, giant maidenhair, scented tree-orchids and crinkled green ribbon of their leaves make a tropic heaven undreamed in the trim and temperate south. But to find it you must follow the rivers.

When the thirty big rivers are on the move, with their thousand creeks, they flow not only to the Timor Sea, but east and west almost to meet each other. Each is the equivalent of five of its size in the south when they "come down" four or five times in five months in the annual deluge of monsoon, lipping the hills miles wide, fifty feet deep in a day. Victoria, Katherine-Daly, Adelaide, Roper, Macarthur, are up to five hundred miles long in the main stream.

Southward are the "silent rivers", flowing into the old Inland Sea, from Newcastle Waters to Finke River, a thousand miles long, but these may run only once in two or three years. Sam Irvine, overland mailman before the Stuart Highway, counted up for me seven hundred creeks and rivers between Adelaide and Darwin, yet you might travel with him half a dozen times and never sight one. When you did you would not forget it. In 1932 I battled with the mail from Alice Springs north for seventeen days and nights through mud and water, and finished up on packhorses across the big creeks from Newcastle Waters to Birdum.

Newcastle Waters were two hundred yards wide for fifty miles, with twenty miles of bog each side. Quite often these Waters are sand. Lake Woods, into which they disappear, in flood is ninety miles round, reflecting clouds of wildfowl and flocks of pelicans sailing. In drought it is a fog of bush-fires. John McDouall Stuart, the path-finder, crossed it twice and never knew it was a lake.

In this country in the old years grey men were walking. Tjingilli and Warramunga blacks, in cold winter winds, coated themselves all over with clay-pan mud, and roamed the earth like spiders or spectres. If you happened to call in on a burial, you would see snow-white nymphs among them, women of the dead men painted from head to foot in pipe-clay, wearing heavy widows' caps of *kopi,* black man's plaster of Paris.

At Alice Springs in winter are golden days and cold nights, at Darwin clear skies and the steady south-easter blowing. The equable Barkly Tablelands, nearly a thousand feet above sea-level, though winds are raw and chilly in July have one of the healthiest climates in the world. At Katherine the thermometer can fall as low as 28 degrees, with three inches of ice on the wells at Wave Hill and Tanami. Only the fringe of the Timor is tropical for two hundred miles deep, with rainfall to a possible ninety inches—average sixty—in four months when monsoon comes frowning in from sea, dry bulb at 95 degrees and wet bulb climbing to 90 degrees. "Lion's breath" of humidity, overpowering heat, is just before the wet season, in October and November, relieved, and then intensified, by sudden cyclonic storms, when five inches of rain may fall with sun or moon still shining.

As I write I see red hills, red leaves, creeks of red sand running through steamy green. I feel the fetor of Territory night under cathedral clouds, with trefoil of coloured lightning, a crack of thunder like a revolver shot, heavy cool drench of rain. I hear loud shouting of a million frogs, monsoon roaring in a black fog through the trees, and the wild-beast breathing of a blackfellow's didjeridoo.

This is the land of strange but true, from islands of an unknown coast with rising smoke of sea-birds to timeless, formless deserts where the red sun bounces like an indiarubber ball . . . meteors falling by daylight.

. . . an isle of skeletons, where some mysterious plague annihilated the people; an isle once of black women, no men. Maria, at the mouth of the Roper, is an isle of the dead, with hollow memorial posts painted and filled with skulls.

On the empty yellow grasslands of Barkly Tablelands, nearly a hundred thousand square miles, you can see a light coming at night for seventy miles; in mirage of early morning you look over the curve of the world.

Quartz hills of the Jervois Ranges are glittering Arctic-white. Burning hills of the MacDonnells smoulder away west to Ayers Rock, Mount Olga, Mount Connor, glazed domes of Venetian red in a level plane of sand.

There, sunsets are like the end of the world and dawns clear and pure as its beginning.

There are tourists' delight of waterfalls, limestone caves, picnic spots, fern grots, panoramas, known only to the bushmen for generations. Elsey Falls, Flora Falls, Katherine River gorges, Melk-chalandu Waterhole of Waterhouse River with its golden sand-beaches, split rocks and thousands of little crocodiles like toy submarines in clear crystal lakes in the heart of a range, would attract round-trippers by the busload. Where Mary River finds the sea are striped cliffs of yellow sandstone, red ochre, white magnesite, grey slate and purple plumbago, beyond, the broken old castled ruins of South Alligator and the dazzling red lily lagoons of Oenpelli and Owai. Here the blacks wander in a wizard world.

Six miles of deep water sixty yards wide run through Katherine town, from the Old Crossing to the railway bridge, but the dejected patch of shacks that is Katherine knows little about it, for the river is netted in by jealous jungle. A lovely sight there is tea-tree in blossom, bend after bend of flowering beauty, crimson or white. On the satin-smooth river fallen honey-blossoms lie like fragments strewn on glass—in the dark reaches a fitting setting for Ophelia's drowned face.

In Kintore Caves near Katherine white-walled corridors lead to a throne-room of coronation drapings and musical stalactites, but the caves, cool as refrigeration in the heat, have not yet been lighted. Petrifaction is rapid in the tropics. One old cattle-man told me he left a lighted candle down there one day, and went back in a couple of hours to find it petrified, flame and all!

At Paragundi Creek of Jimmie Gibb's Roper Valley Station is "the Lighted City", alleged to be radio-active rock with luminous fungus in weird and starry brilliance. Through Hell's Gates to ranges of the Roper, where ledged red crests of Mount McMinn and Mount George look down on that great silver serpent, are caves of aboriginal relic and legend, catacombs that wind under-ground for miles, never yet penetrated by white man or black.

Every backwater and bywater in the north is alight with lilies from May to October. They still the singing of little creeks, crowd pandanus springs, and even stem the tides in the big mother-river, all the nymphs of *Nymphaea* up to giant African nelumbium, twelve inches across nestling in eighteen-inch leaves. Red, yellow, mauve, blue, white, green of the Nile or royal purple, in this land of illusion lily-pools may change colour every year. Fairyland is Blackmore River near Tumbling Waters with carpet of white lilies and canopy of snowy-blossomed paperbark and frail gold woollybutt meeting above. In two lagoons of the Daly and one of Adelaide River the sacred pink lotus of India blows.

No need to promise "white-fella tucker" when lily-time is here. Blacks, glossy as onyx, dive into lagoons, and before ripples have settled the tallest lilies in the patch crack and go under. A couple of hundred yards down-stream ten minutes later, three or four ducks, with flutter and squawk, disappear—pulled under by the legs. With sleek wet heads and broad smiles the submarine hunters, who were breathing through hollow lily-stalks, stroll up the bank with a brace of duck in each hand, wring their necks, and carelessly throw them down to be cooked where piccaninnies are eating lily-bulbs and lubras pounding lily-seeds between stones for daily bread, and with wallaby to make aboriginal meat-loaf, *chintopee*.

Flying-foxes bring twilight to all the gorges in silent flight for hours,

hanging head downwards in billions in the banyans, eating blossom, fruit and seed. Head of a dog with vicious canine teeth, Mephistophelian leathery wings with claws, human breasts to which the young ones cling by their teeth, the flying-fox is something out of hell, with a voice like a squabble between Mickey Mouse and Donald Duck. The white-necked sea-eagle is his arch-enemy, cutting him out as he flies in clouds, gulping him down alive.

Bushmen in dire hunger can eat flying-fox, though its vile odour imparts itself to the body, so repulsive that it keeps mosquitoes away. A boat-party in the Daly River one night, eaten alive by mosquitoes, took on board a black-boy who had been eating flying-fox. All mosquitoes promptly left the ship. At the next landing they put the boy ashore and thankfully took back the mosquitoes.

Birds of the Territory range from the emu, six feet tall, which takes the whole continent in his horny, corny stride, to the sun-bird of Papua, two inches from tip to tip, a flash of water-opal by the springs. There is an occasional glimpse of the ornate pheasant of China.

Quick dawn and sunset along the rivers are a wild life rhapsody. In octopus roots of banyan and dark-green strings of casuarina is a quiver of ripples where blue water-hen are nesting, or where crocodile waits for kangaroo.

Jabiru, *Xenorhynchus asiaticus*, the "policeman crane" of India, five feet six inches tall, in clerical black and white with red biretta, stalks on couch-grass at the edge of the lagoon like an Oxford don in his Oxford gown, or stands motionless for hours like Socrates on a street-corner of Athens. A wise bird, benign, solitary, dumb, when he snaps his beak in irritation even the arrogant brolgas take to flight. That beak is over a foot long, and can sever a man's finger in its snap—with it he spears a diet of live fish and snake. At dusk, with a spread of lazy wings seven feet across, he soars to his nest in a tree. Bushmen tell me that as a meal jabiru will serve, though he has a phosphoric flavour—you can just fit him nicely, with a few lily-bulbs, into a five-gallon can, and the formidable beak thrown out near camp will frighten away the cheeky crows.

Bubbling of gourd music in alto melody descending is the swamp-pheasant. He loves the dank of the banyan and its burst purple figs. White, black and glossy ibis trail their Arabic lettering in the sky. Brolgas begin their mazing dances out on the clay-pans, weaving *Les Sylphides* on rose and blue of south-easter skies, doing all that Nijinsky and Pavlova would have done with a pair of wings. Statuesque Nankeen crane and the snowy spoonbill stand, one-legged, in the shallows, and little jacana, the "Jesus-bird", walks on the water-lily leaves. One of Nature's most delicate fancies, with his long horizontal toes and legs like stems of maidenhair fern, he lives in the world of lilies, and mother-bird sets her eggs afloat on a diminutive raft.

Magpie is there with his organ notes, vox melodia and dulciana. Chief Musician is butcher-bird, small virtuoso gracefully bowing in white tie and tails to his coda of viola and cadenza of flute. Mazes of brilliant finches play kaleidoscope in shrubs where Java sparrows and diamond sparrows—"tin tacks"—rise in twittering myriads with tiny waxbill, "red ochre longa him cheek".

Granddad pelicans touch down in the manner of seaplanes and swim in a Grand Fleet cordon, driving fish before them, and scattering small craft of whistle duck, sheldrake, teal, coot and quail, green pygmy geese in pairs and the wood duck that nests in trees. Kingfisher skimming the river is a streak of peacock colour in all sizes up to kookaburra chortling goodnight for an hour in the last gleam of day. By starlight plover and curlew are crying, and mopoke strikes midnight in some lonely gully among ghostly moth-hawk owls.

White cockatoo and crow, all over Australia, are spirit-fathers of aboriginal tribes. Dancing waves of "greenies", shell parrots, love-birds, galahs, with king parrot, lory, Corella, Rosella, blue bonnet, Blue Mountain, blue-grass parrot—a splash of heaven on the road—the Antioch or golden-shoulder in pairs, feeding on white gum-blossom, lorikeets and parakeets decorative as Hindu tapestries, all these nest in ant-hills or in knots and boles of trees, where they pop in and out like cuckoo clocks.

Down in the ranges of the Centre, peerless Princess Alexandra, Bourke and crimson-chested parrots, unique in the world, weave a prism of opalescent colours in Namatjira gorges, shyly changing their nesting-grounds every year to evade the cruelty and stupidity of man. The voiceless night-parrot that nests in the ant-hills may not be sighted once in thirty years.

Wedge-tail cruises the coast, grim as the golden eagle of Europe, gaunt as the condor, with white-breasted sea-eagle and Caribbean frigate-bird. Snipe and dotterel, nimble as spiders, run along the beaches. All over those pale skies are wheeling brown hawk and brahminee kite.

Koralk-koralk, flood-bird, channel-billed cuckoo, tells the coming of the wet. Autocrat and robber, he pelts the crows' eggs out of their nests to make room for his own. Wherever he flies, a mob of outraged little birds is indignantly shrieking "Stop, thief!" in his wake, but to the bushman at the end of the dry no nightingale music could be sweeter than that ecstatic squawk at piccaninny daylight just one beat ahead of the rain.

Jungle-fowl, modest little bird of big ambition, is first cousin to southern mallee-hen. You may see the brown mother hopping on one yellow leg, carrying leaves and grass in the other to build the crèche fifteen feet in circumference and eight feet high. She lays fifteen or twenty pinkish-brown eggs. The chicks are hatched in the wet, by heat of decayed mould. Pert and sturdy from first kick of the broken shell, they have no need of mother. A jungle-fowl's nest has been found in the north fifteen feet high and a hundred and fifty feet round—nine thousand cubic feet. Eggs are big as a goose-egg, and the bird smaller than the fowlyard hen.

Wood-dove and diamond-dove are singing glees with rose-crowned and purple-breasted pigeons, speckled spinifex pigeons, quaint little top-knot pigeons wearing a tiara, and Torres Strait or black-banded pigeons whose feathers make dainty curio fans, but nest and eggs are rarely found. Here, too, are the peewit, the pert fantail, gentle little blue wren.

Plain turkey is too good a friend to man—with his giraffe neck and bright inquisitive eye, he waits to be shot for dinner. In mating-time turkey-gobblers puff out their feathers and stand for hours in the landscape, stock-still as a traffic cop. Across the hot silence you can hear for miles that curious mating call like the single beat of a drum.

Star turn of all is bower-bird, with his jeweller's shop in miniature wurley of twigs or spinifex, a little Arc de Triomphe all set about with bones, stones, berries, shells, scraps of tin, bottle-tops, feathers, flowers, glass, everything that glitters, in sparkling mosaic round the nest with a reserve stock of bric-à-brac inside. A coloured toothbrush handle or a broken china cup is a precious family heirloom. A Victoria River saddler told me he had to give up business because the bower-birds cleaned him out of buckles.

These speckled brown busy-bodies are in myriads all over Centre and north, and keep up a comic flat wrangling all day. A great game for married couples is to snatch up knick-knacks and chase each other through the arch, ringing the changes on home beautiful with matrimonial chiacking in crack-pot duet. Here and there they tuck a red flower in the thatch, or amusingly arrange white quartz pebbles from a creek-bed into little crazy pavements and bordered paths with a zest worthy of suburbia.

But the big story of bower-bird is not the *décor* of his little stage, but his vaudeville of vocal mimicry and burlesque—never a set performance in camera for art's sake, like the lyre-bird, but a cheeky off-hand badinage as he goes about collecting antiques. He will mimic a corroboree or a circular saw, bark at the dog, miaow at the cat, neigh at the horses, bleat at the goats, then cut in on a quarrel between Missus and Boss in querulous treble and grumpy bass, finishing with a cackle of laughter. If there is a radio around, he will give you racing announcers in good Astrylian, beginning with a leisurely croak in description of the field to the sudden yap of "They're off!", and a nasal *crescendo* running upstairs in semitones all round the furlong posts till it finishes in a winning-post shriek. Nobody with the luck to hear a bower-bird "doing the Cup" can fail to give that jackanapes a hand of hearty applause, except, perhaps, the racing announcers.

North of Katherine, rivers and pools are alive with little Johnson crocs, rarely more than seven feet long, a thrill to behold. Black children bathe among them without fear, and splash defiance at them—they climb out on the limb of a banyan, drop figs into the water, then dive for the rising croc with a fishing spear. Big Indian crocodile is a different story when he cruises up-river from the sea and the tidal waters, seeking whom he may devour. As a rule you are safe from him a hundred miles from the sea, but even then be wary, for often he comes up in the wet season, to lie in a deep pool when the rivers go down.

Territory trees, all over the north, are sylvan glory, bamboo thick and majestic on the rivers for two hundred miles south. Giant bamboo grows on the Daly, up to ninety feet high, its pageant of smoky flowers seen only once in forty years. It is a Burmese superstition that blossoming of the big bamboo is warning of coming disaster—it creamed into a white glory just before the war. The vasty banyan is moored to the earth with its own fibre cables that root into Neptune caves and grottoes with background of leafy Leichhardt-trees and bright yellow satin-wood; and freshwater mangrove, of which the natives pound the leaves and throw them into the water to dope the fish and float them to the top, has doubtless some value as a soporific drug.

Most of the eucalypts, mimosas, acacias and grevilleas of Australia wave their green scarves in those sunny forests—tall carbeen gums with white sculptured limbs of a goddess, snapper gum in black and white—Pierrette.

Here are age-old cycads and zamia palm, fan-palm, cabbage-tree palm, sago palm, feathery casuarina, scented milkwood, graceful nutwood and rosewood, tecoma for handsome furniture; belts of native ebony; beefwood, red and grained as rump-steak; bloodwood, a rich deep red and valuable for tannin; ironbark and ironwood for railway sleepers and bridges; "quinine tree", its chips a tonic in fever; mighty scrubs of lancewood and the hedge-wood, bulwaddi, as you travel south.

In belts along the coast grows cypress pine, Nature's answer to white ants. The wood is too tough and too sharp in flavour for them. A hardy timber for houses and furniture, its oils preserve it from mould and dry rot. Everything in Darwin that survived change and decay is built of cypress pine, and there are railway sleepers in the little permanent way that have stood the weights and weathers of fifty years. Most of the nearer belts were cut down long ago by Chinese coolies, but there is still a good deal left farther out.

Rimming the rivers and in ghostly groves all over flood and swamp are paperbarks, white and willowy, up to four feet through and a hundred feet high. You can peel off countless layers of the light, pliable papery bark, wrappings for parcels of the Stone Age, tissue of rarest opalescent colourings, rose, silver, mauve and white—no department store ever evolved anything like it in silken softness and delicacy for gracing a Christmas gift. The timber and tough outer bark are roof, raft and blanket for white men and black, and a feather-soft pillow for babies.

Pandanus and paperbark are friends. Wherever they grow, there is water. Of picturesque screw-palm, pandanus, the dry trunks, ten or twelve feet long, make a splendid raft. Arnhem Land natives swim miles to sea on a single tree. The fibre the blacks use for their homes, baskets, and binder-twine. They eat the nuts. Pandanus, afire, flames bright as a torch for hours, then takes a new lease of life like the phoenix. The cones make a glowing coke oven for the bushman's damper.

A beauty in all seasons is bauhinia, pale-green butterfly wings that fall and fade and dye the ground to purple beneath a flame of orange flowers and bright magenta seed-pods. This soft, firm bean-tree wood is a favourite of the natives for making coolamons and shields. Nutmeg, not the spice nutmeg, grows round the lagoons, its dry wood quite the best for the aboriginal art of kindling a fire with stick-friction.

Trees, alien and native, that lose their leaves in the dry season, no doubt to conserve water, are poinciana, kapok, milkwood, frangipanni, calophyllum, black acacia, cassia and baobab. Towards the beginning and end of the wet, dense night-fogs, heavy as rain, brim pools and the clay-pans, drip from trees, and may not clear till ten in the morning. I have seen Darwin in April, misty and drear as an English winter scene with fog rising through its leafless trees and swallows wheeling.

In high summer of the wet the bush is sickly-sweet with scents. Down on the Daly when grevillea is in bloom, to walk beneath it when morning begins to grow hot is to suffer a sticky shower-bath of melted honey falling from the flowers above. In the dry, all is brittle brown crackling. Then the grass fires sweep through in majesty, swift flame and suffocating smoke, at night halls of glowing coals and Christmas trees festooned with fire.

The far north has the most sensitive plant in the world, a mimosa that curls its leaves and shrinks in nervous apprehension when you stamp on the ground near by. It was Josie Flynn at Rum Jungle who first showed me a horrible little cousin of the Amazonian flesh-eaters—"chicken-catcher" they called it, but at Maranboy it is known as "crow-strangler". A ground-creeper with fur of minute barbs on the under-side of oval leaves, these tiny cat-claws clutch and hold the down of birds. As the unhappy creatures struggle it tangles them till they die, then feeds on the dead flesh. Patches of the vine are a sickly bright green, strewn with feathers and small bones. It was Jack Mackay, at Mainoru, who showed me an Arnhem Land lily, a withered brown stalk in the dry, that blooms for one night only in the wet season, by moonlight, like the African lily of Malud. That diaphanous white beauty fades in the first rays of the sun.

Flora wears chain-mail down in the Centre, where armoured seed-pods, dew-absorbing leaves, water-holding roots and winged and barbed seeds withstand a drought of years and blow for miles. There the blessed parakelia grows, with watery stems that for months without rain will keep cattle and sheep alive. It takes a fall of three inches to bring up grass on blacksoil plains, but in the great zones of the spinifex and mulga a few points will do it, covering the sands with paper daisies and perfumed "herbage", bright yellow tribulus, pink convolvulus and purple vetch.

Where yellow clay-pan ground is heat-baked in deep cracks, no water for miles, in a Pharaoh's chamber a yellow frog hides, puffed into Humpty-Dumpty, a living water-bag. He can sit pat for a year, goggle-eyed and mum, till the blacks find him by a bead of air on the surface, seize him and drink him dry.

On all the plains between Oodnadatta and Daly Waters, *Phlogius,* barking spider, burrows like a rabbit by day and comes out hunting and hooting at night, mostly after rain. I first heard him in the gutta-percha of Brunette, tucked in my swag with an ear to the ground—that uncanny, small, sharp, ventriloquial bark. Was it somebody chopping in the woods—a goanna?—a frog?—an owl? With a torch I tracked him down in a clump of grass near by, *Phlogius* baying the moon. He belongs to the tympani, his bark produced by rubbing mandibles on hairy little palps—shock tactics, loud as a lion's roar to small fry that are his nightly prey. Banyan spider weaves a strand so long and silken-strong that Wargait lubras bind it round the right forefinger at the first joint to bring about gradual amputation, in the hand-mutilation fashionable with the world's most primitive tribes. A band of women at Point Emery showed me how spider-web was wound round and round so tightly that "finger tumble-down, short-fella, more better dig-em out yam".

The Territory is a land of lizards, from friendly gecko chasing over the gauze at night, his small hands pinkly human and an excited yap like a kitten as he swallows moths and midges, to eight-foot *prenti* of the g.w. spaces, galloping like a brumby, nearly a Komodo dragon. Most diverting are "mountain devils" of the flat sand, pocket dragons painted in fearsome colours, knobbed like crocodile, horned like unicorn, nine inches long—and frilled lizards two feet high, with bright vermilion ruff and gossip's tongue darting in and out. When cornered, he struts and frets like a courtier in a rage.

Snakes are vivid and various, some of them venomous, but the bushman, throwing down his swag for a night-camp, never gives them a thought. He may be watchful for death-adders in blue-bush country. Caterpillars march in armies, or build silken nests over every shrub, a cellophane veil. Some, if they cross your clothing or your bed, leave a viscous trail that gives you a maddening itch. Some build a bag, like a wine-skin, at the foot of a tree, full of a fine grey powder of the same irritant nature, which will cause blindness—"killem eye".

Jumping mice, marsupial, you may see on a wet night hopping four feet high in headlights of a car. Dainty sugar-glider, phalanger, eight inches long, silver-grey, a sweet-tooth after sugar-bag, is flitting from tree to tree, and jumping lizard, built on the same concertina lines with membrane under his elbows, volplanes sometimes twenty feet to lick in the moths and the little fly-by-nights.

Steps and stairs of evolution all the way up creation are found on the beach and in the bush—life-forms between plasm and coral, flower, fish, reptile in tepid seas, reptile-bird-animal on land. Some scientists alleged that among Territory blacks they found the Missing Link from ape to man. This is open to question. With no greed of acquisition, no fret of finance, no tenement cities, no politics, no wars, no taste for alcohol and no bestial crime—a merry soul and a kind one, content with freedom of sunny earth by day, song and dance by a community fire at night—I am rather inclined to place the true Australian as a missing link between the sages and so-called civilized man.

Throughout the land death is not to be feared by violence of wild beasts, with due respect to shark and crocodile, and a sinister jellyfish of Arafura waters known to the blacks as *moya*. Transparent in the water, seeming half vegetable, half eel, like the stone-fish it gives an "electric" shock from poisonous spines that paralyses circulation and checks the beat of the heart. To touch it in diving is fatal within an hour unless help and stimulants are near. Natives of trepang fleets and one or two swimmers in Darwin Harbour have died of the shock.

Out on the north coast, where phosphorescent fins cut like knives through warm oily waters, where crumbled banks of tidal creeks and rivers are a seething of soapy foam rising ten and twelve feet in an hour and travelling at eighteen knots, islands unexplored are white as a snowfall with fairy tern and silver gulls. There the turtle nests, and every coral rock-pool is a kaleidoscope of brilliant sea-flowers and fish. Trochilus bird sits in the crocodile's jaws as he suns himself on the beach, and picks his horrid teeth. Black pearls and pearl-shell abound in river estuaries where tides wash down sulphates and ammonium in carcasses of crocs and fish. On Coburg Peninsula near the sea is a thin chalky layer of edible earth, a third of an inch thick, pigment-white, like cream filling in a cake. Lubras and piccaninnies enjoy this raw earth with the delight of schoolchildren licking a threepenny ice.

Here the dark woodland people, with their keen eyes, track down treasure of sugar-bag, following not the flight of homing bees through the air, but the merest specks of pollen they let fall on leaves and earth. There are five major varieties of honey bees, all stingless, little bigger than house-flies. Usually they nest under the knotty eye of a tree, the sugar-bag up to two feet long with protective wax at the base, then larvae, then honey, then on top the bee-bread. As in garden honey, flavour depends on flowers—nectar from lilies and woollybutt blossom, rank eucalypt honey from coarse resinous gums. Bee-bread is peppery when bees nest in an ant-hill. Some species are earth-bound. There are millions of nests in the limestone cliffs, the rocks and the sand.

All imported animals do well, from Angora goats and buffaloes to pigs and pussy-cats, with the exception of the well-bred southern dog, which dies of heart-worm and heat. Around Port Essington you may see little Sourabaya cattle, big Brahmin cattle, and mobs of Timor ponies, dainty and small as Shetlands, all brought over by early settlers, now running wild. English deer in natural parklands are another surprise, imported from the Sydney estate of Dame Eadith Walker and shipped on a lugger from Darwin.

Because the blacks delighted in these pretty timid fawns, they were always taboo to the hunting-spear and increased till, with their slickness and their sharp little horns, they were driving the buffalo away. Wild pigs abound on Daly River, where hunters can bring in three hundred a week, boars up to four hundredweight of pork. On Croker Island, burrowing in soft sand, the species has lost a snout.

In comparison with North Queensland, insect pests are few, especially now that chemical science, with repellant and DDT, has helped us to annihilate mosquitoes, ants and flies. To keep the white ant company the borer beetle, a miniature brace and bit, perforates furniture in decorative design, holes from needle-point to nearly an inch wide—you can hear the tiny carpenters grinding at their fell work day and night.

Curse of the north is a stranger, smallest emmet on earth, Singapore ant. Processions of countless millions travel in single file to cover in clouds, to riddle and devour, to bite in Chinese torture of red-hot pins—from that dark-brown line of devils, no escape. Carried from Singapore in the bales and cargoes of fifty years, they have invaded stations east and west for five hundred miles. They have eaten out the Darwin railway for a mile each side and sacked the little towns—many a time the people of Pine Creek and Katherine have abandoned their houses to camp on the flat, while travellers at the hotels, the legs of their beds in jam-tins, have fled in their pyjamas, screeching into the night. They demolish everything from day-old chicks to peanuts in the ground. They can survive arsenic, creosote, kerosene, boiling carbolic, flood, fire, and DDT. A king and queen can breed five million in three days. They float across water on each others' drowned bodies, or walk on the meniscus-film, so minute they are, and so light. More than once they have murdered a man—as he lay in a drunken stupor or unconscious from a fall, penetrating through his eyes to his brain. One of the first colonization problems is extermination of that vicious little alien, the Singapore ant.

I have told but a few of the wonders, and one or two horrors, of a fanciful land. Fifty years ago it was described by an "abler pen than mine", and earned the writer the reputation of "the Greatest Liar on Earth".

He was a quizzical little Swiss called Henri Grien, with a face like a Van Gogh self-portrait, who took a high dive to fame in the nineties from the springboard of North Australia, his travellers' tales first published in *Wide World Magazine*. The wide world listened with bated breath. He wrote in the first person, under the *nom de plume* of Louis de Rougemont of Bordeaux. Success was his downfall. After the third instalment he ruined splendid material with tall tales of derring-do to glorify himself—in bringing two whales ashore single handed at Melville Island, in killing sixty-eight black snakes in a cave at Wave Hill. Though white colonization was twenty years old, he wrote of an undiscovered country, and it never occurred to the naïve little man that his latitudes would be checked.

Some are still living who remember him well when he drifted the north in the nineties, an inconspicuous bagman applying a continental imagination to all he saw and heard. It was Mr M. P. Durack who, when he was cooking at Newry Station and plaintively asked for something to read in French, lent him La Fontaine's *Fables* and a battered old school copy of *Télémaque.*

One of his kindliest critics is that authority on the north coast, A. J. V. Brown, who met him on the famous pearling schooner out in the Arafura in 1879.

"De Rougemont," he said, "is fundamentally true. Allowing for author's licence—and he's not alone in that—you can't fault him far. When he talks of building a house of black pearl-shell, that would be New Year Island. He'd have to build some shelter in the wet. There's no timber on those cays but there's heaps of black pearl-shell there.

"Riding a turtle down the beach is easy, but he doesn't say what he harnessed him with to keep him from sounding in deep water. The aboriginal stuff is authentic, all through. Shooting rapids on the Roper, getting water out of a bottle-tree on the Ord, and licking the leaves for dew down in the desert—I've done all those myself, they're nothing new. His pearls and gold and rubies are founded on fact, and there were three white women in the eighties, a pearler's wife and daughters, stranded on one of the islands in the Buccaneers. The petroleum he found in the desert was Freney oil—a big company and a lot of talk today. They laughed about the crocodile fight—while Yamba stuffed a paddle down its throat and gouged out its eyes, he stood on its back and brained it with a hatchet. I've seen the blacks harpoon them in with bamboo, prise a stick into the throat, and go for the spinal cord with an axe. It can be done, but the man I met didn't do it. I was sorry for de Rougemont. He piled it on too thick, but reading through him with a bit of commonsense, you'll find it's all there."

The little more and what worlds away! When gallant de Rougemont, wandering with faithful Yamba and his overgrown pup, Bruno, reached that part of his narrative where Yamba allayed his thirst with milk of her own breasts, and killed and ate her piccaninny, carrying the child's bones round her neck in a bag, the wide world howled him down. Yet this was feasible and possibly true. The magazine apologized for a son of Ananias, and their notorious contributor disappeared from scientific view.

Had he not painted the lily, and strutted as a hero—had he made clear the division of his fiction from his fact—the book of Louis de Rougemont, with a little sub-editing, might be read in our schools today as a standard work on the Land of the Long Bow.

Chapter III

Vikings of The Arafura

UNDER THE casuarinas at Croker Island is the grave of Tingha Dian, last of the Bugi-men of Macassar who, back in the dim twilight of fable, fished wealth in our northern seas.

The Malay, the "gentleman of Asia", was Australia's Marco Polo. He founded the commerce of this continent with a traffic in trepang. In crazy ships of straw sailing under the Yellow Tiger of a rajah, rusty little Dutch guns popping at the prow, he blew in with the wind and out with the wind, selling his cargoes by the picul to shrewd Chinese merchants in flowered silks and skull-caps, counting *cash* under the lanterns in Banjermasin. As the whiff of cloves and pepper led Vasco da Gama and Magellan round the world, so the Manchu's epicurean zest for the musty sea-slug opened our first trade route, from the Celebes to Arnhem Land. Trepang soup was elixir of youth to portly old mandarins, fathers of innumerable sons, and a pick-me-up after the opium pipe.

A few years after Captain Cook skimmed the eastern shores of a large and mysterious isle, the Bugis drifted across the Arafura. If we are to believe Pobassoo, courteous commodore of a rag-tag fleet, who furnished a historical note on the subject to Captain Matthew Flinders when they met in Malay Roads in 1802, the lucky mishap of a hurricane blew the first proa to these shallow shores some twenty years before.

For a hundred years thereafter they were in virtual possession of three thousand miles of coast till a great British Commonwealth had grown up in the south to frighten them off with a warning from White Australia. While William Charles Wentworth and Sir Henry Parkes were haranguing in Parliament the grave and reverend seigneurs, fathers of a nation . . . while five millions were roaming for pastures and gold, building cities, railways, a thousand towns, six States and a Federation . . . while Melba was carolling *Juliet* and Mark Twain delighting the intelligentsia in crowded halls of the south, at the other side of the island the naked betel-chewing Bugis were trading and invading, raping and burning, exacting the law of a tooth for a tooth in what they called Mareega, Black Man's Land.

From Cape Leveque to Cape Arnhem and down into the Gulf, you can still find traces of Malay occupation along the north coast—occasional groves of fine old tamarinds, fireplaces, Malay wells, iron boilers rotted in the sand, graves with Arabic letters fading. Sea-coast tribes from Darwin to Borroloola are half Malayan, with broad shoulders, high cheekbones, piercing eye and "cranky" temper, the intelligence, energy, arts, customs, of Asiatic islands. They were Australia's first ship-builders, of the Celebes dug-out canoe without the outrigger. They decorate spears and shields, plait and paint bamboo baskets in gay design of colour, fashion feather leis and necklaces of berries, bury the dead in Mohammedan wrappings of paperbark. Many of their words are Malayan—they are the only blacks of the continent who easily pronounce the letter "s" in their languages. The didjeridoo, their bamboo oboe, is the Bornean *saru-ling*, transposed to the double bass. But they don't like "men with salt-water in their eyes".

When the *manga-jarawa* came, the blacks went mad on arrack—orgies on the beaches, women shanghaied, boys kidnapped as slaves, men stabbed with a *kris*, or blown up by the old Dutch guns, or more subtly put out of the way with a blow-pipe and poisoned darts. The blacks craftily hid in the scrub when the next proa came along, and with a crew inshore for water it was "Up, boys, and at 'em!"

Macassar-time was massacre-time in the drama of the tropic wet, every Malay literally armed to the teeth with blow-pipe or dagger, the blacks howling like dingoes and crying like curlews at piccaninny daylight, creeping in on the beaches. Vengeance was theirs in a wreck.

Tingha Dian, who died in 1906 and had worked twenty years for white men, winning their affection and respect, came to Australia to avenge the death of his brother murdered at Cape Brogden with a boatload of Malays. Tingha told the story, with relish, that the serang of his proa tricked the enemy tribe out to a sand-spit to gather trepang for tobacco, then opened fire with his two-pounders. Those who made the water were sliced up the middle, "like fish".

Every year with the north-west monsoon came the *betripang prahoë*, *prau*, *proa* or *prahu*—call it what you will—in fleets of from thirty to sixty under a *nakhoda*, each ship with a dozen outrigger canoes, a queer little navy of over a thousand men . . . prow low on the water, high galleon stern, trident mast with two or three head-sails, all sailing together against the high-piled clouds of the wet, in sunrise or moonlight a rakish and beautiful sight.

No charts, they sailed by dead reckoning, a remarkable sleight of seamanship for such bundles of grass adrift on the Javan deeps, or in reefy seas of cyclone and nightly "cock-eye" squall. The hull of the ship was wood, so narrow that it was sometimes hacked from a single tree—the rest a clumsy superstructure of attap and bamboo. She was steered with two wooden rudders at the stern, her wooden anchors weighed down with stones, and her flexible mat sails rolled up and down like the "walloping window blind".

Sixty feet long, from ten to thirteen tons, each proa carried about sixty men, swarming and squatting all over the deck and the bamboo rig—betel-red mouth, blackened teeth, oiled bodies with a belt and a *kris*, wild hair with head-band or turban of red coolie-cloth, some tattooed, with caps of monkey-skin. Clean-shaven, they taught the blacks of the north to banish the "five o'clock shadow" with cuttle or razor-shell. They lived mainly on fish, rice, dugong, turtle, coconut meat and oil, herded like guinea-pigs to sleep in the rickety pigeon-cote aft with a couple of hogs and a crate of Malayan fowls—officers' mess for *nakhoda* and serang—cook's galley a fire burning in a big iron pan of sand.

To call on the *nakhoda* you boarded her at the prow and crawled on hands and knees into his cabin for'ard, a *mia* three feet high with room only to squat and lie down. He wore a sarong with a snicker-snee and ear-rings big as bangles—a cunning trader with kegs of rice-wine and katjes of tobacco, enslaving a human race for the stuff of dreams.

From King Sound right over to Burketown were regular ports of call, and our blacks still remember the Macassar names. Port Essington was their Liverpool, Limboo Moutiara, Port of Pearl-shell. Melville Island, for sinister reasons we can guess, was Amba, slave; Castlereagh Bay, Limboo Tordi; Malay Bay, Limboo Raja in honour of big chief Flinders, who paid the same compliment to Pobassoo in his chart. Cape Wilberforce was Oojoung Turu; Arnhem Bay, Limboo Katona; Groote Eylandt, Pulo Dylompo; Blue Mud

Bay, Churapee; Caledon Bay, Mungoola; Roper River, Wakea; Vanderlin Island, Denna Seeda; Sweers, Pulo Tiga.

Every island, cape and bay of the coast had its name, and every captain, till he made it too hot, had his regular run, each taking a bay to work it. A couple of proas anchored off, canoes paddled in with up to a hundred and thirty men to recruit local labour—boys, old men, lubras and children out on the mud-flats "dry-fishing" for trepang in low tides by day, or diving into shallows for the luminous shade of the sea-slug on sun-rippled sand, hauling bamboo seines by night with paperbark torches. Each proa for the season would bring in about thirty-five tons, for the tribe on shore to cut it, gut it, boil it, dry it, smoke it, boil it again with black mangrove, and smoke it in a primitive smoke-house over green mangrove smouldering for days.

Only grey trepang is found in Australian waters—the red is mandarins' delight—but boiling it with roots of black mangrove tanned it a more or less convincing crimson. The price was £10 a picul—one hundred and thirty-three and one-third English pounds—£160 a ton clear profit, plus perquisites of turtle-shell, pearl-shell and pearls, which the blacks collected all the year round and saved for a barter in red and white sarongs, sugar, salt fish, beads, a chicken or two and a coolamon of rice, luxuries for luxuries, never forgetting arrack and tobacco. Pearls and turtle-shell were sold in Samarinda, so to jewellers at Batavia and The Hague.

The trade was worth millions. By the time Australia woke up to the fact, in the eastward drift of the Dutch empire the proas sailed under the red-white-and-blue of the Nederlands above the red-and-yellow of the rajah, a matter for international agreement instead of a wholesale rout.

Even so, Alfred Searcy, first customs agent up there in the early eighties, in his sprightly adventure books *By Flood and Field* and *In Australian Tropics*, tells of many a gay sortie in the wake of the Wild Man of Borneo, a naked black at the masthead watching for proas hidden in mangrove creeks, an occasional rifle-shot across a smuggler's bows. Elegant in sarong and topee, his right hand brandishing a Colt revolver and his left gracefully waving a palm-leaf fan, Searcy exacted, from those he boarded, all that "England expects". E. O. Robinson, who followed him in the job, at his buffalo camp at Port Essington collected £1000 a year in Dutch gold from proas passing by, duties inward on arrack, square gin and tobacco, outward on trepang and pearl-shell. These two together never sighted a tenth of the fleets.

Only one man in Australia has first-hand knowledge of the Vikings from Macassar in their rococo corner of our past—Tuan Brown of Oojoung-tamba-nounou, out on the north coast from 1879 to 1942, "Mr Northern Territory Brown", the country's oldest living son. His memories, never written, are volumes in history, travel and romance. In civilization a shy and quiet man, on his rare visits to Sydney—two in a lifetime—before coming in to any bar of good cheer to meet friends from the north, he would put his head

CHARLES DARWIN.

round a door, bend a cautious eye on the barmaid, and ask in a fearful whisper,

"Any authors here?"

Alfred John Vowles Brown, son of V. V. Brown, one of Darwin's best early pioneers, and nephew of V. L. Solomon, its first Member of Parliament, as a boy with his father in a blackfellow's canoe, brought in the cash-box and ship's papers from the wreck of s.s. *Brisbane* in Bynoe Harbour in 1880. At the age of ten, four days out alone on his pony, he tracked up his young brother, lost in the bush. Educated at Whinham College, Adelaide, he stroked his school fours on the Torrens, and pranced as the Pirate King in *The Pirates of Penzance* with Adelaide Musical Society. He found it such a glorious thing that he was a pirate king thereafter, gypsying to windward in any old lugger and stroking aboriginal eights all along the trepang banks from Lacepede Islands to Torres Straits. After starving with Kimberley gold rush he spent his life at sea, finding whales and pearls beyond the Buccaneers with Harry Hunter, white king of Cape Lévèque. He landed at Melville Island in 1898, and had to run for his life, then crossed to Coburg Peninsula and the coast of Arnhem Land. For eight years at one time, 1913 to 1921, he was the only white man on a thousand miles of coast between Darwin and Borroloola. He knew the rapture of that lonely shore so well that, where Admiralty charts are dotted lines, he could sail it blindfold. To Darwin he was "the Ambidextrous Skipper", having piloted the little Roper ship, after a Christmas spree, flying before a gale through Cadell Straits, one hand on the tiller, the other juggling a pannikin, a siphon of soda and a bottle of Scotch.

A courtier of the coral reefs, face pleasantly round with neat grey moustaches, benign blue eyes, a gentle humorous bearing, his friends said Alf was

> the mildest-mannered man
> Who ever scuttled ship or cut a throat.

The captain of a cruiser caught up with him in the blue around Elcho Island in 1923, harpooning a dugong through sparkle of foam with twenty or thirty mermaids and mermen—he was quite embarrassed, officers and ratings in tropic white, Trader Brown in his sarong, and never a thread of cotton among his crew. As the Navy swung by on the crest of a wave the songs it sang were "This is the Life" and "I'd like to go to Brigham Young a Mormonite to be".

For fifty years A. J. V. Brown was the law on the north coast, with one trim camp at Irracole near Port Essington—three or four hundred blacks and a couple of hundred Malays at times about it—another at Oojoung-tambanounou in Bowen Straits, but most of the time he was out chasing "Macassars" and trading along coasts where the blacks were bad.

"I was the Commodore Tuan," he told me. "Respectful salaams on all sides when I came on the scene. My little bit of braid and a revolver kept them all in order. The proas were owned by Chinese and Dutch. Their last port of call in the Indies was Kissa, they travelled by compass till they sighted Melville Island, then along Coburg Peninsula to report to me before they began to fish.

"Most of the nakhodas and kapitans were princes in their own country. None of them spoke English. Except for a few villains they were good trustworthy men. They came ashore to my camp, or aboard my lugger, for their 'papers', dressed in red turbans interlaced with silver, sleeveless white jacket, gold buttons, a necklace of red agates, gold rings in their ears, short blue pants and bare feet. It was a solemn official powwow, me in an old Navy coat and white trousers, topped up with Her Majesty's cap. They carried their manifestoes in cylinders of bamboo, written in Dutch—neither they nor I could understand them, but they all paid their customs dues without a word of protest, paid in Dutch gold till our Government demanded English sovereigns.

"Some came to the coast for many years and were my good friends—Duntoona, Reimba, Riola and Bapa Paloe, a regal man. The old Arnhem Land blacks can tell you about them, and their sons are about still. Now and again they brought me down a case of Dutch lager with compliments from the owners, for a toast on the sand to our peacefully allied nations.

"They were all Mohammedans, but I never saw them pray to Allah Before they started fishing, they put over the side a little meal of sugar and rice, bamboo shoots, sauces and garlic to propitiate the sea-gods of the Celebes. The Port Essington blacks looked for them and liked them, but sometimes there was a row, and round the coast, from King River to Caledon Bay nothing but wars and bloodshed. The Macassars disappeared by the boatload. In hurricane-time I've known eleven wrecks in one blow. I used to pick up the survivors.

"So long as the Chinese will eat trepang you can sell it. I myself handled £30,000 worth in a few years. The Malays have taken millions of pounds' worth away. They knew all the banks for the best quality fish, and I've seen thirty-five men bring in thirty-five tons. A white man's lugger, in later years, would get about ten tons for the season, and with freights, tariffs, agents to pay, he wouldn't make more than £2 a ton, not enough for a year's flour and tea. He'd be lucky to get sixty or eighty pounds of saleable turtle-shell where the Macassars went back with three thousand pounds of the best hawk's-bill at £1 a pound. They never showed me their pearls, but they got a good few, and tons of pearl-shell—gold-lip, silver-lip, black-lip—those river estuaries of the north, with the silt and potash of centuries, are full of black pearls. Trocas is always a winner, and down in the Gulf they loaded piles of trocas—it's found in crevices of the reef, they dive and swim in—but though I showed samples to all my blacks, they said there was none on the north coast, and they know everything.

"No policeman ever came round our way, and a white man never had any trouble till the missionaries came, then there was a court case a week. Funny how Christianity sets everybody fighting. The blacks used to love the trepang work—it's their natural life out on the reefs, they were always laughing and singing—but the missionaries collected them up and used to take them to Darwin, the bad boys to trial and jail and the good boys for a treat. After that they were looking for any excuse to get to Darwin, even if it was only murder."

The Macassar-men brought ravage of disease to the lithe dark people of the north coast—venereal disease, leprosy, yaws and smallpox, the dreaded *meeha-meeha*. In sweeping epidemics even the camp dogs died, till the tribes found the juice of a scrub creeper to cure the fatal sores.

Two curious racial relics still survive the old Macassar days—*karda-wogga*, exact pattern of a *kris* in stone found all over the Territory, but used only in mock duels of *makarrata* and corroboree, "playing fight". The other is "blackfella Sunday", an epilepsy half "gammon" that afflicts a boy with sulking, skulking, dancing and yelling fits, twitching and tearing his hair, a sort of devil possession that is terror to the camp for days and nights—in homicidal mania he threatens his friends and relations with axe and spear. It seldom goes as far as a killing, and is obviously Malay heredity running amuck.

Every three or four years Trader Brown sailed in across Van Diemen's Gulf to Darwin with a cargo of trepang, turtle-shell, a few worth-while pearls, and a thousand hides of buffalo or Sourabaya cattle, "to brush up on general knowledge and have a *wongi* with old friends". Then away in his lugger *Essington*, ship's tanks full of tobacco, flour, sugar, red handkerchiefs, scouts' knives, sweets and cheap beads, he would be out through the Vernons to blue days at sea, living on oysters, quail, fish, crab, goose, duck, turkey, pigeon, wild beef, cabbage-palm and yams . . . turtle eggs on damper-toast for breakfast, curried crayfish and dugong steak for supper—"Number One tucker all the year round, free". He might happen to call that year on a buffalo-hunter camped on one of the rivers, or hail a beachcomber at sea. Sometimes closer settlement set in, and there might be four white men, a couple of hundred miles apart, along a thousand miles.

A. J. V. Brown called me his "Legacy Lady". In my first journey round the Gulf, although we had never met—it would have taken that thousand miles in a native canoe to find him—I wrote a story of his remarkable life, a *bon viveur* beyond civilization, "seventy and half-blind, a man who is history". It was brought to the notice of a well-to-do aunt, aged ninety. Alfred had been her favourite nephew sixty years before. Stirred to misguided pity, she made an annuity payable at a bank in Darwin, provided he came in once a year to get it, and promised a place in her will when her wandering boy came home.

At last, blinded by the glory, he arrived in Sydney in 1938, for a surgical operation to remove cataracts from both eyes. In "strange country" of a crowded grey city, bewildered by its faces and voices, threading its devious ways with his cabbage-palm walking-stick, and at the Ophthalmic Hospital, staring into the dark, he longed for his own warm sparkling world, and the black friends who had cared for him, fed him, in his blindness. One eye in service, he could wait no longer. With four pairs of horn-rimmed glasses he was off on the Singapore ship and soon back at Port Essington, "looking", as he wrote to me, "for a few seed-pearls to put under the pot". At the outbreak of the Japanese war he was ordered to proceed to Cape Don—which he did in a blackfellow's canoe—to be carried by Bathurst Island mission lugger to Darwin, and evacuated to Adelaide with the other old hands.

His aunt, now rising ninety-four, lived to welcome him home and died next day, leaving him £2000. Four winters in the south, muffled in an overcoat, riding in taxis, correct, and cold, and lonely. When I last met Trader Brown he was tacking across King William Street, outward bound for a park to shoot the sun and set a course for Oojoung-tamba-nounou.

But he wouldn't go down to Arnhem Land. Never again, he told me. He said the missionaries were too bad.

Chapter IV

Phantoms of Failure

One sunny south-easter day in 1935, Mounted Constable Pryor of the Northern Territory police, off duty in khaki shorts and shady felt hat, went digging in the sands of Melville Island near Point Barlow with a mission black-boy and his tracker. They unearthed, in three pieces, a heavy old goblet of cut glass grained and weathered in the passing of a hundred and ten years.

Encouraged by his find, the trooper went on digging. He carried home a good little swag of the forgotten first chapter of the Territory's past—moulded buttons of a redcoat's tunic, fragments of a Spode china dinner set, a George III shilling and a corroded cannon-ball. He set free a chain-gang of unhappy ghosts, soldiers and bluejackets, men dragging their feet in irons, women and children sallow under their sunbonnets . . . shadows of those shadowless sands.

The relics, only a few feet under, might have been found long ago, but until the first years of this century, when a buffalo-hunter, Joel Cooper, and a priest from Alsace-Lorraine, Father Gsell, each in his own way, made friends of the Mala-ola men with their seventeen-barb spears, Melville Island was no place for digging.

As in that old glass, darkly, what sea-pictures of other years!

Australia's largest island, fifty miles by fifty, blocked to the entrance of Van Diemen's Gulf about forty miles over from Darwin, Melville is our San Salvador, our earliest sea-legend. A hundred years before *Little Dove* turned back at Cape Keerweer, before the Spaniard Torres drifted past Cape York, del Cano, they say, hurrying homeward with ships of the dead Magellan, coasted Melville Island.

Frobisher, with his quill, wrote of Terra Australis in 1578:

"... a great firme Londe, in many places a Fruitfull Soyle and touch'd on the north edge thereof by the Travaile of the Portingales and Spaniards in their Voyages to the East and West Indies . . . in some places reaches into the Sea with great promontories, even unto Tropike Capricornus."

Old Darwin had relics and rumours of Portuguese galleons, guns, coins, buried in Coburg Peninsula sands. I have seen Mala-ola and Wongo-ak corroborees of Melville and Bathurst Islands that, in their amazing make-up of whitened wigs, gigantic feather and fibre ruffs, neck-pendants of powdered fur, hands painted as frilled gloves and decoratively pock-marked faces, in their exaggerated posturing and prancing with rapier-sticks, their processions behind crude crosses, commemorate the *conquistador* priests and duelling grandees of castled galleons sailing a nameless sea.

When melancholy Charles I is carpeted to the throne of England, the Dutch yachts *Pera* and *Arnhem*, under Jan van Carstensz, are cruising Arnhem Land. *Klyn*, *Wesel* and *Amsterdam* name a few smokes as they pass Melville Island. Tasman, in 1644, sails between Groote Eylandt and Blue Mud Bay, charts the north-west point of Melville as Cape van Diemen, thinking it part of the main. In 1700, Martin van Delft corrects him, explores Van Diemen's Gulf. Two hundred years of oblivion go by.

When this Commonwealth of ours is two jails—one at Sydney, one at Hobart Town, fearful to the folk of England—Matthew Flinders, fretting in his whitewashed cell of the old Garden Prison in Mauritius, is first to vision a colony in Capricornia, that "untravelled world" of north and north-west Australia where he longs to finish his survey, perhaps to found a port of the vanished Inland Sea, a "naval station and place to take in spices for China". He wonders if he might be Governor there.

In their small world of the Navy, a little boy in a sailor suit he met at Norfolk Island when he himself was little more than a boy—Phillip Parker

King—whom he meets again in a London drawing-room as the cadet son of a New South Wales Governor towards the end of his own brief life, is chosen by the Admiralty three years after his death to fill in his map of Australia. Once again the Frenchmen are on the coasts—Louis de Freycinet, Baudin's cartographer, sailing the west, Baudin's old track, Dampier's track, but only to reassure France that it is not worth owning.

"*Quel horreur! Quel stérilité!*" de Freycinet cries of those yellow sands that now pasture millions of sheep.

The sealed orders of Phillip Parker King we do not know. From 1817 onward, in cutter *Mermaid*, brig *Bathurst*, any old ship he can find, he hovers between Hobart and Koepang, Mauritius and New Zealand, darting in and out to the Australian coast as a moth to a candle in a miracle of quick explorations. Lieutenant J. S. Roe is his surveyor, Allan Cunningham his botanist. An old friend of ours in the fo'c'sle is Bongaree of Broken Bay, ambassador to the natives on *Investigator* with Flinders, now making overtures to the dark people for another young master. Three times round Australia before 1820, Bongaree on the north coast is not so well received, in his old age less a diplomat than a marathon runner.

Mermaid romps in high tides of King Sound, where Dampier's pirate *Cygnet* drifted in 1688. She is first sail down through the mauve-figured hills of Cambridge Gulf, bats in their silent millions a dark screen over the stars as her anchor-chain rattles away. The blacks set fire to Lacrosse Island till it glows as a coal, reddening the waters to frighten the white invader. King climbs View Hill to see forbidding ranges, "bastions and ramparts" of a land "wild and eerie" that he names for the Earl of Kimberley, ranges to the memory of King Leopold of Belgium. The Bastion and Mount Albany now look down on Wyndham.

Threading the flotillas of Macassar-men faint as pencil-sketches all along the Arafura wash of blue, in another year of his flying surveys he writes many aristocratic names in the map, a river for the Prince Regent and one for Lord Liverpool, nearly a thousand miles of twisted coast between them; for my lords of the Admiralty, Melville and Bathurst, two big islands split by Lord Apsley's strait, which is forty-five miles long narrowing to half a mile wide of channels and mud. For his friend Admiral Sir William Essington he names the grandest harbour in the north, a V-shaped inlet twenty miles deep by seven miles across, "to shelter a navy", commanding the sea-track to those Isles of Spice, the Moluccas, and to New Guinea. He is as proud of Port Essington as Captain Phillip of Port Jackson.

To King in Koepang comes a mysterious letter written in Arabic translating to Malay, lest it should be intercepted by a "foe". It is from Singapore, from Tom Stamford Raffles. For news of the new harbour in New Holland, John Company is awake. Can he sell Manchester and Birmingham—turkey twill, gay chintz for sarongs, hatchets, razor-blades, beads, ear-rings—to the naked-wading Macassar-men for their Chinese trepang, their scavenging of turtle-shell and pearls, and their Dutch dollars?

A trader drifts by in the old schooner *Stedcomb*, rum-running the Arafura to Sydney, a privateer named William Barnes. His talk in taverns of Deptford takes him to Whitehall. To Raffles and to the rag-tag Barnes my Lord Bathurst lends an attentive ear. There will be a settlement in the north of Australia to confound His Majesty's enemies and to fill the coffers of Company.

Captain J. J. Gordon Bremer is hurried across the world in H.M.S *Tamar* to plant a flag—at Port Essington perhaps, or at Liverpool River, or he may move the borders of Cook's New South Wales as far west as he likes. There is room, and to spare, on the sandy shores of New Holland.

Tamar swings south of the continent to Sydney for freight of souls and soldiers to build the fort around a flag of the north. Governor Brisbane shuffles his pack to find them, but there are lawyers in Sydney who warn them they need not go—their legal prison is New South Wales and Bremer travels beyond it. In August gales he sails out of Port Jackson with a fair little roll-call of volunteers, not of nation-builders but of dismal exiles plotting to escape, looking for the road to China.

Three ships travel in convoy, H.M.S. *Tamar*, *Countess of Harcourt*, a lumbering transport homeward bound by Timor—they load her with the lags, the pigs and sheep—also "His Majesty's Tinder-box", Flinders's old friend, the scapegrace *Lady Nelson*, in her last stages of senile decay to mother yet another mournful colony, then to be garrotted by black pirates in a back lane of the Seven Seas up in the East Indies.

Destination unknown, these three ships carry to settlement Captain Manners Barlow and fifty-five rank and file, forty-five convicts, fourteen marines, six ticket-of-leave women and three free men. A quick and lucky journey through Torres Straits—a great seaman is Bremer—they make Port Essington in twenty-seven days, and enter the new harbour on 20th September 1824, with most of the nation-builders in irons. They have shown too strong a tendency to light out and form a settlement of their own on the way.

Limboo Moutiara, Port of Pearl-shell, lives up to expectations—coloured cliffs and glittering bays, splendid tamarinds planted by Malays at the head of the inner bay promising fertility—but four boats in two days can find no fresh water. Over the coast Bremer waves the flag for Britain, fires a *feu de joie* that puzzles the Bijenelumbo people out hunting turtle in canoes, then plants his title deeds in a bottle at Point Record and sails for Melville Island, where he anchors in Apsley Strait on 2nd October. The three ships furl sail near a running stream. *Tamar*, with her twelve-pounders and long eighteens, will stay till the settlers are safe among the natives. King has written that they are not to be trusted—in his word, "ferocious".

Beach and bush are still as a picture . . . no sign of the Mala-ola men with the leaf of the sago-palm burnt in their breasts.

His Majesty's men tramp the torrid shore, tight-buttoned scarlet coats, stiff leather stocks, martinet, musket and shako. Behind plod the Royal Marines, blue jackets and cross-bands, bell-bottomed white trousers, pigtails and little straw hats. After them the chain-gang. A convict with a ball at heel is felling a tree for a flagstaff. He comes loping in fright to tell that his axe is gone. He saw no one. The axe was there!

Soldiers march into the bush and find only a grave—the painted pookaminny post, a painted basket of fan-palm upon it and the dead man's painted spear . . . no trace of the living but a pile of burnt cycas nuts and mussel-shells, and the sheets of paperbark where these sylvan creatures sleep.

Axes and sickles vanish every day as a log fort rises, seventy-five yards square, built of the trunks of trees, with a moat ten feet deep and ten feet wide. Within is a well in one corner, three wooden houses for the gentlemen, a bough shed barracks for soldiers with hammocks under the trees, thirteen grass huts for settlers and seven for Royal Marines. The convicts are building a jetty sixty-four feet long, of coral rocks and rough timber. Beyond, the guardian ships are mirrored in melted silver.

On 21st October Bremer hoists colours. His little fort he names for Sir Philip Dundas, England's First Lord of the Admiralty, and by the power of a spoken word he moves the border of New South Wales six degrees west, from the 135th meridian to the meridian of 120 degrees east.

A six-pounder on *Tamar's* quarter-deck barks a royal salute to the birth of the third Australian State. The woebegone little crowd moves in to the stockade.

Two thousand miles from Sydney through cannibal isles and reefs, twelve thousand miles from home, Fort Dundas watches all day, listens all night. Silhouette on the lightnings of the coming wet, the sentry stands rigid, glint of blue steel the musket on his shoulder, eyes staring under the wide shako. He hears a sound of paddles in the strait.

Bremer and Barlow go exploring in the whaleboat. On Bathurst Island they find a little river, and there come face to face with the Mala-ola men. Eighteen or twenty together, a queer design on the daylight, they stand in the woodland unmoving, all of them six feet high, holding the ten-foot spears with Egyptian markings, five feet of sharpened barbs. Shock-headed, muscular, smoky black eyes and nose-bones a foot long, here are warriors and sailors more warlike, more active than any in Australia—two or three thousand on the two islands, crossing the strait in their canoes, one tribe.

Bremer knows that white and black must be friends if white is to survive. He and Barlow pass guns to the back of the line and make friendly gestures. The native leaders pass back their spears. Bremer offers them Manchester—coloured handkerchiefs and beads on the blade of an oar. They want Birmingham—iron. They make the motion of chopping. When axes are shown they come forward and smile. An axe and a sickle are stolen by two running away. When Bremer demands the return of the axe, they all turn for the bush and are gone. He names the stream Intercourse River, and next day comes back.

The blacks are there, with them a "light-coloured young man" whom they thrust forward, as to his own people. Of what shipwreck is the unknown's strange story?—but "he speaks as one of the rest" and Bremer shows no interest. He may be a half-caste or a Malay. As a matter of principle, Bremer wants the stolen axe. The blacks give back the sickle. A musket is raised to shoot a bird in a tree, but they fail to take the meaning. They bring down a bird with a waddy neatly thrown. Another axe is snatched away.

Bremer is angry, and threatens in signs. As the soldiers march with fixed bayonets, the blacks rush for their spears. As the soldiers fire, they "run for the woods with the speed of deer". The first meeting with white and black in the Northern Territory has not been a success. Guns from *Tamar's* quarter-deck are mounted above the fort in the gloomy mangroves. From now on it will be war.

Alarms, night and day. A hundred savages cross from Bathurst Island—"we chased them in the whale-boat and took their best canoe". An army of sixty blacks attacks a party cutting rushes . . . forty surround the jolly-boat at the landing and try to fire the hut. A midshipman and a corporal of marines run for their lives through showers of spears—a ball from the fort and the flint-locks barking.

"I am inclined to think that more than one suffered," Bremer writes, with the discretion of the white man ever since in chronicle of such matters. But the blacks will play a waiting game. What work can there be in the bush where the bush is alive with eyes watching, hands snatching, and what chance have those old Brown Bess flint-locks of ramrod and rag, powder and pan against silent, swiftly flying spears?

Everything flourishes—for a time. Lieutenant John Septimus Roe is making survey of "forests inexhaustible", under armed escort. Sergeant Robert Charteris has a fine garden of corn, oranges, limes, bananas, sugar-cane, rice near the ponds, under armed guard. The convicts are beasts of burden, dragging the plough, dragging great logs for two miles through swamps full of mosquitoes, under armed warders. The well is dry, and women go down to the little river to fill ewers and water-casks, an armed sentry marching fore and aft.

Tamar and *Countess of Harcourt* pass on. A cyclone sweeps away the wharf, drowns the gardens, flattens the huts. The sixteen horned cattle and twenty-three sheep from Port Jackson are dead from spears and rank weed, while the four dozen pigs run wild over the island—these snouted beasts of cloven hoof the natives of the north will never eat. The settlement lives on fish and plantains, dried pork and pease.

Human strength in these breathless jungles can no longer bear inhuman burdens. Captain Manners Barlow sends *Lady Nelson* to Timor for maize, pigs, rice, poultry, anything to eat, and for thirty water-buffalo, trained to the yoke, to mow a Melville Island meadow. *Lady Nelson* will be mourned and forgotten for fourteen years, and then her story told of the crew killed and eaten in cannibal islands. *Stedcomb*, following on the same errand but without her master, the crafty Barnes, shares the same fate, one child left living to record the massacre when he is a man.

An occasional passing transport anchors outside the reef, her last port of call Mauritius, her next one Sydney, bringing to the exiles once in a year the news from England and "a feast of flour, pickles and dried meat". Slaver-schooners to the islands sell a few pigs, fowls, onions, for Spanish dollars and Dutch guilders, but they are far between. At last Captain Manners Barlow manages to buy from a Monsieur Béchade, a French trader in Timor, a dozen working buffalo, for a hundred and twenty-five dollars each, of which only three are living, on King's schooner *Isabella*, when they land. Monsieur Béchade contracts to deliver three hundred buffaloes a year, but sends, in all, fourteen—that will crash the stockades to freedom and father the first great herds of North Australia.

Soon Barlow has ninety acres cleared and fifty planted, but the rascal Barnes takes an estate on the beach, tries to grow wheat, pays the settlers in rum, and there is no more labour. Mischief and misery—convicts hiding in the mangroves, building boats to sail away . . . every day shots and volleys from the fort.

The blacks! The blacks! They have stolen the hand-cart—a boat—the cross-cut saw! Fires rage all over the island, burning out game in the dry season, but to the desperate settlers with no ship a threat of doom. They parade each Sabbath morning along an earth-walled roadway to their little paperbark church where Captain Barlow feelingly prays to God for another week of their miserable lives. They smell blacks in the night-time and hear that strident singing through all the island hills. Curlews cry about the little tent hospital where women groan in childbirth and where soon five soldiers and a convict lie dead of fever, two soldiers and three convicts of blackfellow spears. Nobody sleeps.

First Lord Dundas and Colonial Secretary Barrow, in their gilded four-posters with lackeys to draw the velvet curtains on their exalted days, read the reports now two years old and congratulate themselves that "there never was so promising a spot". The settlement will continue, but the garrison will be relieved. In 1827 H.M.S. *Slavery* anchors outside the reef, Captain Manners Barlow and his redcoats sail off with a sigh of relief, and from white-anted huts in the walled fort the exiles face a new armed guard. Major Campbell is commandant now, a fiery Scot with an acid wit.

A significant fact has engaged their lordships' attention. In three years never a Malay proa has come near the narrow Apsley Strait though they are scattered about the mainland in thousands. John Company is restive for those Dutch guilders, and pearls, and yellow tortoiseshell. The mountain must go to Mahomet—there will be another trading station in the north.

With the trade-wind again come three ships from the east, under Captain James Stirling in H.M.S. *Success*. They circle Croker Island and make over to Raffles Bay, a Malay village of a hundred proas and over a thousand men, canoes busy in the bay, smoke-houses along the shore like the factory-smokes of a city—here, then, the strand to build the East India Company store.

On a wooded ridge above the mangroves Stirling sets his company ashore —Captain Collet Barker with thirty rank and file of His Majesty's famous 39th, the Buffs; fourteen marines, twenty-two convicts, two women, five children, thirteen sailors and a lieutenant of the Navy on half pay—a band as sorry and as valiant as the first. On 18th June 1827, twelfth anniversary of Waterloo, Stirling declares Fort Wellington with fanfare, colours and guns. He reports that the natives are not numerous, the climate not unhealthy, the soil not infertile, the country not disagreeable—negatives all.

Too soon he sails away, to his already-beloved Swan River, where he will win the honours of empire and the praise of generations, founding the largest State of Australia—nearly a million square miles—kindly land of boundless hope and happy people, the gold-radiant West.

In command of the mangroves he leaves Collet Barker, friend and fellow officer of Captain Charles Sturt, with the same wisdom and understanding of men, the same bright zest for exploration. A little while and Barker, too, is away from the forlorn hope of the north, but only to end his young days by a blackfellow's spear in swimming Sturt's splendid new river, surveying the Murray mouth.

Spices for China! Raffles Bay believes it has found cloves growing in the bush, and the royal nutmeg of Holland—they prove to be only gumnuts. The store does a roaring trade with the Malays in a line of cheap razors for their fighting game-cocks, but the proas fade away with the south-easter. Fort Wellington frets and sweats under a bully, Captain Smyth—flimsy huts on that blazing ironstone ridge, a well of bad water breeding fever . . . squalor, sandflies, starvation . . . guns barking in constant fear and conflict with the blacks.

On a bright moonlight night the whaleboat is stolen from near the commandant's tent, to be found in the mangroves stripped of iron. Why do these savages need iron?—for the tips of their murderous flying spears. They shall pay for it with slug bullets in the lungs. Six convicts are freed to go hunting with the soldiers, and Smyth offers £5 for a nigger, alive or dead.

Beach and bush are a horror of the dying. One tribe they surround while they are singing corroboree and drive them into the sea. Women and children are butchered with bayonets—a poor victory for His Majesty's 39th. A mother is slashed to her death as she stands screaming in the waves with one baby in her arms and another clinging to her knees.

This punitive raid, in time, is dealt with in Sydney, condemned by Governor Darling as "an un-officered expedition of private soldiers and convicts undertaken against the natives upon a promise of pecuniary reward".

Governor Darling regrets that atrocities were committed on women and children, but the natives had brought the trouble on themselves.

Over comes the wet. Forty-nine out of seventy-five are sick in the flooded camp. From jails and barracks of New South Wales to the "lion's breath" of tropic heat, with little to eat, they are black and swollen with scurvy, covered with ulcers, huddled round fires in their stockade, not daring to move beyond it for in their weakness they suffer from night-blindness. The lime-juice kegs are long empty—no hope, through the gales, of a ship. There are many graves.

Surgeon Wood lies listless, in debility from fever, listening to the firing from the fort. A man is brought to him with a spearhead embedded in his back. Too weak to rise, the doctor prizes out the barb, drenches the wound with salt to stop the bleeding, then lies back. England is far away . . . too far. In the rancid yellow sun of morning he asks for his razor, to shave. They snatch it from him as he madly gashes his throat. But it is all equal. In the rancid yellow sun of evening he lies dead, his surgical pins, sharp and deliberate, driven into his heart. The camp of death is left without a doctor.

Over on Melville Island, Major Campbell is crying to be let go, if he should live to go. His men are hopping in wooden clogs, no leather. No food. No medicine. No vinegar for their scurvy. The huts are sodden, the fort falling, the garden a swamp. The hospital tent is full of "putrid diseases" —no wine, no rum, to drive them decently insane. With faded ink on mildewed paper he writes barbed and bitter letters to my lords in London—letters months old before they can be posted with some Portuguese slaver to take a chance round the world, *de profundis* with a daring satire—"my exalted situation . . . marking a site for a metropolis . . . I pray you to release me from this vile island".

Comes Surgeon Gold to call on Major Campbell—a vanity man, a fop in ringlets, knee-breeches, and ruffles once white, his black satins rusted with the salt of his sweat, prattling French and Latin like a ninny—a man whom his soul loathes, as he loathes all these fools and felons penned up with him in hell. Surgeon Gold, whining for cinchona bark, for lime-juice, castor oil, physic, potions, cornflour, when he knows there is nothing but a little sour pork and mouldy pease.

For once the creature has reason for his blabbing. The young wife of Lieutenant Hicks is dead, a gentle lady, an English rose. In her white tent she lies, and the poor little settlement is sadder for her silence. On the morrow all march to her burial, all that can limp along, out from the fort under armed guard. A new grave in the bush. It is a day of grieving . . . and horror.

In the storm sunset a man comes running, a man named Thomas Swan. He saw the blacks. He heard screams. Surgeon Gold is murdered, and the storekeeper, Green. Swan found the bodies, quite dead but quivering warm, the doctor in white shirt with his knees drawn up, his face livid in agony, a spear through the head. a spear through the groin, thirty-one barbed and pointed spears—Green with three in the throat, seventeen mortal wounds and his head smashed in with a waddy. They went for a walk together in the sunset, and they were not armed.

That night the Mala-ola set fire to the islands. The settlers watch from the fort where, bathing their sores, they will be prisoners now till the end.

Gold left a dandy's wardrobe, a library of richly bound books, mostly of poetry, a writing desk of rare woods inlaid, a jewel-case with rich filigree in antique design of coral, sapphires and amethyst, and perfumed love-letters from a pretty mistress in Sydney . . . left them in a rain-rotten shack and is buried by an alien sea.

Such are the figures we see in that old glass, looking backward now a hundred and twenty years.

Dispatches from my lords of the Admiralty, months old, received in March and August 1829, mercifully order the abandonment of the two settlements in the north of Australia. From Fort Dundas and Fort Wellington the condemned are set free. Their graves and their little forts of fear and hunger are washed away in a few years. Their travail for empire has never yet been honoured by a single memorial stone.

England has now relaxed to peace from a century of war. Fife and drum are pageantry, the Navy no longer a shambles but an argosy for colonization and commerce. Wilberforce, Shelley and Tom Paine have won nearer to the rights of man, and the proper study of mankind is soon to become a science.

A ten-gun brig sets out on a voyage round the world, H.M.S. *Beagle* under Captain Fitzroy. Her mission is neither flag-planting nor buying and selling, but quest of the knowledge that is power.

First true ship of science since the *Investigator* of Flinders, she carries a company of intellectual, altruistic, humorous, even poetic young men, product of the schools of peace in England's literary heyday. Among them are Lieutenant John Lort Stokes and Midshipman Owen Stanley. Benjamin Bynoe is her surgeon, her artist Conrad Martens. The naturalist is a Cambridge graduate not quite twenty-three years old, grandson Charles of Dr Erasmus Darwin, son of a doctor, educated for the Church, but by invitation sharing Captain Fitzroy's cabin and cramming it with biological notes and specimens for a life's work to change the course of civilization.

The ship of science spends four patient years on the coasts of South America, a story of high courage, adventure and infinite interest told by Charles Darwin in a world classic popularly known as *The Voyage of H.M.S. Beagle*. Via the Galapagos Islands, Tahiti and New Zealand, she sails into Sydney Harbour in a summer dawn of 1836.

Conrad Martens, in his delicate colours, keeps for us precious memories of that radiant young Sydney, of warehouses, white-winged ships, "beautiful villas" and the "woods, bright and shadowless". Darwin, with a man and two horses, rides over the Blue Mountains to Bathurst, noting a "close resemblance to the English country-side, perhaps the ale-houses here more numerous". He passes chain-gangs of white men under armed warders, crosses the Nepean River by ferry, and meets a party of "black aborigines" who, for a shilling, throw spears to amuse him, ". . . their countenances good-humoured and pleasant . . . far from being such utterly degraded beings as they are usually represented. In their own arts they are admirable . . . their number rapidly decreasing." He sees a platypus and a kangaroo rat. He takes lunch at a lone Weatherboard Inn where now is Wentworth Falls, looks down from Echo Point and Govett's Leap to "immense gulfs" of valleys with broken headlands "as a bold sea-coast", filled with thin blue haze, "extremely magnificent". He camps for a night at Wallerawang when it is a convict farm of forty men, no women, shares the benediction of bright Australian sundown, rides to Bathurst village through a dust-storm and back through a bush-fire to confer with Major Mitchell and Captain King.

For a convict race he can find no purgatory in Australia:

> As a place of punishment, the object is scarcely gained; as a real system of reform it has failed, as perhaps would any other plan . . . but as a means of making men outwardly honest—of converting vagabonds, most useless in one hemisphere, into active citizens of another, and thus giving birth to a new and splendid country—a grand centre of civilization—it has succeeded to a degree perhaps unparallelled in history.

H.M.S. *Beagle* sails for Hobart, to spend ten days in geology and geography in that glorious harbour, then is away westward to King George Sound, where a white cockatoo "corrobery" and an emu dance of the Bibbulmun are highlights of a "dull and uninteresting time" under gloomy winter skies: "Farewell, Australia! You are a rising child, and doubtless some day you will reign as a great princess in the South; but you are too great and ambitious for affection, yet not great enough for respect. I leave your shores without sorrow or regret."

Mauritius, Ascension, Brazil, the Azores, and so to Falmouth on 2nd October, where Darwin leaves the *Beagle*, "having lived on board the good little ship for nearly five years".

She had carried from England a grave young student, uncertain of his path in life. Now he is naturalist, botanist, biologist, "a geologist who has lived his ten thousand years". A great adventure is over, a greater to come—the adventure of thought. He never leaves England again, but marries his cousin, Emma Wedgwood, and settles at Down, Bromley, Kent, to "do his barnacles" in forty years of profound research *On the Origin of Species by Means of Natural Selection, or the Preservation of Favoured Races in the Struggle for Life*, the clearest ray of revelation from a human mind to penetrate the Divine design of creation, but in the myopic theology and stumbling science of the day a blinding light, a percussion terrible as the atom bomb with its radio-active showers of truth, its rolling and vitriolic clouds of contention. Silent, upon his peak in Darien, Charles Darwin, throughout life, for that vision of the infinite gives grateful thanks to H.M.S. *Beagle*.

The "good little ship" comes back to Australia, across the world from Bahia to sandy Fremantle when "you could run it through an hour-glass in a day", then playing hare-and-hounds through hazy archipelagos of the north-west, looking in vain for a gulf to an inland sea. Three hundred miles of new coast she makes her own, discovers the Fitzroy River and Yampi Sound with its red-glowing isles of pure iron, calls to Koepang, returns to the coast at Beagle Bay, and so, with a fund of knowledge, round by the south to Sydney. Her commander now is J. C. Wickham, with Lieutenant J. B. Emery, still with Lieutenant John Lort Stokes, L. R. Fitzmaurice mate and surveyor.

Skirl of a bagpipe along the Arafura—the piper of Port Essington.

The young Victoria is on the throne of England, her very name an inspiration, a reasonably pretty girl kindling in every manly breast the highest ideals of empire. Six Australian States are born, though two not yet christened, calling thousands of free settlers. New South Wales in wide pastures is breeding Macarthur's merino sheep. Stephenson's *Rocket* has found a use for its Coal River coal. Transports, traders, whalers, come down through Torres Straits—six thousand miles sailing from India with never a landfall—in a hit or miss navigation that piles too many up on the reefs. In rumour of a French expedition sailing from Toulon, my lords remember Port Essington, where the Malays have gathered in numbers, and again commission Gordon Bremer to conjure up a settlement there, for defence, trade, and as haven for shipwrecked men.

Bremer dutifully leaves Plymouth, post-haste across the world, standing in to the bright harbour on 27th October 1838, in H.M.S. *Alligator*—Alligator Rivers had been named by Phillip Parker King in 1818. Trader and colony ship is H.M.S. *Britomart*, under young Owen Stanley from *Beagle*. For settlement they bring Captain John McArthur, a subaltern, forty Royal Marines, a linguist, Mrs McArthur and a few brave garrison wives, a regimental piper. Marching ashore with his kilts a-swing to the lilt of "Bonnie Dundee", a piper of Hamelin he is to the musical Bijenelumbo people with their own symphony orchestra playing concerto for didjeridoo under the tamarind-trees.

Nose-bones, necklaces, bangles of bamboo, a wide smile with a tooth knocked out, a merry mob are the Port Essington blacks, portly on fish and turtle, constantly trading with the Malays and not afraid of strangers. One bright boy, Neinmal, appoints himself aide-de-camp to Captain Owen Stanley—so manly, intelligent and helpful they make him one of the gentlemen and call him Jack White. The tribes fluently speak Malay, bring canoe-loads of fish and oysters, show the Macassar wells of laced bamboo in the sand,

and promise, in the coming wet, a stream running deep at the head of the bay.

On the crest of a white cliff—Adam Head—Bremer and Stanley run up stockade and huts, at the foot of it a little stone pier. On 13th December, with march of marines to fife and drum and a delighted crowd of the dusky disinherited, they christen it Victoria, first namesake in Australia of the queen.

Here Australian history repeats itself with startling coincidence, turning back to page 2 over sixty-eight years.

The blacks come running to tell of two big white proas in Raffles Bay—of white men, not Malays—but speaking another language. The French? A party under Lieutenant D. B. Stewart is hurried overland, thirty miles through the bush.

There are the ships with the tricolour flying—sure enough the French, even as Captain Phillip, two days in to Port Jackson, hailed the two ships of Lapérouse. These are *Zelée* and *Astrolabe*, under Dumont d'Urville, rounding Australia, looking for Lapérouse. Once again, Britain is just in time to be a gracious host. *Zelée* and *Astrolabe* are welcomed in to Victoria, and on a wild and lonely shore men feared as enemies for generations prove to be genial and knowledgeable friends. d'Urville sails to death and oblivion even as Lapérouse.

Macassar-men come in to Knocker Bay with the north-west monsoon, campongs and smoke-houses all along the beach under the British flag. *Britomart* travels to Timor, begging through the islands for buffaloes, livestock, fowls and rice, getting precious little. Bremer sails for Sydney to interest free settlers with a prospectus that is a historical gem:

> NOTICE IS HEREBY GIVEN that persons of respectability may obtain town allotments within a mile of the pier for a period of not exceeding seven years and suburban areas of eight acres within five miles—flourishing gardens of plantains, tamarinds, oranges, lemons, maize, bread-fruit, mangosteens—tracts of meadow-land for sugar-cane from Rio, cotton and rice . . . gardens now advancing to perfection.

A few ticket-of-leave men take a chance to escape, the Duke of Newcastle invests a tidy sum, one or two financiers blow another little South Sea Bubble in London.

While Victoria is clearing a space for itself on Adam Head, H.M.S. *Beagle* slowly follows the east coast, sounding and surveying through Torres Straits, standing in to Port Essington for stores. Gaily the flags fly from the commandant's house in the clearing and from faithful *Britomart*, anchored off the little stone pier. There is happy reunion of deep-sea friends and bags of English mail—"in tremulous joy and anxiety they were afraid to open the letters". No ships have arrived, and the cupboard is bare.

The second Singapore is showing signs of life—a street of eleven paperbark huts, Government House high on piles, wells dug, gardens planted, goats browsing, an ox-team grubbing stumps, pigs rooting in a pen of mangrove stakes. All cattle are lost, but a few big Brahmin cattle, a dozen buffaloes and five Timor ponies that *Britomart* managed to land are doing well. In the bay are a thousand Malays, proas at anchor, boilers and huts ashore—so many came at Stanley's invitation that he had to ask the Governor at Koepang to stop them. In the powder magazine at Gunners Quoin are enough balls and shot to rout an enemy . . . but the enemy hiding in the mangroves is not one to be routed with balls and shot.

Captain Wickham lies listless and ill on the Residency veranda while *Beagle* marines help to build the church. The gentlemen, first bushmen of the north, carrying swags and water and sleeping under the trees, explore the "South American forests" of Coburg Peninsula with their freak natural history, the dazzled beaches and mud-flats of weird marine life.

Lieutenant Stokes now writes *Beagle's* story, Stewart draws the maps, Vallack studies the natives, Tyers observes the tides. Their guide is a boy, Marambari, striding ahead with his spear—they call him Alligator for his wide toothy smile. Alligator's wife hugs to her breast their long-dead child, wrapped up in paperbark. Sometimes she kneels and sets the little bones together "with a rapidity that supposes a wonderful knowledge of osteology" and grieves above them with heartrending cries. At Raffles Bay the party find nothing but graves—"the rapid growth of vegetation had swept all else away".

Four boats set out to survey the coast. On a sandy beach below red cliffs Fitzmaurice and Keys dance for their lives. Comparing compasses, they leave their firearms to move to a spot free of iron, and peering through the sextant are suddenly conscious of shaggy heads and jagged spears twenty feet above them, black faces chewing ragged beards in rage. The boat is a long way out. Fitzmaurice drops a courtly bow and whispers to Keys. Handkerchiefs waving, pointed toes, they tread a tense gavotte to the puzzled stare of angry bloodshot eyes . . . each time they *chassé* near the guns a warlike rattle of spears. On with the dance! At last the boat pulls in. In a Sir Roger gallop they rush the waves and swim, the audience hot on their trail in a bark canoe. That place goes down as Escape Cliffs—we shall hear of it again.

Torrid heat and sandflies, poor rations, peril in the water, peril on land, in thirty miles they find their reward, a magnificent new river . . . hiding away in salt-water creeks and jungle of eighty-foot bamboos a seven-fathom channel, deepest in Australia. The forest is full of wild blacks, boats grating on scaly crocodile-backs—a pistol-shot when a snout shows over the gunwale. Fear in the night, but exultation of a new world in the dawn! *Beagle* moves round to the survey . . . a truly glorious river flowing four hundred miles from far hills to Adam Bay, navigable for vessels of six hundred tons fifty miles from the sea to the fresh water, its loamy plains a pageant of fertility . . . a major river, the Adelaide.

Beagle slips back to Port Essington with the cheerful news. No store-ship yet—"provisions short and tempers shorter", *Britomart* alone at the pier, settlers starving, the harbour a gloomy prison in the grey of dusk. But with dawn comes H.M.S. *Pelorus*, a transport China-bound—transport of joy in greetings, stores and mail.

A gala day for Victoria, flags waving, men shouting, boats flitting over the water, white sails of hope in a harbour blue and serene. Up the hill with the stores and the English mail! Sports for the tars, ship against ship in tug-of-war, wrestling, races, the sundown rowdy with cheers . . . a gay little dinner at Government House for the gentlemen, toasts to "The Queen, God bless her!" to sweethearts, absent friends, to the bright eyes of the ladies, those valiant exiles the garrison wives.

Clang of a bell and the town crier calling "Oyez! Oyez! Victoria Thee-ay-ter! Roll up! Roll up! At eight o'clock tonight!" Captain Owen Stanley presents a play—some rollicking farce from a dog-eared book he picked up by chance on Tower Hill and carried with him from Cape Horn to the Arctic Circle. With coloured ochres of the cliffs the gay young captain, a brilliant artist, has painted the scenes himself. It is the talk of the town. The big workshop, under festoon of signal flags, is packed with rosy English faces.

Down the paperbark street comes the vice-regal party, kiltie piper strutting to reel and strathspey, Captain McArthur as host—epaulettes, swords, cockades, white gloves, jewels and laces. Can these ringleted beauties be the poor little garrison wives? The gallantry, the laughter and the glances!—London is very near in this one bright hour. Shadows, multitudinous dark shadows, are crowding in to see them all go by.

Hilarious is Captain Stanley's play—a stout sea-dog in Mrs McArthur's ample satins, waving an ostrich-feather fan and waddling with lorgnette as a dowager in Park Lane . . . a bearded hero waving an honoured sword . . . a mincing spinster who was with Nelson at the Nile . . . the tow-headed, pink-cheeked heroine a piping midshipmite.

Some such, but little we know of that first drama of the north, save that the act-drop was an old ensign, and through it the "ladies" could be seen squatting to take a pull at a cutty pipe, while the theatre whooped in glee. Somewhere, perhaps, in an old sea-chest, is a hand-written cast of characters or a meaningless scrap of pasteboard inscribed in copperplate:

VICTORIA THEATRE

PORT ESSINGTON

24th August 1839.

Where is Port Essington? Nowhere. A few graves in the bush.

Candles shine like stars in the shacks on the ghostly head where the lost are reading the letters from home. Fires of the Bugi glitter all round the beaches. Clear call of a bugle over the water . . . men's voices ring and echo "John Peel" from three English ships black on a road of gold to the rising moon.

Out in the bush the Bijenelumbo are blowing the didjeridoo: *Ebroo . . . ebroo . . . ebroo . . . ebroo*—black man's country . . . life-blood pulsing from the heart of the tropic night.

Within a week *Beagle* sails west, to her discovery of Port Darwin and Victoria River. A hurricane rakes the harbour, smashes Government House, drives *Pelorus* in under the cliffs with twelve men drowned.

The piper of Port Essington is left to dree the weird.

Rains roll over and trade-winds blow in the seasons of seven years. Malays come and go. Gardens flourish and wither, houses rot and fences fall. Arrowroot, sugar-cane, cotton from Pernambuco and Ile Bourbon are fine crops, but who comes to buy? Sweet potatoes from Rio are twice the size of those in Rio. On these the settlers live, with fish and a bit of brahma beef. Sixteen miles from the sea-breeze in that landlocked harbour, idle whites lie in the shade with idle blacks . . . a lotus land, their plan of life forgotten. Reek of mangrove swamp brings fever. Pale and peevish the garrison wives.

In two years *Beagle* is back from a round of the continent, creeping through Carpentaria, on Sweers Island to discover the old Flinders tree with *Investigator* carved on it, and to cut *Beagle* the other side. A precious explorers' tree, on Sweers I could not find it, and feared the lightning had taken it long ago, but I hear the historic slab is safe in Queensland Museum. Two other big rivers *Beagle* writes to her name—Albert and Flinders, a cattle kingdom for Queensland—but for Port Essington, "jaundiced and careworn", she cannot see hope. Not even our gallant and successful little ten-gun brig can see hope in the colony of her friends.

Ships are too few—fourteen months with never a sail. Men and women are sick of the sight of each others' yellow faces. A wreck is a godsend. When *Orontes*, a liner for India, piles up on the reefs, when *Montreal* and *Corinda Packet* founder and run aground, when *Hyderabad* breaks her back on the shoals and seventy ragged men in boats stir those dead blue waters, what rejoicing, what relief! Far sorrier the exiles than the castaways, crying for news, for thoughts of their own world. Now and again a survey ship comes with stores, H.M.S. *Rattlesnake*, *Freak*, *Fly*, *Midge*, *Bramble*, charting Torres Straits and New Guinea.

At Bligh's Booby Island, eighteen miles west of Cape York, where feather of breakers and green of shoal lead in to the reefs and cannibal isles—the most notorious ship-trap in the South Seas—Captain Hobson of *Rattlesnake* has set up a marine post-office in one of the caves. Passing liners leave mail-bags for Sydney or London—the English mail haphazard by any ship—and each a cask of biscuit, if they can spare it, for those in peril on those scintillating seas. The lucky ones row to Port Essington, six hundred miles.

Watchers from the white cliff see strange visitors save many lives, and lose their own for lack of the will to live. The fever is fatal to those in debility of body and mind. There is always sickness after the long loneliness of the wet. The hospital down in the mangroves is the biggest building in town, rain dripping through its rotten roof. Clarke, the doctor, sleeps with a tent rigged over his bed—until he takes his place in the graveyard.

A grey company finds Port Essington one day in 1845, not from the sea but stumbling the cart track round the foot of the hill, spectres of men and horses. They come to the street with its one white house and straggle of coconut-palms. As Captain McArthur rises to greet them, the leader grips him with lean scurvied hand, blue eyes full of tears. He whispers something about God and civilization.

It is Leichhardt, this haggard, ragged creature . . . Leichhardt with his men, first riders to the north. Through the nightmare grandeur of Queensland ranges for a thousand miles, then over sun-raddled plains of the Gulf for another thousand, with nothing to guide them but Arrowsmith's old map of New Holland, they have been riding for over a year and every hour with death. Gilbert, the naturalist, has fallen to blackfellow spears. Well known in Port Essington where he collected birds for John Gould, he is buried by a river that bears his name, first grave of Carpentaria.

To Leichhardt, Essington, with its "snug little thatched cottages", is threshold of heaven. Dried pork is a banquet when you have lived on the entrails of bats. With his lieutenant, John Roper, happy for human companionship, he sits writing for a month on Government House veranda, sketching into Arrowsmith's map the endless feathered line of the Great Dividing Ranges and many big rivers, Dawson, Burdekin, Gilbert, Macarthur, Roper and a score of others, rushing to the Pacific or winding to the Gulf in what was believed an arid land. An unexpected little schooner, *Heroine*, calls in and carries the heroes to hero-worship in Sydney.

Leichhardt will ride again, ride westward out of the world. This nervous inhibited man, for ever trying to prove a courage already proven in resisting German militarism to do some good on earth, will give his life for a new land and perish a whole expedition in a crossing of the continent that cannot be made even yet, their fate an eternal mystery of the drift sand. He will never win the honour that is his due. Wars of a century are stacked against him, the wars from which he ran away, braving the hostility of Nature rather than the malignance of man. He led the way to the north, contributed millions of pounds' worth of knowledge and a homeland for future millions. From his desert failure others will find the right way to go. In death he is for ever Australian.

Views of North Queensland, unveiled by Dr Leichhardt, waft Mr Gladstone and Sir Robert Peel into daydreams of colonization—the top half of a continent, a round million and a half square miles, to be, in Gladstonian rhetoric, an outsize in jewels for Victoria's resplendent crown.

North Australia by and large, above the twenty-sixth parallel, from 17th December 1846 to 5th August 1847, is actually declared and gazetted a Crown Colony. Governor-in-Chief is Sir Charles Fitzroy of New South Wales, Colonel Barney Governor-elect, and capital city on Captain Flinders's wide harbour, Port Curtis, is founded, planned and named for W. E. Gladstone.

Sugar and cotton planted in ten-acre patches—rent-free for three years, with rations and bedding supplied—secure the real estate thereafter, to be purchased at £1 an acre in ten easy instalments. Between Godfather Gladstone and Colonel Barney, volumes of official correspondence on every windjammer are hurried to and fro.

Puzzle, find the settlers. For lack of others, convicts are selected, to be furnished with English wives from workhouses and jails, but Mr Gladstone humanely decrees that they must be classed as "exiles", above the finger of posterity's scorn, and adjures Colonel Barney "that his first duty to empire in the vast unknown is promotion of a healthy moral tone". Colonel Barney modestly applies for a clergyman and a school, for a few sappers to survey, for a sailor and a whaleboat, and for £10 to buy presents for the blacks—the rightful owners, on a walk-in walk-out basis, are expected to sell cheap.

In February 1847 from New South Wales on the *Lord Auckland* with two hundred and ten highly respectable "exiles", the colony sails for Port Curtis, under Capricorn. On the desolate shore of Gladstone, in full-dress regimentals, Colonel Barney makes an impressive stand, but to fervent strains of "God Save Our Gracious Queen" *Lord Auckland*, with the colony, runs aground. In the fall of the Peel Government a few weeks later, Earl Grey vetoes the scheme, ruthlessly throws away the largest pearl in the crown.

Meanwhile, Port Essington storm-clouds silhouette a sail, H.M.S. *Royalist*, first relief in seven years. The garrison sails for England, a second takes its place. McArthur is commandant still. Another piper is calling the tune, a dreary coronach. Of fifty-two Royal Marines, eight are dead of fever by the end of the next year.

The settlement is stifled in stagnation, starving on old naval rations thrown out from the war with China, drowning its sorrows in sailors' grog. The sick are carried to Coral Bay, tents under the paperbarks in charge of A. R. Tilston, assistant surgeon, a scientist forgotten. He is first in Australia to make cajuput oil, of medicinal value, from paperbark leaves. He compiles aboriginal vocabularies and legends, sends the first bower-birds' playground to the British Museum, picks and packs the first Australian cotton for the Manchester market, where it is sold for 6½d. a pound. He makes drawings and collections of shells, birds, and natural history unique, such as the one and only "white-gloved rat" for which, in 1948, Dr David Johnson, a curator of United States National Museum, crossed Van Diemen's Gulf by mission lugger and paddled alone from Cape Don to Port Essington in blackfellow canoe.

Tilston is one of the first to foster the science of dentistry in artificial teeth. He barters with Bijenelumbo braves for the sound ivory incisors gouged out with stone knives in their initiations, and mails them by schooner captains to London where, strung on a wire, they find ready sale, providing gummy old fops with gorilla smiles. But here it is easier to die than to live. Even Tilston loses heart. He is stricken by fever, and lies in the paperbark shade with the first priest of the Territory, Father Angelo. The wild colony of the Coburg was a diocese of the Roman Catholic church in 1845. When Dom Salvado, founder of the great Benedictine mission and monastery at New Norcia near Perth, was consecrated Bishop of Port Essington, he sent to the north, on a schooner, two catechists, Hogan and Fagan, and Rev. D. Angelo Confalioneri, a young priest highly educated, just arrived from Rome, and eager for propagation of the faith. The schooner was wrecked in Torres Straits, all drowned but the captain and the priest, who was rescued by the barque *Enchantress* while clinging to a mast, and came to his parish as a castaway. For two years he laboured, wandering the bush, camped on the shore, the garrison sending him rations as scant as their own. He made valuable ethnological maps of Coburg Peninsula and vocabularies of its tribes. Into the native languages he translated the Lord's Prayer, the Ten Commandments, the Creed, and a short history of the "Passion of Our Redeemer". His papers and maps were sent to Rome, with his chalice, his vestments, and letters to Cardinal Franzoni, in 1847, when crazed with hunger and loneliness in his hut at Black Rock, Father Angelo died.

H.M.S. *Rattlesnake* calls again . . . and once again . . . gallant Owen Stanley her commander, in his surveys from New Zealand to New Guinea and the north coast of Australia. He, too, will give his life for the new land, worn out by privations and explorations, old at the age of thirty-nine, to die by his own hand on his ship in Sydney Harbour. Wrapped in the flag, to the marines' slow march, he is buried at St Thomas's, North Sydney, leaving his name to a high range of gold in the ramparts of New Guinea—name of dark memory to Australians in the horror and grief of wars a century on.

Neinmal, his friendly shadow, "Jack White", with him from this world is outward bound. Neinmal has travelled with his young master to Fly River, Singapore and Java, via Cape Leeuwin to Sydney and north to Port Essington again. As captain's steward on *Rattlesnake*, as Tilston's collector-in-chief of natural history and a clever taxidermist of birds, mammals and fish for English museums, this myall blackfellow in a few years has won the white man's favour and even fame. In aboriginal drama, he dies for his own people.

A Monobar tribesman from west of the isthmus is shot by a soldier when trying to escape. To avenge him the Monobar creep on the garrison, one of them killed in the street by a Bijenelumbo sentry. A life for a life! Monobar men, at piccaninny daylight, rush the camp where Neinmal sleeps with his children and wife. They club him to death where he lies.

John MacGillivray, naturalist of H.M.S. *Rattlesnake*, and Jukes, naturalist of H.M.S. *Fly*, paint a woeful picture of Port Essington, "dormant and retrograde" in the reek of mangrove swamps, "the most heroic and the most hopeless enterprise in British empire history". Courage has evaporated, and energy, and faith.

"Tobacco, drink and disease have decimated the natives and fever has killed off the whites." By 1848, twenty-seven out of the fifty-two are invalided home or dead. The houses on the headland, in stranglehold of the vines, are more like wurleys of the blacks. The gardens are weeds ten feet high. The dozen buffaloes have gone bush with the Timor ponies, the plantations, the English bull and cow. MacGillivray is "glad to see it before it becomes a matter of history, as I fervently hope the abandonment of the place will make it ere many years are gone".

McArthur ascribes the failure to intemperance, but young Thomas Huxley, surgeon of H.M.S. *Rattlesnake*, serving his apprenticeship to immortality, even as Charles Darwin, in a six years' voyage round the world, bluntly remarks that "the commandant made the place as much of a hell morally as it was physically".

Our first Victoria is dying. H.M.S. *Maeander* comes, in 1849, to carry away the living just in time. Captain Hon. H. Keppel communicates to Captain McArthur "the welcome intelligence that we had come to relieve them. While the garrison rejoiced, the natives wept and cut their heads with sharp flints".

Lest the huts should provoke a black war with the jealous Monobar people, or become a stronghold of the Malays, the gunboat stands off the white head and shells the unhappy place to atoms. Wild corroboree keening follows her down the harbour. Eleven years of endeavour are a heap of smouldering rubble and a fade of smoke in the callous tropic sky.

This is the end of the Imperial Government's pathetic bid for empire in the Australian north. Jungle veils it over, pathways lost. Till the turn of the century the Malays come to trade, but from White Australia the proas sail away, leaving a crescent of tamarind-trees by sparkling beaches and a mango-grove by the vanished creek.

For a long time the blacks remembered garrison days and ways. Sad and merry tales were told, and barrack-room ballads sung by the last of them in the nineties—Flash Poll, Jim Crow, Port Essington Mary, Jack Davis and Brassy Bet. Bijenelumbo and Monobar are now an unknown people, and even the Uwaja, who inherited their sunny sea-coast, are a tribe virtually extinct. The piper of auld lang syne is quite forgot. Ruins crumbled through a slow hundred years . . . five quaint conical stone chimneys in a row and the larger chimney of Government House . . . tamarind-roots through *Beagle's* little church . . . the sunken powder magazine at Gunners Quoin near the crest of the white cliff, where the tides bring a lugger once in five years.

Harder to find in the bush is the graveyard with only five gravestones, one tall for an officer, one small for a child. The only inscriptions are to Captain Crawford, and to Mrs Lambrick, wife of the commissariat lieutenant, and her baby. Hers is a noble monument in that silent place to the poor little garrison wives.

Sometimes piccaninnies wander there, gathering sugar-bag—the native bees nest in the tombs. Port Essington graveyard is full of wild honey, the old Greek asphodel of the dead.

Chapter V

Strange Waters

OVER THOUSANDS of miles of outback travel I treasured in my suitcase a split of wood about two feet long. It looked like kindling, and in an unguarded moment, by a Sydney housemaid, was finally thrown out. Given to me by O. K. Samuels, manager of Mount Poole Station two hundred miles north of Broken Hill, it was a piece of Sturt's boat to cross the Inland Sea.

Coracle of a man's dream, Argo of mirage!

There it was found in the sixties by the pastoral pioneers, high and dry at Depot Glen just where Sturt had left it when the sparkling bays that blessed his eyes ebbed into sand, when the desert closed in, when Death signalled him back. Finder of rivers, greatest of all explorers in the great vague of Australia, not his "to lift the veil" on the mysterious centre of this continent, but his to light a fire in the mind of the man riding beside him, John McDouall Stuart, his young draughtsman, his friend.

Nearing the Barrier Ranges of silver in 1844, Sturt wrote to Morphett in Adelaide that he had sent Poole and Stuart to the top of a hill for a view of the land:

> Poole is just returned from the range. He says there are two high ranges to north and north-west, and water—the sea—extending along the horizon from south-west to south, and then north of east, in which there are numbers of lofty islands and ranges as far as eye can see.
>
> What is all this?
>
> Tomorrow we start for the ranges, and then the waters, *strange waters*, on which boat never sailed and over which flag never floated. But both shall ere long. We have the heart of the interior laid open to us, and we shall be off with a flowing sheet within a few days. Poole says the sea was a deep blue, and in the midst of it a conical island of great height.

And again in a letter to Colonel Torrens: "It will be a joyous day to launch on the unknown sea and run away towards the tropics."

From under cathedral rocks at Depot Glen, organ pipes of slaty cliffs dyed red with iron and eroded to gargoyles reflected in the pool, the boat was hung in the homestead for over sixty years, whittled away by a few souvenir-hunters of those far-out tracks till, when I passed by, nothing was left but the keel. First keel of those strange waters, it was a geological joke, fifty million years too late.

Australia's inland sea, like Noah's flood, lived long in the minds of men. Pliny wrote of a South Land enclosing an ocean. Many old mariners sought it. Dampier, at his Rosemary Isles, thought he had found the strait leading in. Flinders, Cunningham, King, Oxley, Sturt, and Cook himself believed that Australia might be an archipelago. A wise man of the Bibbulmun people of the south-west told Lieutenant Roe that beyond the sunrise was a lake so big that if a piccaninny started to walk round it, he would be a long beard on bandy legs when he came back to Perth.

Edward John Eyre, a vicar's son from Yorkshire, was first to find it . . . to find the last sad sunken tides of it, trapped in its own sands, below the level of any living sea, safe—too safe—from restless ebb and flow and the white-caps of emotion. Entombed in alabaster of salt, bones of the great mesozoic lizards bedded in its primal slime, it had been long a-dying. From his dazzled vision of three or four thousand square miles, Eyre named it Lake Torrens after the colonel and, hopeless to cross it, turned west.

For years South Australia's horseshoe of lakes—Torrens, Blanche, Frome, Callabonna, Eyre, Gairdner, "blue as indigo and bitter as brine"—was believed to be one, shallows of a Caspian drowning the heart of the continent, shimmering to a mystical land. Sturt, in his Central Australian expedition, against his better judgment, gave it a wide berth, rode north-west from his own living river, the Murray, to be lost in the maze of the dunes, prisoned in walls of sand.

Following birds to water in dreadful drought, he took his bearings by a Broken Hill of hidden mineral millions, first traveller in realms of silver, opal and gold. He marvelled that his few sheep could thrive and grow fat in "this metalled region", now a vast kingdom of sheep, and saw Dampier's clianthus "in splendid blossom on the plains", an army of green spears and scarlet banners, Australia's most valiant national flower, ever afterwards known as Sturt's Desert Pea.

Chained to a sinking pool between a red hill and a black, seeking that inland sea with Stuart and his men, he rode thither and yon for a thousand miles to find a way through the saddest country in Australia . . . hummocks and dunes, flats of baked clay a mirror of mirage . . . stony hollows once the pebbled floor of ocean, his "steel-shod desert" of gloomy purple hue, an eerie empty world where kites were a design in the sky and the white owl flew in the noonday.

"From what hidden waters come the bitterns, cranes and seagulls?" On beaches ever receding they rode for a year, Sturt's journals an elegy of the weird. They found crabs' claws and cockleshells . . . teeth of the nototherium, *kadimukera,* giant crocodile of ages long ago . . . fretted old hills once islands in foamy drifts of brine . . . the dry channel of many an ocean current . . . swamps of polygonum, withered claws of an old sea-grass.

They built a log fort in a low grey range, challenged the silence with a listless flag. In seven days' riding the stony wastes through blast-furnace of heat, they found the silent rivers—Cooper's Creek, Diamantina, and the far Georgina, Eyre's Creek—next to the Murray the mightiest river system in Australia, a trinity ever dying, ever living, thousand-mile streams that surge and submerge in hundred-mile-wide floods to smother themselves in sand. Thirty miles deep in the Simpson Desert that still is no man's land, Sturt found his phantom sea, a petrified ocean of yellow combers a hundred feet high and a mile apart for five hundred miles—"the sand-ridges in formidable array" fuming in every wind, "the mirage, bright and continuous", false waters glassy blue hazing a million square miles.

Small moving figures in monochrome of earth and sky, they were prisoned in thin air. Over that grid of sandhills the frantic horses no longer would stumble on. At Fort Grey they struck colours, and made it a race with death to Depot Glen, a hundred miles to every sump of slime and shimmer of mud on the long road back.

On the rim of those blue waters Poole died, and Sturt watched him die. He could give his own life for his dream, but not the lives of his men. Seventeen months of superhuman striving, adrift in desolation, he had magnificently failed. Home he struggled to the world again, white-haired and blind . . . yet hopeless never. His prophets were the birds.

> North of the Tropic, I will be bound to say, a fine country will be discovered. Birds always migrate to the north-north-west. Cockatoos and parrots, well known in the colony to frequent the richest and best pastoral vales of the higher lands, would pass in countless flights to that part of the compass . . . the country to which they went would resemble the country they had left, abundance of water, rich valleys and hills. . . .

Terra psittacorum. Colourful land of parrots! Who will find it?

Three years later, Leichhardt was lost out there, his expedition faded away, a legend and a warning. Explorers looking for Leichhardt circled the inland sea. B. Herschel Babbage threaded the salt lakes, found the pass between Lake Torrens and Lake Eyre. A. C. Gregory swung round the continent with Baron von Mueller and eighteen men, a remarkable journey of which too little is said. By brig *Monarch* and schooner *Tom Tough* west-about to Victoria River, he travelled south-west to that silent river, the Sturt, traced it for three hundred miles to the Great Sandy Desert and a northern arm of the old ocean, Gregory's Salt Sea . . . then a thousand miles east across the Never Never, naming Elsey Creek for the doctor in his party, and another thousand south from Carpentaria to the Barcoo. Into Lake Eyre he marked the great river-trend of Queensland, Georgina, Diamantina and Cooper's Creek. The coast of those strange waters at last was coming clear.

Goyder goes down into history as the man who mapped mirage. Beyond Lake Eyre he reported a glorious freshwater lake rimmed by high cliffs and giant gums, grasslands to horizons—a pastoral paradise for South Australia, alas, seen only through the glass, but solemnly charted and named for Surveyor-General Freeling. To sail the lake and survey the pastures for selection, Freeling toted a boat and a punt five hundred miles. The "giant gums" were stunted scrub in eerie magnification, the "mountains" clods of earth, and the gangrenous light of a raddled sun Goyder's "green pastures". Fresh water was certainly there, in swift evaporation—they waded two inches deep for ten miles. Lake Freeling changed its name to Illusion Plains.

Where the purple peaks of the Flinders, ranges within ranges, rise like melancholy thoughts above the desert and its dust-storms, the first shepherds from huts in the valleys were droving the first sheep. The time had come "to lift the veil". Sturt was living in England, but John McDouall Stuart, that steadfast little Scot, through thirteen years of lonely riding, was still dreaming his captain's dream. Like his kinsfolk, Bruce and the Spider, in the grandest epic of patience and perseverance in all Australia's history, six times he would try that far and fateful crossing, five times beaten back over thousands of desolate miles, at last winning through to a living sea.

In May 1858 in earnest he set out with a white man, a black, and half a dozen horses—two riding, two spare, and three months' tucker on two packs —the "expedition" financed by two old friends, William Finke and James Chambers.

From Oratunga Station, through the fiery peaks and white-gum creeks of the Flinders, they lit their first camp-fire in Aroona Gorge, and by St Mary's Peak—Munya-moodla, Cold Nose—and Mount Patuwerta—Emu Feathers—each two thousand feet high, they rode north-west to where the ranges fall in skeleton ribs of quartzite and callouses of erosion to the gibber plains and sand-dunes of that spectral sea. From its false pools of salt they travelled each trail three times, taking the horses back to the last water, then blindly on for the next till the thirsting animals found for themselves the blessed parakeelia—a rambling mesembryanthemum of purpling flowers and lush watery stems, miracle drought fodder of the future—to tide them on over the stones.

Stones! Floor of creation cracked to billions of sharp little stones . . . pale green and sulphur yellow of grass in slanted morning light, at noon an irritated scarlet, gentle mauve at twilight . . . valley after valley, rise after rise, colours and horizons fading down to foreground of stereoscopic brown stones. On the shore of ten thousand square miles of brine, throwing back the heat-waves in silica blaze of light, five thousand square miles of sun-split, sand-polished stones. *Steel-shod desert*—he remembered Sturt's words as day after day the dry wind whistled over the stones and the horseshoes rang on stones.

Time was life in that silent land where rain had not fallen in a year. Water was where you found it, and more precious than gold. Twenty-five miles a day, they slept on stones, scarcely enough wood to boil a quart-pot of tea. While Forster made the damper that was daily bread, Stuart climbed every little rise, watching afar for a flight of birds, a line of trees, a smoke. They dug feet deep in every creek of sand—here a brackish pool, there a soak, to keep the horses limping for three hundred miles, the dip of the land still to the old sea.

Beyond Mount Deception their blackfellow was useless, and in strange country he ran away.

Queer little tent hills swam in sunset light, one like a Chinaman's hat, black band and rocky white crown. They camped at a vanishing water, and a swan came in the night. Promise in desolation? Across the brilliant stars drifted a cobweb of cloud.

All the horses were crippled, shoeless, hoofs worn to the quick and bleeding from that stony grid. Stuart's little grey mare, Polly, was pitiably lame. Relief came with a splash of great drops on the stones. A canter of nearly thirty miles in wet breath of showers, soon they were sinking in slush. A cloudburst came with the dark, washed away their shelter of boughs, soaked the flour and sent them running for a little bald hill, trapped by a creek two hundred yards wide, floundering for days, horses belly-deep in water and bog.

Stuart was worried for Polly:

> The grey mare very bad. I am afraid I shall lose her. If she is no better in the morning, I shall try to get her on a creek running south. . . .
>
> I must leave the little grey mare, for she keeps me back and endangers the other horses. I shall be sorry to do it, for she is a great favourite. . . .
>
> The grey mare quite done—the stones play the mischief with her. I have great doubt of her living through the journey. . . .

There will some day be a statue to Polly along the Stuart Highway, for she weathered that journey and all the others, and carried her master ten thousand weary miles to his dream of a northern sea.

Clouds and rains were gone in a flash, the wet plains optical lenses: "The mirage is so powerful that little bushes appear to be great gum trees. . . . It is difficult to see what is before us, almost as bad as travelling in the dark."

Nights were bitterly cold, frost on the stones, an empty circle of Arctic white. At five miles a day the weakened horses dragged their feet in gluepot of stones and clay. Three nights without water through "dismal mulga scrub", then came another saving rain.

"July 30. Forster baked the last of our flour."

For the next months the two men lived on "four wallabies, one opossum, one small pigeon and a few kangaroo mice, very welcome. We were anxious to find more, but we soon got out of their country". They boiled the tops of the "pig-face" in its own juice, "to a hungry man, palatable", and found a few sow-thistles, "very good".

Harsh, arid hills below the level of the sea—grey hills of opal, but how could anyone know? . . . torture of spinifex and red sandhills led them again to—stones.

"I cannot face the stones again!" cried Stuart. "This dreadful work! When will it have end?"

Where was the land of his intuition, his faith? A sad weather-worn little figure on a sandhill at dawn, staring down on stones . . . to the south a faint blue fringe of mallee. "Not a mouthful for a horse to eat."

Beaten. By stones. The two men wheeled their horses south through the mallee. Nearest habitation was Gibson's station at Streaky Bay—a breakneck ride with no diet but a crow, three days' starve of a hundred miles in to Streaky Bay, the last thirty-five miles a frantic search for a few shellfish along the beach.

To understate it in a Scotsman's words with a nice rolling of the r, "We were beginning to feel the cravings of nature very severely when we came in to Gibson's station for supper, quite a treat. . . ." The wholesome food made them ill for a week as they rode for horseshoes another hundred miles. When they came to Thompson's station at Mount Arden on 11th September, they had ridden a roundabout of a thousand miles with only four days' rest.

So ended the first lesson for John McDouall Stuart, where none but the greatest of bushmen could stay alive.

A summer by the sea at Semaphore, and he was up to the Flinders Ranges and out on 2nd April 1850, from St àBecket's Pool, known to the less literate bushmen of today as Sandy Bagot's Well. With him this time were three men, Hergott, artist, Campbell, stockman, Muller, collector of plants.

From the few inches of merciful rain the stones had lost their horrors. Hergott, looking for stray horses, found in a ragged washaway a dozen flowing springs, "good water, unlimited supply". Hergott Springs went down on the map where now is the railway town of Marree . . . and a few miles on the bountiful Finniss Springs. On the very shores of Lake Eyre, in rock and salt and mud, they found freshwater springs. The Dead Heart was a living world, creeks of last year's burning sand a long chain of shady waterholes with many fires and human tracks. They met blacks carrying spinifex nets and fish. Grid of stones was silver-veiled with salt-bush, a lush green feed for the horses.

"Australia's wells are deep and full," wrote poet Mary Gilmore. One morning Stuart followed emu tracks to a little withered hill, to find the crater crest brimming with sparkled and perpetual springs, green sweep of ripples twenty feet deep and twenty feet across within a swamp of rushes—the grey mare Polly was bogged on top.

So he made the great discovery of the desert's secret waters, those mysterious mound-springs in hazy crazy hills, in whiskered hummocks of sand . . . some hot, some cold, some effervescing with soda and magnesia, or frosted with saltpetre, some running miniature rivers for miles . . . gushers of hope and salvation in drought and despair, millions of gallons a day of pure sweet water where you find it, even in the crown of the Chinaman's hat. This they named Blanche Cup for the governor's lady. Near by is the Bubbler, where brown silting of oily sand balloons above the waters like the blown hide of an old diprotodon and falls in the bubbles again all day.

"This is of great importance," wrote Stuart, a good general of ninety years ago. "It keeps my retreat open. I can go from here to Adelaide at any time of year."

Beresford, Emerald, Strangways, Hawker, Milne, Hope, Hamilton, the big Freeling Springs—thirty to fifty miles apart, they carried him joyously on five hundred miles to Peake Creek and a new river, the Neale, steep banks and flood drift fifteen feet high in the trees, around it meadows of waving grass, "no person could hope for a better country". But again they were down to the last of the horseshoes. Horseshoes were Stuart's good luck—he could never carry enough. "Having experienced all the misery of being without them, I am regretfully forced to turn back. My party is too small to make a proper examination of this splendid country."

On the way back they paid for it in the traditional price of empire, meeting a little wandering tribe. The Old Man came trembling.

He seemed to wonder and be pleased at my smoking a pipe of tobacco. I gave one to him, cutting, filling and lighting. He put the wrong end in his mouth and found it hot. I showed him the right thing. He managed a whiff, but did not fancy it. He was mightily pleased with the pipe, which he kept.

I made him understand that we wanted water, and they showed us a deep hole, but were quite surprised to see the horses drink it all. They would go no farther with us, nor show us any more.

After such poor return for hospitality, can one wonder?

Stuart came home in July and was back in November, with a powerful telescope looking for islands in the blue haze of Lake Eyre, and wading its bitter waters. Again he rode north to the Neale with three men, Smith, Strong and Kekwick.

In hot summer nothing but trouble . . . maggots in the jerked beef, weevils in the flour, sun-heat a couple of hundred degrees. Tricked by vanishing waters, the men refused to live for Stuart's dream. Bad-tempered and lazy, they threatened to leave. Kekwick was his only trustworthy friend. When the other two, in the leader's absence, opened his plan-case and ruined his charts with their "hot moist hands"—a draughtsman's charts exact and immaculate, perfected and protected through rain, mud and cracking sun—he had half a mind to send them walking to Adelaide. He could not trust them to ride for stores, he could not leave Kekwick. Smith ran away, taking French leave with the little grey mare. Having nearly perished them both, he had the grace to leave Polly at Oratunga.

Again on the threshold of new country, Stuart had to bury his gear and return seven hundred miles . . . to find a boom in exploration in the cities.

Trailing behind the Victorian Government—about to launch the grand expedition of Burke and Wills, equipped and financed to the tune of £12,000 to travel from sea to sea—the South Australian Government, with never a thought to McDouall Stuart, his knowledge, his endeavour, proclaimed a reward of £2000 to the man who would cross the continent first, to be paid after the event if he lived to claim it.

The bright-eyed little Scotsman was the only competitor in that wide field.

With two men and thirteen horses, flour and jerked beef supplied by Finke and Chambers, he was riding north within the month, and on 2nd March 1860 threw on his laden packs for the fourth time at Chambers Creek. From now on Kekwick was his second in command, sharing his troubles and his triumph.

It was another good year. Hot-foot over the stones, then up to the saddle-flaps in bog, in heavy rain twisting and turning for miles around the floods, when they came to the Peake, where four creeks meet in a delta a mile wide, it took them five hours to swim across. Water streamed into the saddle-bags, rotted the beef and swamped the charts, the horses threw their packs and smashed the instruments: "All day repairing the sextant, and now I don't know whether it is correct or not. This is a great misfortune." The Neale was a river a hundred feet wide, racing at five knots. Even the salt lagoons of the dismal mulga scrub were freshwater lakes with fish a foot long. Stuart named Lake Stevenson, to the east, from its light mirrored in the evening sky. While he camped to mend saddles and dry out the flour, Kekwick rode ahead and foretold a dramatic change of country—boundless pastures, far winding creeks of many permanent waterholes, blackfellow roads over foothills to a high rocky range!

Through seas of tall mulga they travelled by compass like a ship, then plodded bright red sandhills with eight-foot spinifex yellow as ripening wheat to shadowy groves of the desert oak—casuarina, in widow's weeds mournfully sighing, graceful as a willow-tree.

It was far and hard to the mountains, but a distant gleam of silver called them on . . . a lake? . . . or shallow floods . . . or flowing river? They passed a village of wurleys deserted, the fires still burning. Bright new birds in clamouring clouds led them to the waters, wide, strong and deep, Finke River, that flows, when it flows, for a thousand miles.

"I christened it after William Finke, my sincere and tried friend, and one of my liberal supporters in the explorations I have had the honour to lead. I look upon him as the original pioneer."

The horses reared and plunged in quicksands of the Finke.

"We were nearly across when I saw a black-fellow among the bushes. I pulled up and called. At first he seemed at a loss to know where the sound came from. As soon as he saw the horses he took to his heels and was off like a shot."

So a herald of the great Arundta people, happy nomads of the red crags and misty billabongs in that stormy sea of ranges, ran with the terrible tidings of the devil-riders, man and beast as one, centaurs of another world, crossing the rubicon from time into the dreaming.

Against the mosaic of the desert, sun-bright as a temple of Ra, a "remarkable pillar" pointed to the sky. Chambers Pillar, a spire of one hundred and fifty feet sheer, twenty feet through and only ten feet wide, set on a pedestal hill a hundred feet high, they could see it for twelve miles. Monolith of age-old phallic symbolism, one of the many weird works of erosion in these virgin valleys, to devout Stuart it seemed a covenant of God, gateway to the Promised Land.

By cleft and scoriated cliffs carrying still the scars of sea battles and swirl of the tides, syncline and anticline in corroboree colours of ochre, Ordovician fossils of ferns and fish, they crossed another river, the Hugh, to climb the old residual hills.

. . . crowns, columns, amphitheatres, bosomy curves and towered castles, Pharaoh faces in Egyptian red, fluted cones and knife-cut canyons . . .

smouldering gullies and harlequin heights a sparkle of quartz and mica, or velveted over with spinifex, or veiled in luminous haze, and through it all winding the Finke, river of glittering sand, Larrapinta, White Snake of the Dreaming.

Tall white gums reflected in glorious waterholes, or rooted in rock on the face of the cliff, rose to a hundred feet . . . here a valley of "meadow-grasses ready to cut with a scythe", there "a valley of a hundred wurleys". Tangle of blackfellow pads led to a thousand fires, but always the wurleys deserted, spears, waddies, boomerangs, *pitchi*, forgotten in fear, and fires still warm. From the smokes of the devil-riders the Arundta had fled.

James Range . . . Waterhouse Range . . . still the red mountains rose, five hundred miles east and west, wave upon wave breaking higher against the della Robbia blue of Central Australian skies.

"The country from north to north-east is a maze of ranges, to the south high broken ranges. . . . It is the only real range since the Flinders. I have named it MacDonnell after his excellency the governor-in-chief of South Australia as a token of his kindness to me. . . ."

Happy, now, the hungry naked little Scotsman, his face, hands, saddlebags and clothing ripped by rock and scrub, solitary human figure scaling perpendicular cliffs, clambering down the gorges, sliding the slopes and standing on the rim of the abyss to gaze upon the pageant of his own new world. Kaleidoscope of brilliant wings wheeled in the gulfs of morning, jewelled all the billabongs . . . tossing waves of love-birds, golden shoulder and blue bonnet, Rosella, Corella, galah . . . Mephistophelian black cockatoo, white cockatoo sleek as a magnolia, in brassy-throated choirs. He was first to see the little Bourke parrot, a ball of opal down, and exquisite *Polytelis alexandrae*, which he named after the Princess of Wales, earth's rarest gift to royal lady.

Land of parrots! He had found it!

"My poor little mare has got staked in the fetlock joint and is nearly dead lame, but I must proceed."

Exhausted in February heat and blinded by the flies, they stumbled in to the Valley of Palms, stronghold of the Stone Age with its tall cycads, *Livistona mariae*, to seventy feet high, tufted crown like a grass-tree, a cellular fossil growth so old that it is new. The seas receded, the hills eroded, and here the winds were still, holding Palm Valley out of time.

Three months closed in the glamour of the ranges, not till April were they quit of the cliffs and gorges, leaving "a cone of stones" and a tree blazed "J.M.D.S." at Brinkley's Bluff, about fifty miles west of Alice Springs . . . leaving a new ghost-dance to the Arundta people.

North of Capricorn, they were looking for water again when they came to the dead centre of the continent, where precise Stuart quaintly rebukes the Lord's less careful plan of creation:

April 22. I find from my observations of the sun—111° 00′ 30″—that I am now camped in the centre of Australia. I have marked a tree and planted the British flag. There is a high hill about two and a half miles to the north-west. I wish it had been in the centre, but on it tomorrow I shall raise a cone of stones and plant the flag, naming it Mount Sturt.

Through a publisher's mistake, later ratified by the South Australian Government, the name in the journal was given as "Central Mount Stuart", denying the explorer the right to honour his old leader, immortal and beloved.

On the anniversary of Shakespeare's birth, 23rd April, in 1860, with Kekwick he plodded to the crest of the hill, waved a flag on a sapling, and under his cone of stones buried his papers in a French caper bottle, no more than names and date. Two feeble voices in the silence, "We gave three hearty cheers for the flag, emblem of civil and religious liberty, and may it be a sign to the natives that the dawn of liberty, civilization and Christianity is about to break upon them."

As a red-white-and-blue headband the flag was doubtless worn to a rag by braves of the Kaitish, and civilization was too soon the end of their perfect day. In revenge for the Barrow Creek Telegraph murders fourteen years later, gunfire—not Christianity—was about to break upon them. Men, women and children were shot into annihilation for hundreds of miles around.

The puff of dust moved slowly on over the spinifex downs. Naming all the big creeks—of sand—for Stuart's friends, they rested in the shade of a new tree, butterfly leaves and scarlet pods, known in the Centre as Stuart's Bean Tree. In ordeal of thirst Kekwick found a "hill of water", Mount Denison, gushing springs and deep rockholes brimming thousands of gallons, but steep to climb, three hours' sliding with quart-pot and bucket to water the horses. On for two hundred miles they toiled, digging soaks with an old tin dish—they had lost their only shovel in the ranges.

At Tennant's Creek, named for John Tennant of Port Lincoln, where the horses were nearly all lame and the country burnt black with bush fires, the path-finder himself foretold a future in gold.

"I should think it a likely place to find gold in, from the quantity of quartz, its colour, and having lately passed a large basaltic and granite country, the conglomerate quartz being bedded in iron. The slate perpendicular is a good sign."

This year one mine alone at Tennant's Creek was sold for £200,000.

All Australia's explorers noted wealth, but their quest was the water of life.

Six months' provisions, five months gone, they were starving. "Five pounds of flour a week is too little for many weeks at a time." Stuart was thrown from his horse, suffering concussion, dazed, "seeing gum-trees everywhere, very alluring, apt to lead the traveller into serious mistakes". Too many have followed those false green trees of delirium where Lethe River is sand.

Through sleepless nights they baled with a quart-pot in shallow sumps of mud to give ten gallons each to skin bags of horses . . . men with their throats on fire might go thirsty. If horses were lost it was a long walk home.

In the blind blue of the sky Stuart could see the closing in of the walls. "I must do everything in my power to break this barrier that prevents my getting through to the north. I am determined I shall not give in on the threshold of success." Even he was to learn that the little gods of the old N.T. laugh at determination.

In his headlong ride he had seen nothing of the blacks. Of what nature these mystery men of the north . . . shadows and smoke . . . pixy towns of wurleys . . . their skeleton dead in the trees a clamour of crows? At Kekwick Ponds they met Warramunga the Song-Men, wearing fantastic top hats of padded feathers and painted bark—warrior's helmet or priestly mitre?

"Tall, powerful, good-looking, as fine a specimen of the native as I have seen, their countenances quite different from those of the south . . . I think they must have encountered many white men."

The blacks brought four possums skewered on long sharp spears, and many dead birds, but in aboriginal barter demanded prompt payment, and tried to make off with the canteens. Followed a conversation-piece worthy of study by Grand Masters:

> . . . an old man very talkative, but I could make nothing of him. I endeavoured by signs to get information as to the next water, but we could not understand each other.
>
> After some time and having conferred with his two sons, he turned round and surprised me by giving one of the Masonic signs. I looked at him steadily. He repeated it, and so did his two sons. I then returned it, which seemed to please him very much, the old man patting me on the shoulder and stroking down my beard. They then took their departure, making friendly signs. We enjoyed a good supper from the opossums, which we have not had for many a day.

At a falling creek a quiet camp of blacks watched them water the horses and ride on, but when they returned at sundown three angry sentinels barred the way. Suddenly the scrub bristled spears.

> Every bush seemed to produce a man. I told my men to make ready their guns.
>
> An old man in advance, with his boomerang, made signs for us to be off . . . blacks yelling and posturing like fiends . . . boomerangs whizzing and whirling round our ears. I gave the order to fire, which stopped their mad career.
>
> Some ran to cut off our horses, others setting fire to the scrub and throwing boomerangs. We gave them another reception. It was dark in the scrub, we could easily have been surrounded and destroyed.
>
> I wish I had four more men to stand and fight them. . . . I have unwillingly made up our minds to return to last night's camp.

So the Warramunga triumphed over white men with guns, defending their great tribal stronghold, Itheri-mindi-mindi—Attack Creek. They moved in to the waters oily red with their fires, all night chanting victory over the dauntless three. Morning broke with signal fires all round.

"Had they been Europeans they could not have better arranged and carried out their plan of attack. With such as these for enemies, I must abandon the attempt to make the Gulf of Carpentaria. It would be madness and folly . . . all the information I have already gained would be lost."

Had he come too far? Blacks on their track, waterholes dry, the leader too blind for observations, full of scurvy sores, in agonies of muscular pains, his men "moving like men of a hundred years old".

"O that rain would fall!" When a few clouds drew over, he thought of a lone dash to Victoria River to link, at least, with Gregory's farthest south—"I could kill one of the horses and live on its flesh. . . ."

The clouds were gone. Sadly he turned back.

On the way down they met a little Warramunga hero who well deserves his note in history. They surprised a camp of blacks where the men "made off at top speed" leaving "a little fellow of about seven years old cleaning grass-seeds in a wurley with a child who could just walk. The moment he saw us he jumped up, seized his father's spear, took the child by the hand and walked out of the way. It was quite pleasant to see the bold spirit of the little fellow".

Southward, the waters were nearly all gone. In the desperate ride of the ranges, when death seemed near, two running emus led them to a soak under a gum-tree in a creek. July was bitterly cold, ice in the early morning on the shallow pools of the Finke.

They rode into Adelaide on 26th August dust-begrimed and done, to hear that the grand expedition of Burke and Wills, after all these months of preparation, to the cheering of multitudes and music of bands in gala procession, had moved out of Melbourne five days before. A regiment on the march, with a caravan of twenty-six Peshawar camels driven by Hindus, stores for a year, "everything that logic could suggest and money could buy", the dashing Robert O'Hara Burke, darling of the ladies and leader of men, could not fail. A galloping horseman left Ballarat to give him Stuart's news.

Now that the ragged little rider had added to the map two pastoral provinces the size of France and Spain, the Government of South Australia granted him £2500—ten men, forty-eight horses, six months' bread and beef—to go and find some more. An Irishman and a Scotsman, hare and tortoise, were out in the field together. Everyone, Stuart himself, was quite sure that Victoria's heroes would win the race to the sea.

A few weeks in Adelaide to heal his sores and restore his sight, by November he was riding north through red-hot summer, no shade but the blankets in five hundred miles of stones. Winding the MacDonnells for two hundred miles in January blaze, Polly slipped her foal and close-up departed her endless trudging of a thirsty world. Stuart refused to leave her, and camped at Polly Springs, where nobly she rallied the camp-fires through to the end.

Six hundred and fifty miles of spinifex hills and downs, forty miles to every pool and never a blackfellow in sight, they were in new country at last . . . vast vacant prairies veiled in yellow grass, the horses falling in rotten ground over the black-soil plains to witch-woods ugly and dark. After an eighty-mile ride with never a drink for horses and men, a flight of wild turkeys guided them to lazy grey lagoons a hundred yards wide, seventeen feet deep and smiling for nine miles . . . permanent waters of great significance named for the Duke of Newcastle, Secretary of State for the Colonies. In the drowsy shade of its coolabahs they feasted on ducks and fish among the lively Tjingilli blacks.

Stuart believed his troubles were at an end. He had passed the latitude of Gregory's farthest south and, bound to Victoria River, turned west.

Thus far and no farther. The witch-woods closed in. Between him and Victoria River lay the "horrid forests" of the Murran-ji, sprawling, crawling to infinity in light-red sands . . . lancewood, thirty feet high, straight acacia close as spears, hedgewood thick as a hedge, a gorgon's head of a tree, a matted mass of sombre boughs and murderous dead spikes that staked the horses, dragged shirts into shreds, jagged saddle-bags and spilt the precious flour, wounded the men and ripped up the water-bags—"a fearful country where hoof-marks leave no track".

Through goblin mazes the men doubled, in a few seconds out of sight, lost in a hundred yards. Sullivan wandered for three days within a few miles of the camp, and came back mad. Through eerie nights of listening they fired into the trees. Though they rode for a hundred and six hours at one time they could find no water, only the twisted shadows on the sand. Stuart bewailed that Polly, Bonney and his old friends among the horses, trained in a hard school to live without water, could endure these stifling scrubs for no more than three days. He made a star of the compass, riding north-west, south-west, north-east, south, and circling, for a look-out climbing the lancewood. When a few points of rain passed over, they were up to the knees in slime.

No escape. The malignant scrubs ran on, writhing for sixty miles,

> . . . as great a barrier as an inland sea or a wall built round. I don't like this place . . . if more rain comes it will lock us in with so many blacks about. The horses will not face it. When forced, they make a rush through, wounding us severely and tearing all we have. We are nearly naked, our limbs and faces bleeding, nothing heals.
>
> It would take a long time to prospect this country for water. I have no hope of succeeding without wells, and I have not the provisions to stay and dig.

Thirty weeks' stores, twenty-six weeks gone, and a ten weeks' ride back to the nearest station . . . one thousand six hundred and fifty desert miles.

"Here ends my last attempt to make the Victoria River. Three times I have tried it and been forced to retreat." Stuart won through by knowing when to turn back. "One day's journey too far may perish the whole party."

Within two days of his return to Adelaide in September, the bodies of Burke and Wills, in a dead march of the desert, were carried down from Cooper's Creek. The race was not to the swift nor the battle to the strong . . . time and chance. . . .

In scenes of national mourning, the second historic tragedy of the crossing, McDouall Stuart made ready to go again, by October at Moolooloo Station in the Flinders, mending saddles, salting beef, shoeing horses. He suffered a kick on the temple, and a dragged rope smashed his right hand almost to amputation—he was to ride in agony till he could ride no longer. The men of this last journey were James Frew, Stephen King, John Billiatt, Heath Nash, John McGorrerey, naturalist J. W. Waterhouse, lieutenants William Kekwick, F. W. Thring and W. P. Auld . . . out from Moolooloo on 20th December, the leader on his little grey mare.

High summer once again for winter in the north. Ranges, clay-pans, salt lakes, springs, polygonum swamps, heat-waves over the stones, sandhills, dust-storms, creeks, bogs, bull-dust, mulga scrubs and flies—plagues and patience of Job—the white men's camp-fire twinkled northward with the dark to Finke River and the MacDonnells, razorbacks and canyons, blacks' camps, parakeets, pools and palms . . . then swiftly on over the hills and downs, in May to Newcastle Waters and the labyrinth beyond. Twisting, turning, hacking a way through, they threaded the grisly scrub for weeks, this time due north, slowly conquering mile by mile. On Queen's birthday a tall lancewood was flying a hopeful flag to "a chain of fine waterholes"—King's, Frew's and Auld's ponds—and "delight of a pool half a mile long", Daly Waters, where they camped to catch fish and blaze a "J.M.D.S." tree for victory over the hedgewood scrubs. June brought them to Leichhardt's Roper, the young river of powerful springs and shady banyan groves where Yungman blacks, merry and well-fed, came to borrow fish-hooks and laugh at the horses eating handfuls of grass. One was a "perfect shadow" of a man seven feet high, with legs four feet long.

Fantastic land of raw red hills and glittering fan-palm valleys, quartz and colour of gold, Gothic cathedrals in miniature built by the white ants, sunsets lambent as liqueurs, soon they were on the Timor fall of big impetuous rivers and boisterous creeks . . . elfin springs, lily lagoons, paperbarks crowding the long silver reaches, deep pandanus pools, a green world restless with life and alight with bright wings, water and its blessings all the way.

Strangways, Chambers, Fanny, Waterhouse, King, Flora, a sparkled net of rivers to the Katherine, welling majestic gorges and flowing free for a hundred and fifty miles to meet a greater river, soon they were riding

JOHN McDOUALL STUART.

through grass to the shoulders over a score of streams to the Mary in streaked mineral hills. Where lilies deepen from modest mauve, white and blue to flamboyant rose, tall as a tulip floating on leaves a foot wide, in mid-July they came to *Beagle's* famous Adelaide River, two hundred yards broad through sixty-foot bamboos, shining down through the bush across splendid alluvial plains to marshes and

"The sea!"

As Thring cried out, the canny Stuart gave him a wry smile. All night in the firelight, camped in a tangle of vines to draw maps and mend saddles, he had "heard the wash of the waves from the other side of the valley", steady breathing of a long tide that he had lived to hear. He blazed a tree where he heard that sound. Now on the crest of the dune, aloof, an equestrian statue of himself on Polly, he was at journey's end, "greatly delighted to behold the water of the Indian Ocean in Van Diemen's Gulf before the party with the horses knew anything about it. They were so astonished that Thring had to repeat the call before they understood."

"*The sea!*"

The jocund sea, beautiful to infinity, dancing in morning sun . . . cool breeze to the sweated brow . . . benediction to eyes grown pale from peering through mirage. "Three long and hearty cheers", shrill as the cry of the gulls, faded away with the ebb along the blue mud shallows.

24th July 1862. A ride of ten thousand miles and four terrible years.

"I dipped my feet and washed my face and hands in the sea, as I had promised the late governor, Sir Richard MacDonnell, I would do if I reached it.

"Thus have I, through the instrumentality of Divine Providence, been led to accomplish the great object of this expedition, through one of the finest countries a man could wish to pass."

Latitude 12° 14′ 50″, Chambers Bay, named for Katherine Chambers, eldest daughter of his patron and friend, who had fashioned the silken flag, with Stuart's name embroidered, flying at dawn from the tallest tree along those lonely beaches. The men scattered to collect souvenir shells, a watch over the horses for fear of the sea-coast blacks, heard but not seen.

Nine months in the saddle to one day of rest—a toast and speeches, a handshake all round, they blazed a coastal tree and buried their papers, and on 26th July turned two thousand miles for home. The flag was taken by curious blacks. The blazed tree was never found. The papers were carried away by the tide. Where Stuart looked upon the Timor Sea, a primitive buffalo station is now. A knowledgeable bagman, in a land without monuments doffing his hat to history, once set up a sheet of iron on an old railway rail to mark the unmemoried spot, but that, too, has fallen in the sand. Darwin unveiled a memorial plaque to Leichhardt in 1945, honouring the wrong explorer!

Most fearful of all Stuart's journeys was the road back, through flame and smoke for the first thousand miles, waterholes drying, skeleton horses dying, mischievous blacks all the way. The leader was crippled with scurvy and going blind. He had lived for the work, and the work was done.

"I fear my career is coming to an end. I keep everything ready. My plan is finished and my journal written. . . . Though the moon is full, and shining bright and clear to all the others, to me it is darkness. . . . The nights are agony and the days are long."

Two thousand miles. Lifted into the saddle for eight hours a day, through dizzy avenues of endless trees, a dreary zigzag from pool to falling pool, he was lifted down at night to stumble and grope, twisted in pain, with spongy gums and blackened lips trying to swallow tea and "a little boiled flour". The livid ulcerous flesh sagged on the bones, leaving him as a man of wax with rheumy sunken eyes, toddling and trembling as the very old. In the lag of his afflictions he was always last in, yet leader still, he pointed them to the waters when speech was gone.

No rain had fallen in a year south of Newcastle Waters, big creeks all dry, the men digging soaks. Horseshoes were gone again, none left for the stones, horses dying of weakness, thirst and poison weed . . . in urgency the expedition abandoned most of its gear.

Stuart believed he could never live through the last thousand miles. They carried him into the ranges on a bush stretcher. On 27th October, at Brinkley's Bluff, it seemed that his cone of stones would be his grave.

"I kept King and Nash with me in case of my dying through the night, as it would be lonely for one young man to be there with the dead."

All who were near him that night told that his wasted body was rank with the smell of decay, his breath the breath of death.

Deeply religious, he cried on God "Who has never failed me yet, the only One who can help . . . my only Friend" . . . and Thring found water in a stony gully, ten miles of water, and came back to his dying leader with a miracle in a quart-pot, fresh beef-tea! Already there were cattle in the ranges, strayed from Finke River where settlers were finding their way to Stuart's Delectable Mountains.

"I sincerely thank the Almighty, Giver of all good, that He has given me strength to overcome the grim and hoary-headed king of terrors, and to live a little longer in this world."

For three months they carried him on the stretcher of boughs and canvas slung between two quiet horses, slowly down over the sandhills and the stones. So they returned safely, by way of the springs, to the home ground of South Australia, where John Chambers rode to meet them with the news that his father was dead. James Chambers had not lived to know his friend's achievement. On 10th December they came in to Moolooloo—just a year away.

Welcomed to Adelaide by eager crowds and patriotic bands, Stuart received

£2000 and two thousand square miles of country, Royal Geographical Gold Medal and presentation watch, and rewards for his men. First to make the crossing beyond shadow of doubt, and to be free of tragedy on all his journeys, he had won through by knowing when to turn back. He never cared to claim his grant of the new territory he had "brought to the mind and knowledge of men", but returned to England, blind and ailing. Two years later he died at the age of fifty, and is buried at Kensal Green. His gravestone, erected by his sister, bears one brief claim to remembrance: "First Australian explorer to cross the Australian continent from the South to the North."

Without wife and children, far from friends and home, most of his life a rider in mirage, I think he lies content. All men are born to a purpose, and his high purpose was fulfilled.

In the little old copper town of Blinman in the Flinders Ranges—where faithful William Kekwick is buried, his tombstone erected and inscribed by the Royal Geographical Society—I met a man who remembered John McDouall Stuart. Charlie Roberts, till he was ninety, loved to tell the tale.

"I'm a young shaver of twelve when one day I ride over to Moolooloo with my dad and a mob of horses. There's a big plant on the station creek, and a rough one too. 'My God!' my dad says, 'look at the state o' them horses! Them fellers ought to be shot!' Then he rides up to the government house to see the overseer.

"I'm sittin' on my pony in charge of our mob when I see one of the men walkin' over the flat. First I think he's a nigger. His legs is black and he has no trousers, only a blue blanket slung round, and his arm in a sling and he's full of Barcoo sores. He's got a long beard and a rag of a hat, and under his fly-veil his eyes is red-raw. I don't reckon a white man should get around dirty like that.

"I whistle 'Pretty joey!' and call out 'Scarecrow!' as he goes by me. He don't take no notice. I never see a man walk so slow. I keep on whistlin' and chiackin', the way kids do. Suddenly I get a clip under the ear. It's my dad back with the overseer.

" 'You hold your tongue!' he says. 'Givin' cheek t' y' betters. I'll learn you, my lad, when I get you home.'

"After he sells our horses, we go down and boil the billy on the creek. Dad's all the time eyein' the other party, a big camp layin' off in the shade.

" 'D'ye know who that wuz you gave the lip to?' he says to me.

"I says, 'No, dad.'

" 'Well, that's Stuart,' he says. 'John McDouall Stuart. Them blokes has just come back from a ride across Australia, all the way to the sea. They're the first to do it, and he's their boss. It's worth a couple of thousand. A few around here don't believe him, but when he gets to Adlid he'll get the money, because he done it all right.'

" 'Now let this be a lesson to you, Charlie,' my dad says. 'You quit pokin' borak at anyone around. You don't know who they are or what they been through. And don't you forget this day, neether. When you're an old man you can tell them you wuz one of the first to see John McDouall Stuart, the time he come back from ridin' across Australia, and that wuz here at Moolooloo in 1862.' "

Chapter VI

Pack-Bells of John McKinlay

STUART'S LITTLE grey mare, Polly, carried South Australia north to the Timor Sea.

Within a year a traveller's tale was transferred from Captain Cook's old New South Wales in Letters Patent signed and sealed by Victoria herself:

TO OUR TRUSTY AND WELL-BELOVED SIR DOMINICK DALY, KNIGHT, GREETING . . .

NOW KNOW YE that we have thought fit to annex, and we do so annex, to our said colony of South Australia, until we shall think fit to make other disposition thereof, so much of our said colony of New South Wales as lies to the north of the twenty-sixth parallel of south latitude between the one-hundred-and-twenty-ninth and one-hundred-and-thirty-eighth degrees of east longitude, together with the bays and gulfs therein and all and every the islands adjacent. . . .

Witness ourself at Westminster,
The sixth day of July in the year One thousand eight hundred and sixty-three.

New South Wales, lately shorn of Queensland, watched another half million square miles go west without emotion. Ambitious South Australia doubled its dimension of desert sands and light-heartedly adopted the tropics with no more than a hundred and eighty thousand men, women, and children adrift in a round million square miles. It was the time of gold fever and landtaker greed. The Government was elated, monarch of all it never would survey.

So colonization was to come from South Australia—in its youth the most earnest and ardent of all Australian States, and before Federation the most distinguished in achievement and success. Its people were ever valiant in exploration, leading the way to the unknown world of the Territory, to the desert silver of Broken Hill and the desert gold of the West. It promptly planned the north as a highly-respectable sister colony in its own idealistic, altruistic Edward Gibbon Wakefield Scheme.

Flushed with the success of the South Australian Company, which had begotten a thriving State within ten years, it formed in England the Northern Territory Company, conditions identical, to throw another seven and cash in on the waste places of earth. Half a million hypothetical acres were offered for sale in 160-acre farms at 7s. 6d. an acre, a city half-acre thrown in, land to be occupied within five years. Investors were warned to be quick off the mark—the price would soon rise to 12s. 6d. an acre.

There's a Pilgrim Father born every minute. In the fogs of London, smoke of Birmingham, sleet of Glasgow, sunlight and freedom found a ready sale. By Christmas the company had a working capital of £91,917, a quarter of a million acres allotted to settlers in London, and a ship-list waiting.

Now for the capital city and shires beyond geography. Who better fitted for the immortal quest than Colonel Boyle Travers Finniss, partner and spiritual son of that Raleigh of the south, founder of Adelaide, Colonel William Light? (They thought little enough of him living, but he was a patriarch dead.)

This time the settlement would not be alone in the north, the only dismal dot in the blue from Port Jackson to Port Louis. There would be neighbours a thousand miles each side. Queensland was throwing a line to the tip of Cape York, and a Melbourne Utopia Limited had staked a claim on the wild Kimberley coast at Camden Harbour. Within a year, barques and brigantines were all away on a wave of colonization, John Jardine from Rockhampton with a squad of marines to Somerset, and a noble little band of nation-builders west-about from Port Phillip to Port George IV—they had signed on the dotted line of a mystical shore.

At the end of April 1864 Finniss left Largs Bay in the barque *Henry Ellis* east-about for Adelaide River with two small schooners, *Beatrice*, survey ship under Hutchinson, R.N., *Yatala*, tender, to ply to Koepang for stores and stock. Manton was surveyor-in-charge of forty officers and men, Ebenezer Ward storekeeper, Dr Goldsmith colonial surgeon and protector of aborigines—he soon resigned in favour of Dr Millner. Protecting the aborigines proved a troublesome job. Flocks and herds were twelve horses and four hundred sheep—most of them died at sea.

From Bass Strait to Torres Straits it was a hopeful journey except for a mutiny in which they tried to throw the second mate overboard, and on 20th June squabbling badly, they landed at Escape Cliffs in Adam Bay—where Fitzmaurice and Keys danced their theodolite ballet twenty-five years before. On 1st July they proclaimed a colony around a barrel of beer in a tent. Adam Bay was no more than an anchorage, yet here Finniss hopelessly bogged down.

A camp in the noisome mangroves by a dead coral reef, a well of swamp water and a few log huts were the first great thought for the second Adelaide. While the Colonel drew plans for his capital city before he selected the site, the sailors regaled on rum. One half of the unloaded stores floated away, the rest rotted on the sand—bags of flour and split peas awash in every tide. *Beatrice* and *Yatala* dumped surveyors forty-five miles up Adelaide River, in reek of mangrove creeks to map out country lands.

To young men nicely nurtured in county Adelaide, Adelaide River was a surprise, its waters queasy hot, its banks blazing with blacks' fires and demoniac with corroboree. Unwelcome strangers padded behind them in the bamboos, wearing red ochre and cockatoo feathers of war. Guns were stolen, the watchdogs snaffled by crocodiles. When clothes and stores were ruined and done, these tonies and johnnies of Rundle Street, from dickies and side-burns, stalked naked under their beards, learnt to live without soap, dosed themselves with lamp-oil, and applied leeches out of the river to their festers and swollen eyes. In frustration and tropic languor they lay in their tents till August, and came back to Escape Cliffs without having laid a single chain.

Escape Cliffs was hell in the mangroves—idleness, drunkenness, slander, discontent, rumour, rebellion and spite, the Territory's seven deadly sins. The Government Resident, by popular consent, was allotted the role of the devil—as he has been, for the most part, ever since.

Colonel Finniss, it seems, was allergic to blacks. He herded his men in tents three deep around his hut in the stockade. They lived on salt meat and ship's biscuit, hand-feeding rank grass to a few diseased sheep. Cutting lanes through the stifling mangroves, they were ill of the swamp water. Bastien Boucaut and the cook of the *Yatala* died. The Resident went round with an armed guard, looking for blackfellow tracks. When the poor primitive Woolna tribes, in delight of the colour red, stole a flag at Port Ayers, he wrote it down as defiance of empire, affront to Her Majesty the Queen . . .

and when from the unguarded stores, rotting in the sand, where white men pillaged medicines and grog, the natives, following suit, pilfered a few old bags and empty tins, a punitive party set out with carbine, revolver and sword to "shoot them down".

There was only one casualty, according to his report—and ugly evidence at an Adelaide inquiry that "the poor wretch, riddled with bullet wounds, was finished off by a humane white man who placed the butt of a rifle on the dying creature's chest and leaned on it. Then the party adjourned for lunch and spent the rest of the time burning deserted camps". All witnesses told that the "old man" so kindly put out of his misery had a short stick and a little basket full of roots—obviously a woman gathering yams.

Sir Dominick Daly demanded a trial for murder, *subpoenas* and commissioners tossed back and forth ten thousand miles on the wave. The murderer was acquitted by the Adelaide court, and reinforcements of men and arms sent up to Finniss for his "protection against savage blacks".

Forty additional surveyors, under R. H. Edmunds, sailed in October by *South Australian*, with surveyor F. W. Litchfield and police, J. P. Stow representing English landholders, Mr and Mrs Bauer, first settlers, Mrs Packard, a surveyor's wife, and her child. On 14th December, Edmunds laid the first chain in the Territory, surveying the city of Palmerston a mile up Adelaide River, completely under water at spring tide.

Two women and a hundred men in hunger, hate and fear . . . Mrs Packard soon gave birth to yet another "first white child", Adam Manton Finniss Packard. The natives, "thick as crows", stole axes . . . shouts and shots by night, the white men scaring each other with firesticks in the mangroves. When Finniss led an army, horse and foot, to "shoot blacks where they found them", the terrified women camped out with the men, and the blacks, with more humour than the whites, raided the tents and skipped with the bedding.

Survey parties under Manton and Edmunds sailed a hundred miles along Adelaide River again to plan out country lands. Davey, making fast a dinghy, was taken by a crocodile, Alaric Ward was speared at a well close to camp. So another riding party set out as far as East Alligator River, burning two hundred camps and shooting blacks. For his men's safety Edmunds forbade them to shoot a native within fifty miles of his camp. They quoted Finniss's orders. He warned them that not even a Government Resident of the Territory might command murder of the innocent—but they galloped away, and youth had its fling.

No sooner were surveys completed than they were all promptly rejected by Mr Stow, on behalf of his English clients. In the six months' season of rains nothing whatever was done.

Finniss made an expedition to Sourabaya via Victoria River, to bring a few buffaloes and edible tack. On the way he discovered and named the glorious Daly River, main stream of Stuart's Katherine and half a dozen others. But his brief authority was coming to an end.

From his "reign of idiocy", its "horrors and absurdities", there was conspiracy in the mangroves of fearless young radicals whom idleness and contention had driven slightly mad. With that frenzy to be out of it, alive or dead, that all through the years has been an epidemic of Darwin, seven of them planned to sail off, if need be in a tub.

Arthur Hamilton, J. P. Stow, William McMinn, Charles Hake, Francis Edwards, John White, James Davis—they bought a boat from the barque *Bengal* and named her *Forlorn Hope*, twenty-three and a half feet long, six feet beam and two feet deep, two masts and a sail—they added a little jib. Two hundred pounds of ship's biscuit and twenty six-pound tins of beef they smuggled aboard with a few medical comforts, seventy gallons of water, tracings of *Bengal's* faulty charts of the Indian Ocean coast, two sextants and a pocket compass.

A raucous send-off in the bakehouse, another on the beach, and on 7th May *Forlorn Hope* slipped out of Adam Bay, westward ho! with the south-easter. Her flag was a jester's flag, *Finis coronat opus*. A dinghy with a blanket sail sped her on her way till she was hull down to a faint cheering. Colonel Finniss waved them away with the sardonic nonchalance of Fletcher Christian's farewell to Captain Bligh. About fifty were left in the settlement, but all looked after the little skiff with longing. Away she went for Geraldton, hugging the shore, two thousand eight hundred and fifty-four miles—one of the great open boat journeys of history. Their only port in a storm was Camden Harbour . . . and Camden Harbour could give them nothing but a tale of woe. Already it was bottles and graves.

Where Dampier sailed under the Jolly Roger—where Baudin, Hamelin and de Freycinet fluttered the red flag of Republican France—and where King unfurled the Union in 1819 in a Neptune's court of the Georges, seventeen years later Lieutenant George Grey, in the yacht *Lynher* from the Cape, possessed the beaches of fairyland for "Her Majesty and her heirs forever". He rigged his tent in King Leopold Ranges, discovered the "glorious Glenelg" River, wrote lyrics and panegyrics to "a moving rainbow of paroquets" in rocks, dells and lovely vales, and "grieved that so fair a land should be the home of savage men". There Stokes met him, in H.M.S. *Beagle*.

These three, King, Stokes and Grey, in the fire of their youth, had visions of empire "from under the arched white sails of ships".

Using George Grey's poetry as a prospectus, an altruist named Harvey floated a Melbourne company to subdue five million rugged acres with four million sheep in "paradisal glades three thousand feet high", capital £20,000 in £100 shares. One share entitled a settler to first-class passage in a first-class ship, a year's rations, and twelve years' lease of twenty thousand acres with twenty prize cattle and a thousand well-bred sheep. All shareholders were equal—none could hold more than five shares. So gilt-edged were the baobab-trees of Kimberley that there were seventy-three applications in Victoria alone, all buying for friends and relations. One man, for his wife and seven children, bought forty-five shares. The stockbroker's faith moved King Leopold Ranges two thousand miles south, "only two hundred and seventy miles north of the city of Perth".

In Christmas week of 1864 three barques chartered to carry the Utopians round Australia—*Stag*, *Calliance* and *Helvetia*—sailed the silver mazes of Camden Harbour to find that "glorious Glenelg" River was salt. The "noble forests" had faded into red crags and bush-fires. The "waving pastures" were that Biblical grass "which today is, and tomorrow is cast into the oven". The heat at sundown was a hundred and twenty-five degrees. Men ashore for water had just about perished when the cooing of a wonga pigeon led them to a spring.

There the nation-builders made a tattered camp, swimming horses and boating sheep—but the tumultuous tides of Camden Sound, rising to thirty-eight feet, came in at a bound and swept the stores away. *Calliance* was caught in a squall, and with fatalities turned turtle on a reef. Four thousand sheep died at the rate of a hundred and twenty a night from thirst and poison weed.

Most of the settlers left by the next ship, and those that stayed soon came to grief. In June *Wild Dayrill* carried the last away—for a few months in the wild north-west they had lost all they owned. With the Government Resident, Robert Sholl, sent up by West Australia to found a town, some of them formed a little settlement half-way to Perth, at Nickol Bay—their descendants own some of the finest sheep country around Roebourne today, among them the well-known pioneer family of McRae.

Camden Harbour was beaten by geography, and the worst season of the year. The grave of Mary Jane Pascoe and her baby, on the island where they landed the sheep, still keeps memory of those who died in its few fated months of existence, and when we sailed those channels of glory far from the sea-tracks in a yacht in 1934, after seventy silent years we found the survey-pegs of streets never to be.

When the heroes of *Forlorn Hope* came safely home to Adelaide, Finniss was recalled, and John McKinlay appointed to lead the expedition in his stead. There was news from the north. That sailor of fortune, Captain Francis Cadell, who opened the Murray River to paddle-wheeler trade in the good ship *Lady Augusta*, now in a pearling schooner cruising Carpentaria, had discovered the mouth of the Roper, another grand waterway, and added it to Matthew Flinders's chart.

John McKinlay, from the banks o' Clyde, came out to be a farmer—his old stone farmhouse is standing at Gawler in South Australia still. Ten thousand miles of adventure and a name among the explorers he won in the years between. Searching for Burke and Wills in 1861, he crossed the continent from Lake Eyre nearly to Carpentaria, first to drive sheep and cattle, as stores for his expedition, through the Queensland west. With a presentation gold watch from the Royal Geographical Society he had settled down to a quiet time when the South Australian Government called him to follow the no-hoper Finniss, to find the capital and found the colony in the north.

In cramped meagre notes of his tiny surveyor's diaries, McKinlay was to write the most amazing page in our history of exploration, his odyssey the queerest, his faith in ordeal and resource in leadership second to none.

In November 1865 he left Adelaide with fifteen men, most of them qualified surveyors. Leading citizens fitted them out with a first-class team of forty-five ponies, two from the vice-regal shafts, no less, of Governor Daly's carriage. They would cover the whole coast from the Roper to the Victoria, the schooner *Beatrice* attending them by sea.

New Year in the tents by candlelight, a gay farewell from Davies's shack store bedight with swords and flags, they were out from Escape Cliffs on 14th January for a half-moon ride of reconnaissance south through the hills of Adelaide River, then north-east to Hawkesbury Point, where *Beatrice* would meet them in six weeks' time with stores for Arnhem Land. The wet was down, but this cheered McKinlay. After ordeal by drought in the Dead Heart, he revelled in the rain—or so he thought. In the gig *Julia* he sailed Adelaide River a hundred miles to the depot, the party bringing the horses and sheep on what should have been land.

That night a shower of six inches washed the party away. However, it collected itself, and in three days of deluge crossed creeks, bogs and marshes into heavy sand. Crisp and Mayo went back for a lost dog. Mayo returned alone, and four men went back to look for Crisp. They searched eight days, found his horse, swag and rifle, and were giving him up for dead when they saw him naked and mad, aiming a rusted revolver at them from behind a tree. Restored by black tea and damper, he told of a murderous gang of Malays that had been riding him down for a week, the chief on a grey horse . . . they realized he had been dodging them. A fortnight late at the depot, they loaded up for the bush.

Pack-bells in the jungle, ringing the white man's coming to earth's last wildernesses. . . .

Through weeping rains till the horses, belly-deep in hot mud, could flounder only a mile between sun-up and sundown, on 5th February they crossed a rushing stream in the dark and camped on a flat. It was under water by morning. They swam for a rise and waited a fortnight for floods to go down.

No hope to go back through Adelaide River swamps, two weeks to meet *Beatrice* at Hawkesbury Point . . . digging the horses out of bog they lost one day in two. The sheep, in agony of grass-seeds, were shorn in the steaming scrub and stung to death by mosquitoes. The six weeks' stores were nearly done—tea, jerked beef, medicines, all gone. Each man's weekly ration was nine ounces of flour, ropy and gluey, "a nest of spider's webs". On 9th

March the pack-pony Nigel, hopelessly bogged, was shot, cooked and eaten. A diet of horse began.

Weary miles round every creek, through lanes of twenty-foot grasses, they struggled waist-high in mud, carrying the last of the sheep, the dogs crawling after, soon to die. When the rain stopped, the heat was a hundred and nine fetid degrees in those rank swamps. So they passed from April into May.

Sometimes, to passing blacks, they gave fish-hooks, tomahawks, necklets, for a bit of bush tucker or to keep the peace. Sometimes they caught a fish and drew lots, or camped at a pretty lagoon to live on cabbage-palm and cockatoo stew. One "excellent breakfast" of three kites, two galah parrots, three small turkeys, a sheep's head with the wool singed off and the trotters, was shared by sixteen men. No salt. They craved salt. Crisp cut a rag of sheepskin from under his saddle, stewed it in his quart-pot and gulped that vile liquor salt with horse's sweat. On Queen's birthday, a patriotic gesture, they made a banquet of the Governor's carriage-hack, Daly.

Bags of bones with hollow reproachful eyes, staggering under the packs of their fallen fellows, it was cannibal to eat these melancholy friends, the only friends in a sodden green prison. When the little grey pony, everybody's pet, was swept away in a creek, the party lost a week's meals with relief. Meticulous little ticks in McKinlay's diary tell the doleful story: "Jenkins . . . Bob . . . Wall-eye . . . Ranger . . . Miss Hughes . . . Big Governor . . . Darkie . . . we live on the bones while the meat is pickling." The hides they wrapped on their bare feet over the stones.

The men suffered from mastoid, ophthalmia, dysentery, fever. McKinlay bled them, but they had little blood to lose. He had lost fifty-five pounds weight, but what troubled him most was that his watch had stopped—he could make no observations. Off camp by starlight, steering by the sun all day to a camp-fire in the inimical stillness of the bush, they listened for blacks all night—a shout of alarm and a frantic search for rifles, then the weak and hysterical laughter at their own foolish fright.

June found them nowhere. *Beatrice* had left Cape Hawkesbury months ago, but where else to go?

Pack-bells faltering, fading away, as one by one the horses are drowned at the crossings, smothered in bog on the flats, and shot for food by those starving white men who stumble deeper every day into the quagmire of death.

They had lived on horse for thirty-three days when over bald clay marshes marked with the cloven hoof of the buffalo and the claws of the crocodile they saw to the north a low red range like the ruins of Philae, crested with a broken tor. How far was the sea?

In two days of riding, McKinlay climbed the tor and his heart turned sick. They were trapped . . . right in their path a slow grey river alive with crocodiles, and a maze of impassable swamps all the way, seventy miles, to the sea. He rode back, haggard with despair.

"We killed the mare Millner before we could have supper . . . a nice little horse, but not wholesome as food."

That night, as he rigged his bush net, he spoke to Edmunds, his second in command:

"I have done all a mortal man can do, but fate is against us. In the morning I shall tell the men that each must fend for himself." A bitter admission for a leader. When Edmunds tried to cheer him, he said "Go and see for yourself".

The next day was Sunday. He would tell the men the fateful news after evening prayer. Shadowy circle of faces in firelight of world's end . . . the mournful note of a pack-bell recalling the church-bells of far-away Adelaide, that surely they would not hear again. McKinlay chose Psalm 107:

> They wandered in the wilderness in a solitary way; they found no city to dwell in.
> Hungry and thirsty, their soul fainted in them.
> Then they cried unto the Lord in their trouble, and He delivered them out of their distresses.
> And he led them forth by the right way, that they might go to a city of habitation.
> . . . .
> Such as sit in darkness and in the shadow of death . . .
> . . . .
> They that go down to the sea in ships, that do business in great waters;
> . . . .
> They reel to and fro, and stagger like a drunken man, and are at their wits' end.
> . . . .
> He maketh the storm a calm, so that the waves thereof are still.
> . . . .
> Whoso is wise, and will observe these things, even they shall understand the lovingkindness of the Lord.

His own voice, reading, gave him courage. "Whoso is wise. . . ." He would be leader still. ". . . down to the sea in ships . . ." but how? In God's name, how? On his way to his swag, he passed the carcass of the horse Millner. With curious purpose he bent above it, feeling and testing the hide.

In the morning he said they would build a boat. Of what?—they asked, surprised. Of mangrove stakes and horse-hide. They had lived on horse, worn horse. Now they would sail in horse.

Of the forty-five, twenty-seven were still alive. He ordered that they be shot, and the hides pegged to dry. The party moved on to the river with its steep muddy banks. McKinlay called it Alexandra, but later learnt it was the East Alligator. He sent the men into the mangroves to cut saplings.

Blacks were soon about, sullen salt-water men carrying spears. Two or three hundred gathered, their fires drawing nearer. With nothing to give them, the white men worked in frantic haste, their rifles close beside them. Watts, bringing in the last horse, was yellow with malaria and fright.

Clap-trap, the punt was made—twenty-one feet long, nine feet wide, three deep, hides lashed to the poles with strips of hide, and where the skins were pitiably thin the big tent, which they had so often urged McKinlay to leave behind as cruel and useless weight, was lashed as a bulwark over all. Even so, the craft was too frail for the weight of sixteen men. So they lashed the bottom with whipstick, lined it with saddle-pad. The oars were saplings, the wooden flaps of the pack-saddles for blades. The lead was the shoeing-hammer, the anchor a pack-bag full of horseshoes, and a tether-rope the anchor chain. Not one atom of those ill-starred ponies, presented in Adelaide with so many high-flown speeches, was wasted. The ship was held together with horseshoe nails. McKinlay, not an imaginative man, christened his ghastly Argo *Pioneer*.

The blacks crept nearer in the smoke. A lost tide might mean massacre. Eight hundred and fifty pounds of half-dried horse were thrown aboard, with canvas bags and an air-bed full of water. While McKinlay fired into the thick of the yells, the men rigged a tent sail on a sapling, and Edmunds blazed a tree:

MK
MADE PUNT OF
HORSE-HIDES
TENT AND STARTED
7 TO 29 JUNE
DIG IN TRACK
FOR BOTTLE
8 FEET S.W.
R.H.E.

McKinlay buried a pickle-bottle with his papers eight feet south-west, and a last letter to his wife.

At ten in the morning of 29th June they scrambled aboard and pushed out into the turgid grey river. A hundred miles to go. From the start they baled with pannikins, fending off from snags in soapy shallows, fending off the crocodiles that, three and four at a time, nosed the reek of the rotten hides. At dusk they pulled in to a paperbark swamp and stood guard all night, off again at daylight. Maggoty horse and the water in the vulcanite air-bed made them violently ill, they fell at the oars with no room to lie down. Not one was a sailor. Over the river-bar, five miles wide, they were blown eight miles to sea, where sharks and swordfish took up the running from the crocodiles, sharp teeth and glancing saws a far keener peril to the crazy boat now falling asunder.

As the faint blue outline of Escape Cliffs showed up on the third day, from blackened lips came whispered songs and a soundless cheering. A passing canoe, of the settlement blacks out fishing, turned tail and fled from a ship of the dead. But McKinlay cajoled them back, and on a page of his tiny diary sent in a message:

Expect to be at Escape Cliffs in about an hour. Please have dinner ready. H.M.S. *Pioneer*.

Escape Cliffs was puzzled. No ship had called in eight months, it had precious little dinner, and what was H.M.S. *Pioneer*? Until she arrived in port she was hidden by a belt of mangroves—the blacks rush up to tell of a mob of wild blackfellows coming in from sea.

As *Pioneer* touched land she fell to pieces, she could not have lasted another night. Change of diet to pork and pease after five months' horse, and the pipes of tobacco for which they had prayed, put captain and crew on the sick list for a week. Six months before, they had all been given up for dead.

That was virtually the end of McKinlay's explorations. Though he recommended a possible site for a capital of the north in Anson Bay at the mouth of the Daly, he was not enthusiastic. His ardour was too damp. He found his "city of habitation" in quiet little Gawler, content to sing the Psalms in church on Sunday—he came no more to the Land of Fable. All that was left of Escape Cliffs at the end of 1866 was a cannon-ball and an old tin tank at the mouth of Adelaide River.

Somerset was the only settlement that survived . . . blowing its bugles and marching marines to victory over the Korraregos, chasing wreckers, pirates, head-hunters through the Torres Straits for thirteen years, till the first pearlers moved their schooners across to the haven of Thursday Island. The epic of the Jardine family—of Frank and Alex, the two Sydney Grammar School boys who conquered Cape York jungles—is a feather in Queensland's cap.

Chapter VII

Tree of Knowledge

TALL TALES of heroism and hardship are of lively interest to posterity, but the Northern Territory Company was more concerned with interest in the bank. Finniss's nightmare at Escape Cliffs had cost £100,000, and the McKinlay picnic £10,000. In five years the monsoon clouds showed nothing of silver lining. Landlords of the infinite demanded their money back.

Nobly South Australia faced its responsibilities with the largest and most urgent expedition in Australian history, a Surveyor-General in the lead. G. W. Goyder, that water-diviner of the clouds whose Line of Rainfall decided the future of South Australia's wheatlands, was raced to the north with a hundred and thiry-five men. In the little barque *Moonta* and the steamer *Gulnare*, they circled the coast of West Australia in five weeks without touching land, guided by a star of destiny direct to Stokes's Port Darwin.

On 5th February 1869 Goyder made his landfall in a jungle cove under pied cliffs, and set up his little cannon on a hill to the north—Fort Hill. He looked upon the panorama of that wide bright haven from the diamond-shaped plateau above . . . a harbour within a harbour, shimmering for seven miles from the faint horizon of a Haycock Hill to the ghostly Talc Head, King's

Table a flat-topped isle in middle distance, Stokes Hill to the south, and beyond, the sweep of the bay and the mangroves.

Perhaps he remembered Batman's words when Melbourne was a dream—"This will be the place for a village"—for in sandy scrub of terra-cotta and terra verde, here and there a cathedral banyan or a milkwood-tree in bridal white blossom, he planned the squares and thoroughfares of his capital city, a city majestic as Adelaide, with streets two chains wide and two miles long, and girt with parklands. To be a fortress of defence and a market for the East, it would hold, for a modest beginning, thirty thousand people.

Down on the beach, in a glossy forest of corkscrew palms, the surveyors ran up their tents, candlelight shining with the fireflies in the green lacquered leaves of Port Darwin rains. Tucked under mosquito-nets of fine-mesh book-muslin, with an armed guard on nigger-watch, they listened to the crocodiles coughing in the mangroves.

Shyly smiling through the trees, the Larrakia came to give them a civic reception in sing-about. Expecting some weird atonic saga of the Stone Age, the white men gathered curiously round. They were dumbfounded when, there in the timeless firelight of world's end, the sylvan choral society broke into a lusty rendering of "John Brown's Body", the Glory, Hallelujah! full choir, setting the rocks ringing, and for encore, piccaninnies sweetly joining in, "The Old Virginia Shore". Word-perfect though they knew no English, time-perfect and tone-perfect with no conductor but a shrivelled old beldam beating her yam-stick on the ground, these naked stragglers of an unknown strand might have been a minstrel show in Dixie!

The mystery was later explained away by two young warriors, Umballa and Billiamook—naturally nicknamed Billy Muck—who, fitted out with nagas of turkey red, soon learned pidgin, and became guides and interpreters to the party. When they were asked where they learnt the songs, they pouted their lips to the east—

"White-fella corroboree thatta-way, Woolna been talk."

With the rare musical talent of the Australian blackfellow, they had picked up the ditties from the Woolna, who learnt them lying doggo in the bush round Finniss's survey camps on Adelaide River.

Goyder let no grass grow under his feet. In a few weeks he had charted the harbour shores, rivers and salt arms. He made camp on the beach, with storehouse and stables, built a pile of rocks at the sea's edge to grow up into a jetty, planted the first vegetable garden in Doctor's Gully, and ran up an old twelve-pounder on Fort Hill to guard his little domain. On 4th March he led his parties into the field under Burton, MacLachlan, McMinn, E. Smith and young Dominick Daly, a nephew of the Governor of South Australia.

Wading swamps and thrashing through bamboos to swim many a brimming river, headsmen and chain-men covered fifty thousand square miles, working their way back through hot winds and grass fires. In nine months they paced out half a million acres for plantations in three hundred-and-twenty-acre blocks, they divided the fan-palm and grevillea forest into five counties, and plumb-bobbed the streets of four imaginary towns.

Goyder's lost counties, named for parliamentary peers of England, were Palmerston, the country of Port Darwin and Coburg Peninsula; Disraeli, Mary and Adelaide rivers; Malmesbury, Daly River; Rosebery, Pine Creek; Gladstone, headwaters of the Roper, where Mataranka and the Elsey are now. The streets of Darwin he set down in honour of his own surveyors—Daly, McMinn, Smith, Mitchell and so on—his main thoroughfare, Cavenagh Street, for the Commissioner of Crown Lands.

The expedition was a dazzling success. In a miracle of good leadership and good luck there was no serious illness and no petty squabbling. One man died of old age, and one was killed by blacks.

Pre-war Darwin, sixty years later, made it a pleasant sunset stroll to "the grave on Fort Hill" of J. W. O. Bennett and R. Hazard of the survey party. Bennett was a promising young surveyor-draughtsman, one of Finniss's men from Escape Cliffs, who had helped with the plans of Darwin—one of its streets is named in his honour. At Fred's Pass on the Adelaide River he was speared by a Woolna black-boy caught thieving in his hut. He knew his murderers so well that he could speak their language, and had compiled a Woolna dictionary for his comrades' use. The wounded man set out on the seventy-mile ride for Goyder's camp, but was carried the last thirty miles on a litter of saplings, and crossed the harbour in a dinghy. He seemed cheerful enough, but the spearhead was still in his shoulder. Mortification of the wound set in, and neither of the medical men could save him. He died in the lamp-lit tent by the sea. Maira, Old Man of the Woolna tribe, came to cry at his burial, wagging his aged head in sorrow for the death of a friend. Richard Hazard, who shared Bennett's historic memorial on Fort Hill, was a coloured cook.

At the end of the year the Goyder expedition returned to Adelaide in triumph. It brought a remarkable collection of photographs, commissioned by the *Illustrated London News*, of a new corner of the world. It brought tons' weight of specimens for botanists, geologists and museums, with a whisper of gold at Tumbling Waters on Blackmore River, and blueprints of wealth in the wild.

Too late.

On behalf of English landholders, the Northern Territory Company had issued a writ against the South Australian Government for breach of contract in effluxion of time, claiming £70,000 plus interest. The Government generously offered to double the estates for the money—it could have multiplied them by a thousand and still have had plenty left. The offer was rejected and the company won the case.

First the buyers and no land—now the land, no buyers.

South Australia paid up, but in those pre-Federation days it was not easily daunted. Moreover, from Charles Todd, Government Astronomer, it was hearing rumours of things to come written in the stars.

Striking out the notorious name of Charles Darwin—descended from monkeys—from the plans of the capital city, and placing it under the patronage of the Viscount Palmerston, as a self-respecting mid-Victorian community would wish, it called a half-price sale of the north at 3s. 9d. an acre—less than the price of a yard of stuff. With seven diehard investors and a gallant little squad of local pioneers ready to take a chance, two ships were equipped to found the colony then and there.

The mantle of *Mayflower* fell on the *Gulnare*, under Captain Samuel Sweet. Once a scapegrace slaver of the Caribbean, her hundred and fifty tons so slow that the cruisers always caught her, *Gulnare* had reformed in her old age to a living in odd jobs. Her passenger list was not of Pilgrim Fathers, but a pilgrim family—Captain Douglas, his wife and seven children and their Irish maid

A sturdy old clipper-skipper from the China Seas, South Australia's Collector of Customs, Captain Douglas was appointed Government Resident. Others aboard *Gulnare*, as well as crew, were the schooner captain's wife and baby, an old man unclassified, and an Alderney cow. As they romped and rolled round the east coast of Australia, the cow was washed overboard in storm.

Meantime, Government officials, surgeon, surveyors, storekeeper, a posse of police under Captain Paul Foelsche, settlers and sundries, with wives and children to the number of sixty all told, were mustered aboard the aged barque *Bengal* to take the western half-circle, with one bull, six cows, a hundred and fifty sheep, and two goats, patriarchs of the flocks of Capricornia.

As *Gulnare*, months late, rounded Escape Cliffs, the Woolna kindly paddled out in canoes to warn her of the Vernon Shoals. They need not have bothered. She found *Bengal* well up on the reefs there, and hauled her off at low tide.

On 24th June 1870 both ships entered Port Darwin harbour together. Herald angels of civilization on that picturesque strand were Mrs Mary Elizabeth Sweet, wife of the master of *Gulnare*, and her baby daughter Rose. First of the fair sex to set foot on the sands of Darwin, they lifted their Kate Greenaway frills out of the mangrove mud, and to faint cheering from the ships, sedately stepped ashore.

Captain Douglas ran up the Union on Fort Hill, while the Larrakia, from Stokes Hill opposite, looked on with amiable interest, standing at ease in their human Figure 4, right toe on the left knee, leaning on their spears.

It was a halcyon day for the settlers—boats for the shore in the sequined blue of the bay, Dolly Varden bonnets and stovepipe hats hobnobbing with the savages under the corkscrew palms. In translucent trade-wind beauty of earth and sky, it was more like a picnic than a band of grim-visaged nation-builders five thousand miles from home, with maybe death between. But that is the way of Australians.

Bengal brought Mr Todd's great news. England would speak with Australia in the magic letters B.A.T. The British-Australian Telegraph Company was about to extend the deep-sea cables from Europe and Asia along the Timor floor from Java to Port Darwin. Following the lonely track of John McDouall Stuart, South Australia would erect an overland telegraph line two thousand miles north across the void to meet it. There was even a whisper of a trans-continental railway.

Gaily the settlers congratulated each other while the billy boiled. They had sailed for a blank spot on the map, and here they were, a cable capital, a scientific marvel of the age, right on the world's highways.

"Front Gate of Australia!"—the famous and ironic old phrase was coined that day.

"Green flash" of trade-wind sunset held them spellbound with delight, and low on the northern horizon, as darkness fell, the Great Bear was shining. . . .

Port Darwin a link with England!

If, in the mystery of the tropic night, in that formless shadow of land, warm-breathing, illimitable, secret, they sensed a power impervious to man, a magnitude to mock his perseverance—well, with the Telegraph through, their friends would know when they were dead.

Black forms prancing round the fires on the hill, the Larrakia made a night of it with tum-tum and tobacco, price of their lily lagoons and their heritage of lands . . . the beginning of their end. That week a war-party of the Woolna of Escape Cliffs, jealous of this diversion of the tourist traffic, crept on the camp at piccaninny daylight, killed one and maimed three.

In sunny south-easter weather, the working bees were out from the ships. Log huts sprang up among the corkscrew palms, grey as mushrooms with their paperbark thatch, wooden shutters propped open by a stick, floors of coral lime well pounded, a camp-oven in the open for the sunbonneted cook . . . the old story of happiness in small beginnings and hope.

Gulnare hurried about the coast bringing cypress pine for Government offices and for her own little jetty in the lee of Fort Hill—the skeleton stones of it are still there, last relic of the earlies. Settlers hacked a track up the cliff and over the horehound prairie, dividing the sea-girt plateau in two.

Under a spreading banyan in the heat of day, they had so many theories and arguments about the future of the north, and shouted each other down with such ferocity, that the shady old fig was christened "the Tree of Knowledge". In years to come it sheltered a motley crew.

Land selectors rode and rowed to find their land, and with them the romantic shade of Raleigh. Across the harbour and a few miles up Blackmore River, the first plantation colony Goyder had mapped for them was named Virginia. When the surveyors were there, Blackmore River was a glory. Now it was a mangrove swamp. Some of the blocks had no surface water at all in the dry season, and others were floods in the wet. The only part of the "township" not under water was the wharf, and that was remote in quicksand mud, inaccessible by land or sea.

Fat men physically and financially, the land selectors left in a hurry, but Darwin Harbour raced out to sea and left them on the sandbanks. For three days of sweat and sorrow they dragged their boat from channel to channel over those sandbanks, dodging sharks and crocodiles, all night eaten alive by sandflies.

Hope springs eternal in the Territory swamps. With the riding-parties, lost for three weeks in sago-palm scrub without finding their allotments, they came back to fill the stables with rough trestles and plans, with heated arguments about rice, sugar, coffee, wharf frontages and freight. Then they all left for the south on the barque *Bengal*, and the north to them was no more than a funny story.

A stockman's hut was the first building in Goyder's city. George Dean was the stockman, a dashing young Englishman in blue Crimea shirt and white moleskin trousers, singing a Tyrolean hunting-song as he rounded up the goats from their daily raid on the garden in Doctor's Gully. George was a ladies' man. He made a pin-up gallery of his paperbark hut with actresses and peeresses cut from the London papers. He polished his spurs and Wellingtons, broke in horses for the girls, and escorted them to the beaches and the lily lagoons, a bold defender with a scowl and a revolver.

The garden in Doctor's Gully, in charge of horticulturist Hill, was breaking all records—tomatoes, cucumbers, cabbage, lettuce, twice the size of the ones down south, lemons, limes, bananas, pineapples sprouting to perfection. Somebody measured the melon-vine growing feet in a night.

Captain Douglas moved his wife and pretty daughters into the first little Residency on the crest of the cliffs, a look-out on the lovely harbour. A one-room stone cabin, crazy with outhouses and verandas of *pisé* or pug, it was built by Ned Tuckwell, ship's carpenter, all the settlers sitting round on logs shouting advice. Caulked by sailors of *Gulnare*, with awnings of sailcloth, it looked more like a Malay proa blown inshore.

That poor little Residency was to weather seventy years of change and decay, eternally eaten out by white ants and washed away in the wet, till it became the beautiful old white Government House of today, in colourful tropic gardens on which the Japanese dropped a twelve-hundred-pound bomb in 1942.

An Arcadian track through the jungle, circling the cliffs to the sea by moony grottoes of the banyans and bamboos, was, then and always, Lovers' Walk. Two or three weddings that year, registered by Captain Douglas or Captain Sweet, were a heartening beginning. In one of the paperbark shacks the first white child was born, Palmerston Hayball, named for his native city-that-never-was-to-be.

With a sense of beauty lacking in older Darwin, the pioneers planted miles of coconuts along the harbour shores, but the Larrakia blacks, not interested in picture-postcards for posterity, dug them out and ate them. A few did struggle up, to lend to the grace of casuarina and pandanus the poetry of motion of their silky palms. The ragged coconut avenue at the gates of the Botanic Gardens and the white-anted veterans of Mindil Beach still keep memory of Ned Tuckwell and Surveyor McMinn.

Riding the bush in those sunny days of south-easter was first-footing in paradise, all Nature a novelty. There were picnics to the pterodactyl caves of the beaches, to gather treasures of turtle-shell, coral and little mythological sea-horses, or of spider-orchids, spider-lilies, ferns and lizard lycopodiums from the crystal creeks. Goannas in glistening armour strutted through the scrub, gaudy parrots, silver pigeons and the long-tailed pheasant of a Chinese screen flying above. Brolgas danced their quaint gavotte at sundown.

Gallants at a gallop and the girls side-saddle, mothers and children in the wagonette, in happy excursions they put names on the map—East Point, facing sunset, the St Kilda of older Darwin; Frances Bay for Mrs Chapman of Adelaide; Casuarina Beach for its feathery casuarinas; Rapid Creek and Racecourse Creek for the sulphurous yellow tide rising twenty-eight feet in its seething seventeen knots; Parap Parap from the Malay, Barat; Myilly Point and Mindil Beach *ab origine*—all these to be suburbs and Sunday afternoon trippers' delight for flivvers, trucks and sedans in the pleasant pre-war years, a maelstrom of blitz buggies and marching troops in war.

At night there were glee-parties at the Camp in moonlight bright as day, or an "evening" at the Residency, tenors and sopranos carolling duets to flute and concertina. The Larrakia added to their repertoire "Ever of Thee I'm Fondly Dreaming", and, very appropriately, "Paddle Your Own Canoe" —also, in pure Parisian, doing the actions with a wommera, a clever corroboree of "*Voici le Sabre!*" the dramatic specialty of a fussy little Monsieur Durand, known as "the French Consul".

The Larrakia were already dispossessed. A scandalized Ladies' Guild sewed turkey-red pants and Mother Hubbards for nymphs and satyrs of the woodland. Police-Inspector Foelsche and his troopers put the fear of God into them, riding the billabongs in the dashing blue and silver uniform of an Indian cavalry regiment that was Adelaide's civic pride, and potting the cockatoos with a silver-mounted Colt in warning. Inspector Foelsche had been a colonel of Hussars.

The settlers taught the blacks to fetch and carry, to hew wood and draw water, taught them the Lord's Prayer in parrot repetition, and taught them contempt of their own myall brothers in the bush. For the wallaby hams, fish, geese, dugong steak, wild fowl and wild honey they brought in, they were paid in tea, sugar, flour, tobacco and rum, not so nourishing but more to their liking. When their small but rich hunting-grounds failed in this inrush of population, when the game was scattered by the white men's guns, they dared not intrude on Woolna to the east nor on Wargait to the west, where strange devils haunted waterholes and enemies would kill them, so they gave up hunting, squatted in accumulated dirt on Stokes Hill, and lived on kicks and charity—the old story.

A myall speared a horse in Doctor's Gully, perhaps terrified at sight of the strange brute, or perhaps he fancied its tail for the swing of the bull-roarer. The blacks refused to tell the guilty man, and the outraged settlers proceeded to punishment by a trap. They spread the news of a big hand-out of tucker on *Gulnare*. At the appointed sun-time the harbour was black with canoes, and *Gulnare* with police. Eagerly the natives clambered aboard—to be told by Billiamook they would be held prisoner till they gave the offender up to justice. In panic they raced for the ship's rail—the canoes had been cut adrift—all but two dived overboard. The settlers, also in panic, lined the near shore with guns. Some of the natives swam for miles, and all went bush.

For a time the settlers never ventured out of their huts without pistols, and the story was told in the southern press as TREACHERY OF THE BLACKS. Nothing was said of the white men's treachery, and lack of common sense to see the other fellow's point of view. The "incident" ended when they tamed Maranda, a powerful old man, called him King Solomon, hung the royal tin plate of false pretences round his neck, and allowed him to beg with it for tucker and tobacco as long as he kept his people out of mischief.

Never in seventy years have the peaceful Larrakia committed a serious crime against the white people in Darwin. I doubt whether there is one true descendant of a virile and interesting tribe alive today. There were about a thousand in twenty square miles in 1870.

Making home by the blue of the bay, making their own furniture from the beautiful Territory timbers, with fishing and hunting, no coats, no clouds, no winter colds, the settlers through July and August made holiday in heaven. Then the cool and pleasant trade-wind fell away.

On a hot, still morning in early September, pandanus and coloured rocks reflected in the Venetian glass of the bay, the Camp woke to the glad surprise of s.s. *Omeo* in harbour—a big home mail and celebration. Scores of horses were slung over the side to swim ashore, carts laden with reels of wire floated after them—the telegraph line and the cable had come true. They were all up the cliff-side to build the B.A.T. Stockman George and his goats made room for Her Majesty's couriers under the Tree of Knowledge as the tallest and straightest of the eucalypts came shattering down to be the First Pole.

The fifteenth of September was another gala day of bustles, boleros and pork-pie hats, of trimmed beards and silk cummerbunds, when the white population of a hundred or so gathered on the headland to see a charming and accomplished Miss Douglas plant that First Pole. Her marriage to young Dominick Daly was one of the earliest romances of Lover's Walk, and her book *Digging, Squatting and Pioneering Life in the Northern Territory of*

South Australia, for all its unwieldy name, is one of that sad country's few vivid and valuable old-time records.

Behind the First Pole the stone walls of a post-office emerged like a giant ant-hill from the horehound scrub, with a galvanized-iron roof so new and dazzling that birds of the air alighted there, believing it to be a lake. That post-office was the beginning, and its fall the tragic end, of old Darwin's civil history.

From the Overland Telegraph stables under Stokes Hill, surveyors, linesmen, axemen, teamsters, mechanics, operators and cooks rode off down into the Never Never, trailing the magic wire through the blue. In a blur of bushland, of which so little was known, they vanished from sight.

The climate waxed hot in September—the verb is carefully chosen. Never a drop of rain had fallen from those skies of milky blue. The ferny creeks were rocks and sand. Fan-palm forests dried to brittle yellow, blazed to red in the grass fires, scorched to grisly black. In October the heat was turned on full blaze and action was paralysed. *Gulnare* lay at anchor, a little ship painted on glass. Houses were left half-finished, with holes in floor and roof. The saw-pit was deserted. The axe and the adze lay where they had fallen. Picnics were at an end. There was nothing but talk, and talk a foolish babble or a dangerous flame. Men drank themselves into stupor, and fought, while women fretted at the wash-tub. They were changing their clothes, heavy with sweat, four and five times a day till the clothes were thin and the water from the shallow wells was putrid.

November bowled everybody over. Limbs seemed to be afflicted with locomotor ataxia—the hill was a long way up and the heart failing. Coming out in the cool of the morning with the ants, in the cool of the evening with the crickets, for the rest of the demoralizing day they lay on their backs and stared. Work was damned and left undone. Things that had fallen to the ground stayed there. The settlers dragged themselves round half-naked and could not care.

When the humidity was too oppressive for humans to live through, everything split! The glassy skies cracked in a splintering of hot needles, heavy and gone. Thunder crashing down the canyons of the clouds, in came the storms, the couriers of the rain. They raced across the harbour in olive-green light with the regularity of express trains, and rumbled away to the south through tumbled vermilion towers of tropic sundown.

Purple storms with skyey phenomena terrified the people. High-tension lightning played all night through, played in the moonlight brighter than moonlight . . . neon lightning, green and red, sheet to fork, streak, chain . . . globe lightning, the fireball, uncannily rolling through the bush.

Death came to the little colony, and something of terror. The smiling heaven of yesterday seemed an evil, waiting land.

In full view of the Camp and children playing in the sand, Trooper Davis went for a swim in the tepid, greasy waters of the bay. He swam for a floating log. Sailors of *Gulnare* shouted warning, but with an agonized scream the swimmer went under the oily tide.

White men in boats and blacks in canoes beat the water till sundown, but of the lurking enemy there was no sign. Days later what was left of Trooper Davis was uncovered at low tide in a stagnant under-channel of the mangroves. He was first to be buried in a God's acre of the long grasses that saw the end of many a queer life-story.

Bathing was forbidden for fear of crocodiles, and legendary pythons became bogies of the bush—rock pythons, giant constrictors of the region, measuring up to twenty feet long, awful to behold. They swallow a wallaby and crush a lazy dog, but have never been known, in Australia, to attack the human. When Bob Collard, the jovial armourer and a soldier of the Maori Wars, was found after the New Year revels in a ditch of Doctor's Gully, lovingly hugging the head of a fourteen-foot rock python that had taken a double hitch round a post to pull free, it was one of the jokes immortal of the north.

New Year came in with the north-west monsoon. Rain was a thick curtain let down on the world. Three inches in an hour, twelve inches in a day, it blotted out the little Camp, washed away the huts and gardens. It rained with a helpless hysteria of weeping all through January, February and March, till the cliffs were waterfalls and the tracks running rivers. "Out bush" the Telegraph drays were glued to the axles in ooze, posts floating out of the holes, wires a rusty tangle, starving men swimming for their vanished camps. Valuable horses were shot in bog, drowned in the rising of the rivers. In the few glassy-bright days between the black squalls, it was sweat, sweat and sweat. Nothing could move a mile in that bottomless slag of red mud.

For nine months no ship came in to Darwin's forgotten harbour. Brave horsemen rode and swam to Fannie Bay to watch for a ship, often mistaking a blackfellow's fire on a distant shore for a little steamer, or a drifting log on the sea-line for a sail. The store was empty, no coffee, no tea, rice or sugar, the flour soon to be finished. The blacks brought wallaby, fish and cabbage-tree top, boys stoned geese in the lagoons for supper. The settlers shared with each other. When their flimsy huts collapsed in the floods, they sheltered each other. So they lived on—how, none of them cared.

And the green grass grew all round, sixteen feet high.

Food and clothing, furniture and boots, all the household goods were afloat and ruined, or green with rust and mildew, or devoured by moths and ants. Charlie Fry, a teamster, unpicked a boot and made shoes from wallaby skins. There was not a needle-and-cotton in the north. The Ladies' Guild was trotting round in the turkey-red pants and white calico Mother Hubbards it had sewed with self-righteousness for the blacks, who went joyously naked. Men lived in pyjamas night and day.

Pyjamas, for the next forty years, were the traditional Territory wear for dress occasions. Out bush it was a pair of boots and a big whisker—or a belt and a revolver—or a red handkerchief and freckles.

In April the wind changed—"knockem-down rain"—flattening the long grasses till you could see the next hut. As the swamps dried, the whole colony went down with a bout of fever. Then *Omeo* came back from Java with a few stores and some blessed mail, year-old newspapers telling of the Franco-Prussian War.

In May the healthy trade-wind came rollicking in again, with its song of Pacific surf and cool, cloudless weather. In a glorious land of freedom and singing rivers, hills and valleys a thousand shades of glittering green, fretting was forgotten—the settlers were all friends. They had learnt that God demands of us more than endeavour, that moth and rust corrupt, that nothing matters very much, and that petty ambition has no place in the Divine Architect's plan.

Lazy blue bays and shadowless days, friendly talks in the starlight—after all, they would stay. How could they go away?

The single strand of the Telegraph Line was drifting to the south again, linking the Old with the New, to the exiles a lifeline to their own far-away world.

Chapter VIII

The Singing String

A MIRACLE OF human endeavour and achievement worthy of honour in the history of any nation is the story of Australia's Overland Telegraph and Todd's Men.

Charles Todd was a Londoner, a student of astronomy of Cambridge University, who served his apprenticeship to Time and Space under the dome at Greenwich. From longitude 0° to longitude 138°, from the Pole Star to the Coal Sack, he came to South Australia in 1855 to foster the infant science of telegraphy. Within three months his first ten-mile filament ran from Adelaide to Port Adelaide. Within three years a line was across the Murray River and the mallee deserts to Melbourne. Soon all the eastern States were chattering together in Morse.

Till 1869, all English news was three months old, carried by the little P. and O. mail steamers ploughing round the Cape of Good Hope and six thousand miles across the Indian Ocean, looking for the trimmed lamps of a dim antipodean shore. Kings were buried and victories won without Australia knowing. In those days the oversea ships did not call at Fremantle but came straight on across the Great Australian Bight. Their first signal was a string of flags by day, a lantern winking from the cliffs at night, from the wild lighthouse eyrie of Cape Borda, Kangaroo Island. A blue flag ran aloft on the post-office tower in Adelaide to herald the English mail. When Disraeli bought Britain's controlling shares in Suez, the deep-sea cables came down to India and Java, and company directors in London were conning over the map "to bring Australia in touch with the civilized world".

There were two possible routes and one impossible. The first was from Colombo to Cocos Island and Fremantle, through the deep Indian trench for three thousand miles three thousand fathoms down—a big job for the cable-laying ships. A land-line from Port Augusta on Spencer's Gulf must travel one thousand six hundred miles along the Great Australian Bight to meet it. The second was from Banjoewangie in Java to Burketown in Carpentaria. Queensland telegraphs had travelled as far as Cardwell. The Queensland Government would be most happy to oblige with extension of the line seven hundred miles to Burketown, but the cable must cross the Arafura Sea for two thousand seven hundred miles, in constant risk of coral reefs and shoal water. The impossible route was, from the company's point of view, by far the most attractive—only sixteen hundred miles from Java to Port Darwin, with a land-line two thousand miles south to Port Augusta, already connected with Adelaide.

Was it impossible?

Charles Todd, Government Astronomer, with the philosophic vision of the infinite, denied that word "impossible", but only one man, John McDouall Stuart, knew. Across that almighty desert he had plodded four times. Stuart was dead, but he had given a Scotsman's word to Todd that a land-line could quite easily go through and that, except for one patch of three hundred miles in the dust-bowl of Lake Eyre, the tall Australian eucalypt as a telegraph pole would shoulder it across.

Charles Todd offered to build the telegraph line from Port Augusta to meet the cable at Darwin.

When South Australia entered the lists with this outlandish project, the other States laughed—a hundred and eighty thousand people with more ambition than sense. Queensland, openly rude, denounced it as an "absurdity". Newspapers published a cartoon of Todd in a P.M.G. chariot drawn by two white elephants and supported by cannibal blacks, three insulators on a telegraph pole his trident, followed by gangs of skeleton navvies and a hilarious goanna. In arid distance the ghost of Leichhardt waved a skinny hand. Even the London *Times* raised a questioning eyebrow, with a murmured aside as to "the mysterious interior of the Australian continent". There were some grim prophecies when South Australia was given a chance to try.

Charles Todd was a small man of specific gravity, eyes redeemed from their engrossment with the spheres by a keen earthly perspective and a very human twinkle—a quick assessment of matters and of men. He was no stargazer. This Captain Noel Osborn learnt when he lunched with Mr Todd in Adelaide on his way from London to Brisbane, representing the cable company to sign the contract with Queensland. On his recommendation, the company delayed decision to give the matter very serious thought.

On 7th June 1870 came an announcement extraordinary by Admiral Sherard Osborn, managing director of the British-Australian Telegraph Company, transmitted through the Attorney-General in London: "*. . . the cable will be laid to Port Darwin if the South Australian government will pledge itself to construct and maintain a land-line, to be open for traffic by January 1, 1872, connecting that port with the present system of colonial telegraphs.*"

Eighteen months to conquer the void! Penalty for delay would be £70 a day, and possible cancellation of the contract in favour of Queensland.

Within a week a Bill was drafted and rushed through Parliament, appointing Todd to the office of Postmaster-General and Director of Telegraphs, and granting him £120,000. Within a fortnight he had planned his route by Stuart's map, divided that route into three, and called for tenders for construction of the north and south sections, country known to a few surveyors and bushmen. The third section, virtually unknown, must be a labour of Hercules under his own direction. From Port Augusta to Darwin twelve repeating stations would have to be erected, about two hundred miles apart, and permanently staffed by Australian operators.

The continent seemed a long way across as Todd put in his order for two thousand miles of iron wire and thirty-six thousand insulator poles.

Edward Meade Bagot of Adelaide secured the contract for the southern section, six hundred miles from Port Augusta north to where the last little shack of civilization was Philip Levi's sheep-camp in the yellow sands of the Finke. Darwent and Dalwood, shipping contractors to the poor little tropic outpost of Darwin, would undertake the north, with Goyder's surveys to carry them down through jungle. Between The Peake and Pine Creek—fifteen hundred miles—was nothing but Stuart's map.

In the mosaic hills of Port Augusta in July, wagons, horses, bullocks, carts, drays, poles, wire, insulators, tools and hillocks of stores were waiting. Newspaper advertisements called for men—and men they must be. There were no forms to fill in, no award rates of union hours, no wooden cities of camps to be erected in every sixty miles with water and light laid on, cooks, refrigerators, recreation halls, bacon-and-egg trucks and electric fans. These men were bound out for oblivion with a packhorse and a swag. Two questions only were asked:

"Are you sound in mind and limb?"

"Can you live on bandicoot and goanna?"

Wages were "25s. a week and found". If you were lost you ate what you found till you were found, if you were found.

On the day of applications a multitude rocked the office door off its hinges. Most were South Australians, but there were men among them from all States, of all classes, eager to share an international work no less vital than the Canadian Pacific Railway or the Suez Canal. From the rail terminus at Kapunda, sixty miles north of Adelaide, away they went with swag and pannikin to dig post-holes in the desert, to thread the magic wire across the sky.

Todd's problem was to keep them alive—no cattle stations and never a rabbit out there in 1870. The Government offered £10,000 reward for the first drover across to the north with sheep or cattle. In the meantime, bully beef, the famous Australian "bully" that has travelled the Seven Seas in peace and war, and kept the wolf from the door at the South Pole, made its bow to a grateful world. J. V. Hughes of Booyoolee Station in South Australia packed the first fibre of it in a tin, and fibre it was, but it was meat. Nick-named "red blanket" because of its red label, for two hungry years on the Telegraph Line it was breakfast, dinner and tea for five hundred men. There is a school of thought that the idea and the name were derived from the French *bouilli*, and indeed it was pronounced *bouilli* by pedants of the time, but it was originally written "Booyoolee beef"—the blacks' word is still *belyalie*—and every old bushman of Australia will tell you that "bully for short", the good old tinned dog of the camp-fires, Number One Tucker, first came to the g.w. spaces in the pack-saddles of Todd's Men.

Parties under Todd, Jarvis, Babbage, travelled north to direct the work. In July John Ross, with four others, set out to explore the Centre, and s.s. *Omeo* was off round the east coast for Darwin. Soon the poles were marching down through the ant-hill jungles of the tropics, up over the saddleback ranges, soda flats, gibber stones and sand-dunes of the vanished Inland Sea to meet, in Todd's plan, at Tennant's Creek.

From Darwin Harbour cable ships *Investigator* and *Endeavour* were paying out cable under command of Captain Noel Osborn. The schooner *Gulnare* carried surveyors under MacLachlan and G. R. McMinn round to the mouth of the Roper. In one of the schooner's long-boats they opened that river highway for ninety miles to Leichhardt's Bar. Stores and gear for the hinterland could be landed there by ships, giving the Telegraph teams a short-cut of a hundred and fifty miles south-west to Daly Waters, where the Line would pass.

Exploring and sounding that winding river, trigging the red bluffs and finding a pathway for the wagons, they were through in a few weeks to the interior. One humid night the boat-party was awakened by a scream. Read, second mate of *Gulnare*, sleeping with his feet thrown over the side, was dragged in by a crocodile, blankets, bush-net and all.

John Ross's explorers were away to solve the riddle of the Centre—Ross, six feet of black-bearded Highlander; E. W. Harvey, stocky Lowland Scot; Alfred Giles; W. Hearne, a crippled rider, and our old friend Tom Crisp of McKinlay's north coast expedition, who livened up the lonesome nights with tales of horrors in store.

These five men were first to follow McDouall Stuart. Their story is told in a forgotten small book, *Exploring in the Seventies*, by that hardy old Territorian, Alfred Giles.

For a thousand miles Ross found his way by a prismatic compass, a tracing of Stuart's map, a carpenter's lead-pencil and a two-foot rule. Food in the pack-bags was flour, tea and four hundred pounds of jerked meat—"boot-lace"—a diet varied with boiled crow and nardoo. The medicine chest was Holloway's pills, boracic, eye lotion and castor oil. Each man's home was a tent-fly, a four-gallon bucket, quart-pot, knife, fork and spoon. In mound-spring and sandy soak they looked for water, and carried it on the saddle in canvas bags, sometimes for a hundred miles. When water-bags wore through or ripped up in scrub riding, the men shot wallabies, stewed the meat and made water-bags of the ill-cured, evil-smelling skins. The guns were long-barrelled Colts with ramrods, muzzle-loaders with powder-flasks and buckshot. Once they had no meat for a month but three hawks.

Guided by Chambers Pillar they were the first riders through Heavitree Gap, in the wide central valley of the MacDonnells to find Todd River, rising in runnels and rock-pools, pure cool waters of infinite flow, to weary men a refuge and delight. In honour of Mrs Charles Todd, once Alice E. Bell of Cambridge, they changed the musical Arundta name, Tjauerilji, to the just-as-musical name of Alice Springs. They opened the pass through the rough schist hills to the spinifex plains beyond. On a sandy flat near Stirling Creek they found Stuart's track, a well-marked pad of forty horses that, in that timeless land, was now eleven years old. They found a pair of binoculars hanging on a tree, devil-magic never touched by the blacks.

At Central Mount Stuart Ross unearthed Stuart's papers. Harvey unearthed a bottle of o.p. rum he had carried in his saddle-bag for over a thousand miles so that, sitting on the little knoll that is pivot of a continent, they might lift a glass in the silence to the memory of a fellow Scot.

Through to the north in five months, they found surface waters all the way, and a grand array of telegraph pole gums. Todd marked the site of his stations by their advices—Beltana Gap in the Flinders Ranges; The Peake at Strangways Springs; Charlotte Waters on the 26th parallel; Alice Springs; Barrow Creek; Tennant's Creek; Powell's Creek; Daly Waters; Katherine River; and so to Darwin.

Close behind the explorers came the construction gangs, each with two hundred men, eight hundred horses, two hundred bullocks, stores, express wagons, drays, under R. R. Knuckey, Gilbert McMinn, W. W. Mills, A. T. Woods and Harvey—to each party two degrees of latitude and a little world to learn. The big caravans moved on in mirage, a hundred camels lent by Sir Thomas Elder carrying poles and gear over the sandhills for five hundred miles, Arab and Afghan drivers, in fez and burnous, bowing bismillah to Allah in the Central Australian sundown.

First blackfellow to see a camel-pad on Finke River told a comical story about it in years long after. He had wrinkled his Arundta brow with a lot of hard thinking, then he went back to the wurley, picked up a newborn piccaninny, carried it to the spot, and sat its little posterior in the strange soft track. It fitted like a glove.

"Debil-debil piccaninny walkabout longa sit-down," he informed the astonished tribe, who came to the conclusion there were leprechauns about.

Few Australians know that Charlotte Waters mirror the romantic shade of Byron. That pool of salvation in sandy madness was named for Byron's Ianthe—Lady Charlotte Bacon, who lived in South Australia fifty years after the poet's death. Her son, Harley Bacon, was one of the storekeepers for Todd's Men, in charge of the first two thousand sheep on the Finke.

The Waters were discovered in 1871 by Woods, Knuckey and Gilbert McMinn, riding together on a fierce January Sunday of heat and drought. It was a theme for Byron.

Crossing a flat by the stars, they camped through the blaze of day with no water.

> At sun-down we noticed some bronze-wing pigeons keeping an eastern course. We saddled up and followed. My horse, Bonnie Dundee, the quickest walker, forged ahead and I caught sight of the waters, so clear that my heart went down to my boots. I thought they were salt.
>
> We watered the horses and made some johnnie-cakes, flour, water and a little salt. We called them beggers-on-the-coals. Mr Knuckey was so delighted that he was moved to poetry—
>
> "The greatest enjoyment under the sun
> Is to sit by the fire till the beggers are done."
>
> I named the Waters after Lady Charlotte Bacon, daughter of the fifth Earl of Oxford.

Charlotte Harley was rarely and delicately beautiful as a girl of thirteen years, when Byron met her at her mother's home, Eywood House, Hereford, in the time of the celebrated love affair. Byron was twenty-six. *Childe Harold* was in the publisher's hands. To pay homage to the mother by way of the lovely child, or in minor mood of wistfulness, he wrote the famous dedication "To Ianthe", and commissioned her portrait by Richard Westall, R.A. The engraving has accompanied *Childe Harold* in all editions.

In tender numbers the Great Lover assured Ianthe of a fireproof paternal love:

> Love's image upon earth without his wing,
> And guileless beyond Hope's imagining.
> . . . .
> Young Peri of the West!—'tis well for me
> My years already doubly number thine,
> My loveless eye unmoved may gaze on thee,
> And safely view thy ripening beauties shine.

When she was nineteen, Charlotte married Major-General Anthony Bacon, a hero of Waterloo and the Spanish Wars, and shared with him the perils and hardships of the Siege of Oporto. A brave, bright, intellectual woman, a dashing rider, hers was an adventurous life. She arrived in South Australia in 1860 with her three children as a guest of her friends, the Dalys, at Government House—a fair Ianthe still, but much less ethereal. After three or four years in South Australia, Lady Charlotte returned to England, where she died in 1880, her eightieth year. Her descendants are living in Adelaide.

Incidentally, she left in South Australia an interesting relic, Byron's coach, discovered years after her death by a traveller at Lake Wangary, near Port Lincoln. It was in a fair state of preservation, though dilapidated, with the aura of old romance in the scrolled crest, *Crede Biron*. Alas, in the outhouse of a wayside inn, the fowls were roosting in it. In the grooved leather cushions where genius had brooded lay an egg. So the chariot of Apollo, the most glorious, most notorious coach of London in its day, was left at world's end to ruin and neglect.

Flat desolation is visible to the eye for thirty miles at Charlotte Waters—sixty miles with field-glasses. Mercury in the thermometer may hover at a hundred and ten degrees for ninety days at a time. Rain seldom falls, but the Waters never fail. To the north is the red grid of Depot Sandhills, to the south the blistered brine-flats of Lake Eyre. Many a life have those Waters saved, and thousands of cattle. Brilliant and wonderful birds of the Centre there find "love's image" in a very barren earth.

Ninety miles north are Dalhousie Springs, named for Lady Edith Ferguson, daughter of the Marquis of Dalhousie and wife of a Governor of South Australia—she presented to each of the Telegraph parties a pack-saddle full of books. One of the great spas of the world in one of its clearest climates, there are nearly a hundred thermal springs, some in black whiskered mounds forty feet high, some in naked sand, some with tall reeds and floating reedy isles. They run from thick as mud to clearest crystal. Some are ice-cold, some boiling, some electric, effervescent with mineral salts, or cool and fresh as mountain dew, others sickly sweet. The blacks and, later, the drovers, have long known of their healing. One old bushman has seen a myall lubra carried in from the Musgrave Ranges, a living skeleton, paralysed, with her knees up to her chin. In six or seven weeks of Dalhousie bathing, she walked home, a normal woman of her age.

The crater of the largest spring, in the lee of a hill of fossils about twelve miles from the homestead, is a hundred and fifteen yards by thirty, boiling in the centre, warm at the sedges, where bubbles burst with a faint Debussy music of drowned bells. Another spring, a little river, runs for eight miles four feet deep, to spread out over the salt-pans with the silica glitter of seas in moonlight. Yet another brims a dam thirty yards across. Many are alive with fish—Dalhousie perch, up to six pounds in weight, a titbit of sea-food for passing drovers. In some of the hot springs half-cooked fish are swimming, black as ink. Either as a dose or a dip, the mysterious Dalhousie waters are most healthful and refreshing, with the exception of one or two of severe metallic chill. They are just one of the many wonders of Australian desert sands.

Nearly all the time-honoured names of the Overland can be traced back to Stuart and the O.T. Warloch Swamps in the Centre and Warloch Ponds in the north commemorate a remarkable horse of the exploring party. With a wilful toss of the head, Warloch would start off east or west and find water —twice he saved the lives of the men.

Renner Springs, south of Newcastle Waters, and Doctor's Stones, southwest of Alice Springs, honour genial Dr Renner, who travelled the thousand miles between, up and down with a medicine chest and a bottle of rum in a buggy, to safeguard the health of Todd's Men. Abrahams Billabongs, near the Elsey, were named for the popular Bob Abrahams, and Stanley Billabongs, near the famous old Elsey homestead, after the noble neddy that carried John Ross for three thousand miles. Lake Woods, into which Newcastle Waters flow, was named for A. T. Woods, whose party camped in sight of it for three thirsty days, believing it mirage. One of the men made a delirious bet that it was *real water*, and rode out to dip a billy in a glorious fresh lake seventy miles round. (*Note*: Before you take a header into any lake between Wendouree and Wyndham, paddle first to make sure it is not mirage.)

Through the furnace of Central Australian summer, through Indian red and yellow of the sandhills, stunted mulga forests, whirlwinds of stinging mica dust, all through 1871 the Telegraph teams moved slowly on, leaving the thread in the blue, twenty poles to the mile like masts of ships on a phantom sea. Big blue German wagons bedded down in sand, floated in flood, bogged in black-soil glue. Bullock-teams, horse-teams, camel-strings, goats, sheep, dogs, donkeys followed. Cities of mushroom tents sprang up at sunset and melted away with the morning. Wild human creatures were occasional shadows and smoke, but Stone Age and civilization kept endless watch on each other.

Warramunga of Banka Banka for three generations danced a historic corroboree of Waddilecki the String. When the construction parties hurried through their country, from Attack Creek to Renner Springs, they were away hunting on the downs. They came straggling back in a dry time to springs and rockholes in the hills, travelling as a tribe travels, warriors in the lead, on the flank and in the rear, ready to rush out after an enemy or a euro, lubras in the centre carrying camp dunnage, babies, coolamons, yam-sticks and firesticks.

Suddenly they came to the draytracks, the cleared space, the marching poles and the endless wire shimmering above. They were pop-eyed with fright. They believed that a great and powerful devil had passed that way—and they were not far wrong. *Nyee nyee cooya?* (What animal here?). *Jennanga! Jennanga!* (Back! Back!). *Killeeberta mullooga cooyu!* (Angry big animal). You must never tread on a devil's track or you will draw up his evil through your feet. So they made it a running jump, young men vaulting on spears, lubras throwing babies, the old ones puffing and blowing, clearing it by a whisker. For a long time the Singing String, its poles humming a high sinister note, was a Voice of terror in the bush. But when the telegraph station was built, the Warramunga of Tennant's Creek came in three hundred together, men with their arms above their heads to show they carried no spears, women and children before them, and all holding green branches of peace.

Djauan tribe of Katherine River, in industrious imitation of the white men, went out and chopped trees and put up a jolly good mile and a half of poles leading nowhere, to the confusion of the Telegraph men till they discovered the joke.

By July 1871 Bagot's parties were through the Flinders Ranges, nearing The Peake. A thousand miles north, the Government line was through the MacDonnells and spanning the spinifex hills to Powell's Creek. No news from the far north for five months, but from Darwent and Dalwood's brilliant beginning of ninety miles in their first five weeks from Darwin, Todd fondly hoped that their section was nearing the end. The Telegraph would meet the cable by New Year.

It was a cruel mirage. On a day of sheer panic for the P.M.G.'s Department in Adelaide, McMinn, surveyor-in-charge in the north, came from a ship with the shattering news that Darwent and Dalwood were ruined and gone. Over their head the waves had met in the Territory wet. Wagons were bogged, horses drowned, men starved out. No stores, no ships, no hope. On two hundred and twenty-five miles of broken poles, a hundred and fifty-six miles of sagging wire hung forlorn in the jungle.

Five months to go! Breach of contract for South Australia, a good laugh for Queensland.

No telephones in the seventies—Todd rushed round to the most capable man he knew, R. C. Patterson, surveyor-in-chief and engineer for railways. He promised him a bonus of £1500—worth about £6000 today—if he could finish the northern section by New Year.

Patterson was away with a fleet of five ships, *Omeo*, *Himalaya*, *Laju*, *Antipodes*, *Golden Fleece*—sail, steam or galley slaves, anything in the old Port River. With one call at Newcastle for five hundred bullocks and two hundred horses, they made it a race for Port Darwin with two hundred men, leadsmen chanting, skippers at the masthead, non-stop through Torres Straits. At Darwin the crews came out on strike, they were delayed for a month in landing gear. Then in parties to five sections of a hundred and ten miles each, all went bush in a hurry under MacLachlan, Mitchell, Rutt, Ringwood and Burton.

"If we don't get through
By '72,
Patterson's bonus will look very blue!"

That was their theme-song.

The end of the Line was chaos and defeat. South of Katherine in a dreadful "dry" they were urgently digging wells, sixty feet to solid granite, most of the labour lost. Drays carried more water than gear south from Katherine River. Bullocks and horses died in droves. Huge coils of wire lay by the track. In steep creeks and patches of bottomless bull-dust, wheels came off the wagons, drays fell to pieces, not enough flour and bully to keep the men alive. In October every camp went down with fever.

In frantic haste, Patterson sent *Gulnare* with stores to Roper River to be rushed to Daly Waters. The schooner ran aground on Vernon Shoals. Patterson tried to charter *Investigator*, but the cable company demanded £8000. His only hope was the barque *Bengal*, mooning around Koepang to buy meat for famished Darwin. At last she ambled back and hauled *Gulnare* off the reef.

Patterson bumped five hundred miles in a buggy through virgin bush to Roper Bar. In November he faced the wet there, his stores and transport done. It was J. A. G. Little—later to be Darwin's first postmaster for a long thirty-five years—who carried a life-and-death telegram to Todd, carried it in an open boat across the Gulf of Carpentaria to Normanton then, riding, to the nearest telegraph station at Gilbert River in Queensland. For Queensland, with the end in sight for South Australia, was hopefully extending its own telegraph to Burketown.

"Hungry Patterson" called across the continent for thirty teams of horses, four hundred miles of wire, for lightning conductors, soldering fluid, staples, insulators, food, clothing, medicine, mosquito nets, boots—it was only too plain to Todd that all he had, including hope, was lost.

Charles Todd the resolute, with the stray ships he could muster, set out himself for the north. He loaded up *Omeo*, *Tararua*, and a little old paddle-wheeler known as *Young Australian* that reached the Roper and gave up the ghost—her bones and the last of her brasswork can be seen there today.

Out in the Timor Sea cable ships were paying out cable, *Hibernia*, *Edin-*

burgh, *Investigator*, two-and-three-thousand-tonners under Captain Robert Halpin . . . steadily on, five hundred and fifty-six miles from Singapore to Batavia, one thousand and eighty-two miles from Banjoewangie to Darwin. On 20th November 1871 the cable was through. Captain Halpin from Batavia signalled his greetings to Captain Douglas in Darwin—"Advance, Australia Fair!"

Australia Fair had no chance of advancing. The Big Wet was down, telegraph poles washed out of the holes, telegraph parties on hilltop islands. Under the arch of an inky sky, bogged horses were helpless to cover three miles a week. The Roper was not a river but a sea.

An afternoon's motor-run now from Elsey Station are the famous Red Lily Lagoons—Yaalput—a close weave of scarlet for three square miles, the glory of the Roper. In New Year '72 was written their greatest page of history. Three of the telegraph parties were marooned there, within fifty miles of each other without knowing, living on flour and the last of the bully beef, when into that world of waters came Ralph Milner, first drover from south to north, with four thousand sheep.

His story begins at Killalpaninna on the Cooper, fifteen hundred miles south, a station long abandoned on the shores of Lake Eyre, its fences now buried and its lofty old rooms filled to the ceilings with sand. In 1870 Ralph Milner owned the station and his wife died there. He built a cairn to her memory in the wild-flower sandhills. When the Government offered £10,000 reward for the opening of the stock route from Adelaide to Darwin with sheep or cattle for the Telegraph parties, Milner set out, with his brother John and seven men, droving seven thousand sheep and three hundred horses. The Government changed when he was half-way across, and he never collected the money. His men, like Stuart's and Todd's, were paid 25s. a week. They were Kirk, a ship's pilot, John Thomson, a teamster, Jack Brown, Bill Lamb, Harry Pybus, Jack Wooding and A. C. Ashwin. They carried a year's stores on bullock drays, with greyhounds and sheep-dogs to guard the flock, also a black-boy and his lubra, faithful Charley and Fannie, every night for eighteen months building little brush yards.

From Peake Station in a cruel summer they whipped on the sheep till they were blind under the sulphur sky and crippled from the stones. One stage was eighty miles with no water. On Christmas Day 1870 they stopped at a mudspring to wash clothes, clean firearms and shift the loading. They found some bags of sago soaked through with kerosene, but dared not throw them away. That sago was their Christmas dinner, 1871.

The Finke was a river of sand, its pools all salt, but they dug soaks, and one night the river came down from rains in the ranges. It was two fathoms deep for a hundred miles by morning. They were trapped for a month, horses bogged and wagons floating. Wild dogs circled with melancholy howling.

When the Finke had subsided to a quarter of a mile, they made it a swim

—the first hundred sheep went down to their bellies in quicksand. The men worked the water out of the sand and saved them. A stiff current carried the next lot downstream—all hands and horses swimming. At last they built a bridge, of spinifex and gum-boughs, five hundred yards long, over the quick-sands and the flowing channels and, with a few goats to lead them, seven thousand sheep scrambled across in single file.

Out of the bogs, the next trial was a plague of rats. The men fought them, in moving blur of thousands, to save the flour. Thankfully they rested at the lonely Telegraph camp of Alice Springs, and went on—to a valley of fatal beauty. Beyond the Devil's Marbles the gastrolobium was in blossom, tall as English hollyhocks and softly bright as wallflowers. On a blithe morning the drovers were wearing it in their hats . . . two thousand sheep were dead that night, the pain-maddened bullocks tossing the carcasses on their horns. Gastrolobium is swift and deadly poison to stock—many a mob of cattle has since perished at that spot.

Tragedy caught up with them at Attack Creek. Blacks were mustering for mischief—smokes all round. John Milner unwisely made friends with the natives and brought them in to camp. He was waddied to death while he lay sleeping in the shade, his grave the first of many on the overland track.

By the moon, the mopoke and the dingo's howl, each night the shepherds camped a few miles northward. There was trouble with the blacks all the way, but the dogs were their defenders. One morning they "found a black-fellow with his throat torn out, and many tracks of blood". Grim years, the seventies, in the outback of Australia.

At Newcastle Waters, through dense walls of lancewood, they chopped a passage for the sheep, a long seven miles—you will still find it on the Stuart Highway, known as Milner's Cutting. So they came to the Roper when it was six miles wide—it rained inches every day for the next three months. They still had four thousand sheep, herded on a ridge south of Red Lily, paddocked in natural walls of grass. When the sun came out for an hour they killed sheep and ate them, and bagged the mutton chips—you cannot jerk meat in the rain. Flour, tea and salt were done, they lived on sheep and cold water. The bullocks were bogged miles back, with most of the packs and swags, horses drowned and running wild. They boiled the kerosene sago for a treat on Christmas Day.

By February the plains were an inland sea with breaking waves, crocodiles swimming in the lagoons like sharks in the Indian Ocean. In March the un-merciful rain stopped. Rutt's, MacLachlan's and Burton's parties were a surprise to each other, all starving on flour while Milner's were starving on mutton a day's ride away. They boated over the sheep in an upturned cart, eleven at a time, and that night Todd's Men had chops for tea.

Between King River and Bitter Springs is Providence Knoll, a pretty spinney of pines and jungle where Rutt and his men raced for safety when their drays were under water on the flat. There they lived for six weeks on ship's biscuit, the skeleton horses drowning their heads in flood waters, trying to crop the vivid green grass below. Near by is All Saints' Well, named by Ringwood, which had saved their lives a few months before in the scorched and unbearable dry. Some years ago at Epping, Sydney, I met David Melville, a white-headed patriarch of ninety-five years, who was with Rutt at Providence Knoll and helped to count Milner's sheep. He told me that when hopes were lowest and tempers worst in the accursed rain, he made four sets of playing cards out of bully beef tins, painting them in spades, clubs and hearts. The men played euchre in the dripping bush, good-humouredly trumping each others' tricks till the floods went down.

When the Roper was a river again in a thousand miles of glue, W. G. Stretton, Burton's storekeeper, with eight others, floated in the body of a dray to Roper Bar, and pulled back two hundred miles against the stiff current, bringing the glad news that Todd's ships were in the river, Todd and Patterson on the way up with a hundred and fifty packhorses bringing food and clothing for the camps.

There was a "toff's party" at Red Lily—a razor, a shirt and trousers, a silver-mounted pipe to every man, Milner's roast mutton, a plum duff and a nobbler of whisky to toast the Overland Telegraph Line. It was disastrously late, but so far the B.A.T. had taken no action. The heroes had not suffered in vain. They still might cover the ground in time.

Skies cleared—the wire raced on. From twenty poles to the mile Todd reduced the number to sixteen, to ten. By May, twelve hundred miles were completed from Port Augusta to Tennant's Creek, and three hundred miles from Darwin south to Birdum Creek, named by Patterson for his wife, a Miss Birdum. Three hundred miles to go—the end in sight.

All the world was impatient to hear the first message through. Todd had an inspiration—he would run an *estafette* with four relays of horses, field operators with the construction parties to spell out messages in Morse at each end of the Line.

On 26th June the packhorses of Ray Parkin Boucaut galloped three hundred miles south from Katherine with souvenir cables and the first international news-flash to Australia—that, over the Alabama question, England and the United States were about to declare war. News of the Franco-Prussian War, less than a week old, at Australia's breakfast table was a marvel of the age.

The thrill was brief. Next day the machines were silent. The cable had broken in deep water off the Java shore.

This gave Todd time to breathe—a race, now, between sea and land. John Lewis rode the ponies of the *estafette*—later the Honourable John Lewis, a foundation member of Broken Hill Proprietary of the silver wealth of the south. His son, Sir Essington Lewis, today controls Australia's industry of iron and steel. Through grass fires of the dry, John Lewis and his brother raced two riding-horses and two packs, once a week . . . then twice . . . then three times, as the gap in the Line narrowed down to fifty miles.

The moon of August was lighting the way to victory, the men worked day and night. Charles Todd was riding down the Line two thousand miles to Adelaide and home.

On 22nd August a telegram reached him at Tennant's Creek—eight miles to go. With a grand sense of the fitness of things he asked that the wire should not be joined till next day, when he would make his camp at Central Mount Stuart.

In the hushed Australian noontide of 23rd August 1872 England and Australia were inseparably joined by the twist of an iron wire, three miles east of Frew's Ironstone Ponds. From another old camp of John McDouall Stuart, A. Howley was the field operator who tapped the signal through to Todd. Nine or ten men stood round his shackle-set as back from the silence came the fluent dot-and-dash of the Great Work done. They fired a salute of twenty-one shots with somebody's revolver, and shared a toast and a billy of tea under an ironwood-tree.

That night Charles Todd's message rang out in Adelaide with a peal of the Town Hall bells: "We have this day, within two years, completed a line of communication two thousand miles long through the very centre of Australia, until a few years ago a *terra incognita* believed to be a desert."

In the bleak wind of Central Mount Stuart, Todd sat till daybreak, his camp-fire no brighter than those of the primitive dark people sleeping on the plains about him, his little pocket relay set clicking the world's praise that he had brought civilization and commerce to Australia. Even Queensland could scarce forbear to cheer. The faint thread of iron wire across the red of dawn was a link in the world's thought.

Investigator was still grappling for the cable off the Javan shore, but the Overland Telegraph parties were finished and free. Pack-bells ringing a merry carillon of work well done they were off to Roper Bar, four hundred men singing along. *Young Australian* wafted them to Maria Island, where *Omeo* called to carry them home. She arrived in Brisbane burning her own beer-cases, and in Adelaide to one of the grandest pay-days in Australia's history. Queues of bearded bushmen, in blue shirt and moleskins, lined up at the G.P.O. to draw big cheques for two years of exile. It was a "knock-down night" in Adelaide.

Only five men, of over five hundred, were missing. Kraegen, an operator, wandered and perished of thirst. John Bowman, a teamster, died of sunstroke; Jeremiah Harcus was lost in the bush; Meinaber, a German boy, died of apoplexy; and one other was drowned.

On 30th October the mended cable slipped back into place in a deep-sea ravine of the Arafura. England officially greeted Australia, and the world rang with felicitations. In Adelaide there were bonfires, banquets, public holiday and processions. Todd's Men were the heroes, telling their tales of crocodiles and blacks, flood, fire and desert sands.

Charles Todd was Sir Charles Todd, K.C.M.G. With time signals from Greenwich he fixed the 141st meridian, border of New South Wales and South Australia, and found new worlds to conquer in Overland Telegraph Number Two, to circle the Great Australian Bight for sixteen hundred miles to West Australia. Of the type of the late Dr J. J. C. Bradfield, designer of Sydney Harbour Bridge, who offered his engineering genius to his country in continent-wide schemes of irrigation and reclamation, for Todd the span of a man's life was too brief for all he had to give.

Overland Telegraph Number One cost £479,174 18s. 3d. Within the year, from one cable alone, South Australia cashed in a round £1,000,000. With news to hand of wheat famine in Europe, ships were chartered in India and Java to carry away the first world exportation of Australia's wheat.

Only the wealthiest newspapers could afford cable services, and readers were reminded of the eighth wonder of the world at the head of every item. Till Bentley's beat the minimum with code, it was a flat rate for commerce and the press of £1 a word to London, 1s. a word in Australia. A telegram in those days was a shock. It meant either Big Business, birth, marriage or death.

The saga of the Singing String is endless. It could go on for two thousand miles like the String itself—and every mile a story—of the perishers who shot the insulators and severed the line, and so found salvation in hunger and thirst; of the thousand who followed that shining strand in the gold rushes; of the coming of the cattle-men, a classic in colonization; of the explorers who made it the lifeline when they challenged the unknown, east and west. The telegram boys were naked blacks "foot-walking with a paper-yabber" a couple of hundred miles, carrying the wire in a split stick. It was magic and not to be touched with the hands—if they dropped it they never picked it up. So lonely was that land that telegrams to it might not be delivered for five years, too many of them never.

Till 1930 the Overland Telegraph track was the faint midrib of the fifth continent, ghost of a road, the width of a wagon, running from south to north. The telegraph stations were the great first cause in colonization of a round million square miles. From shacks in wilderness, each with two operators, a linesman, a cook, a box to cover the instruments, and a rifle above the key ready for a raid by the blacks, one by one they became fortresses against the implacable loneliness, citadels of law and order in a lawless, loveless land. To build those old stations Elder's camels and many a bullocky, and Chinese coolies in the north, like slaves of the Pyramids, toiled with the stones in some places for five hundred miles. So firm was their foundation in the realm of illusion that all save one are standing there today.

Beltana, Alice Springs, Tennant's Creek and Katherine are large and thriving towns. Barrow Creek and Daly Waters soon will be towns. The only ruin is Strangways Springs in its weird setting of mound-springs on the zinc-white shores of Lake Eyre. Roofless to the sky and long-deserted, it has no population save night-owls and the dead. There is a graveyard in the drift sand, three or four headstones. One of them bears a woman's name—"Mary . . . Beloved Wife. . . ."

But women played a small part in Overland Telegraph history. That was a fidelity surpassing love of women. The first telegraphists of those incredibly lonely outposts, at 8s. a day and rations, gave their lives to the Line. Most of them died there, forgotten men, but their work is immortal, and their stations were beacons across the empty plains to the dying and the lost. They gave board and lodging, tucker for the track, maps of waters, medicines, news, letter-writings, leg-settings, legal advice, horses and friendship to every traveller in three generations. Their stores were sometimes two years on the track from Adelaide—their mail came with the stores, also their tombstones. The cracked marble tablets "Erected in Loving Memory by Comrades of the Overland Telegraph" are among the few relics of old days along the Stuart Highway.

Out in the wilds writing history in Morse, every night at ten o'clock they received and repeated the news from England for the southern press. Australia never gave them a thought in seventy years.

The struggle with Nature was one long battle. The Line must be kept open for a hundred and eighty-three days of the year, and Australia paid England for every hour lost. White ants ate the telegraph poles, blacks stole the insulators for making their spearheads, the wire rusted and snapped. Cockatoos in myriads played trapeze on it and nipped it through, hurricanes blew it down, trees short-circuited it, lightning struck it, wasps built their nests and frogs electrocuted themselves in the binding wire, causing leakage, sandhills undermined it and floods engulfed it. The linesman would jump on a horse and gallop a hundred miles with swag, tuckerbag and hand-set, camped alone in the bush, swimming horses and camels over the creeks, following the fourteen-mile shackles, and climbing the swaying poles to test and mend.

For the rest, they mustered their few cattle, hoed the vegetable gardens, and in empty hours of leisure called each other to play chess and euchre in Morse over the wire, forgetting the silent miles between. They learnt the bliss of solitude, and few of them would leave it. To work in a row at a G.P.O. seldom appealed to them thereafter.

Many books could be written of Todd's Men and their conquest of wilderness . . . men like J. A. G. Little, fifty years in the telegraph service, twice a year driving down from Darwin in a buggy on his thousand-mile inspection of the Line. Or J. G. Kelsey, with a shackle on the Line and a potato tin for a sounder, sending cables to London of gold in the jungle, calling the doctor at Darwin to prescribe for men gone mad, then riding ninety miles to mend the wire; he retired thirty years later, but died on the ship going south, and is buried on an island of the Great Barrier. There was F. J. Gillen, twenty-five years at Alice Springs—Mount Gillen is sentinel of the bright little capital of the Australian Middle West that once was his dark valley; Gillen put in his spare time "studying the blacks", and to the knowledge he gave to Sir Walter Baldwin Spencer we are for ever indebted for the unveiling of the life and mind of the Arundta people. These are but three of a hundred whose life-stories should be told.

For the O.T. inspired a race of heroes—of dramatic tragedy and of the long empty years. Among the greatest of all were A. T. R. Halls—"Snowy" Halls—Superintendent of Telegraphs, and J. C. Bald, postmaster at Darwin in February 1942. These two, after more years than were fair of outback service, applied to be sent back in peril of war. Good men and kindly—I can see them both still—Mr Bald took his wife and daughter with him to Darwin, leaving a young son at school. Mr Halls left his wife and children in the Adelaide Hills. In the fall of Singapore, four days and four nights on duty with the gallant office staff, they never left the key. All were killed in the horror of the first Japanese raid. It was a transcendent ending to the story of Todd's Men.

The last of the old brigade was out there when I last passed by, Waldemar Holtze, old "Wallaby" Holtze, at the age of seventy-nine years officer-in-charge at Powell's Creek. He joined the service in Darwin when he was fourteen years old—sixty-five years in the silent places. Because he had lived adventure, Wallaby liked it quiet. He applied for a transfer from Daly Waters when the aeroplane called there in 1930, and was sent to the farthest outpost, Tennant's Creek. Fate hounded him down with a gold rush, and soon Tennant's Creek was a town of nearly a thousand people. He went bush to Powell's Creek, with the roar and onrush of war close behind him along the new military road. Wallaby weathered that through, on duty.

Old hands remember a night long ago at Powell's Creek when little Billy Gents, the operator, passed on to a camp of drovers, as the Telegraph always did, the news of the night. Marconi had perfected radio-telegraphy.

"That means you're out of a job, Billy," they said. "The writing on the wall."

"Not so," said Billy calmly. "He'll never get away with it. You can't have the whole world tuning in."

Marconi did get away with it. Now the whole world chatters and sings all day and all night on a radio beam, but Billy's successors are not yet out of a job. Overland Telegraph Number One has been a greater power than ever before in the life of the Australian nation, stone pylons shouldering it over the rivers where once the linesmen swam, Darwin talking to Melbourne on the telephone above the drone of the traffic on one of the great continental highways of the earth.

Look up! The O.T. is a different story from when Charles Todd sent his first message in 1872—why, it has more strings than a steel guitar. One of them is the old iron wire of the earlies. The Singing String of the seventies is joining in the music still.

Chapter IX

Forgotten Gold

THE FIRST news of the far north the Telegraph shouted was gold. The jungle sweated gold.

Where the motor-drome of the Stuart Highway spirals the hills of Pine Creek at seventy miles an hour, swallow-diving through valleys green as Ireland and fan-palm creeks running red, there's a ghost in the twilight wheeling a barrow seventy years ago. In the time of grass fires, glowing logs and trees aflame in the gullies of night keep alight the camp-fire memories of the poor little towns of forgotten gold.

On very bad roads with a very good map you can still find them. Some are on the railway line—that cranky little hairpin gauge of the eighties zigzagging the highway from Birdum to Darwin, plodding the hills the long way round.

Union Reefs, Lady Alice, Burrundie, Grove Hill, Fountain Head, Yam Creek, Brock's Creek, Spring Hill, Howley, Bridge Creek, Zapopan, all the way to Batchelor and Rum Jungle, once towns of many mines, now names in nothing, each one a bottle-dump, an overgrown track to thousands of tons of rust, and a graveyard that only the old hands can find.

Bullfrogs honk in mazes of waterlogged shafts that once floated capital in millions. Bower-birds build in phantom streets haunted by the ghosts of Chinamen and wild-cats.

When I was in the Territory in 1933, Union Reefs, Extended Union and Lady Alice, twenty or thirty big mines within a twenty-mile radius of Pine Creek, were sold for £12 . . . acres of machinery, poppet-heads, steel-lined shafts, two towns and a tramway thrown in, a wilderness of rusted iron and corroded dreams.

The seventies in Australia were a mania of gold. It was twenty years since the Sindbad realms of Ballarat and Bendigo—nuggets weighing a hundredweight and halls of bullion a mile deep—had sent trade routes and populations across vague oceans to a vague land. All over the eastern colonies, chasing the grand illusion or the magic fact, the gypsy legions of gold had left great mines, cities and railways in their wake. Some cashed in their claims for millions, many left their bones by the track, but the caravan went on, ever northward, ten thousand crooked miles across the plains and ranges to another treasure of buried millions at Charters Towers.

Where now? These ragged men, women and children would follow the whisper of gold to death and misery, and after them came the company kings, "experts", real estate jobbers and the wild-cats. The blackfellow wilds of Cape York, the Territory and the West were the next scenes in that stupendous drama.

Finniss's men at Finniss River, Goyder's men at Tumbling Waters and Todd's men digging post-holes at Cullen River, shouted tally-ho of gold. In 1871 E. M. Bagot and John Chambers formed a company in Adelaide that hurried the brigantine *Alexandra* round to the north with a party of nine prospectors, experienced men who knew gold when they saw it. Caught in a willy-willy off the north-west coast, *Alexandra* was crushed to broken wood. Her masts ripped out and her rudder gone, through a whirlwind of birds, butterflies, branches and sand blown from the desolated land in columns about her, she reeled in to Darwin Harbour in March '72. The nine men were Westcott, Noltenius, Houschildt, Roberts, Hylandt, Litchfield, Hulbert, Woods and Porteous Valentine. They floated up Blackmore River on a raft made of casks, and with ten horses and a dray set out south through jungle.

Across black ribs of rock at Tumbling Waters, up and down through bamboo creeks of Adelaide River, for a hundred miles they followed pallid drifts of quartz, finding a few colours to drive them on till tucker and strength were nearly gone. On a reef near Grove Hill, sitting with his mate, Harry Houschildt, in the clammy heat of noon, Harry Roberts viciously threw his pick with a curse on gold.

... *and there it was*, in the shattered quartz, a lightning streak of the fickle gold to a leader of a thousand ounces!

Red-hot along the telegraph wire they sent the news away. A second party rode past them, Adam Johns and Phil Saunders—those two apostles of the rag-tag Round Australia Army who first-footed a continent from east to west. Out among the blacks and bower-birds near a creek of native pines their picks and shovels unearthed five thousand ounces at the dazzling Union Reefs, a lode two hundred feet deep and eleven feet wide for twenty miles, of which John Lewis has written: "You could see gold glittering in the reef seventy yards away, the most magnificent sight I ever saw in my life. I bought a sixth share for £1,000."

Wind of the word brought three shiploads of diggers who sailed right past Port Darwin to Blackmore River, dumped stores in the mud and scrambled through the mangroves, ships' crews after them, leaving skippers with a few kanakas to trim sails. These ships going out met others coming in. The rush was on.

Dragging swags through rivers and over the heights, the first diggers found gold everywhere, in sandstone, blue granite, red ironstone, snow-white quartz and black slate, on the crests of the hills and in the beds of creeks—men in rags, living on ropy flour, every day picking up gold!

Tin dish and cradle, bucket and windlass, dry-blower, shovel and pick—French polishers and photographers were pegging claims among the ant-hills, cooks, doctors, remittance men, miners from gold in the snow at Kosciusko, Forty-niners from California, varicoloured waifs of the world, all starving and all armed against the blacks. They brought back wash gold in bottles, nuggets in dirty calico bags, and gold-shot ore in sacks.

At Pine Creek a pick and shovel ten feet down turned up four thousand ounces; fifteen thousand ounces went by in a cart full of stones from the shadow of Eleanor Hill; from one claim of thirty-eight acres came £38,000 in a few weeks. A Frenchman vaguely known as Louis found a hundred and fifty ounces in one golden lump coated with earth, and a "milk pudding" of quartz where a dozen "plums" were nuggets of pure gold weighing from two to ten ounces.

Eureka, Enterprise, Day Dream, Dog and Duck, Emperor, El Dorado, Sailors' Patch and Pay-me-well, Golden Gully and Lucky Strike—the old names in the litany of gold sprang up in the pandanus, but fortunes were in the shareholders' faith, not in the prospectors' find. A ton of sparkling specimens was rushed to the south to float companies. Roberts sold his jab at the reef for £5000, plus ten thousand shares, plus all stone raised, to be the

Princess Louise Mine. The fan-palm jungle was infested with jackals in goggles, pith helmets and Assam silk suits—mining agents and company promoters. Todd's Men raised their eyebrows at the bare-faced skulduggery that streamed over the wire for Adelaide, Sydney and Melbourne, and by cable for London, four or five times a day:

PEG OUT ANYWHERE CAN SELL ANYTHING REPLY URGENT.

But typhoid is less contagious than gold fever. Todd's Men went bush with a shovel, or signed on the dotted line for shares. Some made fleeting fortunes and came back to the key. McMinn struck it rich in the Britannia. Howley floated the Howley, richest mine in the north for the next sixty years. All banded together in the Lady Alice and the Telegraph. Westcott, Houschildt, Roberts and Noltenius cashed in thousands, put their money back in the mines, quarrelled and sued each other, and the lawyers got the lot.

The Telegraph bullock-team dragged a ten-head stamp battery a hundred and fifty miles over the hills to Lady Alice, and miners carried their stone to it fifty miles. First crushing gave seventy-seven ounces to the ton at Union Reefs, six hundred and nine ounces to the ton at the Telegraph mine, eighty ounces from ten tons of milky quartz for Lady Alice, and a hundred and fifty ounces to the ton from Houschildt's Rush.

Flocks of English and Australian companies came down like crows, each with four or five leases and fifty or sixty men, fares paid, wages £5 a week "and found", east or west round Australia on any ship. Darwin boasted seven shanties and seven stores, a couple of hundred shacks—but soon it was a town of empty houses and gold widows. Even the Government Resident had "gone to the reefs".

A hundred miles to the south of it, Fletcher of the O.T., sitting on a box in the bush with a shackle thrown over the Line, was tapping out fairy-tales while half a dozen towns and thirty or forty big mines were ripped out of the hills all round him, at Brock's Creek, Bridge Creek, Howley, Yam Creek, Fountain Head, Port Darwin Camp, Douglas River, Grove Hill, John Bull—days of frantic digging, uproarious nights of rum. At John Bull a digger rode in, his pack-bags bulging gold—seven hundred and fifty ounces from a crushing of seven tons! They shouted and sang till the small hours, and the packhorse was gone in the morning. It was found six weeks later, straying in the ranges, and returned to its owner with every pennyweight of gold. That is how Rum Jungle received its name.

By October there were a thousand men in the hills and a few scrags of horses staggering over the boulders to the heights, some with eleven hundredweight to carry in the heat. They cost from £50 to £100 each—30s. a day to hire them—and they did not live long. In half a million square miles of rank grasses, the chaff they ate, at £1 a bag, came with them on the ships. Freight on stores was from £70 to £100 a ton—£70 added to the cost of a £20 ton of flour. Bully beef was half a crown a pound, and precious little of it. You would see eighteen or twenty diggers pushing a heavy dray over the jagged hills for a hundred miles, then they "split up" in mates, swags and tucker on their backs, to disappear into the butterfly gullies and burrow out of sight.

Rifts and alluvial, shafts, costeans and dykes, drifts, leaders, pockets of gold, earth pied with gold—and nothing to buy with it. A crop of shanties, like evil fungus, grew up on the straggle of road made by the drays and barrows, bamboo shack and bark hut taking rough gold for grog. The dump in the mangroves where the sailing-ships anchored became the town of Southport, three or four shanties, ten or eleven stores, acres of machinery waiting to go down to the mines, a half-built jetty hanging between earth and sky. Soon Southport was twice the size of Darwin, sixteen ships offshore at a time. There were a dozen shanties from there to Union Reefs, tipsy sheds with no beds, a hurricane lamp hanging to the rafter, drunken diggers lying on earth floors.

When grog was short they made their own, recipes tried and proved on the goldfields of Australia—methylated spirit and kerosene mixed with Worcester sauce and flavoured with ginger and sugar, known to the diggers as Sunset Rum. A bottle of wine—gin, vinegar and saltpetre—would burn the bottom out of an iron bucket in a night. The shanties made a squalid fortune out of fights and madness. Every one of them had a "dead-house" for the unconscious and the mad.

The Big Wet came in with three inches of rain in ten minutes, twenty-six inches in twenty-four hours. Tornadoes blew the tents away and filled the shafts all over the drenched hills and brimming valleys where men were swimming creeks by lightning and wading waist deep for miles over flooded plains carrying bottles and bags full of gold.

The Telegraph Line fell with the first storms. Tom O'Neill, a merry Irish foot-walker, was walking and swimming up to the mines, a hundred and fifty miles in a week, carrying urgent wires and messages from Darwin. He said the Territory was the only country in the world where you could "sweat in cold water".

Then John Lewis, on his way to Port Essington to form a cattle run for Bagot, Shakes and Lewis, put his *estafette* horses on the road to carry stores. The diggers rafted the rum over the rivers, and left the flour and bully.

There was a dreadful toll of fever—starvation, exposure, delirium tremens, everything was labelled "fever". In camps of thirty, five and six died in a week—in drunken brawls, or sunstroke at the claims, of dysentery in their tents, of malaria, wandering in the bush. Sick men reeled out of the shanties and lay all night in the rain—eighteen at Bridge Creek were buried where they had fallen. Some lay under a tree with a mate beside them, who promised to write a letter home, to send the cursed gold to wife or mother, a mate to wrap them in a blanket and dig the grave.

Dalton, a wrestler from Cumberland, was found dead on the road after a downpour of four inches. John Goldie of Dumbartonshire was found in the bush, covered with ants. "Black-eyed Susan", Henrietta Richardson, first white woman of no-man's land, was found dead in her tent, £500 worth of shining little nuggets in a bucket of washdirt beside her.

The warden, J. G. Knight, in his tent at the Shackle, begged them to come in to him while they had strength to do it—he was giving out four and five cases of quinine a day. Dr Millner in Port Darwin sent prescriptions by telegraph. Here is a typical message from Yam Creek:

> MAN BROUGHT HERE PROSTRATE, SKIN COLD AND CLAMMY, PULSE FEEBLE. HAVE GIVEN BRANDY AND EGGS. EYES NOW GLASSY AND VACANT, FANCY NOTHING CAN BE DONE BUT ADMINISTER STIMULANTS. PLEASE ADVISE.

The colonial surgeon replied briefly:

> GIVE EGGS, BRANDY, EXTRACT OF MALT. ALMOST SURE TO DIE.

His name was Richard Whitington, and his mate, John Flack, sat with him till he died.

Falling off their horses, falling off the little ships crossing the bay, some of them reached Port Darwin in time to die there, wandering drunk or mad, too dazed to look for the doctor. There was no hospital shack. They breathed their last neglected in the "dead-house" of a shanty, among scenes of drunkenness and riot, or lay down on the beach and happily died for relief of the sea breeze.

A grim jester was always the presiding genius of Darwin. Somebody found a right boot in the mangroves with a foot in it. They looked for the rest but found nothing, so they buried it in the graveyard with a nameless cross above.

Darwin was a din of pack-bells when the diggers were in to its shanties. There were three iron stores, Skelton's, Adcock and Doig, and V. L. Solomon's, advertising shipments of

> *bouilli*, groceries in tins, tents, tarpaulins, towels, saddles, long-tailed and short-handled shovels, sheath-knives, belt-pouches, tomahawks and hammers, meerschaum pipes, cherry pipes, briar pipes, raven twist tobacco, Yankee felt hats, blue shirts, mole-skin and brown drill trousers, pegged Blucher boots, fine mesh sieves and coarse mesh sieves, tin dishes in variety of sizes, brandy, wines and spirits (in case), Snyder cartridges and all makes of guns.

There you have a full-length portrait of the miner.

The Camp among the screw-palms was slowly climbing to Goyder's city, where the luxury bungalow of the cable company now sprawled next to the post-office—the "B.A.T. Folly", at a cost of £6000 with twenty-two rooms, offices, ballroom, billiard-room, a well, a garden, shower-baths, a carriage-house, stables and a tennis court. Larrakia piccaninnies pulled punkahs over an impressive senior staff with Hindu servants and a sportive crowd of junior johnnies, Englishmen all, from service in the languorous East. When the sahibs went calling on a select few at night in their victoria with prancing bays, the Larrakia walked before them carrying lanterns. Whist parties and tiffin, little white mess jackets, dancing pumps, monocles and after-dinner port, the B.A.T. for sixty years was in ramshackle Darwin but not of it, top rung of that pathetic little social ladder with so many rungs missing and its props in coal tar.

Once in three months a half-caste of steam-and-sail, s.s. *Tararua,* anchored under Fort Hill with mail from Adelaide and stores from Melbourne, Sydney and Brisbane. Her voyage was six weeks of tossing in torture, sheep and fowls cooped on her slant of deck, men, women and children cooped on three tiers of wire racks below. No sanitation, no tables and chairs, they lived on rank corned beef, stale scones and swill of milkless tea, drinking water from the condensers "cooled" in the shade of the wind-sail. A bath, for the fastidious, was a hose-pipe and salt water once a week. For an hour of morning and evening, passengers herded for recreation to a square of deck where the sick, from stretchers in the hold, were carried up for enough fresh air to die. Once ashore in Darwin, few had the courage—or the money—to book a passage back.

The first hotels, each three rooms and a bar, were Pickford's Family—the family came overland in a dray—the Palmerston Club, built by a Norwegian ship's carpenter named Opal, and the North Australian, by a Frenchman named de Brosse, who also built the lighthouse at Point Charles. In the wake of the mining agents two attorneys arrived, Villeneuve Smith and Rudall, fighting cases of "jumping claims" and taking gold in fee. A few wood-and-iron Government offices straggled along the headland with police station and jail, also a bank—English, Scottish and Australian—where the diggers could store the nuggets out of their swags. You could break into the bank with a tin-opener.

The town clock was a ship's bell rung at the B.A.T. Dotted about the scrub were the shack homes of pioneers—a few of Todd's Men and surveyors had brought brave young wives to the new land. Inspector Foelsche and his troopers, when their famous Adelaide greys of Arab strain gave up the ghost in the humidity, were patrolling about on Timor ponies.

Culturally and socially, Port Darwin was progressing. Mrs O'Halloran, in her parlour with a goanna in the thatch, opened a small "Academy for Children of Gentle-folk", as opposed to little darkies running around with nothing on. At Barclay's Room, an old store of Goyder's, the *élite* gathered for dominoes, debates, smoke socials, charades and concerts, sopranos shrieking of marble halls above the roar of rain on its iron roof. Monsieur Durand, now a mining magnate with tamarind-blossom buttonhole and waxed moustache, as master of ceremonies tripped about making everybody happy.

Dr Millner read services in Barclay's Room on Sundays till a Reverend J. A. Bogle arrived, a Wesleyan minister who held a tea-meeting in a tent for funds for a little paperbark church. Finally, Mr Bogle built the church himself—a little bit off the square, but he was proud of it. He gathered the faithful round his harmonium on the Sabbath morn. His church-bell was an iron bar hung in a tree, his bell-ringer a Wargait black-boy, in turkey-red pants, hitting it with another iron bar in measured and devotional ring. But Darwin and the diggers were too much for Mr Bogle. He faded away to a less torrid clime.

At Christmas there was a calico ball to the treacle strains of a concertina—the Residency had landed a piano, but the only pianist was "gone to the reefs". Sports for the blacks were more picturesque than prudent—the spearing of a canvas man and a lubra-race won by Darby, a Larrakia beauty. When Darby "cast her duddies to the wark" and came sprinting up the straight like Venus rising from the sea, the Ladies' Guild fled screaming. They planned the first race-meeting for Boxing Day, on the white curve of Mindil Beach, six-foot jockeys on three-foot Timor ponies—but bookies and jockeys, billycock hats and bustles, were all flattened in rain-squalls. As the little newspaper had it, in the classic diction of the day, "Pluvius was unpropitious, no sign of Old Sol." On New Year's Day there was a regatta on the harbour, dinghies and native canoes in a race from Fort Hill to Myilly Point. It was won by the only ship in it, the B.A.T. gig.

But Darwin's greatest civic achievement in 1873 was the founding, by John Skelton, of the *Northern Territory Times*, strange chronicle. It survived for sixty years where all else wilted, a chiaroscuro of history weird as any in the world. When ships were months late it was printed on blue, beige, brown, green, pink, mauve or jaundice-yellow paper, its tales of Territory life and death to match. Now and again an editor went bush, or on a bender, or off to the reefs, or to jail, but Bret Harte in his Californian days would have envied its copy and its lively literary style. C. J. Kirkland and his son Bruce were its best descriptive writers for nearly half a century, their journals of journeys to the islands and rivers well worthy of a place in the annals of exploration.

Tragedy and comedy capered together in those haywire columns set up by a Chinese foreman and a gang of blacks on an antique flat-bed from some junk-heap in the south. I saw the paper "to bed" in 1930, in its old stone cottage of Primus Alley. A "king" of the Larrakia was printer's devil, asking for time off to organize corroborees. A couple of Wargaits, the opposition tribe, in shorts and red headbands, fed the ink-roller, smacked down the old flat-bed, and carted the edition away.

"Which-way you been look-out longa that-one paper-yabber?" I asked one of the machine-men, and he answered proudly, "Hi been puttem hink."

The editor was always chief of staff, printer, publisher and proof-reader. When they ran out of lower-case or caps, they just boxed on with what they had.

EATH OF ING OF GREEGE

would convey to intelligent readers that a king of Greece was dead. Fs, gs, qs and ps, wrong side round and upside down, and "i" before "e" except after "c" beat all the Chinese typesetters of three generations.

But the *Northern Territory Times*, an epic little weekly never known to the world, reflected Northern Territory times in all their natural glamour and cynical humour, breath of new beauty in a virgin land and its tragedy unique. It grew old with men and women of a supreme courage, and passed away in 1933. The last editor was a woman, Mrs Jessie Litchfield, writer of good verse and prose, press correspondent through meagre years to the big dailies of the south, keeping the land of the lost in touch. Mrs Litchfield knew and loved old Darwin—she went home to it after the war and is still faithful. She has left us an interesting book of her own, *Far North Memories*.

In 1873 the *Northern Territory Times* unfurled the banner of the nation-builders in a lyric leader:

> North Australia now bids fair to take her place among the great colonies of Great Britain, first settlement on the Australian shores of the Indian Ocean. What the Imperial Government has desired for the past forty years, what they have vainly attempted in their settlements at Melville Island, Raffles Bay and Port Essington, has been accomplished by a handful of people from the other side of the continent. To our present population of 1400 will belong the credit of starting the colony on the long career of prosperity that lies before it.

The word "lies" was prophetic.

Gold is always a flash in the prospector's pan. Already the diggers were leaving in hundreds for that fatal river, the Palmer, crazed vision of El Dorado in the ranges and rain-forests of North Queensland. Where Captain Cook beached *Endeavour* was a new seaport, Cooktown, four thousand people in streets of tents with slushlight flares and dance-halls, fighting for food with their fists when the ships came in, wandering the ranges in pitiless and unceasing rain, lost in the ravines, drowned in the creeks, murdered by the blacks. Madness and misery and a river running gold—£3,000,000 in gold in three years. From Pine Creek to the Palmer was from purgatory to hell, but away they went, the maniacs, three hundred and fifty in one batch on *Tararua*, some in boats they built in the mangroves, others riding by way of the Roper and the Gulf, a thousand bush miles.

At Southport, acres of machinery settled down in the mud. No horses. One man skull-dragged a team of buffaloes from Adelaide River, and yoked them to a cart with stores. At the crack of his whip, cart, stores and buffaloes went bush and were never seen again.

Captain Douglas was still at the reefs, working his claims, floating companies, sending ecstatic wires about Midas finds of copper, gold, tin, lead, antimony, bismuth, mica, silver and cinnabar all in one mine together. Then, offered the Government residency at Selangor, he suddenly departed the radiant scene to a nabob's life in Malaya.

G. B. Scott was appointed Resident in his place, to arrive on R.M.S.

Gothenburg, a little luxury liner, five hundred and one tons, now chartered to redeem the north. When Darwin heard the news, *Gothenburg* was due to arrive. A reception committee rushed out the Larrakia to gather festive palms for a triumphal arch of calico and turkey red. It could not honour the new Resident with a dinner—there was nothing in town but flour and bully beef.

The blacks came in like Birnam Wood on the march, but the exiles forgot the celebration in excitement of swarming off to the ship for mail and news. Unable to resist her plush-lined seats and the saucy tilt of her funnels, two hundred and fifty lucky diggers booked their passages south. According to the *N.T. Times*: "The Resident was welcomed by a stack of greenery that turned into a mound of dead leaves, and a few feeble cheers from the population in pyjamas. We did not fire a salute because the white ants have taken possession of our twelve-pounder." Climbing the cliffs in a buggy to Government House, Mr Scott thought it was the blacks' camp. First of his public works was to build a house fit to live in. He then made an official visit to Southport in the cutter *Dot*, wading through the mud with his trousers tucked up to his thighs.

He found "the town busy with a bullock-team moving to and fro". On the goldfields road he found £20,000 batteries, carted up at a cost of £100 a ton, rusted in the scrub for lack of labour to carry them on. The owners of the brilliant bonanzas he had read about were naked and hungry, living in blackfellows' shacks. He saw nuggets of gold pushed into the publicans' hands to buy hope and relief in a bottle of square gin.

It dawned on Mr Scott, as it has dawned on everyone who has seen the Territory, that this is a land of fabulous wealth worthless without at least a million people. The population of the painted East, four hundred miles north, was a couple of thousand starving millions. Science had not yet belittled the work of human hands. Mr Scott implored his Government to give him coolie labour. He was backed up in Adelaide by an enthusiastic party led by Dr T. G. Guy, who wrote spirited letters to the papers and interviewed members of parliament, extolling the Chinese. Without labour, this colony, like all the others, would be gone within a year.

So at a time when the rest of Australia was hounding out the Chinese with the yellow-press warning of "Yellow Peril", South Australia, then a State of independent thought, welcomed them in thousands to its northern province, jobs waiting, passages free.

The first two hundred arrived by s.s. *Vidar* in 1874, human cargo in the hold of a little trading scow. Pigtailed fatalists all, they scarcely knew where they had landed, and every man-jack was an opium smoker. They sat down by the well on the beach, and threw back into it all their dirty water. The outraged settlers scouted them up the cliff, and around the Tree of Knowledge, in the street marked on Goyder's plan for Mr Cavanagh, Minister of Lands, they built their bamboo shacks.

In a month or two the ships had landed a thousand, recruited by Captain Douglas through agencies in Singapore from the ricefields, the riverboats, prisons, of Canton and Hong Kong. They hired themselves out as beasts of burden at 1s. a day, and were boated over to Southport. Slouching along in their palm-leaf hats with shoulder-poles and baskets, they set out to carry stores and machinery to the miner. Thirty Chinamen to a team would carry two tons for a hundred and twenty miles over the hills to Pine Creek in two or three weeks, living on a bag of rice, and dodging wild blacks on the way. They brought back cakes of smelted gold, a white man with a rifle walking beside them.

For these fag-ends of humanity who had never known a square meal in their lives, luck was a fortune. One glimpse of the yellow gold, and with their first week's wages they bought pannikin, shovel and dish, and ran to earth in the gullies. There was no law to prevent it, short of chain-gangs and slave labour. Where the white men, one or two together, picked up malaria, the price of a bender, the news of a better find farther out, the Chinese, rabbiting in hundreds, with pick and bucket ratted every acre, fossicking by the light of sun and moon. They picked up thousands of ounces from under the white men's noses, and kept the white men out by force of numbers—who would camp on a Chinamen's creek?

They came out as beggars and went back to Singapore on the coolie-ships, bound for Hong Kong and the home province in China to be plantation lords and merchant princes. Nobody knew how much gold they carried away, and none of them paid even for a miner's right.

"No savvy. Plenty dig."

The good news in China brought four thousand five hundred by the end of the year, and soon ten thousand, tongs with their leaders, patriarchs with families—among these Wing Cheong Sing, Ping Quee, Man Fong Lau, Yam Yan, Fang Cheong Loong, and, from Ballarat gold diggings, Lee Hang Gon, honoured fathers of Chinese Darwin.

Chinatown had taken deep root under the Tree of Knowledge. It was keeping hogs in the backyards and fan-tan dens in the shacks—pigs, pigtails, fowls, cats, partitions and yen flying whenever the troopers made a raid. A few industrious gardeners and fishermen improved the general diet with vegetables, fish and prawns, brought cypress pine in their junks from Adam Bay and Bynoe Harbour, and cleared the screw-palm valleys for pineapples and bananas, but nearly all were grubbing gold. They hired the blacks to work for them, and paid them with the opium ash out of their pipes. Day after day the shack court-house was crowded with gabbling Chinamen accusing each other of theft of chickens, rice, nuggets and cash.

White folks, with the Larrakia snatching their sweet potatoes out of the patch and the Chinese robbing their hen-roosts, with no coolie cheap labour after all, their town crowded with Asiatics and unwholesome rubbish tips, were having a thin time and restless nights.

A person worn out by the intense heat of the day retires to rest. Mosquitoes sweetly sing their evening hymn, then proceed to a gory repast on his recumbent form. Dogs delight to bark and bite. Friendly rats gambol over his stomach. Stray horses of the coal tar breed scrub themselves against his sleeping caboose, and then go round the corner to dance the fandango on piles of bouilli tins and bottles. He knows that the crickets are devouring his inexpressibles while cockroaches are making a hearty meal on his toe-nails.

That was a little essay on sleep by one of the pioneers.

Elders of the town were much concerned with the need of a jetty and a water-supply, so they formed a District Council in 1874, John Skelton president, J. E. Kelsey clerk of a shire unbounded. They held their meetings in a little town hall "the size of three piano-cases". Not a single investor had claimed his three hundred and twenty acres of plantation land, so to raise money on rates and town allotments—where people were squatting their paperbark huts regardless—the Council took out the elaborate map of Goyder's city. It made the shattering discovery that the B.A.T., the plutocratic Folly, was planked down right in the middle of the Esplanade Reserve. It demanded that the B.A.T., the only building in town worthy of the name, should remove itself forthwith. The cable company registered silent contempt.

As yet little was known of the land east and west of the creeks of gold. Somewhere west was the Daly, heart of darkness, a blackfellow's world. Surveyor McMinn had glimpsed that deep river pulsing down through inky forests and red lilies to the sea.

McMinn had walked delicately among its crocodiles and blacks, blacks in legion eternally warring on both sides of the river from the salt water two hundred miles to the hills, Brinken, Mulluk Mulluk, Waukaman, Angulmeri, Marramaninjie . . . sinister sinuous men wearing red ochre puff-balls of wallaby fur, bamboo bangles and bright-red berries in their hair, women sloe-eyed and slender carrying figs, lily-bulbs and mud turtles in their woven pandanus baskets. Bodies glossy as jet with sweat, they poled their dug-out canoes in myriad up and down river. With their reed fish-spears, hawk-eyed and with an amazing mathematical sense of speed and refraction, they could spear a swiftly moving fish three feet under water. Their weirs to catch the barramundi were a marvellous workmanship of tiny plaited bamboos, a mesh incredibly strong and hundreds of yards long. The lily-leaf was their emblem of peace. All along the river in the night-time the camp-fires glittered like city lights, hills rang and valleys throbbed with the wild cantata of corroboree.

"The blacks was bad on the Daly." Shadowy grottoes of its banyans, yellow mazes of its giant bamboos and the glassy sweep of its lily lagoons were no place for a white man to linger.

To the south of Pine Creek, where the Telegraph Line led the way, Cullen,

Edith, Ferguson, Katherine and Flora all tumbled in to the Daly through magnificent gorges. To the east Adelaide, Mary, Waterhouse, the trinity of Alligator rivers, and dozens of others tumbled into the Timor Sea. Three hundred miles south was the Roper, thanks to Leichhardt, Cadell and Todd's Men, a major stream more or less unknown.

First of the coastal ships was *Flying Cloud*, with adventurous Henry Marsh, a twelve-ton cutter that came scudding before the wind all the way round from Adelaide, and on her John Lewis sailed for Port Essington. Two young explorers set out to ride from the Roper to Port Essington—Permain of the Indian Survey Department, Borrodaile from Africa. They travelled with eight Timor ponies and flour for eight weeks, their rifles to "shoot for the pot". The goldfields gave them a send-off.

So far the blacks, along the white man's line of march, had been quiet. If there was trouble, the records are discreetly silent, but trafficking with the Chinese and motley of gold brought mischief and murder. Four troopers were sent to the road, to Southport, Howley, Yam Creek and Pine Creek, to live in tents and keep order. When Chinamen were speared, nobody cared, but when August Henning, a miner, was waddied to death at Birrell's Gap, the diggers rode the ranges and "the blacks were dispersed".

Then came a shock from the Overland Telegraph Line, a tragedy immortal, the murder of Todd's Men at Barrow Creek.

The old stone telegraph station at Barrow Creek is still standing. It lies near a gorge of Forster Range, heavily fortified with loopholes in the walls, a high-walled courtyard with double gates at the rear. Even then it was known that the Kaitish tribes of those hills, unlike the Arundta to the south and the Warramunga to the north, were dull-witted and ill-humoured. James Stapleton was in charge there in 1874. Among the world's first telegraphists in Canada, in the United States and in Central America, he was one of Todd's most trusted and experienced men. After four years' service in the tropic north, at Katherine River, he was riding two thousand miles to Adelaide to see his wife and family of four young children. At Barrow Creek he found the operator ill, sent him to Adelaide in his stead, and took over the key.

"Do not worry about the blacks," he wrote to his wife. "They are poor-spirited creatures, not like our North American Indians. If they ever gave trouble, my dog would scatter the lot. I may be with you by the time you receive this letter, for the man who takes my place is riding up."

On the hot summer night of 23rd February there were five white men in at the station—a rare event, but the explorer Warburton had just passed that way on his trail to the west. There was even a trooper among them, Sam Gason. They were sitting on the front veranda in the breeze, smoking and yarning, one of them playing the violin. About the place were a few friendly natives.

A rush of shadows, a chorus of yells, a shower of spears! The white men were unarmed. They doubled and raced round the station for the safety of the courtyard. In a second shower of spears the linesman, John Franks, and a native were struck through the heart. At the gateway Stapleton fell, four spears through his body and his breast.

Five hundred miles north on the Newcastle Plain that night, Billy Abbott from Powell's Creek was out mending the Line. He told me that by his lonely camp-fire he longed for company. So he climbed a pole, clipped on the wires of his hand-set, and called AG—Alice Springs. Somebody else was calling the Alice, an insane stuttering in Morse, no hope to understand it . . . then came SOS repeated again and again, and a slow spelling of one word, "blacks". Billy climbed down and looked fearfully around him, at the great silent plain peopled with shadows. He rigged his net, then caught his horse to ride a few miles off, in case. Next morning he tried the Line again, and heard the brief and tragic report from Alice Springs running through to Postmaster Little in Darwin. It came quite clearly now:

BARROW CREEK TELEGRAPH STATION ATTACKED BY BLACKS 8 P.M. SUNDAY JOHN FRANKS KILLED STAPLETON SERIOUSLY WOUNDED SENDING HELP.

To send help from Alice Springs was a hundred-and-sixty-mile ride.

Stapleton was dying. In his last hours, they carried him to the key. He asked for his wife.

Mrs Kingsborough of Adelaide, a daughter of James Stapleton, remembers the day in her childhood when Sir Charles Todd's carriage drew up at the door—sad news not to be told to the children. Their mother left with Todd for the city.

In the Postmaster-General's office the woman listened to death calling, a thousand lonely miles from Barrow Creek. The blacks still besieged the station, but Flint, the operator from Alice Springs, was on the way with a party of men. Dr Gosse of Adelaide had sent urgent instructions for treatment, for the return to the south of the wounded man, but for Stapleton there was no returning.

In Sir Charles Todd's office a faint tapping—the dying man was at the key, lifted up from his bed by his friends. His strength was going, he must needs be brief. Todd told him his wife was there. She waited, wide-eyed with grief, listening to expressionless tapping of Morse. It stopped. Todd gave her the written message:

GOD BLESS YOU AND THE CHILDREN. That was all.

A year or so later came an echo of the tragedy, a message carefully worded:

BLACKS HAVE BEEN FOLLOWED UP VERY SHARPLY AND CONSIDERABLE AMOUNT OF RETALIATION SUPPOSED TO HAVE TAKEN PLACE.

Franks and Stapleton were avenged. The innocent suffered for the guilty. A punitive expedition of police and bushmen, led by a trooper named Wormbrandt, rode three hundred miles, herding all blacks before them, from Ellery's Creek Gorge on Finke River to the Haartz mountains, a hundred miles east of Barrow Creek. Out there a range, for grim and sufficient reason, is on the map for ever with the name of Blackfellows' Bones.

Chapter X

To Let

WHERE THE first settlers had watched nine months for a ship, three or four schooners and barques a week brought hundreds of diggers and carried them back with thousands of ounces of gold. They made straight across to Southport to unload in the mangroves and be off. Summer lightning played about the dumps of dynamite. Hermit crabs thrust a greedy claw into the flour-bags and waltzed away with rusted tins of bully. Sometime a gang of Chinamen, if not speared, perished or drowned, would be along to collect them for the starving miners. Rum was urgent, delivered by John Gilpin express.

Port Darwin was remote as of yore. To make the journey to the goldfields or the south, you drifted to Southport in the little cutter *Dot,* three hours across the bay, or maybe three days in squall, with a passenger list of singing drunks and the dying. There was a snooker saloon at Southport, but no shipping agent. You haggled for a passage with the master of a barque, and followed his erratic course—it might be to blackbird kanakas for the Queensland canefields on the way, or to anchor off the Paumotus fishing pearls.

Dominick Daly, in the startling cruise of *Springbok*, set off to buy machinery for the mines, was lost to his wife and the world for five months, and came back with a master mariner's ticket.

The first mate of *Springbok* was superstitious. On the night she swayed out of Darwin Harbour with a deck cargo of rum and eighty rowdy diggers aboard, he saw the new moon through glass and handed in his papers. The skipper's navigation was three sheets in the wind, but they made the Roper by guess and by God, loaded more barrels, and breasted the bar for Carpentaria.

There *Springbok* lived up to her name, skipping from shoal to shoal, leaping the reefs with grind of coral, churn of foam and a ringing "Wo ho!" of triumph, pelting through uncharted channels and alighting on uninhabited shores, a Nijinsky of the sea. Shy of civilization, she spiralled the Gulf for five months, while savages stared and sharks followed with hopeful eye.

Afloat on sea-chanties, starvation rations and rum, she was bound for the crack of her doom, till Dominick Daly stole a chart from the captain's locker, and studied it by lantern on deck with a brawny second mate, who could follow a course but not set it. These two, the only sober men aboard, dragged her back to the sea-tracks every night while the skipper and the diggers were carousing. At long last they crawled into Somerset. A marine court of inquiry, held by Captain Moresby on the deck of H.M.S. *Basilisk*, then surveying the shores of New Guinea, presented the convivial skipper's ticket to Dominick Daly, with instructions to take *Springbok* to Cardwell. Her last frolic, in hurricanes, was nearly her end. After that experience the northern colonists preferred the miseries of s.s. *Talorua* whenever she happened along.

The wet came again, settlers mildewed into their shacks, living on bully beef. Rivers were up to the tops of the trees, coolies marooned in the foliage, diggers riding saddle-deep on the plains. No gold came in to Darwin, no news from the mines, no stores in the stores, nothing in the main street but a mournful Chinaman, his mangy dog and the skeleton of a horse.

Monsoon shouted on the roof for hours, reducing conversation to dumbshow. Sun and moon were drowned in grey half-light of rain, lagoons brimming, flood waters lipping closer in silver lakes till it seemed that helpless heaven was falling to engulf them. Nothing came to visit the dripping shacks but shadowy trails of ants, millions on the march to every crumb of damper, every treacle tin, and at night a fog of flying things piling burnt wings and wingless bodies feet deep round the lamp-glass. Tarantulas and gecko lizards gambolled in the rafters, where whip-snakes and tropic creepers were green invaders.

The jungle beyond the clearing was alive and alight with earth's refreshment after the long dry, but there were no roads to the beaches in 1875. Horses and buggies would drown and bog.

Then a big ripple broke the protococcus of stagnation. The *élite* in pyjamas were just sitting down to dinner of Bagot's Extract and mashed turnips when bang went the gun.

A ship!

It was R.M.S. *Gothenburg*, her company now subsidized to the tune of £16,000 a year to call every two months. As that modern little five-hundred-and-one tonner rounded Point Emery, a cheery plume waving from her smokestack and all sail set, luggers, dinghies and catamarans were joyously off to greet her. The monsoon raced them home, and tipped them up in the crocodile harbour.

Gothenburg brought everything the heart of man in the Territory could desire—even woman, three of the species. She brought fresh flour, bully and bullocky's joy; Lemon Hart rum, bulk beer, English hams, pickles, onions, dried potatoes and fancy tinned fruits for a belated Christmas; mackintoshes, umbrellas and spirits of camphor for the wet; quinine for fever; oats for the horses; sugar and tobacco to pay the Larrakia for services rendered; indigo cottons and canvas trousers for the coolies; a £15,000 battery for the Lady Alice Mine, and the first commercial traveller to the north—an agent for carbolic soap.

She brought the scales of justice—His Honour Mr Justice Wearing, Mr Pelham, his associate, Mr Whitby, South Australia's Crown Solicitor, to hold the first circuit court in the north. Until now all major offenders, with witnesses, troopers and exhibits, had been shipped to Adelaide—in one case a broken-winded old black mare alleged to have been stolen had made the five-thousand-mile journey to appear in a Supreme Court case as Exhibit A. Another distinguished passenger on *Gothenburg* was Dr T. G. Guy, whose inspiration had landed in Darwin its Chinese coolies. Dr Guy had scores of other bright ideas for the salvation of the north. As colonial surgeon he would replace Dr Millner, faithful for five years.

The ship brought the biggest mail on record, a hundred and fifty new novels, and all the Adelaide papers of the past six months. She even brought £5 towards the building of a church from a lady in England, but since nobody was interested they put that by for a hospital.

Port Darwin was reborn. There was revelry in rain-squalls in Mrs Kelsey's store, a concert in Barclay's Room, and a testimonial to genial Captain Pearce for bringing *Gothenburg* safely through the reefs. When he announced that he would wait a week to give the goldfields time to answer mail, all the Timor ponies in town set off to swim the rivers with laden pack-bags. Batteries at

Union Reefs were crushing night and day to send down an imposing block of gold.

As the legal gentlemen must return with the ship to Adelaide, the Supreme Court was called with an extempore jury of white men, Chinese and Malays. It was the Alice-in-Wonderland fantasy of the law it remained for seventy years.

In a land where murder stalked abroad, there were no murderers on hand at the moment, and no hope of catching them in the wet season—it might take a trooper two years to get his man. A Dane was charged with stealing a tin of bully beef, and a wild Irishman with pointing a revolver. The only conviction was a wicked old Chinaman, Ah Kim, sentenced to solitary confinement for life—in a tin hovel one-roomed jail with fifteen others. Ah Kim escaped soon after with a price on his head, pilfering food round the settlement till he was shot dead by the police in the mangroves, where he was building a boat to sail away. But by that time His Honour, too, had faced the Great Tribunal.

The *Gothenburg* was guardian angel and at the same time a sore temptation to the nation-builders. Her halo of lights at the Gulnare Jetty, the social evenings in her red plush and antimacassar saloon, baritones braying "A Life on the Ocean Wave" and fat matrons obliging with "The Maiden's Prayer" in a jangle on the upright grand, wafted their hearts back home. Diggers waded and swam in from the goldfields. The ship had brought eight passengers. She carried away ninety-two, with twenty thousand ounces of gold, fifty pounds in one resplendent cake from the test crushing at Union Reefs.

R.M.S. *Gothenburg* sailed from Port Darwin at dawn on Friday, 16th February, 1875. The Honourable Thomas Reynolds, John Skelton, president of the Council, Dr Millner, Mr Wells, editor of the *Northern Territory Times,* Mr Justice Wearing and party, with mining directors, honeymoon couples, a family of five, and bearded diggers were all in the happy crowd at her rail as she pulled out into the stream. Monsieur Durand was there, his waxed moustache conspicuous in a ring of moon-faced coolies grown wealthy overnight. He was hugging a heavy black bag.

Cooees and cat-calls, wistfully waving sheets on poles farewelled her down the harbour. With a cheery hoot she rounded Point Emery, bearing the lucky ones out of sight. The exiles trudged home through the mud to read of the Tichborne claimant and the Russo-Japanese War. Someone was gone from almost every shack. So lonely and desolate was Port Darwin that night that three men, led by one Sheppard, set out in a six-ton boat in the steamer's wake. Blown to the west in a gale, they were given up as lost, but turned up at Nickol Bay, a thousand miles south-west, six months after.

February washed itself away and buried itself in the long grasses. Nothing stirred the dank monotony but an all-in fight between Wargait and Larrakia in the graveyard, and the midnight cackle of fowls stolen by the coolies for Chinese New Year.

On 3rd March the Telegraph bell tolled through the rain.

Bad news?

Bad news indeed. An urgent telegram was pasted to the office wall:

R.M.S. GOTHENBURG TOTALLY WRECKED IN CYCLONE ON REEF OF FLINDERS PASSAGE 70 MILES FROM BOWEN FEW SURVIVORS.

Women screamed. Men stood in silent groups. The poor little settlement was crazed with horror and grief, every house a house of mourning. Flags were flying half-mast in Adelaide. Port Darwin looked for a flag, but there was none.

For five days of anguish no further news—in hurricanes on the Queensland coast the telegraph wires were down. Then another telegram on the office wall told the dreadful story, with a list of twenty-seven survivors and one hundred and seven dead.

Rounding Cape York to the South, *Gothenburg* had run into fitful cyclone weather. On the night of 24th February she was heaving down in a rising gale through the herringbone reefs of the Great Barrier. Most of her people had turned in when from rough seas she entered a lullaby calm. Thankfully they settled to a quiet night. . . .

But into their sleep came a long jarred rasping, a jerk and a snap, and a shout from the bridge

"My God! We're ashore!"

Half-clad passengers trooped on deck. The ship was up on a reef, five fathoms under her stern and only two feet for'ard.

"No need for alarm," said genial Captain Pearce. "She'll float with the rising tide."

Water-casks to the after-deck, fore-topsails backed and engines full astern, two or three times they tried to clear her, but she would not move. A double watch was set. Passengers went back to bed, hearing in their troubled sleep the running and shouting of sailors, now and again the pulse and strain of engines.

Towards midnight a snake-tongue of lightning licked along the clouds. The tide was rising, a strong tide. The ship seemed lighter. She quivered now to the pulse of the engines . . . but the wind was rising with the tide, a low whistling *crescendo*. . . .

In rack and rhythm, *Gothenburg* began to pound on the reef. Her people crowded the companion-ways and pushed out on to the deck. Things looked grave. Captain Pearce himself was on the bridge. A passing officer refused to answer questions. A rumour of launching the boats ran through the crowd. Some went below for their children, others for their belongings. The whole ship was awake and frightened, as with black clouds and forked lightning the wind rose, rose to the high shrieking of full gale. Passengers huddled together in the little red-plush saloon, now shorn of all its glory. Outside they could hear only the tumult of storm. So, for an hour, they waited.

The tide was full at one o'clock, but the engine fires were out—all hope of floating was abandoned. The ship thrashed the reef. The order was given to man the boats. One hour too late.

As the people surged out on the decks, with the screaming of harpies the squall was down upon them, and flood-tide swept over the reef. The quarter-boats tilted in the davits, but a mighty wave foamed through and swamped them, sweeping the decks with panic. Men clung to the shrouds, women to their children. Little Monsieur Durand darted about making shrill outcry that somebody had stolen his Gladstone bag with £3000 in gold.

A second wave churned through, deep, cold and overwhelming . . . and running over the rail with it, tossed like a manikin, was the grave and benign Judge Wearing, shouting something that nobody heard, foolishly spread for a moment in that concave of unearthly green, then down into the dark of the sea. There was a long fearful wail in the wind as a baby was swept from its mother's arms.

Madness now! In the valkyrie ride of the gale, the port boats were swung out and swept away. Silhouettes in the lightning, on the crest of the breakers the sailors were vainly trying to pull back. As the starboard boats were lowered, with a horrible crunch the ship heeled over. Frantic women climbed the bulkheads and clambered down the side, to be engulfed in a third great wave that left a sea of heads round the upturned boats and pitiful creatures clinging.

Then *Gothenburg* slid from the reef and went down by the stern in deep water. Captain Pearce and his officers, three figures, were on the bridge at the end.

In the smouldering cyclone dawn only the foremasts were above the pale level of the sea, and clinging there the half-drowned forms of fourteen men. A woman's plaid shawl tied to the yard-arm was signal of distress.

Two days later in calm blue weather a swimmer from the mast righted an upturned boat still tethered to the wreck. The rescue ships from Bowen found four men lashed to spars in the water, a few more castaways on Holborn Island.

In one of the major disasters of Australian seas, John Cleland, James Fitzgerald and Robert Brazel of Adelaide were honoured throughout their lives for conspicuous heroism on that fatal night. No woman or child was saved.

Not only in bereavement was the wreck of *Gothenburg* a grievous blow to the settlement in the pandanus. It frightened population away, and it was the beginning of a tale of woe five years long.

A schooner laden with quartz and machinery turned turtle in Darwin Harbour with the loss of six lives. A teamster named Ellis, travelling to the goldfields, was murdered at Yam Creek, and a trooper, with volunteers, chased the blacks nearly a hundred miles to the Daly. As they "showed no inclination to withdraw when called upon to surrender", the party charged them and killed seventeen.

From Daly Waters telegraph station, the operator, Johnston, set out with

Daer, his linesman, and Rickards, a teamster, to meet the Telegraph ship at Roper Bar. They camped by the river. Johnston was swimming, Daer putting on the billy for tea, when a shower of spears came out of the pandanus. Johnston fell dead, Rickards mortally wounded. Daer, who was badly injured, defended the dead and dying with his revolver, carried them to the wagon, yoked up the horses, and drove night and day without a camp, one hundred and fifty miles to Daly Waters, where all three were buried.

The young explorers Permain and Borrodaile never rode in to Port Essington, where Lewis and Levi had built a sturdy log homestead facing the bay. Out from the Shackle, Lewis led a party of horsemen to find them, with fierce stag-hunting dogs. Riding many days through a lost world of dwarf cabbage-palms, broken ochre hills pitted with caves, slow grey sludge of Alligator rivers—no traces of white men's passing in that grisly clay, only the claw-marks of the saurian and the cloven hoof-marks of the buffalo herds. Inspector Foelsche and Surveyor McMinn set out on a long search. At Tor Rock they found scattered bones of the horses, half-cooked and gnawed, but the fate of the two young Englishmen was for ever unknown.

Of Bridson's prospecting party from the Roper to Blue Mud Bay in Arnhem Land, two were killed, horses speared, and Bridson four months on the way in, walking. Alex MacKenzie came in to the Telegraph Line naked skin and bone. He had walked round Carpentaria. One of his mates, Angus McKay, died ninety miles out. The other, John Barry, was speared at Limmen Bight. MacKenzie had lived for twenty-two days on little else but water.

E. O. Robinson, with his schooner *Northern Light* in quest of adventure on the north coast, had started a little tobacco plantation on Croker Island to trade with the Malays. His mate, Ted Wingfield, was sitting in his tent reading a home letter a year old when his head was bashed in by Wandi Wandi, a bad boy of his camp. Wandi Wandi was brought to Darwin and sentenced to ten years.

Then Darwin's Chinatown was burnt to the ground. Yee Kee was cooking his dinner when a puff of flame caught the horehound weed, and away went the whole settlement in a sheet of flame, pigs, dogs, fowls, cats burnt alive, twenty-five thousand dollars' worth of rice gone in three stores, hundreds of Chinese homeless.

On the goldfields road, James May, a teamster, was speared, and R. E. Holmes, the innkeeper at Collett's Creek, was waddied to death. Holmes had sent out his blacks to collect snakes and butterflies for museums, promising tucker and grog. He gave them grog but no tucker, and that was the end of him. Next year the Wilwonga blacks burnt out a camp of a hundred Chinamen at Pine Creek.

Then a tornado wrecked Union Reefs, by this time a considerable gold town with a population of four hundred whites and seven hundred Chinese. Two shanties and everything above ground weighing less than a ton careered away through the scrub, leaving the diggers lamenting.

At the end of the dry each year the rivers were fallen to a few far holes, all the creeks vanished. Men looked for water and found baked clay. There were many deaths from thirst. Some were so sick that they shot themselves for relief —and now no doctor in the north. Dr Houston died at Tumbling Waters on his way to the goldfields. Dr Guy, all his grand schemes gangrened into bitterness and resentment, on a humid summer morning in Port Darwin punctiliously sent his black-boy to the Residency with his resignation, and, just as methodically, measured for himself an overdose of hydrate of chloral. The tragedy was far greater than his own.

Came a letter from Stapleton to the Resident:

> Can you, dear Sir, induce the government to supply us with a pickle-bottle case of assorted medicines, to be kept by some trusted man, with a code of instructions tacked on inside the cover? In Darwin you have a sea-breeze but the miner is left to breathe his last unattended.

The only medicines were brandy and quinine. An outbreak of beriberi was a grim story, few of its victims buried. Whenever a Chinaman died in his shack, he was left to rot there till the trooper collected him on a sheet of iron and dumped him in the middle of the fan-tan den for his friends' attention. Trooper Woods died at the Shackle, uncared in his shack, with the rain streaming through it. At last, J. G. Knight, Government Secretary and gold warden, moved to pity by the unburied dead in the gullies, built a little iron shack for hospital with the blacks to help him. For the sick and dying, he did what he could.

In Darwin the death-roll was so heavy that they were "jumping" graves. In that hard sandstone the sexton could dig only half a dozen a week and when a funeral arrived, often as not, he found them filled in. Horses charged over the burying ground, and the blacks had many a battle there, for the whites had chosen for their cemetery the traditional convincing-ground of Wargait and Larrakia. A bit of a wire fence was put round, and a gate with a lost key—coffins dumped over the top or sidled through it. No register was kept, and the sexton often grinned to see broken-hearted white mourners kneeling by a heathen Chinee, decking his resting-place with upturned bottles and flowers.

The neglected north had grown cynical about death. One day pall-bearers were about to lower a coffin when a spotted wild-cat crept into the grave.

"Gosh! Look at that!" they shouted. "Quick! Get the dogs. Old Jim won't mind a bit of fun, by golly, he'd enjoy it." The corpse was forgotten by the graveside while the jungle rang with shouts of "Hey, boy! Git 'm!"

A more finicking settler wrote in to the *Northern Territory Times*:

> Let me pray to God to keep me from dying in the N.T. I am not very particular, but I don't relish the idea of being squeezed into a rough box made of bouilli cases with the brand and PRESERVED MEAT FRESH still on the

cover, then taken away in a dirty cart with a dirty driver smoking a pipe, and dropped into a hole on the waste lands. I would sooner be wrapped in my blankets and burned.

Reading these macabre tales in letters and the press, nation-builders in Adelaide lost their nerve. Compared with this land of hoodoo in the Australian north, the White Man's Grave in Africa was a health resort. Tide of colonization was at dead neaps. The pioneers, as soon as they could save a fare, were coming home. The Resident, Mr Scott, had resigned in despair, and his place was taken by Mr E. W. Price.

Having failed to sell the Territory, the Government now tried to give it away—half a million square miles to let. Agricultural lands were reduced to 6d. per square mile for the first seven years. Free and unconditional settlement, with free passages, was offered in Cornwall and Devon—no applications; next to a religious sect of Russians called the Mennonites, fleeing from persecution since the sixteenth century, but the Mennonites migrated to Canada. A Lieutenant-Colonel Palmer of Waltham Cross launched a vain scheme to colonize Stokes's Victoria River. Major J. A. Ferguson was sent to India to try to interest Hindus with a guarantee of cheap living, freedom in their faith and kindly treatment—but to the glories of the Territory the downtrodden hordes of India turned a deaf ear.

Finally North Australia was offered to the Japanese.

The Reverend Wilton Hack, on a tour of the East, was deputed by the South Australian Government to visit Tokyo, "to make known to the Japanese the advantages of the Northern Territory, its climate, resources, laws and regulations. Should they desire to emigrate, the government would pay their passages, but each must bring a year's provisions".

The Reverend Wilton Hack, on his return, reported with regret that the Japanese people were not awake to new ideas in national expansion. Chinese of the merchant classes were also unimpressed. The coolies were scampering in and out in thousands.

During all this time the Territory lived on gold, a thousand ounces a week coming down from the fields until the mines failed for lack of labour. The Chinese, rocking the cradles out in the gullies, got the rest. All else that the country raised was a record number of shanties. They used eighty inches of rain in the year to dilute the rum of regret.

In 1877, when the Russian Bear was bogy in the Pacific, lonesome little Port Darwin arranged its own defence in facetious proclamation:

"As the enemy will hardly come overland from Adelaide, in this momentous crisis the supreme command of all naval vessels in the Territory is vested in our trusty and well-beloved Henry Marsh (skipper of the *Flying Cloud*) hereby appointed Admiral of the Fleet.

"The Government Resident and Inspector Foelsche, holders of nearly all the iron tanks in Port Darwin, have generously placed their metal ore at the disposal of the Admiralty. s.s. *Dot* and the powerful steamer *Darwin* are to be armed as gun-boats. The canoes *Woolna* and *Larrakia* will be plated with corrugated iron, and fitted with auxiliary steam rams.

"Naval defence of the rising and important settlement of Port Essington will be placed in charge of Vice-Admiral Aarons, hereby empowered to engage E. H. Whitelaw as Able Seaman. Talc Head will be reconnoitred by Lieutenant Manson, who is directed to arm his vessel with three of the best Colt revolvers, with triggers, in the Government Store.

"Our army is to be divided into Regulars and Irregulars under Inspector Foelsche. Troops awaiting the oncoming of the enemy will be billeted at the public houses. As there are nearly as many hotels as soldiers, this will not be a serious problem."

So the Front Gate of Australia gallantly laughed away its fears of invasion . . . but there was a more formidable enemy within the gateposts. Besieged by this enemy unseen, unheard, unconquerable, Darwin, like London Bridge, was falling down.

One of the least of God's creatures, blind, defenceless, insensible, was eating away the fruits of all their labours, eating their hopes and their homes to a hollow shell.

White ants. . . .

The discovery of this deep, dark and deadly work was another laurel to the Bard. Occasionally in these years a Dutch ship or a P. and O. mail steamer would call on her way through Torres Straits to Singapore and India, with celebrities aboard. On one memorable night the world-famous Madame Carandini, with a kindly thought of the exiles, gave a concert on shipboard, lifting to those remote stars the voice that princes travelled far to hear. When Morton Tavares, a ham actor of the grand old school, whose wife had eloped with the captain of a ship, found himself down on his luck and marooned in Darwin, the good-hearted little town and its diggers gave him a benefit to raise his fare to Calcutta. He chose the court scene from *The Merchant of Venice*, his utterly villainous Shylock with a B.A.T. Antonio and a portly Portia striding the boards of Barclay's Room, packed to its wide-open galvanized-iron doors.

The Mercy Speech literally rocked the rafters, and in the furore of the final curtain the whole of the front stalls went through the floor!

That was the end of Barclay's Room. The old shack was badly aslant in the morning, and the next Cock-eyed Bob blew it down. Goyder's old storehouse had lightened the meagre lives of the settlers with many a merry night, but Shakespeare was asking too much.

Within five years white ants had reduced the houses of the pioneers to a shell of masticated pulp. They undermined the jetty at Southport—cargoes stored there suddenly fell into the sea. They demolished roots at their foundations—trees and shrubs, while you were looking at them, foolishly fell over. Beds caved in in the night. Tables collapsed during dinner, steps as one ascended, chairs as one sat down. Telegraph poles dangled in the wires, the parties constantly riding to renew them.

These most rapacious of animals, in an ingenious paradox, have no stomach—internal parasites do all their digesting for them.

White ants ate the Residency piano, the mails in the post-office, the pegs of the miner's claims, wagon-wheels while they were standing, blankets of sleepers in the night. They chewed jagged holes in the walls of the court-house and the police station, digested Government records, broke up the jail—a bad Arab named Abdulla, who had given the police no end of trouble to catch him, simply pushed a beam and walked out. A trooper found his trunk filled with sawdust and buttons. A blacksmith reported that they had carried away his anvil, but he found it buried in the rubble that had been the block.

At the Residency it cost £400 a year to keep the Resident indoors—he had a carpenter on the premises renewing walls and floors at regular wages, 13s. a day. One of the Darwin dandies complained that white ants devoured a pair of duelling pistols and his opera hat, then topped up on his iron dumb-bells. At the B.A.T. they regaled themselves on billiard-balls, leaving a hollow globe of paint, then bored through sheets of lead to set the veranda posts aslant. They ate out the strongroom of the bank, and while the bank manager was building another they came up in thousands through the wet cement and twiddled their antennae at him in derision.

A mining director, absent for three months, came back to his home, put his key in the door, and the whole house fell flat. Then the Resident announced that they had invaded his wine-cellar, perforated the metal tops of bottles, polished off the corks. Darwin was on a slant, everything at a stagger, a honey-comb of dry rot.

Of all living creatures, the termite is most destructive to man's handiwork, and of all termites the North Australian *Mastotermes darwiniensis* is most primitive and most ruinous. It virtually owns Australia north of Capricorn, extracting a revenue duty of forty per cent on production. It wreaks more havoc than the earthquakes of New Zealand. Those vast, still, pindan sands of Western Queensland, the Territory and North-west are perpetual motion, millions of mandibles grinding away Nature's eternal building and rebuilding.

Once, in poetic mood out there, I remarked to a bushman the sound within the silence . . . a mighty monotone of hush, a bell-like high note scarcely heard yet all pervading, ringing beyond the silence.

"Y'r quite right, missus," he said. "It's the white ants chewin'."

In an empire of two million square miles, here is the greatest social organisation in the world . . . of sightless workers born to work till death, of cities built of the stuff of their bodies, the endless dwarf cities of tenements and towers red roan as the sand, or ghastly grey as the clay. Termite social law is merciless and blind as humanity in war. There are workers, soldiers, nymphs, a diminutive king and a monstrous queen, the State, mother of a multitude. There are no strategists where all is strategy, no field-marshals in a robot regimentation, no shift-bosses where all is mechanical slavery—but if you destroy the mother of a race, that race is gone.

Kick an ant-hill. See the soldiers rush out to link legs in vicious resistance to block the opening, blind fighters with an armour-plated unicorn head that they flail from side to side, *Flammen-werfer* throwing an acid spray that encloses and corrodes a small enemy. This saliva cements the ant-hills. It is also the secretion that penetrated the Resident's zinc-sealed wine-bottles and the B.A.T. billiard-balls. It can penetrate sheet iron and it can corrode glass. The termite armies seal themselves with it, and become a living wall of mailed heads. Heroic defenders, they never turn their backs to the enemy, because their abject rear is unprotected, soft and grub-like, like a hermit crab's.

When things are quiet, the soldiers stand aside and the workers seal the walls with the secretion. The eternal breeding, building, harvesting, feeding, goes on. These pulpy, veined creatures, half an inch long, fleshy and grey with a head like a wax match, toil like munition workers till they drop dead, to be immediately devoured by their kind—there is no waste in an ant-hill. The queen, when her procreative functions fail, soon dies and is devoured by her subjects—they fly, they swarm, they mate, they destroy each other and are destroyed and eaten. The survivors establish another state, enthrone another queen. After their brief mating flight in the sunshine, they shed their wings and burrow to build and breed again.

North of the Tropic you travel the endless ant-hill cities, varying in colour with earth, and in form with soil formation, and slant of wind. The west of Queensland and the Centre is one vast wilderness of cones and tombstones, increasing in height to the north till at Cape York they are like kiln chimneys. At Pine Creek, the amazing Gothic cathedrals with fluted buttresses and towers are twenty-five feet high. At Darwin slab monoliths, "magnetic" or "meridional" ant-hills, flat-planed north and south, are dreadnoughts in line ahead across the Cemetery Plain; in Kimberley great slag dumps seem to be piled with buckets of wet sand, at Broome are the domes of scarlet clay that Dampier believed to be "the abode of Hottentots in the savannah". Ghosts of the drovers who died out there are the ant-hills of the Murran-ji.

Out below the Granites in the Territory west, and on the road through the rugged red ranges to Borroloola on the Gulf are the most remarkable ant-hill cities that I know, "madman's galleries" surely unique in the world and covering hundreds of square miles . . . of glaucous yellow clay, or slaty grey, or terra-cotta, half-finished effigies of a crazed sculptor whose addled dreams in shrouded sand return ever and again to the Old Master theme of Madonna and Child. In half-formed imagery they challenge the piled clouds above . . . a coronation group, king, bishop, knight and page; imbecile cherubs; Three Wise Monkeys; a leprous torso of Hercules; a cowled pilgrim with a pack on his back; Rodin's "The Burghers of Calais" half melted away; pock-marked

Shakespeare in a broken ruff—the imagination skips from fantasies to fantods as the car wanders through that chamber of horrors that is built with the stuff of their bodies by the white ants.

Chop off a section of those Gothic towers in miniature, and you disclose a marvel of engineering in architecture as complicated as the city of New York, with highways, subways, ramps, bridges, silos, factories, clinics, spiral staircases, mezzanines, cellars, ventilation shafts, air conditioning—Nature thought of it all first. The granaries are packed with grass sawn with minute exactitude in lengths corresponding within the millionth of an inch. There is a dizzying one-way traffic of entities in endless belts of motion steady as the circulation of the blood through arteries, veins and capillaries.

The queen, three inches long and bloated with fecundity, lies in a domed aortal chamber a foot across and inches high. She spends her whole life in a horrible disgorgement of eggs at the rate of one a second, and she lives thirty years; long files of workers stuff morsels into her mouth that have been predigested by their own bodies—anything from sweet grass to historical records—and carry away her eggs to the heated incubation chambers. Beneath her pallid white obesity lies the little king, with her a life prisoner of communal law.

All is the intelligence of faultless instinct. When a nest is blown down, or chopped open in chunks, the workers swiftly cement the queen in a solid block of clay that resists the axe, and within an hour they are on the job again to build a skyscraper about her in a month. Should a spring burst beneath it, these termites develop a waterproof solution to line the nest and turn that hot spring into account in cooking their edible mould and hatching the rising generation. The big shift of workers goes on at night when birds, ants and other enemies are at home in bed. The honeycomb domes and spires grow in the starlight.

Which reminds me of the tale they tell at Pine Creek, of the stockman who stayed too long at the pub, set out to find his droving camp with a rolling gait and a song, and fell by the wayside. He awoke next morning powerless to move, bound hand and foot in earthy darkness, with a tickling irritation all over like Gulliver on the Lilliputian shore. He thought he was buried alive. In cold sweat of terror he groaned and shouted, trying to remember the holy words he learned at mother's knee.

The cook in the droving camp, packing his pots and pans while the ringers were moving on the cattle, was startled to hear ". . . an ant-hill carryin' on like anything, and recitin' the Lord's Prayer! I reckoned the place was bewitched by a parson or somethink, an' by golly I was goin' to hop it quick, an' ole Bert woulda been there yet if I hadn'ta happened to see a couple o' swan-neck spurs stickin' out!"

By the end of the seventies, Goyder's city was a tin can wilderness howling to God and the Government, both too far away. Ten years on bully beef, no roads, no horses, no hope of taking up the jungle, the Territory was living on Chinaman's luck—

"Bimeby Chinee-man no more catchum gold, eat grass all-same horsey," the coolies gave warning.

To keep the wild dog from the door, pioneers were trapping the beautiful little finches, parrots and Torres Straits pigeons to sell for a few shillings on the ships. But ships were few.

"A strange fatality," remarked the *N.T. Times* darkly, "seems to attend all vessels that enter Port Darwin." s.s. *Brisbane*, a passenger steamer, was wrecked at Bynoe Harbour, the schooner *Dawn* went down off Southport, *Wild Duck* piled up on Cape van Diemen, and *Gulnare* rammed through her jetty in a sweeping tide and rotted away on its stones.

Rusty pens and dried-up ink, in long delay of mails, they gave up writing letters. Some held the fort for sanity and progress in cruel isolation, some went bankrupt, some went mad, some went native, and most gave up the ghost.

Vital statistics for 1879 were births 2, marriages 4, deaths 154; for 1880, births 3, marriages 6, deaths 166; for 1881, 100 deaths, 51 of fever.

The population had fallen to seven hundred and thirteen Europeans—mixed—and four or five thousand Chinese. Of these many died of opium-smoking and leprosy, of each other's jealousy and blackfellow spears. With the petering out of the mines the coolies came in droves to Darwin, carrying opium and squareface round the camps in their shoulder-baskets, keeping body and soul together at any job at 1s. a day. Hundreds of men were walking overland to that fatal river, the Palmer, running the gauntlet for a thousand miles of spears. The Woolna and Wilwonga blacks were bushrangers in the scrub, holding them up for "tum-tum" and tobacco with dead men's rifles. Three wandering diggers found the remains of a gang of Chinamen on a Roper River track. On the principle that the Chinese are always smuggling gold, they burnt the bodies and panned them out, and got fifteen ounces!

A few of the best old Chinamen started splendid gardens in the gullies and in the little goldfield towns—one brought in a cabbage four feet across and all heart. An orange-tree planted in Darwin had seventy oranges on it, an olive-tree four years old was eight feet high . . . but there was no peace.

Antipathies took root in that too-fecund earth, the crazy-headed antipathies that have made Darwin a hot-bed for seventy-five years. The B.A.T., with a capital of £3,000,000 and a round-the-world orbit, laid a charge against the South Australian Government for the value of two fowls that flew over the fence and were cooked by the hungry post-office clerks for dinner.

The District Council, with no answers to its bills for rates, was broke—furniture sold to pay its debts.

"Has South Australia ever done anything for the Territory? Will South

Australia ever do anything to effect settlement of the Territory?

"Has a man with a family any chance of permanent residence in the Territory?

"What are our principles of education?—demoralisation and dissipation. Our boys can find a living fossicking and our girls can be sold to the Chinese."

Thus sobbed the *N.T. Times* at the end of the first decade. There followed a news item unique in the news-sheets of empire.

"The morals of our young men have been sorely tried this week. On Monday, kept as a public holiday, the blacks arrived from the Adelaide and Alligator Rivers, hungering for tobacco and camped on the outskirts of the township.

"The women and children were freely offered for purposes of prostitution in the city. The order of doing business was peculiar. They were about in lots of 20 and 30 of mixed sexes, and no sooner did a European stop to look at their uncouth figures than the salesman of the party stepped forward, pointing to the assorted lots.

"Old women were sold at sixpence, the others ranged from 1/- to 2/-, the latter being demanded for quite young children under 10 years of age. Towards dusk their value had depreciated, lower prices obtained and choice specimens were submitted at a sacrifice.

"We have written on this subject in a light manner. There is a darker side to the picture. The effects may be shown in after years."

In the New Year revels, somebody threw a live charge of dynamite over the cliffs into the blacks' camp at Lameroo Beach.

There was a hospital at last, built *ad misericordiam* with the donations of two distant sympathetic women, a Miss Coates of Adelaide and a Miss da Costa, who vied with each other in providing building funds and the wages of a gang of coolies. A mile away on a cliff, it consisted of two iron rooms on cement, one for contagious diseases. Each room held five, blacks and whites, sweating in heat and half-drowned in the wet together—Chinese not admitted by mutual consent. It was in charge of Mr Manson and his wife, good folk, but nobody went to the hospital unless they were carried.

Dr Morice always had a crowd of the maimed, the blind and the halt outside his shack, his waiting-room and surgery the horehound scrub. For ills throughout the Territory in general he prescribed over the Telegraph Line enough quinine and citrate of iron to go on sixpence. As nobody had a sixpence, the measure was more or less.

The mines were already rusted stampers, silted dams and fallen buildings, but the diggers brought in a hundred ounces in their "shammies" to show that the gold left for the Palmer was still there. The miners were starved out, the wagons rotted where they bogged, the shafts were stagnant wells and rushing waterfalls the drives. Miasmic vapours after the wet brought fever again and the dying. In the dry the camps were abandoned for lack of water. Blacks, setting fire to the grass to burn the game out, burnt down the tents and the little shack towns. Soon even the troopers were gone—one inherited £180,000, one died of malaria, and one of d.ts.

For the sixth time in fifty years, a settlement in North Australia was fading down into jungle mould.

"The *Olaf* not having arrived, we are ur able to print our serial, *The Skeleton in the Closet*," announced the *N.T. Times*. A local author was writing a novel, *The Doomed House, or The Whitc Ants' Revenge*.

For the rest, they talked snake yarns, gold, and the dead.

Chapter XI

A Lantern in the Scrub

A FEW MILES from the freckle of house-lights on the headland—the only coastal lights of the continent between Fremantle and Cape York—every night a lantern was slowly moving in a clearing in the scrub, behind it a man with a spade.

Riding on to him through the long grasses, you might have thought him a demented digger, except that his occupation seemed even madder than that. He was digging small holes in the hand-ploughed earth, filling them with a milk out of a can labelled POISON, sifting it in, marking the place with a stick, and moving on to the next. By day the clearing widened about him till his was a task for Hercules. Most nights he worked till the didjeridoo of the Larrakia droned down into sleep.

A foreigner with a flaxen beard and keen, clever eyes, he was one of the hated Russians had they known it, and the time came in the vicissitudes of nations when he was glad to tell them. But he was neither enemy nor madman. He was Dr Maurice Holtze, who had fled across the German border with his wife and young children in one of the endless persecutions of the Old World that populate the new. Destiny and little ships landed him on the Darwinian shore where, the horticulturist Hill having died of snakebite, they put him in charge of the patch in Doctor's Gully, growing cabbage and sweet potatoes for the Government's bully beef dinner.

Holtze was a botanist. With a couple of million square miles of soil and sun to play with instead of a third-story window-box in a snow-swept city square, he germinated ideas. Translating his science from the Baltic into terms of Fannie Bay, he roped in a gang of dumb driven coolies to clear the jungle for nine hours a day at 15s. a week and nothing "found"—not even the coolies half the time. Trenching and planting, he caught up with them at night. His haphazard mail brought seeds and seedlings from all over the tropical and sub-tropical world.

The white poison was arsenic plus potash diluted with hot water into a paste with flour and sugar to massacre white ants—they ate the arsenic and were devoured by the others. When Darwin cynics laughed at Dr Holtze in apparently irrelevant remarks such as "Bats in the belfry!" and "Nobody upstairs", his literal English was the salvation of his faith. At the end of the second year he astonished them with thirty-two acres of radiant promise hidden away in the long grasses.

There were sixteen acres of sugar, the tasselled cane seven feet high grown from rattans, with a hundred and forty tons of cane-heads to give away; eight thousand banana palms in golden bearing; thirteen thousand luscious pineapples; five acres of maize giving two good crops a year; a field of excellent upland rice, another of Liberian coffee, another of English lucerne, an embryo grove of cocoa-trees, almonds, pepper, cinchona, cloves, breadfruit, guavas, lemons, mandarins, oranges, peanuts three tons to the acre, Cape gooseberries, Tahitian limes, litchi nuts, carob-trees and custard apples, African fibre nuts, Indian physic nuts, Chinese oil nuts, sisal hemp, millet fifteen feet high and five or six healthy fodder grasses. Arrowroot and cotton ran riot like weeds. Apples, grapes and pears were pale and seedy, but China Flat and Malta peaches glowed in healthy rose and gold.

English lawn grasses, carefully nurtured, made a green shadow under the milkwood-trees. The decorative indigo, with its small blue flowers and flecked leaves, was five feet high, whereas in India it seldom grows taller than two feet. An indiarubber-tree sponsored by Baron von Mueller shot up at the rate of two feet a year, but in those days the uses of rubber were confined to child's copy-book eraser and aristocratic heels.

Altogether there were five hundred and sixty plants in the clearing, from

China or Peru, thriving with not one shovelful of fertilizer and no watering other than rain or dew.

Of his rich and glossy West American tobacco leaves, twenty-seven inches by eighteen, Dr Holtze presented the Resident, Mr Price, with a box of home-cured hand-made cigars. "Milder than Manila", they were a mystery of the whist-parties, and Mr Price was complimented on his taste in cigars by no less a connoisseur than the *sahib* of the B.A.T. Holtze imported Chinese silkworms to his young mulberry-trees, and evolved several varieties of sturdy fabric or "Fuji" silk by transferring his little weavers to the native bamboo. His cotton-pods carried the blue ticket of first prize that year at Sydney Royal Show, and his upland rice the pink ticket of second prize in Melbourne.

But indeed Dr Holtze, for the next twenty-five years in his Botanic Gardens, was an agricultural show in himself. From his experiments there in poor land by the sea, he recommended sugar, rice, cotton, maize, millet, indigo and tobacco as staple plantation crops for North Australia—with due regard to markets and prices of production.

His lantern shed a lovely light.

The great Queensland sugar zone was then but a few thousand experimental acres on Burdekin River and around Mackay, cultivated and cut by kanakas. South Australia, still crowing over the Telegraph triumph, set out after Queensland again, offered a bonus of £5000 for the first crushing of five hundred tons of Territory cane. An optimist with a ready reckoner worked it out in the newspapers that at the Javan price of sugar, £20 a ton, three thousand acres would return £300,000 a year, the same area in wheat in the south "only £13,000".

The north stirred from its lethal sleep. Shareholders in the Northern Territory Company who had enjoyed ten years' rent free of nothing woke up and demanded their three hundred and twenty acres.

Two men from Clarence River were first planters, Eriksen and Cloppenburg, at West Point seven miles across the harbour, but seven hours getting there in their little skiff against wind and tide. With blacks to clear the fan-palm forest, they put in twenty-five acres of sugar, five acres of sweet potatoes to live on, fifty-six acres of maize, also cotton, tapioca, peanuts, limes, bananas, mulberries for silk, citrons, peaches, figs and five hundred coconuts . . . which the blacks dug up and enjoyed in a camp-fire kedgeree, missing only two. Prize pigs wallowed in lilies in the lagoons, four hundred fowls in the clearing pecked at the white ants. These settlers built themselves a little Tudor manor of galvanized iron, gabled roofs and arched windows facing a glorious sweep of bay, and interior murals of rainbows in the grand manner, in red, white, mauve and yellow ochre of the seashore, no doubt to cheer them through the wet.

Two mates near by, Harriss and Head, banked on maize and cotton—

twenty-five acres of Carolina cotton-seed at £1 1s. a pound. A lone camper, Vangemann, on a paperbark creek, put in two acres of tobacco.

Thirty miles inland, on beautiful springs near Rum Jungle, Poett and Mackinnon made a dazzling success in a few months of Arabian and Liberian coffee, three hundred thousand plants in five hundred acres, with maize, nurseries of cocoa and rubber, and with five thousand cheerful cinchona sprouts, the invaluable quinine that ever before—and since, alas!—has been a commercial monopoly of the Dutch East Indies. Poett was a Dutchman from Amboina, Mackinnon a descendant of the chieftain of Skye.

All the world loves a lottery. The Government received £11,000 that year in rent for agricultural land. Companies were soon hot on the trail. Eleven miles across the bay from Port Darwin the town of Delissaville began—the red glow of the old poinciana-trees still beckons you to it through the bush.

Delissa was a lieutenant of the 78th Highlanders who changed his kilt for a naga to command a regiment of coolies and Maranunga blacks. With an Adelaide syndicate to back him up, he spent £25,000 trying to win the £5000—perhaps he had his eye on the mythical £300,000 a year. His ten thousand acres of tangled green circled a purling rill where the Maranunga tribe took over the tree-felling contract for "sugar-bag" rights, then cleared and fenced for a weekly hand-out of sugar and tobacco. Chinamen at £1 a week were builders and planters—two hundred and fifty acres of cane, every cane dipped in carbolic and set in pounded seashell lime to foil the white ants, every furrow trenched and packed to withstand the wet.

Delissa planned for sugar, tobacco, rice and tropical fruits. He built two miles of road with a hundred-foot cutting through a hill to a jetty four hundred and fifty feet long with a derrick on the wharf to lift six tons. He built a mill of paperbark logs and iron, a hundred feet by sixty-four feet, boiler-sheds and sugar-store seventy feet by thirty feet, with two noble chimneys, sixty feet high, of ant-hill cement and ironstone. He imported a hundred and twenty tons of machinery—rollers to crush ninety tons of cane a day, vats to hold thirty thousand gallons of treacle. There were workshops, stables, hay-ricks of dried grass for fodder, woodstacks, copper coil, rotary pumps, a manager's residence forty feet square, semi-detached houses for a white population in a little main street, with community hall and library. The Chinamen's huts were on one side of the creek, blackfellows' mias on the other. A mill whistle blew daylight, tucker-time and knock-off till the bower-birds made it a byword by putting it on the record at any time o' day.

White population was two—Delissa, chairman of directors, in cabbage-tree hat, sunburn and sandshoes; Sachse, his manager, ditto. Sachse, from his own invention and Territory necessity, had taken out enough mill patents to revolutionize the industrial world. They were considering a plant to make sugar-bags out of pandanus fibre, and a paper mill to use up the sugar-cane brash in printing the *Delissaville Courier*. They overlooked the machinery to turn molasses into rum, otherwise Delissaville might have been a city now.

All cane was luxuriant and seven feet high. A sugar rush set in.

Solar topees floated up the hill from every ship, planters and agents from Java, Malaya, Mauritius, Brazil, St Kitts and the Hwang-ho. They chartered the scow *Maggie* and sailed through shoals of green turtle to flutter the yellow cranes out of the eighty-foot bamboos along Adelaide River, declaring its upper loams to be the finest plantation country in the world. They came back to regale themselves on warm beer under bag punkahs pulled by piccaninnies in the Port Darwin pubs, where they talked in thousands . . . thousands of acres, thousands of tons, mills to be erected costing thousands of pounds to employ people in thousands.

H. W. H. Stephens for Fisher and Lyons of Melbourne took up twenty thousand acres for coffee and sugar at Beatrice Hills, and Sergison fifteen thousand acres. The Honourable James Munro of Melbourne secured ten thousand acres and sent up John MacDonald, a sugar authority of Queensland, who proclaimed that for navigation, irrigation and cultivation the Adelaide was the finest river in the eastern colonies. Soon seventy thousand acres were "gone". So exciting was the land boom that the South Australian Government, seeing this unexpected wonderland slipping through its fingers, passed the Sugar Grant Act, doubling prices to 7s. 6d. an acre, then to 12s. 6d. an acre, and reserving seventy-five thousand acres to itself. In anticipation of an influx of mill-hands, McMinn surveyed the township of Brenda on Adelaide River—where the little police station now stands. The wilderness hills of Mary River are owned by an Anglo-French Company till this day.

Captain Carrington in the steamer *Palmerston* cruised the lower Victoria, reporting a fine pastoral country. Mylrea, MacDonald and Sullivan, on packhorses, rode the upper Victoria. Another party started for the three Alligator rivers, but crocodiles, fierce blacks and sandflies sent them galloping back.

Edwards from Natal and Reece from Fiji sailed the wild and beautiful Daly, where nobody had been but McMinn. Forty miles up they found superlative soils that made the Adelaide look like a gibber desert. Dodging crocodiles in the mud and the Mulluk Mulluk glowering at them over their nose-bones in the bamboos, they took twenty thousand jungle acres for granted and ran for their lives to *Maggie*, leaving an African darkie named Feodor and a pack of Chinese coolies to plant the roots of empire in that dark chocolate mould. They said the Daly was God's garden—but they wouldn't go back there for £1000 cash down.

Doughtier lads were Owston and Spence, for the Melbourne Palmerston Sugar Company in their own small steamer, *Ellangowan*. Six weeks lost in the serpentine of the river, they wrecked the ship, sank stores, nearly drowned seventeen Chinamen, saved the cane, and lived long enough, revolver on hip, to plant twenty of their twenty thousand acres with rattans that having been withered, submerged and frizzled, grew higher than Delissaville's that year.

Ninety acres of aloes were planted for a fibre industry, and a tong of Chinese took up Peron Island in the Daly estuary for vegetables and fruit, bringing their produce to Darwin in a lumbering old Chinese junk with a formidable eye on the prow. Also an affable Mr Hoo Chun, in spectacles and baggy silk trousers, representing the great Yan Woo Opium Company, made a special trip from Hong Kong to see if the Territory had a river to spare for the White Poppy.

With all this Big Business about, Darwin took heart of grace, and began to tidy up its litter of dipsomaniacs, goat-skulls, tin cans, blacks' camps and bottles. McMinn resurrected the plans of Goyder's city, redrew the straight lines of Mitchell, Smith, Cavenagh, Woods, Bennett, Daly and McMinn streets in a staggered square round Chinatown. The Resident set out with the Larrakia, gathering sandstone slabs from the beach to pave the puddles. Roads were ripped through the scrub by chains of coolies carrying rocks and dirt in their shoulder-baskets, blasted along by Kelly, a wild Irish ganger known as Ah Bang. A few new Government buildings and bungalows of cement and iron, painted white, were run up with prison labour by the Government Secretary, J. G. Knight.

Knight had been a lecturer in civil engineering at Melbourne University, one of the architects of Melbourne Parliament House, a foundation member of the Society of Arts and the famous Yorick Club, where he was friend and kindred spirit of Adam Lindsay Gordon, Henry Kendall, and Marcus Clarke. He came to the north in a fanciful moment in 1872, and his was the most beneficent influence the Front Gate ever knew. Knight's Cliff alone now bears his name.

Knight and Holtze together planted the thousands of tropic trees, shrubs and creepers that in their brief season of flamboyant blossom made poor old debilitated Darwin a joy to behold, the most vivid splash of colour in Australia.

Where are they now, those labyrinths of loveliness where we walked like sultans in a scented tapestry under canopies of scarlet and gold? In the malignity of sixty-three bomb raids and the rude excavations for fortifications of war, that delicate veil of enchantment was torn from an embittered earth, a bright raiment discarded with the old dreams.

When Darwin was a Turkish bath from September to January, in five minutes you could lose your sweaty self-consciousness, the enervation of the straggled streets and the tipsy commonplace of the hotels in paths of frail colour leading to grottoes of leopard sunlight with caladiums like toads and wayward trails of bougainvillea, purple, red and white. You need go no farther than the jetty or the Baths, where, to quote an Australian poet once of Darwin, Frederick T. Macartney:

> The bay, madonna of drowsy love,
> With the beach for halo, holds time asleep.

Nature and Knight terraced the headland and the cliffs with Persian fabric of eternal weaving. All over the tawdry town the poincianas were a spill of red ink, frangipanni a candle-flame, allamanda ringing bells of yellow. Tall tamarinds from the Orient threw down into pools of shade their crinkled brown fruit, dryly refreshing. The *Cassia fistula*, its blossom like a giant yellow wistaria, proffered long cylindrical beans with horny layers of sweetmeat black as liquorice. Amaranthus crimson as a frilled lizard's ruff, sun-spotted crotons, lycopodiums of copper, gold and silver, and ferns from the creeks where blacks and crocodiles smile found coolness under hedges of plumbago, blue and white, and musky oleander, that wears its blossoms as a native girl sets flowers in the darkness of her hair.

Gay little legume creepers and starry garlands wreathed the trees with grisly python vines and yellow-red banners of the mistletoe. By impromptu waterfalls the donkey orchids cocked their pretty ears at rare and diaphanous Malayan lilies that bloom for one night, and fade like a cobweb in morning sun.

In December every garden in Darwin was a kaleidoscope mirrored in silver pools. The humblest half-caste shacks sported their snowy sprays of inquisitive clematis, dreamy purple sprays of bougainvillea, bright-pink sprays of Honolulu creeper—or Mexican rose, or bridal shower, or coral vine, or maiden's blush—everyone has a different name for it, but the botanists call it *Antigonon,* and it is beloved of the bees. Everywhere was the mosaic of lantana, the coronalled hibiscus in a thousand velveted colours from the fluffed pink skirts of a ballet girl to imperial cerise and ivory white, everywhere the Japanese jasmine, quis qualis, millinery posies of small chenille flowers that changed from passionate magenta to palid white when the sun is set, as for the death of love.

We who knew the old Darwin, and loved it for all its sins, will never forget that wilful waste of colour—bamboo lattices a quivering prism of leafy light, the road to East Point splashed red with poincianas reflected in the pools, the Indian weave of Vestey's Gully, the grand march of the coconut palms to the technicolour Gardens. There was a flowering henna at the post-office gate that perfumed all the rain-time, and the little stone Church of England on the headland, dressed in gypsy red and yellow, was more like a pagan shrine.

How often on those rank sunny mornings with thunder rattling its chains in the dungeon of monsoon clouds away to the north, I have wandered in a mist of green butterflies, gathering Dutchman's pipe and Chinese lantern creeper in the pearly shivery grasses around Knight's old "Mud Hut", which was really a Moorish palace of whitened adobe, with its broad balconies under the palms, its flat roof overlooking the bay. The only graceful architecture old Darwin ever knew, it came to no good end. A mob of Government clerks batched there in 1930, and it was burnt down soon after.

Knight built a new Residency around Captain Douglas's one stone room, and his design for Government House is the rambling white mansion of today. He built the first swimming-baths, of stone and mortar, crocodile-proof, with a picket fence above that to keep out the sharks, through which the twenty-eight-foot tides came pouring and roaring twice a day in a lukewarm Nyanza that was the joy of youth, the relief of age, the delight of wayfarers on passing ships for half a century. Wild beasts of the Arafura Sea could find no entry there unless the sluice-gates were carelessly left open—as they were half the time. More than once when the tide went down a fourteen-foot crocodile was found meditating in the mud.

But I left my Chinamen sixty years behind, just at the moment when the philosophers' stones in their shoulder-baskets turned again to gold.

David Tennant, surveying plantation lands on Margaret River, kicked a six-pound nugget. Seven hundred Chinamen were there in a flash, swarming hill and gully, living on rice-biscuits, pelting white men out with sticks and stones. The Margaret River washed down gold in pounds, not ounces, twenty-, forty-, eighty-pound nuggets all ready in a glass case, curiously enclosed in thick crystal quartz. The Chinese got the lot. They herded together in tongs, jostling and squabbling, jumping claims and jumping on each other, snatching washdirt in showers. Macao men rabbited a patch just left by Cantonese, and raked off a hundred and fifty ounces. The Cantonese rushed back, and the Battle of the Margaret was on.

It raged for four days and three nights, the whole field whacking at it in close-up fights of tomahawks, nailed sticks, dolly-pots, dinner-knives, pistols, short-handled shovels and sharpened bamboos, billies of boiling water and flying buckets of ore. One tall Chinkie like Ajax felled everything around him with a long-handled pick. When a band of white miners came over the hill to legislate for peace, they were belted back by a howling mob of a couple of thousand Mongols, throwing rocks. A dispatch rider set off for Lucanas, the trooper at Pine Creek.

Lucanas was a direct descendant of the centurion who witnessed the Resurrection—at least, according to Lucanas, and none could say him nay. Unarmed and without a hat he leapt into the fray, and quelled it with a yell. In fear of his brass buttons it dissolved like froth on the river. So ended the Battle of the Margaret, with five of the generals tied to trees.

It was followed by Saunders's Rush. On one of Phil Saunders's old claims a coolie waist-deep in a waterhole fished forty-five ounces in a day, six hundred ounces in a week. With a fourteen-pound nugget his secret was out—a thousand of his countrymen were round him, and the waterhole, the only water, was gone.

Eyes glazed with thirst, Chinamen staggered about with buckets of gold. Ah Loy drew up a hundred and seventy ounces in the hoist of one bucket. There was a run of luck everywhere in a ringing oratorio of ounces to the ton. At Wheal Margaret, near their Extended Union the indefatigable three, Houschildt, Landers and Noltenius, hit a shoot of gold fifty feet wide compressed in small rich leaders, and then a glittering ridge seven miles long at Houschildt's Rush. Twelve hundred men came racing back from the Palmer.

The companies swooped like chicken-hawks. Southport was a town again, and the blind tigers of the road a blaze of rum and glory.

A hundred and fifteen thousand pounds' worth of gold went to Melbourne in a few months. W. G. Stretton and Lucanas formed a gold escort, bringing in eleven hundred ounces every week in a buggy through the bush, six thousand ounces to every ship, and three times that amount was smuggled out by the Chinese, and with dead Chinese travelling to China. The diggers were still swimming the creeks with pickle-bottles full of yellow treasure. On the fields there was nothing to eat but bad flour and brahminee kites. One man sat in his tent with a twenty-two-ounce nugget, a salt-cellar of gold in perfect natural formation. It held half an ounce of salt with nothing to salt. The few teamsters charged £80 freight for a two-horse drayload of stores. But the Chinese, beggars on horseback, now had the cash to import horses, and put teams of their own on the road in cheap opposition. In an outburst of White Australia fury, their huts were burnt down and they were frequently waddied to death "by the blacks". When £750 in rough gold disappeared from the safe in Southport police station, an astute trooper arrested a gang of coolies for the crime . . . and was himself arrested by a more astute colleague. He was sentenced to imprisonment for seven years.

Gold was again a curse instead of a blessing. Not a horse nor a coolie could be found for love or money. The plantations were deserted save for tribes of obliging blacks who cut the corn and ate it, who cut the sugar-cane and went bush with the cane-cutting knives to make shovel-nose spears. The nurseries were never planted out. At Delissaville a magnificent crop was left in rotting stacks on the beach and by the silent mill—only seven tons of treacle from a hundred and eighty-two tons of first-class cane. The acres of maize at West Arm stood yellow and ripe till a dark cloud of grasshoppers ate them all in a day. At Beatrice Hills the Adelaide came up smiling, drowned the plantations three feet deep in a night. Out on the Daly the Mulluk Mulluk, hiding in the nine-foot cane, speared Owens the manager. Coal-black Feodor came up in the Chinese junk to say that he was "the only white man left on the river".

No hope of beating the jungle without a multitude of men! To save the plantations, the South Australian Government rushed through Parliament the Hindu Coolie Immigration Bill. Poett of Rum Jungle and Sergison of Adelaide River sailed for Ceylon to bring back Malabar men and ghee buffaloes, the patient little humped beasts of Indian ox-carts that might prove more amenable than the myalls from Malaya. Da Costa, labour agents in Colombo, promised to deliver thousands of both. They sent five of each, turbaned Tamils who camped for a month with their charges in the Resident's tumbledown stables till they were suddenly suspected of smallpox and huddled across the harbour to quarantine. While they were cutting timber to build themselves a shelter, they discovered the sacred Bo Tree of Buddha growing wild in the Australian bush, and spent the rest of the time salaamed in solemn prayer. They knew only three words of English, drilled into them in Ceylon, "Port Darwin, go!" After being delivered several times to Darwin, and hustled out of it, they mingled with the blacks to add a few more genealogical twigs to the aboriginal tree. Stockdale bought the last of the ghee buffaloes, and took them down to Sydney with some crocodiles for Coogee Aquarium.

Until this time Darwin had been a free port of trade with the East, its list of exports and imports, other than foodstuffs, largely confined to the Gs—Out, Gold; In, Gin. Pioneers still date their chronologies from "the old A. V. H. days" of loving memory when you could buy a case of Dutch squareface, the world's best, fifteen bottles for 30s. But now South Australia appointed the postmaster, J. A. G. Little, to be Sub-Collector of Customs, with a list of excises and imposts tacked to the office wall. It made no appreciable difference save that the shanties doubled the death-rate with home-brew vitriol of Sunset Rum, and that an inspector of Her Majesty's Customs sat in a shack on the beach cracking open the bones and skulls of dead Chinamen to find a golden marrow.

A couple of Acts of God had occurred in the Gulf of Carpentaria. *Lalla Rookh*, a blackbird schooner from the New Hebrides with kanakas for Queensland canefields, sailed into Burketown under the yellow flag of fever. In a week of horror the plague was away. Seventy died in two months, the dead lying in the streets. The living fled in panic to Sweers Island, a hundred miles offshore, where they formed a little settlement they called Carnarvon, their stores coming from Normanton by schooner. They left behind two drunks who missed the boat. Three months later, when they dared to reconnoitre, those drunks were hale and hearty, tenants of a town. The next year a cyclone blew Burketown away and flattened Normanton to the ground with the rise of a tidal wave and the loss of seven lives. These ill winds made Darwin, for a while, the only port of the north coast.

The gold-seekers were drifting farther and farther out into the ranges of the wild blacks, with no fires and no bells on their horses, hearing the cry of a night-bird and wondering was it a murdering party. Immense lodes of silver lead were discovered at Eveleen and Coronet Hill near Pine Creek, immense lodes of tin at Mount Wells, at Finniss River and Bynoe Harbour, stream tin at Mackinlay River, eleven hundredweight to the ton.

Houschildt, Roberts, Landers and Noltenius sold their dazzling shafts and ridges to a Swede named Jansen, and cradled their way through the fan-palm creeks to Daly River, where a bald hill of the Hayward Range looked uncannily green. It was a hill of pure malachite. One stroke of Houschildt's pick opened a mighty copper blow, with ores of grey steel, red oxide, bell metal and rich carbonates—a range of copper running for four miles, next to Cobar the mightiest sweep of high-grade ores in Australia, and close to water-carriage with all the wood in the world for smelting! Camped that night in silence by the eerie river, their own Wilwonga blacks from Pine Creek, fearful in strange country, huddled in beside them and starting at every sound, these four white men dreamed their dreams. Next morning they rode for Darwin to tell the news and float companies.

Prosperity swept up in a tidal wave. An English company offered to build a railway to Pine Creek, and to spend £200,000 in development for alternate square miles on either side of the line, and fifty acres in Darwin. The Government, which five years before had tried to give the Territory away to Hindus and Japs, coldly declined.

An election was held in the south, and the incoming Government, in faith and fervour, unfurled for its banner the colonization of the Vast Empty North, the building of a trans-continental railway across Australia from Adelaide to open the Front Gate! V. L. Solomon was first member for the North, and now it was represented by a Minister of the Crown.

The Territory was to be called Alexandra Land in honour of the Princess of Wales. In the pubs of Alexandra Land £1600 was lost in a night in quoits and gambling. The coolies wrote home for their friends and relations in thousands to come and build the railway. The District Council came to life again. Men who had sown their wild oats in the spinifex became pillars of the State.

A cynic who signed himself Donald ap Donald wrote in to the *N.T. Times*:

> I had a dream that was not a dream. Tall ships went in and out of the harbour of Port Darwin. The flag that braved a thousand years the battle and the breeze floated everywhere, mixed up with the Stars and Stripes of America, the Eagle of Russia, the Dragon of China, the Yellow Horse of Norway, the Red White and Blue of all countries in the world.
>
> The tall lofty rocks of Port Darwin were extinguished. A broad level terrace stretched across to the majestic slopes of Stokes Hill, and huge docks reflected in their tranquil waters the busy shores, while the rush of mighty locomotives, the scream of the engine, the stentorian voice of the railway guard shouting "*MacDonnell Ranges-Adelaide*" filled the astonished mind with thoughts that gleam, and hopes that burn, and aspirations that leap upward like old boots.
>
> The *N.T. Times* was a vast journal, three-quarters of an acre in size, printed in blood-red ink and burnished with gold. Mr Bogle's chapel was broader than the Coliseum, and all along the Esplanade was one vast range of palaces designed by Knight. Between Darwin and Southport great steamers conveyed the lords of the soil, owners of the rich gold mines, proprietors of sugar plantations, masters of swarthy crowds of human beings whose voices echoed along the silvery strand, singing ever and for aye:
>
> *"O this is the country of lovely banannas,*
> *O this is the land of good cheer!*
> *O this is the region of breezy pyjammers,*
> *And cold bottled beer!"*

Before the echoes died away, the vision had departed, leaving a bad headache.

Two new little ships, *Busy Bee* and *Aphis*, were flitting about the harbour, their names indicative of their size. Melville Island was mooted as a health resort for jaded citizens of the new Darwin—visions of old ladies in bathchairs pursued by stripy cannibals with spears on that hostile strand. Ten pounds was subscribed to start a library, £500 for a new town hall, and £5000 for a new jail, to be built at Fannie Bay, providing prison labour for Holtze's gardens, the white hope of the north. Knight was the architect of Fannie Bay jail, the old stone pile that stood for seventy years, a queerer gargoyle of human nature in its tragedies and comedies than any other jail in the world. Because water was scarce, its prisoners, black and white, went surfing in Van Diemen's Gulf. When Lawrie, first jailer, died they all marched to his funeral, freed of their chains, to pay homage to a good friend gone.

The first missioners to the blacks arrived. Under an old-man banyan that shaded half an acre at Rapid Creek the Society of Jesus established a monastery in the open air, eight priests and brothers, black-robed and black-bearded, under Father O'Brien and Father Strélé, pacing natural cloisters of the great hanging roots, picaninnies singing "Ave Maria" in a little bark church. Only two of the priests spoke English, and none of the rest spoke each other's languages, but they learned Larrakia, and for their quaint parishioners, in very quaint translation, they told the story of creation and of One Who Died to save the Larrakia. Their mission proved of little avail so near the devious ways of Darwin, where there was an aborigines' ball that year. One-eyed Emma was the belle, as the *Northern Territory Times* described her, "gracefully, modestly and becomingly attired in a pocket handkerchief".

To entertain expected visitors, a Mr Christoe started a little zoo with a crocodile capable of swallowing a child. It got loose in the dead of night, patrolled the luckily deserted streets, and looked in on the B.A.T. on duty.

For the first time, Christmas brought good cheer. Shirtless diggers and the *élite* in pyjamas gathered in thunderstorms to drink good health to the railway, singing "Christians Awake! Salute the happy morn."

In New Year '82 the newly elected Minister for the Northern Territory, the Honourable J. A. Langdon Parsons, set out by ship from Adelaide on the five thousand-mile journey to find his electorate.

The Minister had travelled *en prince* with three Members of Parliament in his suite, also Professor Ralph Tate of the Chair of Natural Science at Adelaide University, and Mr William Sowden of Adelaide *Register*—later Sir William Sowden. In a rare little book, *The Northern Territory As It Is*, he has left us a graphic description of the Northern Territory as it was.

As s.s. *Menmuir*, after many adventures, crept inshore under the monsoon, carefully avoiding the kerosene tins on sticks that at full tide marked the submerged jetty, she was greeted by a drunk in pyjamas sailing a dug-out canoe. He asked for a light for his pipe—all the fires in Darwin were out and all its matches mildew. He begged to inform the Minister that in the wet season the Territory was wholly dependent on passing steamers for a light.

On shore a bedraggled little mob read a damp illuminated address, and invited the party to a bully beef banquet, but business before pleasure, the Minister said. He set out across the bay in squalls, his colleagues sitting on the boilers of the *Maggie* wearing singlets and Wellington boots.

"Ip! IP! OOLAY!" shouted Chinese and blacks as they scrambled up the jetty at Southport, to a welcome dinner at Hopewell's Hotel in din of a gale, corroboree and crackers, with a health to the "not far distant day when thousands of toiling mechanics and the smoke of many factories" would pollute the pure glory of Southport's clouds.

Next morning they mounted old hat-racks of horses and went bush with Mr Knight through a realm of rain to the mines. The Minister travelled in tweed trousers, singlet, black umbrella, long white oilskin leggings and slouch hat with fly-veil. Statesmen of girth and dignity, plodding plains and swimming rivers, over bogs and boulders they rode three hundred miles—now and again a horse fell flat.

Through fairy vales of emerald and silver, through crystal sun-showers and sunsets of Olympian splendour, they took up the white man's burden of fret and sweat, and in that world of wildering beauty learned the weariness of being. Grass-parrots of heavenly blue, and that brilliant mite, the sun-bird, flashed above the coloured grasses and the crowded graveyards of gold.

Through Gothic towers of ant-hills and mazes of butterflies "like animated pansies" they came to stricken little towns of pestilence and neglect "where even the strongest man in the place has lustreless eyes floating in a sea of yellow". They saw the straggled mines, the shafts of drowned wealth, teams and wagons months' deep in mud, a million pounds' worth of machinery run to rust. They camped at the shanties, herded in with drunks, blacks, pigs, fowls, Chinamen and bats to a shouting of frogs and racket of pack-bells all night, while wind whistled through the bamboo walls and rain poured through the roof.

They listened to delirium of ounces to the ton, received deputations in the lightning from mandarins in red silk robes and white men half-naked who gave them nuggets of gold for their watch-chains. They heard "stranger than fiction", grave and gay, met characters unique in this world, among them four white women, far apart and unnamed, who had crossed a continent with the camp-fires of gold.

At Adelaide River they met Cocky Haynes, the most versatile bird, sulphur-crested—or if not, he should have been. No trooper ever swore like Cocky Haynes, famous among the bushmen even yet. Cocky was star boarder, barman, mail-driver and chucker-out at the little pub at Adelaide River kept by Charlie Haynes, who bred him from a chicken. On duty in the bar, he shouted the diggers' orders with sound-effects of popping corks, fizzing bottles and guggling of beer. He would holler a stave from a sea chanty whenever he called for rum, take a long gurgle with an appreciative "Ah-h-h!", would deliver a blurred speech about the north, sing, stagger, cheer, and bet any bloody man a bloody pound. His one-man concerts included a frogs' chorus, a dingo howling and a parson preaching, though Cocky had never heard a parson preach. He would dig for gold with his claw, find it, yell "Eureka!" and call a shout for the boys, writing his cheque with his beak dipped in beer and a shout to Charlie, "Fill 'em up again!"

His favourite game was to perch outside, starting the teamsters' horses, cackling demoniac laughter when the teamster rushed out, and he refused to have a —— nigger about the —— pub, screeching them out with Billingsgate and a few parting shots of a sharp-shooter. Every second week when Charlie drove to Southport for the mail, Cocky flew eight miles to Stapleton to meet him, putting in the time in a gum-tree giving lessons in advanced English to a mob of myall cockatoos. When Charlie hove in sight, he flew down on the seat, reached for the reins, and with terse biographical sketches of passengers and horses, drove the buggy all the way home. Lord Brassey, on a tour of the world in the *Sunbeam*, offered £100 for Cocky Haynes, but Charlie wouldn't have sold him for *Sunbeam* herself. So remarkable was the bird's talent with the banjo that the diggers subscribed a fund to send him south for lessons on the piano. In Adelaide Cocky attained fame and fortune, giving recitals, monologues and music, for charity, admission one shilling. The day after Charlie Haynes died, Cocky dropped dead of a broken heart.

The ministerial party spent five weeks in the north. Driven back by gales and floods from an attempt to reach the Daly, they sailed Adelaide River, visited Delissaville and all the plantations, made friends with the lonely, shared their hospitality and their troubles. They glimpsed the pastoral pageant a hundred million acres unknown.

The only need of the Promised Land was a trans-continental railway. The Minister announced at his farewell banquet that that was now to be built. (*Loud and prolonged cheers.*)

The party left by steamer for the south, rich in knowledge, firm in faith, singing the praises of a land of hope and glory. As the green cliffs of Darwin faded to the blue of the Arafura, the Minister surprised himself and his colleagues with the announcement that he would soon come back.

Now came news of a big mob of cattle drifting across the downs. The Age of Bully would soon be over.

Chapter XII

The Conquistadores

GLAMOUR OF gold and golden fleeces, Australia in the seventies was a landtaker's paradise. Phillip's patch at Port Jackson had widened to a continent of six States, with telegraphs and railways, three or four million people settling down. Cockatoo squatters, growing beef and mutton for mushroom towns and cities, had become a landed gentry. Some retired to mansions at Potts Point and carriages along St Kilda Road. Others sold on the boom, and with unlimited backing for their properties and propositions at the too-numerous banks, moved farther and farther out. A rush of pastoral companies was formed, looking for new worlds to conquer—the new worlds the explorers had found in years of lonely riding.

The Territory was a new world with a vengeance, where areas vast as a

European kingdom could be taken up for a lifetime by a swing of a surveyor's compass on a totally blank map. Rents were nominal, the only condition that they must be stocked within three years. The overlanders stocked them, travelling by mariner's compass, two years out with cattle, finding the way and the waters, their home a swag.

First man to bring cattle to the north was D'Arcy Wentworth Uhr, "blind-stabbing" for fifteen hundred miles north-west from Charters Towers with four hundred bullocks for Darwin in 1872. Nobody knew he was coming till he rode in with the first fresh beef they had seen for two years. He told his story as the bushmen do. A friend met him in Port Darwin.

"Hullo, D'Arcy! What are you doing here?"

"I just came across the Gulf with cattle."

"Go on! Had any trouble?"

"No. Got along well."

Some say D'Arcy Uhr shot his way through the blacks. He stockwhipped one of his drovers, who charged him with common assault, first civil action in the Territory, heard under a banyan-tree at Roper Bar. Patterson of the Overland Telegraph gave a verdict in favour of Uhr. The stockman had pulled a gun on his boss, who flicked it from his hand with the curl of a whip, and laid down the law in a good sound thrashing. Mutiny was fatal on the trail of Carpentaria in those days.

Dillon Cox travelled Uhr's track with three hundred horses to the goldmines. The drover who followed lost all his cattle and starved to death in the ranges of Limmen River.

On a hot day in '75, R. R. Knuckey of the Telegraph Line, now a travelling superintendent, from the veranda at Daly Waters saw a bushman stagger out of the scrub, leading a skeleton horse. His name was Leonard Elvy and he carried a rag of paper, an urgent telegram to the Resident in Darwin:

> OLD FRIEND IN SAD DISTRESS LEFT IN BUSH QUITE EXHAUSTED NO HORSES SEEK YOUR ASSISTANCE.
>
> WILLIAM NATION.

These two were last of a party of drovers for G. D. Latour that left Charters Towers with a mob of five hundred that dwindled to a hundred among crocodiles and bog. The men quarrelled, died or turned back—one wandered with the blacks for three months, tracking and spearing his own cattle, living on saltless beef. Nation and Elvy reached the Limmen in sweeping flood, and made for the ranges, where Nation became ill. Elvy had found his lone way three hundred miles to Daly Waters. Knuckey rode back with him to that lost world, to find Nation eleven days dead. He had killed his riding-horse for food. His will was in his pocket: "My saddle I leave to Leonard as I feel sure he will have done his best for me." Well-known in South Australia, he had been aide-de-camp to a Governor. Knuckey named Nation Creek for the lonely grave, and Rosy River for his own sister.

In 1877 came one of the greatest bushmen Australia has ever known, Nathaniel Buchanan, "Old Bluey". Camp-fires of the continent north of 28° shine bright to his memory, explorer, path-finder, first pilot for hundreds of thousands of cattle, patron saint of the drovers.

"Far-Away" the blacks called him, from his own favourite phrase, a man whose heart was ever in the distance, who found the waters and formed the largest cattle runs in the world. He never strived for money, but was loved and revered by whites and blacks through all his life, as now they honour him dead. His life-story has been outlined by his son, Gordon Buchanan, in a good book, *Packhorse and Waterhole*. Still faithful to the outback, his grandson, Gordon Buchanan, is the friendly voice over the pedal radio at Wyndham.

A Scotsman from Ireland—the ideal mixture of endurance and intuition for the Australian bush—Nat Buchanan as a young man rode the Gulf country with Landsborough looking for Burke and Wills. With Cornish in 1861 he explored Diamantina River, and formed Mount Cornish Station near Longreach for the Landsborough Pastoral Company, then the biggest and farthest-out cattle run in the world. He married Katherine Gordon, formed Bowen Downs, and in 1877, riding with Sam Croker, was first to cross the Barkly Tablelands from east to west, where Avon Downs, Austral Downs, Alexandria, Brunette and Alroy Downs are pastoral wealth today. The two brothers Prout, in a tragic endeavour to cross, had perished out there the year before, but Buchanan came through to Powell's Creek, and telegraphed Adelaide to take up country on Buchanan River. The explorer was too late—it was all taken up "on the map". He led the first cattle to the Territory, and across the continent to Kimberley, and again across the continent southward through the west. As an old man he was out with his bluey in the Great Sandy Desert alone, looking for new waters still.

A story is told that when Wave Hill was a great station, mustering its eighty thousand head, the bookkeeper was surprised one day by the arrival of "an old city josser, sitting on a camel under a green umbrella, with a myall nigger and a camel-string in tow". He had come, he said, from Tennant's Creek and was making due south to the South Australian border.

The bookkeeper was at home alone, a newcomer to Wave Hill. He invited the visitor to lunch.

"You give that country a miss," he said. "Take my advice."

The old josser twinkled.

"Why?" he asked innocently. "Are the blacks bad?"

"Never mind the blacks. You won't find any water."

"Ah, well. I'll take a chance on that. I usually do find water."

He loaded up with stores, filled his leather canteens, had a word or two with the old ones in the blacks' camp, and with his black-boy and his camel-string vanished into the sunset.

When the manager came in with the mustering camp and heard of that old city josser under the green umbrella making off into the desert where nothing lives,

"He's Malley's Cow," he said. "He's a goner. We'd better go out and get him, or we'll have to go out and bury him."

They found him a hundred miles down, camped under a tree with plenty of water and quite happy. He was grateful for their attention, but amused.

"I told them my name was Buchanan," he said. "I forgot to say it was Nat."

The station manager stared. "Not . . . Bluey?"

"The same."

Whites grinned, blacks grinned, even the packhorses grinned as they shook hands. For years it was a joke against Wave Hill, for back in the dim twilight of fable Bluey Buchanan had formed Wave Hill, had named that curiously striated hill cresting Victoria River like a wave breaking from infinities of earth and sun. He had likewise forgotten to tell them that he came from Tennant's Creek with his lone black-boy, not round by the road through Katherine but north-west across desert.

No man has followed him yet on that trail to the pale horizon of the Buchanan Hills. They say he dipped his pannikin into a soak and drew it out filled to the brim with magic yellow gravel. The legend of Buchanan's Pint-pot will live out there for ever, though maybe Old Bluey would smile to hear it. Every five years or so a couple of prospectors load up a truck with food, water and shovels, and make a dash south of Inverway to look for the creek of Buchanan's Pint-pot of gold.

Glencoe was first station in the Territory, screw-palm jungle and grass flats of Adelaide River near Brock's Creek, taken up in 1878 by Travers and Gibson of Punjaub Station near Aramac in Queensland. Buchanan was pilot for twelve hundred cattle and half a dozen drovers—his wife's brothers, Hughie and Wattie Gordon, Travers, Bright, Hume and Brebner. Three drays carried flour, tea, jam, rice, dried potatoes and dried apples, food for twelve months. North through Cloncurry then swimming the cattle across the Gulf rivers and stringing them over the ranges, Buchanan opened the Old Coast Road, followed the Roper for three hundred miles and turned north from Elsey River. Each day he rode ahead to find water, blazing trees with distance and direction, a black-boy picking up his track and the drovers bringing on the cattle. Never in his life had Bluey Buchanan any trouble with wild blacks, though he fired over their heads once or twice.

One morning in a Limmen River camp, a dell of glory by a spring, Roderick Travers stayed back to make the damper. They found him beheaded with his own axe, his head in the dish with the dough. After the long and dangerous droving, the cattle were delivered to Glencoe—it was, indeed, to be a Vale of Weeping.

While Nat Buchanan was blazing the trail from Queensland, across the dry downs and mud mazes of Carpentaria, other path-finders came from south and west. In September '79 Alexander Forrest, with Fenton Hill as

nearer till the Dark People ran for the hills and lay flat on the rim of the cliffs, peering through veils of spinifex to see the Animal that Falls to Pieces.

Eagle eyes watched the packhorse come in to the waterhole, saw a figure alight, throw off packs and saddles, undo girths and water-bags, tucker-bags, billy-cans, swags . . . saw it light a fire with a flash, make a mysterious meal without hunting, set up three spears with points together, squint to the horizon as though for ghostly kangaroo, then pace and prance and curtsy, trailing a hair-string on the ground. When the creature took off its skin, popped a firestick into its mouth, sat under a tree smouldering, writing *millee-millee* in a small white square, the marvel was complete. Then the litter amazingly welded itself into one again, and was off at a kangaroo-bound, leaving a four-footed track iron-sharp and deep but too far and too swift to follow, leaving an altar of stones to some ungodly worship on top of a hill. This visitor from Queer Street took a lot of thinking out.

In 1883 David Lindsay, that rider of a continent, was twisting about in the bamboo creeks and debil-debil plains of his first survey in Arnhem Land. With three white men, two black-boys and thirty-two horses he spent five months out there, and crossed the perilous region twice, riding north of the Roper to Blue Mud Bay and over to Castlereagh Bay. The blacks speared his horses and set the country on fire. On Goyder River the party was attacked at night by an army of three hundred. Those who believe that Arnhem Land was penetrated for the first time by an expedition of the Royal Geographical Society in 1948, I would refer to David Lindsay's journals of 1883, and, again, of 1917.

Captain Carrington, in the Government schooner *Palmerston*, surveyed all the river estuaries from the Roper to the Victoria. John Carruthers, T. E. Day and others, two years camping in the sand, marked down the Queensland-Territory border by the slant of the stars. W. J. H. Carr Boyd, with Larry Wells as surveyor, bushman Billy O'Donnell, Linacre, O'Malley and Wall, on twenty-five packhorses, were out for a year of reconnaissance through the bristled Kimberley Ranges, and so was Stockdale's party, both financed by Melbourne firms. Mulcahy and Ashton, of Stockdale's men, stayed out in those ranges looking for gold, and were never heard of again. McIlree, his surveyor, died of exhaustion, and a man named Pitt went insane when they came in to Springvale. A thousand miles south, Ernest Giles, with ten camels, was setting out from The Peake in a desert trek of fifteen hundred miles to West Australia.

D'Arcy Uhr and Jock McPhee rode the north coast from Victoria River to the headwaters of the Macarthur, sailing the rivers in blacks' canoes, made into sleds on the swamps and clay-pans and hauled by their horses. Mair and Harriss rode from Elsey River to Limmen Bight. Adam Johns and Phil Saunders left Darwin in the little schooner *Prospect* for the west, sailed a thousand miles to Nickol Bay, discovered the gold of Ashburton River, the copper of Whim Creek—then, along the Eighty Mile Beach, the Fitzroy

River, and over the formidable King Leopold Ranges they rode three thousand miles back, bringing the first tidings of Kimberley gold.

These men looked upon a virgin land, saw the wonder of its rivers and fine pastoral country, now offered by Government on a forty-two years' lease at peppercorn rentals, no taxes, no fences, no drought in an annual rainfall monsoon country. Following a disastrous drought in the south, the early eighties saw a grand migration of cattle across a continent unrivalled in the world's history, a classic of flocks and herds right out of the Old Testament, but on a mightier and more heroic scale.

Soon the black-soil and Mitchell grass plains of the Barklys were all taken up. Avon Downs on Shakespeare Creek and James River, just over the Queensland border, were occupied by Thomas Guthrie of Melbourne, the first four thousand sheep a year on the way from Victoria. The pretty old white homestead and its golden prairies are heritage yet of the Guthrie family. Rocklands Station was pioneered by McCulloch and Scarr. To Austral Downs, rich country on the head of the Georgina, came fourteen hundred cattle and nineteen thousand sheep for Richardson, Little and Carr. Kilgour, the surveyor, took Lorne Creek, McPherson the headwaters of Buchanan River, and E. W. Lamb Alroy Downs on the edge of the big desert. North Australian Pastoral Company formed Alexandria and its out-station Sudan on the Buchanan, Playford and Rankine rivers in the years of the British victories over Arabi Pasha—three thousand five hundred cattle and seventy horses overlanded from the Collins estates in Queensland. Today the finest cattle run in outback Australia—eleven thousand eight hundred and ten square miles of beautiful country with sixty-two thousand pure-bred Shorthorns on surface waters and sub-artesian bores—Alexandria, or "Box-A Ranch", as American servicemen called it, is the largest cattle station in the world.

Harry Readford, "Captain Starlight", alias "the Dodo", brought the first cattle to Corella Lakes and Brunette from Albilba Station on the Barcoo for MacDonald, Smith and Macansh. West of Anthony's Lagoons—Kul-kul-quadja, twin waters—Bowstock of Melbourne formed Eva Downs, Tom Nugent, leader of the Ragged Thirteen, bringing the cattle out. Brodie and de Salis sat down with their mob at Creswell Downs, and on the Barkly fall to the Gulf ranges and rivers the brothers Christian formed Walhalla Downs.

From Ernest Favenc's reports, Amos brothers and Broad took up Macarthur River, twenty-two thousand square miles. Tom Lynott formed that station in the frowning Clyde Ranges swarming with wild blacks—twenty thousand cattle and a fine homestead of Oregon pine sent up from south to provide a feast for the blacks and the white ants.

On Limmen River, wilder still, Alf Scrutton, a rider with the Jardines to Cape York, called his forest run Bauhinia Downs. Koop and Lawrie camped with their cattle on Tanumbirini Lagoon, Mason and Shepherd on Hodgson Downs, while John Costello, pioneer apostle of far west Queensland, leased all the big rivers of Limmen Bight beyond the Four Archers of Leichhardt, his far homestead at Albinjula, Valley of Springs.

Farther out even than these, Macartney and Mayne from Waverley, near Broad Sound, leased Florida, on the Goyder, in Arnhem Land, building a homestead of cypress pine with Chinese sawyers by the glorious horseshoe lagoon near Lindsay's Mount Delight. For them it was hell's delight. Terror stalked the mangroves, in constant slaughter of the Malays and blacks all round. The white men lived one day at a time, never without their nine-inch Colts. Alf and Dick Randall managed the run. Epworth, an English johnnie, was head stockman, whipping his thoroughbred through the swamps, dressed in gay hunting rig and waving a riding-crop. There was a French chef in the kitchen, Louis Fayre, making *vol-au-vent* of liver and lights and *bouillabaisse* of barramundi—but E. O. Robinson, creeping across Castlereagh Bay in his lugger twice a year with stores, never dared to come near the house till he fired a shot and was answered, in case they had all been done in.

Florida was deserted in a hurry within two years, the white men "borderline and over", and most of its cattle killed by blacks. Macartney and Tom Hardy, who had brought those cattle out, gathered what they could of the mobs still alive, and drove them a thousand miles west, to Auvergne on Baines River, where the blacks were nearly as bad. Acres and Suttor, of Sydney, sent five thousand cattle to the Alligator rivers, but had to vacate on account of buffalo flies. Armstrong and Lawrie, on Adelaide River near Darwin, formed Humpty Doo station and Marrakai.

From far across the continent came the MacDonalds from Goulburn, New South Wales, and the Duracks from Cooper's Creek, three years on the trail to Kimberley. The three MacDonald brothers lost their cattle, their wagons, stores—lost everything, even their diaries. They had to turn back and make a second journey, winning through at long last to Fossil Downs, near Fitzroy Crossing, one of the best stations in West Kimberley, with a beautiful modern homestead for the third generation of MacDonalds today.

It was in 1865 that the Duracks had left Goulburn, New South Wales, inspired by the lone and splendid explorations of their kinsman John Costello, to make their home in an unknown land, where rivers were a hundred miles wide in flood, out in the Queensland west. There were five patriarch Duracks—Patrick, Jeremiah, and John and their cousins Patrick and Michael. With Patrick Tully, Ned Hammond, and other brave Irish families of the clan, they colonized all the country from the Warrego to Cooper's Creek, and founded the towns of Quilpie and Windorah. Patsy had settled at Thylungra—now the greatest sheep station in Australia—Jerry at Galway Downs. A remarkable colony they had conjured up, linked to the world by Cobb and Company coaches, within that twenty years.

The explorations of Alexander Forrest, in 1879, called them north-west again, to what seemed the end of the world. In partnership with Solomon Emanuel of Sydney, Patsy financed a schooner expedition to the far coasts of

Kimberley to inspect. Michael J. Durack was leader, and with him Tom Kilfoyle, a cousin, Sydney Emanuel, John Pentacost, surveyor and geologist, James Jose, and Tom Horan. They landed on the uninhabited shores of Cambridge Gulf, at View Point near the mouth of Ord River, and set out on horseback across the rugged King Leopold Range. Looking for Forrest's landmarks, a redbutt and a blackbutt tree, they named the Dunham, Bow, Durack, and Pentacost rivers. Along the Ord and the Fitzroy it was five months' riding to Beagle Bay, where they arrived starved and barefooted. With the well-known pastoralist Lumley Hill of Queensland, Michael formed Lissadell Station on Ord River, second pastoral lease in East Kimberley. Patsy and Jerry Durack shared a great swing of the river between them.

No hope of landing the cattle from ships, they must bring the herds from Cooper's Creek, carry their own food and find the way.

In June 1883 M. J. Durack led off with two thousand two hundred cattle from Mount Marlowe on the Barcoo. Patsy, Jerry, and John followed from Galway Downs and Thylungra, Tom Kilfoyle and Tom Hayes bringing up the rear—good-bye to civilization, across the Diamantina plains in drought, with many a fifty-mile dry stage and many a midnight rush. Four months to the Georgina River, on Parrapitcherie Waterhole, they camped for another three months waiting for rain. Here two men died. The Burke and Georgina rivers were an inland sea when the rains came, and from there men and horses, to save the cattle, were swimming for miles. At Nicholson River pleuro broke out in the herds. Every river-crossing from there to the Roper was a half-mile swim—a ten weeks' rain-camp on the Rosy. On the Roper their ringers were delirious with fever. Jack Sherringham shot himself, Joe Urquhart died. At last they passed the Elsey to the Overland Telegraph Line. Across the Dry River to the Victoria at a slow ten miles a day, they came at last through the red ranges to the Ord. Here the story of their first beginnings was told all over again, ten thousand square miles of range and river redeemed from wilderness into six million-acre border stations controlled by the pastoral firm of Connor, Doherty and Durack for sixty-five years--Lissadell, Ivanhoe, Newry, Bullita, Auvergne, and, head station, Argyle.

East and south-east of the Ord, Kilfoyle, Hayes and Jerry Durack formed Rosewood and Waterloo. A hundred miles west of Katherine, Syd Scott brought the first cattle for Cooper and Stuckey of New South Wales to Willeroo. Connor and Doherty took up Newry on Keep River, between the Victoria and the Ord, and over the western border, far out on that "silent river", the Sturt, which flows into Gregory's Salt Sea, Foster, Weekes and Stretch formed Billiluna, two hundred miles south of Hall's Creek. Stretch was a brother of the Bishop of Newcastle, Weekes had been an artist in Montmartre.

There was a woman out there in the earlies, an English woman, Mrs Stretch, dressing for dinner and reading the *Tatler* in an iron shack in tune to the biggest corroborees in Australia throbbing all night, six or seven hundred blacks. There were other women in the half million square miles—maybe five. The wisest, and luckiest, of the pioneers—Nat Buchanan, the Duracks, John Costello—had wives that would follow, to rear white children and make a homestead home.

Pity it is that the diaries of those stations, each one the nucleus of a province in times to come, in a blind neglect of history and callous indifference to human fibre were left to the white ants. They were a classic of cast-iron courage, romance in desolation, of pitiful hearts and pitiable days, long nights of ordeal, months of starvation, years of loneliness in a land with little enough to give. They held memory of an epic quality in the spirit of man, and woman, unsurpassed in the records of any people on earth.

The early station-owners settled a boundary by mutual consent. To form a station you bought a few thousand cattle and swung them clear of the world to new waters. If there were blacks round the waters you moved them over with a gun. The homestead was "a bit of hurry-up", beefwood posts with a brush roof wire-netted all over to make it spear-proof, as Jack Mackay's at Mainoru in Arnhem Land is wire-netted today. You put it on one of the lesser waterholes and kept the best for the cattle, and you never lived there unless you had a wife. It was to shelter the flour while you were out for two or three months, running cattle to the waterholes and branding calves.

If you had a mate, he was camp-sergeant in charge. When the blacks, watching from the ranges or the creek, saw one man ride out—"White-fella sit down longa himself"—there might be trouble, so he sat up all night at the "station" and was looking for tracks all round it in the morning. The man out with the cattle had just as little sleep. He would camp and boil the billy before sundown, then smother the fire and ride five miles in the dark so the blacks couldn't track him. If he felt "windy" he put a shirt round a pack-saddle and a hat on it, and sat it up against a tree with a gun on its lap while he had a cat-nap, his revolver strapped to his wrist, ready to fire at a sound. He kept waterbags full and the horses tied close by, and he was gone from every camp before piccaninny daylight.

To the new station you brought working blacks from some far country—no conspiracies, they were terrified of the "bush niggers", and for protection of your "muckity", musket, never ventured out of your sight. There was "quiet nigger" country and "bad nigger" country, but on most of the far-out stations cattle-killers were a grievous trouble for thirty or forty years. Not only did they kill for the tribe's meat. In at the waterholes they speared for sport, drove the cattle into the swamps, cut off a rump steak or a tail for a fly switch, and left the beast to bleed to death. Running them on the plains, they set fire to the pastures for miles and reduced the mobs to skin and bone, eyes starting out of their heads, mothers standing over their stillborn calves till they dropped dead. If you let them kill your cattle, the bushmen believed that for sheer mischief they'd come in and kill you.

John Durack was speared at Rosewood, Tom Hardy at Auvergne. Syd

Scott, manager of Willeroo, was stoned to death, John Fraser killed at Macarthur River, a man named Ross at Alexandria sinking the well, Perry at Creswell Downs. But every station has its tragic first graves. A big item on the books was ammunition, and it was not for shooting kangaroos.

Here is the order you put in to the store when you were stocking up wilderness:

40 fifties of flour;
12 seventies of sugar;
6 fifties of rice;
10 lb. bicarb. soda;
20 lb. cream of tartar—to leaven the daily damper;
20 lb. dried peaches;
20 lb. dried prunes—these for "health";
2 tins dried potatoes;
50 lb. Derby tobacco;
1 case assorted jam;
1 case treacle, bullocky's joy.

That diet was yours for a year—luxuries in at the homestead, salt beef, damper and jam out on the run. Horses came next:

4 doz. hopple-chains;
10 cwt horseshoes;
12 packets shoeing nails;
30 yards collar-check and saddle-cloth;
12 sides of harness leather;
4 lb. beeswax;
15 balls hemp;
1 ball collar-twine.

Now for the blacks:

12 gins' dresses of striped galatea;
2 doz. wooden pipes, clay pipes for the ladies;
1 doz. shirts and trousers, all sizes, for the boys and girls you would catch and train as stockmen;
1 doz. cheap felt hats;
4 doz. kangaroo hides for whips;
½ cwt blackfellow tobacco, nigger-twist.

Off you went into the blue, with your new home on packs.

For fifty years the cattle-men of the Territory were a lost white race. They met at a muster, three or four together, a yarn by a billabong once in a couple of years. For the rest, they lived in a swag. In time they built a house, or engaged a passing bagman to build one according to his lights. In a moneyless land they paid him in heifers, so many for a kitchen, so many for the house. As builders' labourers he press-ganged a mob of blacks to chop down trees, mix ant-bed into adobe cement, and cart rocks.

The homestead of a lonely man looked out on the plains like an empty skull—with ever-open doors, a stretcher of plaited rawhide on saplings where he slept when it rained, a couple of beer-cases for chairs, his riding-boots in a corner, a bridle hanging over a pile of bills on a nail. Earth floors. The veranda was held up by trunks of trees, and pack-saddles straddled the beams.

The kitchen was well away from the house, an open fire, a camp-oven, an old black billy hung on a hook, half a kerosene tin for boiling the beef and a barrel of brine. A bush table was rooted in the ground with a form at either side—knife, fork, pannikin, chipped enamel plates, salt, pepper and sauce. In drab frocks down to their ankles the lubras trailed round, doing a greasy wash-up, watering a patch of garden for greens.

A Kaffir kraal of a meat-house, hooks under spinifex thatch, and an anvil in a bough shed that he called the saddler's shop, comprised the rest of the "buildings", the only ones in from two to ten thousand square miles, and beyond these the stockyards, the blacks' camp down on the creek.

Such is the homestead still on some stations I know.

If he had half-caste children, they lived with their mothers in the blacks' camp till he could teach them to ride. Then they helped him to make the station a property worth while, proud that the "old man" was white, proud of his knowledge and his praise. To replenish his stores he rode with a pack-team maybe once a year, three hundred miles to Katherine or some half-baked little town, for the bush races, a bit of a bender and a yarn about cattle with the boys, then he was riding the long way back to the shack he called home, and from there out to the cattle again. If he wrote a letter it lay coated with dust in the dry or went mouldy in the wet, unless a rider came by. So he rarely wrote letters, even to his childhood's home. Urgent notes to the stations, about horses and cattle, he sent by a foot-walking black-boy, addressed with the station brand. He put in the wet mending saddles and "doing the books" by a slush-lamp at night. For the rest of his life he was out riding tracks.

Two or three hundred thousand cattle were moving across the Territory in the early eighties. Pilots met the mobs at Settlement Creek, to lead them to waters and river crossings all the way to Kimberley. Between Cloncurry and Darwin on the Old Coast Road the only sign of civilization was Burketown, a dead horse village in miles of clay-pans, until Mickey Cronin, "Mickey the Priest", out from "the 'Curry" with a bum-boat of grog for the border, camped on Georgina River near a lagoon of white lilies known to the blacks as Camooweal. There Mickey's wagon took root and became a pub built by a man named Bowman, the wildest pub in the west, which opened the Tablelands track through to Anthony's Lagoons via Alexandria and Brunette.

Horse-thieves and cattle-duffers followed the drovers out. At the first waterhole eight miles across the border they were safe from the Queensland police—hence Happy Creek. Over the downs, with gambling rings by the wells, they rode the ranges to the Gulf to meet the big mobs passing there, and camped on Macarthur River near a freshwater creek, Booroolooloo, paperbark. An old man, Billy Macleod, in the schooner *Lucy and Adelaide*, came across from Normanton with stores and grog, sat down on the river bank with a double-barrelled gun to guard them from the blacks, and Borroloola was on the map. Into the river sailed Black Jack Reid in the schooner *Good Intent*, with a cargo of Thursday Island rum. He dumped a tankful, worth £700, in charge of his wife under the Leichhardt trees, and made off with the rest to catch the mobs at Roper Bar, where Billy Hay was starting a "blind tiger" and a store. In those days there was interstate excise to pay. Alfred Searcy, the Customs agent from Darwin, arrived by lugger express at Roper Bar, seized the rum in Her Majesty's name, painted a skull and cross-bones on *Good Intent*, arrested Black Jack and sailed for Borroloola. Three hundred and seventy pounds was owing to Her Majesty from Billy Macleod's little dump, but Billy had pooled the lot in a spree, and died in the general bender. As Searcy loaded the contraband for Darwin, along came Mrs Black Jack, tearfully pleading for an old accordion that once had belonged to her pa. To the first white woman of Borroloola the gallant Searcy yielded it up, and away with a party of drovers she hied to the west, cheques for £700 safe in the old accordion with the wild colonial songs of long ago.

Hardly were the stations stocked up than a hoodoo fell over the land—the gravest calamity in Australia's pastoral history, and a problem to the Governments even yet. It was a little bloodsucker no bigger than a bug—cattle tick.

The fatal vermin was first seen at Glencoe in 1880 by Alfred Giles, on a few Brahmin cattle imported by the B.A.T. from the East, to be sirloin roasts for the staff while Darwin was living on tinned bully beef. Lawrie noted it in Darwin stockyard in 1881, and gave due warning. Redwater fever swept the station, killed half the stock in a week. In a year it had spread to the Roper, to the big mobs fattening at Red Lily Lagoons, travelling in to civilization and out to colonization. Travelling cattle died in thousands. By 1883 the plague had reached Wave Hill in the west, and was over the Queensland border to ruin hundreds of pastoralists and to move steadily down to menace the dairy herds of New South Wales. It cost Australia millions till, by the simple process of establishing a dip—submersion in strong carbolic with inoculation for redwater, at first on private properties and later on the stock-routes—it was brought under control. Meanwhile the name of the north was accursed and its markets were lost.

Half the big companies threw in their leases and sold at any price. Dr Browne sold Newcastle Waters to Steve and Harry Lewis, cattle at 3s. 6d. a head, and walked off the other properties, writing off £80,000 as a bad debt.

North Australia Pastoral Company gave up ten thousand square miles of their country in a day. The little men starved on their own worthless beef.

There was not only cattle tick. The pioneers learnt the lessons of the country in a cruelly hard school. In some regions horses died of swamp cancer and walkabout disease, wandering mad. Ruined by walkabout and the cattle-killing blacks, John Costello abandoned Valley of Springs, which had cost him £30,000, and again, with his family, in an epic of droving, crossed the Territory from north to south, to form yet another new station in Georgina River's healthy clime, just over the border from Queensland, Lake Nash. Bob Farrar, his helpmate and overseer, moved in to the Roper and pioneered Nutwood Downs.

While John Costello was building the first homestead at Lake Nash, his nephew, M. P. Durack, a thousand miles north-west, was riding the bush at Argyle. Mr Durack remembered a dramatic moment of the time. Camped with his uncle, John Durack, at a waterhole of the Ord, he went to fill the billy in the dusk, and was excited to find a white man's boot track there. There was too little light to examine it then. What bushman, they wondered, was in these forests of their far country. Nearly three years on the outward trail with cattle, and making the journey around Australia by ship, they had heard no news of the world.

By daylight they were amazed to see boot tracks in dozens. Wheelbarrow tracks, dray tracks, rags of shirts on bushes, broken buckets, bottles and cans profaned that silver billabong, and away from it led a road running for miles. The Duracks looked at each other with a wild surmise. Fifty miles on, they caught up with the packhorses racing night and day for gold.

It was the vanguard of Kimberley rush, making for Hall's Creek.

Chapter XIII

Gold-Mine in the Sky

TWO THOUSAND miles the diagonal of Melbourne is the wilderness village of Hall's Creek, nine iron roofs simmering in the heat in a web of packhorse trails.

The jail door of a mountain, Pandora, shuts out the breeze by day and a patch of stars by night from that rift of human living in the range. Its red crest gathers the first clouds of the wet in thunder of November noon. It rises from a maze of hills and creeks where the blacks still wander, and it is slashed and gouged all over as though by the knives of madmen. And so it was, some sixty years ago.

From Pandora's Box of elusive gold came a crazy multitude stumbling in poverty, thirst and fever, in blindness, hunger and fear; came ships groping to nameless harbours; roads that circled a continent, leading nowhere; towns, to be forsaken save by their own dead.

Jack London and Robert Service have told the world the story of the Trail of '98, of gold in the ice-grip of the Yukon. Australia's Trail of '86 is a story not yet written, of a ragged battalion of ten thousand men and women, eyes bright with desire, following a will o' the wisp for ten thousand crooked miles to a gold-mine in the sky.

The diggers! All the pathos and pageantry of gold are for ever hidden in that casual name. The sons of Australia and New Zealand, through two great wars, have been proud to hark back to it in an ideal of comradeship new to the world. It belonged to the fathers of the Anzacs, who made Australia a nation. An expeditionary force against Nature, they stormed the rocky fortresses and conquered the desert in slow, painful advance. They, too, had their roll of honour. Together they faced the ultimate, mates for a day or a lifetime, in travail, in triumph, in the dark hour of death standing by. They travelled through many a Golden Gate to the old grim story of dreams and starvation. Money meant nothing. Love could not hold them. They lived and died for the pot of gold at rainbow's end.

One half of the continent was still virgin earth in the eighties. When West Australia, left behind on the national vaulting-pole to wealth and population, offered £5000 for the discovery of a goldfield, the towers of El Dorado shone in the setting sun.

An impish gleam flickered in a valley far out of civilization, in the trackless wild of Kimberley that Alexander Forrest had just sketched in the map. In a lone ride from Roebourne to Port Darwin those path-finder prospectors, Adam Johns and Phil Saunders—Don Quixote and a sick Sancho—dollied a few glittering ounces at a night-camp in a range. The surveyor Hardmann, galloping through wild nigger country, thought he sighted a quartz vein.

Pilgrims of gold love the danger to perish in. One Charlie Hall, his mate Slattery, and three others set sail in a skiff from Roebourne, a thousand miles to the new little cattle-landing of Derby, and rode five hundred miles east along Fitzroy River for the ranges. The world told them good-bye.

They were there and back at a gallop, a hundred and six ounces in nuggets wrapped in the miner's "shammy" inside their shirts. X marked the spot where they found it, in the dark sands of Black Elvire River, a stream of the Ord. God—or was it the devil?—had guided them straight to that spot.

Overland Telegraph Number 3, creeping north through the sand-wastes of the west coast to Derby, stuttered in Morse a dramatic demand for Hall's Reward, £5000. The crazy legion heard it. In that vast unhuman wilderness, where the patriarchs were driving their first flocks, they cropped up out of the spinifex like the armed men of Cadmus, with pickaxe, dolly-pot and dish to scorch to the gorge of gold.

They dared not stay long. Five came back at hard riding with four hundred ounces and a nugget a pound in weight. A fatal telegram from Derby was published in the southern press, predicting rich reefing and the biggest field in years. The wild-cat was out of the bag.

That Cortés of Australia, W. J. H. Carr Boyd, with a literary love of the g.w. spaces and an eloquent flow of hyperbole, was on the spot in as near to a flash as time and space could make it. He said there was enough gold in Kimberley to reduce its worth as a precious metal throughout the world. They named a patch of the range in his honour when he freighted four tons of rocks three hundred miles through it on packhorses, to a ship waiting at the mouth of the Ord to carry it south, six thousand miles to Melbourne to a battery. Six of his ponies were drowned by the weight of their golden stones at a river crossing. Two tons of rocks crushed in Melbourne gave twenty-eight and forty-three ounces to the ton.

At a banquet in Perth Sir Frederick Napier Broome, poet and nation-builder, Governor of Western Australia, and John Forrest, explorer and statesman, innocently put the finishing touch to the fantasy afar when they raised their glasses in prophetic, if premature, celebration of a western Ballarat.

Kimberley . . . a diamond magic in the name!

Away went the gold rush—bearded prospectors with memories of the treasure snatched out of their hands on every field in Australia . . . youngsters who had never sighted it except in fobs and sovereigns, tailor, teamster, lawyer and clerk, the well-to-do and the waster, fathers deserting their families, sailors deserting their ships.

Non-stop to the river of romance, the barque *Wistaria*, less fragrant than her name, was first off the mark from Fremantle, three hundred diggers aboard. Lunatics at Pine Creek and the fabulous Palmer River left their proved claims to the Chinese coolies for a breakneck ride of one or two thousand miles after a bird in the bush. A regiment was riding the coast from Perth, and another from Adelaide following the Overland Telegraph Line, that gossamer strand in the blue. Storekeepers made fortunes fitting out schooners in every port of the Australian coast . . . buggies and bullockies were ploughing a road from Queensland . . . some took the hypotenuse from New South Wales and Victoria by no road at all.

It was a proud day for the brand-new port of Derby when s.s. *Triumph*, direct from New Zealand under special charter, six thousand sea-miles behind her, landed five hundred men and a cargo of splendid Clydesdales, with coloured ribbons in their manes, in the grey tidal mud. They were off, with never a day to spare, along four hundred and seventy miles of the winding Fitzroy River.

And to beat them all to it, sixteen ships a month—steamers, schooners, brigs, ketches and luggers—swung to anchor under the red bastion hills at the unsurveyed mouth of the Ord. They shouted contempt at Darwin, passing by—at the barques there, a hundred and twenty-one days from Antwerp, unloading steel rails and fish-plates for the Territory goldfields railway, when on the Territory goldfields there were only Chinamen left.

Four hundred men, seven women and six children they dumped on the marshes, to scale the walls of sandstone ranges, to hack a highroad through those frowning gorges that had known no more than a blackfellow's pad. Jock McPhee, a stockman of the Ord, was first man out. He brought back a pannikin full of nuggets. Bushman Billy O'Donnell led the gold-rush by Jock McPhee's track. It shortened the distance from the Kimberley coasts to a mere three hundred miles—if they came through alive.

At the end of 1885 there were two thousand miners around Hall's Creek living in bough shades like the blacks. When they ran out of tucker they ate their candles. When they ran through their boots they hopped barefooted. Rifles beside them, with the faith that moves mountains they dug, then raced back to the ports with gold for grog, to forget the hunger and the horror in fevered raving of the find. Marriott was the first man killed by the blacks at the Sandy Elvire. Two hundred blacks died to avenge him, trapped in the cliffs of Mary River Gorge. They picked up the bodies of the dead as shields against the bullets of the white men.

McPhee's Creek, Donkey Gully, Hourigan Gully, Spear Creek, Barney's Patch, Brockman, Mount Dockerill, the will o' the wisp danced till the labyrinth of the range was pegged for five hundred miles. Leaders, shoots, nuggets and slugs, streaks in quartz and powder in pipe-clay, gold and rumours of gold . . . two thousand ounces in swags thrown on the deck of *Dickie* leaving the Ord for Darwin, a thousand ounces handed in to the Derby pubs, and how many smuggled away? Peruvian legends were sung in the south of creeks running gold, of savages wearing studs of gold in their noses.

Drays in the marsh at the mouth of the Ord had become a little town to the eternal glory of Lord Wyndham . . . shanties and stores of hessian and iron where horses champed and miners stamped, waiting for flour, tea and sugar to be off. Ships were arriving every day with hundreds of men and nothing to feed them. A storekeeper's letter from Wyndham gave warning:

> "All the men who come in have gold with them, but they keep dark, and only change enough for their needs. I bought 84 ounces from a man yesterday, and know a party with over 400 ounces, some pieces weighing more than a pound.
>
> "To go to the fields men must have six months' provisions and good horses. The spinifex is like a well-sown field of corn, you can't walk through it. Mosquitoes are murder by night. Gales are terrific and the blacks dangerous. Native rats, with tufted tail, destroy everything and eat the stores. So do the white ants. *There are crocodiles in the rivers and snakes in the bush*. In the rain the road is 300 miles of bog, in the dry you can perish on it.
>
> "There is going to be an awful rush. There will be heaps of gold found, but there will be dreadful misery."

Misery in a golden frame—who cares for misery? On they came—in ships with no navigator, no "ticket" and no chart, following the coast. They sailed the Ord and the Fitzroy till their little boats grounded in the mud, and they ran the rest of the way. Five men travelled the Ord in half a tin tank as far as House-roof Hill.

But on the Derby road at the end of the dry Fitzroy River had shrunk to a chain of waterholes thirty, fifty, miles apart. The splendid Clydesdales of the New Zealand contingent, perished of thirst, speared, or poisoned by strange weed, were fly-blown carcasses grinning at their masters circling in mirage. Unburied men lay on the plain.

On the Wyndham road, through sylvan glory of the ranges, the granite pylons of Pompey's Pillar beckoned the pilgrims on—Ngumuluwalli, Head-in-the-Clouds of aboriginal legend, his stolen lubra in travail of childbirth in the rolling boulders at his feet . . . and sylvan glory was grid of the hills, jump-up and go-down of prickly scrub at a slow ten miles a day, leading into Hell's Gates, where the blacks lay in wait to spear a sleeper and pillage his packs for axes and sugar.

Beyond lay twenty miles of hour-glass sand, the shifting Cockatoo Sands, pale red, with mocking effigies of stone—a fiendish trap of bull-dust where the drays sank out of sight, its fringes of pandanus and quinine-berry trees a toss-up between the mosquitoes and the blacks. The wise were a meal for the mosquitoes. They rigged a net and slept away from it there, so that spear and *kaili*, at piccaninny daylight, whicked into an empty swag.

Creeks had vanished in glaciers of stones, stony cliffs above them . . . day after day on blistered feet, leading the laden horses, straps buckled crosswise over the prospector's pack with its dish and short-handled pick, dry-blower, cradle and swag . . . road of heartbreak to the Valley of Hope. Three hundred hot and hungry miles!

At last the smoke of little fires, a tent or two in the brush.

The Fields!

Fields of the blazing yellow spinifex . . . men naked to the waist in torment of flies and blinding sun, digging . . . begging flour from meal to meal. No meat, little water, only flour. Dry-blowing out on the tumbled red hills in whirls of dust, carrying their dirt twelve miles to a rockhole to wash it, these living skeletons prattled of nothing but gold, listened for the sound of it in the dry-blower, peered in the dish in the gloaming for that Tantalus gleam of "colours".

The madness was upon them. They spied on each other and fought. A German named Hornig murdered a Swede, Johannsen, his mate. On the bank of McPhee's Creek he showed Johannsen where he had seen colours, and set him to dig . . . to dig his own grave, for he shot the man dead on the edge of it, and Johannsen fell foolishly in. Hornig rifled the pack for a few poor nuggets, and made a break with the dead man's horses, to ride alone two thousand miles to the south.

Along came "Peter the Greek" to McPhee's Creek. He noticed the bare patch of something hidden—the miners, mad of a new rumour, would often bury their bags of flour and run. Peter the Greek, a hungry man, began to dig. He found Johannsen two feet under. Trooper Paddy Troy caught up with Hornig five hundred miles away on the Eighty Mile Beach, and Hornig was hanged.

A man at Mount Dockerill, somebody said, dollied ten thousand ounces in a week, and Mount Dockerill was the cry. Slaves to their own delirium, they ran this way and that, digging. Hills of drought smouldered into flame of bush-fires. They went on digging in hell.

Then Pandora gathered the clouds to its crest in thunder of November noon. The copper sky of midsummer cracked. Down came the wet, a deluge a day, the valleys of spinifex brimming, the Ord with its rivers and creeks in raging flood. The diggers starved in their shacks while the rain fell for five months and washed the gold away.

And still they came—in droves. The Big Rush was on the way. Eighteen-eighty-six was the terrible year.

In that year five thousand landed at Wyndham and fifteen hundred at Derby. Coming across from Queensland was an endless procession of riders, spring-carts, wagons, drays, buck-boards, buggies, gigs, Afghans with camel-strings, bullockies cracking the whip, strong men wheeling barrows, foot-walkers travelling a swag and water-bag, women wheeling perambulators, children, goats, fowls, dogs, donkeys—the cortège and the camp-followers of gold. One man walked a thousand miles from Katherine to Kimberley with a bag of oatmeal, a swag and a billy-can, no gun. He lived on thin gruel. Another came in to Katherine after a three hundred-mile walk. He had lost his horses, everything gone but his coat and billy-can. He was skin and bone. For sixteen days he had eaten nothing but grass-seeds.

Burketown, on the clay-pans of Carpentaria, was dead end of civilization. From there, two thousand three hundred miles to go—two thousand three hundred miles of nothing.

Playing hare and tortoise, where the cattle-men had been years on the trail, some of these made it in weeks. Too often they travelled in dead men's tracks. Many perished of thirst in the dry, hard-bitten old Forty-niners and adventurous young Englishmen among them. Known and unknown were drowned in the wet, horses' tracks leading in to a river and never following out. Women slept under the wagons at night. Babies were born, and buried, by the roadside.

Jack Forsyth and Charlie Goodliffe—who later found fortunes at Norseman, West Australia—rode ahead of a little rag-tag mob to find water, and were lost. They shot their horses and filled the water-bags with blood that clotted in the night. They cut the bags open and lived on that for three days of wandering till they were found, crawling on hands and knees. The answered shot of a revolver saved them. A fair-haired young Englishman named Nash, six feet one and twenty-two years old, with his mate Bayles, perished on a Macarthur River track—his mother's address in Cavendish Square was found in his pocket-book with a cheque for £60. The black-boy guiding them through had run away, afraid in strange country . . . the brimming river was only three miles on. A man named Orr, stooping to drink at Leichhardt River, was taken by a crocodile. Three in one party were murdered by the blacks at Limmen Bight.

Travelling five hundred together or one alone, the cavalcade came on, unsheltered in heat or storm, singing by the billabongs of evening like the blacks, or clapping a concertina to a step-dance under the stars, to forget the debil-debils of fear and despair in a madcap quest. Sundry little schooners sailed up the rivers with stores, and "blind tigers" sprang up in the bush . . . two kegs of rum under a tree grew up into a shanty, a wagon-load of flour to a store, a beef-gallows to a butcher's shack, a forge to a saddler's shop. So towns are made.

Oblivion has taken the Old Coast Road, and most of its people and its memories . . . thirteen rivers to cross before you came to the Roper, to travel that winding waterway for three hundred miles.

Out from Burketown across the Nicholson and the Gregory rivers, at Turn-off Lagoons where the policeman was murdered, the road swung west across ant-hill wilderness to Wollogorang, a fort against wild blacks, and on to where horse-thieves and cattle-duffers were hopping the border at Settlement Creek . . . from there to Calvert River, Skeleton Creek, the Robinson, Foelsche and Wierien rivers to the glorious green valley of the Macarthur, where the multitude sat down for the wet. They left behind them Borroloola, two pit-sawn shanties, an iron store and a Chinamen's garden with a light-tower rigged up, where the sons of Sam Lee kept a night-and-day watch on whites and blacks with a double-barrelled gun. Greens were as precious as gold in the Kimberley rush.

The big rains over, with flour for daily bread and brandy for Dutch courage, they made on over Batten's Creek up into the walled gorges of Limmen River, where four were speared, then down to the salt-pans of the Roper and the three hundred-mile trail of its beautiful paperbark reaches to the grandeur of Red Lily Lagoons, full of leeches and crocodiles, and a Hades of mosquitoes. A man sold his net for £10 one night, and tried to buy it back for £20 in the morning.

Through the swamps of the Elsey to Abraham's Billabongs and Bitter Springs, then up over the pindan plains of the O.T. Line, at Katherine River crossing they joined up with the thirsty crowds who had ridden the desert from Adelaide or Cloncurry, bullockies and barrow-pushers, packhorses, wagons, camping in their hundreds round the telegraph station and Barney Murphy's shack pub.

All in together for "the bad thousand miles", they thrashed on over Vampire Creek, King River, Sardine Lagoons (a sardine tin), Brandy Bottle (a brandy bottle), Flora Falls, where the blacks were so bad that you could smell them and never see them. It was two hundred and fifty miles to the nearest white man at Victoria River Downs, then two hundred and fifty miles across the black-soil plains to the West Australian border. One more river to cross, the Ord, men and horses swimming, for the last hundred miles through the tumbled hills to Hall's Creek and Black Elvire.

On that last hundred miles they met the vanguard of disillusion coming back.

Hall's Creek was a town—of wood, stone, canvas, kerosene tins, bag, bark and spinifex—with a restless population of two or three thousand digging the hills to honeycomb, here today and gone tomorrow, like flocks of parrots chattering, screaming gold. They dragged twenty-head stampers and tons' weight of machinery up and down over the bristled ranges, floated companies for hundreds of thousands of pounds, tore angry gaps in the hills for the Sydney, Melbourne and London mine agents and managers hurrying to bury money there. H.M.S. *Myrmidon* surveyed Cambridge Gulf and buoyed it for big steamers. The Government was putting through a telegraph to Hall's Creek, but as soon as they got it up, the wild blacks took it down—they built that line four times. A surveyors' camp up in the ranges was planning a new road, and even a railway to Hall's Creek. There were eight hotels and twelve stores on the Wyndham marshes, under the red ledged hills, also warden, postmaster, sergeant with seven troopers, bakers, tent-makers, butchers buying mobs of cattle from stations along the Ord.

Nineteen ships in a month unloaded twelve hundred passengers and a thousand horses. The Wyndham road, where M. P. Durack the year before had wondered at a white man's boot track, was a chain of shanties—piles of bottles under the bottle-trees—and a high-road of teamsters and packers goading their heavily laden mules, horses and camels over two hundred and fifty rugged miles, twenty horses strung together, each carrying two hundred and fifty pounds, the men walking beside. They charged £40 a ton for freight in the dry season, £120 a ton in the wet. A Sydney company, backed by Anthony Hordern, with English capital, petitioned the Colonial Secretary for the right to build a railway through the west from Albany on King George Sound to Wyndham on Cambridge Gulf, asking a grant of twelve thousand acres for every mile of railway and a hundred and sixty acres for every immigrant they could bring out. The Governments were merely annoyed, and this "enterprising dealer in tapes and ribbons" was told to mind his own affairs. The two thousand miles of railway was estimated to cost £10,000,000.

There was a murder a week by the blacks along the line of the Kimberley rush—and not without reason. A sentence from old records tells that from Burketown to Wyndham the blacks were shot along that road "like crows". When Barnett, a teamster, was killed beside his wagon at Bow River, seven spears through his body and the stores stolen, seven horsemen from Queensland rode out through the ranges and "dispersed" a mob of six hundred natives, "Queensland fashion". Those blacks were allegedly a race of giants, seven feet high.

Hall's Creek was lively with two hotels, police, post and gold warden, small stone cottages and hundreds of humpies in the hills. In gambling rings by the lily lagoons they played for nuggets, shirts, gold-dust, horses, flour, meat, tea and wives. They held a race meeting that year, the Miners' Chamois a five-ounce nugget, the Ladies' Bracelet of purest Kimberley gold. That was the last flutter of the will o' the wisp. The rich little pockets of alluvial were found no more, and reef lodes were small.

From 1885 to 1888 ten thousand came to Kimberley. You could follow the trail for two thousand miles by the meat tins, rags on bushes, and old pack-saddles. Hundreds never sighted the goldfields, thousands drifted quickly away. When the enchantment of distance was gone, those hills of savage heat in summer were no longer blue.

Horror set in with the outward rush when the waterholes were drying—in scurvy, thirst, malaria, heat apoplexy, dysentery, hunger and delirium tremens. Wrecked wagons, dead horses and graves became names and land-marks of the Australian bush—the long track back of broken bottles and broken dreams. Some of the men could never get back, though they crawled on hands and knees. Here is a letter of that time that I found in old police records at Hall's Creek:

> "Let whoever gets this first help himself to what is in the box, and then do what I want you to do. It is only to write a letter to New Zealand and tell them I was lost and starved to death. Tell them the plain truth and nothing more. My mate's name is Bob Dove. Bob, if this gets to you, please send that hair chain to Rose, and oblige a dying man
>
> "Good-bye, mate. . . ."

In the box were four ounces of gold, a diamond ring, an address in Christ-church. The bones were scattered by wild dogs.

In every police station over a million square miles, a great rhomboid of wilderness marked by Burketown, Alice Springs, Roebourne and Wyndham, such records are commonplaces of the Kimberley rush.

By the end of 1886 two thousand were left in the maze of the spinifex valleys. Then Jenkins, Carey and Wilkinson, steering by the sun across five hundred waterless miles of sand to the south-west, sent up a shout from a blackfellow creek called Nullagine. The will o' the wisp again, Little Hero nugget, four hundred ounces!

A thousand Kimberley diggers were there in a week. Ted Francis un-earthed its mate, the Stray Shot nugget, on the bank of Coongan River at Marble Bar. Pilbara was the hue-and-cry. Dreams and hunger again . . . writing names on the blistered parchment of another desert map, they were out on the road of gold to rainbow's end, Coolgardie—to Kalgoorlie, the western Ballarat. They had taken the long way round.

Kimberley was forgotten. The mines, Lady Broome, Lady Margaret, Ruby Queen and Lady Carrington, produced four thousand eight hundred and seventy-three ounces in 1887, and in 1888 three thousand ounces. One mine manager from London, Hamilton White, was drowned while swimming a creek, his blueprints, papers and wages cheques swept away in his hat, his body caught in the fork of a tree. His rival, Captain Eddy, dropped dead of sunstroke at Wyndham . . . a hard land for the English stock exchange clubman, and too high the prices it calls. So the fabulous reefs of the prospectuses were never found, the "million in sight" never sighted. They are still a hatter's rhapsody, for a few old "woolly-nosed prospectors" ever lingered on.

They dollied a poor living, and now and again struck it rich for a bender with a little find, a secret. They lived like wallabies in "them thar hills", and the cattle-men had the laugh on them that there were dingbats in Kimberley's caves of gold. But I am not so sure. In a recent year, Northam Crowther, who knows the vagaries of gold, with his young wife and a mate, out in the old haunts of Lilli Pilli and Brockman, has had the luck, in a few months, to "loom" a couple of thousand ounces.

The first gold of the Golden West was no more than a drift of alluvial, a flash in the geological pan. Sixty years ago, the blacks came creeping back to camp in the deserted villages of Brockman, McPhee's Creek, Donkey Gully, and Black, White and Sandy Elvire, but Hall's Creek remained a small citadel of white men and women. In the red shadow of Mount Pandora it loves to sit and yarn of the grand old days.

For out of Pandora's Box, with that mad rush of fools for fortune, came human courage and kindness beyond belief, romance in love, nobility in death, and though many tears, much laughter.

The Trail in '86 was a world's epic of gold, a living drama of rare characters that must not be forgotten. Leading them all down into history are those laughing cavaliers who rode a couple of thousand miles together, highwaymen of the spinifex, their wild oats the camp-fire legend of half a continent still—the Ragged Thirteen.

The far lost places of Australia have their hero-worship, no less than the cities, their mythologies, founded on fact, of "men like gods". Wherever the drovers camp by the billabongs at twilight, you are bound to hear of the Ragged Thirteen. A Robin Hood and his merry men of a million square miles of greenwood, their fame in the Territory, Queensland and the West is equal to that of the Twelve Apostles. They put the town of Katherine on the map.

The Ragged Thirteen were neither supermen nor bushrangers. They were just light-hearted scamps riding together, gentle grafters of the Great Unfenced, soldiers of outback fortune and in that hungry country out for all they could get. Their meeting-place was the Overland Telegraph Line when there was little else in the Centre, and when they crossed the Tropic they left the law behind. An Englishman, a Scotsman, two or three Irishmen, a runaway sailor, a cocky farmer, a prizefighter, and an old convict, the rest wild colonial boys, they were the usual band of mates that rides in any day to any goldfield, to camp on the creek and fade away forgotten.

To haggle about the true identity of "Will Scarlett", "Little John" and "Tom the Tinker" is to nibble away the lily-leaves of romance, but there has been such endless argument and so many false pretenders to the honour of the ragged banner that the list, as given by the leader to my old bush friend, Billy Miller Linklater, and written down by him in 1902, is here given in full:

The leader was Tom Nugent "brumby-buster" and great bushman. He learnt his bushcraft—and craft was sometimes the word—from "Long Tom" McNiven, Harry Readford, Thurston and the poddy-dodgers playing ping-pong with the police across the Queensland-Territory border.

The twelve were Hughie Campbell, who left his sailing-ship at Port Augusta, and set his course due north across the vanished inland sea; "Sandy Myrtle" MacDonald, from Myrtle Springs in South Australia; "Wonoka Jack" Brown and his brother George from Wonoka, South Australia; Jack Dally, a farmer of Terowie; Jim Carmody from New Zealand, brother-in-law of "Black Jack" Reid, the "Maori Smuggler" of Borroloola; "New England Jack" Woods; Bob Anderson, later founder of Tobermory Station, Northern Territory; "Larrikin Jack" Smith, one of Major Colles's orphans from his Norman River settlement in the Gulf; Jim Woodroffe; plain Fitzpatrick; last and least, "Tommy the Rag". It was originally "Tommy the Lag", but the Territory was kind, and never held a man's ball-and-chain against him. The others were all fine men of unblemished character except in the matter of horses and beef. A man must ride and eat in the Kimberley rush.

To the cattle-men stocking up the top million square miles, the Thirteen certainly brought bad luck. All the way up they duffed for the tucker-bag. Bluey Buchanan, to his sorrow, watched them camp near his mob one night at Frew's Ponds. In the morning they were gone, "borrowing" two of his best night-horses. Bluey counted them up, and told them they were "the devil's number". At Abraham's Billabongs, passing by, they snatched a newly killed beast from the gallows, and had the butcher on their track. At Katherine they tried it out again. Cashman, the butcher there, searched the camps of the river, with wrath in his eye, looking for "the Thirteen".

"Which thirteen?" he was asked.

"Tommy the Rag's—the Ragged Thirteen."

So the immortals were born with a bad name. A trooper was stationed at Katherine River to keep watch on the Ragged Thirteen, and the telegraph station became a town.

The Thirteen shared their booty with their comrades of the track, and nobody ever put them away. One was a champion wrestler, one an exhibition rider, one a first-rate marksman, another a genius at crib. One could recite poetry with the best, one could box, another would scratch-pull any man, and yet another was an artist with a stockwhip. When they were challenged, they offered the man out, to beat him at his own game, and settle the argument that way. The Ragged Thirteen won. If they didn't, they fought it out with fists, all good fighters, even Tommy the Rag.

Their tucker-bags filled at Springvale, in the moonlight, lasted two hundred and fifty miles to Victoria River Downs, where they camped on the creek to muster for themselves a sirloin roast. The manager, Lindsay Crawford, was out with the cattle, only the storekeeper, Lockhart, at home. Tom Nugent rode up to "government house" and introduced himself as a "speculator looking at country", which was literally true. While he and the storekeeper played cribbage, the twelve played havoc in the store. They ripped a few slabs off the side of it, and helped themselves to flour and five hundred horseshoes, where horseshoes were money in the bank. In a midnight flit, they had fifty miles' start towards the border when the crime was discovered in the morning. That was the only really black mark against them, though the traditions of the Territory have handed to them, on the drover's tin plate, a hold-up drama at every waterhole, with the knavish tricks, the politics, the two-gun glamour and the Dick Turpin rides of every rapscallion who passed that way in sixty years.

They salted the bullocks of the Ord with Ord River salt, but at Hall's Creek they did penance for their sins, and turned over a new leaf. Tom Nugent rode back a thousand miles to be O.T. linesman at Tennant's Creek. Galloping to mend the Line, he took up a "nice little pocket of country"—about two thousand square miles—at Banka Banka. With a bough shed by its never-failing springs, he rigged a bush net, formed his station from calves dropped by the drovers, and became a pioneer of the Great North Road.

Sandy Myrtle MacDonald, a bootlegger in elastic sides and concertina leggings, "ran a bum-boat" of rum a thousand miles from Katherine to the ruby rush in the Haartz Ranges of Central Australia. He defied any horse in the Centre to buck off his twenty-three stone till he died in his pub at Arltunga, when that was another deserted village of gold. Woodroffe finished up at Alice Springs selling meteorites to museums.

New England Jack Woods, after his five thousand miles of riding from the east coast of Australia to Kimberley, made it three thousand miles of the west coast to Coolgardie, then a canter to Port Augusta fifteen hundred miles east, and another fifteen hundred miles up the O.T. Line to call on his old chief. He had a rendezvous with the unknown. He borrowed a pack-team from Tom Nugent and set off north in a hurry. Neither he nor the pack-team were seen again.

Larrikin Jack Smith was one of the first prospectors of Bulolo in New Guinea. Hughie Campbell sailed to his native Scottish heath. Jim Carmody was drowned in Katherine River. Bob Anderson, remembered yet in a land of great riders, has the pioneer's grave at Tobermory, north-east of Alice

Springs. Wonoka Jack Brown died on the Maude Creek goldfields, and Tommy the Rag just blew away.

"The Last of the Ragged Thirteen" will be introduced to you on nearly every station camp in the Territory, Kimberley and the Queensland west. In point of fact he was Jack Dally, who lived as long as two men, and was still living in Charters Towers a few years ago when I passed by.

Tom Nugent, when he died, left Banka Banka to a sister he had not seen in thirty years. Her two sons, Arthur and Paddy Ambrose, said good-bye to the city for the saddle, and rode to find their little run in the big warm heart of Australia. They were fine stockmen and popular station-owners for another thirty years. Many a pickle-bottle of nuggets, slugs and mystic stones was brought to them there by passing prospectors and wandering lubras, predicting Tennant's Creek gold and the wolfram of Hatch's Creek.

The bearded men and bonneted women of the Kimberley rush, with their hand-carts and wagons, made the first road west, the Old Coast Road from Burketown to Derby, but few are living to remember who they were. Esau, an Afghan hawker, set out from Hughenden with camels, and gave an old woman, "Mother O'Neill", a hump of a camel to ride on for over a thousand miles. At Black Gin Creek she was lost. They found her waving from the top of a hill that is still on the map of Victoria River Downs as Mother O'Neill's Knob. It was a tenet of Esau's religion, which he faithfully adhered to, never to refuse a fellow human in need of food, shelter and clothing—a tall order in the Kimberley rush.

When she came to Hall's Creek, Mother O'Neill did odd jobs about the town, and was its only midwife. Her language as rough as her complexion, she would ride or walk forty miles to a sick prospector, to give him a bit of mother-love and Billingsgate. When he died she laid him out, set the blacks to dig the grave, and shed a tear above him for his own folks. She was the Lady of the Lamp on the Hall's Creek diggings.

Not such a shining light was "Mrs Dead Finish", a shrewd old Gagool woman who started out with her husband and a load of stores on a mule-team. When the old man died she brought the mule-team on with blasphemies just as effective, and her prices for flour and whisky were twice as high. For many years after the rush she lived on at the Brockman in a bit of a shack with her dog Boss, which she trained to go down with a bucket to the waterhole and fetch up her water and wood.

There was no Jake the Half-breed, with a knife in his teeth, no dance-halls of hooch and vice, no Lady that's known as Lou on the goldfields of Australia—the Australian bush is too far and too wholesome for that. Only the fittest survive out there, where sunshine warms the heart and mind to lazy good-humour. There were scores of women in the spring-drays, somebody's wife or mother, and two or three in the wheelbarrow brigade, maybe a foot-walker, with a baby in the swag. "Till death do us part"—every now and then a birth or death on the road, and at the end of the track an occasional wedding before the warden. The first bride in Hall's Creek was "the Long-Handled Shovel"—in those days a woman was known by her "lines"—and the second "the Scrub Turkey", who married the Wild Scotchman. "The Mountain Maid" travelled from Queensland with a party of prospectors including six Afghans and fifteen camels, and a woman named Mrs Reilly camped one night at Abraham's Billabongs with five hundred men.

At Calvert River was a bit of a store run by one Mackie, a descendant of distillers of Dundee. When the cattle and gold mobs were passing by, Calvert River crossing was like Pitt Street at peak hour, but when there was no one for months at a time, Mackie went about, revolver on hip, drinking his ancestral whisky to keep up his spirits. Peering through the slats of the store one night, he saw black shadows creeping from the river. He put on his kilts, snatched his bagpipe, and proudly stepped out. Pacing and skirling to the pibroch o' Donil Dhu, he scattered the blacks of the Calvert from that crossing for years.

"The Orphan" took over from Mackie, a well-known character of the north whose real name, Christian or surname, was Martin. Educated for the priesthood, he could babble a bit of Latin. As poddy-dodging butcher to the pilgrims, he made a small fortune in the station-owners' beef—the nearest court was Darwin, a thousand miles away. They decided it was quicker to buy him out than to charge him with duffing their cattle and offered him "so much for the store, so much for the yards, and quit".

"That's all right," said the Orphan, "but I've worked up a good connection. How much for the goodwill?"

There was, too, "the Indian Chief", with method in his madness. When his little garden failed, he turned highwayman of the Turkey Creek road with no raiment but feathers in his hair and a handful of spears. The Wyndham doctor certified him as a lunatic for free transport to the south, and he finished up with a nice little fruit farm in Victoria.

King of all barrow-pushers in the world's history was "Russian Jack", who wheeled his way from Victoria to Hall's Creek, and then down to Coolgardie. But Russian Jack went farther than that. When his mate on the goldfields was dying, he loaded him into the barrow with food and water for two, and for two hundred and fifty hard and lonely miles of the hills he wheeled the sick man, fed him, defended him, and camped beside him at night, on their way to seek help from the doctor at Wyndham. When Wyndham blossoms in civic pride, and honours the great men of the past, I think a statue is due to Russian Jack.

The only one of the pilgrims who left memorial of his passing, beyond a broken wagon or an unknown grave, was H. Dowd, a monumental mason of Adelaide who travelled up the Overland Telegraph Line. At every one of his Sunday camps from Adelaide to Kimberley, he cut a shield or scroll on a tree. These tree-scrolls are still to be found by the track here and there, if you know where to look for them along the Stuart Highway.

H. DOWD
OVERLANDER
1886

An epic year forgotten. Perhaps the bark has overgrown the letters.

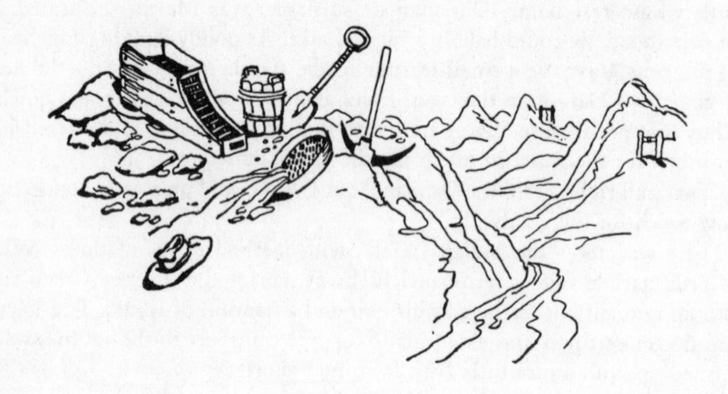

Chapter XIV

Rich to Rottenness

THERE IS a black lagoon on the Daly. No fish swims there, no lily blows. No wallaby bends to drink his own tawny-gold reflection in those bitter copperas waters. Never do you see a homely ring of camp-fires, lubras pounding the brown lily-seed for dampers, old men strutting with their babies on their shoulders, the boys in the billabong after duck. The tribes make a wide circle of the haunted water, though they have forgotten why. Only the swamp-pheasant, in his Hamlet suit of glossy black, calls a descending scale of low minors plucked on the strings of a harp, a ventriloquial chuckle like something wandering mad. There was a day when the lagoon was dark with the bodies of the dead.

In 1884 Houschildt, Roberts, Noltenius, Landers and Schollert worked their miracle copper-mine with their own Wilwonga blacks, who always carried spears in case of attack by myalls. The white men had a big house nearly built, a vegetable garden, an orchard of papaws, oranges and egg-plants. They were clearing a road to the river for a wharf under the banyan-trees. Soon there would be mules in thousands, as at Burra in the south, bringing down the copper of the greatest mine since Burra, nothing like it in Australia.

C. J. Kirkland of the *Northern Territory Times* rode three hundred miles from Darwin to write lyrical articles of the lodes of wealth by special request of the southern press. "The miners," he finished up, "have not the slightest trouble with the blacks."

When that sentence was printed, all save one of the miners were dead.

Harry Houschildt saddled up and rode in with Kirkland to Pine Creek for stores. On a bright September morning Roberts, Landers and Noltenius were deepening their open cut and piling up copper while Schollert cooked their dinner.

It was an idyllic scene, white flutter of tents under the casuarinas, a creek with a velveting of blue lilies, the copper crags shining with malachite. Noltenius held the drill. Landers, a Nordic giant bare to the waist, was striking. Roberts, sorting and dressing, bent over the scintillating ores. The steady ring of the drill was music.

Roberts heard a shout. He looked up to see Landers throw a hammer . . . then the great body lunged forward, a spear through the hairy breast. For Roberts the world went dark—he was felled by a rock. Noltenius raced for the hut . . . then sprawled and crawled, a barbed spear in his back. Over the rocks and through the trees the blacks vanished, not the Daly River myalls they feared, but their own Wilwonga boys.

Noltenius and Landers reached the hut. There Schollert lay dead, a stone-headed spear jabbed under his ribs and through the heart. A little while later Roberts, who had been left for dead at the mine, groped the door, his head split open and his eyes full of blood.

He tried to take out the spears for his mates with a butcher's knife. Landers was nearly done. Noltenius endured an agony of cutting and probing, but the shattered barb was still in his chest. Roberts stopped the bleeding of his own battered head with a handkerchief and flour. Now and again a spear rattled on the sloping iron roof. Long hot hours dragged by. Sundown was quiet. The living made themselves a billy of tea and drank it there with the dead.

In late twilight they crept out to try to make a cattle-camp forty miles away, but Landers tottered and fell. They set him up against a tree with water-bag and revolver, and went on. In nine slow miles Noltenius stopped every hundred yards to fight for breath. They came to a streak of silver reflecting trees and stars—on Tipperary Station you will find it, Noltenius Billabong, named for the night when Roberts left the dying man under his bush net with a gun in his hand beside those waters.

At the next billabong Roberts heard horse-bells and found Houschildt's boy, Nammie. Nammie said his master was sick at Rum Jungle, and had sent the horses back. It was a lie. Roberts told him to go to Noltenius, but when he and Sachse rode back from the cattle camp, Noltenius lay there alone, only his eyes alive. They lifted his head for brandy, and he died. Landers was dead, his body mutilated with spears . . . and Schollert in the hut. All the Wilwonga blacks were gone. And what of Houschildt? Decoyed by his blacks with a tale of gold in the ranges, he had ridden out with Nammie . . . and while he was sleeping Nammie had driven a stone-head spear through his throat.

The Daly River murders and their aftermath were notorious in the north for fifty years, held up as an example of the traitorous nature of all Australian blacks. If there was reason for the crime, the one white man left alive, in loyalty to his dead mates, did not tell. The Wilwonga people of Pine Creek were practically wiped out. To quote records: "The horrible crime aroused the wrath of all residents and fellow-miners, who set out in several parties and severely punished the natives, who tried to escape by seeking shelter in the waters of the billabongs."

The affair took two years of "bush riding" to clear up, until there was a storm of protest in the south at "cold-blooded mass murder of the blacks", with formation of native protection societies shouted down in the north with vehemence and vituperation. There was talk in the Territory of importing that horror of Queensland, the Black Police. "Here noble pioneers," wrote one of the noble pioneers,

> "are hurled into eternity by blood-thirsty savages without bell, book or candle. We don't want the Native Women's Protection Society to preach to us who live in the bush about the modesty, purity and chastity of degraded creatures known to us as black gins but who the city association greets as 'black sisters'. Well, I do not envy them the relationship they covet, but when they tell us that nearly all the murders of white men in the Territory may be traced to abuses of the women, they lie."

Unfortunately the missions and associations, in sweeping indictments and thunder-and-lightning damnation, repudiated the brotherly love they counselled—as they sometimes do today. Anger and resentment rankled in the north where the lonely white man far out in the bush was never sure that he would wake up in the morning. Slanders levelled at him from the safe and well-fed south, whether he was guilty or not, intensified racial hatred, sometimes with tragic sequel for the ignorant, mostly innocent, blacks.

When Lenehan, head stockman on Macarthur River, was killed while hunting down cattle-killers—when "Kid Gloves", a man who manicured his nails with a pocket-knife, was speared while fishing on a creek of Victoria River—when Koop was maimed for life near Calvert Downs, Marstin in the cutter *Spey* murdered in the mangroves near Borroloola, Captain Thoms waddied to death on his lugger at Carrington's Landing of the Macarthur, there were ruthless and terrible ridings. The Mbiah tribe of Macarthur River was annihilated, leaving one little girl and boy hiding in the trees. They grew up to be Kitty Karlo Pon of Darwin, and Jupiter, a stockman of Macarthur River Station, both loved and respected by their white friends through life. Many a cave of blackfellows' bones all over the north harks back to the old punitive raids.

Outside the zone of the law the hunt of human game was free for all where nobody knew about it. Depraved and vicious white men shot women. "Go for the breeders!"—that grim phrase is still remembered in the north. Pot-shot murderers were few and far out, very seldom the pioneers or bushmen to whom the blacks were help and companionship, wife, home and human fibre—the only comradeship of life. They were rotten driftwood, morons with a "cowboys and Indians" complex, or blind, bitter self-righteous men who looked upon the natives as wild beasts.

With one of these a true bushman, Billy Miller Linklater, author of *The Magic Snake*, was riding one day in the eighties, out north of the Roper. They heard a faint chipping, and saw a very young mother, with a baby, chopping out a "sugar-bag". At sight of the white men she dropped the tomahawk in fright and climbed a tall gum-tree, her piccaninny on her back. Outlined in gold sunlight, they were gentle and pretty as a koala bear and her baby.

"Give us a cartridge, Billy," said the riding-mate. "I'm goin' to drop her."

"You'll drop me first," said Billy, "or, by God, I'll tell the world."

"Nits is lice," said the riding-mate. "Them brutes cleaned me out o' my station in Queensland, and I get 'em wherever I see 'em."

"The only cartridge you'll get from me," said Billy, "comes quick out o' this gun. For God's sake come on, and let the poor little blighter alone."

That story is typical of both points of view. The newspapers openly incited to "dispersing the blacks Queensland-fashion". Not only Queensland and the Territory, but every State in Australia has its crime sheet in callous inhumanity to the blacks.

The problem is a complicated one. Before we throw stones at the old-time punitive raids, let us remember that the Vanishing Race—with all the Native Affairs departments, anthropologists, philanthropists, psychologists, pathologists, research officers, patrol officers, missions, compounds, school, clerks, typists, advisers, wages awards, clothing, housing, rations and medical care provided—is vanishing rapidly today. The numbers of half-castes and mixed races are certainly increasing, but the true Australian native and, among these, the authentic tribesmen, are few and far away.

The Duke of Manchester, on a tour of the world, arrived in Darwin just after the Daly murders. At a calico ball and a Brahmin beef dinner, he referred to the four brave pioneers. Through cable misconceptions, the *British-Australasian* scooped the London press with a startling announcement that "during his travels in the Northern Territory his party was attacked by blacks and some of them killed. The Duke himself had a narrow escape. He speaks with enthusiasm of the fertility of the Northern Territory".

The fertility, as usual, was measured by feet in a night. Holtze made the Gardens a glory, over a thousand plants thriving, forty varieties of maize up to nine feet high, nineteen varieties of rice, for which he was offered up to £8 15s. a ton in Sydney, the grocers willing to take an annual twenty thousand tons. With no labour, he longed for machinery. Sea Island and Carolina cotton were excellent crops, also Japanese clover, millet, paspalum, Rhodes grasses, Panama palm for hats, jute, flax, ginger, sago, tapioca and ramie fibre. Reece at Beatrice Hills surprised them by getting the blacks to work well, fencing and planting Para and Castilian rubber and coffee. Otto Brandt took up Shoal Bay for sugar, and with eighty coolies looked upon a planter's dream, fifty acres of ideal cane. He was importing a mill from the south.

Delissaville and Poett's plantation were deserted, but Owston's on the Daly was thriving with an experienced manager, an exact and elderly man. MacKinnon from Rum Jungle was his overseer. There was actually a white woman living on Daly River, the manager's young wife, with her four-year-old child, keeping house in a trim little shack. Her stepson, her husband and MacKinnon to guard her, she was not afraid of the blacks. A few miles away a big white and Chinese community worked the copper-mine, forty or fifty men there, one tunnel two hundred and thirty-six feet deep at Solomon's Wheal Danks yielding a thousand tons of rich ore that year. The scow *Maggie* and a Chinese *sampan* carried it away.

Darwin now wore a tiara of pearls. Into the harbour in 1884 came a ship of glamour, Belle of the Beach or Queen of the Sands, the pretty *Sree pas Sair*, a brigantine of a hundred and twelve tons under Lieutenant Edward Chippindall, R.N., with a crew of eighty wild-haired Solor men, bound for the north-west coast of Australia to fish pearl-shell and pearls for Bond Street and His Royal Highness the Prince of Wales, a shareholder in the enterprise. The only other white men aboard were H. E. Streeter, son of the well-known Hatton Garden jeweller, and the supercargo, Moss. From Banjermasin, after cruising among the pirates of North Borneo, she anchored a mile from Fort Hill, and with swimming divers from eight of her boats had gathered sixty pairs of prize pearl-shells within three hours, a hundred and seven pairs at the end of the day. Broome and Thursday Island pearlers swiftly followed her in, Captains Miller, Parks, Riddell, Frank Biddells, James Clark and Edwards, from the Darwin banks bringing two thousand tons to the shell-shed for shipment to London that year, a sparkling new industry to be for the next half century near the top of the list. With the invention of the Bampton rubber suit and Heincke gear for deep-sea diving, the pearlers indented Koepangers as crews and Japanese divers who lived with their women ashore, Miss Ocheo, Miss Osiya and Miss Otama, the professional beauties of Chinatown.

A radiant land awaited its trans-continental railway, already creeping up over the sand-wastes of South Australia on the first thousand miles to Oodnadatta. Millar brothers had the contract for the north, Bagster their superintendent. Barques and brigs were racing from Europe with hundreds of tons of rails and gear, unloaded in the mangrove mud till a jetty was built, one thousand one hundred and twenty feet long, of "white-ant resisting" jarrah from West Australia—it was eaten out in its first ten years.

In schooners and sampans the Chinese shaved the nearby coasts of iron-bark, paperbark and cypress pine for sleepers while ten thousand of their countrymen came in a steady stream to build the line. To feed the multitude Chinese gardeners were getting £25 a ton for all the corn they could grow, 2s. more a bag for Territory rice than for the Chinese variety, and the fishermen made a fortune salting and smoking fish.

What a rosy glow was the railway! Disillusioned diggers waved the picks and shovels dedicated to gold in cuttings and culverts, grubbed stumps and carted stones with the coolies on a big weekly payroll. Towns on the surveyed line, and some imaginary ones, sold half-acre blocks for £20. Mining shares, and energies, soared, seventy thousand ounces that year declared through the Customs, new mines and old wild-cats floated in London. From the Eleanor Mine alone Olaf Jansen dug seven hundred and fifty pounds' weight of gold, and Maude Creek, near Katherine, was discovered in another little rush. Great quantities of silver, lead and copper were found by Tom Lynott near Borroloola, and tin on the headwaters of Limmen River.

Eveleen on the Mary—"grandest silver-mine in Australia"—opened up with a manager at £1000 a year, two assistant managers at £500, captains and bosses driving round in buggies, twenty white foremen, two hundred coolies delving, and a hundred and fifty black charcoal-burners setting fire to their totem-trees. Eveleen produced five tons of silver from the first fourteen tons of ore, £3000 in a month, then £20,000 in bullion from two thousand tons of ore that gave fourteen thousand ounces of silver. The Leviathan Tin Mining Company was to open big mines at Bynoe Harbour, and forty-eight tons of pure tin came from Mount Wells, tallest mountain in the Territory, which soon would have its own little town, Burrundie, on the railway.

Darwin had a brass band. s.s. *Darwin*, sixty tons, was sent up to trade with Singapore and Manila. Mrs Pett came to be school-mistress to motley. The *Northern Territory Times* was a four-page paper with a "reptile contemporary", the *North Australian*. The District Council was asking £2500 for rubbish dumps and bush blocks it never could sell for £5. Hopewells of the Club Hotel made a magic block of ice, sold it in chunks, and sent twelve tons by a steamer to Wyndham as lordly gift from the metropolis of the north. In Smith Street, beside a row of little shack shops and Jolly and Luxton's store, a new hotel was rising, brick by brick, two-storied and modern as any country pub in New South Wales—the old Victoria, still there today, with sixty years of harum-scarum memories.

Some beautiful yachts in the eighties furled sails in that *eau de nil* harbour, among them *Undine*, once Baron Rothschild's, bought by Millar brothers to carry timber along the coast. Schooner-rigged, a hundred and fifteen feet long, her millionaire luxury tarnished, she was later sold to Streeter as a pearling schooner, and wrecked in King Sound.

On *Cushie Doo*, W. F. Osmand called in the course of a trip to the East via his station at Ord River, with him his sister and niece, Mrs and Miss Booty, among the first white women to land in Kimberley. *Cushie Doo* unloaded stores for the Ord at View Point in Cambridge Gulf, and Sandy Maugher left the yacht with a seaman and two horses to "ride to the station up the river and let Bob Button know the stores were here". *Cushie Doo* blithely sailed away. Sandy Maugher rode for two hundred and thirty miles in twenty-three days through the ranges before he came to "the station up the river". In the wet season, he and Bob Button rode and swam for three weeks before they could get back, to find the stores all eaten, as a hand-out from Providence, by the sea-coast blacks.

Lord and Lady Brassey called in *Sunbeam*, the third *Sunbeam*. For Lady Brassey, happy pilgrim of knowledge and adventure who made home for husband and children and wrote books on the Seven Seas, Darwin was last port of call in the world she loved so well. She died on *Sunbeam* seven days out from Darwin, India-bound. She established St John's Ambulance in many far places of earth. Soon after her death *Sunbeam* was sold to Savile Kent, the naturalist, who later sold it to a north-west pearler. The famous yacht sank at her moorings in Admiralty Gulf in the early nineties, and, to quote the *Northern Territory Times*, "is now the sport of the natives so wild in that region".

Lord Brassey wrote to the London *Times*: "Port Darwin is a noble harbour in an important strategic position. In time it will become a port of English and European mails to Australia." He could not vision that those mails would travel by air. *Sunbeam* presented to the little town hall bookshelf three books, of which Darwin City Library, when there is a Darwin city, will some day be proud.

An agent of Barnum and Bailey came, with crates of apes and jaguars on the deck of some old schooner, to collect, at fair prices, half a dozen blacks —the Wild Man of Australia for the Greatest Show on Earth. If he shanghai'd a Wargait corroboree for the big time in New York, history is discreetly silent.

There arrived in the Territory in 1886 a distinguished scientist in the robes of a priest—Dr Julian Tenison Woods. An eminent churchman, Father Tenison Woods worshipped God in Nature. He relinquished the position of Vicar-General of the Roman Catholic Church in South Australia "to be a pilgrim", and enriched every State with contributions to its natural history. He also travelled extensively in the East. In botany, geology, palaeontology and marine zoology he is one of the greatest of our early scientists. Fellow of the Linnean Society, gold medallist of the Royal Society, much of his valuable data was collected on long journeys on horseback through the Australian bush. To his chance meeting, in the eerie woods of Mount Gambier, with a restless and melancholy stock-rider brooding in Byronic numbers, we are indebted for the first recognition and encouragement of the poet Adam Lindsay Gordon.

As the most noted practical geologist of his time, Father Tenison Woods was invited by the Government of South Australia to travel the north, to tell the truth of the Jack-in-the-box bonanzas, and to guide the Government in the development the railway should bring. By packhorse with the surveyors and on flimsy little ships, he travelled thousands of miles of gruelling hardship, and in the course of a year sent down the first comprehensive and authoritative report of a vast mineral zone in an uncivilized country. The Tenison Woods Report—twenty-one thousand words over the wire to Adelaide—was the longest telegram in Overland Telegraph history. Broken in health from heat, fever, bad food and arduous journeys, Father Tenison Woods died in Sydney the following year.

His "Memoir of the Geology of the Northern Territory", published in the *Proceedings of the Royal Society*, 1888, is rich in description and scientific fact.

> "I confidently assert that the Northern Territory is exceptionally rich in minerals, only a small portion of which have been made known to the public.
>
> "I do not believe that the same quantity of mineral veins of gold, silver, tin, copper and lead, will be found in any equal area of Australia.
>
> "In fact, I doubt that any province will be found in any country so singularly favoured as Arnheim's Land in respect to mineral riches.
>
> "Of the mines that have been worked, in gold especially, they cannot be said to have gone to any depth, and nearly all of them have shown unusually good ore.
>
> "Of two things I am convinced—first, that not one of the mines hitherto worked or abandoned has been exhausted of the gold; secondly, not twenty-five per cent of the auriferous reefs of the country have been tested.
>
> "Years will not exhaust the discoveries to be made here. When the difficulties of labour have been solved, it will be one of the greatest mining centres of Australia."

When Father Tenison Woods made his report, £3,000,000 in gold in a few years had come from those rifts in the Pine Creek hills, most of it on the prospector's shovel. With the exception of Jansen's Cosmopolitan Mines, which, in a brief development of the eighties, yielded £1,000,000—to help to build Tivoli Theatres in the south—his observations regarding development may, for the most part, stand as truth today.

No sooner were they published than, in exciting verification, came the discovery of rubies in Central Australia.

David Lindsay, in his four-thousand-mile camel zigzag of unexplored country from Hergott Springs to Carpentaria, when a hundred and twenty miles east of Alice Springs in the rugged gneiss gorges of the Haartz Ranges, followed Elder River in search of a native soak for water. Scratching a hole under a cliff in creek-sand glittering tinsel-red with corundum and mica, he drew forth a handful of red gems. The lambent little blood-red stones were everywhere, washed down by heavy rains in the dry creeks, Lindsay named the place Glen Annie Gorge for his wife, and rode five hundred miles in three weeks back to civilization with the news.

Ruby rush! Hundreds of men over thousands of empty miles challenged the desert with horses, camels, hand-carts, carrying food and water—some perished. Camels streaked back with packs full of rubies in parcels weighing seventy to ninety pounds, to every parcel a thousand gems of rich colour and fire. Posted off to lapidarists in London, mainly to Streeter, godfather to Australia at the time in opals, rubies and pearls, at first they were hailed with delight, valued as highly as £21 a carat, said to be indistinguishable from the priceless "Siams".

Twenty-three companies were floated and the ruby rush redoubled. Afghans packed stores on camels over the rough ranges, bum-boats after them with grog. A hundred men were scratching their finger-nails away all down the Hale and Florence rivers. Central Australian rubies descended in such coruscating showers on the London market that quantity obscured quality, and the jewellers took fright. Chemical analysis carried out by Cannon and Newton showed only 23.44 per cent of crystallized alumina in "Alice Springs rubies" as against ninety per cent in the oriental, seventy per cent in the spinel. It established the fact that they were rubies, not garnets, in that they were not fusible, as garnets are, under the blow-pipe.

"Time alone," wrote the non-committal analyst, "will show the value of these Australian stones."

Time showed that Australia would spend millions in semi-precious stones and gimcrack from Europe but would never consider her own. The first prospectors kept sugar-bags of rubies in the chicken-house for years, then gave them away by the handful to friends and relations. In necklets, pendants and rings they are always much admired. At any rate, they put Alice Springs on the map—William Benstead applied for the licence of the Great Northern Hotel—and with a bottle of beer in Australia a town begins.

For Queen's Jubilee exhibition in Adelaide, Darwin's leading citizens arranged a thrilling Northern Territory Pavilion, pillars of gold, silver, tin, copper, ornate and beautiful woods, Malays from the jail were taken to dive for coral, and seventeen Chinamen serving six months for fan-tan plaited bamboo and native grasses for a decorative roof. Everything that grew under the Territory sun from Dr Holtze's Gardens, a retorted cake of gold from Pine Creek grand as an imperial throne, a half-ton block of pure tin from Mount Shoobridge, silver from Eveleen, buffalo horns and boomerangs, birds, butterflies, dugong oil and dugong ivory, live blacks and dead crocodiles, palms, turtles, pythons and albino kangaroos—with Mr Knight to sing the praises of the north in symphonies of sugar and poems about pearls, the Northern Territory Pavilion was the hit of the whole show, surrounded day and night by surging crowds. Householders sold up their homes and set sail. The track was full of swaggies, who faded away in the first hundred miles. Adventurous lads vanished overnight—the last of them still living are the wise old bagmen of today.

Wonderland was wanderland. While hundreds were riding north, hundreds were riding east to rubies, west to Pilbara and Ashburton gold.

Otto Brandt crushed twenty tons of sugar in the first year at Shoal Bay, but his mill had not arrived till after the cane had flowered and thirty acres was swept away in a bush-fire. Next year he planted two hundred and fifty acres, and had ten tons crushed when a cog-wheel broke—in delay of mails and ships, no hope for another year. The next year his milled sugar, in a lugger for Darwin, went under the wave in a squall. So he abandoned Shoal Bay, where he had lost thousands, and grew prize tobacco at Rum Jungle—with no factory to cure it. He inherited a fortune he richly deserved, and bade the Territory a fond farewell.

The *sampan* came in from the Daly with the manager of the big plantation aboard, to give himself up for shooting his overseer. It was the old story—old man, young wife, young lover. MacKinnon was dead. With the first miners of the north in the graveyard of tragedy under the banyan-tree they buried the son of the chieftains of Skye. The plantation was abandoned for lack of white labour, offered to settlers in thousand-acre blocks, but no settlers applied. In heavy floods the copper-mine was idle. The Daly went back to the blacks, who killed a few Chinamen, broke into the store, and were *dispersed*. To redeem them the Jesuit Mission moved from Rapid Creek to ten thousand acres at Serpentine Lagoon. Fathers Strélé, Marsohner, Conrath and Eberhardt, with Father McKillop as superior, built a church and planted four acres of excellent cigar-leaf, with orchards and stock. Soon they had the baby Brinken, all proper in little pants, sitting in a paperbark school. With pride Father McKillop showed to Darwin the letters they wrote:

Dear Reverend Father,
At your arrival we will be happy to sing you nice songs.
Armand. Nimbali.

Enlightenment! In such a few years.

But now it was found that a black shadow had fallen over the land. The Chinese coolies and Malays of the coast had infected the aboriginal people with leprosy and venereal disease—a curse that has increased as a menace to colonization through the years.

Building of the railway was so long-drawn that great expectations died. There were endless delays at appalling expense, waiting for ships with gear; five months gone in every year waiting for rivers to go down; only forty per cent of human efficiency in "lion's breath" of heat. With huge stony shoulders of hills to circle on a grade rising to six hundred feet, creeks, swamps, rivers all the way, bull-dust and rotten ground, to cover a hundred and fifty miles took nearly four years. Many Chinese were killed on the line and the gangs ran off to gold. White men drifted away from the mines. Sweating all day in the shafts and all night in their shacks, with no recreation but rum, in that climate they died. Graves were yawning—the grave-digger now took contracts for a dozen at a time.

There was still only one doctor, in Darwin, and no hospital in the north with accommodation for women. W. H. Light, the young telegraph operator at Daly Waters, died in a buggy on the way to medical care—a five-hundred-mile ride. Gillespie, a young prospector at West Arm, accidentally shot in the shoulder, bled to death. Fred Pearce, a teamster nineteen years old, was crushed by his wagon at Cullen River, and for three days crawled with a broken thigh. As he was making splints of his tucker-box, a wild buffalo came near and pawed the ground. They found the boy, but he died.

In 1889 at last the little three-feet gauge crept up to Pine Creek. For the gala opening of the trans-continental, Mr Langdon Parsons named the day.

The Iron Horse! There it stood in the railway yards in a triumphal arch of flowers, Darwin's dream. It looked like Stephenson's Rocket, but for many bush-dwellers it was the only train they would ever see. To christen it *Port Darwin*, Mrs Pater, the judge's wife, over its girders cracked a bottle of champagne.

Made by Beyer and Peacock of London a century ago, that noble little locomotive is still in Darwin railway yards, but now they call it *Sandfly*. For the heroic lives it has lived, it should be in Canberra National Museum. As the *Northern Territory Times* proudly described it on that great day, it has a "six-wheeled coupled bogie of outside cylinders of 12″ diameter and wheels three feet in diameter. The foot-plate is covered with a neat cab to protect driver and fireman . . ." perhaps from a shower of spears. There was an adventurous little jaunt for all social Darwin as far as the engine-yards "with not the slightest mishap", and a banquet in the white-painted iron shack, "head northern station of the trans-continental line".

"Magical change!" How they cheered in the morning when *Sandfly* made a cyclonic rush of twelve miles an hour, killing a few more Chinamen on her way to Pine Creek. She came back loaded with navvies and diggers on a spree, the brake-van shining like Aladdin's cave with two thousand ounces of Pine Creek gold and two hundred ingots of silver from Eveleen.

Alas, to the Land of Upside Down, it brought only ruin and grief. To a howl of dismay the Government announced that the railway could not continue its painful progress beyond Pine Creek. At Oodnadatta, fifteen hundred miles south, it had stopped dead in the sand—a gap that was never to be bridged by rail, nor by road for fifty years.

Poverty instead of prosperity came to Darwin with that trans-continental rainbow's end. It could mean nothing to the cattle country, falling a hundred miles short. Freights were too high and the line too small to mean anything to the mines. Hundreds who had drawn good wages, or made small fortunes catering for the men, had the money to go, and went. Coronet Hill and Eveleen, with all their new machinery, closed down for lack of labour, also Mount Wells. One by one the English companies gave up the ghost, always in the hope of starting again this year, next year, sometime, never. Southport, when the line was through, vanished in a year.

The coolies, as tributers, swarmed all over the mines. Tong Hing Hong bought Eureka for £1100, made £500 in the first week in gold-dust left on the plates, and crushed from five to forty ounces to the ton. Lee Hang Gong, with Chinese labour at Bynoe Harbour and West Arm, made £20,000 from tin in a few years.

Darwin was in debt. A schooner put in to Fannie Bay and carried off a horde of stowaways owing thousands of pounds. Ships to the south were crowded.

"The more gold we get," wailed the *Northern Territory Times*, "the worse we are off, for the population has the money to leave. If this sort of thing goes on, we shall soon have only Chinamen and blacks left."

The Government Resident, Mr Langdon Parsons, who had fought so splendidly for the railway, in bitterness resigned, and the South Australian Government could find no one to take the job—one Wigley, to whom it was offered, turned it down. At last Mr Justice Dashwood was appointed, of a well-known administrative family in the south.

In March 1891 the Earl of Kintore, Governor of South Australia, was first of His Majesty's representatives to cross the continent, mile by mile. With an interest in this queer Dominion, to gain first-hand knowledge he sailed five thousand miles to Darwin for a hazardous trip in a buggy south for two thousand miles, his companion Professor Stirling, later Sir John. Rumours of his coming were months old when the B.A.T. flag gave signal of his steamer sighted from the jail, and warned the *élite* in pyjamas to dress. A multicoloured little crowd made for the railway yards, and as His Excellency, elaborate in white and gold, alighted from a flower-decked dog-box, the reception committee opened fire with an illuminated address in Chinese inks mounted on stout card, to ask him to finish the railway and to wish him safe journey through perish tracks and wild blacks. The little town hall was hastily decked with turkey red and Chinese lanterns, a banana-grove on the dais and WELCOME written in Dr Holtze's cotton-pods, for a banquet of

SOUP: Gravy.
FISH: Soused.
REMOVES: Sirloin of beef.
POULTRY: Roast fowl.
SWEETS: Plum duff. Tinned peaches.

"Not bad for a community as modest as our own," said the *Northern Territory Times.*

Even the rain stopped as His Excellency rose to speak.

> If you require accurate information, there is nothing like going for it yourself. Therefore I have travelled five thousand miles to undertake another two thousand. (*Cheers.*)
>
> Although I have heard so much of the Northern Territory from old Territorians in Adelaide, none of them agree upon anything, and all information is most conflicting. (*Laughter.*)
>
> I know well the infinite resources of your country. I want to help in development of labour and markets, and see how capital can be attracted. (*Hopeful silence.*)
>
> Dr Stirling accompanies me to the south to inquire into diseases of your cattle—a tragedy to Australia. (*Groans.*)
>
> I shall say no more of the difficulties of government from two thousand miles away, but I suggest reference of all your problems in the near future to a Federal Government of Australia, for I believe such government will be in existence before long. (*Loud and prolonged cheers.*)

As they faded away down the little Chinese street, there was yet another rainbow in the sky.

Having cheerfully inspected all Darwin could show him—the B.A.T. at work, the Botanic Gardens and the leper camp—the Earl attended a corroboree and a calico ball, sailed on the midnight tide to Adelaide River on the launch *Victoria*, just in from Port Essington with a tribe of live blacks and one dead one. Having shot the traditional buffalo for souvenir horns, he came back to a Chinese banquet of roast pork under silken banners in a tin shack and was away to the mines on the Iron Horse, to climb down shafts of the Union at his peril on rope ladders, to watch the coolies washing gold in the creeks, and to swim horses over the rivers. At Springvale, Alfred Giles named in his honour the remarkable limestone caves eight miles west, Kintore Caves, which even yet are known to very few.

Katherine, when the party arrived, was holding a race-meeting so rackety and rapscallion that vice-regal patronage was regretfully withheld. As the buggy with the gilded crown slipped by, it was followed by a galloping highwayman, well under the weather, who held it up for a race club donation. His Excellency was not amused, but Dr Stirling emptied his pockets and found 30s., a joint subscription. So derisive were the beery bushmen at the reproof unspoken that they made it the trophy for the donkey race with black-boy riders. The donkey race at Katherine is the Kintore Stakes to this day. The buggy battled on for fifteen hundred miles to the railhead at Oodnadatta, its incredible adventures recounted in detail by the London and Australian press. The Earl of Kintore believed that the Northern Territory, a stranger to the rest of Australia, should be made a Crown Colony forthwith.

Down on the stations redwater was raging. Mobs of a thousand head waited months for rain, and to avoid the heavy border tax on cattle the drovers were turning back. It was shortly after this that the magnificent properties of Dr Browne in the west were advertised for sale. Harry Gosse, son of the explorer who found Lake Amadeus, had perished on Delamere. Willeroo was nothing but a haunted hut. The big blue and gold void of the Barklys was a hell of brown drought, cattle, horses, goats and even the native blacks dying in droves. White men died of thirst, among them David McKay, between Alroy and Brunette, only fifty miles. They found him wrapped in his blanket in a wide and irregular circle of fourteen horses and his own two black-boys dead. Charles Deloitte and George Clark were killed by the blacks on Creswell Downs.

Stores for the big runs of the Tablelands, to avoid customs duty, travelled a thousand miles by sea from Darwin to Borroloola, were floated up the Macarthur, and then the horse-teams dragged them six hundred miles through Anthony's and Brunette to Alexandria and Avon Downs. Borroloola at this time consisted of two hotels, three stores, two or three Government buildings, the library and a permanent white population of fifty, with eight or nine teams always waiting for the boat. A town was surveyed, but whenever a trooper rode down to arrange a census for a packhorse mail, three-quarters of the population, horse-thieves and dead-beats, went bush.

The wet came in with ruin. Borroloola was three feet under water. A tornado blew down Burrundie in eight minutes, the whole street careering through the scrub. Five inches of rain fell in twenty-five minutes at Union Reefs. The Overland Telegraph Line was in such a state that the Melbourne Cup news did not come through for three days, an outrage that brought the exiles the sympathy of all Australia. The Postmaster-General promised that the line would be renewed with copper wire and iron poles.

The railway and rushes for rubies and gold had left paperchase of bad cheques drawn on banks in Rockhampton, Melbourne, Adelaide, often two years before they came back marked N.S.F. or R. to D. One morning in 1893 the warped doors of the "stone bank and the tin bank" in Darwin did not open. Sensational rumours from the B.A.T. proved to be truth—the Bank Smash in the south, thousands ruined, Australia's credit a byword. The north was stone motherless broke, living on barter and the Chinese storekeepers, who banked in their own back yard. Now Coolgardie boomed in the West, and all the white diggers were gone, riding across desert. Jansen's Cosmopolitan, the last gold-mines in the Territory, closed down. There was not £5 in cash in five thousand square miles. Cattle tick and the bank smash had ruined all the stations. With no work, the "Bagman" came into being, from waterhole to waterhole living on the blacks, "just ridin' around".

All industries had failed. There was talk in Darwin of exporting pineapples to the south, "for here they grow like a weed", but pineapples were rotten pulp before a ship came in. A Manila-man, Antonio Carlos, brought in a little blue he made from indigo growing wild—he said he could make four hundredweight in a day if anyone would back him. Christie at Point Charles Lighthouse made some matting from plantain fibre, and tried to market that. The old lads down on the rivers trapped dozens of twenty-foot crocodiles and wrote to Bristol to find a market for the hides. Receiving no answer, they mounted the teeth in Coronet Hill silver to sell to tourists on the Singapore ships.

Darwin was Chinese. The Front Gate of Australia looked more like a back street in Pekin. Population in pigtails was five times that of the *élite* in pyjamas—scarlet banners, god-shrines, the analects of Confucius and reek of opium all down the main street, drugged blacks lying about the dirty shacks, old men smoking the water-pipe and parading the josses in palanquins whenever the gold or the fish was short. When the new joss-house was opened, with its beautiful fretwork teakwood doors that cost £1000 in Hong Kong, there was a Chinese procession over a mile long, gongs beating for three hours, a couple of thousand decorative devils frisking behind a yellow dragon belching fire and glory with his tail out of joint. The hungry Northern Terrors were glad enough to be guests at the feast of the "yellow peril" that night, trying to recognize their own stolen chooks in festive *kurri kai*—but the coolies had stolen the fowls and vegetables from the garden of Fannie Bay jail. There was a gambling club for white men in Chinatown, fines paid out of a common fund. Maranda, "King Solomon", only five years before a great hunter and leader of the Larrakia, had lost his sight in disease caught from the Malays and Chinese. Though he had never seen the streets of Darwin—it was all bush in his day—he could carry messages, feeling his way with a wommera as any blind man with his stick, and recognised all his friends by their footsteps and their voices. He loved to stand and beg outside the bank, laughing and yelling to hear the chink of money. Alas for his downfall. He was fined £4 for assaulting a policeman when crazed with opium, sentenced to three months in Fannie Bay.

Darwin was diverted one day to see a mob of eight naked myalls, trailing in neck-chains and leg-irons, to be tried for the murder of a proa full of Malays at Malay Bay. The ringleader was Wandi Wandi, who had killed Wingfield at Croker Island and served ten years in jail. Mr Justice Dashwood sat on the Bench, and one of the jurymen was stone-deaf.

At Cape Brogden the natives had found a wrecked proa and six Macassarmen wandering the beach for water. Feigning friendliness, they led the Malays to a lagoon, waddied the lot, burnt the proa, and stole the arrack and rice. No evidence was called for the defence. The dread death sentence was read eight times in eight minutes and the interpreter, Mamitpa, a white man's boy, translated to his father and brother, standing in the dock, that they were condemned to die. It was a case without parallel in British law. In

Wandi's case the sentence was to stand, but for the seven myalls it was commuted to imprisonment for life—they all escaped a week later, and were caught in the tree-tops at Rapid Creek, climbing for sugar-bag.

A budding anthropologist in Adelaide now induced the Government to have native murderers hanged in their own country as a demonstration to their relations that crime does not pay. Wandi was taken by lugger back to Malay Bay, and with tucker and tobacco a trooper gathered the tribe. When they understood they were there to gaze on death, they shrieked and fled. Wandi dangled in the breeze for a long time, and for many years his gallows, black and grim, was the only sign of civilization on the north coast of Australia.

At Cullen River in 1894 Bob Richardson found a diamond, "the size of a revolver bullet and of a pale-green flash—when rubbed with a file it rasped the steel". He said there were plenty of Koh-i-noors about, and one he sent to London, three carats, "a bright diamond of the first water", was valued at £60. Diamond rush! Four or five companies pegged, but found only quartz crystals and soon petered out.

The old pioneers were dying of disillusionment, among them Edward Mackenzie, one of the earliest and best, with his wife and baby, and G. L. Barrett, who owned what is still the richest little pocket of tin in the north. A settler for seventeen years, he had worked night and day unaided for the sake of a little daughter in the south. He had just sent away fourteen tons of tin oxide worth £800, which he mined himself through cruel years, when he dropped dead of heat apoplexy in the streets of Darwin. A fifteen-year-old boy, Harwood, was stung to death by a poisonous jellyfish in the swimming-baths.

To brighten the sad monotony Mr Justice Dashwood started a literary magazine in manuscript, a debating society, a dramatic club playing *Weak Woman* in a thunderstorm. When the Earl of Jersey and his lady called, they took them to see the murderers at the jail and the Botanic Gardens cultivated by jail murderers. When the Countess of Kintore and her daughters, Lady Hilda Keith-Falconer and Lady Ethel Keith-Falconer—later to be Lady Stonehaven, wife of a Governor-General of Australia—came by on s.s. *Catterthun* for the East and England, there was a corroboree and a ball, with "seventeen varieties of Europeans present to the number of two hundred", reported the *Northern Territory Times,* "and the inevitable medley of Chinese, Hindus, Japs and various other descriptions of mixed humanity common to our free and enlightened community. Lady Kintore and the girls claim to have enjoyed the dance immensely, and the fact of their having sat it out for over an hour was gracious guarantee of the fact".

A Mr Watanabe from Tokyo came to learn of Australia for settlement of colonies of industrious Japanese. When New Australia, in *Royal Tar*, set out for Paraguay, the neglected north wanted to know why. Those gallant followers of John Lane, with their splendid energies, their sincerity and fidelity, might have found a New Australia nearer home. But after all, who cared? All the rivers were in flood again, and over their heads the waves had met too many times.

In 1897 the worst cyclone in all Darwin's history blew the pack of cards down. Twenty inches of rain fell in five hours in a circle of gale and lightning. Blacks were blown over the cliffs. Nine white people and many coloured died of exposure. Twelve luggers of the pearling fleet were lost. Forty Chinese were never found in the town. Only one house escaped destruction. The Residency was unroofed, the Government offices wrecked and most of the records destroyed. The Roman Catholic church collapsed and killed two blacks who had taken sanctuary there. The gale struck the dead-house behind the joss-house, with all its mortality jars of bones, shanks, skulls, carefully pickled to reconstruct the bodies for transport to China, a frightful spectacle of cadavers whirling in the air by night, a horrifying shambles in the wan light of morning.

Port Darwin was an abject and pitiable ruin. The settlers stayed on because they had no money to go—sat and stared at the ruins from their waterlogged wrecks of homes in the long grasses. After nearly thirty years of the mad zigzag up and down, they were right back where they started. It was a long time before they had the courage again to take up the white man's burden.

Chapter XV

Dots in the Map

COVERED-WAGON pioneers of America travelled like the Children of Israel in a great community pilgrimage of caravans together, roads and railways soon to follow. Pioneers of Australia rode alone, or with wife and babies in a spring-cart, out of the world's ken.

It was a long ride to the north in the nineties, and for thirty years thereafter, when Oodnadatta was head-of-the-line from Adelaide, and scarcely a house but the telegraph stations from there to Pine Creek. A rickety heat-cracked train crawled once a fortnight to an angle-pole just north of Oodnadatta, in those days a camel-camp of Arab, Turk, Afghan and Hindu, dirty tents, a mosque with its *Mullah* and *muezzin*, and a date-palm or two mirrored in mirage.

It was the age of the camel in Australia. From the South Australian railway they made east to Broken Hill, west to Coolgardie and away to Marble Bar, north-east to Innamincka, Birdsville, Bedourie and Cloncurry. Long strings loped over the sandhills and gibbers from Oodnadatta three weeks to Alice Springs, then over the spinifex hills and downs another five weeks to Newcastle Waters. They could go no farther north, for the ironwood-tree of the tropics is poisonous to camels, but they took the track eastward to Brunette and Camooweal, west to Wave Hill and Wyndham . . . billowing nose to tail for years, with a vindictive Afghan driver and a few fly-blown blacks, each beast laden with seven hundredweight, twenty miles from the morning star to a camp-fire in the void of night.

Till 1927, when the train came through, overland travellers joined up with the Afghans or rode their own horses three hundred and forty miles from Oodnadatta to the Alice, crossing the border at Charlotte Waters. There the telegraph men held an annual race-meeting with stakes to £500 and some of the finest horses in the world, in from Sir Thomas Elder's stations on Cooper's Creek and Finke River, where he was breeding cavalry mounts for India and carriage pairs for Rotten Row.

Crown Point was a slanted shack under a red coronet hill. Augustus Elliot's little bush store at Horseshoe Bend of the Finke sold flour and tea, blue shirts and blue blankets to stockmen and explorers. Idracowra was a station then, formed by Major Warburton in 1875, and about a hundred miles apart Erldunda, Tempe Downs, Joe and Alan Breaden's Todmorden, Ellery's Creek, and Henbury, where a meteor falling had slashed the earth for ten square miles. At Mount Burrell the Hayes family were picture-book pioneers, across from Queensland in an epic droving of father, mother, boys and girls with cattle. The girls shared mustering, fencing, branding, building yards, and riding "outside tracks" on a run of a thousand miles.

In a bad year when rivers were sand, between Oodnadatta and Alice Springs were only Alice Well, and Deep Well two hundred feet down, half the time the bucket broken and the water full of dead turkeys and wild dogs. Old hands followed emu tracks to the springs, or went in to Ooraminna Rockholes, deep caves snow-white and cool, with aboriginal drawings, in weird mottled towers of hills near Doctor's Stones—one of the beauty spots of the old road, now quite forsaken.

Over the Depot Sandhills, fifty feet high, a mile apart for thirty-six miles, summer temperature up to a hundred and sixty degrees in the shade—no shade—you came at last to the foot-hills of the MacDonnells and Owen Springs Station, where Sir Thomas Elder was running eighteen hundred thoroughbred hacks. So through Heavitree Gap to Alice Springs.

The Alice was a roof or two in a dreamy valley, the telegraph station near the springs. There were drovers' camps and bullock-drays on the bank of the Todd around Wallis Fogarty's little log store. Even then the Alice was noted for its race-meetings and sprees, and the telegraph men were the best euchre players in Australia. A half-caste cricket team played on the green on Sundays. All over the valley and at the glorious gaps in the ranges, the Arundta sang and danced corroboree every night. Camels and pack-teams came winding in with Haartz Range rubies and Winnecke and Arltunga gold. Poddy-dodgers had their hidden yards in the ranges, running wild cattle and so-called brumbies wearing the world-famous T.E. brand.

A spell at the Alice and you were goading your packs over the spinifex plains past Love's Creek, where Louis Bloomfield was a lone pioneer. Connor's Well was often a slime of dead snakes and owls, but Boothby Rockholes, south of the Woodford, brimmed cool water for months after rain. You would see the pack-teams sliding and clambering up, horses drinking from a camp-sheet cupped in the stones. The Dutchman was best, but so high that only a barefooted man could reach it. Many perished on the road when five miles from it this remarkable rockhole held twenty-five thousand gallons. It was wise to be wary of blacks. At the foot of the rocks grew a tasty yam, and the place was a great old corroboree haunt.

Central Mount Stuart was a favourite bullocky camp, and a trig on a hill led you in to Barrow Creek. A hundred and sixty miles from Alice Springs to the Barrow, and another hundred and sixty to Tennant's Creek. In the dry you carried water on the saddle, in the wet you bogged and swam for weeks. Taylor, Wycliffe, Wauchope, Bonney and Gilbert are all big creeks—you might have to ride thirty miles round the swamps. The Bonney is a hundred and twenty yards wide with many channels, a danger to men and horses swimming. God's break in the grand monotony were the Devil's Marbles—those remarkable sandstone rocks like huge skittles, balanced and piled at angles, one at forty degrees overhanging the road—and Little Edinburgh, an ant-hill city sixty miles across, the horses shying and stumbling all the way in bull-dust.

Crossing Attack Creek you came to Banka Banka—Warramunga word meaning "many bees"—where Tom Nugent, leader of the Ragged Thirteen, lived in a little log hut—one box, one form, one table—by a spring. His walls were plastered with newspaper prints of prizefighters and jockeys, W. E. Gladstone and Banjo Paterson holding pride of place. Tom was farthest-out in Australia then, whether you travelled south from Darwin or north from Adelaide.

Renner Springs was a ruin with two graves, Hammond, shot in a gambling row, and one of the Telegraph men, Alan Giles, whose story, in *The Great Australian Loneliness*, I have told. Powell's Creek, the roomy old telegraph station built by Chinese coolies, had always the finest garden of the line. Newcastle Waters was Newcastle Station, owned by the Lewis family, Steve and Harry, since it was first taken up and abandoned by Dr Browne.

After a thousand miles of mulga you were now in the lancewood and hedgewood scrubs, ninety miles through to Daly Waters if you had luck, and from there steep-banked creeks, screw-palm forests and lily lagoons a hundred miles to the Elsey, then eighty miles to Katherine, the only store in eight hundred miles. Mrs Murray, who made the world welcome at the telegraph station, was first white woman to live in Katherine town.

Those last little wharves of civilization, Oodnadatta, Camooweal, Darwin and Wyndham, sent out mails by packhorses when floods were not too deep, or when there was water enough on a five-hundred-mile trail to keep a man and his horses alive. For half a century the bush mailman was a lone camper in the vague. One of them rode from Camooweal to Borroloola, across the golden downs and the red ranges full of wild blacks, six hundred lonely miles. There were no mails to the west—Wave Hill and Victoria River might not get a letter in a year.

The Government Resident's report for 1899 showed an income of £84,000 in gold from 2740 acres of mineral lease; £86,000 in pearling; 187,000 square miles of pastoral country occupied and 27,500 square miles of it stocked. About 30,000 square miles were surrendered because of cattle tick. Ten thousand cattle were shipped to Singapore.

High floods that year drowned the work of human hands in a green glass world of tree-tops and hill-top isles. Jack McCarthy, the telegraph teamster on the top thousand miles, floated his wagons across the rivers, tribes of blacks swimming behind to push. At Bradshaw's Run a crocodile swam into the homestead yards and seized a seven-hundredweight cow. The Daly swirled through the Jesuit Mission, swept away gardens, fences, cattle, and marooned eighteen hundred goats on little islands, Father Mills and Father Fleury boating for miles to hand-feed them with banana palms. The Jesuits spent £15,000 in fifteen years on the Daly, but after the 1899 floods they abandoned the place. Bitterly they recorded that they had not made a single convert in all those fifteen years. They left another deserted village for the bower-birds to play with—a lofty ten-roomed mission house, workshops, servants' quarters, machinery, water laid on, fruit orchards, four acres of prize tobacco, plantations of bananas and rice, piggeries, poultry, stock, even the two fierce staghound dogs that had defended them from treacherous blacks at night.

The Society of Jesus, which conquered the Americas, was vanquished by the north of Australia. All trace of the mission is long gone, but in speckled sun-drifts of the river paths you still may meet an ebony Armand with his Julie, or Léon with Antoinette, you still may hear in a Hermit Hills corroboree a Mozart *Kyrie*.

In Darwin a Chinese opera dragged its slow length along in an infernal caterwauling nights, days and Sundays. "Mother of Ten" and "Pro Bono Publico" wrote to the paper about it, but art was long, and it miaowed on the midnight air till invaded by a furious neighbour known as "the White

Frenchman". Mobbed by actors and audience, he went down in a volcano of dragons and three-legged stools.

The harbour swarmed with crocodiles, for the blacks, "living white" for a generation, had given up hunting their eggs. They sunned themselves on Mindil Beach and came nosing around the swimming-baths in droves. A Larrakia boy named Mubbleburra, from May's pearling fleet, was clawed from a canoe and carried off in a clamp of jaws. The boy gouged his fingers into the crocodile's eyes. As it relaxed its grip, he dived for the bottom, swam a few strokes, came up near the canoe and scrambled in, beating it back with his paddle. Mubbleburra's photograph was published in London papers, but he was modest about it:

"I think that-one old-fella. S'pose him quick, might-be I die."

Shipping cattle from Darwin was one of the sights of the world. They were goaded down the hill, slid down the race, lassoed and dragged through the waves for half a mile to the steamers, clawed into the air by cranes—a bullock roped by the horns, climbing in space, madly pawing the sky—then swung over the bulwarks to the ship. Captain Joe Bradshaw had to swim three Arab stallions ashore, taking the chance of crocodiles rather than a lugger and the certainty of broken legs.

Through the fag end of the century the Territory lived on the white hope of Federation. A few adventurous stockmen went to the Boer War, but there was more local interest in a Chinese war of picks and shovels at Wandi, the wounded carried by the cartful into Pine Creek.

Nineteen hundred and one rang the bells for the old order drifting into the new, stars of the Australian flag shining on the horizon. Chinatown at New Year was a blaze of coloured lanterns and a throb of gongs. Japs of the pearling fleet on the Mikado's birthday strung wires across Cavenagh Street for a pyrotechnic Son of Heaven nine feet high, green, yellow and red, with wickedly winking eyes. "Japanee all-same debil-debil!" the blacks fled squealing.

Poor whites raised their glasses to the Commonwealth-to-be, to all the promises for the grand awakening of the north as the crown of a White Australia. For the Federal Parliament, in confidence and pride, had pledged itself to take over the Territory, with its national debt of £3,000,000 for a thousand stony-broke people, and to build the trans-continental railway to open the Front Gate.

As Darwin mourned the death of Queen Victoria, the Duke and Duchess of York arrived to open the first Federal Parliament of six States, prosperous and united. Of the blaze of ducal glory in the south the outcasts read with pathetic enthusiasm, in papers from two months to twelve months old. There was no celebration for Federation, except that a band of festive blacks broke into the Club Hotel, stole a case of gin, and rambled the streets that night, singing "Rule, Britannia!" Their patriotism landed them in Fannie Bay jail.

Now up went the graph again, of the "infinite resources". Ultima Thule was a land of promise overnight. The old mines at Pine Creek were stirring up the dust. Horatio Bottomley floated companies for £6,000,000 on Howley, Zapopan and Eureka, London Stock Exchange singing another anthem of Northern Territory gold. According to Bottomley there was enough gold in Howley mine alone to pay Britain's national debt—£4,000,000 in sight in the surface workings, untold millions underneath. Retired colonels in Surrey and doctors' widows in Bloomsbury furnished the spot-cash to dig it out.

Sandfly towed down trainloads of mining machinery, eighteen trucks for Howley in one week and as many for Grove Hill. All the other wild-cats came to life, pumping water out of the shafts, mine managers from England in elegant tussore suits, pugaree and *topee*, four or five thousand Chinese building offices and houses. One company spent £80,000 in a year. Brock's Creek became a town with streets of stores and houses, hospital, tramway and telephone to the mines, forty or fifty white men, five white women, and last, not least, the Federal Hotel.

The mines made a powerful stride onward. New batteries crushed low-grade ores to big values, shafts were put down on brilliant mullocky leaders, and thousands of ounces of gold were reclaimed by cyanide from the old slag dumps and tailings. Elsinore Mine yielded a cake of pure gold, seven hundred and thirty-four ounces from thirty-four tons of ore—the publicity was grand. Thousands lost millions in Bottomley's companies, and when his story was told in years long after, Northern Territory Gold Mines were the darkest page in the ledger.

Next bright flash of excitement was the Eastern, African and Cold Storage Company with English capital, £500,000, which set out to develop the "eastern shores of the Gulf of Carpentaria" and acquired all vegetable, animal and mineral rights of Arnhem Land—cotton, sugar, rice, cattle, prospecting for gold. With Captain Joe Bradshaw as northern manager they bought Wollogorang, Hodgson Downs and other runs on the Roper, moving twenty thousand cattle to a brand-new station at the mouth of the Goyder, Arafura on the Arafura Sea. Bradshaw put up a fine homestead, boats on the lily-lagoons, thoroughbred horses and dairy cows in the paperbark shade. Lugger-loads of Chinamen came from Darwin to plough the fallow flats of the Goyder and Maroonga Island for Sea Island and Egyptian cotton, sugar, maize and rice. *White Star*, sixty tons, came up from Melbourne, smartest little steamer ever seen in the north, to colonize the coast, her white-coated stewards serving Port Essington oysters, turtle-egg custards, baked fish, quail, duck and rib roast of Arafura beef.

Arafura was a pageant while it lasted. It lasted two years. Drovers and cattle were lost trying to reach it. When the Chinese coolies and nearly all the cattle were speared, the white folks fled.

"Up at the Kathe-rhyne" Tom Pearce grew a 127-pound pumpkin and made a one-man town. Next to Barney Murphy's old cabin at the crossing, he built a new pub with a mob of blacks to help him—a Grand Hotel, fourteen galvanized-iron rooms like horse-stalls, and four of them with beds. The bushmen camped on the river and nobody slept in the beds, but that pub rooted Katherine deep. Tom later took up Willeroo, a ghost station, abandoned since its blackfellow murders, and made a success of horse-breeding, with seventeen thoroughbred stallions, Arab and Suffolk Punch. He put seven teams on the road from Katherine to Victoria River Downs.

An enterprising settler named Niemann moved in to the old Jesuit Mission on the Daly, and gave one of the best examples to date of maintaining a family "on the country". He trapped birds, snakes, spiders, crocodiles, and sent them to museums—for a stick of tobacco the Brinken would bring in enough to sink a ship, while keeping the family in fish, game, geese-eggs and Daly wild apples for pies. He cultivated the fruits of the old garden and with black miners worked a silver lode thirty-six feet deep. In the wet he set the natives spinning wild kapok, and sold it in Darwin for 8d. a pound to stuff beds and pillows.

This wild-kapok tree grows all over the north, to about sixty feet high, with waxy yellow flowers and decorative pods a fluff of cotton. The wood, like South American balsa, is one of the lightest, and seldom eaten by white ants. With a little cultivation and liberal pruning the tree gives a heavy yield of good kapok.

A long yam, *yeelik*, grows on the Roper and Daly in immense beds. The Chinese paid Niemann 4d. a pound for it, and 2s. a pound for the seed to send home to China. He sold Daly pea-bush for fodder and, being an analytical chemist, extracted a pitch from the Leichhardt tree, stewed acacia bark for tannin, and brewed a solution from one species of mangrove that cleans copper on the bottoms of ships. He pointed out that Daly River could glut the world's market in crocodile hide and snakeskin for shoes, that in vegetables and fruits it could supply the Territory and Queensland, that white mulberry-trees flourish there for silkworms, that the natives are good cheap labour in easy work such as growing tobacco and tapping rubber-trees. His Tahitian limes and oranges were of beautiful flavour and big yield, and wild rice grows everywhere on the flats.

A new arrival in Darwin, in 1906, was a quiet young priest from Alsace-Lorraine, Father Francis Xavier Gsell. He realized that the Jesuits could never redeem the natives depraved in rum and ruination, and with five Manila-men in a ten-foot lugger he sailed to Bathurst Island, where the tribes were still hostile to white men. For a while he slept on the lugger at night, then carried his stores ashore to a little hut he set up on the beach, of pandanus and cypress pine. Chancing the ten-foot spears, he said his first mass on a wooden bench in the wildwood. As he turned to bless an invisible congregation, black shadows darted and fled out of the trees. There was a Mala-ola man behind every tree on the next Sunday morning, to see this mysterious white man without a double-barrelled gun, content to "corroboree longa himself".

So began the well-known aboriginal mission of Bathurst Island, where Father Gsell devoted his life for the following forty-five years. He became Right Rev. Bishop Gsell of Carpentaria, famous throughout the world, in a newspaper jest, for "buying black wives". From harassed fathers out hunting for all the "in-laws" of fifteen or sixteen wives, Father Gsell bought the new-born girl-babies that were destined to be the wives of old men. He paid for them in turkey twill, tobacco, tomahawks and knives, and bought over two hundred babies, each to the value of £2. So he triumphed over age-old tribal custom. He reversed the usual order of collection-plate, presenting to every native who attended mass on Sunday a pound of flour and a stick of tobacco.

A busy colony evolved with black labour. The young generations of Malaola and Wongo-ak became a race of devout Christians and active workmen, educated by missionary priests and a valiant little order of French nuns in residence on the island for many years under the guidance of Mother-Superior Geraldine.

As yet the only sea-light on the coast was the watchful eye of Point Charles on Darwin Harbour. In 1904 the French barque *Calcutta*, with a cargo of rice for Saigon, and in 1906 R.M.S. *Australian*, from China to England, piled up on the same rocks at Vashon Head. This led to the building of the lighthouse at Cape Don.

Out on the tracks the bushmen were still cutting their throats in despair, shooting themselves in thirst, and being speared by blacks.

"A few well-directed bullets," advised the *Northern Territory Times*, "will rid the country of these pests."

On King River, Moore and Mackenzie, buffalo-shooters, kidnapped lubras of the Yerrakool tribe. One little girl they called Jungle Lily tried to run away. They hoppled her with iron wire and thrashed her because she "all-time cry". Jungle Lily died. Her boy, Nappaloora, and her brother, Kopperang, killed Moore and Mackenzie, and were sentenced to death in Darwin, but there was an outcry and they were set free.

"Brumby" Clarke was shot by his boy, Jingle, at Settlement Creek. As evidence the trooper carried his head, boiled with eucalyptus leaves to preserve it, two hundred miles in a meat tin to Burketown. Mulligan and Ligar were speared in Jasper Gorge, Mildwater at Top Springs, and "Paddy the Lasher" at Pigeonholes on Victoria River. When Jaddeadda and Wallagoola, convicted of this crime, were asked by His Honour in Darwin court, in the terrible legalities of the black cap, if they had anything to say, the interpreter told them, "Talk-talk". The condemned yabbered loudly with each other, and burst into merry laughter, no doubt at the whole show.

Tribal murderers lay in the jail for months while the Government in Adelaide was wondering what to do with them. Murderers of white men were hanged at the scene of the crime until, from the Roper, the story was told of the dance of Mooloolooran.

At Crescent Lagoon, a half-moon of white lilies under a red cliff, a Chinaman was found with a spear through his throat. Mounted Constable Stott rode the river and brought in Mooloolooran, sentenced to be hanged as a lesson to the Jungman people. To the white lilies and the tree-shadows Mooloolooran came home, chained to the trooper's stirrup-irons by neck, wrists and ankles. Stott sent his trackers for fifty miles to gather the blacks with promises of tucker and tobacco. In mobs they camped at Crescent Lagoon. After the hand-out the trooper explained, through an interpreter, the capital crime of murder, their guilty kinsman now to pay the penalty of the law.

"Him killum dead-fella that-one Chinaman. All right. White man all-same killum dead-fella this boy.'

The backs sat in the shade of the trees, patient, puzzled, waiting. At sundown a rope was thrown over a branch. Mooloolooran stood on the tailboard of a cart, a noose about his neck, a yawning hole dug in the earth beneath him. Stott gave the signal. The tracker let down the tailboard and drew the cart away.

It is not sweet with nimble feet
To dance upon the air.

Mooloolooran, like King Charles the Second, was an unconscionable time dying. A boy of strong muscular reactions, his contortions were frightful. Quite unaware of the horror, his friends and relations roared their hearty laughter, mimicked the death agonies, held their sides and rolled on the ground in uncontrollable glee. When the limp body was carried away they shrieked for an encore, bundled another boy to the cart—one of their best dancers—and made signs to Stott for more tucker and tobacco. After this grim fiasco, closely following the brutal conduct of white men at the gallows on Bradshaw's Run, the Adelaide judiciary wisely decided to delete from the list of penalties such psychological atrocities as "execution at the scene of the crime".

The first new deal from the new Commonwealth was the Alien Immigrants' Restrictions Act of 1905—"White Australia". Believed to be a safeguard to the south from the "teeming hordes of Asia", to the north it was a knock-out blow. The Chinese in thousands were sent home, or went, to China—no labour for the mines. English companies forfeited their leases. El Dorado faded again, the batteries were rust, streets, mines and houses empty. Vats of deadly cyanic crystals were left at Brock's Creek and Pine Creek for drunks to commit suicide, for Asiatics to poison each other and the blacks. Only a few of the old Chinese were left rocking their cradles in the gullies. Pearling revenue fell from £86,000 to £12,000—no crews, no divers. Most of the pearlers "turned Dutchmen" and sailed for the Aru Islands. To save the industry the Government was later forced to sanction indentured Asiatic labour.

With mining and pearling gone and the stations at their lowest ebb in drought and the cattle-tick hoodoo, the outlook was hopeless. As a last resort the Resident sent to Manchester some sample pods of cotton from the neglected crops of failure, running wild. The quality created such interest in the British Cotton-growers' Association that the Territory was offered, in five-thousand-acre blocks for plantations, wages to the blacks to be a few sticks of tobacco. Nobody wanted an old Kentucky home. Mr Justice Dashwood resigned. He believed in a great future for the north—but too far in the future for him.

Many interesting pilgrims crossed the country at this time. Some were scientists, renouncing comfort, home and friends for hard living and hard riding to gain knowledge of a fascinating land.

H. Y. Lyell Brown, in 1895 at Victoria River, began his mineralogical surveys and explorations, a ten years' trail of every known reef and lode in the western half of Australia, his maps and reports the invaluable foundation charts for the Department of Mines. Sailing in the lugger *Venture* along the dim coasts of Arnhem Land, or chopping away at a crag in the Red Centre, "Mr Geology Brown" was revered by the bushmen, who learnedly discoursed of "dy-rites and py-rites" for the rest of their lives.

All over the central deserts with packhorses, Alan Davidson, for an English company, prospected for gold. As early as 1901 he discovered Tennant's Creek, Kurrundi, Tanami and the Granites, and recommended every one, but they were too far out of the world for other men to follow. Davidson died in Africa at the White Man's Grave.

Sir Walter Baldwin Spencer, in 1903, travelled with F. J. Gillen *Across Australia* from Alice Springs to Borroloola, in a wagon loaded with mirrors, beads, tobacco and knives, to trade for the literature and religions of an unknown race and its varied people from Arundta in the MacDonnells to Anuella in the Gulf. Their driver and cook was a South Australian trooper named Chance, who later made a study of the Dieri tribe in the sandy wastes of Lake Eyre. Lighting their fires on the plains at night, these three men "held converse with the aborigines", and gained a wealth of knowledge of its own dark people for Australia.

A seeker of God in the wilderness, Baldwin Spencer was not alone. On the way he met a cloud of dust—a bishop in a buggy. First cleric to offer a prayer under those pale inland skies, Bishop Gilbert White of Carpentaria, from his little Quetta cathedral at Thursday Island, travelled across the great Gulf and jogged south in the buggy to make the rounds of his diocese of a million square miles. A strange journey it was for a peer of the Church in broadcloth and gaiters, "swamping" with J. A. G. Little, the Darwin postmaster, on his half-yearly inspection of the Overland Telegraph Line, four white men and twenty-six horses riding and running alongside. Scattered were the flock. When they heard there was a bishop on the track, most of the pioneers went bush. There was one white man at Union Reefs with over four hundred Chinese. At Pine Creek he watched the coolies sweeping up the dust in the street and washing it for gold. At Katherine corroborees were in competition with Sunday vespers, and much better attended.

The mantle of Dr Livingstone fell on Dr White when the blacks of the party, in strange country, ran away for fear of *kurdaitcha*. One morning His Lordship discovered a skeleton in a blue shirt sharing their night-camp. Through whirlwinds of grass-seeds and bush-fires the buggy went on down, a hundred and eighty miles between stations, to find nobody home but a Chinaman cook, hospitality of bread and beef, but, "No savvy". On the whole trip from Darwin to Oodnadatta they met only thirty white men.

His Lordship was gravely shocked at the tragic living of these forgotten men—he denounced from the pulpit the callousness of Governments to the shame and sadness of outback stations—and if he divined more of human nature than can be cut and dried in the Articles of Faith, nature was his refuge and his strength. He came to preach, and he remained to pray. He has written a book of that trail in all its courage and wonder—"a harmony of desolation". Of Central Australia he has written: "I think many of the psalms, with their nature voices, must have been written in the open air in a land like this."

Coming in to Oodnadatta at last, he went up to the station with a pleasant smile:

"Good morning. When does the next train leave for Adelaide?"

The man answered him without a smile. "Tuesday week."

In Savage Australia on the Daly, Knut Dahl had his camp, professor of piscatology from Oslo University studying the crocodile. He spent three years with blacks in bark canoes, and carried back to Norway seven tons of scientific wealth, and one of the best books ever written about the region.

Practising taxidermy in bough sheds in the wet, the Tunney brothers, collecting for the Honourable Lionel Rothschild, who joined them for a time, travelled in a wagonette from Ord to Alligator rivers, and sent a thousand birds and four hundred mammals to the Rothschild Museum.

Richard Thewell Maurice, that lost genius who spent the months between remittances out in the vague of Australia, with a South Australian surveyor, Murray, and a black-boy, on camels crossed the trackless deserts from Fowler's Bay to Wyndham. The Horn expedition travelled the rugged western MacDonnells for hundreds of miles, while the ill-fated Thorold Grant expedition traversed the eastern MacDonnells and "tramped the funereal wastes to the gold country of the west at a funeral pace of two miles an hour for a thousand miles".

Banjo Paterson came from Sydney and wrote articles for the *Bulletin* about the "Land of the Cycloon":

> They start drinking just before breakfast and stop just before. Everything good is going to happen 'after the wet' . . . a wild land full of possibilities, millions of miles of splendidly watered country where the grass is sour,

rank and worthless; mines of rich ore—that it does not pay to treat; quantities of precious stones that have no value. The pastoral industry and the mines are not paying, and the pearling has got into the hands of the Japanese.

The hordes of aliens that have accumulated here are a menace to White Australia. The white folks are hospitable to a fault, and strangers have not a dull moment, nor a sober one.

I would give a lot to be back at Port Darwin in that curious luke-warm atmosphere, and watch the white-sailed pearling-ships beating out to sea, to see the giant form of Barney Flynn stalking emu-like through a dwarfish crowd of Japs and Manilamen, to be once more with the B.A.T. and the O.T. and the G.R. and Paddy Cahill while the cycloon hummed and buzzed on the horizon, or to be in the buffalo-camp of Rees and Martin, shooting the big blue bulls at full gallop, or riding home in the cool moonlight, the packhorses laden with hides.

A man who once goes to the Territory always has a hankering to go back. Some day it may be civilized and spoilt, but up to the present it has triumphantly over-thrown all who have tried to improve it. It is still the Territory. Long may it wave.

THE BANJO.

In a diversity of creatures a quaint little Frenchman named Etables roamed the north for thirty years, trapping birds, camped by the lily lagoons in a covered cart noisy with parrots. They were shipped to bird-fanciers in Europe at the rate of nine thousand a year. Across the Barklys from Camooweal came Monsieur and Madame Gilbert with seven horses, riding round the world for a bet. A child was born to them at Powell's Creek. From Katherine to Victoria River they rode on west and out of ken. s.s. *Ching-tu*, Singapore-bound, showed the first motion-pictures, in 1904—a railway train in America, head-on to the audience, sent the blacks pale with fright, but a Jack Johnson prize-fight revived them.

Next distinguished visitor was Sir George Le Hunte, Governor of South Australia, his vice-regal tour something new under the sun. When he arrived by s.s. *Eastern* in 1905 the lugger *Midge*, the only ship in harbour, fired a Martini-Henry in welcoming salute. All Darwin greeted him on the white-anted jetty in peril of its life, Chinese merchants in silken robes and pepper-and-salt schoolchildren of the colony garlanding his buggy of state with hibiscus and oleanders.

Sir George was a sportsman. He shot wallabies, geese, jungle-fowl and pigeons all round the town, graced an open-air banquet on Mindil Beach, and sailed for Adelaide River where, knee-deep in mangrove mud through clouds of mosquitoes he shot pythons, buffaloes, crocodiles and duck. He landed on Melville Island, hoping to see, though not to shoot, wild blacks. He bathed under a garden hose on the lugger to Victoria River, threw pipes and tobacco as a hand-out from His Majesty to a school of cannibals swimming around Point Pearce, and blandly acknowledged "God Save the King" as curtain-raiser to a corroboree at Bradshaw's Run. Near the Depot, where he alighted, his aide-de-camp, Hood, blazed a baobab-tree in his honour. It is still there, known as Governor's Tree.

Through Jasper Gorge, that bottleneck of peril, His Excellency drove a buggy and slept in his swag for ten days and nights on the way through wild Willeroo and Katherine back to the railway line. The blacks pushed his buggy through all the steep creeks. The population at Katherine, five all told, had gathered to sing "God Save", but the bush horses shied at a waving Union Jack and His Excellency passed at a flying gallop. Sunburnt, travel-stained and stiff, the vice-regal party looked more like a perish party just in from the desert, when Pine Creek, in its honour, in the dining-room of the pub, staged the only play in its seventy years of history, a little comedy called *Barbara*.

Sir George was not to be beaten, his head was bloody but unbowed. He set sail for the Daly, romped up-river in a squall, bumped over snags and sandbanks, and waded to the copper-landing waist-deep in the dark. Looking through his binoculars in morning light, he counted thirteen saurian shapes on the bank.

"By Jove, they're crocodiles!" said Sir George Le Hunte.

A hundred half-wild natives with great fires burning met him at the copper-mine, white teeth and nose-bones flashing into smiles for 'bacca. The Governor made them an eloquent speech, with elegant play of a monocle that was a Brinken corroboree for years. He asked them as a special favour not to drink rum and smoke opium, and assured them of His Majesty's good faith. Mulluk Mulluk and Marramaninjie sang the National Anthem for tea, flour and tobacco, and a good time was had by all. No spears were thrown. The tour ended with a Chinese banquet in Darwin. His Excellency departed for the south with a wry smile for the Empire where the sun never sets.

His Majesty's good faith carried some weight. One day to the Residency came a humble deputation, a straggled mob of the Larrakia headed by Nellie, Blind Solomon's daughter, to ask the king to stop the Chinese and Malays from catching black women, whipping them and giving them disease, from taking them to the pearling luggers, never to be seen again. All over the Territory the blacks were half-fed slaves.

In these first years of the century so pitiable was the condition of the blacks, whipped out of their country and wandering like pariah dogs, in disease a menace to the community, that letters were published in London *Times* crying shame on Australia. The authorities were forced to take action. Reforms were enforced from Adelaide and resented by the apathetic north. A Protector was appointed and a new Act became law. Where they had been at the mercy of every wanderer, and regarded as the property of employers, a permit was now made necessary, controlling conditions of labour. It was no longer permissible to take them a thousand miles from their homeland and leave them to die among strangers. Care of the old and the sick became a government consideration, and several missions were established. White men were not allowed to give them liquor, nor to take and abuse their women, nor to employ a woman without her man—they were also forbidden to appropriate their blankets, "which remain the property of His Majesty the King"—! Though these laws were more honoured in the breach than the observance—the poor dumb creatures knew little enough about them—they were, at least, the beginning of a recognition of human rights.

Ring in the valiant man and free,
The larger heart, the kindlier hand,
Ring out the darkness of the land . . .

A champion of the Australian blacks, true-hearted and kind, was Lord Tennyson, a governor of South Australia and son of the poet who wrote those lines. He was a powerful ally, and stirred up a righteous public resentment of inhumanities and injustice, an outcry against atrocities. On a tour of the railway to Oodnadatta, he addressed a vast crowd of natives who greeted him with a corroboree. Wearing full dress uniform—cocked hat with cock's feathers, gold epaulettes, the gold and silver cord of office, he turned gravely to the old men in their symbolic head-dresses and cockatoo plumes:

"Heads of the native tribes," he said, "and all other natives of Central Australia. Thank you for having brought together in my honour so large a corroboree, wearing the adornment of the different peoples. I hope you will continue to preserve these marks of your tribal distinctions.

"My pleasure is great in being among you, for I come to you as representative of our great and beloved sovereign, with a deep and sincere interest in your welfare and happiness.

"I beg to assure you that we shall faithfully keep our promise of protection to you all. We shall enforce with absolute strictness the laws to guard your rights. Any native who appeals to me, or to the government through me, can appeal with the certainty that the strong right hand of justice shall guard his tribe and his liberty from the greed, the violence of selfish and evil men."

It was a championship timely and splendid, but the country was too vast and lonely for the laws to be carried out, and to that sanctuary of justice and protection for the unlettered black-fellow there was no bridge.

W. G. Stretton was appointed to be protector of Aborigines, a man of long experience, understanding, and genuine sympathy with the blacks. He made amends for many wrongs, and tried to better their conditions. No longer could a "nigger", like a wild dog, be shot at sight.

From 1902 till 1905 the skeleton grip of drought had paralysed Australia, the most terrible drought in our history . . . from Queensland to West Australia pallid earth, pallid skies, a horror of dead sheep. South of Katherine the country was bare of feed and water. Jerry and Jack McCarthy, the telegraph teamsters, where they used to swim horses and float wagons, now faced a ninety-mile, sixty-mile, eighty-mile dry. On the Barkly Tablelands the blacks died in droves, and the cattle in thousands.

F. A. Stibe, the mailman who rode from Powell's Creek to Anthony's Lagoons and back before the Fizzer's time, perished on the Downs, with a white man named Hehir and a lubra. Corella Lake was dry. Koolinjie Waterhole was dry. Too far to go back, with three quarts they rode on.

Harry Readford of Brunette, riding north to shift cattle, found the bodies, fingers worn to the bone from digging holes in the hard ground, two dried water-bags and a horse with its throat cut on a mad circle of tracks, only five miles from permanent water. Six miles from Rankine River he found a drover, Hopkins, and his son, heads resting on their swags, four horses with their throats cut, the hair torn from a horse's tail to mop up the blood for the dying men. It was the same grim story everywhere. The west was a land of dead men. The Territory was a land of living ghosts.

A world traveller who passed at this time has left on record these words: "Never have I seen a country inhabited by the British where so much worth while in empire-building was thrown away."

Chapter XVI

On the Victoria

GRANDDAD OF all Territory streams is the Victoria, ambling down five hundred miles from the spinifex desert to the Timor Sea, where it gobbles in the big tides twice a day with a mouth twenty-six miles wide.

Nubian nymphs in sun-flecked jungle and Solomon's glory of lily lagoons are harder to find on this old brown river slothfully moving through a pliocene world. The Victoria is Jabberwocky. Gargoyle ranges and split cliffs above the white-hot glitter of its salt flats . . . echoing gorges shouting back thunder in titanic laughter . . . goblin galleries of ant-hills and dwarf baobab-trees . . . and a battering-ram of a tidal bore, horribly foamed like boiling yellow glue, that surges up-river twice a day, could find it a place on a map of the Inferno, to say nothing of its crocodile hatcheries and the torture of Mosquito Flats. The blacks call the lower river Wongawalli, devil talking.

Even so, it has its reaches of conventional green and silver beauty, forests of grey box and gracefully drooping nutwood and bauhinia hung with scarlet mistletoe and alight with movement of parakeets and painted finches. On either side is an infinite realm of grassy plains and rolling downs, guarded by the broken forts of hazy red ranges, jewelled with pandanus springs and a hundred singing creeks. To the cattle-men who pioneered this vast region of the western Territory, for seventy years it has been the crowning blessing. The Victoria is navigable for seventy miles by ocean-going ships, for a hundred and twenty miles by flat-bottomed craft. Its watershed is ninety thousand square miles.

Through all the years there were but two white men's dwellings on its banks, the old homestead of Wave Hill and, two hundred river-miles away, the little slab store at the Depot.

Under the unassuming name of Catfish, the source is a sand-creek in those stark plains below Wave Hill where Keith Anderson and his mechanic, Hitchcock, perished of thirst in their aeroplane search for Kingsford Smith in 1929. A trefoil design of many creeks comes in from the tumble of unexplored ranges to the west, and by the time five or six rivers join up—Armstrong, Gordon, Wickham, Buller, Baines and Norton Shaw—the broad stream is worthy of the majestic name conferred upon it in a moonrise of a hundred and twelve years ago, when Victoria was still a blushing girl. Lieutenant John Lort Stokes writes of that night in 1839:

> Wickham, Keys, Fitzmaurice and I were out in a boat from the *Beagle*, running before a north-west breeze . . . suddenly the moon above the hills in all its glory shed a silver stream of light on the water . . . under our keel the ripple and swell of a river-current, marble-smooth. . . .
>
> It was indeed a noble river, worthy of doing honour to her most gracious Majesty, the Queen.

Four men in a boat, they raised their glasses in a tot of medicinal brandy to the young Victoria, and the benign moon above them, a single star in attendance, was a smiling empress in a robe of cloud. This was twelve years before the naming of the Australian State.

Beagle groped her way for fifty miles up-river, and spent a stormy October there, surveying. The explorers dined on crocodile steaks and quandong peach pie—their excursions make lively reading. Out on a sandbank after geese, Stokes, while swimming a creek, nude, white and inviting, was chased by a crocodile—an electric snap of the air behind him as he scrambled up the bank. At Point Pearce he was chased by very wild blacks. Running for the boat with a spear through the shoulder, he fell twice, but just managed to make it—Treachery Bay. Believing the river a major discovery, as valuable to the north of Australia as the Murray is to the south, he wrote most of the names in the chart that are names in wilderness today. As he planted a bottle with documents at Indian Head, he visioned "cities and hamlets on the shores of this new-found river, and smoke arising from Christian hearths where now the prowling savage lights his fire". The prowling savage still lights his fire there without putting a penny in the gas-meter, and though the few white wanderers who happened along were Sherlock Holmes for bottles, I never heard of anyone unearthing *Beagle's* bottle at Indian Head.

It's an eerie world, the Victoria, right out of the world. Sailing down from Darwin in the erratic little twenty-five-tonner that was sole guardian of Territory coasts before the war, at the mouth of the river you pass magnificent groves of tamarinds planted by the Malays over a hundred years ago. Where sickly yellow ochre hills rise from the viscid grey of mangrove jungle is the sinister profile of Point Pearce and Port Keats—"perilous seas in faery lands forlorn"—scene of many a massacre of white men and Japanese by the blacks.

Among the Neanderthal coastguards of Port Keats, in 1906, Dr Hermann Klaatsch, a globe-trotting German anthropologist, discovered a Missing Link —a hairy ape-man with receding brow, protruding jaw, a splendid clamp of blue-white gorilla teeth, his big toe set far back from the others, which were long, lean and efficient as fingers in picking up small items from the ground. Photographs and plaster casts of this native, taken in Fannie Bay jail, where he was one of the Alleluyia tribe charged with the Bradshaw murders, were sent by the professor to Heidelberg. His fellows said there were others of his kind.

The little boat carries you on, engulfed in red whirlwinds, or, if it is nearing the wet season, through green lightning and torrents of hot rain. You sail at the whim of the tide, tossing stern first or broadside on before it, then motionless in the mud of the ebb for hours, perhaps for ever. The river changes its currents every day, building new sandbanks and hollowing out new channels, as the wrecks of luggers far inshore can tell. The ugly white tidal bore that rips through Queen's Channel is ten miles wide, at spring tides covering the islands to the tops of their trees and travelling at twelve knots.

Turtle Point is a turtle graveyard, a sandy mausoleum of whitened shells and skulls where countless generations of hawksbill, greenback and loggerhead have come in from the sea to die. In the mystic circle of Blunder Bay—an amphitheatre twenty miles round of writhing baobab-trees, grotesque ant-hill sculpture and rocky murals of aboriginal art—you lose the river in a fold of the hills, to find it again, as broad, and deep, and confident of fame. Holdfast Reach, where *Beagle* lost two anchors, clawed down and snapped from their chains in grisly mud, is a mile wide and twenty-two miles long, dimpled with greasy whirlpools and flanked by scowling cliffs—you have to pull up the anchor every few hours or it will hold fast in the slime till doomsday. Shoal Reach is a mocking hall of echoes. Clouds of cannibal bats fly over at dusk with the whistling scream of Hallow-e'en witches, and yellow dogs wail on the yellow hills.

Around you dances Curiosity Peak, east, west, north, south, playing pea-and-thimble in the winding reaches and puzzle ranges. You track it up, to torment of Hades at Mosquito Flats, a dense black veil of mosquitoes shrouding the tide-flats for eight miles where three rivers meet. Heaven help you now if you are becalmed. Every beach and every waterhole in the Territory in summer is a Chinese torture of mosquitoes, but there is only one Mosquito Flats.

An awe-inspiring sight here, at top springs, is the incoming tide, a flood of water running uphill two feet at a bound, seething over the quicksands with leprous streaks of foam, silting up the old channels and gouging out new. It rises twenty feet in two hours. Once one of the little ships was stuck in the mud and, to float herself off, unloaded two tons of stores on an island with mangroves eight feet high. In came the tide. She could never find island or stores again, only a floating crate of drowned fowls.

The remarkable sugar-loaf of Curiosity Peak and the equally remarkable Dome on the other side of the river are gates of a mighty cattle kingdom. From now on, prairies of reddish Flinders grass are blowing for shadowless miles to the far purple shadows of knobbed and castled hills swimming in those filmy sunlights as though through water. Since the eighties, four great cattle stations have divided the river between them. South-west, on the Baines tributary, is Auvergne. North-east, on the Ikymbon or Norton Shaw, is Bradshaw's Run. Then flanking the river on both sides for about three hundred miles is the biggest cattle run in the world, Victoria River Downs. With 13,150 square miles until this year, it had an area larger than Belgium, and a steady population of about eight white men as compared with Belgium's eight millions. The head station is on Wickham River, seven miles above the meeting of the waters. With a hundred and seventy thousand cattle, a hundred and fifty black stockmen, and six out-camps—some of them sixty miles from the homestead—the Big Run covers the maze of ranges and creeks in mid-river. Another hundred miles south, on the headwaters, is Wave Hill, seven thousand square miles, with as many more as it likes to adopt, up to half a million, of the Great Sandy Desert below.

Not one of the homesteads is built on the Victoria bank. Wave Hill used to be, but they moved it eight miles east on the plain in 1924. In the same year that Anderson and Hitchcock met their deaths by thirst, a flood swept everything away. Donkeys, huts and cases of jam floated for forty miles. In an avalanche of waters, fourteen men were marooned on the roof of the wagon-shed, singing "Abide With Me".

In early years both Wave and V.R.D. would brand their twenty thousand calves in the year, and together set seventy thousand steers on the road to market. Ever noted for its demigod riders is the Victoria—they muster in the limestone ranges and over the Bay o' Biscay Downs, through sliding gorges and slippery creeks down to pandanus pools and paperbark springs hidden away in pockets of giant boulders. Madly they race the mobs in "debil-debil" of the black-soil plains, pitted through the long dry season with the cloven hoofs of the wet, the pads baked into cast-iron traps where man and horse may crash at any moment. It is one of the few stations in Australia where you can still see a thousand cattle in the yards at one time, with two white men and twenty or thirty blacks to rope-and-throw and brand. Many of our greatest stockmen, famous throughout the continent, have made history there. At sundown, in the smoke of the billy fires, some grand old ghosts arise.

Lindsay Crawford formed the Big Run for Fisher and Lyons of Adelaide in 1884. One of Todd's Men, telegraph operator at Daly Waters, he left the key to explore with Favenc the Macarthur River country, then rode a thousand miles east to meet Bluey Buchanan with the mobs for V.R.D. His first slab hut homestead was "a bit of hurry-up", stores landed at the Depot, sixty miles away. He spent eleven years out there riding blacks and cattle, and when he went back to the Telegraph Line the west gave him a send-off, and a purse of two hundred and fifty sovereigns from five or six white men. Camped in a big wet on the rim of Newcastle Waters when they were seven miles wide, he died of fever—his grave is there by the Stuart Highway.

The station was sold to Goldsbrough Mort in 1895. Enter "the Gulf Hero", Jack Watson, a d'Artagnan of the north, second manager of Victoria River Downs. On a lugger in Carpentaria once, he saved the life of a sailor chased by a shark by diving straight on to the shark and ripping it up with a knife. His star turn after that was to dive at crocodiles in Gulf and Territory rivers, with a direct hit to the jaw to knock out the croc. From Cape York to Kimberley his name was a byword for lunatic deeds of derring do. It was also a terror to the natives. There is a story—I do not like to believe it true—that hearing of a Burketown station pestered by cattle-killers, he promised to set the matter right. Riding back in a week he threw eleven skulls on the table with a jaunty "There you are! No more trouble out there!" The Gulf Hero boasted that he never carried a gun. What he did carry was a sinister mystery. One of his favourite exploits at Victoria River Downs was to race his horse down the narrow tongue of land where the Wickham and Victoria meet, with a thirty-foot leap down into the rivers. His black offsider, Queensland Mick, was famous as a fire-eater. It may have been magic or leprosy, but for a stick of tobacco to amuse a droving-camp, Mick would chew live coals.

No gravestone commemorates the Gulf Hero. The crocodiles won. At Katherine River crossing on April Fool's Day 1896 the river was in high flood, a brawling torrent a quarter of a mile wide and seventy feet deep. It swept away the telegraph line. All the Katherine blacks were marooned on little islands. A big crowd of cattle-men was in at the pub, and boats were taking stores across to their camps. The Gulf Hero elected to swim to and fro. In that big swirl of rapids, they were cheering his bobbing hat. He was nearly over for the last time when, a few yards from the bank, the hat blew off. He turned to reclaim it, and went under . . . for good. They never found his body when the river fell, but they did find an eighteen-foot man-eater in a pool near by. It had cruised up from the Daly in high tides, an evil fate lying in wait for the Gulf Hero.

Bob Watson, his brother, took over the management of Victoria River Downs, and "Mrs Bob", a sterling woman of honourable mention in *We of the Never Never*, was first white woman to live there. The two women who followed her died. Goldsbrough Mort, in the nineties, sent up two thousand sheep to those infinite pastures. Though they doubled their number within two years and gave excellent wool, shepherding was too difficult in the great unfenced. They were sold to Captain Joe Bradshaw, who landed them farther out among the wild blacks and wild dogs, and lived to rue the day.

For the first thirty years V.R.D. was writing off seven thousand calves a year, speared, stolen or strayed. Those gay adventurers, the poddy-dodgers, had their cattle-duffing units in the ranges. There was no mail, and telegrams, contracting for thousands of cattle to be delivered by a certain date, were left at Katherine or Wyndham till somebody was going that way—a two-hundred-and-forty-mile track through bad blacks' country either way. White men rode together, and took their firearms to bed. One night Charlie Rix heard a mysterious sound, and got out of his mosquito-net to listen—his gun went off and killed him as he was crawling back.

The tick menace of northern cattle to the great herds of the south brought stern prohibition of shipping. With thirteen thousand square miles of good country and fifty thousand cattle, there were times when the Big Run "couldn't pay the cook's wages". It was once offered for sale for £22,000. Later, Forrest and Emanuel bought it, with a small export trade of cattle to Manila to keep it alive. But the blacks and the dingoes faded away, the cattle increased, and when Bovril Estates, London, bought the station in the first great war, it is said that they paid £200,000. Even then, most of its stock for many years was driven to Wyndham meatworks, to be turned into beef extract at rarely more than £2 a head. Well might the cattle kings of Argentine, looking to Australia, quote the old slogan, "Alas, my poor brother!" Following Tom Graham, manager for Bovril Estates for more than twenty years, was Mr Alf Martin, with his fine little wife and big family in residence, watching the Big Run grow from a remote outpost into what is now virtually a little town.

Richard Townshend was manager for seventeen of the hardest years, from 1902 to 1919. His wife died there, a poignant tragedy involving the death of the Fizzer.

The Fizzer, Henry Ventlia Peckham, will live in our school-books as a hero for all time—a mailman who gave his life for his mail. The story of his riding alone the Dry Downs, in ninety-mile stages to the broken wells with the mail to Anthony's Lagoons, was told during his lifetime by Mrs Aeneas Gunn, in one of the finest chapters of the literature of Australia. His death is an epic she has not written.

The Fizzer was haunted by fear that he would die of thirst, that death, in the dust of the downs, was drawing near. He had good reason. Once, with his horses lost, he crawled in on hands and knees to water. Stibe, the mail-man before him, with a white man and a black woman, had dug his own grave out there. So he left the stark plains of his horror, after a brief period as manager at Auvergne, to ride the mail to Victoria River Downs. It was five hundred miles on packhorses from Katherine and back, calling at Willeroo and Delamere.

On his first journey, April 1911, he arrived at the Victoria at the end of the wet. Mrs Townshend was seriously ill. A letter was posted in his canvas bags, calling for the Darwin doctor. Twelve miles out, he found the river in high flood at Campbell's Creek crossing. His only companion was a little black-boy. He sent this boy riding back with a note, asking if any matter in the mail were urgent. If not, he would camp a few days and wait for the flood to go down. The answer came—the letter to the doctor for the sick woman was most urgent. That was enough for the Fizzer—he would swim. With the black-boy in the lead, they whipped the horses in. Two of the frightened packs doubled back in midstream. In heading them on, the Fizzer fell from the saddle and was tossed away in a drowning current.

"Save the mail!" he shouted to the black-boy. "Save the mail!"

The little fellow got the packs across, and rode up and down, calling . . . but the Fizzer was gone, so he hoppled the horses, swam the river again, and rode back to the station. All night they searched, with fires lit on the bank and the blacks swimming. The floating bodies of horse and man were found next day.

"Save the mail!" The echoes are ringing still along the Victoria. They will ring on through history.

The Fizzer's grave has, regrettably, been removed to a Never Never memorial graveyard two hundred and fifty miles east, to right on the Stuart Highway. It belonged to Victoria River. For thirty years it was a landmark of a very lonely land. On the east bank near Campbell's Creek, just above the crossing, fenced in from the cattle, was the gravestone carried by packhorses two thousand miles from Adelaide, a bas-relief in bronze of packhorses against a setting sun. The most conspicuous and the most carefully tended grave of the whole of the Australian outback, it was always painted a dazzling white, a labour of love by the bushmen, who every year carried a pot of paint in the saddle-bags from Katherine, so that no one might pass without knowing. Few of them knew him in life, but bagman, swagman, parson and poddy-dodger would doff their hats to a memory in the Land of Forget, as they took the turn-off by the Fizzer's grave.

Hills and valleys westward are a Cretan labyrinth of creeks—Skull Creek,

Bare-back, Pint-pot, Black Gin, Camp Oven, Surprise, Water-bag, Snake, Cow and Sundown creeks, Revolver Creek winding round and round, Battle Creek—a battle of boomerangs and guns—Timber Creek, where A. C. Gregory cut the timber for his schooner *Tom Tough* when he sailed the Victoria in search of Leichhardt in 1855-6, camped for eight months at the Depot, and blazed his famous tree, LETTER IN OVEN, carved on a baobab.

Most spectacular is Jasper Creek, leaping down through Jasper Gorge, thirty miles north-west of V.R.D. and right on the road to the west—a canyon slash of pied and jagged cliffs nine hundred feet sheer and four miles through, a ravine of great boulders tumbled down by the blacks to trap the cattle and bar the white man's passing. A few years ago romance was bulldozed out of the picture, and a good road now runs through Jasper Gorge.

In 1895 it was the scene of a sensational ambush. Jammed in among the mountains, a funnel of cliffs leads into the pass from the west. Mulligan and Ligar, two teamsters with a wagon-load of stores for the stations, camped with their few blacks at sundown at the T.K. Boab—a baobab-tree marked for Tom Kilfoyle. A tribe of myalls came in, wanting tea, tobacco and rum, and joined Mulligan's blacks.

They were all singing corroboree and the white men making tomorrow's damper by the fire when the singing stopped. A shower of spears came in. Mulligan was slashed through the thigh with a murderous "shovel-nose" made of sheep-shears stolen from Bradshaw's Run. Ligar had a stone-headed spear through his back and a glass-head embedded in his nose. The two men crawled to the wagon, dragged the tarpaulin over them, groped for their revolvers and spent the night shooting at shadows in the dark.

At piccaninny daylight the blacks showed up on the cliffs, pelting stones, rolling rocks, throwing an occasional spear. The men made a barricade of their bags of flour and answered with rifle fire. By nightfall they were nearly done. The spearhead had penetrated Ligar's lung, and he was coughing blood. At sunset, dragging saddles, they ventured out together, shooting left and right. They managed to catch a couple of half-draught horses, and painfully rode the sixty miles to Auvergne, where the manager, T. K. White, heard them calling across the flooded river. Ligar was delirious, Mulligan crippled for life. T. K. White applied first aid, and rowed them forty miles down Baines River to wait for the Victoria ship, but the *Ark* was down-river, waiting for the tide, expected to float in five or six days, so he carried them on to Bradshaw's Run, and there met the Victoria River policeman. It was a month before the wounded men reached Darwin and medical care.

The trooper, with a party of seventeen bushmen, rode the range, a grim memory for the seventeen bushmen. The blacks had rifled the wagons of all save wine and rum—not being able to read the labels. Saddles, guns and tobacco were found in camps away up in the ranges. After a year in hospital in Sydney, Mulligan came back and died at Ferguson River. Ligar, a comedian of the north, for the rest of his life delighted to frighten the girls in Darwin and Pine Creek by pushing a peg or a hat-pin through the cartilage of his nose, the hole made by the spear.

Where all the creeks of all the ranges leave their water-lilies, their bluebonnet parakeets and their dancing brolgas to join the grand march of Victoria River, there is the Depot, for ever known to old hands as Matt Wilson's store. Matt was a kindly deaf old bushman when I met him, universal provider for the drovers in the only store in the Territory west of the O.T. Line. His free circulating library circulated farther than any other on earth, via the billabongs for two thousand miles right down to Bourke and back. He would always accept books for a beer-bill, and lend them out to the wild and wide for love of them.

He lived all alone in his shack on the river, pannikin and billy for the family plate and a beer-case for a chair, but, make no mistake, his turn-over in good years ran into thousands. There might be no customer in two months, no stir of dust on the plain except a whirlie-whirlie. Then the boys would ride in in batches of six to thirty, from all the mustering and drovers' camps from the Ord to the Georgina, £400 orders to give, £200 cheques to knock down.

Matt had a gallon licence, and they drank by the gallon, but he had also a reputation to keep up. There was a notice in the store:

NO BENDERS ON THE PREMISES

←←←———→

BOTTLE TREE FOR DRINKING

A gnarly old boab on the river bank was Grand Hotel, saleyards, hospital, town hall, polling booth, convincing ground and grandstand in the far-famed Depot races, where once a year the station nags and blackfellow jockeys held tourney on the clay-pan, horses and punters from Queensland, Alice Springs and Marble Bar—the Victoria Cup £200, and the betting thousands all told. It was also the court-house on the rare occasions when Captain Joseph Bradshaw, J.P., arrived up-river—generally at race-time—his Bench a beer-case, a bottle of Scotch at his elbow to regale the whole court, prisoner included, while he banged for Order! with a loaded ten-inch Colt.

Matt Wilson banked his takings every year or two in Darwin, and cheques were sometimes two years in transit before they were honoured. Blacks were the only ones who paid cash, when the drovers set them to do their washing, and threw them a two-shilling piece. Matt would always put an extra scoop in for the blacks for auld lang syne. He also traded with them in kind. When they brought in a big barramundi,

"What-name you wantum fish?"

"Wantum plour, tea, tchugar, toe-bacca, wantum lolly all-about."

He weighed and doled out. When salt-water blacks were around looking for trouble, he did his bookkeeping with a rifle on the counter.

White men's orders were nearly as simple in a simple life—

"Fifty or sixty quids' worth o' stuff, Matt, anythin' you got, and a couple o' gins' dresses, and a couple o' gallons o' square."

Pack-saddles and horses were often traded in instead of barramundi. The stock ranged from eye-lotion to horseshoes, from pants to pickles, all on one shelf. Matt was a shrewd and enterprising buyer, but one line he never stocked—ties. He did speculate once in a lady's tailored coat and skirt from T. C. Beirne's in Brisbane, but it got into the hands of the wrong people. There were so many corroborees in it and so much gambling about it, so many broken noses and lubra fights and *yacki* up- and down-river, that he had to trade for it back and burn it before he could get a bit of sleep.

He ran a few hundred horses and cattle, and when the local crocs were patrolling the landscape in the wet, he might be away for weeks, rounding them up. The store was never locked. A droving-plant can't ride three hundred miles to find a store locked. He would come back to empty shelves, and a stack of cheques and chits on the spike nearly a foot deep. The only trouble with the bookkeeping was that the cash was always more than the sales recorded. Matt trusted the whole world, and his wild corner of it would never betray a trust. After 1930, when the motor-trucks brought strangers from civilization, it was a different story. He had to put a notice in the *Northern Territory Times*: "Old hands still welcome at the Depot, but dotted-line merchants, blow-ins and boomerang cheque artists take another track."

The wicked little love-god spreads his wings even with the bower-birds and flying foxes. When Matt was sixty-seven, Cupid hit him with a glass-top spear. On his annual trip to Darwin to bank his takings, he lost his heart to a waitress. Watching her little butterfly bows flitting round the dining-room of the Victoria Hotel, he longed to transfer them to Victoria River. The ministering angel was uncertain and coy, and undoubtedly hard to please. She was twenty-three. Twice he rode and paddled a thousand miles, there and back, for the wedding—she kept him missing trains, at one a week.

She refused a ring of Chinese gold—he dutifully sent to Sydney for a diamond cluster. His idea of her trousseau was a riding-skirt and spurs, but she wanted £200 worth of frills from the fashionable south, a £50 three-tiered cake, and a photograph of it. So far, so good, but when she insisted that Matt tie up to the altar-rails in black suit and gardenia, he saw breakers ahead, and rang down Both Engines Full Astern. He said he would get a new blue shirt if she wanted—nothing more. There were scratch-pull arguments in Lover's Lane in the gay tropic sunset, his lady-love shouting a monologue into Matt's good ear.

On the eve of the wedding she told him to take his feet off the table, and cut him to the quick with the public rebuke that he had had too much whisky. He knew, then, she could not be a soul-mate.

"Never had too much whisky in my life, my dear," he answered her sadly. "My trouble is that I can never get enough."

She went further, and demanded that the wedding-breakfast, with fifty guests invited, should be teetotal.

Matt said that was unthinkable—why have a wedding at all?

Darwin rocked with laughter when the first breach of promise case in the Territory was listed, *Blank v. Wilson*, damages, £2500—Matt's money or his life.

A gallant old bushman, with his beard trimmed and the new blue shirt bought for the wedding, Matt told the court it would be presumptuous of him to link his worthless life with that of an angel. He was an old man, crotchety, he said, shivering with malaria, lame in the left foot, deaf in the left ear, and he did what seeing he could with the right eye. He could not see what a beautiful girl like that could see in a feller like him. He had worn out the seat of his pants sitting on stones to be lectured, but it was no good . . . too old to change. If he did propose, and if she did accept, he never heard it . . . it must have been his offside ear. The Depot was no place for a lady.

Plaintiff assured the court of her willingness to be a pioneer. She knew nothing at all about Victoria River, except that someone had warned her that in that wild spot the ladies were all black ones. Nevertheless she was ready and willing, as Mrs Matt Wilson, to honour and obey.

The judge thought that would be taking devotion too far. As Matt left the court, shoulder-high, on a big wave of laughter, the lady proffered him his ring.

"No thank you, my dear," said Matt. "You keep it. I'm through with those for the rest of my life." He made it a hand-gallop home through Jasper Gorge, where he was safe among the eagle-hawks and the myalls.

Every three or six months the little ship from Darwin hove out of the mud with supplies. Towing a flat-bottomed boat, she was a week or two in the river, picking the tides. The Depot, ninety miles up, was her only port, and Matt was the Depot. Fencing wire, petrol drums, pumps, machinery, bore-piping, flour-bags and iron-clads, all the loading came through him for Victoria River Downs, Willeroo, Wave Hill, Limbunya, Auvergne, Newry, Bullita, various little stations and the police at Timber Creek.

The boat was always a week or a month out of schedule. You listened for her hoarse little hoot. She kept enough steam for that, though it might be her last gasp in the middle of the night. Matt woke, made a mental note, then turned and snored again.

"Early-fella morning-time" he was out with a gang of black wharfies to the white-anted landing in the mud, the crocodiles poking inquisitive noses through the planks. The skipper of the "flattie" was usually a Malay or Jap, dumping tons on the jetty till it staggered, presenting manifests and bills of lading he had no hope of reading. Bashau or Nogi, as the case may be, he spoke very little English, but Matt made up for that.

The cargoes out, branded for the stations, the blacks undid the slings. Matt checked over, to see how much flour and square-face the crew had borrowed while they were stuck in the mud. Then he signed the manifests, and signalled the boat away to slip down-river with the tide, a silhouette in the glassy red dawn. If she didn't get away with the same tide, she might be there for a month.

Pluto, general manager, clad in a spotted handkerchief, brought up the lorry with three horses, to drive everything into the bough shed, out of the wilting sun and soaking rains, while Matt made breakfast for the black wharfies—a hunk of salt beef on to boil, a big digger's dish of damper, soddy in the middle so it would stick to their ribs and "tuck-out longtime", a couple of quart billies of rice, two buckets of tea, strung by the handles on a sapling, and two sticks of tobacco each all round. There was no strike in that Waterside Workers' Union. Matt himself was the proud possessor of No. 1 union ticket in the Queensland A.W.U.—he had burned down a shearing shed to get it. All was fair and square in his camp. One of his boys was a cripple, who sat down keeping a fire going in the open, where all could see the tucker for share and share alike. That work made the crippled boy a good provider, earning his bit. Matt Wilson understood the blacks—or he would not have lived for thirty-five years in his store alone on Victoria River.

In God's good time, out of a big dust came Burton Drew . . . in his little 'roo-skin cap, three huge creaking wagons behind him. They were drawn by a couple of hundred donkeys, spares and foals running alongside.

Burt Drew was Donkey King of the north. Year in, year out, at three miles an hour, he carried the loading to the stations, three months out and three months back, via Victoria River Downs to Wave Hill, with a branch line to Delamere and Willeroo. His big iron wheels made most of the roads up that way, and made them too wide. The motor-trucks following cursed his gauge, but Burt didn't care. Before they were thought of, he had travelled these tracks for eighty thousand miles—he liked to reckon it as the equivalent of three times round the world, and three times round his world it was. He sat on the leading wagon all day, and slept under it at night, outspanning the donkeys at sundown. A couple of black-boys had the tricky job of catching them in the morning.

It was one of the sights of the north to see the big teams moving and they got there. When the motor-trucks were stuck in the creeks, along came Burt's donkeys and hauled them out.

It took him a couple of weeks to load up at the Depot. Burt was as deaf as Matt, and could carry on only a one-man conversation. But both were well-read men, and entertained each other at meals pointing out patches of Gibbon and Carlyle, nodding appreciation together over the salt goat. Once Burt traded in half a dozen donkeys for Buckle's *History of Civilization in England*. Matt sold that book four times, but it always came back in exchange for beer. He called it the "boomerang edition"—it was too solid a dry stage even for the salt-bush historians of the N.T.

There were plenty of boarders, off and on—men in from the stations with fever, a broken leg, a cheque to knock down, a spear embedded in the chest, or various other reasons for catching the boat to Darwin. They might have to wait for it from three to thirteen weeks. Matt made them welcome, free, gratis and for nothing, but some could not wait—there is a fair-sized graveyard at the Depot, and there, now, Matt Wilson is host among the shades.

He said good-bye to the world on his own account a year after I passed by. Old and failing, lame and nearly blind, he was unwilling to leave the place or to be a burden. His leave-taking was a Territory classic.

Happy to the end, he was sharing a celebration in the Christmas wet with one of his cronies. The boat was very late that year, the grog was running short—not enough left for two.

Matt reflected. Eventually, why not now? . . . finish up the year. His singing-companion heard the crack of a gun.

Under the old bottle-tree of so many songs and revelries they laid him to rest.

Greater love hath no man, that he lay down his beer for his friend.

Chapter XVII

Bradshaw's Run

AWAY DOWN-RIVER, where the Baines meets the Victoria under a cloud at Mosquito Flats, in the lee of the Ballyangle or Pinkerton ranges, is Auvergne. The French name of the station is a mystery. It was formed by Macartney and Mayne in 1886, when the blacks chased them out of Florida in Arnhem Land.

Some stations, like ships and men, seem foredoomed to tragedy. Auvergne has collected more than its share. Twenty thousand cattle are running in the river-scrub, and the homestead on the bank of the Baines is pleasanter than most, but with a melancholy history.

The first manager, Tom Hardy, was speared there. A thousand miles with

Macartney's cattle he had travelled the Territory from Blue Mud Bay, and built a slab hut by the river. One piccaninny daylight he went down to fill the water-bucket, his rifle in his hand. The early morning cool was very still. River-sunlights rippled up the white trunks of the ghost-gums, and from the rushes came the chuckle of a swamp pheasant.

Hardy put down his rifle and turned his back on peril . . . a spear whistled through the rushes and caught him in the throat. He crawled up the steep bank to the hut. When Billy Frost and Tom Chapman, his stockmen, came back, they found him dead in the doorway.

Three adventurous years passed. One night the salt-water blacks crept in from the Ballyangle Range, and sent a shower of spears over the men sitting on the veranda at tea. The only fatality was a canvas water-bag hanging over their heads. There was a ride-out through the ranges, and the blacks paid for that water-bag.

Sam Croker was manager now, "Greenhide Sam", with a brave heart and a bitter tongue. When the year's work with the cattle was over, Greenhide was in at the homestead with his head stockman, Jock McPhee, and Ah Wah, the Chinaman cook. A half-caste rode in, looking for a job. He was Charlie Flanagan, a psychological problem in half-castes, a black white man, with a black skin and a white mind. Flanagan was a fine athlete, a wonderful jockey, a good worker and honest as the day. He had four or five good horses. Greenhide gave him a job.

The wet came down. The station blacks sang thankful corroborees while the men in the hut played cribbage, a rifle on the table every night in case of a wild blacks' raid. Flanagan was a poor player but he liked gambling with white men. It amused Greenhide to whip the boy with gibes at his dark blood. The half-caste grew vicious and sullen.

In a humid night of ill humours they cut for partners. Greenhide cut Flanagan. He refused "to partner a nigger—let him play with the old Chow". The boy's eyes narrowed black with hate. He played badly, a target for Greenhide's caustic wit. At a cruel jibe, he snatched the gun and shot Greenhide dead. The slush-lamp crashed to the floor.

Ah Wah skipped out the window and raced for the river, where he spent the night knee-deep in mud. Jock McPhee followed and hid in the dark. It was ninety miles to Victoria River Downs, and suicide to travel through Jasper Gorge unarmed. All bridles, guns and tucker were in the hut. They ventured back in the morning. Flanagan ran them round at the end of a rifle, one to cook his dinner, the other to dig the grave. He himself sewed Greenhide up in his camp-sheet shroud and twisted a coffin of galvanized iron . . . but he was uneasy and slept not a wink that night. The black in him dreaded the place of the dead.

He rounded up his horses and rode away next morning, first demanding his cheque from McPhee, and making out a receipt for it, with duty stamp attached, as a white man would. He rode west to the Ord, to a white man he liked and trusted, F. C. Booty.

Booty was breaking horses in the yards when Flanagan rode up, the rifle in his hand and a dangerous brooding eye.

"I just shot old Croker, Mr Booty. What d'ye reckon I better do? I'll shoot any ——— that tries to take me."

Mr Booty thoughtfully stroked his beard.

"Well, now," he said in his pleasant English drawl, as though shooting old Croker were no more than shooting a cow. "Well, now, you'll have to report it, Flanagan, you know. The police will have to register the matter. Jack Kelly's going up to Hall's Creek—you can ride in with him if you like, and he'll explain to Sergeant Brophy."

So Texas Jack Kelly took the half-caste to Hall's Creek, three days through the lonely ranges, camped with the murderer at night. From Elvire River, Kelly rode ahead to "explain", telling Flanagan to follow and "sign the statement". As he walked into the police station, a constable and a tracker grabbed him from behind the door.

The half-white man was condemned to death by the white man's law. He said not a word in his own defence in Darwin Supreme Court, and was first to be hanged in Fannie Bay jail, where he lived for six months in shackles waiting for the order for his execution to be signed by the Governor in Adelaide. His only desire was to die game. He laughed at the chaplain's consolations.

"They'll make me a stoker in hell," he said. "You won't see me hanging round here with a pair of wings on."

The *Northern Territory Times* records that under the black flag "he walked to his execution stoic as an Indian and with as firm a step as a man set free". And so, indeed, he was, set free from the dark prison of his own mind.

At Auvergne, the bad beginning was almost forgotten in tranquil years that followed. A white woman, Mrs Skeehan, and her children were living there at the beginning of the century, when Jerry Skeehan, the manager's brother and head stockman, was killed in the Bradshaw massacre at Port Keats.

The Fizzer was next manager, and after him came Archie Skuthorpe. Out after cattle-killers, he was speared in the shoulder. With the spearhead in the wound, he rode two hundred miles to the doctor at Wyndham, but, rather than face an operation, rode home with the spearhead still there, and was killed a few weeks later by the flying heels of a colt.

Neil Durack went out to manage the run. At the beginning of the wet his young wife left the station to meet the ship at Wyndham for the journey to the south. Neil rode over to the Depot races, and won £600. Eager to share the good news with his wife in a land without a telegraph, he started back for Wyndham. The Ord was in flood, and in swimming the crossing he was drowned. A blackfellow recovered the body next day, with the sodden roll of cheques in the pocket. Every one of those cheques was rewritten for the wife.

Many a stockman has lost his life in a crash on the debil-debil plains of Auvergne—it is the worst country for stock-riding in Australia, an average of a fall a week. In 1919 a returned soldier, Alex MacDonald, just back from five years' service, was killed by the Ballyangle blacks. His grave is on the road, eight miles from the station. He had just built a stockyard, finished the job at sundown, and sent his black-boy for the horses to ride in. The wild blacks came down from the range, creeping behind trees. MacDonald saw them and ran to the tent for a rifle, too late. He was dead, and the stores gone, when the boy came back with the horses. In his swag they found letters from a sweetheart in France.

For many later years the manager of Auvergne was Harry Shadforth, a cattle pioneer of the Queensland north. His brave and busy little wife was often alone at the homestead for weeks with the blacks. Harry Shadforth, too, met death by misadventure. He was charged by a maddened bullock in the stockyard, and injuries were fatal.

Reginald Wyndham Durack, third generation of the great overlanding family, has managed the run since then, with his young wife and family, sometimes with one, or both, of his well-known and talented sisters to keep him company. The valuable and delightful books of Mary and Elizabeth Durack—*All-about*, *Chunuma, The Way of the Whirlwind*, *The Magic Trumpet* and others—written by Mary, illustrated by Elizabeth, of delicate legendary grace and rare poetic insight of aboriginal life, are among our happiest, most human and most authentic studies of the black Australian.

With pedal radio and the Flying Doctor, with a main road passing Auvergne today, and hundreds of travellers in the year, the old hoodoo is forgotten. It is no more than a tale of old times.

At Whirlwind Plains, near the mouth of the Victoria, is Bradshaw's Run, farthest cattle outpost in Australia. So far is Bradshaw's out of the world that two lone riders, Byers and Inwood, have disappeared on the way to it, never the sign of a camp-fire, never a horse track found. This is uncanny where the white man's presence, the white man's tracks, are landmarks. One is more easily lost in Sydney than north of 28°.

"Cap'n Joe" Bradshaw was one of the greatest nation-builders the north has ever known—he lost about £200,000 there. First mate of a British India ship in the days of sail, he put no stock in imaginary railways. He believed that the Territory was best colonized by sea. In 1890 he bought the pearling schooner *Gemini*—in the land where a spade is a spade she was always known as *Twins*—and the once-beautiful yacht *Red-gauntlet*, to cruise the shores from Dampier Land to Arnhem Land in quest of a kingdom.

His first empire was an unbounded station holding on the Prince Regent River of the Kimberley coasts for sheep, a startling novelty in that razor-back region.

In an April sunset, from cliffs a thousand feet sheer, I have looked down on this secret and glamorous corner of the continent that Phillip Parker King dedicated to the court of the Georges . . . Brunswick Bay, Hanover Bay, George Water, Prince Frederick Harbour, Augustus and Coronation isles, Glenelg River and Rothesay Water, to the south-west Port George IV and Camden Harbour.

With a bold front to tranquil seas of a myriad coral islands, the King Leopold Ranges mount southward in crags and valleys of grape-bloom blue, in never-ending tiers. So rough and raddled are they that not even a pack-horse can find foothold on the steep spurs and broken limestone ridges receding for two hundred miles. This far north-west coast between Derby and Wyndham, split into a thousand fiords breathtaking in their colour and beauty, is far and away the loveliest in Australia. It will one day be a world-famous tourist resort. Now it is known to few.

Sails curved white as a nautilus-shell drifting through levels of sea-light, *Gemini* sounded her way through coral reefs into Prince Regent River, which is navigable for fifty-seven miles, fifteen fathoms deep, and bold water flanked by four-hundred-foot cliffs.

With Cap'n Joe were his bride, his brother Fred, and Aeneas Gunn, writer, naturalist, navigator, a cousin of the Bradshaws. He and Cap'n Joe, as adventurous boys, sailed their boats together. To him these uncharted seas over the rim of the map, these new lands of the north, were life's best gift. He has left us vivid pen-pictures of a very strange world.

Strange company, but good company, were the schooner's crew, now turned land-lubbers and hewers of wood. There was Hughie Young, head stockman, a skilled musician on every instrument under the Prince Regent moon; Philp du Bois, the French storekeeper, with his housekeeper wife; "Bill Johnson, sah, from Greenock", comic West Indian negro, *maestro* of the mouth-organ in tunes of all nations; Dan Darroch, a Hebridean sailor; Francisco Blanco from Spain; José Anto from Brazil; and a Chinaman cook.

Paddling through the mangroves at low tide they carried on their shoulders fifty tons of iron and stores. They built a little homestead of cypress pine, with the men's tents about it, and called the station Maragui. Across the bay of burnt red islands they could see the mouth of the Glenelg River, where the salt-water blacks had murdered the crew of a pearling lugger a few months before they landed.

Maragui kept an armed sentry on watch night and day. One night, Aeneas Gunn tells us, there was a queer mopoke concert in all the boab-trees, question and answer of owls in the moonlight. In the morning there were many tracks and the bottle-dump had vanished to make glass-head spears. These glass-head spears of Kimberley, delicately chipped with a quartz chisel and glittering like faceted beryl, are the most deadly of all. When the spear is pulled out, the splinters of glass remain in the wound.

Bradshaw bought four thousand sheep from Victoria River Downs when the Big Run gave up breeding them. Aeneas Gunn drove them over the border, and shipped them on the schooner at Wyndham in hurricane weather. Maragui was not a good country for sheep. In the dry its imposing forests and grasslands were prickle-bush and stones. In the wet, the cattle had to hook down the high grasses with their horns. Bradshaws were early routed, not by the blacks, nor the country, nor the isolation, but by red tape. West Australia imposed a stock tax of £2 a head on animals crossing the border. Though there was no surveyed border in the north, and the station a couple of thousand miles from where it mattered, this law was enforced. Rather than pay £9000 the brothers abandoned the run, and no one has taken it up since.

Cap'n Joe commissioned Captain Carrington, in *Red-gauntlet* with Aeneas Gunn as navigator, to reconnoitre the Western Territory coasts. They entered the lost world of the Victoria, and from Mosquito Flats north to Fitzmaurice River they called the fretted old hills and the Whirlwind Plains their own. A shack was run up on Ikymbon Creek, just where the explorer A. C. Gregory had camped his few sheep in the *Tom Tough* expedition. Aeneas Gunn drove the big flock back across the border, while the brothers moved everything round by sea—station buildings, windmills, furniture, sawmills, engines, stores—to begin again. They landed on the bank of the Victoria, under the Dome and across from Curiosity Peak. A third sentinel of the dun-coloured range, a sharp razorback hill frowning down on the river, was then without a name.

Shepherding their sheep from wild dogs, building the house, guarding the stores from wild blacks, so "Bradshaw's Buccaneers" formed Bradshaw's Run. Under their flag of all nations they enlisted a Russian named Egoriffe. Known to the whites as "Ivan the Russian", he became Ivan the Terrible to the blacks. His vicious tyranny and brutal treatment of the natives brought death to the white men of the outpost in one of the grimmest tragedies of the north.

The border-hopping sheep came to no good end, though their breed was improved with thirty-three of the stateliest rams from Victoria. They were worried by wild dogs and burnt in grass fires. In the first year they gave hundreds of bales of fine wool that was tossed by floods into the tops of the trees. The blacks stole the sheep-shears to make shovel-nose spears, and speared the rest of the sheep and ate them. So Bradshaw swung the station over to cattle, and looked for fresh fields.

Old Territorians ever lovingly remember Cap'n Joe. A member of the Melbourne Stock Exchange and Royal Melbourne Yacht Club, a man of financial integrity and far vision, in his smart little steam launch *Wunwulla* he led the way into many an unnamed inlet of North Australia, floated his companies on its sluggish mangrove tide. Ever a sailor, when he put on his "admiral's hat" the blacks knew he meant business.

Standing on *Wunwulla's* foredeck as though it were the bridge of a liner,

"Stand by, me lads," he'd bawl, "to heave up anchor!" or "Go out on the bowsprit, Mister, and make fast your jib." None of the crew wore trousers, not even Mister. Then the "Old Man" in weighty solemnity, would retire to the sanctuary of a stateroom two by two to write up his log, while the good ship *Wunwulla* grounded in the mud and tied up to a coongaberry bush. He was a Nelson tableau in the willie-willies, in sea-boots and sou'-wester, spy-glass to his eye . . . or in the Turner sunset of some tropic river, shouting "Hard aport!" to the blackfellow at the wheel, and aiming at a crocodile's eye with a Mauser pistol out of his belt.

The Run was a great success in the nineties, when Aeneas Gunn was manager—forty thousand cattle, Arab stallions and stock of high degree imported from the south and taking the five-hundred-mile trail from Darwin. Bradshaw's Buccaneers cantered the coast in their steam launch through the cyclones five or six times a year. They carried mail and medicine for lonely settlers, never a beacon on those dim shores to guide them. The exciting old diaries are still out there—history left to the white ants, as it is in so many towns and stations of the outback, much of it lost for ever. Headstones in that far-away graveyard tell of a number of men and two women who died far from help at Bradshaw's Run. Among them were Palmer, a stockman, once manager of a bank, who dived into the river and was mauled by a crocodile; also Mrs Pounds, who came across from Queensland with her husband in a dray, a married couple to a lonely job. In her last illness, no hope of medical care.

Another buried there is Hughie Young, who planted the boab-trees at Katherine from Victoria River nuts. He would ride in four hundred miles from Bradshaw's, and make for the piano in the pub where all others made for the bar. It was a poor crack-pot old piano, salvaged from the wreck of *Brisbane* in the eighties, but when Hughie played, the bearded bushmen, pipes in hand, would gather round him spellbound. What he played we do not know—it might have been Beethoven, or vamp, or *Maritana*. Music was not of their world, and all they remember is that Hughie could "make it speak". The piano was dusty and dumb when Hughie died of fever.

Aeneas Gunn, F.R.G.S., "the Maluka" of *We of the Never Never*, died at Elsey Station in 1903. In compliment to his wife's great book the Commonwealth Government has made an historic memorial park about that quiet bush grave that now is a tourist interest of the new Stuart Highway. Beyond the classic character portrayed by his wife as "the Maluka", little of Aeneas James Gunn is yet known. A great writer and historian was lost to Australia when his letters and diaries of exploration were thoughtlessly destroyed by a company winding up an estate. Worthless vouchers and receipts were carefully preserved, but Gunn's wealth of records was destroyed as personal and insignificant affairs. Stray passages of his graphic and poetic descriptive writing are still to be found in odd corners. Here is a word-etching of a mangrove swamp of Victoria River, written on a bush trail after black cattle-killers:

> It was an uncanny underworld, a vast shapeless vault of fantastic device of the gnarled and knotted trunks . . . slender buttresses fallen away in a long series of elliptical arches . . . a jungle cathedral conceived in delirium, and built by unseen, silent, thinking, feeling beings capable of action, the contorted boughs and branches stretching out hideous mud-stained arms to catch and hold one in their loathsome embraces.
>
> The atmosphere was stifling and hot, the silence intense, broken only by the gasping of shell-fish in the mud or clinging to the trunks of the mangroves. So still it was that one could almost hear the moisture exuding from the ooze, the sap coursing in the veins of the trees.
>
> No vista, no distance, no perspective, only the gnarled, knotted and twisted trunks, a tangle of boughs, branches and roots, roots, branches and boughs . . . above, a roof of leaden leaves, underfoot the noisome ooze of decaying leaves, roots, shells and mud.

And here is a human note, the death of Ebeemelloowooloomool, an "old man" of the Elsey:

> The king is dead. Long live the king.
>
> Old Ebeemelloowooloomool, alias Goggle-eye, is dead, king of the Elsey tribe. In his place reigns Tchunbah, alias Billy Muck.
>
> They were tired of the old man for a long time, and singing him dead—the aboriginal form of the curse of bell, book and candle in the dark ages. He was sung so that he might waste slowly to death. All food was sung so that it might not nourish him. His various organs were sung so that they could not perform their functions. The sun was sung so that it should not warm his wasted frame. The night was sung so that he should not sleep, the water that it might not quench his thirst. Other black-fellows were warned that if they gave him food and shelter, they would be sung dead.
>
> In his extremity, Goggle-eye dragged himself to the station camp to get the aid of the wonderful white people who could conquer everything but death. But it was too late. The curse had done its work. The white man's magic could only prolong for a few days a life fast ebbing away.
>
> Mrs Gunn took the chance of being sung, and gave him porridge and arrowroot, stayed beside him and comforted him with tobacco, but at cock-crow this morning the king was dead. It was suspected that he had been the cunning organiser of many a cattle-raid, and was not above running the rule over a traveller's swag.

The Maluka himself died at the Elsey soon after that little requiem was written, even there, in the wet season, beyond hope of medical aid.

Cap'n Joe was at that time in England, engaged in vast developmental schemes for the N.T., mainly for Arnhem Land. He had taken up Hodgson Downs on the Roper, Wollogorang in the Gulf, and the Arafura country at the mouth of the Goyder River for the Eastern, African and Cold Storage Company. His drovers were delivering tens of thousands of cattle, his coolies planting hundreds of acres of cotton and rice, and his new steam yacht *White Star* and launch *Bolwarra* were waking the Arafura shores to lively interest when a series of sensational events began at Bradshaw's Run.

The schooner *Twins* was sold and *Red-gauntlet* wrecked at Vashon Head. The only link with the station on the Victoria was the launch *Wunwulla*. With Ivan the Russian at the helm, Bradshaw's Buccaneers were sailing into danger.

One pearly morning the lugger *Minnehaha* from Darwin, ploughing the lower reaches of Daly River on her way to the Jesuit Mission and the copper-mine, discovered Ivan adrift in a dinghy without oars and without food. He alleged that blacks in the night had boarded *Wunwulla*, knocked him overboard with a murderous blow, then tomahawked old Larsen, killed the Victoria River crew, and seized the ship.

Constables Stone and Stott girded up their gun-belts and set out from Darwin for the Daly. They travelled first to the mission, and with the Jesuit fathers' good Christian boys and girls as guides and interpreters they cruised down-river interviewing the salt-water tribes. They pretended to be settlers looking for country, and they were "prop'ly good-fella" to the blacks, giving them plenty tea, sugar and tobacco for news.

In a camp-fire under the paperbarks they told Ivan's story and asked about the boat. The blacks came to light with full confession. Two strapping lads, Kammipur and Mungkum, proudly announced that they were the guilty party. Alone they did it.

A lubra called Eileen was interpreter for the police, one of Father O'Brien's most pious pupils, who never told a lie. Through her, the Daly boys said the white men had called them to bring women to the launch, promising tobacco, but no tobacco was paid out. So in a "little-bit row" they hit Ivan with a waddy. He jumped overboard, climbed into the dinghy, cut the painter and made off, leaving old Larsen to his fate—this item was true, for the painter was cut low down with a white man's knife. They then showed how they had killed Larsen and the three boys from Victoria River, and had thrown them to the crocodiles and scuttled the ship. They led the police to the battered and stripped *Wunwulla,* heeled over and hidden in the mangroves.

At the coroner's court in Darwin, Kammipur and Mungkum again confessed their guilt, and acted it all in detail. They were remanded to the Supreme Court on a charge of wilful murder. Ivan the Russian went home to Bradshaw's Run. He came back hot-foot with the surprising news that the Victoria boys, the crew of the launch, were the murderers of old Larsen.

They foot-walked home from the Daly, carrying bloodstained axes and gear from the ship, boasting round the camp that the hated Ivan and old Larsen were "finishem up dead-fella", and that Daly River blacks, merely lookers-on were going to be hanged.

Father O'Brien held a a long court of inquiry at the mission. He elicited the astounding fact that the Daly boys had given themselves up to fool the policemen, that Kammipur and Mungkum had put their necks in the noose for a joke on Stott, because "that fella too much gammon he savvy ebery-ting allabout". The whole river, including the mission blacks, was laughing at the corroboree of the mountie who got the wrong man.

A similar incident once happened on the Roper where a tribe in possession of shirts, knives and tin dishes gave such a convincing reconstruction of their brutal murder of two prospectors that they were arrested. They were chained to trees at Roper River, awaiting transport to Darwin, when the "murdered" men walked in—they had given their gear to the blacks. Truly, these innocents should never be tried in our courts.

The Daly jest had a terrible sequel. Not to be fooled again, Mounted Constable Stott landed his police party at Bradshaw's Run. The launch boys vanished. He rode to find them, and Ivan the Russian rode with him. They caught Little George along the river, and tied the boy to a post at the station. They daylighted the tribes for Dick, and galloped him down through a mob of sixty wild blacks, all armed with spears. Then Stott and his tracker Dandy set out for the citadels of the old red hills to hunt down Big George, the ringleader. Over the raw, stony ridges . . . down into the crumbling ravines . . . and up the cliffs where horses had no hope, they travelled for days on foot, following the wild man to his lair over a hundred miles away, by the blown ashes of a fire, a faint footprint, a broken twig.

Suddenly they faced him. Big George was crouched in a rift of the cliff, eyes wide with hate and terror, spears and wommera in his hand. He leapt five feet down under cover of a crag, and turned on them, raising a spear, but his foothold was slipping and his marksmanship bad. The spear slashed into the dust.

Dandy fired. Big George sprang forty feet down the face of the cliff, stumbled twice and, leaving a trail of blood, staggered for the scrub. Dandy fired again. Big George shot forward and pitched on his head dead.

Dick and Little George were taken in chains to Darwin, and Dick was condemned to be hanged at the scene of the crime, as an example to his people. A gallows tree was rigged at Bradshaw's Run. The blacks all fled. Trackers went out but the hills were empty. The policeman was due back in Darwin, so the boy was strung up for the entertainment of the white men while they sat at breakfast. Ivan the Russian enjoyed that joke, but there was no laughter among the blacks along Victoria River.

In December 1905 Cap'n Joe came back from his tour of the world with promise of boundless capital, energy and hope for the transformation of Arnhem Land. First item in the programme was that his brother Fred should meet him with the launch *Bolwarra*, and take him home for a Christmas reunion at Bradshaw's Run. Day after day Cap'n Joe waited, as everything waits in Darwin, but the launch *Bolwarra* did not come. Then Postmaster Little opened a telegram from the postmaster at Brock's Creek:

TERRIBLE TRAGEDY FEARED MASSACRE OF WHITE MEN ALL BELIEVED DEAD AT BRADSHAW'S RUN.

It was true. Only Williams, the cook at the station, survived. Fred Bradshaw and the three other white men had been slaughtered weeks ago on *Bolwarra* as she lay at anchor in Port Keats. Two drovers, Benning and Flinders, had first heard rumour from a Victoria River black-boy who was frightened, and ran away.

The launch had left the station on 12th November, the cook alone at the Run. Fred Bradshaw, Ernest Dannock, a stockman, and Ivan Egoriffe were aboard her, with an Ikymbon River crew. As usual they ran across to Auvergne to see if there was an errand of mercy they could do for that station in Darwin. There was. Jerry Skeehan, head stockman, had broken his arm in the stockyard, and set out only that morning, with the bone protruding, on a two-hundred-mile ride to the doctor in Wyndham. As the launch trip to Darwin would be less painful, with hospital attention there, *Bolwarra* waited while black-boys rode thirty miles, bringing Skeehan back to join the ship of death.

At this time, following the suggestions of H. Y. L. Brown, the noted geologist, who had discovered traces of coal reefs on Victoria River, there was a Government boring party of seven white men putting down a drill at Port Keats. The launch, on her journey down-river, put in there, to find the southerners terrified at the mischievous mood of the blacks all round them. They were stealing knives and axes, and the day before had burgled one of the huts, hopping off with everything, including some family photographs and washing left soaking in a bucket. They were all about the camp now, appearing and disappearing in the bush.

On the sunny beaches of Port Keats, over a hundred naked warriors were on the move, with spears and without their women and children, a bad sign. Ivan said he recognized many runaways from the station. Jerry Skeehan, with his arm in a sling, warned the borers to "look out",—he "didn't like the look of things at all".

When Fred Bradshaw pulled back to the launch, the crew had deserted. He and Ivan went back with guns to find them, and failed, so they hijacked five Port Keats boys, and took them to the ship, in leg-irons. The boring party kept a watch that night, but the prehistoric army had vanished. That was all they knew.

The launch was lost and the hunt was on.

Inspector Waters himself, in *Wai Hoi*, with a big posse of police and trackers, sailed from Darwin for the Victoria in storms of the wet. Two luggers, *Coral* and *Turquoise*, borrowed from a pearler, scoured the low yellow-red cliffs covered with ant-hills and stunted scrub rising to thick jungle. At Cape Dombey they saw a naked blackfellow with a suitcase and an umbrella up, streaking along the beach like Apollo out of the Art Gallery running to catch a train. Trackers landed and ran for miles, but the trail was lost in jungle. All they found was a frying-pan hidden in the vines.

Troopers at the bore camp had better luck. In a mangrove swamp by lightning they heard a shrill cooee and ambushed eight blacks, great sleek men with many tribal scars and kangaroo teeth twisted into their hair. Among them were Kumbit and Dongbol, two of Bradshaw's boys from the launch.

With revolvers at those glistening backs, the police marched them miles into the bore camp. When they saw the chains and handcuffs there was a mad rough-and-tumble. Champion natural wrestlers with trick grips and oiled bodies, the police were no match for them—they were gone, but before they reached the beach two were shot dead. Another dived into the sea and escaped through a hail of bullets and a big funnel tide running. Three raced along the beach for the jungle, their leisurely lope swifter than the wind—the running stride of one man's footprint in the sand measured nine feet.

Of the eight prisoners, only two remained—a remarkable stand for the Stone Age, unarmed. The two were chained to a tree, and a two-hour watch was kept. In the brutal third-degree of the bush, they were tied so that they could not sleep and were given no water. At last they told the story of the Bradshaw massacre in dumb show.

The launch had anchored at Cape Scott on the night of the murder—(long sinuous arms and pursed lips pointed to Cape Scott). Ivan the Russian (a moustache) and Fred Bradshaw (a pointed beard) rowed ashore to a native well on the beach there, dipping water with a billy into a bucket. The angry blacks crept along the shore from Port Keats following the ship and their kidnapped friends. They sent a shower of spears at them through the trees ("*Swish! Swish!*") The white men fired ("*Boong! Boong!*") Then they rowed back to the launch, and pulled down a little way, the blacks slinking after them along the shore.

That night *Bolwarra* slept with all lights burning. The kidnapped boys were in leg-irons and no watch was kept. About twenty blackfellows (fingers of both hands opened and closed twice) swam out and climbed on board. They clubbed Ivan the Russian to death where he was lying with three of the blacks in the engine-room, aft. Skeehan and Dannock were waddied on the head through their mosquito-nets on the prow. Fred Bradshaw, sleeping in the hold, stood up and looked out. He was felled by a stone axe. The blacks then loosed the leg-irons from their comrades, and plundered the ship, taking everything ashore in the dinghy, even the lamps still burning. The boys pointed to where the scuttled ship would be found.

On Christmas Day, in a dreary vista of paperbark swamp and mangrove, the ghost of *Bolwarra* lay with bloodstained decks and smashed compass, fretfully tossing in the tide. On the previous Christmas Day, at Cap'n Joe's farewell party before he left for England, the pretty little launch had carried all fashionable Darwin to a picnic down the harbour, queening it over the pearling luggers with her newfangled engine. The proud old master mariner "out of sail" was extolling the speed of those modern engines and the beauty of her twentieth-century lines. Now on this desolate beach, as he kept vigil beside her, a savage came out on the heights above, insolently waving her Union Jack.

With the turn of the spring tides the bodies of the white men were washed in—little more than a few bones. Cap'n Joe was chief mourner at the strangest funeral ceremony ever known in Australia. The coffins of crude beer-case, with naked blacks as pall-bearers, were carried up the shadowless cliffs to the crest of the nameless hill, for ever after known as Bradshaw's Tomb. Looking down on a lost world of eerie splendour, it recalls the resting-place of Cecil Rhodes on the Matoppo Hills.

After another long man-hunt of swamp and range, five salt-water tribes of Victoria River were represented at the trial in Darwin. Tall, powerful men with long womanish hair and strangely intellectual and benevolent faces, they looked round the court with the startled eyes of trapped animals. Kujuru of the Alleluyia was their head man, their counsel, a wise old Moses with a flowing white beard. Through an interpreter, he told of the cruelty to his people for many years by Ivan the Russian. That was their salvation. Two boys, Kumbit and Dongbol, known on the station as Calico and Blanket, with Mybilla and other Ikymbon boys of the launch who had led the murdering-party, were sentenced to imprisonment for life.

For Cap'n Joe, the death of his brother Fred and of his friend and cousin, Aeneas Gunn, at the Elsey, were the beginning of the end. In two unlucky years eleven thousand of his cattle were speared by blacks and lost in the swamps of Arafura, crippled by the curious blue mud of the Goyder River plains that in the wet season expanded in their hoofs and burst their feet. Although the river-flats were ideal for tropical agriculture, with their phenomenal all-the-year-round rainfall, Chinamen were attacked while planting and ploughing, and many of them killed. The station was abandoned through the ferocity of the blacks, and within a few years there was not a stick of it left.

The Elsey, Hodgson Downs and Wollogorang were later sold. When the leaky old steamer *Wai Hoi* fell to pieces a second time, the Government replaced her for the Borroloola run by buying Cap'n Joe's *White Star*. She was the darling of his heart, but he had little heart now. The Eastern, African and Cold Storage Company in London had written off Cap'n Joe and North Australia. There remained to him only Bradshaw's Run, but his Arab foals were worried to death by the wild dogs, and soon it was just one of many cattle stations on a rapidly falling market. With various managers, the fine old pioneer spent his last years out there. His first manager, Byers, riding out to the station with a mate, sat under a tree in the heat of the day, dizzy with fever. When he did not come on, his mate rode back. He had vanished from this earth, and they found not a track.

The Dome and Curiosity Peak still look down on Bradshaw's Run as far out of the world as ever—the Fogarty boys, Territory born and bred, are there now. Though it had its share of tragedy, the remote station was not a melancholy one. At one time it was known as "the Singing Homestead", a joke of the north.

When Ivan the Russian was killed by the blacks he had just completed a water supply and irrigation system, a mile of pipes leading to a spring in the range—not for Cap'n Joe the time-honoured Australian laziness of a lubra with a bucket. Byers arrived out there to find the homestead badly white-anted, and for his wife and family began to build a new one. For beams and uprights he had the bright idea of using Ivan's old iron pipes.

The new house, with its white-ant-proof beams and foundations, looked fine . . . but one dark night, in the first storms of the wet, it broke into a deafening chorale and town-hall-organ tooting to the skies. Every hollow pipe was packed with frogs that hibernated in the dry and came to life in the wet.

Tenor, soprano, alto, bass, the glee club hammered away night after night, quaver, crotchet, minim and breve, triangle, oboe and bassoon. The white people, living in a bell foundry, went mad for lack of sleep. They moved into the store, leaving their new house to nightly revels all through the wet.

The blacks of the station, Numba, Minda and Alleluyia, fled in fear to the ranges. With all the devils of the rain and the dark, Ivan the Russian had come back in his pipes. He was singing them . . . singing them dead.

Chapter XVIII

White Ants

OLD HANDS of the Territory love to look back on "the good old South Australian days" of friendliness and freedom, but the callous neglect of the last five years of South Australia's administration was a national crime. So long was the new Commonwealth in adopting into the family its brilliant but unmanageable child that South Australia, without responsibility, left it to the wild dogs and the myalls.

From 1890 till 1905 the white population had hovered around two thousand. In 1908 it had fallen to a thousand, seven hundred of these about Darwin and Pine Creek. The rest were scattered out in the void, with no regular transport of food supplies and mails. In the whole Territory not ten miles of road were passable in the wet season, and no ship on the coast was worthy of the name.

Outside Darwin there might have been ten white women, a thousand miles apart, in the half million square miles.

There was only one doctor, in Darwin—death still their familiar. There was a madman a year for nine years, fourteen deaths from thirst, murder fourteen, suicides ten, accidents twenty-four.

Mr Justice C. E. Herbert was Administrator, vainly knocking at the gates of Governments while his people died unburied. Down south, Australia was a self-confident young nation, precocious in cities. Up north it was stark tragedy in oblivion—"that great and glorious north", to quote the newspaper clichés, "with its mighty tracts of pastoral lands unrivalled in the world, the boundless agricultural resources of its countless rivers, its mineral wealth unknown".

There was no labour whatever. Thousands of able-bodied Chinese had been sent back to China, leaving only the opium wrecks, a few patriarchs and the young Australian-born, who started laundries, stores and tailor-shops in Darwin, stores in the tiny settlement towns. Hang Gon's Wheel of Fortune at West Arm, where, with thirty Chinese, he had mined £20,000 in tin, was buried under jungle mould. Owners of tin and gold shows in the hills worked their mines themselves. Humorously known as "Ah Bell" and "Ah Brown", they worked like coolies, humping their water in shoulder-tins, dressed in cabbage-tree hats.

Down on the Daly, with three thousand tons of ore on the surface, the Government smelter was idle, waiting for spare parts that never came. The blacks picked over the dumps, loaded the ore into an old canoe, tipped in a few buckets of water and agitated it round, threw the best copper into a barrow and wheeled it to the heap on the bank to wait for a lugger that might come in three months' time. Once she was stranded on a sandbank for a fortnight, all passengers starving, a woman and child aboard.

The Government party boring for coal at Port Keats struck promising shale, then lost their rods, waited months for more, then ran out of food and drifted away.

Dead weight of years dragged on in false faith and fantastic rumour. Alan Davidson's journals and H. Y. L. Brown's reports brought occasional epidemics of mineral madness, prospectors far afield. Gleam of silver, smell of oil in a paperbark swamp, glister of gold where cannibals dance, could bring them riding a thousand miles . . . in the poor body's weariness and thirst forgetting their quest, and forgotten.

Near Wandi, W. A. Thompson discovered rich deposits of an unknown mineral that proved to be wolfram, then realizing a price in Queensland of £105 a ton. He sold the mine to W. H. Brock who, with three men in crude mining and bagging, made £12,720 from the claim that year. Brown, Burns and Coggin, at the Crest of the Wave near Pine Creek, found hundreds of tons of wolfram on the surface, the biggest tungsten drift in Australia.

There was a silver-lead rush to Boolman in Arnhem Land in a sixteen-foot lugger, a radium rush of five on packhorses to Tanumbirini Lagoons of the Limmen River. A man named Hedley set out to find El Dorado at Cape Wilberforce with notes of an old diary in the Adelaide Lands Department, written by a Sindbad named Raymond forty years before. According to Raymond, those mythical Arnhem Land beaches were "scattered thick with quartz studded with gold." Hedley had no luck. His lugger was swamped in a squall. Another party, on the mere wind of the word "auriferous" in H. Y. L. Brown's reports, made out west to Fitzmaurice River with two savage dogs—that barked them up one daylight in time to see a band of warriors hopping at them with spears. What happened to the warriors is not stated. The party spent five weeks on the river, and found colours of gold but no more.

The Administrator pleaded for the appointment of a metallurgist to identify specimens, for the diggers were always finding new metals and minerals—they tried to identify arsenic by grinding it up and tasting the powder! No battery in the north was in working order. Two cargoes of ore were shipped five thousand miles to Adelaide to be crushed. Bearded hermits were "sitting down" on copper shows all over the Territory from Wollogorang on the Queensland border to Bradshaw's Run, where the myalls brought in coolamons of stones showing tin, silver, lead, tantalite, tourmalines and gold.

There was always gold—mad hatters out in the ranges for ever "chasing the weight". Any blackfellow from Pine Creek to Arltunga, with a tin dish in the bed of a creek could wash three pennyweights a day, collecting an ounce a week in a bottle to bring to the nearest fossicker for a stick of tobacco or a two-shilling piece to buy opium ash out of a Chinaman's pipe.

These shameful two-shilling pieces for the past forty years have been a depraved white man's traffic to the black for the loan of his woman, for his labour and his gold. More than once, storekeepers have shown me the pennies that come in, coated with silver to trick the ignorant black foot-walking for hundreds of miles to spend them at the store.

Gold is never "where you find it" to the Australian digger, but always far away. Down in the dim deserts below Wave Hill, at Tanami Rockhole—Chan-a-mee—nearly a thousand miles south-west of Darwin, a rift in the red sands where the wild blacks crept in on hands and knees to drink at a pool in the boulders, Alan Davidson, in 1900, had marked X for treasure. Travelling west from Tennant's Creek, where he sank two hopeful shafts, a blackfellow led him to Tanami Rockhole, and was killed by his tribe for showing it. Davidson dollied a few stones hurrying through, and reported a leader of twenty ounces to the ton.

Eight years later Bill and Jack Lawrie, with "Little Jack" Brown, hoppled out their horses to scour that wilderness of scalded earth for gold. Seventeen miles south-west of the rockhole they scratched a thousand ounces—three hundred ounces in one hit of the pick, and the next uncovered a nugget weighing one pound.

Mulga wires raced them to civilization. Sixty men and two hundred horses came in a nine days' rush from Hall's Creek, one of the madmen's tracks of Australia, no water in the last two hundred miles from Gordon Downs. In the shade of the solitary bean-tree they threw down their swags and began to crack up the boulders. The Lawries' shaft, eighteen feet down, was, in the grand old phrase of gold, "a jeweller's shop". All eyes turned to Tanami. Lionel Gee, the mining warden, came out five hundred and fourteen miles from Katherine on a bicycle, through Wave Hill and Inverway and south through nothing but that lair of the myalls, Frog Valley, to declare and control a goldfield, and to pay over Lawries' Reward.

When the rush of men and horses drank the rockhole dry, Bill and Jack Lawrie carried their shovels from the golden claim to dig a well of sweet, dark, evil water a hundred feet deep, soon putrid with vermin and the carcasses of wild dogs. Many died looking for that well.

George Doyle fell dead from his horse, of sunstroke. Bryant, a mining agent, was found thirty-six miles out. Bannigan put himself nicely to sleep among his saddles, neatly tucked in his bush net, and in the throes of thirst shot himself. Stephen Pearce died of fever. Frayne perished. At the Granites, seventy miles south, Stuart was speared for his trousers and his gun. Barnes and Leahy were speared at their little gold show in the turpentine scrub, and Jack Rooney, chipping away at a reef alone ninety miles south-west, was knocked on the head by a waddy. They covered the country, those "woolly-nosed prospectors" of Tanami and the west. New generations will take a fair while to beat their farthest-out.

There were two women in the rush—Mrs May Brown, six hundred and fifty miles in a buggy from Pine Creek; Mrs Christina Gordon, the Grand Old Lady of Darwin, who travelled with her husband, his twin brother and her two young sons, Cookie and Wallie, in a spring-cart with goats and fowls over a thousand miles to Tanami from Bamboo Creek in West Australia. The diggers shared their precious water and moved off from the bean-tree to give the women the only shade.

Mrs Brown returned early to her wolfram at Pine Creek, but Mrs Gordon stayed. Such is the rare chivalry of the Australian miner and bushman that the Lawries, leaving for Sydney to knock down their reward, called the two Gordons aside:

"While we're away," they said, "you can have all the gold you can get out of our claim. We've got plenty. You take it for the missus and the kids."

Of thousands who have known and loved Mrs Christina Gordon in her many years as proprietress of the Victoria Hotel in Darwin—and many world-famous names were written in her visitor's book—few heard the stories she might tell of a heroine's life on Australia's trails of gold. Regal, gentle and kind, as she listened to all the adventure stories from air, land and sea, she never told her own. She crossed the continent more than once in a buggy, with her young sons on her knee. Through later life she was the friend of all Darwin, and, after the war, returned to the ruined seaport with the first of its faithful, ready to begin again at the age of eighty years. We shall ever remember her Mona Lisa smile.

Tom Pearce put down the wells on the track from Katherine to Tanami. With nine well-sinkers, two black-boys, two carts and a cook it was a six months' crossing for his five camels, cutting down trees for a road till trees faded into shrubs and bald desert. The first well was forty miles south of Wave Hill, and he sank two others in the next hundred and fifty miles. He found five hundred men on the field, their well and rockhole nearly dry, and worked day and night to sink another to save them. They beat the vanishing rockhole by three days.

For twenty-two months Tanami lived on bandicoots and flour, sometimes they caught a wallaby at the rockhole. There was never any meat or milk—goats perished on the way to the place. When a man came in with a bullock-team they levelled a rifle and shot the leader on sight, cut him in hunks and gorged on fresh meat, all violently ill from rich tucker for three days. They were crouched in spinifex huts in the unmerciful heat.

It was seven hundred miles to a doctor. "If you pulled your shoulder out," said Tom Pearce, "you pulled it in again and went on digging. If it was sickness, you died. We had boiled flour for dysentery, and a tin of corned beef fat for healing ointment. One man started a little garden of pumpkins and seven-year beans after we put down the well, but it was too late, they were all rotten with Barcoo rot. Later on, a couple of horse-teams went out there with stores, and bum-boats with grog, and that was the finish. White men couldn't weather it. There was only the track from Gordon Downs and the one from Wave Hill—no road from the Alice those days. In two years the first rush was starved out and gone."

So much for the mineral "wealth".

Agricultural lands, offered forty years before at 3s. 9d. an acre, were down to 1s. 9d. For a while there was interest. Maurice Holtze had been appointed Curator of Adelaide Botanic Gardens, his son Nicholas curator of Darwin in his stead. He won high praise in 1908 from the British Cotton-growing Association for twelve varieties of Territory cotton. He could not recommend it as a crop, for though there were mobs of singing darkies, they were not of the cotton-picking kind. He did recommend rice, which on the river-flats never failed—a Chinaman could throw out a handful and reap a harvest. Also, studying markets, he recommended tobacco, sisal hemp, arrowroot; patchouli and citronella for perfume oils, indigo for blue, anatta for dye; the coca plant, six feet high in the Territory and seeding several times a year, for cocaine; also cloves and cola nut. Had he thought of Coca-Cola, he might have made a fortune for the poverty-stricken north.

On the north coast at Shoal Bay, W. B. F. Pruen started a cotton plantation. A quaint Kentucky it was, his canvas house in a kapok grove of bright blossom and bursting pods of leafless trees against the jade of mangrove swamps and the white curve of beaches, north and west a sweep of lonely sea. There was a brushwood fence to the plantation, where cotton-shrubs were soon seven feet high, and a glittering forest of coconut palms swept down to the water's rim. Pruen was an Englishman, much-travelled and well-read. Living there quite alone, working with his blacks by day, studying botany by candlelight to the barking of crocodiles in the salt creek near by, he built a little wharf, and sheds of iron and cypress pine for storing, ginning and baling. He ordered a hand-gin to weave his cotton, and wrote to Liverpool to arrange a market. In the second year a tidal wave washed everything away. Pruen stayed there till the end of his life in 1938—a white man's ghost under the rags of coconut-trees.

Paddy Cahill took up the fertile lagoon lands of Oenpelli, and planted acres of sisal hemp, with a sturdy homestead for his wife in the wilds of East Alligator River. Upland rice was thriving on five half-hearted plantations between Darwin and Adelaide River, and a couple of optimists at Katherine, with Government assistance, started an experimental farm. They planted wheat, oats and barley, which grew to perfection till August and withered in September. The optimists were discovered "gone troppo" in their shack with no tools and nothing to eat.

Roberts and Thomas started tobacco on the Daly, in fine style with a house built on piles. The Mulluk Mulluk helped them to fence twenty-four acres of promising sprouts, brought them fish, game, eggs and yams, and put up the sheds for curing and drying. In "beautiful loams twenty feet deep of inexhaustible fertility" they planted also rice, rubber, arrowroot and maize, all doing well, and raised goats, fowls, pigs and horses, making ensilage of the grasses for their stock. Of their first tobacco-curing, they made tribute to the Old Man of the Mulluk Mulluk, a connoisseur in tobacco.

"Py Crise, good-fella!" he said.

In November the Old Man and his people were dead in droves in their wurleys from eating rotten fish from the squalid river pools . . . and in February the Daly rose ninety feet, washed the settlers out of their houses, and swept away the farms.

History repeated itself with the same fiendish precision . . . every year the wet, imprisonment, mould, the labyrinth of the long grasses, a wide world of waters . . . every year the perish plains, dazzle of brown stones, the grass fires. The blacks exulted in burning out the game, and the white men no longer cared. In any case the flood and the jungle would take all their labour. *Nature was never cut and trimmed to man's little pattern of profit and loss in this passionate land that held their hearts in thrall with the pagan glory of its rolling jungles, its silences, its freedom. They were married to it for better or worse, in the acquired taste of their own solitary life and the joys of eternal roaming.* Wanderlust . . . walkabout disease . . . call it what you will. They called it "ridin' around".

The age of wheels was coming—a flash of headlights through the dark. Dutton and Aunger, in 1908, were first across the continent by motor-car from Adelaide to Darwin in an English Clement-Talbot with twenty mechanical horses under the bonnet to spurt them over the gibber plains, jib in the sandhills, bog in the creeks, jump through the MacDonnell Ranges and canter the spinifex downs. Lost to sight in the lancewood scrubs, rearing at ant-hills, diving into rivers thirty feet steep and roaring out of them to wind through jungle green, they put two thousand three hundred miles behind them in many a lone night-camp to open a motor-car road across Australia. Their horseless carriage a wreck, they trundled at last through the lily lagoons to Darwin. The bushmen said they were mad. Pack-bells ringing by all the rivers would be the Territory's theme song for a long time yet.

Other trans-Australia pilgrims followed—Francis Birtles, aged twenty-five, described as an artist from Melbourne, with his camera strapped to his bicycle. It was his first appearance in the outback, of which he became a lifetime photographer and writer. Also on bicycles came the O'Neill brothers and Blakeney, fifteen hundred miles from the opal-fields of White Cliffs, the tale told long after by Fred Blakeney in a good book, *Hard Liberty*.

It was a literary year for the inarticulate north. A modest book was published in London, a series of rare descriptions and portraits from a lost land in Australia, weaving the story of a woman's happiness into that bright pattern of the Territory bush. Best-loved of all Australian books for the next three generations, it was *We of the Never Never*, by Mrs Aeneas Gunn.

Pastoral settlement was at a standstill except for one brave family, the Bohnings, who came from a thousand miles away in Queensland in a spring-dray to take up the country of Helen Springs above Banka Banka, and build a homestead that was Australia's farthest-out. Today the run is right on the Stuart Highway, but the family, educated by the mother, lived out of the world for years. Among them was Elsie Bohning, whose poems and writings in childhood, for a newspaper two thousand miles away, are still remembered in the Territory from when she was "A Little Bush Maid".

Darwin had settled into mould. Nothing had been rebuilt since the cyclone except a very good jetty of West Australian jarrah. The children went to school at peril of their lives—school, teachers and scholars might any day collapse in a white-anted heap. Every roof in the town leaked, every house decayed. The Residency was not fit for a white woman to live in—the Resident slept on the veranda. The hospital was a nest of open drains, nurses paddled in the wards in the wet. There was still no sanitation, no water supply. Slums of Chinatown would have embarrassed an Asiatic city. As the medical officer pointed out, the tropical clime of North Australia must be particularly healthy, for Darwin was always free of contagious diseases where any normal community would have been wiped out by plague.

The faculty of philosophy in Darwin's university, if ever it has one, will include a post-graduate course in cynical humour. Its people could always laugh at their plight in the bandy old houses under the bougainvilleas, furniture falling, piano a hollow shell, cupboards alive with Singapore ants. To drive a tack to hang up a picture was to bring the whole caboose about your ears.

Now and again Joel Cooper brought a cargo of cypress pine from Melville Island in his lugger *Buffalo* to Sam Olsen, the carpenter, hand-sawing in his shack near Gulnare Jetty. Sam's ambition was "a modest little engine and a saw-pit", but nobody had any money to pay him. Newcomers built their houses of scrap-iron and kerosene tins. To gladden their hearts there were beautiful tropic gardens and vivid blossoming trees, all grown in hollow logs or in tubs standing on sheets of iron, safe from white ants. When the big storms came, they hastily moved the garden to a sheltered side of the house.

Tricksy beams of hurricane lamps were the only harbour lights, and people farewelling the ship often fell from the jetty among the crocodiles and sharks. When *Chang-sha* landed two white women it was hailed by the newspaper as "the most important addition to European population in the Territory recorded in a long time". The only steady increase in population were the Chinese smuggled down from Singapore with a bribe to cook and steward, or a false back to the bunk. The most profitable import trade for years was opium, thrown overboard in crates of tins with a floater at Point Charles, picked up by Chinese fishermen, passed on to coolies at the mines and carried overland, hidden in swags and accordions for seven hundred miles from Katherine to Cloncurry. From there it travelled three thousand miles in passengers' luggage by train to Sydney's Campbell Street or Melbourne's Little Bourke, a long roundabout for the drug of dreams never suspected by the interstate police.

Someone foretold a fortune for buffalo-leather boots—high, wide and handsome, so tough they never wear out. Billy Grote, a sailor, and Fred de Warr, a blacksmith, between Mount Norris Bay and Raffles Bay shot a thousand buffaloes and tanned the hides for a conditional market in London, sales depending on samples. It was a hungry year of hard work in a shack, not even a horse to help them. They burnt coral for lime and made a good job of the tanning with wattle and black mangrove. At the end of the year they shipped their hides to Darwin on the little schooner *Kingston*—she was never heard of again.

A. J. V. Brown remembers another Arnhem Land enterprise of the time. "About 1906," he told me, "a German steamer with German officers but owned by Chinese in Hong Kong, was chartered by de Courcy Hamilton, who took out timber rights for cutting cypress pine in Malay Bay, which I had leased. I gave them an axe licence and they were to give me royalties of 1s. a log—they had a contract for three thousand logs. Hamilton brought his wife out from Darwin to get the timber ready, and they built bark houses and lived for a few months on that lonely beach—she was one of the only two white women we ever saw on that coast. Charlie Pfitzner, Paddy Cahill, Joe Cooper, Billy Johnson and I were all around at the time, and there was no fear of wild blacks.

"They sent the Chinamen in to cut the timber and pile it on the beach, but pulling big logs they couldn't get within two miles of the shore and were such a long time doing it that the twelve days the steamer was allowed were up, the demurrage so high that they couldn't pay it. The steamer went off with five hundred logs instead of three thousand. Hamilton and his missus were stranded there till I took them, with the coolies, in to Darwin. Before the steamer left the captain died, and the second mate stowed away on my schooner. In burning-off the blacks burnt all the timber they left piled on the beach."

Roads had gone back to jungle and sea-tracks were lost at sea. *Lone Hand*, a little oil launch, went out to Victoria River about twice a year, and *White Star* to the Roper and Borroloola till her Captain Harry Lawson took up one of the Goulburn Islands for stock-breeding and landed there with a flock of goats. *Wai Hoi* was put on the run, a lumbering old trader from Rhio Straits. On her first trip she failed to find the Roper—a cyclone had blown down the landmarks and altered the coast for miles, so with mails and cargo undelivered she came back to Darwin, leaving the settlers down there to starve on cabbage-top and kangaroo. On her next trip, carrying silver-lead ore from Borroloola, she ran up on a sandbank in the Roper, and stayed there for three years. The crew came back on packhorses three hundred miles.

Goats were a white hope of industry. Alf Brown stocked Croker Island with a colony of pure-bred Angoras from the stud of a Californian "Uncle Sam", and Tom Flynn introduced them to Adelaide River. Several companies were formed for breeding Angora goats, but they were killed for tucker before they came to mohair.

In 1908 the first packhorse mail set out for Victoria River Downs. Urgent telegrams regarding the sale of stock were carried by packhorse courier from Wyndham or Katherine at a delivery cost of £25, and well worth it, an eight-hundred-mile round trip, three weeks' hard riding with luck, a night-watch for bad blacks and carry your own water. It was world's record for a telegram boy and something of *A Message to Garcia*, a wire for V.R.D.

Another classic of that track was the death of Jock McPhee. Madrill, the mailman, passed a white man's camp deserted, pack-saddles and swags. A tin match-box, set up on a stick, was scrawled with a pin, "I will be back with water". Half a mile on a dead man was a moving mass of flies, gripped in one shrivelled hand a purse of notes and gold. A pair of trousers, a water-bag and a hat were found in a wide circle. The mailman rode on to Willeroo.

There Tom Pearce told him that Jock McPhee, with four horses, had left ten days before, and with him a sick man, a foot-walker named Schwarz from a little tin show at Golden Gully—to see the doctor in Darwin he was carrying his swag two hundred and sixty miles to the railway at Pine Creek. Jock McPhee went with him to help him, and gave him a horse to ride, but the horse, with hopples and bells on, had come back. The dead man was Schwarz—his friends at Golden Gully said he had a mother somewhere, but nobody knew where.

A search party set out to look for Jock McPhee, "Tam o' Shanter" in *We of the Never Never*, one of the greatest bushmen of the north. Twenty years before he had led the Kimberley gold rush to Hall's Creek, and he knew every mile of this western country.

They found him at Scott's Creek—a foot in a boot, ribs, a shoulder-blade, farther away a head. The wild dogs had found him first. His worldly goods were a keep-sake threepence, a Browning revolver and a pocket-knife. Scott's Creek was dry. He had perished looking for water for a mate, and his grave is there.

A year later the same mailman found a pair of trousers on the track. He knew they were white man's trousers for in the pocket was a plug of tobacco, and no blackfellow would throw tobacco away. Tracks led him to a couple of skeletons sitting together under a tree, the bones picked clean by crows, the swags eaten by white ants. They were Temple and W. E. G. Cockburn, last seen riding donkeys in to the Katherine from Willeroo.

The exiled women of Darwin in 1908 were among the first in the world to vote, for South Australia led the Empire in women's franchise. A school of ten scholars was opened at Pine Creek, first school outside Darwin, its teacher Mrs Niemann. Two or three drovers brought their families up from Katherine to camp on "the royal road". For white children only, its orbit widened in a peculiar way.

The swarms of young Chinese in Darwin had never attended Government school—they lived, dressed, and talked Chinese. Their acclimatization as Australians began at Pine Creek. The teacher who followed Mrs Niemann—we shall call her Miss Trim—boarded with a railway fettler who thrashed his wife. Miss Trim complained to the police. The fettler's revenge was subtle and original. He interviewed an old Chinese storekeeper with twenty-seven grandchildren running with the chickens through the shop, and brought to his notice the beneficent British rule that made the trousered hopefuls Young Australians, entitled to attend school—in fact, breaking the law if they did not attend school. He told him to pass on the word.

On Monday morning Miss Trim was indignant when a mob of small-size Orientals stormed her citadel and squatted on the schoolhouse floor. She bundled the lot of them home. That set fire to all the crackers in Pine Creek. The fettler wired the Administrator, who informed Miss Trim that the fettler was right—no teacher could refuse to teach the Australian-born. For Miss Trim it was resignation or—resignation.

So Darwin Public School doubled its attendance, all the little Wings and Hops with their earnest clever faces coming to lisp their ABC. For thirty years afterwards, teachers of infinite patience taught them to speak English, awarded them prizes for dux of the school and transformed them into the present generation of mechanics, warehousemen, secretaries, and clerks that are Darwin Chinese today.

The convent was established in that year, with sisters gentle and kind to reclaim the half-caste children from the blacks' camps, and find them a place in the world. Roper River Mission was founded by the Church of England, in the "Hundred of Flint and Glynne"—away in that wilderness they still held to the old South Australian land divisions.

From Humbert River far west came the beard of "Brigalow Bill". Brigalow Bill was a bagman of idle life and a long black beard. He "travelled a lubra" named Judy, horse-girl and slave. A drover stole her away, with his blacks and his plant, a thousand miles to her homeland, Borroloola. In the lovely river-world of the Macarthur Judy married her "proper boy". But Brigalow Bill was on her track. He followed to Borroloola and whipped her back. He had to tie her up at night, she was always running away. They rode a thousand miles to Humbert River, where he built a hut. One day, going down for water, Judy slipped the white man's revolver into her bucket, and sat by the billabong, silently talking finger-yabber into the dense scrub.

Brigalow was burning off round the hut when the blacks circled in with their shovel-nose spears. He raced to the hut for his gun, but it was gone. A firestick flew into the thatch and the hut burst into flame. Brigalow ran, and they riddled him with spears.

A year or so later Mudgella and Wolgarora boys were brought in chains to Darwin. Brigalow's body was never found, but among the exhibits on the courtroom table was a bull-roarer strung on long black human hair. Judy identified this as the beard of Brigalow Bill.

Forty miles west of the Humbert, at Bullita, the same tribes, grown bold with the murder of Brigalow Bill, attacked Harry Condon. Making motions of loading and aiming a gun, he chased them in the moonlight, with a spear through his chest—and lived to tell the story fifty years after.

But the inoculation of civilization was slowly having effect. After the Burns-Johnson prize-fight the blacks, watching the white men, were boxing all over the bush, "the sweet science" a new departure in aboriginal warfare. Paddy Cahill's boys, in Darwin for the wet, introduced billiards to East Alligator River, a table of tent-fly stretched on packing-cases, holes for the pockets, marbles for balls, and a spear for a cue. Elbow Davie of the Larrakia came in to the police station with a playing-card in a cleft stick, the three of hearts inscribed with turtle and crocodile in fearsome tribal challenge. He wanted the police to deliver it as a "chummon" (summons) to an enemy in camp. Davie had served two years for the nulla-nulla murder of a Woolna boy who ran away with one of his wives, and now he was ready to abide by the white man's law.

There was a plague of crocodiles in the wet. Gore, at Marrakai, killed forty-two, and at Katherine crossing they were taking the drovers' horses—old hands measured tracks and swore they were four feet wide. On the Daly one settler lost eleven horses, another fourteen. A croc waddled up into Behren's camp, and snaffled his kangaroo-meat hanging on a tree. Next night he heard a clatter in the bark kitchen, and found a sixteen-footer rummaging among his pots and pans. The shots and the yelling woke the blacks' camp and the dogs, and there was big-fella *yacki* "Down on the Daly River O".

Nineteen hundred and eight was a bad year for fever. Dr Strangman was doing his best by telegram. Ten men lay in an iron shack at Katherine with malignant malaria, and the telegraph master was out of quinine. A sick woman travelled five hundred miles in a buggy from Victoria River. J. Munro, inspecting pastoral lands, died in a buggy on Bradshaw's Run, Fred Long on the Borroloola track, Alex Steele on Valhalla Downs, two unknown men together at Anthony's Lagoons, Reilly and "Sailor Bill" at Roper Bar. Fred Anderson wandered—only his packhorse was found. A drover injured in a rush at Victoria River was eight weeks in agony before the boat came to take him to Darwin.

Sick men from the Government smelter at the Daly were carried over the river in cut-down tanks and native canoes. Five times in the year Captain Webber, foreman, read the burial service over his men, among them Max Wolff, an Austrian count from Klagenfurt. They were buried in the old graveyard of jungle drama.

In fever and fatality Umbrawarra broke out—"broke out", that apt Australian phrase that holds the heartbreak history of all our great mines, irruption of the wealth of earth in desolate places, pestilence and death to the first brave pilgrims.

Umbrawarra, a dazzling gully of stream tin in the hills near Pine Creek, was a massacre, not a mine . . . the bush has obliterated all trace of that gully of graves. Tin was a fortune, and there was a tin rush, two or three hundred men riding across from Queensland. Five perished on the Barkly Tablelands in the dry. Others died on the way. A few were from New Guinea. With these came the deadly malaria, or perhaps blackwater fever—there was never a diagnosis except by telegram.

In Umbrawarra Creek the crude dams were alive with mosquitoes. Under a hot sun, waist-deep in squalid waters, the men shovelled tin gravel from daylight till dark. They lived on salt beef, damper and jam. Bum-boats came out from Pine Creek with grog. In debilitation and neglect the malignant malaria spread—twenty-seven out of the fifty were dead in a few months, forty-four out of a hundred and thirty in a little over a year. Nine thousand pounds' worth of tin was bagged, but only £320 worth of tin was sent away. With the men who had given their lives for it, it was soon overgrown in the jungle.

Kitchener came to Darwin in 1910, down from the East—H.M.S. *Encounter* in harbour, bright with flags and merry with bluejackets, a nineteen-gun salute from Fort Hill, a motley crowd on the beach to gape and cheer. It was a proud day for the rickety little Front Gate when the tall Field-Marshal bowled in a buggy through Chinatown, sitting beside him the Ace of Spades, crack black-tracker of the Larrakia, dressed in khaki and scarlet to be his escort. There was a Kitchener Ball at the Residency, Chinese waiters, Chinese lanterns, dancing on the tennis court, Darktown dodging in the undergrowth to see "big boss white-fella savvy plenty fight". Wheel tracks of the hero's buggy were whittled into a road from the jetty to Fort Hill, and preserved for posterity as Kitchener Drive. I fear posterity has already forgotten it.

Northern Terrors put in the years reading. The monthly ship brought five hundred novels, sold in bundles of twenty—you paid your money but you had no choice. They were sold out early and travelled far, till the white ants inherited them in some deserted shack.

There were only ninety-nine rate-payers in Darwin, thirty-five of them Chinese.

The revenue in 1910 was £13,780 for three thousand-odd people—and they were odd people. The hardy little newspaper kept up their hearts by telling them how to preserve prawns for export, but it was having a hard time—no press telegrams without cash down and a new Chinese printer. Came a letter from Pine Creek:

> The Editor. Sir,
>
> You tlak about a Great Tin Feild and then a Graiter Tin Feild but how about our grait Nusepaper neglected? The last three weeks the printer cow must of been on the boze. What is he a bloming Chow? I can't read the rag and I don't want it any more. Thanking you and dissipation.
>
> BILLY BILLABONG.

An agent in real estate tried to sell the north coast for mangrove bark. Nobody bought the north coast. They stayed home and read the Crippen murder, and watched Halley's Comet from Fort Hill. That comet of fate, the Arabs say, into all human lives brings change. A change was coming.

The new Commonwealth became suddenly and nervously conscious of the top half of Australia. Came a call to the nation, "Look to the North!"—a sequence of thrilling articles published in J. F. Archibald's *Bulletin* magazine, the *Lone Hand*, prophecies in fiction, drama features of imaginary war with startling illustrations, landing of dark hordes of Japanese by night, heroic deeds of Australians in the jungle, with hidden treasure of statistics and information to inspire the public mind with consciousness of the mighty, unmapped north. All the other newspapers beat the big drum. The Commonwealth Government, ten years late, was goaded into action—to rope in the great wide spaces, to light the darkness, to build the trans-continental railway promised half a century before. While parliamentary draughtsmen prepared the complicated constitution of the first Federal Territory, engineers and surveyors were out mapping the railway on the lonely overland trail. Rolling stock worth £10,000,000 was ordered in Canada, England and the United States for a national work to electrify the world till the sands of that desert grow cold.

Old hands held their horses. They had heard this sort of thing before in the Land of the Great Might Be. Some who had hopelessly drifted away hopefully drifted back. If all else failed, they would jump the rattler home.

Chapter XIX

On With The Motley

THE STAGE was set. Spotlight played on the half million square miles. In the Northern Territory Acceptance Act of 1910 the Commonwealth rang up the curtain on the transformation scene of the Vast Unwanted.

One flick of the Federal flag over the timeless void would disclose a model State moving to quick-step of commerce . . . blithe little towns, like beads on a string, threaded on road and railway, mines belching smoke, green fields growing, factory whistles blowing, plate-glass windows and sixpenny pops. Now for the trans-continental railway. Now for another Conquest of Peru—the stockbroker and the savage, each for all, lying down together in a swag of brotherly love.

Australia was thrilled and gratified. "Front Gate" open at last. For the first time in their history, Northern Terrors had a front seat. All the lugger captains, in festival beer spilt on the bar counters, were drawing docks in undiscovered harbours, station-owners mapping tracks of trains through their country, diggers shouting prophecies in ounces to the ton of the mineral millions in "them thar hills" where you had to push back the gold to grow vegetables.

On 1st January 1911 the first Federal Territory was born.

Cap'n Joe Bradshaw and the diggers wanted to call it Aurania, land of gold, but the majority favoured Kingsland, a consort to Queensland near by, and a coronation dedication to George V. They asked for a royal visit for the christening, to follow the Grand Durbar, Darwin to be the New Delhi of empire in the south. But there was no rechristening. The Northern Territory was to battle along under the old bad name.

John McDouall Stuart was resurrected as the Founder, to be immortalized in plays, pictures, pageants, oratory and oratorios, but in the wet season history and histrionics ran to seed. When a party rode out to set a plaque on the sole remaining "J.M.D.S." tree near Chambers Bay, it had been burnt out by blacks.

At an impressive little ceremony on New Year's Day, Mr Justice S. J. Mitchell, last of the South Australian Administrators, unfurled the Commonwealth flag. On this day of days it was discovered, to Darwin's confusion, that there was no blue ensign, civic standard essential to the dignified occasion. Cap'n Joe was reminded of the old blue ensign of Royal Melbourne Yacht Squadron, mildewed but saved from the white ants in a locker of *White Star*. Skipper Harry Lawson willingly produced it, intending, as he told me, to souvenir it back as a museum piece, but when he sent his blackboy up the flagstaff after dark the historic scrap of bunting was already souvenired, and it never came to light.

Wing Cheong Sing waved a scissors all that night to make a flag of Australia in turkey red and coolie blue, his nineteen grandchildren asleep on the floor beside him while, with the fine national frenzy of a Betsy Ross, he cut out a seven pointed star. When Papua was tranferred to the Commonwealth, nobody reflected that the Australian flag should now be an eight-pointed star. The star of the north is missing still.

First year of Federal control was spent in heavy deliberation. A galaxy of distinguished scientists and an army of engineers and "experts" were hurried north to tell the Territory's fortune. Foremost among them were Dr J. A. Gilruth, noted authority in veterinary science and all matters pertaining to stock; Sir W. Baldwin Spencer, world-famed anthropologist, to advise as to conduct and contact with the Vanishing Race; Dr Breinl, specialist in tropical diseases, hygiene and conditions affecting white colonization; Dr W. G. Woolnough, then Assistant Professor of Geology at the University of Sydney, to make a geological survey; Walter Scott Campbell, a former Director of Agriculture in New South Wales, to discipline the jungle; Gerald Hill, entomologist, to study the buffalo fly and the white ant.

Two American visitors were William Halley, a railway authority, and an agriculturist, A. Toy. They spoke in superlatives . . . "Some of the most fertile country it has ever been my lot to see, far and away ahead of the cattle lands of the United States." Wave Hill they compared with Santa Clara Valley, the lower Victoria reminded them of Mississippi delta. On the Barkly Tablelands they visioned ten millon sheep, half a million cattle on the Victoria River fall. Daly and Adelaide rivers took their breath away, and there irrigation would be simple in a second Florida for sugar, fruits and fodder grasses.

All the mining companies were rampant. There was even a packhorse expedition through Arnhem Land, led by a knowledgeable prospector, W. J. McCaw, W. Murphy second in command, four stockmen, two black-boys, thirty-two riding horses and fourteen packs. Five months on the crossing, they did not wait long to dolly out gold, but all five got home alive.

The various commissions spent the pleasant months of the year in travel and research, and foretold a glamorous future for the unwanted child.

The land of paradox was relegated to the care of the Department of External Affairs—it is now administered by the Department of Territories. Chosen Administrator was Dr John Anderson Gilruth, a New Zealand Scot of unbounded zeal and vision, of proved ability and practical experience in Australia down south. At a salary of £1750 a year, his task was to develop the north regardless of expense, his position more regal than vice-regal. In a curious slant of Australian democracy, parliamentary franchise was now taken from the Territory people. Gilruth was absolute. He would reign by the divine right of kings.

Preceded by nine glorified departments established at a cost of £100,000 a year, Conjuror Gilruth made his bow in May 1912. He came overland from Adelaide by motor-car—the second car to make the journey. It cost £300 in benzine, and he was dragged out of bogs and creeks all the way by camels and donkeys. His chauffeur said he rooted out the same ant-hill a hundred and forty-seven times, and it was still there.

From Pine Creek the goldfields road had gone bush, so on the little *Sandfly* His Excellency made triumphal entry into a Darwin that covered its sins with turkey red and tropic flowers. The tiny train was crowded with sightseers from all over the Territory—about twenty-five aboard, including blacks.

Mr Justice Mitchell thankfully handed over the pandanus strings of government. The shabby old Residency, as the new Administrator crossed its threshold, blushed under its bougainvilleas in new dignity of a Government House. Official and parliamentary parties arrived by steamer, and at the court-house Mr Justice Bevan presented to Dr Gilruth His Majesty's Commission. Whites, blacks, Chinese and what-not made cheerful racket of cheers.

His Excellency hastily tidied up Government House and held an official banquet, where the gentlemen made rousing speeches, tapping the great resources, reining in the rivers, offering 335,116,800 radiant acres to humanity at large. The Director of Lands offered "magnificent pastoral country", leases for a lifetime at an annual rental of 1s. per square mile, "today's special" for pioneers, reduced from 2s. 6d. The Director of Mines promised the hatters the riches of Ind from the tangle of rusty machinery and rotten shafts of the old bonanzas, and "all the great mineral fields that extend from the Gulf of Carpentaria to Victoria River, from Arnhem Land to Arltunga". The Director of Agriculture invited a legion of small farmers to sixty-seven million acres of inexhaustible fertility, rent free for twenty-one years, the Government to guide and finance them with roads, tools, telephones, regular shipping, schools, hospitals and the establishment in their midst of three great Government experimental farms.

"To the trans-continental railway and the dawn of a new day! To White Australia Felix in the north!"

There at the Administrator's table, parliamentarians and pioneers charged their glasses. The lives of failure and the lonely graves forgotten, they visioned the weekly train from Adelaide across desert, whistling in to cities in the sand . . . ships calling to wharves and roads all along the big rivers . . . a railway from Katherine to Camooweal . . . a second Riverina of wheat and sheep on the Barkly Tablelands, towns on those plains where the Fizzer rode alone . . . a railway to Borroloola from Anthony's Lagoons and the deep-sea port at Vanderlin Island . . . a new country of Arafura between the Roper and the north coast, the Mary, Alligator and Goyder, a pastoral, mineral and agricultural heaven . . . another deep-sea port at Blunder Bay in the west for the Victoria's millions of cattle and sheep, coal, oil and Tanami gold . . . big barrage at Katherine Gorge for orchards and irrigation . . . another on the Daly . . . Flora Falls, Elsey Falls, harnessed for electric power . . . water supply, good housing, a high school and cold storage in the garden city of Darwin . . . dairy cows for butter and cream . . . water, water everywhere on perish tracks in the dry.

. . . but, above all, people, and their children in thousands—the Territory's own white children to lighten the eternal loneliness of the bush and grow up in the love of their homeland . . . panorama of human life down through the generations, the dream that has no ending.

Parliamentarians and pioneers joined in ringing cheers.

One of the visitors inquired if they would be good enough to leave one strip of virgin bush in the half million square miles for visitors to see.

Among the guests at the Administrator's table that day was a tall and thoughtful Presbyterian "parson" from Central Australia, where he travelled about on camels, mainly in the interests of a medical mission known as the A.I.M. He listened attentively—the Reverend John Flynn.

The great day ended in a corroboree. Parliamentarians set sail for the Daly River on the good ship *Wai Hoi*, fished out of the Roper where she had wallowed for three years, and fitted up for the occasion. On the way back they sheered off the map for a week's fishing at Melville Island. Rumours caught fire in Darwin, and were telegraphed to the south, that they had all been speared by blacks!

Festivities over, Conjuror Gilruth rolled up his sleeves, monarch of all his surveyors had surveyed—and he carefully pointed out that they had surveyed only one-seventeenth of his Territory. Administrator's Report of 1912 was a historical classic, shaming South Australia as the base Indian who threw away the pearl, and finishing up with expensive coloured plates of the various horse diseases of particular interest to Dr Gilruth.

Directors and Commissioners of Mines, Public Works, Customs, Education, Agriculture, Veterinary and Stock Department, Lands and Survey, Post and Police with their staffs moved in. In the old Government offices on the headland, still a ruin from the '97 cyclone, the white-clad bevy of the Commonwealth's elect settled down to work, very superior to the poor pioneers in that their weekly living was assured, with tropic allowances, and homes to be provided by the Government. White-anted beams above their heads hanging like Damoclesian swords, the "nine choirs of angels" tried to un-gum the O.H.M.S. envelopes hermetically sealed in the wet, fished moths and dead beetles out of the ink-wells, and started in on the transformation scene.

Judge Bevan held a Supreme Court for two unfortunate blacks who had awaited their trial in Fannie Bay for six months. The Commissioner of Railways made a grand tour of inspection a hundred miles on the *Sandfly* to Pine Creek. The Director of Mines was deep in the problem of thousands of feet of piping to pump millions of gallons of water out of the old shafts, where diamond drills now proved the prospect to a thousand feet. The Commissioner of Police organized an opium raid in Cavenagh Street, then went outback and inspected the police stations, often a tent in the brush. The Director of Agriculture sadly reported that agriculture had gone bush. The Director of Education read a roll-call of sixty Chinese and fifty European children at the white-anted school. The Health Officer condemned the whole town, including Government House, as unfit for human habitation, and the Public Works Department made blueprints of the third New Darwin.

There was a marathon dash to achievement in that first dazzling year. Darwin Botanic Gardens were such a pageant of glorious growth that Gilruth ran special trains to the gates when the Singapore ships were in so that tourists might inspect. Nicholas Holtze, with a gang of myall murderers in a chain-gang for his gardeners, was carrying on the splendid record. By a Sydney firm, C. E. Waters, he was offered a market for twenty thousand tons a year of his sample of best Territory rice, if it could be delivered as a regular order, at the top price of £8 15s. a ton. To all intending settlers he suggested they try rice for a beginning, with starch plants and fodder grasses.

Field-work of the scientists was the farthest-flung in the world. Covering that mighty field, Dr Gilruth and his advisers rode thousands of miles, every professor a bearded bushman, and often his own camp cook, with nothing but bully to cook. Dr H. I. Jensen, Director of Mines, Dr Woolnough and Edward Copley Playford made tangents across the Territory on horseback from Tanami to Borroloola, justifying the faith in old finds and bringing news of new. Rich reef tin was discovered by Sharber and Richardson at Maranboy in 1913—ten tons of pure metal from two hundred and fifteen tons of ore; wolfram at Hatch's Creek in the Centre in 1914, and later at Wauchope Creek, and large coal areas at Borroloola with wealth of copper and silver-lead. All Maranboy needed was a battery to make it one of the greatest tin-mines in Australia—and this battery the Government would provide, at a cost of £22,000, with a manager at £600 a year.

Professor Baldwin Spencer, at his own request, was appointed Special Commissioner and Chief Protector of Aborigines. From the Chair of Biology at Melbourne University, he rolled his swag for another year in a buggy through the trackless bush, in hardship and privations devoting his life to knowledge of the blacks in their country. The broad principles he laid down are foundation charts of the Commonwealth Government schemes today—except that Spencer, in the matter of reserves, was opposed to any form of white domination. In Darwin he rescued the town blacks from their appalling dirt and degradation on Lameroo Beach to a new Kahlin Beach compound, planned with respect of family life and tribal traditions. Half-caste children he brought in from the blacks' camps to learn to "live white".

No anthropologist has left us such a complete and authentic study of the wild man of Australia, laws, religion, the index to his mind. None has made wiser deductions for the preservation of the race among us for as long as may be—for Baldwin Spencer thirty years ago, as Charles Sturt, the explorer, fifty years before him, could foretell the inevitable end. Spencer computed the black population of the Territory in 1912 as about fifty thousand —today it is estimated at thirteen thousand.

Baldwin Spencer's many books are neglected on our library shelves, yet for the student of ethnology, theology, philosophy, for the poet and the imaginative writer, there is wealth in every line. Some of these books were compiled in stress of a three-thousand-mile trail in a wagon, some written in collaboration with men such as F. J. Gillen and Paddy Cahill, who spent a lifetime studying the blacks. Here is the very essence of the old Australia, distilled from songs, dances, ceremonies, laws and legends, the natural life of its own wandering people since human life began.

In the little old pub at Borroloola they treasure a merry memory of Baldwin Spencer. Injured at Melville Island, after two months' medical care in Darwin, he travelled the three Alligator rivers by lugger and pack-team with the Kakadu tribes. He then set out by primitive motor-car through Newcastle Waters and Anthony's Lagoons to Borroloola, to study the Gulf natives, returning along the Roper to Katherine—a bush trail of twelve hundred miles.

In the black silence of world's end, Borroloola, as he sat one night with Tom Lynott, Alf Scrutton, and one or two other great bushmen, "talkin' blackfella" by hurricane light, along the grass-grown track from the river came the measured tramp of a regiment of armed men, left, right, left, right.

The bushmen gripped their pipes and gaped a hole in their beards. Were they dreaming?

"Halt! Order-r-r arms!"

Click of rifles. Bump.

"Stand-at . . . ease!"

The bushmen crept to the door, Tom Lynott with the hurricane lamp held high. Outside was a squad of thirty marines with a naval officer, all dim and ghostly in tropic white.

A lieutenant mounted the broken steps, his gold epaulettes gleaming in lantern light. He greeted Tom with a neat salute. Tom returned a limp salute and an astonished grin.

"Good evening, sir!" rapped out the lieutenant. "Can you tell me any thing of the possible whereabouts of Sir Baldwin Spencer?"

"Eh? Spencer? Yair."

Tom shuffled around.

" 'Ere y'are, Perfessor, there's a whole bloomin' army askin' for you."

The professor emerged, surprised.

"Ah, sir, glad to see you," said the officer with relief. "Our ship was detailed at Thursday Island to make search for you in the Gulf, where it was believed you had been molested by natives, and detained against your will."

Bushmen and marines shared the professor's hearty laughter. The party was from H.M.A.S. *Brisbane,* anchored in the Gulf. The men had sailed the Macarthur in a pinnace, and landed in the dark under the Leichhardt trees. The old pub that night entertained its biggest crowd since the days of Kimberley gold rush, their host the lost professor, certainly not detained against his will.

At about this time Sir Baldwin Spencer's recognition of the nobility of a fellow man won a myall boy the Albert Medal, a King's decoration unique in the history of the black Australian race.

Hunting cattle-killers on Roper Valley, Constable Johns—lately Commissioner of Police in South Australia—rode back with three natives in neck-chains to Wilton River in flood. The blacks swam safely over, but Johns's horse went under and stunned him with a kick. Neighbour, a prisoner in chains, dived for the drowning trooper at risk of his own life, brought him back to consciousness, and rode sixty miles to get help from the nearest white man.

At Government House drawing-room in Darwin, in quite a little ceremony, His Excellency pinned the Albert Medal on Neighbour's dingy breast. Judge Bevan, Professor Baldwin Spencer and Bishop White of Carpentaria patted him on the back, and his photograph was published in London papers. His name is still world-famous, though the story is one of thousands typical of the helpfulness and broad humanity of the aboriginal race.

Finest rapture of the year 1912 was the founding of the Government farms, and the fable of the Magic Pumpkin—the Biggest Pumpkin in the World.

When everything in the Territory's garden seemed lovely, W. S. Campbell, Director of Agriculture, in three months had made three selections of first-class farming country—at Batchelor, sixty miles south of Darwin, the second on Daly River, and the third on the Katherine. To these Dr Gilruth later added a fourth, for the breeding of horses and sheep, the wholesome pastures and miracle springs of Mataranka, two hundred and fifty miles south and eight hundred feet above sea-level . . . there he would establish stud stock and fodder fields. Mataranka was to be the inland capital. Applications for land were legion, some from New Zealand, from England and India, but the first step was to set up the Government experimental farms.

In the green valley-folds of Batchelor—where old Jack Cameron, alone in a grove of blossoming trees, ponders on the past today—two thousand six hundred and fifty acres of woollybutt forest and pandanus swamp were mapped for high endeavour. A traction engine and two forest devils trundled down to clear it, the first consequential machinery the north had ever seen. Scores of farm-hands came from south by steamer, fares paid, high wages. Mowing a meadow that bobbed up again behind them overnight, they managed to get twenty acres ploughed in six months, a Territory record. Also they fenced two and a quarter miles—and here I quote the report—"with the exception of the wire netting which is not on hand". They planted two acres of cowpeas and pumpkin to sweeten the earth.

So delighted was Dr Gilruth with the girth of a giant pumpkin that he worshipped at its shrine, mentioned it in dispatches, published its photograph in the southern press—the famous Batchelor pumpkin of bitter flavour to Dr Gilruth and the Territory's undying shame.

A signpost on the Stuart Highway with a pointing hand, a deserted little railway shack in the long grasses—not even a notice to WHISTLE—is Batchelor now, only that and nothing more, but every passenger that travelled on Leaping Lena in the past thirty-five years, soldiers in their tens of thousands whooping by in blitz-buggies, half-castes, tourists from the south, old women and babies, greet it with a knowing smile.

"Ah! Batchelor!" they say. "This is where they grew the £65,000 pumpkin."

A pumpkin splendiferous as Cinderella's coach, the truth of it now is lost in fairy-tale, but Tom Flynn, the grand old ganger at Rum Jungle, remembers it well. Tom has, with his own eyes, seen it, the girth of a tank in his garden, he guarantees.

"A mammoth cattle-pumpkin, it was four feet six inches high by five feet six inches wide, in circumference fifteen feet handsome. Four men could just roll it."

Tom Flynn's word along the railway line for fifty years has been taken as Bible truth.

The pumpkin was stolen from Batchelor siding, even as Mona Lisa from the Louvre, while it was waiting for a truck to Darwin so that it might stagger the Doubting Thomases down there. Dr Gilruth offered £15 reward—vain hope. Even as Cinderella's coach, in the dead of night the light of his eyes was gone, spirited off by an ungodly gang on wheels. White detectives and black trackers failed to uncover it. Months afterwards one of the conspirators led Tom Flynn to wreckage in the bush. Too late. The seeds, two and a half inches long, had rotted into mould. Never again on earthly soil would the giant produce its kind.

It is not true that Batchelor pumpkin was the only product of the Government farms that cost £65,000. They grew quite a number of things that had been successfully grown before, but at a sensational cost.

Aristocratic bloodstock arrived by the ships to the value of £12,697 10s. 6d. The Scottish Earl, a noble Clydesdale whose forefathers fought at Bannockburn, cost three hundred guineas, and his fourteen Clydesdale mares seventy guineas each, all from Victoria, with two of Australia's royalty merino rams valued at hundreds of guineas, eighty maiden ewes of the best families, twenty-six Berkshire and Tamworth boars and sows, Ayrshire bulls and dairy cows—the poddy-dodgers decided to live on a bit longer—right down to prize Orpingtons on tick-proof, snake-proof roosts, supercilious collie-dogs to shepherd the sheep, pedigreed turkeys and a colony of Ligurian bees.

A model tropic bungalow, at a cost of £1200, was erected for the manager, recreation huts and dormitories for forty white farm-hands, quarters for the blacks cutting fence-posts and slabs for stables to be gauzed against March flies, also for cowsheds, sheepfolds, poultry pens with concrete floors.

Meanwhile the glorious Daly sprouted surveyors' camps for a hundred and fifty miles. Bosky dells of Leichhardt pine, paperbark and bamboo patterned the little white tents. Cockatoos, ibis and wild geese screamed in kaleidoscopic flight over the chain-men marking and measuring empire. They slept on bunks above the carpet-snakes wreathing and writhing, rifles on the ridge-pole ready for "cheeky" blacks, salt beef hung high in the trees out of the crocodiles' way. Lights glittered in the jungle at night where the white men played euchre under their mosquito-nets and the blacks the didjeridoo. In the moonlight they all went fishing, black and white together, out in canoes on the broad shining river among the crocs for barramundi.

Progress was the usual Jack-and-the-Beanstalk on the Daly. For the first time in twenty years wagons found the old tracks from Brock's Creek, twenty-three horses dragging five tons, with Berkshire boars tethered on top and Ayrshire bulls tied behind. At the experimental farm the house was built, a thousand acres cleared and some planted with maize that grew twelve feet high and produced two crops that year.

Thousands of acres of dense jungle were rapidly allotted in five hundred and forty-acre blocks, and the first ten families were out with the blacks burning off and planting. They put in maize, tobacco, sugar-cane, pineapples, everything they could think of, and it all came up overnight. Here, as the pamphlets said, "luxury living would be the cheapest in the world from Nature's generous hand", and the Government would provide everything else.

Already there was a good little wharf, a store, a harvester, hay-press, pigs and prize poultry, seedlings of everything under the sun, and science at their side. They had no horses—they dragged logs and made trenches for planting in sweat of the brow. They cut fence-posts in thousands—and there was never any wire-netting. They built a little school, and the Government appointed a teacher. The children crossed in native canoes and trotted the jungle paths with black guides till their fathers built them a swing bridge of steel cables, eleven chains long, over the crocodile river.

Private enterprise took heart of grace. Pearce started a plantation of plantains and coconuts at Shoal Bay. Milton, at Stapleton, and a Dutch engineer, Verburg, at Adelaide River, had fields of waving rice and maize, all vegetables, all tropic fruit. With a few blacks to help him, Verburg constructed a grand little weir in the Adelaide River that cost him £3000. All over the Territory groves of golden citrus shone in gold harvest of lemons, oranges, grapefruit and limes.

A man named Zakharrow started a Daly River Farming Company and got in a few more settlers. Roper River Concessions, a Melbourne company with a London capital of £50,000, would lease six thousand square miles for rubber, tin and gold. Far out on the north coast, Elcho Island Petroleum Company, with £200,000 capital in £1 shares, was floated on the wave of the Arafura. There was at one time an iron shack on the sands of that desert isle, with a notice:

ELCHO ISLAND PETROLEUM CO.
OFFICE HOURS
11 a.m. to 4 p.m.
Every fourth Thursday.

Passing the Wessel Islands, Alf Brown called in in his lugger one fourth Thursday, but the managing director was out.

A cannery was to be established for buffalo beef. Gibson, Hollowood and Sullivan were granted a twenty-one-year lease of Woolna Reserve to yard, brand and domesticate the wild mobs galloping round Lake Finniss. There was even talk of putting buffalo butter on the market!

A. J. Cotton for thirty years was owner of Brunette, and has published a book, *With the Great Herds of Australia*. He drove the first car over the rugged ranges to Borroloola from Anthony's Lagoons, the tyres lashed round with buffalo hide. Before that, the journey from Mataranka to Borroloola, with buggy or dray, occupied the best part of a year.

Wonders would never cease. The world-wide English beef-baron firm of Vestey bought in to North Australia in a mighty sweep of cattle-lands that in area rivalled the Argentine—from the Fitzroy and the Ord rivers in Kimberley in one unbroken sweep across to the Katherine River and Marrakai on the Adelaide. George Seal galloped four hundred miles from Katherine with the telegram when they closed the deal with Buchanans for Flora Valley, Gordon Downs and Wave Hill. In all, they acquired forty thousand square miles of long-term grazing country, and announced the immediate construction of a £1,000,000 meatworks in Darwin, where their Blue Star line of ships would call to carry beef to Britain. After poverty-stricken years in their far-out shacks, watching the sky-line with no market for their cattle, the station-owners were jubilant to sell for countless thousands. They took the cash in hand and waived the rest.

In 1914, War.

Vestey's began to build their £1,000,000 meatworks. The Government began to build the trans-continental railway. The pig began to go over the stile. The Territory was coming home.

Sons of adventure, sons of the pioneers, were away to the war.

Thousands came to the north, wages sky-high, fares paid, barracks and good living guaranteed. They were labourers from all States, sent up by the unions. Hundreds of others were foot-walking across country.

William MacGregor, a compositor, walked overland two thousand miles from Adelaide, wearing greenhide leggings through the spinifex, carrying food, swag and water all the way. He was ten weeks on the trail, about forty miles to each water, though once he covered a dry stage of a hundred and five miles, and another time walked ninety-four miles in two and a quarter days.

It was the willy-willy season in the Australian Workers' Union, the most stormy period in its history. With all the gangs came union organizers and strike agitators to see they got their rights.

A cosmopolitan horde of meat-workers came with the ships, Greeks, Bulgars, Turks and Siberian Russians, with motley from South America, socialists all, vociferous for the brotherhood of man. From eternal poverty and persecution in their own countries, within a few months they were Marxian fighters in fairyland, shouting out the battle-cry of freedom in broken English, demanding £8 and £10 a week, with annual holidays to Sydney, fares and wages paid. Slaughter-men made £25 a week. The humble ringers of the drovers' camps trebled their wages to £1 a day, with overtime for night-watch—and well they deserved it. Even the Darwin Chinese joined the unions with a vim—"No more workee, plenty overtime, plenty money bime-by? Alli!"

Down on the railway line the gangs cutting sleepers and plate-laying represented every race on earth, working together happily in the brotherly love of the Australian bush while their nations were at death-grips, then spending their wages in the shanties of the line that took hundreds of pounds in a day.

Settlers were arriving by eastern and western steamer and overland in drays, camped in an immigrants' depot of iron near the jetty, and in tents under the palms on Mindil Beach, waiting for their land. They had sold up their homes in the south for a bird in the Territory bush, among them one Perreau from Melbourne, with his wife and ten children bound for the Daly. Twenty-six families were waiting to go to the Daly—to that luxury living from Nature's generous hand. They were five months trying to get out there, and four years trying to get back.

For the Government farms were doomed to shabby failure. They came to nothing in the first year, and were mercifully drowned in the next monsoon.

At Batchelor the Clydesdales fretted and sweated in their stalls, hung down their heads in expensive hay and died of heat and sunstroke. The mares gave birth to premature foals. The Scottish Earl sickened and was hurried to Willeroo, where he fell over a cliff. Farm horses went galloping mad from the stings of March flies, burnt their hoofs off standing in smoke fires to get away from mosquitoes, stood belly-deep in water for coolness till they developed swamp cancer, suffered from moon-blindness and walkabout disease. Those that were left had to be worked in the cool hours, when the men wanted their time off.

Crops withered in hot winds, then rotted in wet ground. They were riddled with pests and smothered in weeds. Science could not save them, for all solutions washed off in the wet, and there was no hope of driving back the weeds. Everything useful was overrun by everything noxious. Even pumpkin vines were devoured by pumpkin beetle.

Prize fowls gave up the ghost to water-snakes and goannas. Berkshire and Tamworth boars and sows from Hawkesbury Agricultural College burrowed away bush, a hundred and thirty-five dairy cattle put through the dip were lost by negligence. The Ligurian bees were gobbled on the wing by the bee-eater, that cheeky little Territorian in olive-green coat, white shirt and bright-blue cap, swift as a slant of sun, that scotches all efforts to make it a land of honey.

Nature was less distressing than human nature. The men, too, had walkabout disease. Scandals, squabbles, drunkenness—of eighty white men employed at the two farms, eleven were left at the end of a year. Illness, resigned, dismissed, none of them stayed. The country of endless frustration made the best of them restless. One contractor started fencing with a team of thirty men, and in a few months he was working alone.

Things were worse still out on the Daly. A herd of five hundred dairy cows died on the ship and on the way out. Calves were bloated big as their mothers within a year, and all dropsical. With no transport, the settlers still waited for tools and fencing wire. A traction engine and boring plant landed in Darwin rusted at the railway siding, no horses to drag it on. Buildings fell down before stock could arrive. Ploughs could not clear the native grass, ink-weed. Then the river came down in flood, rising eighty feet in two days, the farms twelve feet under. The settlers ran for their lives to the high rises, dead kangaroos and live crocodiles floating past them in thousands. The store and the irrigation pump, the wharf and the little shacks of homes, the bridge where the children crossed to school, were tossed away like toys. Several women and children died, flood-bound and far from help. Their men filled in the graves under the banyan-trees.

It was stark tragedy on the bad and beautiful Daly, where wily Nature is ever working to the defeat of man.

After the wet some died, some left, a few began again. One or two of cast-iron courage, or no money, stayed for four years, among them the Dargeys, in a hard life-story back on the Daly today. The settlers grew one-year harvests—peanuts, rice to eat, millet for brooms to make a clean sweep. Parry, a returned soldier there till the end of his days, in 1916 introduced to the Territory the Rhodesian peanut that on the Daly is two and a half inches long and five inches through—the finest-flavoured and most prolific peanut in the world, but too far out of it for market.

Mataranka, at a cost of £17,000, had six managers in five years. Two thousand sheep, with wool of finest crimp, were brought over from Avon Downs, with twenty Wanganella rams. They travelled a year to get there, and with twenty-seven inches of rain in a month they died of pleuro-pneumonia, were lost in the long grasses and drowned in the creeks and springs. They carried three times the weight of their wool in grass-seeds, the barbs penetrating to their entrails, and their plight was horror. In the grass fires the wool was black as charcoal, or a tangle of sun-perished staple.

The few that survived were sold to J. T. Beckett, who drove them down the Roper and shipped them to Vanderlin Island. When he abandoned Vanderlin, they were speared and eaten by blacks.

All was fiasco and failure. Trans-continental, first section, creeping down from Pine Creek at a cost of £8000 per mile, travelled sixty miles in three years to Katherine River, where it was abandoned after the building of the bridge, that arch of triumph to the future, to the bushmen a marvel of engineering, Katherine River bridge, a quarter of a mile long and eighty feet high. Many a man has fallen from it, carrying a case of whisky inside or out. It was ten years before the railway lagged the last hundred miles to Birdum.

In place of the £10,000,000 rolling stock contracts with Canada and the United States for a Sante Fé express, old engines and trucks came from Chillagoe in Queensland. The *Sandfly* moved out for Leaping Lena, still on the run today. One carriage was labelled FIRST for Government servants only, another FIRST LADIES for Government servants' wives.

One day Jack Pannikin dumped his fifteen-stone missus in there with her pups and piccaninnies, a swag and a cutty pipe, a string bag full of horrors and a bit of bad carpet-snake to eat on the way. The horrified Government wives shrieked for the guard.

"Here y'are, Jackie," he shouted. "No good this place belonga lubra. Him prop'ly rubbish. Garn! Get her along to the back of the train."

Jackie was aggrieved. Pointedly he looked up to the notice LADIES, then sheered his pipe at the old girl.

"What's a matter him?" he demanded. "Him all-same belong-ta woman, ain't it?"

Which was obviously true, but in the Territory the colonel's lady and Judy O'Grady will never be sisters under the prickly heat of their skins.

Vestey's, now, was a roar of machinery killing five hundred bullocks a day—forty thousand cattle a year for Imperial Army contract, trains down to the jetty extended to meet liners of fifteen thousand tons. There was a daily train from Katherine, one on Sundays. Hundreds of humpies of tin and sack on Bullocky Point were merging into an unbeautiful pile of galvanized iron overlooking the bay, with manager's villas, barracks, slaughter-houses, canteens, canneries, a chef to every hundred men and a waitress from the south to every thirty. Three times a day they served New Zealand tinned beef and stew—the Territory never tasted its own bully. There were concerts, tennis courts, dances, picture shows, a football ground and lively matches with teams of all colours.

In the high tide of war population soared to eight thousand, nearly all men and herded along the railway line, as many coming as going on the ships. Darwin, with only a hundred and seven houses, was a dirty huddle of huts and camps emptying rubbish on vacant lots, no water for baths, no sanitation, little naked Chinese, what-nots and whites running round the muddy streets. Dr Mervyn Holmes, Director of Health, again condemned the town. He removed Malays and half-breeds to the Police Paddock two miles out, where they took root as a polychromatic suburb of the wildwood. Chinatown blandly refused to go. Cavenagh Street, for all its sins, could never be evicted. Health officers and police officers, in raids of fumigation, backyard fires and orders for rebuilding, did reduce it in time to a reasonable standard of Asiatic living.

In the White Australia fury of the moment, Japanese, Malays and Filipinos were scouted off the pearling ships for union crews and divers. Of six naval divers who volunteered, two were crippled with paralysis and none could stand the life. So the perilous quest of pearls under sea went back to the dark races. No Chinese was allowed to hold a fishing or gardening licence—they were hunted from two miles of gardens and all the harbour beaches to make room for White Australians, who never arrived. In a reported outbreak of citrus canker, all orange- and lemon-trees in the north were ordered to be destroyed. For the next thirty years there were no fresh vegetables, except by the monthly ship at fantastic prices, and few fresh fruits save the mangoes, pineapples, papaws and bananas that grow practically wild.

Gilruth was challenged—he clung to his preconceived ideas and continued to rule by divine right of kings. Each week in the Government *Gazette* rules and regulations set sedition ablaze. The Government owned one half the town, the unions the other. Pioneers were rooted out for the new order. Myilly Point—Dead Horse Ranch—became the Toorak of Darwin, Government officials only—wooden villas high on blocks with balconies and ferns. But the blacks' camp at Kahlin was right beside them, monopolizing the beach, and there it stayed for thirty years.

In the first fall of white ants and dust in Mitchell Street and Smith Street, the District Council held indignation meetings—and was abolished out of hand. When Judge Bevan complained that, from Territory juries, he could never bring in a verdict of guilty in the courts, trial by jury was abolished except in murder cases. At these high-handed actions there was always a community howl, but when he descended on the pubs, controlling hours and prices, Gilruth waded through beer to a throne, and Magna Charta raised its hoary head.

While Mrs Gilruth stimulated social prestige by giving calico balls at the Residency—a tactful courtesy to those with nothing but calico to wear—morale had fallen through the floor at the white-anted hotels, where ducks and blue-tongued lizards roosted in the boarders' rooms, where melted butter was set on the tables in cracked saucers, where Christmas was bully and green pickles and a bushman's plum duff. Only the Victoria, the "stone pub", had a staff to keep it clean, and there men and women crowded together on balconies to sleep, and the rain fell through the roof.

So mad were the nights in those unregenerate bars, so acidly humorous the distinguished visitors, that the Government was forced to take over the hotels in the name of civilization. The Fisher Labour Government, in 1915, at the "old Vic" in Darwin, was first in Australia, by proxy, to stand behind the bar. When it assumed control of the other two, the Palmerston Club and the Terminus, all were declared black in a six weeks' strike. Government officials scattered to the Chinese restaurants, or went batching in shacks—so Primus Alley, a lane off the Esplanade, received its name.

From now Gilruth was a marked man, all his minions hated. Darwin could live without house and home, without food and the franchise, in mental, moral and physical decay to shock an outsider, but not without its beer. There was open rebellion against the Administrator. He was heckled in public, threatened in private, taunted by the newspaper week by week as "His Obstinacy", "Kiltruth", "Gilruthless", "the Administraitor"—an autocrat of Government stroke at the Sign of the Cloven Hoof. The new editor of the *Northern Territory Times* cared not a jot for the wonderland of birds and rivers. He specialized in lampoons, cartoons, contempt, scandal—for there were very serious Government scandals. He published nothing but veiled libels, and vinegar dreams.

The big maritime strike of the south brought disaster to the north—no ships for three months, the whole country starving. The little skiff *Leichhardt*, in union sympathies, did not sail for the Daly, and a year's harvest rotted on the bank. At Maranboy a hundred men had nothing in the store. A miner wrote to the paper:

> Johnnie-cakes are a thing of the past. You could not buy flour if you offered a guinea a pound. The cupboard is bare. The last of the macaroni was sold for the price of gold, and now there is only canary seed left. Well, I bought a few pounds, and the last bottle of croton oil. I shall stew up the old bullock hide I use as a door mat.
>
> This is unlike the Bible—your bread shall be given you and your water sure. The water is sure enough, but there's nothing to mix it with. Can the government take over the stores as well as the hotels, and instead of giving us something to drink give us something to eat?

Now the Territory, like all Gaul, resolved itself into three—always excluding the exclusive B.A.T. There were the Government officials from the south, intent on their own brief authority, gravitating in cliques according to salary, for the most part a dull, myopic people, openly contemptuous of a poverty-stricken hotchpotch in which they were doomed to spend three years. There were the unions rampant. Ignored by both were the old pioneers. While all the others were paid to stay there, they had no money to go.

In daily strikes, stop-works, sit-downs, lock-outs, marchings, meetings, demonstrations and deputations, Vestey's were having a lively time. Rumours spread that they had bought the Territory for £2,000,000 and that Gilruth was their agent.

The union weekly and the *N.T. Times* lived by scurrilous attacks on bosses and administration, public and private exposures till Darwin was a hotbed of personal spite—as one of the time has written, "a fetid immorality of slander surely unknown among white people anywhere else in the world". With no respect for women, life became squalid. As the direct result of vicious gossip, more than one husband shot his wife.

Contamination seeped into high places. The Government was overbearing, self-centred, vindictive. In the camps there was idleness, discord, bravado, until those who wanted to work, or who held their own council, were hated as "scabs" and "black-legs". It was bruited around that Vestey's were importing five thousand Italians to beat the strikes. The unions threatened revolution. The fact was merely that the Government had offered sanctuary to a colony of Welsh settlers from Patagonia, followers of Henry George who, like New Australia, had failed in South America.

These Welsh settlers from Patagonia, after adventure on the high seas, at last turned up, but little they knew of Llanfairpwllgwyngyllgogfrych. . . . There was not a Llewellyn nor a Jones among them. They proved to be: Spaniards, sixty men, ten women, fifteen boys and twenty-six girls; Russians, forty-five men and one woman; Italians, thirty men; British, eleven men, three women, nine girls.

How green was their valley! Yet they made good settlers, and a few are in the Territory still.

The five hospitals promised by the Government were no more than a nurse and a first-aid man for railway-workers at Pine Creek. The high school was J. L. Rossiter, M.A., who came to conduct classes "in higher education", and left for lack of classes. For lack of labour to build houses and roads, the paper alleged that the police were arresting the blacks—aboriginal owners of Australia, nomads by nature—on charges of vagrancy, and having no visible means of support, and when convicted, as they invariably were, chaining them up as slave labour.

Whenever an editor was held to have libelled police or Administration, he retired into Fannie Bay, from which he was rescued after public demonstration and carried back to Darwin shoulder-high. Fannie Bay was still the tragicomedy jail of Australia, wistful strains of corroboree floating out on the night air with now the sturdy beat of the Marxian anthem in defiant chorus:

"Though *cow*-ards mock and *ty*-rants jeer,
We'll keep-the-*Red* Flag flying-here."

Prisoners were sent to the town each day in work-gangs, blacks on chains with an armed warder, white men on their honour to be home by eight o'clock at night. One night *the late ones were locked out and climbed the iron wall to get in. The second time the gates were locked, prisoners trooped back to town in a body and put in a protest at the newspaper office at the dastardly high-handedness and inefficiency of the Administration.*

Gilruth's annual reports were now brief and doleful. He admitted that the farms were "unfortunate", took refuge in statistics, and staked his faith on Maranboy tin and Daly River copper. He had an apostolic faith in Daly River copper.

Each year the rains rang down the curtain on endeavour. Nineteen sixteen was a tragic wet, eleven inches in a day, thirty-five inches in a week, no news in five months from Daly River settlers. Edith, Cullin and Ferguson rivers drowned the railway camps, drowned some of the men, among them "Peter the Viking", a Nordic giant out in a boat saving life. Katherine River was four feet deep in the street of Katherine, the Roper seven feet deep in the mission house, the Limmen rushing three feet deep through Tanumbirini homestead though it was built on a high rise. The mailman to Borroloola for thirty-nine days waded and swam with his horses between Hodgson Downs and Roper Bar. Wagons from Brunette and Alexandria were five months on the track to Borroloola to meet the ship with stores. Eleven men died of starvation, beriberi, drowning, on the Roper and Macarthur that year.

Gilruth knew nothing of all this.

George Lawrie of Tanami rode in from the west with the same terrible story. In union troubles the ship had not gone to the Victoria. For four months there was nothing in Matt Wilson's store but pickles, dried potatoes and square gin. Eight men, from various unnatural causes, were dead out there, in a population of about twenty. A man named George, on a prospecting trip of eight hundred miles alone, went blind. His packhorses carried him back to Hall's Creek through a hundred miles of limestone walls and split rifts of the ranges. He cured himself with eye-lotion, and rode to Inverway, "submarining" for miles through the long grasses. Here and there mineral wealth mocked him—hills of silver-lead, ranges of iron, copper and tin shining in the bed of the creeks.

South-east monsoon dried the high grass to sere and yellow, bush-fires raging, stagnant scum and animal dead breeding fever. Many more died, without food and without help, no doctor outside Darwin. Some reached Darwin Hospital, among them Captain Joseph Bradshaw, grand old Cap'n Joe, five days tossing in a lugger from Bradshaw's Run, trying to bathe and poultice a foot far gone in gangrene. They amputated the foot, but Cap'n Joe died.

Now fever broke out at Maranboy—malignant malaria, or blackwater, or yellow fever, nobody knew which, but ninety men of the hundred were stricken down, many deaths. The Territory heard again of John Flynn, the pilgrim "parson" of the Australian Inland Mission, who set up the second of his hostels in the great outback at Maranboy in this time of urgent need. Two nursing sisters came from the south to care for the sick. The Australian Inland Mission was not concerned with Territory politics, nor with what John Flynn has called "the tragedy of progress". It was there to help the human being, white or black, in need. John Flynn would achieve in colonization where Dr Gilruth miserably failed.

Poor little figurehead of pygmies in that cosmic drama of the clouds, he had no hope of controlling Nature where Nature controls man. There was strike after strike, flame after flame. Vestey's hive of industry became a hive of stinging bees.

The Territory's own folk were not closely involved in union uproar—they relished and resented it, both at the same time. They had no respect for the Administration. When a story went the rounds that a big consignment of opium, without Gilruth's knowledge, had been smuggled in his luggage to the Chinese at Pine Creek, they preserved it for posterity with gusto. When the Administrator made a survey of his wide domain by motor-car, a hundred and fifty miles from station to station, they will tell you that every station-owner in six thousand miles was "out", nobody home but the Chinaman cook to greet him. The twisted road built by prison blacks from Darwin to the meatworks, with more humour than enmity, they christened "Gilruth's Neck", and Gilruth's Neck it is today.

The population had fallen to 4883—3500 British assorted, in eleven white races and seven coloured. Official report shows a roll-call at Darwin school of fifty-one white Australian children, fourteen Greek, sixteen Spanish, forty-six Chinese, fifteen Malay half-castes, five quadroons and sixty-five half-castes. There was no future worth while for any of these children.

In Chinatown girls were sold for £10, fan-tan and opium raids—all along the beaches poker and prostitution. The home for half-caste girls was a wicked joke, the new blacks' camp as dirty as the old. Fabric of colonization was riddled with white ants. Darwin was written up in the press of the south as

DARWIN THE DAMNED

LAST RESORT OF THE AUSTRALIAN DERELICT.

Whipped into shame, a few bright spirits formed a Progress Association to ask for a general clean-up, lights at night, a water supply, decent town-planning and better transport. The only progress association poor Darwin ever knew, it was laughed to scorn by the rabble as "the Goose Club". After the first public meeting in Larrakia Square, a howl of misery and contention raided by drunks and dispersed by the police, only two members had the courage to attend, Mr R. I. D. Mallam, then solicitor, and Freddie Thompson, an editor of the *N.T. Times*. One or two weathered the ridicule, with solemn and regular meetings on an esplanade seat in the evening cool, till the seat was tossed over the cliff by a rowdy. Though progress was always a forlorn hope, the faithful Freddie, twenty-four stone, was the Goose Club till the day he died, all by himself in the moonlight, plaintively airing wrongs, picturing, to anyone who would listen, the Darwin of his dreams.

In the wet of 1918 the big storm, of long threatening, broke in comic fury.

The war was over. Armistice was signed. Darwin celebrated with a bun-feast on the Oval and a corroboree in the compound. The heat was "all-same hell". Hundreds of meat-workers were idle, waiting to go south. Steamers were crowded, six to a two-berth cabin, stretchers all over the decks.

H.M.A.S. *Brisbane* and some cruisers called, and drank Darwin out of beer. When the town got down to rum, there were orgies and brawls in the streets. Gilruth, like Canute, tried to hold back the tide.

When the next ship came in, beer was rationed . . . no alcohol to be served by State hotels except on production of an affidavit made before a police officer that it was required for medical use only, and for personal consumption by the undersigned. Customs duty increased the price of beer from 1s. 6d. to 1s. 9d. a bottle.

Last straw! Yours for the Revolution!

The unions and the town stood hand in hand. State hotels were declared black in another six weeks' strike—noble renunciation in the cause of liberty. Barmen slept on the bar-counters. Never a meat-worker, never a buffalo-shooter, darkened a pub door. Fires of rebellion glowed in the red of the poinciana-trees, even at the banks and the B.A.T. Vestey's Vesuvius was smoking for eruption.

Gilruth's Scots blood was up. The State, 'twas he, and after him the deluge. The Christmas ship came in with seven hundred cases of Melbourne Bitter. He refused permission to unload—it went on to Singapore.

News-sheets announced that the Administrator was about to depart by car for the south, leaving the Territory beerless for Christmas and New Year. Railways refused to carry him up-country. The Chinese refused to do his washing. A meeting at the meatworks rumbled things to come.

At dawn on 21st December the Singapore ship came back. She berthed at the wharf. Would she unload the beer? Gilruth gave no sign.

Over Darwin the storm-clouds gathered. Out towards Vestey's lightning flashed and thunder rolled.

And has he fixed the where and when?
And shall the north be dry?
Eleven hundred union men
Will know the reason why.

It was only a matter of hours now, to the Fall of the Bastille. By noon, rumours of an army on the move.

With the march of the afternoon storm came a march of men under the red bannerol of the A.W.U. behind Harold Nelson—Horatius leading his legions over the Daly Street bridge. Seven hundred from Vestey's were joined by four hundred in Darwin, men of all shades of complexion and all shades of opinion. They waved placards, brandished nailed sticks and nulla-nullas, some said they carried guns. They bore aloft a guy of Gilruth to be burnt at the stake. Nelson's Warriors, men of mettle, ready to die for the Cause and the Working Man's Beer. Through Chinatown came the rebel tread as they wheeled round the headland to the Government offices, doused in a sudden squall but their ranks unbroken.

Government wives rushed for cover. The police rushed for their batons. His Excellency hastily retired into Government House. At a minute's notice, seventy Government servants were sworn in as special police on guard in the garden. All the blacks came running to see the war.

None has a more solemn respect for law and order than your true Australian democrat. Had the French Revolution been staged here, every *sale aristocrate* would have had "a fair go". Instead of a riot, a meeting was called at Government House gates.

In a stormy sea of placards and sticks, Nelson read the indictment, as many accusations as the American Declaration of Independence against the English king. When a motion was put to the meeting, all in favour shouted Aye.

It was demanded that the Administrator should now mount the beer-case to give an account of his stewardship in the past five years, that he show cause why he should not be deposed. "Failing this, is he willing to leave the Territory by steamer, and remain away until a public commission is held on his administration."

His Excellency remained remote and mum.

Armed police and special constables threaded the crowd, led by Commissioner Waters and Paddy Cahill. Two deputies carried an ultimatum to Gilruth to appear within five minutes—it was bruited he was hiding in the cellar. A final deputy gave him one minute—deep, dark alternative not stated.

On the last tick of the second hand a portly figure in white appeared on the lawn, in uproar of threats, catcalls and jeers. Invited to the beer-case, His Excellency preferred the glory of the garden. He was about to begin a speech when a brawl broke out in the mob, Paddy Cahill in the thick of it, waving a shillelagh. Somebody shouted,

"Hop the fence!"

As the mob surged forward, the white-anted shell of a fence fell down. Six feet three in his socks, Gilruth doubled his fists and challenged a thousand angry men. Behind him an echoing chorus of Government officials pranced about like boxers on the lawn. For one sharp moment the battle was touch and go, but each army was held back by yells of its leaders to leave it to a higher power, to *keep within the law*.

As urgent telegrams flew to the south for special police and Riot Acts, the uproar turned to a jeering laughter. The revolution was over with the passing storm. A few black eyes were taken to hospital, a few hot-heads and half-castes hustled into jail. His Excellency, with dignity, retired to Government House, where he remained in a state of siege. The dauntless thousand retired to the Government office verandas where they camped with billies and swags, the union in possession of the town. The crowd went down to the Singapore ship to see it unload the beer, and the red sun sank in a dazzled calm.

Paddy Cahill was leaving for the south that night with some rare specimens for Sydney Zoo, among them that marvel of Australian fauna, a pair of sable kangaroos. For his perfidy with the shillelagh, Paddy's luggage was declared black. A jester opened the crates on the wharf and let the specimens go, frilled lizard, spotted pythons, black kangaroos and pink-eyed wallabies from Alligator Rivers creating a merry panic among the crowd.

Streamer sensations in the southern press were shouting DARWIN REVOLUTION and the peril of Dr Gilruth. The gunboat *Una* was detailed to the scene, her marines marched to the Residency as guard. In fellow-feeling wondrous kind, all shared the Christmas beer. When H.M.A.S. *Encounter* steamed into the harbour a few days later, Dr Gilruth was smuggled aboard and thankfully sailed away.

Pending the Royal Commission, an advisory council governed the north,

H. E. Carey, R. J. Evans, T. J. Oliver, with two union leaders as members, H. Nelson and H. Ryan. A private and confidential letter that fell into Nelson's hands disclosed certain discreditable mining deals and dummying in land. The chairman of the Council, the Government Secretary, and the Justice of the Supreme Court, under threat of another uprising, were forced to resign their positions forthwith, and to leave the town. Ordered to be on board s.s. *Bambra* for the west at eight o'clock that night, they walked to the jetty through a silent crowd. Waterside workers stood guard till the ship carried them out.

Another bombshell in the south, shades of Eureka! But when Dr Gilruth appeared in Darwin with his cronies a year or two later to give evidence at the Royal Commission, under police guard, old scores were already forgotten. The town was much more excited by the arrival of the two "lady typewriters" that accompanied the Commission, a novelty from the south.

The verdict was "agin the Government", strongly in favour of the unions and the Territory people, in that neglect and self-interest had incited them to action, their indignation justified, their allegations, for the most part, true.

In 1919 Vestey's meatworks closed down. Captains and kings departed. Away went the unions to the south, leaving Darwin with just over a thousand white people, including two hundred and eighty-nine unemployed and a hundred and sixty Government officials. Greektown, Tokyo Town, Little Russia, a Latin quarter of Spaniards, Italians and Maltese were dotted about the headland with a Manila Town, Malay village, some new tints in half-castes and the usual straggle of blacks.

The Gilruth régime had cost £8,000,000.

Where were the ships, the roads, the telephones, the colleges, hospitals, railways, seaports, cities? Where were "*the torched mines and noisy factories*"?

Echo answered, Where?

Capital and Labour together left not a trace.

Honourable Miles Staniforth Smith was the administrator who followed Gilruth, pending the appointment of F. C. Urquhart, a former Queensland commissioner of police. Harold Nelson, leader of the rebels, even as Peter Lalor after Eureka Stockade, was elected to parliament, first Federal member for the Territory, and held the seat for many years.

Vestey's big pile at Bullocky Point, overrun with white ants and goats, remained a dismal monument to industrial strife for the next thirty years. The trans-continental railway was a wash-out, the Government farms jungle, and forty-two farms deserted. Of all the dairy herds was left one solitary cow. Still no water supply. Prospectors financed to the tune of thousands, companies to tens of thousands had vanished from the mines, the same old Chinese rocking their cradles in the gullies.

Down on the big stock routes the drovers' mobs still perished on the broken wells . . . no industry in the whole of the north but cattle, population, as usual, one to a thousand square miles. No market now, the stations were broke—not even a new homestead on the company runs, where managers were left to brood, nobody around but the blacks.

William MacGregor, the compositor, who had walked two thousand miles from Adelaide, with high hopes to Darwin, now walked back. At the cattle stations and the telegraph stations all the way south, he counted fifty-eight people.

Darwin owed so much to the Chinese storekeepers that it had no hope of leaving. Absconding debtors were hauled from every ship. Man Fong Lau, Yam Yan, Fang Cheong Loong and Wing Chong Sing, with others in dingy Chinatown for the next fifteen years, by giving generous credit in stores, meals, clothing, to wear and the laundering of it, kept the town on the map. No one had any money.

Except for new Government offices and a new school, there was nothing to show that anything had happened. There was only a fortnightly, instead of a weekly, train to Pine Creek. Holtze was gone, the Botanic Gardens were a wreck. For months the departments had no leaders, no protector for the blacks. The other States of the Commonwealth paid the maintenance of the Territory in taxes, and from now on it cost £1,000,000 a year.

Land of milk and honey—goats' milk and wild bees' honey. In yet another twilight of blighted hopes, the *N.T. Times* kept up the hearts of the pioneers by printing directions for making jute out of eucalyptus fibre and tanning with mangrove bark.

The old hands, all alone again, living with the blackfellows on goose-eggs and cabbage-tree top, sat back in their bough sheds by the billabongs and, like little Audrey, they laughed and laughed.

Chapter XX

Travellin' Cattle

CRACK OF a whip and drumming of hoofs, the mob wheels in to water. Shadows of the paperbarks are long on the pool, the glare of day is ended, and it's sundown on the Georgina road.

The cattle wade deep in the river-cool. Dusty and stiff with riding from the dawn, ringers and wingers swing down out of the saddle, rubbing their insteps where stirrup-irons have bitten in deep.

The cook has pulled up his dray in the curve of a coolabah-tree, Bedourie ovens, flat-side billies, canteens and tucker-bags, in his wide alfresco kitchen, efficiently ranged around. He wears no white cap, but his fame may be continent-wide for all that. The clatter of his pans and pannikins is a cheering vesper sound. His black offsider, bare feet immune to prickles and burrs, gathers firewood, claws kindling to the pile, and sets a match. As a thread of smoke rises, he is off with billies and canteens to fill them at the pool—a reach of the river eighteen miles long, but they call it a "pool" in the outback. It's a big country, Australia.

The boss drover, at the tail of the mob, still sits his mount, with a ringer on duty. He fans his sweating face with his wide-brimmed hat. There's a patch of "storm" where a passing shower has fallen about a hundred yards away. It's "dead sweet" for a night camp, green feed for the cattle and rest for tired men—perhaps. As the last few stragglers climb out of the pool, he and the ringer head the mob in. With a quick canter round for the lay of the land in case of a midnight rush, he takes first watch, riding in narrowing circles to close the cattle in and steady them down.

The horse-tailer hopples out the riding-horses and spares—jangle of bells up- and down-river in the dusk. The men build saddles and packs into a breakwind and swags are unrolled in a half-circle on the dray side of the fire, boss drover and head ringer to sleep nearest the cattle, this also in case of a rush. The fire will be a protection. For safety and convenience nothing is left to chance—trim as the architecture of a house the traditional drover's camp.

"Righto!" The cook calls dinner—curry or corned beef, flapjacks, stewed prunes and rice, or a more elaborate menu according to his lights. Each one comes to the camp-oven to ladle out his own, or to "cut off" with his clasp-knife. Sauce bottle inverted over the plates, they place them on the ground and sit in the stockman's squat, quart-pots within reach at the rim of the blaze. The blacks have beef, damper, a big billy of sugared tea and perhaps a tin of jam at a fire of their own, calling distance away.

Hungry men have little to say. They eat and drink quickly, though this is the only "sit down" meal of the day. While the cook makes tomorrow's damper and buries it under the coals, they jest with each other, roll cigarettes and thumb their pipes. One of them bends to the flickering light, reading a letter from his girl. With the same smiles in the same places he reads the same letter every night.

The horse-tailer brings in the night-horses ready saddled, and tethers them to trees on the head ringer's side. Ten o'clock watch turns in and the others soon after, in trousers and boots, sometimes spurs. The cattle are quiet, their eyes shining like lamps in weird horned masks of faces, and the trees beyond are changing shapes and shadows. Red glow of the burning log, the hump of sleeping drovers, night-horses with their heads down, brooding—it might be a picture by Goya, who painted the devil's mules bewitching men. There's a tenor voice singing across the silence of the bush, "Ma-axwelton braes are bon-nie," a lullaby to the cattle, and away down the river the tonging of a Condamine bell.

Such is any drover's night-camp on the Georgina road, the great arterial stock route of Australia that is no road at all.

By the end of April general muster is over on all the northern stations from Lawn Hills over to Lissadell. Stockmen, white and black, have been out for weeks "riding tracks", mustering, branding, camp-draughting. First mail after the wet brought letters and wires from the companies and owners regarding mobs and drovers. At an appointed waterhole and yards the head stockman meets the boss drover to hand over. The cattle are counted and checked, receipts showing number, brands and descriptions. A ringer riding ahead, wingers on the flank, and the boss drover behind, they string out and move off, maybe five months on the track, maybe ten. In the days of the overlanders, from Wave Hill to Wodonga, from Ord River to Bourke, it might be two years. The men were as far out of the world as old-time mariners on the sea.

The boss drover is responsible for every hoof and night-camp. He used to be paid £1 a head for delivery at the railhead, £1250 for the usual mob of twelve hundred and fifty, but now agreements vary. He provides the "plant" of from four to eight ringers, white and black, a cook—always white—a horse-tailer—generally black—anything up to eighty horses—a dozen night-horses, twenty or thirty packs and the rest riding or spares—stores, drays for calves and gear. He knows the waters, feed, good camps, easy going and dry stages—he knows all Australia by night. His is the psychology of men, horses and cattle, for he has to manage them all in finding a way across a million square miles. When settling day comes in the trucking yards, it is a bad day for the drover whose mob is fallen by the wayside. His story will be told in mournful numbers in all the outback pubs. Except in an outright Act of God, his reputation, his livelihood, is gone. No excuses. He should have known. A captain has lost his ship.

First mobs leave the north at the end of the wet. Strong green feed and stinging flies, thunder and lightning, floods, have made them restless and unruly. The rivers are still "running bankers", they zigzag the crossings or swim forty feet deep—all you can see is their horns in a swirl of muddy waters. Sometimes they ring in midstream, or scatter when they reach the bank, which makes adventurous riding, gallop and smash through the scrub to "bend" them.

It is the law that through all the pastoral holdings they travel at ten miles a day, lest they eat the station-owner out of house and home, and drink his waters dry—he comes around to see that they keep moving. While the stars are still shining the camp is astir to the cook's call of "Daylight!", horse-tailer already out for the horses and the cattle rising and browsing here and there. If there is a waterhole handy the men plunge in, if not they tip a canteen to the dish. A pannikinful is a bath on a dry stage. Breakfast is a thumb-piece and a quart of tea, standing up. Bright morning, burning noon to drowsy afternoon, no dinner-camp for a ringer—his "scran" from the saddle-pouch he munches when the sun is high, with a quart-pot of water from the horse's neck-bag to wash it down. It may have been a quiet ride with only a few fizzes, it may have been a "hell of a day" in bush-fires or in bog—he must stand his two hours' watch at night.

All things of idyllic seeming in this world are the most difficult—a windjammer, a genius, a beautiful woman, gold. Prose and poetry glorify the drover's life into "vision splendid of the sunlit plains extended". Romance glows in the camp-fire light and rings in the rhythm of the riding. I doubt whether there is a more arduous calling. Truly it has its poetry, but the men are too weary to find it. To them the "everlasting stars" are only sleepless nights.

A running river of red and white, the mob goes drifting down, through the pindan, light scrub in red sand, "Bay o' Biscay" country, raggedy gullies and hills like tumbled waves in a big sea, "drummy" country, a crust over limestone where their own hoofs with a sound of drums terrify the cattle, and black-soil "debil-debil" of hard-baked holes hidden in long yellow grass, over the sandhills into "mickery", soak country. Waters range from swift creeks and quicksand billabongs to boiling artesian bores and a nightmare of filling troughs in the dark from wells with broken buckets and frayed ropes to waters a scum of dead snakes and wild dogs two hundred feet down. At their windmill, whim and whip-spring wells the stations charge 3d. a head, with a "cattle-barman" camped there to check the mob through. In a very dry time they may refuse water.

Cattle on a dry stage are travelled day and night, with brief spells for feeding. On the third day they walk with a low moaning, and on the fourth go into a dazed stagger with dry throats gasping, a terrible sound and a terrible sight. Thirsting cattle will mob the drover's night-camp, catching the scent of water pouring out of his billy. The poor demented brutes come round the fire to lick the flames.

Nearing the waterhole at last, a drover shows his mettle, heading them away from the wind and in little batches into the pool—otherwise, when the leader raises his head with a joyous bellow, the mob will race, trampling down the weak, half of them bogged or drowned. The ringers spread them wide and hold them. Eighty-mile dry stages are not unusual, even today. Odds in the earlies were much longer. Dogs have never worked cattle in the north, they could never live through the stages.

A watch must be kept for belts of "poison weed"—nux vomica and gastrolobium—the oft-told tale of five hundred dead in a night. The wise drover knows the perilous places. He steadies the mob down beforehand, lets them "fill themselves fat", then whips them over with no time to snatch a mouthful.

The rush is real trouble. With nervous cattle a double watch is set, and that is why the ringers keep singing, or playing a tin whistle, or reciting poetry in a monotonous chant, to reassure them in the little noises of the night. They never camp where stones rattle, or twigs break, or dead branches may fall—black ground is better than red. The mob may be peacefully lying down asleep when a clap of thunder, a moth or an owl or nothing at all sends them pelting for the river. The ringers, shirtless, leap on the night-horses, plunge in, hang to their tails and swim, scramble into the saddle again and thrash through the scrub, whips cracking. Night-horses know more than the ringers, flying to close the outside wings in on the leaders and head them and ring them. They may be away for days, weeks, after a thousand head or a wing. To wild cattle at night there's a blackfellow with a spear behind every bush. The uncanny stillness of moonlight nights is just as bad as a thunderstorm—they listen, and for no reason whatever they're up, and off, and gone! There are no piebalds, skewbalds or greys in a droving-plant—too ghostly. Old hands will tell you that grey horses have a peculiar smell, and even a phosphorescence that attracts the lightning—"you can see devil-lights playing around their ears". One big stampede to unnerve them, and the cattle are off every night, "hell, west and crooked".

Before the wells and the Government bores the drovers had stories to tell. "Don't talk to me of the drovers of today," said Tom Pearce. "They leave hundreds of dead beasts at the bores, and they're picture-show heroes. With their records we'd die of shame. We stood our ground on a long job, and if a man couldn't deliver without five per cent losses, he was out for keeps. We had bad cattle where the blacks were bad, and hundred-mile dry stages, and no stores for rations. Yet I wonder will they know the peaceful past as we old-timers know it?"

Wave Hill to Wodonga—six thousand five hundred head on the road in six mobs, and Jack-Dick Skuthorpe behind them. In lightning and storms, rushes every night. One night in the gallop Jack-Dick's horse reared back. He goaded it on—with a somersault in a gully it fell on him fifteen feet down. He mounted, rounded up the breakaways, and rode five weeks to Katherine with a broken ankle. At Elsey yards, two thousand had to be inoculated for redwater. The weakened beasts all bogged in the crumbling banks of Bitter Springs.

"We put the leaders on the crossing," Tom went on. "They went straight as the shot of a gun till they reached a mud-bar formed in the last floods. Then they began to ring. Swimming our horses, we threw out a wing to give a lead to the others. Round they rung, spinning till the mud boiled. God help the bullocks that came down in that mad swirl. We were the centre of a double ring spinning against the bar, with whip and voice forcing them back. To straighten them up was the work of a few long minutes. In a few more we had the river cut asunder with a line of cattle from bank to bank, like Moses with his mob of mixed Israelites crossing the Red Sea. Only seven were glued in the mud, and five we pulled out with the help of a mob of myall blacks. Two we had to leave. After that the nervous brutes rushed every night. Were we glad to see the roof of Daly Waters glinting through the trees!

Walter Rose, a year later, tried that track in drought, camped for weeks on low waterholes before he could move on. Four months from Wave Hill to Katherine, he then tried the Coast Road, to be driven back by drought. Taking the cattle south to Powell's Creek he was again turned back by drought—four hundred miles and three months' travelling lost. Over the ninety-mile dry to Eva Downs, and across the Barklys with eight drinks in five hundred miles, he hadn't lost a living hoof when he hit the Georgina road. That was the spirit of the old Australia. The drover may die in his tracks, but the cattle must go through.

There are three great stock routes from the north to the cities of the south. Reading from left to right on the map they are the Canning, the Great North Road, and the Georgina, the big cattle highway of the continent, every year for eighty years moving with fifty or a hundred thousand head. It gathers in most of the cattle of the north, from Normanton over to Wyndham, and follows the big river systems of western Queensland down for the populous cities, Brisbane, Sydney, Melbourne and Adelaide. After their first straggled thousand miles across the Territory, from Victoria River to Katherine or Newcastle Waters, Anthony's Lagoons and the Rankine, they join the Georgina road at Camooweal on the border and thread the river—a pearly river in sand for soft going—for five hundred miles, down through the little cattle outposts of Lake Nash, Urandangee, Boulia and Bedourie. From Kuttaburra crossing at Glengyle the river swings west to join the Mulligan and so down to Lake Eyre. The stock route runs due south, with an eighty-mile dry stage to Birdsville on the Diamantina. Georgina and Diamantina rivers were named after Georgina Diamantina Bowen, the beautiful Greek wife of a Queensland Governor, her Christian name shining for over two thousand miles to redeem an Australian desert.

From Birdsville the stock route may either travel south over the sandhills four hundred miles to Marree, the railhead for Adelaide, or it may take a right-angle east for the grand old Cooper, the Wilson, Paroo, Bulloo and Warrego rivers to Broken Hill or Bourke. Nowadays the big mobs of the Georgina rumble away on wheels from all the railway towns from Cloncurry to Moree.

The Great North Road runs from Katherine to Alice Springs, a three months' stroll for a thousand miles, with Government wells in every thirty, then three days' train journey from Alice Springs to the fattening paddocks of Adelaide.

Far from all the rivers and pastoral holdings is the Canning stock route of West Australia, a trail unique in the world. From Hall's Creek to Wiluna it winds for nearly a thousand miles with never a hut and not a head of stock on either side within five hundred miles. It crosses the Great Sandy Desert, of two hundred and fifty thousand square miles, peopled by a few wandering tribes of utterly uncivilized blacks.

A. W. Canning three times opened this route. The explorer-surveyor told me the story himself. With South Australia's Larry Wells, he was the sun-tanned quiet type of path-finder whose love of the work was its own reward.

When shipping was prohibited to East Kimberley cattle on account of cattle tick, A. W. Canning, Government Surveyor, suggested this route, following David Carnegie's track through *Spinifex and Sand*, and so open a market with the goldfields. Even Kimberley pioneers believed him mad.

In 1906 with eight men and eight camels he set out from Wiluna. After the first two hundred miles there were no known waters, but wild blacks led the party to their native wells, rockholes and springs. Canning drew maps for them in the sand, and, with no link of thought in language, timing distances by the sun, the naked hunters pointed and marked down the number of days with their spears.

"I found their directions remarkably accurate," Canning said. "When we deepened these crude wells they 'made' copiously, the least of them three hundred gallons an hour. At Wardabanna, in an indistinct creek, there were twenty thousand gallons in a natural rock tank. We found water in stages of about twenty miles."

Patiently breasting sandhills fifty feet high and seven to the mile, skirting the dazzled brine of Lake Disappointment, they also found fodder for travelling stock in belts of rubbly mulga scrub or low wattle and quandong. Groves of the beautiful desert oaks were occasional blessing of shade, those sombre boughs a sanctuary for noisy thousands of white cockatoos, bronze-wing pigeons and crested spinifex doves. Where fauna was stunted and small, mainly kangaroo rats and bungarra goannas, Canning discovered a pocket-edition dingo never known to science. Unfortunately a camel fell on the packs, and killed the specimen he was taking to Perth Museum.

At Waddamalla, a well in a white clay-pan, Michael Tobin, foreman of the expedition, was killed by a treacherous black. He drew his revolver and shot the native as the fatal spear was thrown. Canning later set there a marble cross that marks one of the loneliest graves in Australia.

In 1908 he set out from Wiluna again, with twenty-six men, sixty-two camels, two wagons with stores for two years, and eight hundred goats for meat supply. This time they put down fifty wells in eight hundred miles. Working in fierce heat of summer they timbered those wells from twenty-five to a hundred feet deep, and equipped each one with whip, windlass, buckets and forty-eight feet of troughing. The desert oaks provided the hardy red wood for the job, sometimes carted by the pack-camels over the sandhills for a hundred miles. The water was rarely brackish, and it now "made" at the rate of a thousand gallons an hour, to provide for mobs of eight hundred passing through.

Two years without meeting a white man, the party arrived at Flora Valley. They had proved there was no "waterless desert" in Australia, and the stock route was declared open—to tragedy. Thompson and Shoesmith, first drovers, were murdered by the blacks, their camp looted and their cattle eaten.

The hoodoo was lifted by young Tom Cole of Kimberley, who brought a mob safely through. Jim Wickham and Frank McManus followed a few years later, but the blacks had stolen the ironwork of the wells, and sands of the desert were filling them in. The cattle had to travel in small mobs, two or three days between them, waiting for the water to make. For twenty years the blacks and sandstorms were left to their own sweet will.

In 1930, when Wiluna was opened up as a gold-mining centre, a big union population to be fed on Kimberley beef, A. W. Canning led his men out and opened the stock route again. Dick Rowan brought mobs from Sturt River, Bickley from Flora Valley, and Darchy chose this route when he delivered nine hundred Kidman cattle to Perth from the abandoned run of Glenroy in King Leopold Ranges.

In the last war the Canning was a recognized track of the West, but still a lonely one, of camp-fires in the silent sands for four long months. It is the only trail of the continent where camels and cattle travel together—horses are too thirsty, and of those gridiron sandhills and of *munjong* blacks with spears they are shy.

The stock routes of Australia are a long chain of graves. One stormy night in western Queensland a mob rushed camp and killed four men. They were driving old pikers through thick scrub, a troublesome mob with double watch, and camped by the buckboard in the rain, unable to light a fire. At a clap of thunder the mob wheeled in and smashed the buckboard to matchwood—no time to climb trees, the men were trampled to death where they lay.

Dunbar's droving to the Arafura will never be forgotten. With sixteen hundred cattle from Wollogorang for Captain Joe Bradshaw in 1903, Dunbar set out from Burketown along the Old Coast Road with four white ringers and a cook. One died of dysentery, one wandered and shot himself before they reached Hodgson Downs. Dunbar's grave is at Roper Bar, where he died of fever. Sweeney went on with the cattle north into Arnhem Land. On the upper Wilton River he lay under a tree and died, and a black ringer, a woman, buried him at Ahcup Lagoon. The cattle were all lost and speared by the blacks.

But the ghost road of the drovers is Murran-ji Track.

Wild dogs howl and the hedgewood groans,
A night-wind whistles in semitones,
And bower-birds play with human bones
 Under a vacant sky.
The drover's mob is a cloud of dust,
The drover's mob is a sacred trust,
Where the Devil says "Can't!" and God says "Must!"
 Out on the Murran-ji.

Cattle still rush there in broad daylight. Horses shy at their own shadows in the black tangle of its bulwaddi scrubs, and a ringer sleeps uneasily if he knows that he lights his camp-fire on graves.

From Newcastle Waters to Wave Hill on the long ride to the west, the first hundred and forty miles is Murran-ji Track, the northern rim of nothing, most notorious dry stage of Australia in the number of its deaths by thirst and fever. There were three swiftly vanishing waters about fifty miles apart, hidden away in eerie empty bush—never, in sixty years, a friendly bough shed there of white man or black. The desert is an angry haze to southward, all the way down to the trans-continental line, nearly a thousand miles. The Track comes out at Top Springs of Armstrong Creek, eight miles from Montajinnie—aboriginally Meanta-jinnie, wild dog's track—farthest-south out-station of Victoria River Downs. From there Wave Hill is another hundred miles south-west.

Today the Murran-ji is a highway. In one week of June we met sixteen drovers with twenty-two thousand head, bound over for the Barklys and the Georgina road, and travelling west the road-trains with ninety tons of stores for the border stations. There are well-equipped Government bores and tanks in every twenty miles, and through the worst of the nightmare scrub they have bulldozed a stock route nine chains wide. A graded road is that winding pad where once in five years a packhorse pilgrim carried his life in his water-bag, and lay unburied if the Murran-ji was dry.

Nathaniel Buchanan, when he formed Wave Hill in 1883, pioneered this track for cattle travelling west, taking a chance on poor waters to cut off a thousand miles round through Katherine, Willeroo, Delamere and Victoria River Downs. Riders to Kimberley gold, in 1886, followed his horse-pad through the wooded mazes, and perished if the waters were gone. A man named Prosser took "the first pair of wheels across" in 1887, a bullock-wagon. Big Jim Kennedy from Camooweal took two wagons across and sold them to Mulligan, a teamster, who used them as a fort when, with George Ligar, he was besieged by blacks in Jasper Gorge. Steve and Harry Lewis, from Newcastle Station, drove cattle over to the west, and Tom Deacon went through with two wagons to Waterloo. These made the road.

North-west from Newcastle Waters, twenty miles across open coolabah country and lightly timbered plain, you come to a ragged creek, Iandra-kootcha, bird-devil, night-owl, where the Tjing-illi blacks made secret and ceremonial journeys to gather the silver night-owl feathers they wore in their man-corroborees. Nat Buchanan left an old iron bucket upturned there on a stump, and to bushmen the creek was known as "the Bucket" ever after.

From here on you are in the scrubs, lancewood, *ka-now-in-ja*, spears, —and hedgewood, *allumbo*, the "bulwaddi", already described, those "horrid forests" that trapped McDouall Stuart on his fifth journey north, and sent him riding back fifteen hundred miles. Those gnarled dark woods are of the hardest timber on earth—when very old it will break and burn, but it never bends. A rush in the hedgewood was slaughter, the cattle ripped up and impaled, an easy trail to follow of blood and broken horns. A fire in the hedgewood was suffocation.

For over a hundred miles the western road is lined with this forbidding scrub, dense for forty miles north and south. Even today you can't ride through it. The path was burnt out in early years, and hacked with axes.

Deep in the maze, fifty miles from the Bucket, is the waterhole that gives the Track its name—Murrunjai, frog—no more than rain-water shallows in grey clay, seventy yards across, with ramparts of the sinister soundless scrub. No wind comes here. Rimming the waters are wizard box-trees hundreds of years old, mal-formed dwarfs of the kindly coolabah, and their snaky reflections.

A backwater of Lethe, weird as a Gustave Doré, with the red flicker of firelight in its natural graveyard of ant-hills, the place is alive and creepy by night. It is still and ghastly by day. Even when the wattle is a field of the cloth of gold, and tawny wood-duck skim the silver shallows, it is beauty in a minor key, and when spear-shafts of late afternoon sun slant through the lancewood on to its shrouded ant-hills, the cathedral silence is melancholy . . . fey.

Stifling heat and stagnation here bred fever. A long way out in the Territory, by the time the riders reached it, on poor food, hard going, and the canteens rattling dry, too often they were done. Sleeping close to a dead water, they sickened and died in their swags.

There are eleven white men buried around the Murran-ji. A small deep hole to one side is where the drovers made their camp, and had to guard it well when a thousand frantic cattle came thundering in, wallowing the big pool into a black mist of mosquitoes above a quagmire of evil-smelling mud.

Murran-ji Bore now blesses the traveller with pure and healthful water only fifty yards away.

Hedgewood scrubs crawl on for a long fifty miles—ten miles a day with cattle—to Yellow Waterholes, at their best a broken creek with a few spectral gum-trees and etiolated yellow lilies, but most of the year a sulphur-coloured clay trampled by cattle and baked and glazed like pottery in the sun, on the edge of a dreary ant-hill plain. The native name is Ben-cook-we-charra, lily-seed water, or, to the Tjingilli people, Ben-kootch, devil-water. Its blacks were "bad", the wild Mudburra people, hunting down from the ranges, and jealous of this water. Two or three white men were speared here. One, Hardcastle, was ambushed on a cold winter's night. The spear penetrated three rugs and the double of a camp-sheet and entered his lung—he died in Wyndham.

It is ten miles to the Jump-up, where you leave the heavy walls of scrub and go down a rugged escarpment two or three hundred feet steep with one of the loveliest panoramas in Australia, rich rolling downs that remind you of "Macarthur's New South Wales", the country around Camden, but in fiercer sunlights, the wide and lonely valley of Armstrong Creek, black-soil plains. There, in a labyrinth of ant-hills where three tracks meet—to Pigeonholes and Victoria River Downs, or by Dry River to Katherine—the Murran-ji ends in a glad surprise, pandanus palms a-shimmer by a miraculous little river thirty feet deep, seeping out of a cleft in the rock, pretty with ferns, bottle-green and brimming for miles, never known to be dry, Top Springs.

The drovers are casual about it now, with bores all the way over from Newcastle Waters. Top Springs is just a picnic and a swim. In the hard old days it was salvation of God. Some still living have galloped a hundred miles to it, trying to beat the water-bags, trying to beat delirium, finding the Murran-ji and the Yellow bone-dry. They were out of the wood when they reached Top Springs. Some have crawled in there on hands and knees.

Montajinnie homestead is eight miles away—still one of the solitary outcamps of Australia. Mrs Norton was living there when we passed by, with three babies, often for weeks "on her own" when her husband and his black stock-camp were out on the run. With hospitality for everyone who passed by, she was unafraid, the homestead lamp shining far out to the silent tracks either side, and down below the big desert "where nobody lives".

From Montajinnie past Lonely Springs and Kurrenjacki Stones, you follow down Armstrong Creek, "beautiful water" for ninety miles to the Victoria valley and its golden prairies, the biggest of all Vestey stations and, eight miles farther on, on the river bank the little police station, the quaint old Afghan store for the drovers, and the floodswept ruins of Nat Buchanan's homestead, first in the western Territory, under the Wave Hill.

For ten years there were only occasional horsemen and "foot-walkers" along the Murran-ji, bound out for West Australian gold. Many died. Next year's rider found boots and a belt, maybe a swag—the sandy desert is a breeding-ground for wild dogs. One man, Beale, had walked from Oodnadatta, eleven hundred miles, to perish between the Murran-ji and the Yellow. A big Welshman, Llewellyn, left Newcastle Waters wheeling a barrow with an eight-gallon drum of water. It lasted a hundred and ten miles—both waterholes were dry. They found him between the Yellow and the Jump-up. The barrow, hung in a tree, was his monument for years.

In 1904 Blake Miller, for Kidman, brought from west to east the first big mob of a thousand cows. Following him came the Lewis brothers and "Jumbo" Smith, each with a thousand head. These opened the stock route for big mobs travelling east, in a good year a short-cut through for drovers bound down to Oodnadatta and Charleville from Kimberley, Victoria and Wave—if they were game to try it. When the three waterholes were full it cut out a thousand miles, three months' travelling, but there were no pedal radios, no telegraphs, no stations, no people, no "mulga wires" to tell when they were dry—in that fearful scrub a "perish" for beasts and men. In the best of years, with rain all round in the sky, the Murran-ji and the Yellow lasted only seven months, and two or three mobs in front of him finished a man's chances. Once out on the Track there was no turning back—it was go or die. Jack-Dick Skuthorpe, in 1905, whipped his cattle over without a drink for a hundred and two miles, and then with only half a drink for another fifty miles.

But all-time cattle dry-stage honours for Australia belong to the Farquharson brothers of Inverway. On the Murran-ji Track in 1909, from Top Springs to the Bucket, they travelled a thousand head for a hundred and twenty-five miles without even a smell of water, flogging the poor brutes on all day lest they should break back to perish, and leading them on with hurricane lamps all night. They counted at Newcastle Waters and had lost only five. Harry and Hughie Farquharson, of that great droving, are dead, but Mr Archie Farquharson, aged eighty-eight years, nephew of Nat Buchanan and one of the Territory's immortals, still lives to tell their story.

The ringers faced terrible odds, away for weeks after a rush with a water-bag alone through the hedgewood scrubs, or ninety miles down into the desert, living on flour and beef, doing long stretches without sleep for fear of attack by blacks. Of sunstroke and fever they died, and the wild dogs found them.

"You couldn't bury them deep with the cook's old fire-shovel or a hedgewood stick," one of the oldest riders told me. "There ain't no time for a funeral on a dry stage."

"Mulga Jim" MacDonald is one of the few with a grave, a tidy tombstone. He gave his head ringer instructions to carry on with the cattle, and lay down in the shade—his last shade. Hussey is out there somewhere, and Billie Leanie from the Orkneys, one of Todd's Men. Dan Sheahan is buried at the head of Armstrong Creek. Murdoch Macleod, whose brother was a barrister in Sydney, after "doing a perish" on the dry stage was drowned in Armstrong Creek, his pocket full of sodden £5 notes where a £5 note was never seen in years. But old-timers can count twenty and more who rode that way out of the world, and the others were men unknown. Jack Scott strangely disappeared. With a thousand head on the road, he grew dizzy with heat and fever.

"I'm crook," he said to the ringers. "I'll spell for a bit. You get them cattle on."

They were only six miles from Murran-ji, and Murran-ji was full. A ringer rode back with a water-bag, found Jack's horse tethered to a tree, but nobody ever found him. The blacks could not pick up his track. He must have wandered through the hedgewood, and that way madness lies.

The men of the Murran-ji had to keep faith with the cattle, but the name of the drover I shall not write who, with fever in camp, kept faith with cattle. He left three of his men, two white and a black, to die . . . left them with stores and a couple of drums of water to last for two or three weeks till his next mob came by. Sick men cannot boil the billy and fend for themselves, and they had no quinine. The following drover found them. One had travelled in circles till he fell. The others, a white and a black, sat back to back under the same tree in the listlessness of the dead.

From Kimberley over to Queensland, from Darwin to Bourke, the drover is known even yet as "Murdering Charley". He never came back to Murran-ji Track

Hedgewood writhes in the dark o' the night,
Ant-hills glimmer a ghostly white,
The cattle are galloping mad with fright
  From where the dead men lie.
The drover's mob is a fateful trust,
The life of a ringer less than dust
When God says "Can't!" and the Devil says "Must!"
  Out on the Murran-ji.

Chapter XXI

Poddy-Dodgers

When the moon has climbed the mountains and the
stars are shining bright,
We'll saddle up our neddies and away,
And we'll steal the squatter's cattle by the
bright moonlight,
And we'll brand 'em at the dawning of the day.
Ah, my little poddy calf, you may at the squatter laugh,
For he'll never be your owner any more,
When you're running, running, running, all upon the
duffers' green
Free-selected by the Newmerella shore.

Old Australian Song, "The Poddy-dodger's Lullaby".

AUSTRALIA HAS elevated her bushrangers to the rank of heroes. Still we glorify in prose and verse the misguided young gangster, Ned Kelly, who was hanged seventy years ago, and not without reason. We make a shrine of the "last stand" of Dan Morgan, Ben Hall, and other murderers who terrorized the pioneers, who betrayed the trust of the kindly bush and the open road. Bank robbers, intimidators of women, common thieves of the highway, a shabby set of national heroes they are.

If we must have crime in romance, I sing the poddy-dodgers, worthy of a poet's pen.

Scamps of cattle-duffers were the poddy-dodgers, but they never harmed their fellow man. They rode hundreds of miles to help him, and lent him hundreds of pounds in his need. Newmerella is now a highly respectable dairy valley of Gippsland, and indignantly repudiates "The Poddy-dodger's Lullaby", but from the Snowy River to the Ord its legendary sons have travelled far, and played a part in the founding of five great pastoral States.

"Over the range" from the farthest stations they found new pastures and hidden waterholes for the little mob of cleanskins that the big runs never missed. "Running wild cattle", who was to care if they did chase a few tame ones? They were Bushmen. In the great outback, there is no higher praise.

Even yet from the wilds of Queensland, the Territory and the West, occasional press-wires in our metropolitan dailies headed Wyndham, Cloncurry and Alice Springs, bring rumours of masked stockmen and muffled horse tracks on the boundaries, heavy penalties for unauthorized sales. But now the guilty are no more than cattle-thieves. The supermen are gone, those who rode the ranges "out where the blacks is bad".

Not so long ago an aeroplane pilot around Wave Hill and Victoria River Downs happened to mention a bird's-eye view of a mob moving in lonely country. Victoria had no musters in that direction, neither had Wave. Advised by pedal radio, the police rushed out in motor-trucks—the cattle were scattered and the stockmen vanished.

So science has tricked the poddy-dodgers. Gone are the days when their hearts were young and gay, but they have not lived in vain. Some died in the odour of sanctity, leaving a chain of great station holdings and towns that began with a string of motherless calves mustered on a nameless creek.

Harry Readford, who formed Brunette Downs, was demigod cattle-duffer of the world's history, the man who stole a thousand head and drove them fifteen hundred miles through an unmapped desert land. Readford is "Captain Starlight" in Rolf Boldrewood's Australian evergreen, *Robbery Under Arms*. From his little run, Wombunderry, near Jundah, Queensland, in the seventies he lifted a thousand bullocks from the back country of the big Landsborough station, Mount Cornish. Down along Cooper's Creek over the sands where Burke and Wills could not keep a camel alive, he delivered that thousand head to the saleyards in Adelaide, opening up a great continental stock route, the Cooper, the Diamantina and the Birdsville track. Three white men were with him, not knowing the mob was stolen. They found the waters and travelled by the sun. It was a wonderful season, sands and stony steppes covered with herbage, the lakes full of vervein and clover.

Telling the story in years long after, when it was safe to tell it, Readford said there was only one bad moment on the journey. Looking back from the crest of a sandhill, he saw a dark regiment of mounted police galloping in his wake. No hope to hide a thousand head, even in the Cooper sandhills. He sat down to await his fate . . . suddenly the black cavalry wheeled off over a clay-pan. It was a flock of emus.

But fate was on his track in the shape of an old white English bull, which joined up with the cattle in the farm country of Kapunda. Twice they drove it away, twice it came back. Reported missing, it was recognized in Adelaide saleyards. Readford was arrested. The horns of one dilemma multiplied to a thousand when his mystery mob was traced to Mount Cornish by the Queensland police. He was tried in Roma, verdict "Not Guilty", and carried from the court shoulder-high.

"The verdict, gentlemen," said judge to jury, "is yours, not mine, thank God." His Honour strongly recommended that no further cattle-stealing be heard at that time in Roma, where fellow feeling made them wondrous kind.

Harry Readford redeemed himself when he took three thousand cattle from Albilba Station on the Barcoo, and formed Brunette Downs, where he stayed as manager for McAnsh Estates through long and lonely years, and was later in charge of Macarthur River, in the Gulf country farthest out. He returned to Brunette an old man, to find he was not wanted there by the manager he had brought in as stockman.

"It's a fine day for travellin'," they told him—the time-honoured phrase that all over the outback is notice to quit.

With two or three packhorses Readford rode out on the run that he had formed from nothing. He had been "the bank of the north" in his day, never known to refuse a bagman a hand-out and a horse, or a friend a cheque for £100. Now he was a bagman. He camped at the Armchair Waterhole—the Armchair Bore of today—which he named in his heyday, camped there with his ringers, lying back in the pack-saddles with a billy of tea and a pipe, reciting "The Old Armchair". Then he had been a cattle king. Now, with a swag for home, he made up his mind for a last camp with an old pal, Tom Nugent, at Banka Banka. He could tell Tom of an acid he knew that would cloud any brand—a secret too good to let it die with him. A hundred miles of riding across the Dry Downs, but that was "a dog's trot" to him.

It was not such a fine day for travellin'. Corella Creek was rushing deep in flood. A riderless horse came through. Big 'Melia, a half-caste woman, found Readford's body when the flood went down. She and her old black mother buried him in his camp-sheet. That was forty years ago.

A giant of a man he was, with a white beard a foot square, a polished bald head, and the bushman's blue eyes a-twinkle. Miss McPhillamy at Eromanga still treasures his photograph in a group of the town's elders. A friend of mine met him at Burketown races.

"That's Captain Moonlight," she nudged her companion.

With a courtly sweep of his cabbage-tree hat, he uncovered his shining pate.

"Not Moonlight, madam," he corrected. "Starlight."

So he joins the immortals. A tourist trip at Longreach now is Starlight's Look-out on Mount Cornish, while Jundah proudly shows his Burnt Yard. Starlight's Grave on Brunette is to be restored at the request of the late Sir Fergus McMaster, who was a chairman of directors of Qantas Empire Airways. An old blackfellow led them to the grave on Corella, of which only a charred post remains.

There were no stations between Mount Cornish and the Indian Ocean when Readford made his haul, but they were dotted over the million square miles within fifty years—a happy hunting-ground for the poddy-dodgers. They took up pockets of country on the rim of the runs, gathering in calves dropped by the overlanders and cleanskins straying on the back creeks, and they had secret yards up in the ranges for branding. Some of these were real little fortresses with a look-out for many miles. When a dust on the horizon warned that boundary riders or troopers were on the trail, smoke signals went spiralling up that the blacks knew nothing about.

At one time there were seventeen squatters in a fairy ring on the boundaries of Ord River, good folk all. Their motto was, "Honesty is the best policy, but never pass an Ord River calf." The Ord was sold on a book-muster of a hundred thousand head, but the new owners could never tally more than sixty thousand.

In those grand old days of the open-hearted cattle kings of open country, only the most barefaced or the meanest spirited of the poddy-dodgers were hauled in by the dragnet of the law. Out in wild country they were "steadying" the black cattle-killers, and were allowed a commission because they were hard to catch. On runs such as the Ord and Victoria, where half a dozen stockmen ran a hundred thousand cattle in ten thousand square miles of steep ranges, there was no time for following tracks of fifty or sixty weaners eighty miles through the gorges—with a spear for a hatpin at any minute—to where a branding-yard had been swept with bush-fires, and then riding six hundred miles to prove in Darwin court that those fires were not an Act of God. The calves, by the time they got there, would be "hell, west and crooked", innocently wearing the brand of the Newmerella shore.

The poddy-dodgers were hard-living, hard-riding lads, out in the wet and the dry, "moonlighting" and "coaching". Two white men together, or one alone, with a string of horses and a few blacks, were lost to the world for years. Mustering cows and cleanskin calves just old enough to wean—the "poddies"—they headed them up into the ranges, with a long gallop "chopping back" the branded strays and the mothers. They tailed them till the coast was clear—"wait-a-whiles" they called them—otherwise the hide-out might be besieged by a mob of bellowing cows demanding their offspring, and a stockman demanding explanations. After they branded, they set fire to the yards. Sometimes they branded five hundred in a night. Moonlight was the poddy-dodger's high noon.

Coaching was rougher riding. In remote country like Mulligan River, Macarthur River and the Victoria, where cattle have run wild for generations, it is still a feature of legitimate cattle work. You take a couple of hundred cattle on to wild cattle tracks, circle the outlaws and work them in to the coaches, lying down along your horse so that they will not see you and fly. If they do fly, you are after them, thrash and smash. If one breaks, you chase and throw him. Watching for the split second when he turns to horn you, you vault out of the saddle, grab him by the tail, and while his front legs are in the air, swing him off his balance, and bring him down thud. Rapidly, with strap or handkerchief, you tie a front and hind leg together, and leave him lying till you head the mob past him, when you let him up and ring them till he settles down.

There seems to be a psychology lesson in that you can't throw quiet cattle, only a mad galloper. It is all knack, not much strength is needed. In cattle camps where whites and blacks are throwing twenty and thirty in the day, you will often see a skinny fourteen-year-old piccaninny, with a twist of the wrist, bring down a thousand-pounder. Sometimes men work in pairs, one to throw and one to tie, but to make it a one-man job is the stockman's pride. There are some "pretty throwers" in the Territory and along the Georgina.

The poddy-dodger paid for his ill-gotten gains. Travelling light in no-man's-land, he lived on flour and the beef he killed, three yards of Birkmyre for a home. In those "wild nigger hills" nobody knew if he was dead. He kept his rifle handy, and slept with one eye open. If his own blacks "got windy" and ran away, he held the mob himself, riding them day and night in floods and thunder—you can't follow tracks in the wet.

These men swung wide of the stations and the out-camps. Their only sailing directions were the mud-maps of each other—

"Fourteen mile down Bareback Creek there's an old stockyard an' two little flat-topped hills. Take 'em on your right shoulder for ten mile to the jump-up an' a bit of a scrubby gorge—gener'ly a big mob of myalls round there, but they're sweet for tabacca. Foller 'er up about four mile till you come to a whitewood tree on a rise o' red ground. Leave it on your left hand an' you'll hit the go-down, an' three or four bush mile on you'll pick up a couple o' big ant-hills and a bottle-tree. Stab straight sunset till you spot a little knob standin' out in the saddle of the range across a jam-tree plain. Hold that fair between the eyes for five mile, an' you'll come to a rockhole in the limestone—you'd never find it if you didn't know it was there. Now take the moon on your chest, an' three miles in is this 'ere creek I'm tellin' you. If there's any water in it, there's a fair mob out there with an old bally bull—least there was when we made our cut last year."

So does the path-finder lead the pioneer.

Shoeing up for a poddy-dodging was an expedition in itself, in the gullies where horseshoes were wealth. Many a drover has cursed to find his mob barefooted in the morning. Riding along a river, the dodgers would silence the horse-bells, file off the clinchers, prize with the pincers, filling a bag with shoes and nails for their own brumbies. Kicked and buffeted in the dark, they reckoned they earned those horseshoes. Their nags were sure-footed in terrible country, and you can't let dumb animals suffer. Besides, the drover would soon be where he could get more, and the poddy-dodger would not—not if he could help it.

But the high-water mark of the duffer's genius was his brand. His future as a successful pastoralist depended on his brand.

An artist in classic monogram, at some little rocky forge in the hills beating away at the red-hot metal of stirrup-iron, fencing-wire and broken hopple-chain, he worked out intricate designs of cross-branding that would be innocently clear to a galloping horseman as his own registered brand, and at the same time guiltily cover that of the rightful owner. It might have to cover the brands of three neighbouring stations, at the same time being a distinct identification under the Act.

With the ten Arabic numerals and the English alphabet, with hieroglyph, digit, device and symbol distorted into three flaming irons, the smithy under the boab-tree was a Cellini at large. He spent a large part of his life practising the art of embossing bullock-hide.

Records of clever brand-faking would fill a large book. On Territory stations in the lamplight, when delf mugs and enamel plates are stacked away, when the cook sits down with the young ringers while his bread is rising, "poddy-dodging" is the popular game, merrier than noughts and crosses.

The Old Man, with a pencil on the back of the only letter that came in the mail, sets them a poser—a two-figure and one-letter brand, or vice versa.

"There! Cover that. It can be done, for I know the man who done it, an' done three years in Port Augusta jail."

Shouts of laughter at their efforts till the Old Man takes the pencil and, spectacles on nose, shows them how, with a tale of a trooper and a dodger long ago.

Cattle-brands are forgery-proof today, and applications scrutinized by stock inspectors and pastoral boards, sometimes submitted to the neighbours. Each year more symbols are used, clear-cut single identifications such as the Box A [A] of Alexandria, the Axe head of Brunette, the Bull's Head of Victoria River Downs. But a man could do something with the clumsy old three-figure-and-letter brands, even if he couldn't write his name.

For instance, a shrewd registration of B94, with a reasonable allowance for a slip of the iron or slight growth of hair, would obligingly cover

RGI or D27. The famous E of Sir Thomas Elder has done duty as Triangle B, D A B, and B B. The Diamond Tail of Innamincka has burgeoned into W over Y. One owner who registered)I(was beaten by a Lyre and Undoolyas's Legs of Man by a bandy Y. Wave Hill in the old days thought it had the dodgers tricked with 62U until a stranger camped on its boundary with Boomerang 2. Ord River's O55 was a heaven-sent gift for Ps, Qs, 3s, 8s and Bs. On the outskirts of Newcastle Waters, Wine-glass or Spur, , a set of unregenerate scamps tried to register Pitch-fork Double One ψII.

Those well away from police patrols, or in a hurry to deliver a mob to a not over-conscientious butcher, were content with the good old Frying-pan, a blotch. As one ex-poddy-dodger, virtuous in the days of his white hairs, disclosed to me, 2W8 with a script W will blotch anything. He went on to redeem himself with a quotation from the poet:

> I can throw an' rope an' tie 'em,
> But, by God, I'd sooner buy 'em,
> Though I've done my bit o' dodging in my day.

The true poddy-dodger had contempt for the Frying-pan. He was in the game for the skill of it, and the fun, not for the money. He liked the scent of danger out in those wild nigger hills, and if he couldn't twist a brand to puzzle a boundary-rider at the canter, he deserved to go up and do time. Dewlap and earmark were easy—you left a calf less of its jowl and its ear.

The police called a muster when the stations complained. They shot a beast with suspected brand, and took brand and earmark. There were various ways of getting it back. One was to put a sharp stone under the police pack-horse saddle so that it would bolt and be caught by a sympathetic hand, a "clean" brand substituted for the shady. Another was for the dodger to send his blacks to the policeman's night-camp, to entice his trackers to corroboree while a change-over of the branded hides was made. There was great excitement around Skull Creek and Tommy's Hole when the troopers were about, freshly branded little mobs racing for a distant pocket, and on Wyndham and Katherine stock routes many a crooked mob went bush from the approaching dust of Victoria Regina and Edward Rex.

In the earlies these "outside" men, and, indeed, most of the drovers and stations, worked their cattle with lubras, quicker to learn and more to be trusted than the men of their race. The price of a good lubra was beyond rubies. Leading the white path-finders to aboriginal waters, she colonized the country and, with her piccaninny on the saddle in front of her, she was one of the world's best "stock-boys".

Playing "Lochinvar" with lubras of the myall tribes, teaching them to ride, to rope-and-throw, muster, cut out and brand, to take a man's place in the stockyard, was only another injustice to the Vanishing Race—the law will not allow it today.

Here is the story of the "Lochinvar" told to me by one of the very oldest bushmen, his memories back in the beginning.

"Ridin' round in a gully out there, you'd hear a dog bark. That means blacks on walkabout. Put in the double of your whip and race down, cuttin' out the lubras—the bucks keep on gallopin'. Then you take your pick and swing her up on the horse behind you, put a surcingle over her knees and give her the reins to hold. You give her a good tuck-in that night, and a mirror to look at herself, but keep her tied up, and keep a good watch for her friends and relations. Next day you try her on a horse, put your seven-foot whip through the ring o' the bit and lead her. The day after she's much better, and the day after that she can ride. She learns by watchin' you, they're the best imitators in the world, and learn all the arts by watching. If she was sulky at first, white tucker and tea soon give her a smile.

"She tries a gallop round the cattle—you see her comin' with a flowin' sail. The horse wheels and she falls on her head, and jumps up laughin'. She loves goin' along on a horse, and seein' the country, protected from strange blacks by a white man's rifle. She wouldn't go back into the gullies if you paid her.

"Of course you have to dress her. A flour-bag with a couple o' holes punched in, with a string to draw it in round the neck, was Eve's first costume out in the N.T. You'll see a lubra with BRUNTON'S SUPERFINE written all over her till her boss can get a roll of galatea sent out from the store, with a packet of big-eyed needles to do a bit o' wire-fence dressmaking. Once she gets clothes-conscious she'll never be without them again, not like the city girls on the beaches.

"Lochinvars sold the women to the drovers and the stations at £10 a head, but they didn't have it all their own way. A good few were speared. It was a dangerous game when the men follered in. Once two brothers, 'Jimmie the Cruiser' and 'Wonditta Joe', ran a pack o' lubras in from Lake de Burgh, roundin' them up with the old Snyder. A Burketown blackfeller was with them. That night the lubras began dancin' corroboree, all happy and friendly . . . dancin' closer and closer to the white men at the fire. Suddenly they snatched the rifle and gave a holler—the blacks hidin' in the scrub rushed camp with nulla-nullas and boomerangs. They killed the Burketown boy. Jimmie and Joe jumped on their horses bareback and beat it for their lives."

While the cities of Australia were spreading over smug suburbs, universities, parks, picture shows and chain stores, such were the little dramas of progress enacted in the wild and wide.

In a mustering camp on Brunette, in 1889, was a fiendish duel between a white man and a black. Sam Muggleton, head stockman, had ridden out after cattle with the boys, leaving no one in camp but Hamilton, the cook, and a trusted lubra named Myra. They had killed a bullock for meat and Hamilton was cutting it up when a half-civilized boy, Caliph, from Borroloola, walked in. He was cheeky and spoke good English—a type the bushman hated. He asked for beef. Hamilton refused it. He put out a hand to snatch, and Hamilton viciously slashed the hand with his knife. Caliph picked up the steel, and they fought like devils. Myra ran after Muggleton's horse tracks for fifteen miles. When they came back to the camp it was silent. Caliph was dying, a frightful sight, cut to pieces. He had driven the steel down through the white man's throat.

All through the eighties and nineties a steady stream of stolen horses made west across the Territory from Queensland, wearing the brands of Sandringham, Idamere, Glengyle, and other big runs of the Georgina and the Gulf. Once over the border nobody worried about hieroglyphs on horses, a thousand-mile ride to Darwin to give evidence in a Supreme Court case. A trooper meant a scatter of station hands where station hands are few. Even a Justice of the Peace has a broader view of the world when his patch is ten thousand square miles, sixty thousand half-wild cattle and three stockmen. British law on the Tablelands has some precedents unique. One sentence never listed in Q.B.D. was that of a felon convicted of horse-stealing to "six months' cooking on Eva Downs".

On Eva Downs, Corella and Brunette at this time were three old pastoralist philosophers, great friends. Within a hundred miles of each other, they often rode over to pass the time o' day for a week. The owner of Corella was Justice of an infinite Peace.

Bowstock of Eva Downs, with one stockman left, badly needed a cook. Harry Bates-or-Bathern was the stockman, later the famous "Bulwaddie" Bates, pioneer of Beetaloo. Harry boiled the beef and baked the brownie with his spurs on, afraid it should be bruited abroad he was "cookin' on Eva Downs", and ruin his reputation—no stockman under the age of seventy-five will tolerate the rounds of the kitchen. Finally, he gave the old man notice.

"If there ain't a cook here by the end of the month, make out my cheque. I quit."

No dust of a cook showed up on the Downs. Not wanting to lose a genius of a stockman, Bowstock rode over to stay with McAnsh at Brunette. He knew Harry would not leave without his cheque.

One day as they were sitting on the veranda listening to a cockatoo symphony in the creek, a trooper rode in with a hang-dog stranger and two of Brunette's best buggy-horses. The stranger claimed he had bought them, but could show no receipt. McAnsh was outraged—he hadn't even missed them. The man was arrested, and a black-boy sent riding to Corella with a note for the J.P. The case was heard on Brunette veranda—guilty! and court adjourned to consider sentence, the trooper in conference with the philosophic three.

"Now, my man," said magistrate to prisoner, "you have committed the serious crime of horse-stealing. I can remand you to Darwin, where you'll probably suffer the full penalty of three years' hard labour. But Mr McAnsh, with his horses returned, has agreed, on one condition, to take no further action. I shall release you on a six months' bond, provided you spend it in the employ of Mr Bowstock here, cooking on Eva Downs. Now what do you say?"

"Cookin' on Eva Downs," gulped the grateful prisoner. Old Bowstock rode back with a cook, and Bulwaddie Bates was free.

The Monaghan case at Anthony's Lagoons was another smile in Tablelands law. Also arrested for horse-stealing, Monaghan attacked a trooper, tied his hands behind his back, shot the tracker and fled. He was never found. An inquest was held on the body of the native. "German Peter" and a man named Gilbert from Borroloola were called to the coroner's court. Hairy bushmen, they turned up bare to the waist.

"You can't come in to Her Majesty's court without shirts," said the policeman.

"We got no shirts," was the terse reply.

"I'll lend you one of mine," offered the policeman.

"Te hal mit ye courts o' law!" shouted German Peter. "Take us like ve are, or you don't git us."

The trooper appealed to the magistrate, who made a rapid study of the Statutes, the chapter on court procedure. He screwed up one eye and scratched the back of his neck.

"From what I see here," he told the policeman confidentially, "about what has to be worn in Her Majesty's courts of law, there's nothing to stop these blokes coming in naked."

Of the flying horsemen of the Tablelands, a popular hero was Ben Bridge, who covered half a continent in his flight, twice broke jail, laughed with the police in many a bush camp, and laughed at them for twenty years. Back in New South Wales in youth, Ben was a Wild Colonial Boy. A friend leased him some horses for a race meeting. When the horses lost, Ben seems to have sold them to his landlord and then returned them to his friend—he knew all the old tricks of muffling their hoofs with greenhide, or with bedsocks of blanket that last for twelve miles. His own tracks were harder to cover. Sentenced to three years in a country jail he scaled the wall with a vaulting-pole, and landed a thousand miles away in the north countree. But his "brands and descriptions" were there before him. Arrested at Riversleigh in the Gulf, he was taken to Burketown jail.

Burketown jail went up in flames that week. Ben was rescued by the sergeant and tied to a post, but while the sergeant put out the blaze, Ben and the post vanished. In heavy irons he swam the Nicholson and Gregory rivers, and walked sixty miles to a camp where post and irons were filed off. This feat made every man his friend, and on the Gulf stations they will show you his hide-outs, where he was well-fed and given horses for the journey on. At one homestead, while she made the trooper a cup of tea, the station-owner's wife hid Ben under a bed.

Across the Territory he worked his way, a "young man going west". MacDonald was the name. If the station managers knew more about him than he thought, it never dawned on him till one day while he was at smoko in the men's huts, a trooper rode in without his knowing. The boss called him up with a whistle, and spoke slowly, with meaning:

"I say, Jim, this policeman here is looking for MacDonald. Now you ride down to Blue-bush for him. Tell him to get those horses into the *Big Paddock* quick as he can. We'll be waiting for him *here*. Off you go!"

"Jim" understood. He made for the Big Paddock with his horses double-quick time, and rode, with a mate, the lonely Murran-ji Track. When the mate died there of fever, Ben rode all the way to Victoria Depot to report the matter to the police at Timber Creek, and give them the mate's papers and gold watch to send to his mother. He camped for a week with the policeman, who liked him so much he gave him a racehorse. Ben won a £100 bet with it from a West Australian policeman, for by the time the Territory knew it had entertained an angel unawares, he was over the third border, asking for a job at the Ord.

"Can you ride?" they asked him.

"Never been on a horse in me life."

They put him in the kitchen as cook's offsider. One day an outlaw threw half a dozen stockmen and broke the horsebreaker's leg. The kitchen boy was excited.

"Sling us your spurs," he said. "I'll fix him."

With laughter, they flung him a pair of spurs, and he gave them the prettiest one-man rodeo the Ord has seen, gave them the horse back "quiet".

"You're not a man!" they clapped him on the back. "You're a bit of sticking-plaster."

He grinned. "Keep it under your hat."

You can't keep a rider's reputation under the old felt hats of Kimberley. Sergeant Brophy of Hall's Creek called at the Ord, with a keen interest in the kitchen boy, then approached with a pair of handcuffs and a reverent aside involving the Queen's name.

"Not this time, old man!"

Ben dashed for the open, caught a horse, and was away over the river, not to be sighted officially in fifteen years.

Out in the Osborne Ranges, "playing ping-pong over the border" with the Territory and West Australian police, he was discreetly referred to as "Billy" or "the Coon". When a trooper asked questions about a packhorse going out with a load of stores, it was, "Just a coon I've got out there, gettin' a few cattle."

The whole of the Never Never was loyal to Ben Bridge. He came in and out of the stations as he pleased, made £300 a year in dingo-scalps to provide for his wife and children in the south, and was concerned in various deals with cattle. Once he was seen at Wyndham races, mingling with the crowd. In an occasional police chase, Ben always made it—black trackers had a blind spot in their eye for the Coon's horse-pad.

But a young English trooper named Freeman came to Wild Dog police camp, and swore he would get Ben Bridge. Some say that he was no longer playing the game, and that a station-owner put him away. Some say he was tired of being a bagman out on the ranges, and wanted the Government to pay his fare south to see his wife and children, left so long ago in that north coast town.

Freeman, the English trooper, rode in to the Dunham one morning, and saw a horse tethered to the paperbarks down by the river. He set his tracker to guard it.

"If a man runs out," he said, "shoot the horse. I'll get the man."

There was no shooting. The outlaw, the notorious Coon, was quietly taken into custody in the homestead kitchen, from behind nothing more sensational than a plate of bacon and eggs.

He was extradited to New South Wales to stand his trial for a jail-break of twenty years before, but a round robin from Kimberley set him free. With five hundred signatures gathered in over a year of riding, headed by the imposing flourish "Alexander Cockburn Campbell, Bt", it guaranteed that Ben was a jolly good fellow. The magistrate was much impressed by testimonial of a baronet in Kimberley.

Ben returned to the bosom of his family for the rest of his life, in that north coast town. There I saw him before he died, droving a little mob of cows and calves half a mile to the local butcher—and not a cleanskin among the lot.

Chapter XXII

The Diamond Eighty-Eight

In a Dante's hell of sandfly swamps at the mouth of the King River in Arnhem Land is an oval of stones that marks a white man's grave.

Not many white men have seen it, and even the blacks have forgotten the name of the one who sleeps beneath. The whispering tides and the cry of a gull are the only sounds there, and in "big moon" nights of rain-time the haunted wail of corroboree.

The loneliest grave in the whole three million square miles of Australia, it is the resting-place of Jim Campbell, outlaw, poddy-dodger, path-finder, one of the roving brotherhood of the lost who galloped away from the police to the conquest of a continent. His life was high adventure and his death Greek tragedy. Even in the mad mosaic of human life in the Territory, it stands out in a bas-relief unique.

Like Jacob for Rachel I waited seven years for this story, dovetailing it together little by little in curious places and sometimes from curious people. Among them are cattle men who moonlighted cleanskins with him "out in the wild nigger ranges"; a Member of Parliament who knew him in their little home town of New South Wales as a bad lad of the border; a trooper who hunted him for three hundred miles, but in the wrong direction; a trepanger who carried a bag of gold to him where gold means nothing; and a black woman who shielded him from the police, shared his exile in a kingdom of the dead, warned him of peril on the fatal night, and plucked the spears from his body where it lay in the mangrove mud.

In 1893 Jim Campbell came to Katherine River after a thousand miles of riding from the Finke, with a mob of thoroughbred horses branded W-circle, Ⓦ. Even the Territory laughed, though it was used to horses sensitive of scrutiny wearing many a strange device. For W-circle was the registered brand of Major Peter Egerton Warburton, Australian explorer and South Australian Commissioner of Police. In a country without a catechism, whether those horses were bought or caught, Jim sold them to the Chinamen scratching gold around Pine Creek, to whom hieroglyphs on horses were not significant. He made a lot of friends at the Katherine pub, and started on the thousand miles back.

Even as the elephant, which should have been part of its fauna, the Territory never forgets. When that cheerful moon-face draped its elaborate golden moustaches over a pot of beer in the same pub three years later, it received a vociferous ovation.

Jim was a four-square Australian Scot with a flaxen forelock and a neck like Annie Laurie's and the swan's. His cabbage-tree hat was always glued to his head, his blue shirt buttoned up to the chin to guard him from the tanning of Territory suns. This was no land for Dandy Dicks, and in any other stranger that schoolgirl complexion would have called for prompt attention by the boys, but W-circle was Jim's letter of credit, his merry blue eyes and his hearty gusts of laughter made friends of all his foes, and he was a magnificent bushman.

"*He could ride like a centaur and track the Holy Ghost through a thundercloud*," as his friend, Billie Miller, expressed it.

He might have been twenty-five or so when he first checked in at the Katherine, but he looked much older, as the men of those days did—they had lived a fair slice of a lifetime in their teens. His name was neither Jim nor Campbell. It was Ernest Clare Muir. He was no Little Lord Fauntleroy, and Ernest Clare he renounced very early in life in favour of "Sonny". One day a trooper called on his father in matters relating to a poddy calf, and

Sonny left home in a hurry on the back of an unbroken colt. His only luggage was his hat, and he was using that as a whip.

Muir was left behind in Boulia, where the legend of the masked stockmen of the big Queensland runs originated. A sudden scatter blew those masked stockmen over the nearest border and out of ken. It was one Jim Campbell who rode the Toko Ranges in the devil of a hurry, and though there was nothing out there but a brolga dance, rode on, still in haste, dead west. He skirted the Simpson Desert and became a brumby-runner with the famous Jim Cummings out in the eastern MacDonnell Ranges, one of the best and the lonesomest horse-breeding regions in the world.

A breath of old romance disclosed Jim's incognito very early, even where the world is so wide.

His riding-mate on his second journey north was Jack Macleod, then just a lad. They camped one night with Tom Nugent in his farthest-out Central Australian shack at Banka Banka, yarning as bushmen do, the hurricane lamp on the beer-case table, the old black billy on the fire. Jim was describing deeds of daring round the Alice, galloping wild horses over the ranges and racing through the gaps to head them. Tom Nugent watched him thoughtfully, puffing at his pipe.

"Look here, Campbell," he said at last, "are you sure your name's not Muir?"

Jim stared. "Why do you ask me that? I've never seen you in my life before."

"That's true," said the older man. A pause. "Well, I'll tell you. When I was a boy, over in New England, I had a sweetheart, name o' Jenny Carmichael. Jenny wouldn't marry me. She married a feller named Muir. That's one reason I'm out here. Now you're the dead ring o' that girl, and you speak the same. I reckon you're her son."

"You're right," said Jim. "My name is Muir. I am her son!"

Jack Macleod never discussed that matter till he told me a few years ago, but Jim, in his lifetime, often did. What's in a name in a country where half the population changed its name at every waterhole? Campbell's Springs, Campbell's Knob and Campbell's Retreat know nothing of Ernest Clare Muir, and on the map of the Territory they stand.

There was an incident on the journey typical of Jim. All the way up he had given his young friend a rattling reputation as a rider. A crack rider then was a public idol, even as the flying aces and cricketers today. The only autograph books the Territory ever knew were the bottle-trees, otherwise Jack would have had a busy time signing.

At Pine Creek the boys were in drinking a mob of cattle, and they wanted to test Jack. They dragged a buck up to the yards and challenged him out. The youngster was nervous and shy. He refused to get up. Laughter was loud and hostile, and the boy blushed red.

Jim came to the rescue. "This mate o' mine is well brought up," he said.

"He don't ride for a mob o' drunks, specially on a Sunday." Nobody knew whether it was Sunday or not, so they had to let that go. "But what sort o' knock-kneed brumby is this to a breaker like Jack? I could fix this poor cow meself. Give us a go!" He raced for the buck and clawed into the saddle.

The nag was a "dingo" with plenty of devilry. It waltzed on hind legs, dug for yams, danced like a dervish, curled up like a cat, went into a spinning buck, and crashed over a wire fence to scrape Jim off on the stockyard rails. He riveted it with his spurs, crashed it back over the wire fence, sat it to a standstill and tied it up to the veranda-post to loud beery cheers. Then he put a hand on Jack Macleod's shoulder—

"And I'm not fit, me lads," he said, "to put this bloke's saddle on."

It was not strictly true, but it assured Jack's future north of 28°. He was never thereafter out of a job, although their ways divided, and was soon on his way to immortality as horse-breaker at the Elsey, "the Quiet Stockman" of Mrs Aeneas Gunn.

Just at this time the Overland Telegraph was being renewed with iron poles and the second copper wire. Tom Pearce, of the Katherine Inn, managed to get a Government contract for the carting, but Tom had too much work in the bar to leave it, and teamsters were scarce. There were only the McCarthy brothers, "the Irish Macs", plodding up the Telegraph Line once in three months with their bullocks.

Since Jim's horses were shy of Central Australia, he offered to do the carting for Tom Pearce. He was off riding five hundred miles to Brunette to collect a team of bullocks, drive them three hundred miles down through the Abner Ranges to meet the Telegraph ship at Borroloola, and return with the loading three hundred and fifty miles to Daly Waters. On the way he called at Renner Springs.

Only the stumps of the old station are standing now, and the grave of Alan Giles, whose story I have told. When Jim passed by, Renner was a big cattle run. Among its black "stock-boys" was a wonderful rider, a girl named Rose.

Most lubras, in the eternal feminine, once they taste civilization, want to wear a dress and sit down in a wurley, and drink tea and gossip, leading a white woman's life, but Rose was content in trousers and shirt, astride of a horse for ever. She was happier racing on a breakaway than plaiting herself a bamboo bangle. A tall lithe girl from the bad lands of the Ballyangle Ranges out beyond Auvergne, she had been Lochinvar'd early, and trained well. She could sit a buck and drive a team as well as any man, she loved horses, and she was always laughing.

Rose suited Jim. He wanted her in his camp. *Vae victis!* He fought the head stockman for her, and won her by a bang on the jaw. Across the Broad Downs they rode to Brunette, yoked up the bullocks and took them to Borroloola by way of Creswell Downs. Loading up under the Leichhardt trees from the Telegraph ship anchored in the river, they set out through the ranges for O.T. Lagoon and so to Daly Waters.

Two trips a year with luck, slow travelling, Jim had over a hundred horses to catch every morning, two teams and the others running spare. He had five tons on each wagon, poles, wire and stores. Rose was his right-hand man.

She was more than that. The second year out, at O.T. Lagoon, their son was born. Rose just slipped off into the bush, as the lubras do, but she did not come on next day, as the lubras will. Jim was anxious. He rode back.

In that country of human need, human need is often sadly primitive. Rose was "close up finish". She was that rare specimen, an aboriginal woman who suffers in childbirth. Jim never smoked, so he carried no knife. He severed the umbilical cord between a stone and a stirrup-iron, wrapped Rose and the child in his wet-weather coat, set them in front of him and rode back to the wagons.

It was a strange fatherhood. He called the little boy O.T. after the Overland Telegraph Lagoon—a little boy with nothing but initials. Rose liked that name. In blackfellow lore, that was her son's country.

On the next trip, Billy Miller, from running wild cattle on Limmen River, cut their tracks when the big wagon was axle-deep in bog. Jim's bullock-driver was a Tjingilli boy from Newcastle Waters, melancholy eyes, long hair and a Mephisto moustache. The literary Billy christened him Svengali. In ten months this boy had not uttered a word. Not dumb, he yet not speaketh.

Svengali was under a ban of silence. He was passing through that degree of initiation of a young man of the Tjingilli when he may not speak for many moons until, in age-old ceremony of the bushland, he is baptised with the running blood of his brothers, and until the Old Men in senatorial session in their white-hawk down and ochre, have each in turn solemnly bitten the palm of his hand. Not even to the white man who employs and feeds him may he speak.

"*And drivin' bullocks?* That's funny!" said Billy. "Don't he swear?"

"Not a bloody bloody," said Jim. "It's one o' these here abo hoodoos. The old men have put it across him. Till he gets another sort of haircut, he's dumb as a jabiru. He's a good boy, strong as an ox for heavy loadin', so I don't sack him. He'll come right in time."

"But how does he get the bullocks along?"

"He don't," said Jim. "Take a look at us now. We're like that half the week."

"I to you, Jim Campbell," said Billy, "am God's good gift. You can put me down on your pay-sheet as co-director. When occasion arises, such as bog around bullocks, I'm the champion blasphemer of the Gulf. It comes of havin' a strict Presbyterian father who made us learn a chapter o' Scripture every night. You gotta have a good foundation in the Scriptures to be a professor of blasphemy. Anyway, a nigger wouldn't have the vocabulary for bullocks. I'll soon shift 'em. They'll listen to me."

Whereupon Billy drove them forth with blasting and with mildew from the Book of Haggai, and out of the bog the big team churned on. Billy threw his packs on the wagon and joined the staff.

Picture the cavalcade plodding eight or nine miles a day through the castled red ranges, across the dry downs into the stifling lancewood scrub, the only motion in ten thousand square miles of haze. Jim rode ahead with the first team. Svengali, mute but resolute, whipped on the second. Rose cursed the third along. A lubra called Nellie, who cooked the damper and boiled the salt beef, squatted up on the loading with the baby in her arms, Billy entertained the bullocks in the rear with variations on a theme by Zechariah. Behind him Wijialungamo, Widgee for short, a little naked black-boy, came running with the spares.

It was a queer turn-out for the Telegraph Line and empire, but so were the roads of the Northern Territory made.

When they steadied the teams to go up a blow, Rose would take her child to her breast. She loved little O.T. and so did Campbell. In that big silence, what else was there to love? The baby had Jim's braw Scottish frame and fair hair, his mother's dark skin and laughing eyes. He was just one of the quaint little misfit pilgrims on the many strange tracks of this world.

Resting during the heat of the day, travelling all night in the cool, they put the slow miles behind them. Rose had a bad leader, Model.

"Come along, Billy," she would screech. "You killem this cheeky-fella Model!"

Billy would whack Model along—a slash of the whip, a spasmodic bump and a clank of chains, and so lumbering on to a dinner-camp under a bean-tree. One sundown there was trouble. The long steel pin of the shaft, the split-lynch, fell out. Nellie was holding up the shaft and Rose putting the split-lynch in when Campbell rode back. Thinking Model was causing the hold-up, he shouted and put the whip in to the horses. They plunged violently forward and threw Rose down in the sand. The wagon with five tons' weight went with a sickly crunch over her thigh.

They lifted the injured woman up on the loading—only a faint whimper of pain and her mournful eyes in the dusk, then she was happy with her baby at her breast, runing it a little corroboree song. No help could be given, and she expected none. Nellie took the reins. When the teams were unyoked at Wanalyuru Waterhole at daylight, Rose crawled under a tree. They bound up her thigh with saddle-cloth and camped there five weeks till she was hopping about, one leg shorter than the other. One stirrup shorter than the other, Rose still could ride.

Wanalyuru was clay when they left it, on an eighty-mile dry stage to Beetaloo water—Jim knew of none between. On this stage he showed the genius of bushmanship that would carry him far from the fellowship of men.

Rose's accident made them dangerously late on those sallow plains where many perished. Half-way over, the water-drums were rattling dry. Svengali made a vague uncertain gesture to the south. Somewhere there he had heard of a native well or soak—piccaninny water, he showed them with his hand—but this was not his country, and he shook his head. It might be there, it might be gone, they might never find it.

It was their only hope. Billy slung canteens and water-bags over a few failing horses, and motioned Svengali to lead. Jim stayed with the wagons. In seven or eight miles the black-boy left the road, blind-stabbing for twelve miles through dense lancewood scrub. By watching birds at sunset they found the little spring—a thick grey sludge. It made a few gallons by night that evaporated by day. Two nights they stayed to get enough to water the horses and fill the canteens, no fires for fear of blacks and the horse-bells muffled . . . a bad year to be stealing the last of the tribal waters.

On the second midnight there was a crashing in the scrub. Billy sat up and grabbed his gun—but a horseman was outlined on the stars. He gave a "Hoy!" and heard Jim's answering shout. Afraid they were speared or lost, Jim had left the wagons at nightfall to be defended by Nellie and Rose, and had cut the diagonal through the lancewood scrub. With no tracks to follow in the dark, he had ridden straight as a die to the spring he had never heard of. Such is the bushman's instinct. This water is now on the station map of Beetaloo as Birriadidj, a good spring for seven months of the year. Jim and Billy put it there, thanks to Svengali.

Forty miles on to Beetaloo Waterhole, thirty miles down Newcastle Creek, then sixty miles south, they dumped the loading at Powell's Creek, known to its own black people as Pommoyou. Then they turned back for Borroloola, four months away.

In three years the Telegraph contract was fulfilled, six hundred miles of iron poles and copper wire standing the siege of white ants and weather. There were plenty of jobs for Jim as stockman or drover, horse-breaker or station manager, but he was a poddy-dodger born, one of "Diana's foresters, minions of the moon". The boy in him loved duffing cattle, loved it for the devil in it, for the jest of robbing Peter to pay Paul. Around Katherine he was in the right country for it. In the split gorges and hidden pockets of the ranges east and west, little mobs were running not sighted in years, from Dr Browne's Springvale herds and others around. Jim saddled up for the ranges with his crippled lubra Rose.

He was one of the first white men in to those glorious gorges of the Katherine, Edith, Cullen, Douglas, Waterhouse and Ferguson rivers, which with the Mary, the three Alligators and a score of others have their source in the hills to the west of the old gold road. There was the life for Jim Campbell—a camp-smoke in the hills, a gallop on the cleanskins in a valley. He would turn up in Katherine or Pine Creek once or twice a year with a little mob to stock up the stations of his friends, or cash down to a Chinese butcher. If there were a few vealers wearing initials on their rump, they were rump steak by morning to a smell of burning hide.

Rose left her humble name on the map. Where now is Rose's Creek, Jim was taken into custody by a trooper for an unlawful kill. The black woman shadowed the pair to Pine Creek. Each night the trooper slept with his head on the pack-bag where he had stowed the brand and earmark that would be Jim's undoing. Jim slept on the other side of the fire, the tracker twenty yards away.

On a windy midnight of many small noises, the crippled woman crept in . . . on hands and knees behind the sheltering saddles, moving with the stealth and patience that only the aboriginal knows. When a stick cracked, when one of the dogs stirred, she held her breath for minutes. At last her long, sinuous, slow fingers were busy with the straps of the pack-bag under the policeman's head, her eyes on his tracker beyond. It was a full hour before she crawled as quietly away.

When the trooper went to prepare the case against Jim at Pine Creek, his evidence out of the pack-bag was the head of a horse decayed and grinning. The pubs of the north rocked with unholy laughter.

A year later, at a spring on the bank of the Katherine, Campbell's Rose died at the birth of her second child. White men and black gave her a great wake. A square of stones above her was piled by Jules Baumard, a Frenchman far from home. A couple of miles below the township, near the low-level bridge of the Stuart Highway, the old hands can show you Rose's Spring at Katherine today.

Jim had ambitions for little O.T. Trapped by the rising of the rivers in the wet, he studied by slush-lamp in his tent, the half-clad child asleep in his swag behind him while he bent over stock-maps and a queer figuring in pad and pencil, page after page of treble hieroglyph. In the daytime you might see him at a camp-fire in the open, heating a bit of hoop-iron with a hammer. He did very little work that wet, but he found what he wanted.

Out beyond the Murran-Ji by Lonely Springs was a pocket of country taken up on the map by a man named Kirby, of Collarenebri, New South Wales. Kirby had neither seen it nor stocked it. Between Victoria River Downs and Wave Hill, it was four hundred square miles of steep creeks and wild blacks.

Jim wrote Kirby a letter, with much licking of pencils and blind-stabbing at spelling, pointing out that the lease would be "four-footed" if not stocked, that he, Jim, had some cattle to "ejist", and was willing to take the country and pay "anual rentle". He signed himself, as he always did even when promising a man a bang on the jaw, "Your sinceer freind, E. C. Campbell."

In overdue course a letter arrived for Jim—a local sensation. They asked if he had been left a fortune, as indeed he had. Kirby was willing—he had forgotten he owned the place, registered as Illawarra Springs. He hereby transferred the grazing lease. Jim was a station-owner.

The cattle that formed Illawarra were a mythical mob. Negotiations consisted of a cheque—never presented—and a receipt from a cattle-dealing friend that "Jim Campbell has this day taken delivery of five hundred mixed cattle of various breeds and colours"—the usual poddy-dodger legalities to stave off pertinent questions.

Jim mustered his phantom herd, and with stores for a couple of years on the old bullock-dray, headed west. Nellie and her boy Dick, with a few cther blacks, followed on with O.T. and Jim's little dog, Whisky, all piled on a white-anted baker's cart that had come overland from Sydney in the Kimberley rush. Just as they were leaving, Whisky was detained by the arrrival of a large family, also of various breeds and colours. Jim was a lover of dogs as well as of other people's poddy calves and horses. He patiently awaited Whisky's convenience, then added her family to general cargo aboard the baker's cart.

A month or two on the westward trail, he cued his bullocks at Cueing Pen Spring—that fairy pandanus pool that he named you will find on the road near Willeroo. Surveys were wild and woolly but the boundary of Kirby's country was roughly set down on the chart as Mount Compton. Jim selected a convenient hill to be stand-in for Mount Compton, unloaded the blacks and the baby by a billabong, and built a bough shed—later discovered to be nine miles in on Victoria River Downs!

Over his shadowy herds he waved a magic wand, and lo! they were. The brand of Illawarra formed a station overnight. It was the brand of genius—◇88. Curlicued and flattened, or elongated into angles, or placed with a slant and a slur, or trimmed with a plucking of hair, the Diamond Eighty-eight would cover anything in Australia, from O55 of the Ord right down to Cobb and Co.'s station on the Warrego, COB. With a little close attention to branding-irons, all would be beef on the hoof that came into Jim's net. Wherever he travelled, like Aladdin with his lamp, one rub of the Diamond Eighty-eight would make him a rich man.

But the GIO of Victoria River Downs it fitted like a glove, and his spiritual home was in those knife-cut creeks far out—thousands of clean-skins gone bush in unknown country, no need for cross-branding. Over thirteen thousand square miles, the Big Run had spread out too wide. Soon Jim, with a spear through his hat now and then, was mustering where no stockman had ever set his elastic-side boot, where no packhorse had ever cast a shoe.

The natural increase of Illawarra was unnatural increase. Within two years there were five thousand calves of the G Ten running for the Diamond Eighty-eight, and Jim was a pastoralist of promise . . . but he put no stock in that, it was no fun. Once he had his brand on a beast, he never thought of it again. "Something lost beyond the ranges" was what beckoned him. He took in a partner to look after the sales and the station while he sported by moonlight.

Only once he was caught by a trooper, with a little mob of cleanskins on Black Gin Creek. He was "hauled before the Beak", the case to be tried under Matt Wilson's old bottle-tree at Victoria Depot by Captain Joe Bradshaw, J.P. Along came Ben Martin, a buffalo-shooter from the Mary, who looked on Illawarra and saw that it was good, provided Jim's genius was not "cabin'd, cribb'd, confin'd" in Fannie Bay. Ben offered to take the blame and do the time, his buffalo horses and his cheque for the year's hides thrown in, if Jim and Mick would give him a share in the station.

The Campbell case was a great day at the Depot. Cap'n Joe sailed up-river with his naked navy, wearing his admiral's hat and his nine-inch Colt. Dicky Townshend, manager of V.R.D., was there with his stockmen to give evidence. The boys from Wave and Auvergne were in, and all the poddy-dodgers of the border came to learn of the master. Sundry bagmen swelled the crowd. The temperature by Matt's thermometer, hung in his bit of a bush store, was a hundred and thirty-five not out.

Proceedings began with a round of drinks on the magistrate—all hands to the bottle-tree with prisoner, trooper and cook. Matt Wilson followed with a shout on the house. A vote of thanks to all concerned was proposed by prisoner and seconded by plaintiff. Then there was a round on Wave Hill, another on the trooper, another on Billy Biffin, bagman.

Cap'n Joe banged for order—banged with the nine-inch Colt on the beer-case Bench, dislodging a couple of white ants and a red-backed spider.

"Boys," he said, "we're all friends. It's not often we get together. I see some pretty good horses on the flat. A damn pity we have to waste our time in litigation about cattle—we see enough of cattle all the year. Now if plaintiff here, and defendant—that's you, Dicky, and Jim—I say, if you two like to settle this argument out of court, I have power to quash the case and we can get right on with the races. How about it?"

All hands in favour shouted "Aye!" and "Squash the case!"

"But remember!" boomed His Worship, waving the nine-inch Colt, "if there's any shooting to be done, I've been in California, and I'm the man to do it!"

He pocketed his gun and poured himself another with a stern judicial air. Somebody woke the trooper up and told him. While Jim squared up with Dicky Townshend for the cattle by means of Ben Martin's cheque—it later came back marked N.S.F. and no harm done—the black-boys lined up the horses on the flat for the start of the first race. So they saved the honour of Illawarra, and a good time was had by all.

But too many cooks spoil the poddy-dodger's oxtail soup.

A three-cornered partnership of Mick, Ben and Jim meant argument in camp. Victoria River Downs formed Montajinnie—aboriginally Meantajinnie—the out-station on Armstrong Creek, to watch Jim out there. Paddy Cahill took up Old Delamere, and Tom Pearce resurrected the ruin of Willeroo. Jim was a lone rider. Neighbours a hundred miles away gave him claustrophobia. He sold his share in Illawarra to Mick and Ben, and with five hundred heifers moved out to Battle Creek, in a wilder pocket still. With a sense of humour, he called it the Retreat, and carried with him the Diamond Eighty-eight, all rights reserved.

It was just another bough shed in a gully, a couple of bags of flour, a saddle hung in a tree, more like a blackfellow's wurley than a white man's homestead, as the first beginnings in Australia always are. A pack of yapping dogs kept the Mudburra blacks at bay, Whisky's descendants to the fifth generation—Rum, Brandy, Gin and Porter . . . Toddy, Nog, Sherry and Shandy . . . Hock, Cocktail, Sake, Hooch and Vodka . . . right down to Kümmel and Curaçao, which Jim, when sending the pup to a friend, spelt with a Q.

Jim was mostly far from home, and little O.T. was his father's mate in many a moonlight camp. Rose's dark young son had already learnt to throw-and-tie, to race on a breakaway astraddle his pony without stirrups. Jim made him a "balance rider", as dashing as a circus bareback. It was his dream to see O.T. a head stockman of V.R.D., a crack jockey at the Depot Races, and a winner of the Darwin Cup some day.

Nellie and Dick were with him still, and he tamed some myalls. The horsetailer was a deaf-mute lubra of the wild Mudburra tribe whom he picked up on the Murran-ji Track, a screwy little hairpin of a girl about nine years old. They called her Dummy, but she needed no calling. Jim's were the slickest blacks in the north at running cattle, at building a little yard and branding up and burning down.

Out there in the ranges the Diamond Eighty-eight had "open slather". If the Victoria River stockmen cut Jim's tracks, which is unlikely, there are none so blind as those who will not see. If Dicky Townshend sometimes wondered—well, Campbell was outside the boundary, getting cattle never on the station books and pretty game at steadying the blacks, which cost the station a lot more in beef than he did.

Jim became king of the poddy-dodgers from the Elsey to the Ord. Racehorses, stud bulls, heifers, mules, donkeys—they reckoned he would put the Diamond Eighty-eight on the Lamb of God. He never mustered from a "little man", and he never duffed Wave Hill—no poddy-dodger calling himself a man would brand a calf of Nat Buchanan, the path-finder, the bushman they loved and respected, Old Bluey, riding along under his green umbrella. Jim collected from the big companies, "bloated capitalists", lords of the inkwell and the cheque-book in a city office, with managers sent up from the south by "parcel post" because they played golf with a son of the firm or married its daughters. Duffing to "the Diamond" was still a game. He loved running Victoria River cattle with Victoria River mules. When chased by the police, he would head out the elegant G.R. horses into a pocket of the range, and lend the trooper a cross-branded crock to save his life on the hundred-mile walk home.

Alone in his lair on Battle Creek or whistling along to the merry old hills, he was the best-humoured of brigands, with hilarious yarns for the lads at Katherine when he rode in there to sell a mob and shout for the town. Some said Jim only duffed to tell the yarn.

Billy Miller camped with him again on a Dry River track, Billy the Bibliophile, rejoicing in an old mission Bible, sun-blistered and chewed by white ants, which he picked up by a billabong, where someone had thrown it out of the pack-bag.

"Layin' off" in the smoke of a dinner-camp fire, away from the flies, their blacks and horses in siesta under an ironwood-tree, Jim tipped his hat over his eyes in doze while Billy intoned the old Hebrew poetries of the Forty-three Divines. He turned to the Book of Job.

"God, this feller could write!" he said. "Listen!" He addressed the ant-hills and the heat-waves in rolling elocutionary chords: "There was a man in the Land of Uz, whose name was Job. . . . His substance also was seven thousand sheep, and three thousand camels, and five hundred yoke of oxen, and five hundred she asses. . . ."

Jim sat up with one of his hurricane gusts of laughter.

"Ha-ho!" he shouted. "Job's the man for me. I could camp on his boundary! I reckon he'd forget his boils!"

Success has been the finish of many a good poddy-dodger. Jim had three good bad years at the Retreat. The banker doffed his topee when he came in to Darwin with more money than he could spend there, and the *Northern Territory Times* made him a social note: "Our well-known pastoralist, Mr E. C. Campbell, is among passengers listed for the south to attend the Melbourne Cup."

A cheque-book is the world's best visiting card. Seven ports on the way to the south, Jim, for the first time in his life, tasted the luxuries of civilization—the minstrel shows and the menus, first-class hotels and barmaids with their hair in golden rolls, boots cleaned in the morning, a Gladstone bag instead of a swag, a lackey to carry it for him and call him Sir—a great joke to the Man from Murran-ji. In Sydney he ordered an evening-suit with tails and lashed it round his waist with a stirrup leather. A guest at the Metropole Hotel, each night he borrowed the housemaid's brooms, and with one at the head of his bed and one at the foot, he rigged his bush-net and turned in without a revolver, to rise at "piccaninny" and wake the cook with a shout of "Daylight!" to put on the billy for tea.

There was a shipload of Northern Terrors down for the Cup that year. Each morning they met at "the Stockyard", the gardens in Wynyard Square, time-honoured meeting-place of Territorians for the past fifty years. A glass of beer and a counter-lunch at a "billabong" near by, and they are off in mates to cut the track of adventure, to watch the "big mobs" galloping past like a bang-tail muster, to run into other Territorians and stand in the street for hours, talking beef on the hoof the livelong day.

Jim's mate was his mother's old sweetheart, Tom Nugent of Banka Banka. They sat on the grandstand at Flemington together—the dream of Jim's life come true, to see a Melbourne Cup. It would last him out in camp-fire yarns for years. If he mercifully spared the favourite that year from bedsocks of blanket and the Diamond Eighty-eight, he hit the high spots of Melbourne and Sydney so high that he had to borrow £400 from Tom to square his bookmakers and take a ticket home. He promised Tom to return the £400 within a year, in calves at £1 a head.

With the boat-journey back to the waving palms of Darwin the crowded hour of glorious life was over. Now for the five hundred miles of lonely ride to the Retreat. On the way he delivered two beautiful little Arab stallions he had been commissioned to buy in the south for Tom Pearce at Willeroo. Jim reckoned it was madness to buy a horse, but Tom insisted on receipts.

Ruminating on his sins in the city, Jim rode the long trail. Like all good bushmen, he hated a debt. He would rustle every hoof on the Georgina road, but no man would say Jim Campbell owed him £1, no storekeeper waited for his cheque. Before he branded a hide for the Diamond, he must get those calves to Tom across the Murran-ji.

Things had been happening at the Retreat, blacks, stores, and horses gone. Nellie and young O.T. came out of hiding in the bush to tell him.

"Bad blackfella, Jim. Been killem two-fella white man longa Pigeonhole. That boy Alligator Tommy. Him ride this way, catchum tucker, catchum horse, catchum eberyting belong you. We all-about frighten, runaway bush. That boy gottem gun."

"Him killem white men dead?"

"You-i. Two-fella proper dead. One-fella white man been run."

"Which-way that blackfella go?"

"Riding sunrise. Policeman come up, been look-out that boy."

Jim slept with his gun handy that night, in case Alligator Tommy paid another call. No myalls are half as dangerous as a civilized boy "gone bad". The Retreat blacks came back next day, glad that Jim was home. A week later a white man rode out of the gullies.

He was a runaway sailor of some Teutonic breed, tattooed and flat-footed, with lashless yellow eyes, known as Dutchy. Of no particular calling and of no good reputation, he had worked around on border stations, but stayed long on none. Dutchy knew all about the murder. Of three white men building a yard at Pigeonholes out-station of Victoria River Downs, he was the only one alive.

He told a sordid story of the camp of white and black. Alligator Tommy, brooding over his wrongs, had snatched a rifle at the camp, and shot Jim Frost and a lubra dead. Then he rode after Harry Edwards, who was carting posts in a dray, and shot him through the heart. He chased Dutchy, firing shots, but Dutchy caught a horse and galloped off. Tommy then made for Campbell's Retreat, held up the blacks with the gun, stole stores, horses and cartridges, and rode out east towards the Alligator rivers, his country. The trooper from Timber Creek was on his track.

Jim could see that Dutchy was as much to blame as any. The man carried some nasty scars of earlier conflict with the blacks. He was never tired of showing a horrible gash in his stomach where they ripped him up with a shovel-nose spear out on Waterloo. Mrs Deacon, at the homestead there, had saved his life by pushing his entrails back and sewing him up with a needle and cotton.

Dutchy had just been sacked again, from Victoria River Downs. A good renegade, he knew where calves of the G Ten were easy to find. He offered to give Jim a hand to muster and brand up.

"No good comin' to me," said Jim. "I've got no money."

"Dot's all yight mit me, Chim. I take my lot in de heifer-calfs after ve get de mob in."

Jim hesitated, and was lost.

His friends thinned out, now that he rode with Dutchy. They were making the game too hot. They had abandoned the Diamond Eighty-eight for the Frying-pan, a botch. No longer moonlighting cleanskins in a sporting chance, they were duffing the station mobs in broad daylight, chopping off a wing here and there. It would not do. A couple of Jim's pals rode three hundred miles from Katherine to tell him.

"You're not a poddy-dodger," they said. "You're a snake of a cattle-thief. Why don't you rat the hen-house for the missus's chickens at V.R.D. while you're about it? And ridin' with a swine like Dutchy! He's no bushman. Couldn't find his way out of his musquita-net, couldn't track a tram. Bush-spielers, that's what you are—lettin' us down."

Jim was ashamed of the turn-out.

"Oh, this is just a bit of get-rich-quick," he said. "I've got to put this through."

"Get-rich-quick ends in Fannie Bay," they told him, "and once you come down to the Fryin'-pan, Jim, that's the proper place for you. Look here! You get into the peter over a ding-dong job, and from Kimberley over to Queensland every man's your friend. We'll run the station and brand up for you. But you go up for three years for a job like this, and you're out for keeps. We don't want to know you."

Jim laughed it off, but he was a bit windy at mention of Fannie Bay. He lovingly stroked his long golden moustaches, his only vanity, flaxen silken curls nobly curving from his top lip like a miniature pair of buffalo horns.

"Is it right," he said, "that they shave a man in jail?"

There was a shout of laughter.

"Look out for your whiskers, Jim. They shave you clean as an egg, and take y' photo."

"You'll never see me in Fannie Bay," he told them. "No cop will shave me *while I'm alive*."

He threw away the Frying-pan after that. He instructed his solicitors in Darwin, who had helped him out of one or two tight places in the matter of yards, to register a new alternative brand for the Retreat, the Diamond Forty ◇40. It was plain to a child in pinafores that this was a quick and bare-faced cover of the G Ten, but at least it was not anonymous. Before Jim knew whether the Stock Department had granted it or not, he was back on the job—a bad job now, but if he could get the calves away by the desert track to Banka Banka, Tom could run them out to the back of the run.

Dutchy was a poor mate out in the ranges. He had no camp-fire conversation but mean "nigger-talk"—scandal about the blacks—no comic yarns or old colonial songs, he could never see a joke. In work he was a moaner and a drone, he was greedy and he wouldn't cook. He held the bat over Jim with sly talk of Fannie Bay, and Jim was sick of the sight of him. They were branding up the last of Tom's four hundred, ready for the road, when the partnership ended in a row. Dutchy demanded his two hundred heifers "out of dis mob, now, on dis spot here, or by Got I squeal on you". Jim knocked him out and told him to squeal to hell. Dutchy threw on his packs and rode in—rode straight to the government house at Victoria River Downs.

Dicky Townshend sat on a bullock-hide deckchair under the veranda, reading a six-months-old copy of the *Northern Territory Times* and seeing red. The mulga wires had reached Darwin. Two items whipped him like barbed wire: "A well-managed station should have no cattle-stealers round it. The stock should be kept well mustered and branded up. Victoria River cattle are out of control."

The significance of the second item was plain to him as a white bull in a bog: "We hear that Mr Tom Nugent is making many additions to his promising little Central Australian run."

Here Dutchy rode out of the dust with a tale for the boss's ear.

Townshend listened. He called up his head stockman and threw him the copy of the *Times*. The head stockman flushed angrily while the ingratiating Dutchy grovelled on the ground making a mud map, with this yarn and that yarn, telling them where to ride.

Dicky glared at the head stockman. "You get out with one of the men and follow Campbell and get evidence. I'll go for the police."

The head stockman shook his head. "I'm not a detective. My job's cattle. If I don't suit your cattle, make out my cheque."

Townshend himself, with one of the ringers, rode out through the ranges. He caught Jim Campbell red-handed, bound for the Murran-ji Track with a mob of four hundred young heifers and steers wearing the Diamond Forty and the Frying-pan.

Jim tried to bluff through, with his hat on the side of his head and a welcoming smile. He could have bushed the cattle and run for it days before, knowing Dutchy, but he was not the sort of man to run from Dutchy. The manager of V.R.D. curtly turned down his offer of a "drink o' tea", and circled the mob slowly, with grim-set lips and an all-seeing eye.

"You'll hear more of this!" he said darkly, as he wheeled in the direction of Timber Creek, the warrant and the trooper. The ringer in his wake cantered past Jim with a malicious grin and a contemptuous thumbs-down.

The game was up, well up. The brilliant career of the Diamond was botched by the Frying-pan.

Sultry silence in the rocky valley as Jim thought it out . . . no rain yet to wash out tracks. Back in the hills they would find the burnt yard, the beefwood posts still smoking. In two or three days the trooper would ride in to his night-camp, asking questions, writing the answers down. . . .

A ride to Katherine between the trooper and his tracker, in handcuffs if the old ballyhooley liked to be smart, and he would be, because Jim had so often made a fool of him.

The Supreme Court at Darwin, a mob of the cattle-men there, and His Honour in his wig, listening to Dutchy . . . but Townshend they'd believe all right, and on the polished table a square of cross-branded hide, botched hide, and Townshend's solicitor wetting it well and holding it up to the light to show His Honour the G Ten. . . .

Three years. . . .

The cart for Fannie Bay, piled up with wild niggers, room on the driver's seat for a white man and a warder.

"Our well-known pastoralist, Mr E. C. Campbell, recently retired"—retired into Fannie Bay.

Jim laughed. Not on your life!

His world was still wide. East to Queensland, west to Kimberley, south for the desert? They couldn't beat him, he was a bushman. But he must not call for tucker at any of the out-stations, getting the white men into trouble, and caught sooner or later, for blacks tracked and blacks talked. Where would he go into smoke for the rest of his life, and live on a white man's tucker, where there were no stations, no trackers?

He looked at the hazy purple crags, looked across at young O.T. stringing the mob on with Nellie and Dick, his son now a swarthy little ringer at a hand-gallop, heading back a wing. . . .

Life wouldn't mean much to Jim, wherever it was, without young O.T.

Very thoughtfully he stroked his long golden moustaches, curled, as the boys said, like a pair of buffalo horns. *Buffalo horns* . . . the buffalo country!

Nellie and Dick savvied trouble come up. They were watching Jim, awaiting a change of plans. He called them with a wave of the arm.

"Catchum horses, pack on all-about tucker. Little-fella sleep today, then boilem up billy. Tonight all night we go."

"Which-way cattle?" Dick asked with an anxious backward glance.

Jim Campbell threw the world away.

"Bush 'em," he said.

The trooper and his trackers found nobody home at the Retreat but a little Mudburra lubra, and she was deaf and dumb. A polite and intelligent child, when they pointed to Jim's old hat on a nail, and made the blackfella sign of "Which-way?"—the quick twist of an opened right hand—she nodded and smiled, and pouted her lips to the north. They killed a few of the cross-branded cattle in the ranges, cut the hides as evidence, and, with Dummy as guide, went on to collect Jim. A few storms had fallen, but Dummy apparently knew where he was, she never stopped to look for tracks on the way.

For three hundred miles she led them through stony creeks and canyons, through sharp spinifex, round the crags of the ranges by jump-up and go-down, out across the debil-debil plains—through stagnant waterholes to dry stages so long that some of the horses perished—through rocky strongholds of the Wongawalli blacks, the fierce salt-water men—on and out into the broken red hills of the sea-coast bordering Bradshaw's Run.

Where the cliffs were too steep and stony for horses, they climbed on foot, Dummy in the lead, perpetually smiling . . . in thirst by day and nigger-watch by night till trooper and trackers were ready to call it off and ride pell-mell for home. But not Dummy. Excelsior! she pointed them on. It was likely that Jim would make for a hide-out on the coast where he could pick up a lugger, and why should they doubt this little black rag of humanity whose silent lips had never learnt to lie?

It speaks volumes for the trooper's self-control that Dummy is alive today. For when she led him to the top of the stoniest hill in the raggedest range of the cussedest land on earth, his boots and his temper long worn through and his tucker miles behind, she threw up her skinny arms and blew in the air.

Tracks gone!

Jim, like Elijah, had been taken up to heaven from there.

Jim was reading the tombstones at Port Essington. An endless blur of weeks and miles, swinging wide of everything human, with Nellie, Dick and young O.T. he had ridden north-east across many rivers to the old military settlement on the north coast, where no police patrol was likely to cross-examine the dead. He was the last to make a home in that forgotten haven.

Once again a white man's camp-fire glowed in the ruins, above the Uwaja fires in the dark crescent of Knocker Bay.

The hue and cry for the Diamond became an epic of the north. A cross between Ned Kelly and Robin Hood—in all the bars and shanties they swore he would never be taken alive. Imaginative drovers told Deadwood Dicks of hoofbeats that frightened cattle, of a black mare, and a masked rider, with a gun at the draw.

From Chambers' Pillar to Cape Don, from Burketown to Broome, he bobbed up everywhere. All the old Campbell yarns of mild jokes on the police with his little mob of poddies were double-dyed to dastardly crime. Often a misguided trooper crept into a cave, revolver first, or scaled a peak—to a blackfellow's fire.

Of all this the genial Jim never heard a word. At Port Essington for a long time he was canny. With the dawn he vanished, and an old red blanket sprouted on the bushes by the powder magazine of the redcoats long ago. At the faintest spiral of smoke on land or a patch of sail on sea, Nellie would take in the red blanket. Jim never rode into camp unless it was there.

But as days drifted into years over the old memorial stones unmemoried, the kingdom of the kindly dead became his kingdom, and he and young O.T. on Timor ponies trotted round the coast unafraid.

O.T. was a son of the sun, happy as the little blacks who rafted and raced with him about that glorious harbour. But a white man can never go native. He carries his own world with him, pattern of life in pros and cons, in profit and loss, in habit and in the curse of constant thought. He deals in yesterday and tomorrow where the black man spends today. He swims against Nature, where the black man drifts with that abundant tide. He may live in a cave, but he shuts out sun and rain, sets locks and keys to his treasures on earth where the black man merely borrows from Nature for pleasure or gain. He may eat lizard, but he fillets it, salts it, toasts it on a twiggy toasting fork and sets it for himself on a bark plate. He may go naked, but he keeps one shirt and trousers for ceremonial meeting with his fellows. His feet can never develop the blackfellow's leather sole—he must have crude sandals. He cannot sleep, as his dark friends do, curled up like a cat or flat out in fatigue on Mother Earth—he must have a built-up pillow of sand or leaves, and, under or over, a blanket. Without a daily job he dies. No matter how hard-bitten a bushman may be, born in a hollow log, these are his hereditary needs.

Jim, at Port Essington, lived like a lord, on fish, oysters, geese, quail, turkey, duck, beef and buffalo roast and wallaby stew, yams and lily-bulbs for his onions and potatoes, cabbage-palm top and lily-root to grind for his flour, figs and wild honey, pineapples, plantains and mangoes from the old plantations. Some Kakadu blacks wandered across from East Alligator River, among them Barney Flynn's Ada who had learnt to cook for the buffalo camps.

In a bountiful Nature, with his living provided by so many friendly hands, there was no need for Jim to do a hand's turn, indeed no purpose in his labour, but he was a cattle-man and in this timeless paradise he kept the cattle-man's day. He mended up his saddles, made new ones of buffalo-hide, and rode out on Timor ponies "looking at country". He rounded up the wild horses that Cadell and D'Arcy Uhr had left on King and Liverpool rivers, and broke in these brumbies to be his "plant". He mustered the wild cattle left by Cap'n Joe Bradshaw at Arafura, and drove a little mob back to Coburg Peninsula—he would have liked to brand them with the Diamond Eighty-eight, but thought better of it.

Soon he was a capitalist without a bank account, a pastoralist on a station a blank in the stock-map. He had a matchbox full of seed-pearls tucked into his sarong, and a stack of buffalo-hides, contributed by the Kakadu, down on the beach. He might never buy or sell again, but his was the white man's burden.

One day a lugger came into the bay.

The old red blanket, Nellie, Dick and O.T. faded away, leaving Barney Flynn's Ada, well primed, to claim the camp and the buffalo-hides.

But this was no police boat. From cover they saw the Uwaja prancing along the shore with delight and falling on the necks of the crew. It was the good ship *Essington* come home from scouring the isles of Carpentaria, her skipper Trader Brown. Jim and Alf were old friends.

"G'day!"

Alf started to see a familiar figure in blue shirt, wide felt hat, low-slung trousers and elastic sides, large as life, under a tamarind-tree.

"Jim Campbell! What are you doing out here?"

"Glad to see you, Alf. I'm in smoke."

Neither of these two had spoken with a white man in two years. Trader Brown, sailor of uncharted seas, had heard nothing of the manhunt for the Diamond till he heard it from the Diamond himself, with the old hearty laughter at Jim's yarns, and a wag of the head for a good man gone wrong.

Alf was bound in for Darwin. It was not likely that he would be asked questions, so he need tell no lies. For whites and blacks on the lonely strand it was a night of reunion. Alf had a gramophone aboard—first to be heard along the Arafura—its shrill yapping through a frilly tin horn to soothe the savage breasts of the Arnhem Landers who brought him trepang, now and again a pearl.

In the lost silver circle of Port Essington that night Harry Lauder was "R-r-roamin' in the gloamin' ", and Trader Brown to this day remembers Jim, with spurs on, teaching a dark lassie of the Uwaja to dance the Merry Widow Waltz.

Alf stocked the castaway with flour, tea, sugar and tobacco—the white man's well-being—and carried in to Darwin Jim's seed-pearls and buffalo-hides, to sell with his own. He left two or three of his blacks to go overland with a mob of a hundred Timor ponies that Jim had broken in, believing they might be saleable as Shetlands to zoos and beaches in the south. Alf promised to call back "after the wet".

"What's the date?" he asked in leaving.

Jim hung his head in two minutes' silence.

"Nineteen hundred and nine," he said.

After the wet, Alf came back to tragedy. O.T. was dead.

The lad had been cleaning his father's rifle, a forgotten cartridge in the breech. Ada heard a shot, but took no notice. It was too late when they found little O.T.

Jim buried his son at the edge of the lagoon near the five old gravestones of the English exiles of long ago. He spoke so little about O.T. and thought so much, that Alf suggested a cruise in *Essington* along the coast of Arnhem Land.

Jim said, "Thanks, but he didn't go much on the sea." Then Alf remembered that he and his brother were interested in a silver mine at Mount Catt, on the Wilton River, far down inland. He suggested that Jim should lead an expedition, consisting of himself and Jim, two hundred miles of riding south-east from King River. Jim said yes, he'd "like to have a look at that country". Aboard the lugger they shipped half a dozen of his brumbies and his blacks. It was the end of Port Essington for Jim. He was fading farther still out of the world.

Alf Brown told me the story, with the bushman's true modesty, of his trail across Arnhem Land in 1910.

"We left *Essington* at King River and rode across country to the head of the Wilton to take a look at the silver show. We had some Liverpool River blacks to guide us, but our blacks let them into the know about the tucker we had. They were a sly and savage-looking mob, so we slipped them up in stony country, and Jim was our bushman to find the place.

"We crossed Arnhem Land in about a week's riding, beautiful rivers, well-grassed plains and as fine a pastoral country as anywhere else in Australia, and many ranges. Every night after sundown camp, we had to make up into the rocky hills where the wild blacks couldn't track us, and sleep without a fire, and we kept our horses tied up, ready. We were going like smoke. It wasn't safe then, and it isn't safe now. We picked up a cube of silver-lead out near Mount Catt, but the nearest water was fifteen miles, so we condemned the show. Even if the place was another Broken Hill, you couldn't run it out there—the blacks too bad, and too far away, no tucker.

"Jim had a lot of Sydney flash in him, and he didn't care what happened after he lost O.T. I reckoned he might shoot the police—he didn't want to lose that moustache, like Samson. There wasn't a soul at Port Essington, but it was too close to Darwin, if the police wanted to come out. So I got him interested in trepang, and borrowed an old lugger from Smoky Bill, and settled him down at Malay Bay, the best bay for trepang in the north.

"I was afraid my blacks would talk in Darwin, and they did. A feller came to me one night on the jetty, just as I was putting out to sea, with a bag of six hundred sovereigns. He said would I give it to Jim and tell him to make a get-away to New Guinea. All Jim had to do was to sign for the money, that it was a receipt for his station, the Retreat. I said if I ever met Jim Campbell, I would, and the feller nodded. He knew.

"I delivered the bag of sovereigns, but they were no good to Jim. We laughed about it at Malay Bay. He said there were no poddies to rustle in New Guinea, so no future in his profession there. He told me to give them back the bag of gold and let the station rip, so I did. Those chaps were only trying to cash in on Jim being in trouble. Bovril was buying Victoria River, and they wanted to sell them the Retreat."

Trader Brown made his camp at Bowen Straits, the old Malay well under the tamarind-trees, Oojoung-tamba-nounou. He saw Jim about once a year, when Smoky Bill's lugger brought in cargoes of trepang for tea, sugar, flour and tobacco to pay Jim's blacks.

The outlaw spent most of his time "riding around looking at country". In 1911 Bill Murphy met him—Alf Brown and Bill Murphy were the only two white men he spoke to in his seven years of exile. Sitting on the veranda of the old Victoria Hotel one stifling night in Darwin, Murphy was telling me of his long rides as Protector of Aborigines out along the north coast.

"Did you ever happen to meet Jim Campbell?" I asked.

"I buried Jim Campbell," he said, "and I met him once living. The tales about him are all moonshine. He was just a bushman, one of the best-natured I ever met. I was riding out to Cadell Straits with a good plant of Government horses, all branded G.R. for the King, and a fair little camp of uniformed blacks. We hoppled out in a creek of the Frederick Hills, pretty far out. Half a mile away we heard horse-bells. I sent the blacks to see who it was. They came back and said 'Jim Campbell'.

"I don't mind telling you I was windy. I'd heard all the yarns about the Diamond shooting a policeman on sight, and my plant was mighty like a police-plant. I was finishing up supper when the boys said the white-fella was coming across the creek. I sat tight, without a gun.

" 'G'night!' he said. I said good-night.

" 'Brought y'a couple o' ducks.' He threw them down.

" 'Thanks,' I said, 'I'm Murphy. Native Affairs, you know.' I got that bit in early. 'Sit down,' I said. 'Care for a smoke?'

" 'No, thanks. Don't smoke. Just came for a yarn. The name's Campbell.'

"I can see him now as he stood in the firelight, a stoutish man in a cattleman's get-up, spurs and all, with a rosy face well shaved except for a big fair moustache. There was nothing bitter or queer about him, though he'd been out on his own for five years then. In fact, he seemed to be having a darned good time. He knew every inch of the country, where the buffaloes and wild cattle were and what the rivers would carry. If I didn't know we were three hundred miles out in the blue, I would have taken him for a station pioneer with a homestead over the rise—there was nothing but a star over the rise. He talked of Sydney and Melbourne and the Cup, and told a lot of good yarns over a bottle of whisky I had in the packs. He was a natural actor, he could 'do' a barmaid in Sydney or a drover out west. I never laughed so much. We yarned till two in the morning.

" 'Well, I'd better tell you,' he said when he was going, 'I'm Jim Campbell, the outlaw.'

" 'I know,' I said. 'As a matter of fact, Jim, I was worried about you. I reckoned my life wasn't worth a damn when you saw these horses.'

"He was puzzled. 'Why?'

"Well, they look like a police-plant, and they reckon if you sight the police, you shoot to kill.'

" '*Me!*' He had a great laugh. 'They know me, and then put round a yarn like that. If the police came out, I wouldn't show up, that's all. I know a few cracks in the hills where they'd never find me. But I reckon they don't want to. They've got me yarded where I can't give any trouble—no poddies to dodge out here!'

"We shook hands. I heard him whistling across the creek, back to the blacks and his wild life, whistling the 'Merry Widow Waltz' that he heard down south the only time he ever went to a show.

"Soon after that the manhunt was over. Bovril Estates bought Victoria River Downs, and Dicky Townshend, leaving the north, withdrew the warrant against Campbell. Jim was free to go back, and to take up another little pocket for the Diamond Eighty-eight if he wanted, because nothing had ever been proved against him. Alf Brown brought him the news, but he said he had all the pockets he wanted. He was only forty, but he had learnt to live without civilization.

"I looked forward to meeting him again. When I did he was dead. A couple of years later I was riding that country when a big mob of bush niggers came round us at nightfall—the only scare about blacks I ever had in my life. There was a nigger behind every tree, and they wouldn't come into the open. The boys camped close up, terrified, and I sat up all night with my gun handy. When the moon rose after midnight, the myalls started a big *yacki* of corroboree, throwing firesticks in the air. At daylight, I sent over some tucker and tobacco. They helped us catch the horses, but they wouldn't come into camp.

"When we set off on the trail, they followed, friendly, but keeping a good distance. Suddenly, they were gone—into a billabong, under the water, and out the other side into the scrub. There's mischief when blacks disappear like that. I told the boys to watch, I reckoned they'd meet us in ambush farther on. I gave rifles to one or two I could trust, and told them to fire into the trees, good and hearty, if they saw those bush niggers coming back.

"Over the next rise a little mob came riding towards us—Campbell's blacks. Our myall friends had seen them coming and hopped it. They had good reason.

" 'Which-way Jim?' I called out.

"They rode right up close. 'Jim pinish, boss!' Dick whispered in a scared sort of way, looking around him.

" 'Campbell dead!'

" 'You-i.'

" 'How long?'

" 'One night sleep, night before. Bush blackfella been killem.'

" 'Good God! Where?'

" 'Longa salt water.' They pouted to Guion Point and the sea. Nellie and Ada burst into a long shrill wailing. I wheeled my boys and horses for the coast.

"In the mangrove mud of a creek we found Jim, wrapped in his blanket. His face was peaceful and pleasant as I remembered it in the firelight, but in his head and chest, broken off at the haft, were five stone-head spears.

"He was dressed in a clean white shirt and a pair of new trousers bought in the Katherine long ago, and carried in his swag through all the exile for when he should come again to the fellowship of his friends. There was something pitiable about those clothes, they held the creases of years. When I asked how he came to be wearing them over the spears, Nellie and Ada said they dressed him. When the bush blacks killed him, he was wearing an old red naga, 'all-same blackfella', but they said: 'Him likum more better shirt-and-trouser.'

"I was touched by that, knowing their fear and horror of the dead. They knew that Jim, at the last, should be found as a white man by his own people. When I met them they were risking their lives in strange country, going to tell a policeman—a three-hundred-mile ride.

"The myalls that came to my night-camp were the ones that killed him, the Yerrakool, always a dangerous crowd, but they were not morally guilty. It was the queerest story I ever heard.

"There was a boy named Nundil with Campbell's blacks. I had not seen him before, but he was full of information about how these bush blacks did the job. He spoke very glib English. He seemed to me to know a bit too much. I asked Nellie about him. She said he had worked for Jim 'two moon', but they had a row and he ran away. When Jim was dead he came back. I decided to keep my eye on this lad.

"The tides and quicksands at Guion Point would have taken the body, so we wrapped Jim in his camp-sheet, and in Smoky Bill's old lugger we carried him over and buried him at King River. We gathered his few possessions from the smokehouse on the beach at Malay Bay. None of the tucker had been touched, except that his own blacks had taken some to come in with, and Dick had his rifle for protection. There was never any 'lubra trouble', Nellie said—the bush blacks had never been within two miles of the camp. I wondered what was the motive, because Jim never had any trouble with wild blacks. He knew them pretty well.

"We all made for Darwin. A trooper went out in a lugger to get the murderers. Nundil went with him to point out the ones that threw the spears. When the policeman landed on the beach out there, two of the guilty men came to see what he wanted. They admitted their share of the killing, and brought in the others."

The police lugger came back with thirty of the Yerrakool, murderers, witnesses and their wives and babies. Witnesses were kept in the Kahlin compound, where at strange fires and under the evil eye of other tribes, they were frightened and shy. Prisoners were given a shirt and trousers, and kept about the police station on an anchor-chain till the weird story of the white man's death was told to a judge and jury. It was a sensation, the end of "the Diamond". So that was where he had been, out among the myalls, and the police never did take him alive.

In the Supreme Court of Darwin in 1913, eight Arnhem Landers crouched in the dock, charged with the "*wilful, malicious and felonious slaying of Ernest Clare Campbell, trepanger, at Guion Point in the Northern Territory of Australia*". They were wild creatures of the woods—Namarangeri, Whar-ditt, Meebooliman, Lamaribi, Terandilli, Angudyea, and Daroolba. With them was Nundil, a sly civilized boy, the only one who understood a word of the English language. It was a remarkable case of murder by inciting to kill, a crafty imposition of white man's cunning on the receptive mind of the black. Because the guilty never suffered the penalty of the law, it was, in its way, a perfect crime.

Nundil, a detribalized boy, had worked for a ship-builder in Darwin. He drifted down the coast on Smoky Bill's lugger to Malay Bay, where Campbell was fishing trepang from native canoes. Nundil offered to build him a dinghy for half a pound of tobacco and half a bag of flour.

The dinghy was built, and Nundil was paid. He hung about the camp, making trouble—blacks will not work when others about them are idle. Jim told him to work with the mob or get out. Nundil considered himself skilled labour. He refused to gather trepang. When his tucker cut out, he cadged from the camp. Campbell threatened to thrash him if he did not work or go. He stood up and defied Jim, saying he had not been paid in full—he wanted a pound of tobacco and a whole bag of flour.

Jim lost his temper. The "Sydney flash" came out. With a heavy right to the chin, he knocked Nundil backwards into a trepang pot of hot water. The water was not scalding, there were no scars on Nundil at any time, but it was a bad action. Jim's justification was the theory still prevailing throughout the north that a white man must never "take cheek from a blackfella". If he shows signs of weakness when he is far out and alone, his number is up.

Nundil took to the bush, but did not go far. Being a civilized boy, he was not a good bush provider. He still cadged tucker without Jim's knowing.

When clouds of monsoon darkened the Arafura, the Yerrakool came into the coast for corroboree. With the Melville Islanders, these salt-water tribes of the far north alone, in tree-post monument, in drama and in song, honour the dead. When the changing cycle of the year brings memories, in screaming saga and barbaric ballet, they, too, "praise famous men".

Night after night the beaches rang with their yelling, a hysteria of history and old grief.

"Willing-gurree! Willing-gurree!
My father!
Swimming-man.
Raced the swordfish in storm seas
Crested white and flying like cockatoos.
White cockatoos of the sea!
Willing-gurree!
Where?"

And then:

"Kunu!
Eyes seeing-far.
Our brother Kunu.
Quick spear!"

The dance of Willing-gurree . . . the dance of Kunu . . . by men streaked white, the woebegone wailing of the women, the beat, beat of cupped hands on bare thighs, the dusty drum of bare feet.

To Jim in his tent on the sands it was only a hell of a racket. To Nundil, hiding in the bush, it was an evil thought. He camped with the myalls, shared their fish, learned a little of their language, sat and watched the dancing with the women and the old. When they cried for vengeance on the devil robbing them of their loved ones, Nundil motioned them to the light far down the lonely beach.

Kambil!

Kambil killed Kunu. Chased him up a tree, and set it on fire. Nundil saw him do it.

Kambil killed Willing-gurree. Dived from the lugger and throttled the swimmer, held him down to choke—like this!—in the dark water. Nundil saw that too. Saw Kambil rip up Nappaloora with his knife. Saw him smother the sleeping Biambil. Even if Kunu died of dropsy at the age of eighty, and Willing-gurree of appendicitis fifty miles inland, this imaginative race, bewitched by its own dreams, believed Nundil . . . believed, in time, that the innocent Jim had done in every man and woman of the Yerrakool for five generations. With Nundil supplying the scenario they enacted his frightful deeds in a series of firelight dramas, in the corroborative evidence of corroboree.

And in corroboree they began to kill Kambil. . . .

An ochre-coloured Kambil with bright-red cheeks and grisly hair of treefibres, weedy yellow moustaches like a pair of buffalo horns curled back from a whitened mouth.

Jim, sitting in his tent mending saddles by slush-light, making hopples and halters of buffalo hide for a "ride around", never knew that the black men striped with white were singing him dead, dancing him dead. Each night they killed him in his pale and painted effigy, stabbed him, smothered him, held him down to drown, around the red fires in their Stone Age rhythm and chanting, levelling their painted spears at the tent-light ghostly as a glow-worm far down the beach.

Vengeance was forgotten when the show was over. Theatrical grief and hatred faded with the stars. Kambil the White Devil, the corroboree-man, died with the daylight. He was merely the theme of a ding-dong dance. There was no animosity in the world to Jim Campbell the white-fella, pottering about his trepang pots—as well might actors and audience wait outside the theatre to lynch the villain of the play.

Nundil was very sly. When the men were out fishing, he laughed about them to the lubras, pointing out Campbell with derision of all the big talk and the dancing.

Kill Kambil? Ha! they only gammon. No guts. Can't kill Kambil proper. Tonight him die, tomorrow him walkabout. That-one properly cheeky, him all-about killem you-fella.

The lubras jeered at the corroboree now, shrieked with scorn when the corroboree-man was speared, and stabbed, and cleft to the brisket. Only gammon. No guts. Kambil walkabout.

The dancers began to murmur, and the Old Men nodded. For two or three nights the beaches were silent, no singing. Nellie and Barney Flynn's Ada were scared. Be wary when the blacks are no longer singing. They warned Jim. He said damn good job, he could get to sleep. They came in every year and did no harm.

A grey evening with the wind blowing cold along the Arafura . . . tide-flats in the twilight, bare in the ebb. A good night for trepang. Jim mustered the camp to bring the canoes and the dinghy round to the salt creek. Nellie brought his rifle.

"I don't want the gun. Put it away."

"More better you take him, Jim. Might be trouble."

"You do what I tell you. Put it away."

At the salt creek between Malay Bay and Junction Bay they lit their paperbark torches to wade slowly down the shallows with the outgoing tide, stopping to pick up the trepang two and three feet under water. Jim, Barney Flynn's Ada and Little Jacky were slowly pushing down the boat in midstream, Nellie, Dick and the others bringing the trepang to it. Once Nellie stopped and listened . . . sucking of the mud at snaky mangrove roots and the crackle of marching crabs. Soon time to go home and camp—Nellie would be glad.

"Arr-h! Arr-h!" Half a guttural breathing, half a shout.

They held the paperbark torches high.

The mangroves were moving . . . men coated with grey mud, men striped with white.

Spears!

Campbell's blacks shrieked, then crouched and ran, Barney Flynn's Ada fat and stumbling through the mud, yelling.

Jim tried to run. He tore a spear from his breast, and hurled it back, and stumbled. He grabbed Little Jacky's arm, dragged himself to his knees, faced the painted men and cursed them. . . .

They were closing in, grunting like animals, swinging high their spears. . . .

"Oh-h-h!"

With a hoarse, gurgling cry, Jim Campbell fell on his face in the mud.

Little Jacky raced. Dick and the boys were swift as shadows down the beach for the rifle. The women hid in the mangroves, holding their breath. When the boys came back the painted men had gone. They fired a shot and crept across to Jim. He was dead.

All night while the fires burned high to the demon-screaming of corroboree, they kept watch at the white man's tent, lightless, flapping in the wind, dim as a spirit on the sand.

At dawn the three faithfuls crept through the mangroves, washed Jim's body and dressed it in the clothing of its kind.

Nundil came back. He said they should wait for Smoky Bill's lugger, or Alf Brown—plenty tucker and tobacco in the tent. Dick said no, they must catch Jim's horses and ride for the police. Dick was boss, because he had the rifle.

This evidence was given in Yerrakool language through an interpreter, also in pidgin, in dumbshow and finger-yabber in the Darwin court. The seven men of the Stone Age, with their claw-like gesticulations and bewildered dark eyes, nodded that they threw the spears.

"You-i. Been killem that cheeky-fella Kambil. Him been killem my brudder before," each told the court through the interpreter—a brief and childish summing-up of all the sagas of their race and Nundil's lies. Nundil went scot-free. On Lamaribi, Terandilli, Angudyea and Daroolba the sentence of death was passed, commuted to ten years imprisonment. Under such aliases as Left-handed Harry, Terry, Digger and Nut you would probably find them among the old police-trackers or in one of the compounds today.

Some of the other blacks are still living, dark threads in the weaving of Jim Campbell's destiny. Dummy, when last I heard of her, was an intelligent house-girl at Auvergne, silently moving about her chores in a red-yoked frock of galatea, with no remembrance, it seemed, of the little black rag of a horse-tailer that once led a trooper so far astray.

On a rainy evening, I was sitting typewriting in my angle-iron room at the little old pub at Katherine when a lubra, swift as a shadow, drifted in behind a broom. She picked up my travelling clock of imitation grained marble, and turned it over curiously in her long fingers.

"*Binka!*" she said with a smile. "Rainstone."

"What name you?" I asked.

"Me Nellie. Two-fella Nellie belong this pub. Me Campbell's Nellie."

"Jim Campbell, longa Retreat, longa Malay Bay?"

"You-i, missus!" she laughed in delight. "Which-way you savvy that-one? Me long time stock-boy longa him."

Draped on her broom, quite often Campbell's Nellie came to "yarn longa that-one". His name she would not mention, and of his "pinish" at Guion Point she would not speak. I looked for Campbell's Nellie when I went back to Katherine, but the "kings' camp" under the river pandanus, and all the Djauan people, were herded into compounds and gone.

The Retreat is part of Victoria River Downs, also Illawarra. Far out on the north coast of Australia, around Malay Bay, the crew of some navy or survey ship, ashore for oysters, may some day wonder to find two or three branding-irons, perhaps a pack-saddle tree, rusted in the sand, a symbol strange on those beaches, of a cattle-man's life. They may even read numbers on the branding irons, corroded by sea-salt, ◊88.

A queer life it was for a merry fellow, a lonely one from boyhood, for Sonny Muir was "in smoke" most of his forty years, from the empty prairies of the Queensland west to the red MacDonnell Ranges, from the wilds of the Gulf to Victoria River, his last seven years out in the Arafura blue.

In smoke, too, is his memory. Drovers from Wave, and all the old hands from Kimberley over to Queensland, sitting around the camp-fire for the evening pipe, will tell you why Victoria River Downs changed its brand from the G Ten to the Bull's Head when Jim Campbell was a rider of the Murran-ji.

Chapter XXIII

Blackfella Dreamin'

IN THE days before the Stuart Highway a State Governor and his adventurous wife made the journey overland from Adelaide to Darwin, seeking knowledge of Australia. Braving the dust and the distances in two high-powered cars, they travelled *en suite* with a professor of a southern university, an aide-de-camp, a secretary and two chauffeurs.

From Newcastle Waters, then only a cattle station and a store, the transcontinental road was lost in black-soil bog and strangers would never find the washed-out crossings of creeks, so an old black Henry was called up to be escort to the party for the eighty miles on to Daly Waters.

A fine patriarch of noble brow and gentle bearing, Henry was bathed and shaved, tricked out in new shirt and trousers, hastily coached in vice-regal etiquette. With his hat in his hand and a deferential air, he was introduced by the manager of the station as a novelty in guides to interest Their Excellencies.

His Lordship was not so sure. He surveyed Henry as if he were something new in the zoo.

"Mm," he reflected. "Er—do they understand English?"

"Oh, yes. Henry speaks English well."

"Are they accustomed to riding in cars?"

"Henry can drive one."

"What do you feed them on?"

"Bread and beef, tea—anything you're having yourself, sir."

"Do you cook the beef, or do you give it to them raw?"

Henry blinked. The station manager laughed.

"Henry'll cook yours if you like. He's a good clean cook."

His Lordship was still uncertain.

"Mm. Very well. You're sure he knows the road, and that he won't get up to any mischief or run away?"

Henry lost patience. "Look here, boss," he said earnestly, "you think I'm bloody myall like a kangaroo. I been ridin' this country an' workin' for white men porty-chickty year. I savvy all-about motor-car an' cookin' beef an' white missus don' like swearin'. You talk you king belong you people. All right. Me king belong my people all-same you."

His Lordship blinked. Henry joined the party with dignity as a peer of a peer of the realm, and was its shining light as far as Daly Waters, a merry companion and an authority on bush lore, with wit and wisdom for those morocco-bound diaries with a coronet on the cover.

His Excellency would not realize that a history, tradition, law and religion far older on earth than his own were expressed in this traveller from antiquity, this ethnological curio, sitting so quietly in the luxury car regarding his horny feet. When they camped under a gum-tree with a tiffin basket for lunch, and Henry sat, his back to the party, with his hunk of bread and mug of tea at a respectful distance, His Excellency noted with approval the deference due to his own exalted station in life. In point of fact, Henry was afraid of the Evil Eye.

For too long the Australian blacks, by friend and foe, were looked upon as something less than human. If a quick adaptability to environment is the test of intelligence, they are the equal of any race on earth. The Arnhem Land myall with his bamboo bangles, his sporran of fur, his shovel-nose spear in hand and his little crochet string bag under his arm, can make in less than a year the long journey from the Stone Age in comprehension and acceptance of our time in all he needs to know.

In the art of enjoying life, the aboriginal is ahead of us. He hunts his food when he is hungry, and with the sun and a fire to warm him, Mother Earth is his home. His time is the circle of the sun, the changes of the moon, and the season of rain.

In the simple tenets of Christian living he is far more Christian than we are. The vilest crimes and degradations of our cities are not within his ken. If he is, occasionally, a ritualistic cannibal, has not Bernard Shaw denounced our slaughter of animals and appetite for flesh as "cannibalism with its heroic dish omitted"? The case for cannibalism is not proven. Never yet in our courts has he been charged with the crime. So far as I know, he has never been caught *in flagrante delicto*, taking a bite. There is nothing but hearsay evidence—of the man who knew a man who said he saw it, as in the matter of the ghost. We must hold him innocent till he is proved guilty.

His was the only race on earth that through thousands of years could be completely and ecstatically happy without alcoholic stimulants and adventitious aids. As Sir George Grey remarked, he is quicker in intelligence than the average English peasant. He has no head for mathematics—his counting was one, two, two-one, two-two, hand of five fingers, many—but he has a remarkable gift of tongues, and can speak five or six native languages, with English and Malay thrown in, at his own fireside. He has a ready and true sense of humour. His art, his music, his dancing will enrich the thought of the world.

The white man has never known—and now never will know—this silent, sensitive, long-suffering people.

"Observe," wrote Carlyle, "that of man's whole terrestrial possessions and attainments, unspeakably the noblest are his Symbols, divine and divine-seeming, under which he marches and fights, with victorious assurance, in this life-battle. . . ."

Aboriginal symbols are kindred with our own, but so old that now they are alms for oblivion, "blackfella dreamin' ". All over the Territory and south to the Great Australian Bight you will hear that curiously beautiful phrase denoting the farthest shores of memory, *antiquis temporibus*, from the most ancient times.

Laws, legends, languages, the corybantic corroborees, every tribal rite and belief belong to "blackfella dreamin'—before old man, before grandmother, too much long-time I can't savvy, too much old-fella".

The law is the law—why, nobody knows—handed down the generations in songs and dances, in crude glyptic carvings and childish codex of lines and circles on elliptical tablets of wood. Each tribe of a thousand tribes had its own dreaming, but, though they had practically no association with each other, they were all dreaming much the same dream. North of the 28th parallel of south latitude, the blacks of Australia were one great homogeneous group, their babel of languages and all their laws and customs forming one distinct and characteristic national language and mind. They covered and used the whole continent far more equably than we have done without one blemish of nature, without wreaking the vengeance of erosion.

Their mirror of truth was shattered into these tribal fragments heaven knows how many centuries before the white man came. All aboriginal countries were clearly defined in the dreaming, virtual States, to be governed not by hereditary rulers, nor in the haphazard of popular election, but by councils of the Old Men after many graduation years of disciplinary training and initiation to the mysteries of life. No doubt the rigid border-lines and

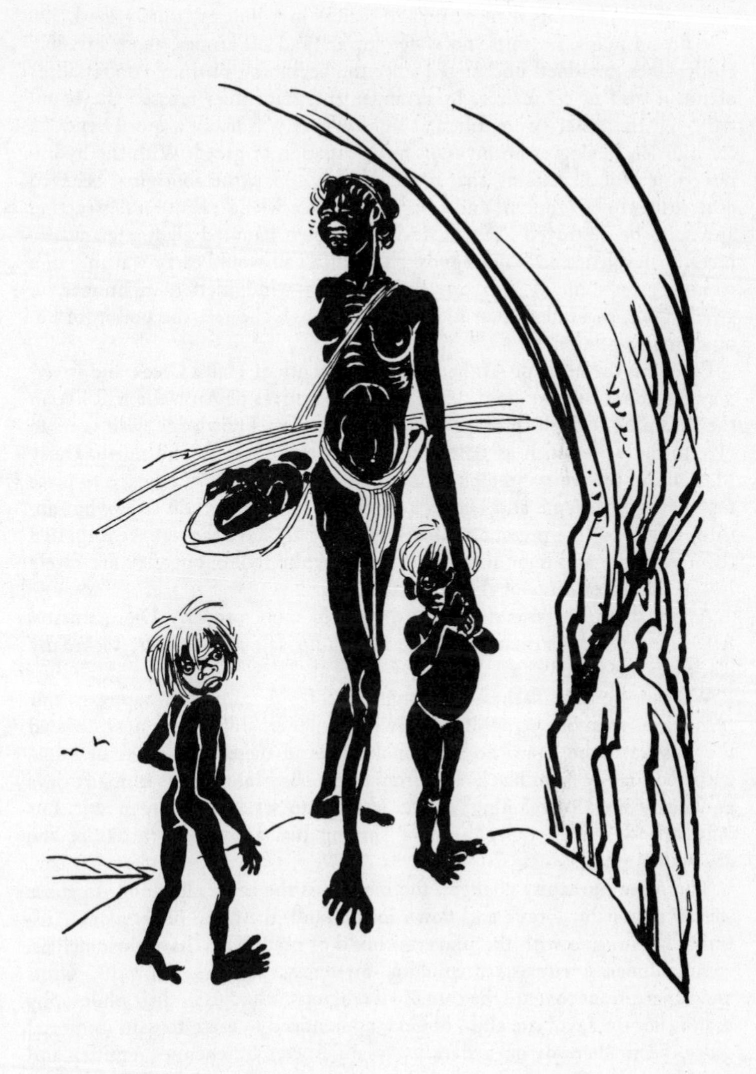

antipathies were a subconscious sense or a conscious ruling to preserve for each nomad group its own game and waters in a hungry, thirsty land.

With no maps, no forts, no watch-towers and no armies, those invisible border-lines remained unchanged since the beginning of time. Ambassadors of music and of commerce, by arrangement, sometimes crossed the boundary, but trespassers were killed at sight. There was many a quick vendetta for murder, but never an invasion for occupation or greed. With the hydra-headed fear of all nations, that is such a bogy today, the aboriginal believed other tribes to be ignorant and savage, "bush blackfella", bent on destruction and so to be destroyed . . . but devils unknown haunted all foreign water-holes, malevolent and jealous gods. Every bird-call would carry warning of a stranger, the scent of him travelled in every wind. Better, in hunger, to swallow lumps of clay than to draw up through the feet the poison of another man's ground.

Except in the heart of Arnhem Land and south of Hall's Creek and Inverway for about five hundred desert miles, no natives of Australia still live in the dreaming. Up till thirty years ago seekers after knowledge with years to give to the work, such as Baldwin Spencer in the Centre and north, Daisy M. Bates in the west and along the shores of the Bight, did manage to piece together, with rhyme and reason, part of the story of certain tribes, but anthropologists of the present are too late. Not only have the natives forgotten their own lore and logic in assimilation of white living, but they are rarely full-blood descendants of the original tribes.

As an aboriginal friend expressed it, "No more properly Dieri, missus. All-same Afghan-German-Japanese, mixem-up salt and pepper, too many blackfella, no good."

We can see only flashes and fragments of old traditions, happy in our researches when one scrap of a jigsaw fits another. Impossible, now, to read the Rosetta Stone. I am no anthropologist, and these stray notes of mine, gathered mainly from blacks and from a few observant whites in many days and many ways of roaming, are no attempt to set a figure in mosaic, but only a bower-bird's playground of shining bits and pieces, facets of the aboriginal mind.

The more humanity changes, the more it is the same old thing. In those sheeny sago-palm forests and down in the sand, the mind of the dark Australians is in tune with the universal mind of man. They have their deities, commandments, rituals, ceremonies, mysteries, parables, proverbs, saints and superstitions that are the core of all religions. Though in their philosophy man is not the favourite child of God, apprenticed to earth to gain immortal glory, he is "here as on a darkling plain", beset by enemies, entities and supernatural powers in but one phase of that eternal living of which, in a broad view, they share our various theories.

Death, always a black brew of man's deliberate evil, is never the end. The soul, in sorrow or in anger, haunts for a while the place of earthly dying, and then may vanish into upward air—the Dieri heaven is *piriwilpa*, the sky, and Melville Islanders have the same word, *wailani*, for "ghost" as for "air". In an amazing flash of poetry the Pitjantara and western people say that the dead walk backwards . . . into the past. All over the continent to name the dead is to call them, as in Maeterlinck's Land of Memory in *The Blue Bird*, but theirs is no happy memory. The dead are vindictive to the living, having been robbed of life.

In many coastal tribes the soul travels to a heaven over the sea, to come back as a turtle, or dugong, or fish of the totem, or *oolkoolpa*, foam. It may rise from the ground in the spirit of a tree or animal, those "little brother" and "big brother" affinities close to the old Egyptian symbols and to the Hindu doctrines of transmigration. This nature-kinship with animals, birds, lizards, trees is very near to the Greek theosophies and to Darwinian theories of evolution. Some call it pantheism. The soul may be born again in a black child, as in sequence of Buddhist reincarnation—spirits avid for life are waiting to leap into a lubra and be reborn, and where she feels the child quicken, that is its spirit-ground. Or the soul may come back as a white man from the place of the pale shades. Australia's explorers by land and sea were all believed to be the dead returning.

Not only a shade is the spirit, but a shade with a shadow, which may guide and guard its loved ones after death. Every tree or animal of the totem has its shadow, a second spirit, from which the old men give the newly-born their secret name, which women never know, but all is "registered" in the totem boards, spoken only in the council meetings. This totem-board registration is to safeguard against intermarriage with forbidden skins.

Among Alligator River people the shade is Eeyalmaru and the shadow Eeyu. In the beat of wings of a passing bird, or a cloud over the sun, a hunter or a lubra will sense danger, and pause, and creep back into the jungle. Eeyu gave warning. In raids by enemy whites and blacks, mothers would hide their children in a tree of the totem. The guardian angel is there in the bush. Some spirits are evil. How often in a native murder case a boy will say, "I been sleep. Debil-debil talk that way longa my ear."

Empty sunlit Australia was peopled by these shadows and sprites. The old-time bushman, riding the track, travelled a haunted world and never knew it—faces in the rocks, a bunyip in every waterhole, a banshee in the cry of a crow, witches in the whirlwind, in every bush a leprechaun, in every cave a *Doppelgänger* or poltergeist hiding. Everywhere was the half-human of kindred Greek mythologies, the centaur, the satyr, the men with crocodile heads or with emu feet.

There was a sermon in every conspicuous stone. This broken limestone crater was the hole the rainbow came out of. That crag of a hill imprisoned Bilbilgie, grandad of all grasshoppers. The red peak beyond was a *minna* or totem-spirit mountain where Old Man Eaglehawk speared Old Man Kangaroo and ate him and turned into stone when both were men. The serpent plays a leading part in aboriginal theology, just as he does in Genesis. Crawling from the sea to the land he made the rivers, and fathered creation on earth.

If many of their customs are of the Brahmins and Parsees, many of the laws Semitic, and the symbols of Egypt, most of the legends are purely and idyllically Greek. The one-eyed Cyclops in the waterhole, the warriors that spring from the pandanus nuts, the spirit-gods and animal-gods that lie in wait for women to beget a child—you find these everywhere. Star-legends are often identical. Orion the Hunter, spear in hand and dog at heel, nightly follows the Pleiades, who are always young girls. From the Centre south-west to the shores of the Bight, Venus is a woman of many lovers, and she eats them all; in the Gulf country she is Kooterincha the Crab, with sparkling claws of light. A falling star is a devil that feeds on the dead. Jove throws his thunderbolts in the Australian bush—in storms the blacks cover their fires so that the lightning cannot see them and strike, or they rush to the waterholes and duck under.

Had the first bushmen regarded as human the fauns and hamadryads they dressed up as scarecrows to be their willing slaves, they would have left us a library of the world's first folklore, a remarkable psychological graph of the childhood of man, but "Blackfella business is not my business," they said. "Never talk to your niggers or you're in for trouble."

The writing of aboriginal legends in Australia at the moment has become a literary vogue. Many books are produced of native lore, some gaily illustrated fairy tales for children, some in erudite scientific manner, some as popular romance. Among these are the valuable books of Mary and Elizabeth Durack, of the Territory's own Bill Harney, author of *Taboo* and *Brimming Billabongs*, and of W. Linklater, author of *The Magic Snake*. Such as these know and understand the blacks, in the casual and friendly association of many years.

There are others, with far less opportunity, who appear to have been lucky in research. I have been twice round Australia by land, clockwise and anti-clockwise, on varying routes in hard monotony of miles. I have been three times across it from south to north, many times east and west, and once by the diagonal, with spider-web journeys from almost every outback town as far as I could travel—all this apart from journeys by sea and air. I have spent months among some of the groups of natives, collecting vocabularies—the only way to translation—and quietly looking for legend and lore. Yet never could I unearth stories one half so fashionably romantic as those I hear over the radio from Melbourne and Sydney. To me the best stories from a literary view, which does not exist in the aboriginal mind, flashed in no more than a few words and were gone, usually with a moral, never with the conventional beginning and ending, never with a plot.

Those trim little fables of why the brolga dances and why the kookaburra laughs never came my way, nor the dusky princess of the lily lagoon, renowned for her gentleness and beauty. The race knows nothing of royalty, and beauty is neither admired nor required where a wife is betrothed to you before she is born or soon after, merely as woman and to scout small game and vegetable tucker. If she is "sulky" or "cheeky", you take it out of her with a waddy. The only reference I ever heard to beauty, as such, was the male of the species described by laughing lubras as *nooroo*, pretty-fella, nose squashed flat. With the blackfellow, as with the lyrebird, it is the male who dresses up and dances, but not when courting, for there is no courting. When he was a boy of thirteen or so and she was a teething baby, a marriage had been arranged—or if she is a widow, toothless and shrill, whom nobody else wants, he can have her till he is allotted his own wives. Even in runaway affairs he puts no stock in romance. He is primitive man.

The better the story the less authentic the legend. The real ones fade in and fade out. Self-respecting authors, even the scientific, cannot abide these half-told tales and half-baked mythologies, so the writers write in a plot and too often the scientists apply their own theories. Often enough the mixture of tribes, fauna and flora in so-called legends is a complete cover of the continent, customs, costumes and aboriginal words picked up from anywhere and from Captain Phillip's time onward, wombats, crocodiles, koala bears, pythons, boomerangs and gum-leaf bands all in together. The gum-leaf band is not aboriginal, but a trick taught by white men.

We have even seen aboriginal poems translated to three columns of Swinburnian sibilance and Shelleian fire, apostrophizing the breeze and the trees and the good old days gone by.

Pure poetry is theirs, but only in a flash of imagery or a heart-pang of grief. There are no aboriginal poems much longer than the distich of corroboree. Man-corroboree songs are abracadabra of the dreaming. Play-corroboree songs are plain statement of fact, such as "turkey for tea", or "lizard been walk along", or merely, as they will tell you, "language", words for the sake of the music. To ask the blacks to translate "language" is like asking us to translate "Hey diddle diddle" or "Ta-ra-ra boom-de-ay".

It is the Australian poet's rightful licence to translate our inarticulate dark people, and we rejoice in all writers who weave their fact and fancy to express and to help those who are with us still, but let us leave a life-mask for future generations to see, and not a cook-up of *Hiawatha* and the *Just So Stories*.

Among the Territory tribes with whom I have made contact are Malaradharra, South Australian border to MacDonnell Ranges; Pitjantara, west of them from Musgrave Ranges to Ayers Rock; Arundta, Finke River and MacDonnell Ranges; Luritja, west of Arundta; Allowera, east of Arundta; Kaitish, Barrow Creek country; Warramulla, west, Landers River to Granites; Bingongana, Tanami and south of Wave Hill; Waggire, north-east of Barrow Creek to Alexandria; Warramunga, Tennant's Creek country; Pintubi, east of Tennant's Creek; Tjingilli, Newcastle Waters country; Agoquila, north-west of Newcastle Waters to Dry River; Yungman, Elsey River; Mungurai, upper Roper; Nullakan, mid-Roper; Mara-mara, salt-water Roper; Djauan, Katherine River; Wogguman, Dilik, upper Daly; Mulluk Mulluk, Brinken, mid-Daly; Marramaninjie, Anglomarie, Ponga Ponga, salt-water Daly; Marununga, from Daly River to Delissaville on coast; Waugite, Delissaville to Darwin; Larrakia, Darwin country; Woolna (Punmurlu), salt-water Adelaide River and Gulf; Minnachee, mid-Adelaide River; Mejeelie, East Alligator River; Kakadu, South Alligator River; Mala-ola, Wongo-ak, Melville and Bathurst islands; Uwaja, Port Essington; Yerrakool, King and Liverpool rivers; Arrarapi, Arnhem Land "sandstone" tribes to Goyder River; Ungurula, Arnhem Bay; Ritherunga, Boolman to Caledon Bay; Remburunga, Wilton and Mainoru rivers; Agrighula, around Pine Creek; Alloha, Limmen River; Anuella, Binbinga, Macarthur River; Karra-warra, Robinson River; Mudburra, Wadduman, Victoria River; Uranara, Toko Ranges, the pituri country blacks; Wonkorunda, Simpson Desert.

With a few others in Arnhem Land, the far north-west and the Sandy Desert, these comprise most of the great tribes still left in Australia, and some of these have faded out of ken in the past fifteen years, not a full tribesman living at the old hereditary waters, nor indeed in all the camps and compounds that gather them in to die.

Tribal areas vary in size according to water and food. The Larrakia (pronounced Larra-kee-yah) of Darwin and many northern tribes were confined to about twenty square miles of sea-beach, river country and lily lagoons, rich tucker. Down in the Centre the Arundta, Warramulla, Pitjantara and others had right of way of over a thousand square miles where waters were intermittent. They were composed of affiliated groups, enemies in good times with a cessation of hostilities in drought.

On the Barkly Tablelands when waterholes dried up, their people could be guests of those with the big permanent pools till the rains came, hunting for themselves and sending back scouts to their country to watch for the waters. As the Crusaders in their "truce of God", they were morally bound not to raid camps nor to steal women, but with the lubras out digging yams and chasing goannas there was many a lovers' tryst and plans to flit. When the time came to go, their hosts gave them a grand send-off corroboree and twenty-four hours—"one night sleep"—to make the border. Away they went, and half the wives after them, the warriors on their tracks by piccaninny daylight, and devil take the hindmost.

Of each major tribe there was a well-defined border never crossed till the white man came, and carried his henchman with him willy-nilly. In Central Australia you will often hear of a "blackfella post-office", a banal misinterpretation of the old Greek rite of placing tokens of a green branch to propitiate gods and men. One of these so-called post-offices was near Koporilya Springs of Hermannsburg Mission. There women for centuries, at the entrance of a cave, placed votive offerings to the spirits of birth when they wanted children—the way of all women of all religions since time began. Another, of a different significance, was on the road from Alice Springs to Winnecke. To our ignorant gaze it was only a pile of dead leaves. The Arundta, passing into Allowera territory there, plucked a branch and added it to the heap, a passport, and giving courteous notice to the Allowera, a co-related tribe, of their coming through in peace. An Ilperra boy from Bond Springs, who travelled with us on one journey, asked the driver to stop.

"What! That old blackfella post-office!" the driver teased him, and the boy grinned. "You don't have to worry. When you're on a car, they can't track you."

"Him savvy all right," the boy smiled and nodded.

"Talk debil-debil, eh? You frightened?"

"You-i."

The driver slowed up at the place and the boy hurried off through the bush, climbing aboard again in the time it takes to roll a cigarette. He had arranged his *visa*.

Scattered and dispossessed within the past twenty years, at first by the traffic in Tennant's Creek gold and then by the war traffic along the Stuart Highway, is one of the most remarkable tribes of Australia, Warramunga, the Song Men, masters of music and mysticism, the people that manufactured Halley's Comet and produced the wisest woman in the world.

H.M.A.S. *Warramunga*, a destroyer of the Australian Navy, was named in their honour, but the Warramunga know nothing of ships and the sea—the "g", by the way, is a singing g and not a hungry one, Warra-moong-a.

Their country is in Central Australia, north of the Tropic from the crested old red Davenport Ranges, about two hundred and fifty miles north of Alice Springs, across the spinifex downs beyond Powell's Creek. To the south of them are the Kaitish of Barrow Creek, always a surly, silent people; to the west the wild Warramulla of Landers River; to the east the Waggire and Pintubi, and to the north the Tjingilli of Newcastle Waters. While all these tribes were obsessed with black magic and family wars, the Warramunga were a merry people, more interested in music than in murder.

They were famed throughout the Centre for soaring oratorio, symbolic legend and fandango of the dance in décor of red and yellow ochre, glistening gypsum and a Masonic regalia of hair-string and tree-fibres geometric on sticks, body-designs in coloured down and charcoal, cockatoo feather helmets and branches rustling at the knees. But above all they were famous for their fire ceremonies and corroborees of brilliant pyrotechnics. They would set a forest ablaze for a stage effect. The tribes all round watched with awe and interest these fiery extravaganzas, a glow in the night skies of those low levels visible for a hundred miles.

When Halley's Comet spread its peacock tail of light across the stars in 1910, Billy Miller was camped with cattle at O.T. Lagoon far north-east of Newcastle Waters. One night, hoping for a legend, he motioned to the comet and asked one of his Tjingilli stock-boys, "Which-way that fella been jump up, Tiger?"

Tiger knew the answer. "Tennant's Creek blackfella makem that one," he said promptly—a foregone conclusion that it was a Warramunga show.

Tennant's Creek was a stone-country Broadway. The best corroborees were carried post-haste to Carpentaria and Kimberley by an entrepreneur wearing a hair-belt only, a "dancing man" from tribe to tribe who would have been speared at sight on any other mission. Arundta of MacDonnell Ranges, Pitjantara of Ayers Rock, Dieri of Lake Eyre, Yandra-wandra of Cooper's Creek, and even Wonkurunda of Simpson Desert, bartered for Warramunga operas, chanting to those haunting rhythms an unknown language of the dreaming, just as we sing Wagner and Verdi in German and Italian. Black man's copyright in wives, knives, pituri, fish, red ochre or whatever there was to offer was willingly paid for the performing rights.

The copyright of corroboree is as jealously guarded throughout Australia as that of Gilbert and Sullivan. The country of origin, if not the author, is always punctiliously acknowledged—"that one Wyndham", "that one Borroloola"—and of infringement of rights the blacks take a very serious view. It was often a killing matter. Pirates please note.

When they were asked why they liked the *derradah* or play-corroborees of the Warramunga better than any other, some blacks five hundred miles north-west said because these songs of the Song Men, "long-way makem", were soft to the mouth, not "crooked longa tongue" like "nudga one language", and because "them boy that country all-time dancing, him savvy proper good-fella"—the reason we sing in Italian and import the Ballet Russe. The *derradah* is *jarada* south-west to the shores of the Bight.

But the Warramunga were not only "show people". Spencer and Gillen describe them as the most imaginative tribe in Australia, and the only people with a purely mythical devil or god—Wollunqua, a huge water-snake coiling out of the bowels of earth in the Murchison Ranges to spiral through darkness into the skies. Wollunqua is the father of snakes and all men are his people.

It is of this tribe that John McDouall Stuart, first white man to meet them, writes the amazing incident of the Masonic sign made to him by an old man at Phillips Creek, and twice repeated by the old man and his two sons. When Stuart returned the sign, they stroked his beard and shoulders with delight, and treated him as a brother.

They made good little beehive wurleys with waterproof thatch of spinifex and clay, and an arch for the door in some idea of architecture. Men shaved the upper lip, in long and painful process of nipping out hairs. A woman wore head and neck-bands of plaited grass. For her initiation into sexual life, she was coated all over with fat and red ochre, decked with bands of string and feathers, and wore a head-dress of tail-tufts and berries—the only approach I know to dressing up a bride. When widowed, she wore the widow's cap, *mungwarroo*, of *kopi*, the heavy plaster matted into her hair and fitted to her head, a weird effect with black eyes peering out. On the tenth day she could smash it at her feet and go to her next husband.

For industry, apart from hunting, in low hills a few miles east of Renner Springs, Benarraban, is a mine centuries old, of a veined quartzite that, when hit in one direction, flaked into small flat spearheads, and when knocked from another, fractured into sharp three-bladed knives. Designed for devilry, like the dagger of Macbeth, were these Warramunga white knives with haft of hardened spinifex gum—I once possessed two of them, but gave them to friends. In stealing a wife, or reclaiming a stolen wife when the little families were out hunting on *muncrow*, the downs, they were the tool of many a horrid murder at piccaninny daylight, the killer creeping on a sleeper, striking the knife into his brain, then taking the woman. The Warramunga were expert with these knives, and they were top price in barter for the lancewood spears of Newcastle Waters, the ribbon-stone rainstones of Anthony's Lagoons, the pituri tobacco of the border, and the pearl-shells of the salt-water blacks that occasionally found their way down from the north coast to be worn as a sporran or clicked as castanets in the corroboree orchestra.

As well as the gift of music, the Warramunga had many beautiful myths and legends, some fortunately preserved for posterity. There is no word for truth in any aboriginal language—as Pilate said, "What is truth?"—but *yoonga-munna* is their word for a lie, gammon, in other words, literature, romance. They were *yoonga-yoonga-munna*, for ever telling the tale . . . of Thabbala, Laughing Boy, chuckling in the wind and shouting in thunder through the rocks of Yappakoolinya, the Devil's Marbles.

. . . of Pittongu, Bat Man, father of the tribe. He lived alone by a dark waterhole, and travelled *kanguroo*, south, where he took the shape of a dog chasing a goanna into a cave, trapped two *wommalli*, young lubras, who followed him, and wanted to take them back to his own country. They said no. So he snatched their long hair and twined it in his spear-thrower and drove them before him. Twice he stopped, and knocked out their two front teeth to make them Bat Women. Since then all Warramunga men and women must have their two front teeth knocked out.

. . . of the two old Rain Men sitting on Mount Samuel—and this brief poem I like best—cutting off scraps of their white beards to float away as clouds.

In that country where they are always looking for rain, a cloud is *ngapa-murrila*, water-shade, and so shy that the slightest sound frightens it away. In drought summer the big woolly flocks of monsoon come rolling down from the north, the rain-dogs running before them, but while you are waiting for the first drops they veer and vanish away. Big rains mean big waterholes and plenty of vegetable tucker, and hunting for the little groups far out on the downs where they cannot travel till rain falls. So when clouds gather and all the piccaninnies in camp are racing round playing and yelling,

"*Jamba koola nienta!* Shut up and sit quick!" the men will shout, and a dead hush comes over the camp under grey curd of skies. They have a quaint idiom, "legs of rain". Here is a Warramunga dialogue:

(Joyously): "*Coot-thara ngapa waili!* Two water legs."

(With excitement): "*Abrie è ban?* Coming here?"

(A tense pause, then sadly): "*Warrakoo abrie è ban.* Not coming here."

(Wistfully): "*Unda abigella?* Which-way walk?"

(Glumly): "*Karu.* West."

They have the points of the compass—*kajenu*, north; *kanguroo*, south; *karkoru*, east; *karu*, west—but like all other aboriginal people they have no head for figures. *Yanni*, one; *coot-thara*, two; *coot-thara yanni*, three; *coot-thara coot-thara*, four; *taka*, hand, five; *waukabi*, plenty, big mob. But the blackfellow can count to any exact number for you simply by taking a stick or drawing a line for each item or man.

Born to the ages before mankind foolishly began to measure the hours, *kilyeree*, sun, expresses daytime, and *tabingarra*, black, the night. They have the same word for yesterday and tomorrow, *wanniberta*, another time, realizing in their native wisdom that we live only today. They have the same word, *biandi*, for new and today—a lesson there for those who have sorrow or trouble piled too deep in the past.

Even as the readers of our women's journals, they believe in the direct influence upon human life of their own hazy zodiac and the wheeling spheres, in the vengeance of a falling star, *looguna abigella*, star-walking. When a black Caroline Herschel in the telegraph camp at Tennant's Creek discovered a little comet with a tail, there were shrieks of woe and fear.

"*Looguna looguna! Abojera! Ballandee!* Stars! Stars! Fall! Kill!" sang an old man at Banka Banka when his daughter was dying, crying upon all the stars of heaven to fall and kill everybody to be sure of catching the murderer who was singing her dead.

Magellan's Clouds, they say, are the camp-fires of the dead, who go long way, make big fire, go little way, make little-fella fire, and then must cover their fires, for those on earth shall never know the way they go. You must never point a finger at Magellan's Clouds, or you will bring down all the curses in the calendar on your head. A lubra will brush your hand away, and whisper in terror of "Trouble come up quick-fella!"—they cannot say how or why, "That one belonga dreamin'".

When *koonkoo biandi*, new moon, is in the skies, corroboree-time begins —*derradah*, play-about, *boorchallie*, the bush corroborees out in the hills, and, in its due time, *kooroongooroo*, the women's corroboree of love and purification by fire, peculiar to the Warramunga, and one of the few Australian aboriginal rites mentioned in Frazer's *Golden Bough*.

In *kooroongooroo* the women come dancing with mop and mow, circling their arms to draw love towards them, singing in low, luring tones. They sit in a line, heads bent to the ground. In come the men with green branches, light them in the corroboree fires and go dancing past the women, shaking the burning bushes over their bare backs and shoulders in showers of red sparks. If a woman flinches or cries she is laughed at for days. *Kooroongooroo* ends in orgy.

Of the many dreamings of children and child welfare among the tribes of the continent, the *kurninando*, emu, rite of these people, and of those south and south-east of them to Lake Eyre and Cooper's Creek, is most poetic. When a baby boy shows signs of walking, his mother, *naminee*, takes him along to an old *boondoolka*, witch-doctor of the emu men. With his mouth close to the baby's knees he sings the age-old chant of the emu totem. This makes the boy a steady, untiring runner, not rushing hither and yon like the kangaroo in panic, but with the easy steel stride of the great bird, keeping it up for hours without falter for breath. So will he run from his enemies when he is a man, till nightfall or till he finds shelter, murmuring as he runs the emu chant to invoke its power and speed. The mother pays tribute, *warela*, to the old man for his services, as white mothers pay the family physician for inoculations and such. Once she would bring the chitterlings of a bandicoot or other tasty dish, but prices went up in civilization to two sticks of tobacco (£A2 10s.).

But the most remarkable feature of Warramunga women is their long silences. When husbands, fathers or uncles die, a ban of silence is imposed, generally for about two years. They manage to survive quite well. Like all other blacks they are well schooled in "finger-yabber", the universal sign language, and this serves every purpose even to a ding-dong go.

Once four men died in the camp at Banka Banka, and so complete was the circle of relationship that not a lubra on the station could utter a word. An old hand told me, "I saw two gins having the row of their lives in finger-yabber. They were surrounded by the whole mob of the station gins, and not a sound out of the lot of them. My boy's Borroloola girl interpreted for me, and I must say it was jolly expressive."

To be freed of the silence the lubra must go out on the downs and hunt a certain species of goanna called *lilpariji*. She breaks its legs and brings it back alive to keep it fresh—the black man's refrigerator—then cooks it and offers it to the old man of her totem. He bites the palm of her outstretched hand and she is "mouth open", free to speak.

Polly, the old goat-shepherd at Banka Banka, had not spoken for ten years. It kept her out of a lot of trouble, so she never bothered to go and get her goanna. Then one day she filled in the necessary forms unbeknownst to anyone, and, chasing goats out of the garden, electrified the station at the top of her voice in a repertoire of all the latest swears. Tom Nugent told Baldwin Spencer that one of the old myalls out there had not uttered a word in twenty-four years. Her wisdom was superhuman and all on its own in the wide, wide world.

The first weeks of the wet were a festival for these quaint sylvan people. How green was their valley! Stuart's Bean Tree, with its merry scarlet pods, and broom-bush in blossom, splashed the stony ranges and sandy creeks with colour vivid as the red and yellow ochre of corroboree. All the tribes trailed over the downs gathering coongaberries, *managoodyu*, and wild oranges, *buntchilli*, with many a feast on the young of the shell parrots from their nests in the hollows of the silver box-trees, and of *barraban*, seed of the nut-grass. The brolgas love *barraban* as much as the blacks do—you will sometimes see eight or ten of the tall graceful birds in a line, forgetting their dignity, digging like navvies. After the feast, for the brolgas and the blacks, it was On With the Dance.

For long sunny centuries there was no jarring note of the white man's trade or tyranny in this far-away country, and even till the nineteen-thirties nothing but Tennant's Creek telegraph station and, fifty miles north of it, the little log shack of Banka Banka. A few riders drifted up and down the Great North Road, then but a track in the grasses. Ten years ago it became a thoroughfare, five years ago a highway. How many of the Warramunga, and what faint echo of their songs, will you find up there today? One of the last at Banka Banka was an old lubra whom Tom Nugent had christened Kitty O'Shea, and her boy Parnell. Kitty's native name was Kandoongalli, meaning jet, "black shine", and she was believed to be a changeling child of the coongaberry people, because in her girlhood her eyes sparkled black as coongaberries, when they are ripe. Kandoongalli died blind.

I have made this little sketch of the Warramunga from a few stray facts on hand, but they are only one of the interesting tribes that might have inspired volumes in popular romance. Australia rang with music at night in those old years—her own eerie music, purely symphonic, not radio records from Europe and the United States. So much there was for us to find on the long serpentine of blackfellow roads now faded into bush.

The jumbled gneiss hills of the Alice were a great place for corroborees, plenty water in the springs, plenty euro, ceremonial grounds and bush corroborees on the bank of Todd River where the train comes through at Heavitree Gap. At Emily Gap was the *nanja* rock of Intwailiuka, grand old man of the witchetty-grub people of Alice Springs. When I tried to elicit the Arundta legend of creation I was told that an old lubra came up from Oodnadatta and had a little boy—"longa himself, no father". They travelled round the waters in the ranges and chased away the devils till the boy was a man. He died. His mother buried him but he came up again after "three night sleep", and both went to camp at Hermannsburg Mission. Here I woke up to the fact that I was listening to a version of the Virgin Birth and the Resurrection, as taught by the first missioners seventy years ago, now garbled into the *alcheringa* dreaming.

In Arnhem Land is a lake of legend behind the marshes of Caledon Bay where two lubras with long hair play about the rocks at sundown. They "belong no country", and if you chase them they always run away, leaving no track. Believing they might be a link with the story of the two white women of the *Douglas Mawson* wreck alleged still to be wandering in Arnhem Land, through Short-leg of the Ritherunga with Yellow Bob as interpreter, out at Mainoru, I made inquiries as to whether they were "properly black". They were "properly black" and very ancient history.

"My father been tchee-um that-time he little-fella," Short-leg told Yellow Bob. "Old man been tchee-um behind my father, old man behind him. I think them-two lubra properly old-bugger now."

It was in this country that Billy Farrar, riding with a black-boy seventy miles north of the Roper, stumbled on a Stone Age knowledge of erosion. As they passed under a red-ledged cliff, two hundred feet high, falling sheer to the sandy plain, the boy pointed to the crest of it and said, "My father before father, long-time father, him sitting down up there fishin' ".

Everywhere are relics of the old stone symbolism peculiar to Aryan worship throughout the world from Stonehenge to the Pyramids, from St Peter's to Easter Island. Peaks, pillars, monoliths, crude natural statues in niches of the cliffs, rocks jutting out of the river, whispering gorges and echo galleries, all belong to mythology and nearly all point a moral. But where we immortalize saints, emperors, poets and politicians, they perpetuate the evildoer as a horrible example.

Twin peaks brooding in the haze, such as Hyimio-mandit in Arnhem Land or Barri coot-thara on the Upper Victoria, are always two sisters or two brothers who ran away with wrong skin lovers. The profile above the pool is the boy who ate kangaroo in secret. Boulders at the feet of pillars or hills are bad little lubras who let themselves be stolen, and were petrified on the spot, like Lot's wife.

Mooloolooma, a beautiful waterhole near the junction of Batten's Creek and the Macarthur, in its still waters flecked with white lilies reflects two "crocodile stones". The boys said that crocodile man and woman foolishly left their own country and came up-river in the wet. They found plenty tucker but when the floods went down they could not get back. The salty bitterness of their own tears transmogrified them into rocks, and in the creek waters falling over them they were, like Niobe, "all-time heart-crying longa country".

Not far from Mooloolooma is Numby Numby, to occasional aviators five thousand feet up a remarkable landmark in a remarkable land. Only eighteen miles from Borroloola, but through rugged trackless bush in a bald plateau of sandstone, it is a deep volcanic crater with steeply shelving conical sides and bottle-green waters that, like the Blue Lake at Mount Gambier, have a mysterious rise and fall in suction of a strong underground current. For many generations it has been a place of fear. No blacks will go within a

N

mile of it, or talk about it. When it is mentioned they are silent and wary—a scare in the air.

Back in the dreaming three young boys killed, cooked and ate a kangaroo there, though well they knew they should bring it to the Old Men. A great snake came winding after them from the sea and made Macarthur River. Numby Numby opened and swallowed them up. *No one must ever drink of the waters of retribution, and around them is poison ground.*

A few years ago an Annuella lubra of Macarthur River stock-camp rode in there. Her horse was found running with the others, but she vanished from the face of earth. Perhaps she died of fright in that eerily silent place or, falling from the steep sides of the pool, was drowned. The trooper found no trace, and none of the trackers or station blacks would follow the hoof tracks in. Numby Numby devil is still alive.

Kooloondoonyoo, on Cave Creek, near the head of the Roper, is a tunnel said to be twelve miles through. According to the blacks it comes out at Red Lily Lagoons, but none of them have been through it—"prop'ly debil-debil, all-time ground been jump up, piccaninny crying". An earth tremor is naturally the worst kind of magic.

Not all caves are "debil-debil". Some are aboriginal art galleries, some the hiding-places of the sacred totem boards, and some the vaults of the dead—but these are never too deep in.

Baldwin Spencer tells of an immemorial shrine of the dead in the fretted old castled hills above Oenpelli, and out on Roper country, near the tributary Mountain Creek, is another such cave, Walgandu, discovered by Billy Miller Linklater in the nineties.

"I had picked up a station boy and his woman," he said, "to pilot me through. We came on camp, threw off the packs, and hobbled out the horses. While the boy cut mosquito pegs the gin went down to the creek to dig yams. I put some salt beef in the billy to boil for supper, then lay down with my back to a tree and my nine-inch Colt on my chest, reading in the last of the afternoon light.

"The boy came up. 'S'pose I show you hole belong blackfella?'

"It might have been a good waterhole, and I always believe in gathering knowledge. The blackfellow went silently ahead and I followed. We crossed the creek to a native pad worn deep through hundreds of years to the crest of a limestone hill and a sandy plateau with a weather-worn monolith of stone about nine feet high.

" 'Him belong barramundi people,' the boy told me. 'S'pose him tumble down, no more fish, no more barramundi people.'

"While stands the Coliseum, Rome shall stand
When falls the Coliseum, Rome shall fall.

"A huge cave ran into the hill, with a right turning and a dead end. We lit firesticks. In the dark vault at the end the ground was three or four hundred years' deep with trampled bones and skulls. I could see dim rock-drawings of turtles, men and women, kangaroos, and above our heads on the roof the white waves in pipe-clay of an enormous snake.

"A hollowed gum grows in that country that the blacks call *colla berra.* Three trunks of it, about nine feet high and a foot wide, leant against the walls, the hollows filled with thigh-bones, arm-bones, ribs and skulls crumbled white.

"The boy showed no fear. He said that long time in the dreaming a mob of blacks on the plain killed and ate a snake and made corroboree. They saw a great storm coming, and raced for this cave, Walgandu, but a crack of lightning came in and finished the lot. The lightning was a friend of the snake they ate, and since then lightning men are friends of the snake men, who always buried their dead in the cave after putting them in the ground till they were bone and the debil gone away.

"There were fresh ashes about, and he said yes, his people made their sleeping-fires in here in the big rain. They were not frightened of the dead-fellas nor of the big snake up top, because he was father of the river, and it was all too long ago. There are no ghosts in Westminster Abbey.

"A mile from Macarthur River Station, on a ridge that is foot-hill to a fair range, is a high flat-topped boulder, a natural altar. When you sit on a horse you can just see over the top of it. I found thirteen stones there, pudding stones from the river, all oval in shape, heavily greased and obviously arranged. I pelted them off. A week later they were back. I pelted them off again, and again they came back. I asked one of the station boys. He said 'Egg belongta emu people, makem tucker all-about'. They were the Egyptian egg-stones of fertility.

"Over on the Victoria side, fifty yards from the bank of Battle Creek, was one of those peculiar phallic stones we call 'blackfella monuments'. It was about three feet high, for centuries engrained with bands of red and white ochre in curves, convex and concave. It may still be there. All the stones were gone from around it, though it was in basalt country. The blacks would never put their packs on the ground near it. One day, riding with six or seven boys, I turned out at the water-hole and thought I would bring it in, but the boys were very much against it. They refused to look at it, and said 'No more! Him belonga dreamin' '. They couldn't tell me anything more. I would have had to get it into a bag, and load the other one with stones, and carry it on horses three hundred miles to Katherine, so I left it.

"But the bush was full of such things up to thirty years ago. We could have got drayloads, not this carved boab-nut trumpery and Birmingham boomerangs, but tree-drawings and cave-paintings, *mourra* stones and poison bones, letter-sticks and corroboree gear, everything in wood and stone and feathers and reeds that they use and wear from the cradle to the grave, the real Mackay in science, but we couldn't carry enough to eat on our horses, and you get no thanks for silence. Some anthropologist just collars it. They're out of the universities and we're out of the gullies, but we've got more respect for the Ten Commandments. They'd hold you up at the point of a rifle to get anything good. I've known them offer a half-caste five quid to go out with a shovel and dig up his mother's skull. Don't talk to me about the scientists, they're worse than the poddy-dodgers. If any of them come around me, I'll take a couple of killer-boomerangs and give them a demonstration of nigger law."

"Nigger law" is a thing of the past. Without its symbols no race can survive. The first strength the blacks lose in civilization is control of the young men. The cry of the Old Men is the cry of a doomed people—"Him no more hearem me, d'reckly me die."

As from the Aztecs and Egyptians down through the ages to our senates, councils, judiciaries and courts, the law and the administration of the law were vested in these old mystics and gnostics of avuncular authority. Their rites and rituals are loudly denounced by the missionary as heathen. On the cattle stations initiations and "blackfella business" are often laughed to scorn, tolerated only in the wet season far out on the run when the year's work is done. Totem foods have given way to the white man's beef and flour. Marriages are no longer made in the aboriginal heaven, but "catch as catch got a mind to", in the old Cornish phrase, in camps made up of mixed breeds, strangers and once-forbidden skins. Even their music, in their own country, is forbidden in most towns and on many stations by "bosses" with no imagination and no musical perception—"Cut that infernal racket and get to bed." In one generation the black becomes a miserable shadow of white, and a sycophant, afraid. . . .

A wild life protection society in itself, apart from its religious significance, is the law that none may kill and eat of his own totem. Often when a boy comes asking his employer for meat, the white man will say, "I've got no meat for you. Go and get a kangaroo", or "Can't you catch a fish?" or "I'll give you the gun and you can shoot a turkey".

When the boy replies, "Can't that one. Him brudda belong me," the white man loudly laughs, and the boy goes hungry. Neither will they kill an animal, such as a goat, for which they have developed a familiarity or affection, or perhaps a prejudice. The blacks of the north coast would never eat pig, though they would hunt it and kill it for Chinese and white men.

Inexorable were these food laws, *murrian* on Alligator rivers, *tajee* in Kimberley, a different name in every tribe but the laws strangely uniform, provision and division of food according to totem and age. Many a bushman was killed in the earlies because when employing lubras he refused to allow them to take tucker back to the men of the tribe. Taboos, akin to those of Semitic and Hindu races, seem to have been rigged by the old wiseacres of the dreaming to get the best for themselves when they were beyond the age of hunting. There was a lot of dietetic propaganda—if a youth eats kangaroo tail, he becomes prematurely aged, a creature of palsied limbs and impotence. To gobble up a nest of young parrots would send a lubra bald, and the only part of the eaglehawk they could pick and gnaw without fear of withering thin was its corny legs. Dinner in the blacks' camp is much the same as dinner-hour in our cities, where those who work hardest too often get least and those who do nothing tuck out on the turkey.

A bad little Mollie on an outback station said she was under a *tajee* ban from eating beef, and giving the cook a bad time demanding goats' milk, cake and potatoes to make up her diet. While she got the good things she kept the *tajee* going till the old cook did a spot of anthropological research on his own account. He learnt that the way to lift *tajee* was for one of the old men to anoint her face with the fat of the forbidden food. When vegetarian Mollie turned up in the kitchen next day, demanding milk and cake, he grabbed her by the hair and rubbed dripping into her complexion till she yelled for help.

"Now," he said, "the *tajee's* off. You take your beef and go."

You still may see an initiation if you travel far enough in the north, but now they send telegrams to save the traditional journeys of the boy and his "huncles".

BILLY INK AND SPRINGVALE HARRY,
COMPOUND,
DARWIN.
YOU TWO-FELLA COME UP MARANBOY BUSH CORROBOREE MY BOY FACE-ACHE BRING TUCKER.
JACKIE BOB-TAIL.

The ngungas or uncles board the train, and the doctor arrives by plane from Alice Springs, whither he had gone with a drover.

Instead of his age-old stone knife, he brings a pocket-knife in a suitcase with priestly regalia of white-washed hessian, wood-shavings, a pot of red paint, some yellow wool, a ball of string and a feather duster all wrapped up in a brown paper parcel. Indeed, through many years Northern Territory Medical Services have induced the tribal elders to have the boys circumcised in the operating theatre at Darwin with a whiff of chloroform to boot! Departmentalism is without a sense of humour, and the glory has departed from the aboriginal world.

There was much to learn from their medical science. They had remedies for all ills, quite apart from the hanky-panky of the *maamu,* or magic, doctor who, in pure psychopathology, produced live frogs from a patient's mouth and sharp stones out of his armpit or ribs with the professional aplomb of our surgeons extracting an appendix or gallstones. There were Harveys and Listers among those old Coués of the Stone Age, and even a Howard Florey.

Penicillin has been in use for countless centuries by the aborigines of Australia—mould of the pandanus and of other selected leaves and roots applied to their cuts and sores. A small shrub with faint purple flowers, not unlike a thistle but thornless and smaller, all over the Barkly Tablelands, Centre and north, is blackfellow's antiseptic. Pounded up with water in a *pitchi*, and applied to a wound, it cleared up the "poison" and kept the flies away.

Cauterization and the ligature were in common use, presupposing an instinctive knowledge of circulation of the blood. Many berries, roots, grasses and certain mineral waters were of proved curative value, and smoke of certain green leaves served the purposes of our hot compress. Long before plasters and antiphlogistine were the order of our day they knew the drawing, healing and setting virtues of packs of heated clay. They could diagnose an irritable liver—"bad binjey" for bad temper, and a murder was often ascribed to an affection of the brain—"me been losem longa my head", though the only brains they knew were *koomboomba*, animal's brain.

A woman friend on a north-west station, when the boss was away, sent an old blackfellow out for "a killer", the nearest he could find. He duly brought the beef without the brains, a titbit he kept for himself.

She called "What have you done with the brains, Tom? I want them for tea."

Tom had the answer: "That-one poor ole workin' bullock, missus. Nuttin' gottem brain."

In psychiatry by suggestion the savage is, of course, all-powerful—kill or cure. *Wuruguru*, the death-bone, or anyone singing him dead, provided he knows about it, will kill a healthy man in a week, while an old man never dies till he gets the idea "Me pinish". In a buffalo camp a Kakadu boy had eaten a fat and tasty, but forbidden, snake. He brooded over his crime in secret, with nightmares and remorse. One morning he showed violent symptoms of snakebite poisoning, writhing in agony, tearing at his throat. They ran for the old doctor, who hurried up and began a frenzied dance in front of him, with motions of uncoiling a snake from his own throat. The boy gazed at first with hopeless dark eyes that showed hypnotic fascination as the skinny old man, in contortions of terrific strength, wrestled with coil after imaginary coil, and finally threw the invisible snake away with a triumphant yell. A few minutes later the boy rose to his feet, quite well and smiling, but very shaky.

On the East Alligator in 1888 Matt Connors saw a myall sprinting along on a homemade wooden leg—his own had been taken by a crocodile. This boy had had no contact whatever with white men—the idea, and the design, were his own.

Sometimes a simple diagnosis and treatment by "blackfella doctor" put our own medical methods in the shade. A lubra at Pine Creek developed acute and painful irritation in the ear. Twice it was examined and poulticed by a nursing sister and by a passing doctor, but the pain and inflammation increased. She was told to go down on the next train to Darwin for treatment, when a whiskered old medicine man from Wandi wandered in. Without any dance or incantation he carefully examined the ear, packed it with earth and told her to keep it well watered. In two or three days a green sprout appeared. He let this grow long for a grip, then pulled it out attached to a sharp grass seed that had penetrated deep. Pine Creek had a good laugh at "the gin with a garden in her ear".

In obstetrics the black woman leads the world. There is no languishing through months of delicate health, no diet, no rules and regulations of antenatal care. The child she bears is as little burden as the fruit to the flower. She never knows she is pregnant till spontaneous movement makes her acutely conscious of her surroundings—that place is her child's spirit-ground, where conscious new life, a human soul awakening, comes not of earthly fatherhood but of the old devil-divinities of the dreaming.

When her time comes she slips away into the bush and, in a kneeling posture, delivers herself. She may have an old woman with her, to help with a girdle of arms in pressure. So is the black baby born, naturally as any other healthy little animal, to lie on the warm earth—no sickly aura of anaesthetics, no "confinement" for the mother beyond a day's rest in the shade.

An epic experiment is on record when a scarcely civilized lubra, who had borne other children unaided and with ease, was brought from her country to a maternity ward of a large city hospital, that professors and students of pathology, physiology, gynaecology and obstetrics might observe the sequence of pregnancy and an aboriginal birth.

The poor creature was so overwhelmed by the unfamiliar surroundings, rigid routine, caustic cleanliness, strange food and frightening odours of the hospital, the observation to which she was subjected with black magic of thermometers, stethoscopes and so on, that she failed to give birth at all! An overgrown child, perfect in form but a stillborn abnormality, had to be surgically removed towards the end of the tenth month. It had no natural impetus to enter such an unnatural world, and the mother was lucky to escape with her life. The only place for such observations is the bush.

The umbilical cord is never cut, but bitten to eight or ten inches long. The mother anoints it with fat where it joins the navel, leaving the rest to dry up. When it breaks, she wraps it in paperbark and keeps it as safely as English mothers once treasured in a locket the first curl. This is for the little one's well-being. If she loses the *waddilecki* string, he will be a peevish baby, "all-time cry", and grow up to be a bad-tempered man. When lubras are minding fretful white babies through troubles of teething and wakeful nights that black ones never know, or even when they are told off by a grumpy "boss", I have heard them explain,

"Him prop'ly cranky-fella. Mudda been losem string."

The little blackfellow is thoroughly spoiled with lenience and love. His mother gives him everything he wants to eat, and he grows *joonee-bulga*, big tummy, to an alarming degree. Her baby-carrier is the best in the world, a coolamon or a curve of bark with a fibre strap over one shoulder, so that he lies flat at full length away from the heat of her body instead of huddled in her arms—she has her hands free and carries his weight on her hips. When he can sit up he rides her shoulders with a good grip of her hair. If there are two "close up" her boy takes one on the hunting-trail—no woman can carry two babies, chase bandicoots and goannas and dig for ants' eggs and yams.

Paddy Cahill tells of a remarkable case of a lubra in his camp. A girl, Kranmeer, died, leaving a baby a month old. Her sister, Murraburra, who had borne two children eleven years before, both dead, took the baby and fed it with the milk of her own breasts.

"I saw her feed the child myself," Paddy Cahill wrote. He goes on:

> I thought the baby was only holding the breast in its mouth, and made her put the milk on a leaf. Surely enough, she had a good flow. They take a bunch of green leaves and heat them in the fire, and when it is as hot as the lubra can bear it they put it on the breast and hold it there to cool. They do this several times till the breast begins to swell and the sucking does the rest.

I have recently encountered a similar case in Broome, where, to restore milk, these leaves were applied to a mother's breast.

Seldom have I heard of insanity or imbecility among the myalls. Physical freaks and deformities are also rare, though among the civilized the ravages of blindness, epidemics and diseases inflicted on the race by whites and Asiatics are too often a horror. Never have I heard of an authenticated case of suicide. An emotional people, quickly moved to tears, fears, ecstasy or laughter, they are too volatile for long periods of deep mental depression. A smile of greeting, a merry-thought, a little gift or exciting news will put them on top of the world again. Like the Irish, in bitter tears they will suddenly laugh at their own destitute plight. Again like the Irish, they are gifted with conscious and unconscious humour, full of spontaneous wit that they appreciate themselves.

Intensely they live, yet swiftly they react to every passing impression. Two A.I.M. sisters, travelling by car, called in on a death-wailing at one of the camps—to which some of the blacks, by the way, had flown a few hundred miles by plane. The girls sympathized with the grief-stricken relatives, smeared with the clay of mourning, beating their heads with stones, cutting their faces with tins, keening and grovelling in the dust in their Biblical woe. As the car was leaving, the whole camp quit mourning to give three hearty cheers for the sisters, then turned again to the wailing and the grief.

As knowledge in their medicine, so logic in their law. Murder is always a capital crime with capital punishment, not, as we ignorantly believe, the homicidal mania of a prowling savage. When murder is discovered they are as much horrified as we are, and there are other capital crimes. The Old Men, sitting in conclave—our judge and jury—pass sentence of death and appoint, as we do, the sheriffs and hangmen, usually two or three to share the onus of dispatching the condemned man, as in our firing-party. In Central tribes, where they wear the silent, trackless ceremonial feather-slippers of *kurdaitcha* —*jinna arbil*, the hidden feet—the death sentence is, "*Meeri poongandago yarra*. The man . . . go away . . . kill".

In lesser crimes, stealing a wife or assault and battery, the Old Men set plaintiff and defendant in front of their fellows, as in a boxing ring, with boomerangs and nulla-nullas. While plaintiff throws, defendant must dodge without moving the feet, twisting, writhing, bending, warding off the blows. If it is a serious crime, they close in and stone knives are drawn, but they must carve only the buttocks and the limbs, not stab in a vital place. The umpires closely watch the play. Even when a boy has served five or ten years in Fanny Bay for wounding a comrade, he must go through this ceremony when he returns to his own country.

Most remarkable of all is the *makarrata* or war-guilt rite of the north coast, practised for centuries where feuds are many and willing, but a traditional peace-making, not a total vengeance on the war-lords. The offending tribe allows the offended to have shots at the ones on whom they claim vengeance. It rarely ends fatally—in fact, it is a foregone conclusion that it is but to be a blood-letting.

The two parties stand about two hundred yards apart, and the named offenders must run between them, always accompanied by men of the other side, white-ochred all over in colour of peace so that it cannot be serious warfare. Spears are thrown by twos and threes, and the runners avoid them with slickness and sleight of body to send them glancing off. About six spears are thrown by each of the accusing warriors, and if a runner escapes the lot he offers a leg or arm to be punctured. When blood is drawn, the feud is healed. A good *makarrata* runner is as famous as Don Bradman. Still remembered is Riola of Arnhem Land, who once made a spear glance from his hip to penetrate the leg of the whitened tribesman who ran with him—from both sides came loud and resounding cheers. He later surrendered for the blood-letting. In the case of a wild and incorrigible killer, the blacks will not agree to a peace-making. Such was Riola's arch-enemy, Parr-Parr of the Goyder.

There is always method in their magic, and often their superstitions are first cousin, or even identical with our own. Human excreta must quickly be buried, lest an enemy should burn it with evil intent—the instinct of bush sanitation. Scraps of meat and bone round a fire bring ghosts.

Never throw your hair away lest it should be burnt—an Irish hoodoo. No discard of the body must be burnt, or the body itself will suffer the same pain —an idea in common with ours in the burning of the effigy or guy.

A whistling woman is bad magic—they don't worry about the crowing hen.

Never walk under a dead tree—even as some of us refuse to walk under a ladder.

New spears must be smoked free of bad luck.

At a clear pool, if you drink of your own reflection, you drink death.

If anyone steps over you, you will die.

A woman must never step over anything that belongs to a man, or let her shadow fall upon him.

Never point to a shadow, it is your own dark soul and can be a thing of fright.

Birds bring messages. When the mopoke is calling around the camp at night, someone is stealing a lubra.

Even as Uncle Remus's Jack Sparrer, our willie wagtail—Cooper's Creek *mejinteree*, Roper River *jinteree-jinteree*—is the busybody mischief-maker, the tattler. You will hear a lubra say to the pert little black-and-white visitor, "Clear out from me! All day you lookem, lookem, all day you been hearem. Tellum lie belonga me! Tellum plenty, that-one. *Get-away!*"

A crow crying above a new-made grave is the curse of the departed—time to quit.

There were trade routes of inter-tribal commerce all over Australia, where chosen ambassadors of regular barter approached the boundaries at certain times and with certain ceremonies, powwow of mystery and even disguises—they must never be seen.

When a patch of pituri had been stripped of its leaves a few hundredweights of red ochre appeared on a dry grey earth. When a log of mulga, favourite wood for spears, was found standing against a tree, a block of quartz for spear-heads, or a lump of *minderee* gum, or perhaps a ribbon-stone for a rain-stone, would be left in the fork of that tree. They might be there for a year, then one day they vanished. Nobody looked for tracks, and fires were never lighted—commercial travellers of the Stone Age, outside their own country, had need to be discreet. The aboriginal never received anything without giving its value in return, nor would he barter food. There was never a murder for trade or gain, only revenge for murder, or punishment for crime.

His educational systems were exactly the same as ours, in their own environment. Even yet you will see the little girls out with the lubras, learning to track lizards and to gather nardoo or lily bulbs, and looking after the babies, while boys at the age of six or so, with a handful of playing spears and a little play boomerang tucked in the back of their hair-belts, come under the authority of uncles and fathers. They have their traditional games, and sit up at the corroboree in lively interest as our children sit up at the pictures. They sing with gusto, and everyone laughs when a toddler joins the dance. As they grow up they graduate in all life's lessons till the boy, in the great silence of the bush, enters his novitiate for manhood, and the girl, after initiation, is given to the man who earned her in many years of hunting for her parents, provided he is qualified, in his degrees of initiation, to take her as his wife.

Incredible as it may seem, there was even a "Rhodes scholarship". A chosen man of powerful physique and intelligence, a hunter of note, a fine athlete and dancer, would be sent on a long journey through affiliated and friendly tribes to learn of their hunting, their country, their various arts, crafts and dances. He would be expected to share his own knowledge. His coming was made known. He carried a letter-stick—a letter of introduction, as it were, though written in antique signs. He sat quietly on the outskirts of the camp till bidden by the Old Men to enter. Though he shared food, and hunting, and might wander with each tribe for months, he remained aloof, a guest. To the presence of the lubras he must be utterly blind. If he skipped off with a strange woman his life was forfeit—he dared never go home.

Humanity runs to pattern, and is not made moral by Act of Parliament, even by the sages of the dreaming. Too often a dusky Romeo and Juliet risked all for love and fled by the light of the moon. Every man's hand was against them. They kept on running to lonely waters, hiding in the bush in perilous lands, watching for avenging smokes, sleeping with guilt and never daring both to sleep at the same time, waking in terror of devil-magic and man-magic, sometimes for years. If they had the luck to survive, they formed their own little families, carrying "wedges" of languages and customs from one side of the continent to the other.

But for ever they were outcasts, for ever wandering, desert rats and to be destroyed. The white man's coming saved many an outlaw from annihilation —and hurled the whole race, as a race, into oblivion.

Chapter XXIV

Bos Buffelus

DRIFTING LIKE cloud-shadows across the open plains of Arafura, the herds of buffalo are slowly feeding on . . . black, roan, blue, white, a blur in yellow haze.

A black-boy rides out on the flats, bareback, naked save for a naga, a centaur in bronze. At the crack of his rifle the mob, like a big wheel turning, goes lumbering away to the scrub, hoofs over the clay-pan the roll of a drum.

Four other horsemen now, white boss, half-caste and two blacks, are racing on their flank. Shots ring out. The buffalo leader falls, a thousand-pounder roan bull paralysed in the hindquarters, feebly pawing the ground. Twenty-seven dead and dying in the rush past, the mob still stumbles for the scrub where foot-shooters are hiding.

The white man is scrambling on hands and knees through the long grass. Black heads pop up like golliwogs out of bushes. Boughs crashing, horns smashing, the buffaloes break in, mothers bellowing to their little skipping calves, wounded bulls looking for fight. Spinifex bushes burst into flame, rifles bark, every tree is a gunpowder plot. Thirteen shot in the scrub—forty hides, call it a day.

The skinners come up, lubras in ragged shirts with or without trousers, boys in red handkerchiefs and old felt hats. They shoot the dying buffaloes and skin while the carcasses are warm. At sundown the camp straggles home to a bough shed on the rim of the plain, seventy-pound hides slung over the packhorses. These hides will be dipped in crude preservative, and shipped down-river in cargoes of a thousand or so by some little skiff in the mangroves when the shooting season is ended. A grim life, and for their sins the hunters live in a purgatory of small stinging flies.

Home is the saddle, a different camp-fire every night. Heat of day is heavy as lead, and on those fetid river-flats of mosquitoes, flies and sandflies, fever lies. Scratches fester into sores, and among the blacks now leprosy is rife. Food is poor, carried on packhorses for three or four hundred miles. There is no shelter for months but a few boughs.

The buffalo in Australia is only one of the many strangers from the four other continents that happily settled down. Even as human races, he has thrown off the yoke of slavery in our New World. For a hundred and twenty years *Bos buffelus*, Indian water-buffalo, beast of burden from Italy to Malaya, has galloped wild over the flats of Melville Island and North Australian rivers, at home in a patch of Australia that nobody else wanted, a belt of swampy prairie unfit for the breeding of any other beast on earth but crocodiles.

From Humpty Doo and Marrakai on Adelaide River south-east of Darwin, out east over the Mary, the three Alligator rivers, the King and the Liverpool, is the buff country, from Van Diemen's Gulf to the edge of Arnhem Land, and for about a hundred miles south of the coast. They do not intrude on the cattle lands, and are seldom sighted west of the railway line except for an occasional old bull in melancholy exile, rambling the rushy flats to the lower Daly.

Compared with North American bison, the Northern Territory buffalo is more of a heavyweight ox, with elongated horns in reverse like the wings of Mercury's helmet. Tip to tip, those horns measure from six to eleven feet. Herds run from six to ten thousand to a river—once sixty thousand to a river. In the floods of the wet they live in the bush, cleverly sidling long horns through the trees. In the dry they come out on the plains, and so do the hunters.

First man to see leather in those rolling herds galloping downwind was E. O. Robinson in the early eighties, a Buffalo Bill dressed in a strap and revolver hunting with wild blacks. A stocky man, trim beard and silver hair, brown face netted into a lace of lines, it was said that he never closed his "shooting eye". He walked for years barefooted through scrub and burning stones, and once, from the wreck of his lugger with a crew of nine blacks, swam eight miles—all but one lubra reached the shore.

Robinson opened up vast tracts of unexplored country, and bought from other hunters in the slaughter of hundreds of thousands of buffalo within ten years. Two coloured men, Tinga Dian, Bugi, and Levuka Billy, Fijian, were with him when he began shooting on the Adelaide River in 1885. A few adventurers, one or two to a river, followed him out, among them Fred Smith, Harry and Joel Cooper, Barney Flynn. The others were killed by blacks, among them Moore and Mackenzie at King River. Moore was a circus rider, standing on his horse at the gallop to frighten the tribes.

These were "foot-shooters", running the mob in the marshes and scrub. Famous Paddy Cahill, on his equally famous St Lawrence, introduced horse-shooting in the early nineties. King buff-shooter of all time, he shot fifty-eight bulls with fifty-six bullets, three hundred and sixty buffaloes in twenty-eight days, all weighing over three-quarters of a ton.

Paddy was Darwin's darling, and always a friend to the blacks, an anthropologist in his ramblings over many years. The knowledge he collected on Alligator rivers was the foundation of Baldwin Spencer's book of "salt-water" life and legend among the Kakadu tribes.

Here are a few stray memories from Paddy Cahill:

"I had some difficulty in schooling my favourite horse, St Lawrence, to gallop right up to the buffalo, but later he revelled in the sport, racing from one beast to another for me to shoot them down. A swift, intelligent horse is gold to the buffalo-hunter, and Larry gloried in the job, notwithstanding the knocks and busters we had together. It was all clear on the plains, except that grass sometimes hides a dangerous hole. In the timber the horse is trusted to pull you through tight places. As most of my shooting was done with a carbine almost touching the animal's head, and at full gallop, the horse learns to swing clear when the rifle is fired. Larry, for all his perfections, sometimes came to grief.

"We shot up to forty-six buffs in a day, sixteen hundred skins for a season, March to October, including loss of time through fever and waiting for cartridges. Blacks are not good shooters, they fire too often, wasting ammunition. As skinners they are expert.

"Once Larry and I felled one buffalo and had ridden on a second when the first recovered and came after us. We both went skyward. Another time, he and I and a buffalo bull went down together in a deep hole hidden in long grass. I was two yards from the buff and took a shot, but so thick was his skull that the bullet flattened on his forehead and only dazed him—last shot in the gun. Luckily when the old man got his bearings he turned to charge Larry, who dodged, giving me time to load and finish him off.

"Once a cow put a horn through Larry's chest, ran me round and round a little shrub a dozen times, then stood back and made straight for it and me. She got it and missed me, and I got her.

"While Larry was convalescing, I was mounted on a hard-mouthed brute that had won the Darwin Cup—Centipede. We came on a mob of six hundred, and Centipede bolted through the mob! I slung the reins over the knee-pad and shot as he raced through. Just as a cartridge blocked in the rifle, we collided with an old bull, and went down. I crawled out, but the winner of the Darwin Cup was no more.

"Once Barney Flynn wounded a bull that charged him, put his horns between the horse's hind-legs, and horse and man took a double somersault ten feet up in the air. Harry Cooper was horned twice while shooting on foot. I've seen many a boy tossed and come down dead. Joe Cooper had two horses ripped up, and one shot dead under him when his rifle exploded against a tree.

"The funniest sight I ever saw was a myall blackfellow up a tree, with a horse on a halter below and a bull buffalo coming full charge—the nigger was trying to pull the horse up the tree out of danger. I shot the buffalo for him, but he was a proper myall. At dinner-camp one day he tried what bread and rac-a-roc oil was like, and promptly passed away.

"Three of the boys and I were sitting on a dead buffalo cow. I was sharpening a knife and they were rolling cigarettes. I started skinning at the back of her neck when she jumped up and threw us all off. My rifle was handy, I finished her, but the cigarette-makers skedaddling for safety was the joke of the season. When we rode over to where Johnstone was shooting, one of the boys was telling him about it, with suitable antics. Seizing a rifle to show how it was done, he shouted, 'This way been shootem!' and put a bullet through the rump of Johnstone's best horse.

"First storms along the East Alligator, we would be swimming the horses and wading for many miles with water up to the knee-pads in the black-soil swamps and flood drift. We used to put in the lunch hour on the bank shooting crocs. All we had to do was to sit still, and they'd rise to the surface, hearing the horse-bells, to go down with a bullet behind the head. At one dinner-camp we shot twenty crocodiles. Next day we rode forty miles to the South Alligator, to be welcomed to dinner by a hundred and fifty wild blacks, who had roast duck waiting, as much as we could eat. The wildfowl and game at that lagoon were a sight indescribable—we couldn't sleep all night for the noise of the waterfowl flying overhead.

"It was four hundred miles of riding, mostly through water, to Union Reefs and home—we could have come straighter, but our horses were without shoes (!). We saw many traces of tin and silver-lead, and nearly every gully of the upper rivers gives promise of gold. This is the most interesting part of the Territory, and ought to be better known. It is a splendid country for prospectors, with wild cattle for beef. I don't want to pose as a prophet, but a big mining field will be found here some day."

Paddy arrived in Darwin that year just before the wet, in time for his own wedding—merriest wedding in years. He was honeymooning in his new home when "a nigger came foot-walking with a paper-yabber" to say his mate Johnstone was in a bad way, gored and trampled by a Sourabaya bull. Through all the rains, Paddy rode back. Johnstone was "close up finish", with only the blacks to care for him, where he lay in a clump of corkscrew palms. They had bound his crushed head with their nagas, and strapped his broken limbs with saddle-straps. "You could see his heart beating," said Cahill, who carried him to Adelaide River on a bush stretcher, sailed him down to Port Essington in a dinghy, then brought him to Darwin through cyclone seas, a hundred and fifty miles in a launch. Larry was the hero—he had galloped two hundred miles in three days, through thick scrub in the rains, to save a life. The old horse won many a race in the Territory, and died at Delamere when he was twenty years old.

Of all the buffalo-hunters, Joel Cooper is most deserving of a note in history. Single-handed, Joel Cooper conquered Melville Island.

When I knew him in Darwin he was a tall grey old man, marking up billiard scores as he had never bothered to mark up his big buffalo tallies. He sought no audience for the adventure tales of his youth. A South Australian, born on 29th February, he celebrated a birthday once in four years, with a few old hands yarning over the earlies. "My word, Joe," they would say, "you've had a remarkable life." Joe never could see it. It was just a living. He died in 1940, soon after his twentieth birthday, at the age of eighty.

Forty miles across the Gulf from Darwin railway station, Melville Island was still a land of some two thousand hostile natives and mythical herds of buffalo in 1895, when Joel Cooper and Barney Flynn landed at Cape Gambier from a pearling schooner, with two or three horses. They had big camps of buffalo blacks on the mainland, but dared not bring them to certain death among strange tribes. They ran up a log and flour-bag hut on the beach, and began shooting—buffaloes, not blacks.

They were lucky. The men of Cape Gambier were all away at corroboree. Their first visitors were two inquisitive small girls, followed by an anxious mother. Joe put his shirt on the woman, gave her a cup of tea and a box of matches, and to the dusky little girls handfuls of boiled lollies. Laughing, they ran away.

Next day three men came down the beach, wearing the amazing regalia of pookaminny, which lends colour to the legend of Magellan's Spaniards landing long ago. Hair teased out and thickly powdered with white ochre, like a wig, ruffs of whitened fibre and cockatoo feathers, bamboo bangles and pendant puffs of dingo-fluff on a hair-string round their necks, their hands were painted white to simulate gloves. Carrying spears as lances, and stepping with elastic grace, they looked like courtiers of Velasquez, except that the only other article of wear was a puzzled frown. White men in squads with guns, from the old military settlement days, their fathers had remembered, but two white men on horses, shooting the big clumsy beasts that had overrun their country, were something new. The pale strangers gave them a bucketful of tea—plenty sugar—and a rib of roast buffalo. Until this time the natives of Melville Island had no idea that buffalo was good to eat.

A truce was declared, both sides watchful. When the schooner called back at the end of the pearling season, Flynn and Cooper were still alive. They stayed on the island two years, and shot out six thousand buffalo.

Joel Cooper had taken a girl of the Mala-ola as his wife. More than once she warned him of a planned attack—he was outside his hut with a gun when the blacks crept in at piccaninny daylight. Then the inevitable happened. While Barney Flynn was in Darwin, Joe was catching his horse one morning when a seventeen-barb spear embedded itself in his back. He broke off the haft, waved an empty revolver, and ran back to his hut and a flour-bag siege. His little Pocahontas, with remarkable love and loyalty, that night from her angry people stole a bark canoe. Her mother ran away with her, to paddle the sick man across to Darwin, a place unknown to them. A day or two later they were picked up at sea by the coastal lighter *Ark*.

Joe married his Mala-ola girl with bell, book and candle. He came back to Melville Island three years later with the two women and his own big native camp from South Alligator River. The islanders claimed their long-lost relations, home from the land of white men, with screeches and tears of glee. They gave "Jokupa" a place in the tribe, and there was no more trouble.

In a green valley like the valley of Typee, six hundred feet above sea-level, he built his house by a beautiful pool too cold for winter swimming, Melville Island shooting-camp on one side, the mainland camp on the other. For the next ten years he was lord of the isle. On Bathurst Island near by, the solitary French priest, Father Gsell—now the famous Bishop Gsell—founded his mission in 1907, but Cooper was the only white man ever to live on Melville in over a hundred years.

They were prosperous days of buffalo-hunting through unexplored valleys, hides by lugger to Darwin, then to Singapore and London. Of three or four half-caste children, his eldest son, Reuben, a boy of fine character, intelligence and physique, was sent to college in Adelaide. He became a noted athlete, and was once chosen to represent Australia as a runner in Olympic games, but in the colour-line prejudice of those days was not allowed to make the voyage to Europe. The founder of football in Darwin, where he was employed for years and always respected, Reuben wearied at last of the racial superiority of the whites, forcing him back to the blacks' camps. He married a good half-caste girl, and formed a fine little colony of half-caste settlers cutting cypress pine in a sawmill village far out on the north coast at Mount Norris Bay. They built two schooners to carry the timber to Darwin, lived in comfortable houses, bought a plant for electric power and light, and were thriving at the outbreak of war. Their schooner, *Prairie Flower*, sailed into Darwin Harbour on the day of the tragic raid, its crew among the heroes. But a few months later Reuben Cooper died. While death notices half a column deep told his life-story in the press of the south, his mother's dark people, crossing in bark canoes from Melville Island, danced round his grave in the greatest death corroboree ever known on the north coast. This boy, between races, is a study for novelists of the future. A born leader, he was honoured by whites and blacks.

If Paddy Cahill and Joel Cooper hold pride of place in the old days, best known of the later buff-hunters was Cecil Freer, once of Wildman River, now retired to a fashionable flat-building in Macleay Street, Sydney, where he can look out on the big mobs galloping for the shadowy jungle of the nightclubs, and the swamps of the submerged tenth around King's Cross. Other outstanding men of recent years were the Hardy brothers of Burrundie on Adelaide River, Hazel Gaden on South Alligator, and George Hunter, of Woolna Reserve. Hunter and Gaden for years carried their wives and each five children in a wild and roving life. For ten years at a time the families lived in one bough shed after another, out of touch with the world.

Modern buffalo-hunters developed a new technique—"You race on to the buffalo till your horse nearly touches him, run him till he's tired, then swing in the saddle and with a sawn-off shotgun shoot backward". It is not so adventurous as it sounds, for the buffalo is a slow, lumbering brute. Indeed, at Vestey's Marrakai Station, a hundred miles from Darwin, a buffalo-shooter on a bicycle has made himself a front-page story.

During the war, though they were occasionally bombed and machine-gunned from aeroplanes in target practice, the big mobs of the north "bred up", and hunters and tourists are out on the trail again along those far rivers. But the industry gives poor reward for a brutal and arduous life.

Horns, polished and mounted as curios, have been sold for £20. Boots and saddles of buffalo-leather will never wear out. The milk is heavily rich in butter fats, but I never met anyone, black or white, who had bothered to try it—the Territory drinks very little milk. Hoofs have also a market. In recent years the use of arsenical solution was prohibited in treating the hides, because confectioners bought the hoofs for gelatine and jubes.

Small Peter, with his all-day sucker from the school tuckshop, little dreams that once it galloped the Alligator prairies of romance.

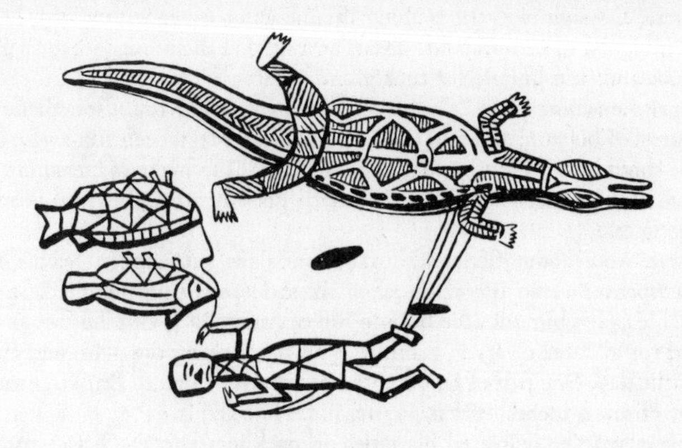

Chapter XXV

"Chokey"

ONE OF the darkest threads of human nature in the history of North Australia was Rodney Spencer.

In the old gold days of the Territory, when the Chinese were ratting the gullies of wealth and undercutting the teamsters in their £100 a ton racket for freight, eighteen horses and two mules were found dead in the Finniss River one morning—a ghastly pile, hamstrung, with their throats cut. Worth £1500 where there was so little transport, they were the property of a gang of Chinamen about to begin the year's work of carting machinery to the mines.

The police arrested three white men at the Shackle. Rodney Spencer, the ringleader, was known for his savage vendettas against the Asiatic—he had several times been charged with burning down a Chinaman's shack. If these men were guilty, they must have ridden eighty-six miles in a night for alibi. They had. They boasted of it. One of them turned Queen's evidence in bravado. So intense was the feeling against the Chinese, as it then was on all goldfields in Australia, that no verdict could be given against them.

Even so, in a land where men loved and respected their horses, their very lives depending upon them, the fiendish act set the Territory aflame with anger. Spencer and his mates were out for keeps. For them there was no place at the camp-fire, no fifty-of-flour for the pack to tide them on, no one to shout a glass of greeting when they rode in to a shanty. Where so much is forgotten, "the Finniss River turn-out" was never forgotten, and in the big bond of mateship in the bush there was no room for them. One went south and one went pearling. Spencer drifted to the lone life of the buffalo prairies. "Daylighting" tribes along the Alligator River with a .303, he mustered a big camp of boys and lubras, and herded them out to Scott's Plains, to shoot and skin buffalo for tucker and tobacco.

A grim customer was "Rodinee". When he glared round on them along the barrel of his gun, and told them "S'posem one-fella been run-away, quick-time I shoot him!" with a volley over their heads to make his meaning clear, they shivered in their hair-belts. He made good his threats where dead men tell no tales.

There were about fifteen thousand buffaloes running on Scott's Plains when Spencer came there. He shot six thousand, single-handed, in three years. He called himself "the Buffalo Bill of Australia", with the foot-shooting record for all time of seven running with the mob on the plain and twenty-six in the day. One pair of horns of the hundreds he sent to Darwin measured nine feet seven inches. It was a cruel life. He liked it.

Once a year he delivered his hides on packhorses to E. O. Robinson, the Customs agent buying for Goldsbrough Mort at Port Essington. Port Essington was a lively spot when the trepangers and buffalo-hunters put in there for the wet. The white men celebrated Christmas together with a case of squareface in the old Lewis shack on the headland, while on the beaches about them the blacks celebrated peace treaties, initiations and "all-about" corroborees. Just before the wet of 1889 E. O. Robinson went for a trip to China to investigate the trepang market. He left his trusted old Macassarman, Tingha Dian, in charge. That year Spencer was first in. He put up at Robinson's camp, a luxury usually denied him, for Robinson hated the sight of him, but with a "coon" in residence a white man takes command. They were joined before long by a Rotumah islander, Smoky Bill, his trepang lugger anchored in the bay.

All night the blacks were dancing, Uwaja, Bijenelumbo and Kakadu yelling *yacki*, jumping like pantomine devils in the light of the paperbark fires in a clearing about two hundred yards from the house. Later they would move round the beach out of earshot for the "man" corroborees, but as yet the dance was free for all, including lubras and strays.

One piccaninny daylight, from the veranda, Spencer saw a native running for the scrub. He whistled up his horse-boy, Mamitpa.

"What name that blackfella been run-away?"

Mamitpa's eyes grew wide with fright. "Can't savvy."

Spencer reached for his whip, hung up with his rifle and bridle. "You savvy all right. Come on! What name?"

The black-boy looked uncertain. "Might be—"

"Might be Mamialucum?"

"You-i."

"Him come up last night?"

"You-i."

"Every night?"

"You-i. Night-time Mamialucum sit-down, catchum lubra belonga him, catchum tabacca, sing-about corroboree. Morning-time been run."

Spencer's eyes narrowed. "Him come up tonight?"

A slight nod. "Might be."

The white man hung up the whip. Mamitpa made for the door.

"Here, you!" The boy stopped. "That time Big Swamp, Mamialucum run away from my camp. Him been stealum rice. Which-way I been talk longa you boys? . . . Eh?"

The dark aboriginal eyes became heavy with an effort of memory. "You been talk . . . 'No matter. Let him go. I get that fella all right.' "

Spencer smiled.

"Rodinee always get 'em. Now you savvy this-one properly. Tonight Mamialucum come longa camp." He held up two fingers, and named them as he touched them. "Mamitpa, Narrambil, you two-fella, catch Mamialucum, sing out longa me. That's all. No gammon. No yabber." He gave the boy a vicious twist of the ear. "Savvy?"

"You-i, Rodinee." Mamitpa was gone.

Spencer sat down to his breakfast of dugong and damper.

"Had a bit o' trouble with a boy last year," he explained to Tingha and Smoky Bill. "Name o' Mamialucum. Galloped away with half a bag o' rice. I didn't bother to track him. I've got his lubra skinning in my camp . . . just kept a watch on her. Now he's knocking around at night, comes in to be with his woman, an' smoke a pipe, an' see the corroboree. Ha!" He sucked his teeth and smiled. "*I'll* give 'em a corroboree, you watch me. I told the boys I'd get him."

Tingha and the islander had nothing much to say.

That night the Asiatics were smoking in silence under the veranda, the white man drinking square gin and reading a year-old paper in the shack, the corroboree hammering out its savage cantatas round the paperbark fires on the flat when they heard a shrill calling of "Rodinee-ee! *Koey!*"—Rodney! Come!"

Spencer ran to his swag for his gun, a .45-calibre Colt, ran towards the blacks, still dancing.

"Hold him, my boy!" he shouted. As he strode into the camp, a lubra screamed.

Mamialucum was down on his knees, the two boys, Mamitpa and Narrambil, holding him in a vise-grip. He was wrenching and writhing to break free.

The white man took hold of the black by the black matted hair, put the gun to his temple, and said "Good-bye, old man!" He fired, and the boy went down.

The corroboree stopped, all the painted clownish forms with white eyes staring.

Spencer tossed up the revolver lightly, caught it and fired again, into the middle of the dead man's back. "He'll steal no more rice," he said pleasantly, put the smoking gun in his belt, and swaggered away. Mamitpa sprinted after Spencer.

A woman crept forward, wailing like a wild dog, and covered Mamialucum with a sheet of bark, to keep away Yumburbur, the shooting-star devil that feeds on the entrails of the newly dead. Then the blacks ran from the place, whispering and crying. Where all had been dancing and laughter, the paper-bark torches flared on death, alone.

Narrambil's body, riddled with spears, was found in the bush a few days after. Mamitpa went in to Darwin with Spencer in Smoky Bill's lugger, and changed his name to Tim Finnegan.

When E. O. Robinson came back from China he reported the story to the police in Darwin. The launch *Victoria* went out to Port Essington, and brought back an aboriginal skull with a bullet-hole through the temporal bone. Spencer was arrested.

For the first time in Territory history a white man would stand his trial for the wilful, malicious and felonious murder of a black. The case was a sensation, particularly among bushmen of the north and missions of the south. His Honour Mr Justice Pater, who had just returned from Darwin to Adelaide after five years' service, was hurried back five thousand miles to sit in judgment, with a carefully chosen jury of respected pioneers.

Spencer had no money, but the only solicitor was briefed by his supporters, colour-line fanatics who rose in a shouting crowd. The solicitor advised a plea of guilty, on the grounds of self-defence, in that Mamialucum was a rebel element following the buffalo camp for revenge. But the evidence for the prosecution was lengthy and damning . . . no hope of confusion of a long list of myall witnesses, who acted the crime in court.

The brutality of the murder was a little too much, even for a Territory jury. They returned a verdict of guilty, with a strong recommendation to mercy in that accused's life among wild blacks was one of perpetual peril. His Honour pronounced the sentence of death.

Outside the court there was uproar. The Territory was outraged. You couldn't shoot a nigger any more! What would the white man's life be worth in the country of hostile blacks when they knew he would be hanged if he used his gun? The solicitor was assaulted—he lost his left eye in a brawl, and his career was ruined. Members of the jury were lashed with such vitriol of contempt that they begged permission to reconsider the case. They said they had not realized they could have brought in a manslaughter verdict. His Honour advised them that a manslaughter verdict would be as grave a miscarriage of justice as an acquittal.

Standing between his warders, waiting for the cart to Fannie Bay, the prisoner was a fine figure of a man, sun-tanned, sturdy, intelligent, hook nose, a cynical slit of the lips, defiant eyes above a reddish beard, blue eyes slanted close together. An exhibition rider and a bull's-eye shot, in the glamour of the gallows his vices were forgotten. Other men shot blacks. Why should he be made a horrible example? From being a pariah, he became a hero. Endless discussions and newspaper letters were in his favour. Because he did not smoke common tobacco, the condemned cell was weekly furnished with a box of the best Havana cigars. Large subscriptions were raised to finance an appeal, to brief the leading K.C. of Adelaide, Sir Josiah Symon, to champion White *v.* Black before Full Court, High Court, Privy Council. Sir Josiah Symon declined.

Fresh evidence was brought forward . . . that Spencer's father and brother had been killed by blacks in Queensland . . . that the dead tribesmen of Alligator River written down to his account in the past were killed by Kopperapo, a bad blackfellow in his camp, who stole his rifle and bullets to do it . . . that Mamialucum had brought to the corroboree that night a handful of spears, and that Mamitpa and Narrambil were double-crossing, pretending to hold the boy and calling Rodney to the camp to turn on him and kill him. It was also loudly rumoured that Spencer had been framed by other jealous buffalo-hunters who wanted him out of the way—that they set up an old skull on a post, fired a shot through it, and rehearsed the aboriginal witnesses—that the solicitor was in their pay when he advised a plea of guilty, knowing that no Territory jury would otherwise convict.

Legal matters at that time were sent by ship mail to Adelaide. For six months of suspense Rodney Spencer waited in the condemned cell at Fannie Bay, which overlooked the grim foliage of the gallows tree. At last he learnt that his sentence had been commuted to imprisonment for life. Before being removed to a southern prison he asked that his four-year-old son, wandering with his black mother on Alligator River, might be cared for by the Jesuit Mission priests at Rapid Creek.

He was gone, but not forgotten. Petitions for his release were continuous, signed by leading colonists over a thousand miles. To no avail. As martyr to a principle, Spencer was an unfortunate choice. In the south, and indeed, among many in the north, his crime was regarded as an atrocity—not the rational defence of the white man in a land of primitive law, but callous and cowardly murder, premeditated, of a helpless human creature. Two successive Governors, the Earl of Kintore and Lord Tennyson, refused to intervene.

Many natives were convicted of murders of white men in the following twenty years, a few executed at the scene of the killing, a few at Fannie Bay, the majority imprisoned for years. Whether they were innocent or guilty it was difficult to say. Many were "shot while resisting arrest". If there were murders of blacks by whites, there is no record till 1911, and after that the verdict "Not Guilty" is so monotonous that it seems a matter of course. *No white man has been hanged in the north or north-west for murder of a native.*

Ten years in the narrow stone walls of Yatala, the Buffalo Bill of Australia died a living death. Rodney Spencer became a pallid oldish man, pottering about his jobs. If the black streak of his cruelty had gangrened into hatred of himself and humanity, nobody knew. He was lighting the lamps in the jail one Sunday evening in 1899 when a warden told him to get his clothes and go. The lifer was free.

Hearing that this final successful petition had come from ever-faithful Darwin, and that his friends there had subscribed a fare to New Guinea or New Zealand, where he could start again, he made his decision. The best years of his life and the only thing he loved were of the Territory—he would go back there. He was galloping in his dreams that night to the lagoon at Oenpelli, with his little half-caste son, Jack Bulanda—Jack White Man—on the saddle in front of him. He was shouting to his boys across the salt marshes, and hearing an old blue bull thrash past him in the scrub.

So the shadow of Rodney Spencer came again to Darwin, to find that Darwin was not so pleased to see him after all. A young generation on the stations had grown up with the blacks and liked them. Then again, his record in retrospect—slaughtered horses and dead niggers—was not a pleasant telling. A martyr in Yatala jail was one thing. Rodney Spencer reeling through Chinatown was another.

He felt the aloofness. He thought it was because he was a jail-bird, forgetting those who had sent cigars to a condemned cell. He grew more bitter, drank heavily, and became a quarrelsome, an even dangerous man. There was nothing about him to suggest the young Spencer but his eyes. The suntanned skin was unhealthily wrinkled and whitish, the swagger had become a shuffle, the insolent smile an unpleasant twitch of thin lips over the artificial teeth they had given him in jail, little rabbit teeth. He had silent moods of bile, and drank alone.

"Don't be seen talkin' to me!" he would shout to the men in the bars. "I've been in chokey, see . . . for killin' a nigger! By God, I'll kill a few more!" Nobody was impressed. He was no longer a hero.

He was looking for Jack Bulanda. The Jesuit priests had gone from Rapid Creek to Daly River. From there he reclaimed his son. Jack Bulanda, almost a man, alone was proud of his father. The mission priests were not pleased when Spencer took the boy to share his haphazard life.

He did no good in Darwin. He would not work for wages. Paddy Cahill on his famous horse, St Lawrence, was now playing his game of St George and the dragon out among the crocodiles and buffaloes of the Alligator rivers, and on the Mary and Adelaide four or five horse-shooters had their camps. The technique had changed. They could get forty and fifty buffs a day. He wanted to be quit of his fellows, and all their moral codes and their yabber.

So he took an old dilapidated lugger, *Nebraska*, and he and Jack Bulanda drifted east to the last coast on earth. Outcast among white men, down there they would be respected as white men.

Beyond the Customs camp in Bowen Straits was nothing—no missions, no mails, only the sea and the low smoky shores of oblivion.

The acute angle of Arnhem Land was *Nebraska's* beat, from Cape Wilberforce, where the Macassars had a depot called Limboo Papa—a few old boilers on the sand, a well and a tamarind-tree—to Caledon Bay. Sun-tanned again as his son, with something of his old-time "flash", Rodinee recruited his blackbirds from King River and Goulburn islands, so that they could not run away, and set them to scour the further reefs and islands. With the loud voice of authority, and a shrewd sense of values—not to mention the .45-calibre Colt—he bargained his trepang and pearl-shell to the Malays. He hated all coloured men, but he liked to strut among them as Supreme Being, to exercise over them, on these ever-lonely beaches, the right of life and death.

The blacks were easy. The tough customers from Asia, ships armed, men armed, were not so quickly tamed. However, his cunning was superior to theirs. He had his own methods of blackmail and extortion. When the praus reported to young Tuan Alf Brown, who had taken Robinson's place as Customs agent at Bowen Straits, for reasons of their own they made no complaint.

A white man's lugger, *Venture*, did venture as far as Cadell Straits soon after Spencer made the coast his own. It belonged to Gore, a pearler, one of the men involved in the affair at Finniss River seventeen years before, the one who had turned Queen's evidence. The Arnhem Land blacks came off to *Venture* in canoes in the night, they speared Gore through the port-hole of the cabin, and were boarding the ship when they were discovered . . . oiled bodies slipping through the hands of the crew. The serang, a half-caste French Malay, was killed, and Gore seriously wounded. *Venture* went back to calmer waters and was seen no more.

The Arnhem Landers grew steadily more vicious. Rumours of praus looted and burnt, of massacre on the beaches, and of dark deeds generally, filtered through the native tribes to reach, in time, the buffalo-camps and Darwin. In 1902 a wounded Malay, Amat, staggered into A. J. V. Brown's camp with a grisly story. His *prau*, under an Arab captain, Delah Ahmed, with a crew of ten from Bandu to Ceram, cargo of sago and arrack, had been blown south and wrecked near Cape Wilberforce. The blacks were friendly at first, then they came in a war-party of fifty, and massacred all but Amat, who escaped with a spear in his side. He had walked the coast for sixteen days, living on sea-food. But when A. J. V. Brown delivered him in Darwin to make his declaration, he said he had forgotten the place of the wreck and would not know the natives. The police were not visibly cast down. Search-parties in Arnhem Land were nobody's week-end. Spencer and his variegated friends were left to their own vices.

In 1903 "Cap'n Joe" Bradshaw, that Daniel Boone of savage coasts, made the dramatic announcement that, with £450,000 to spend, he was about to colonize twenty thousand miles on the Darwin side of the Gulf, with headquarters at Arafura, a million acres on Goyder River. *White Star* appeared on the north coast, terrifying the natives with her devil's feather of smoke, racing at twelve knots through channels uncharted.

Civilization was on Rodinee's track . . . but he was still a long way in the lead.

One morning in 1904 a rag of a lugger with a crew of wild blacks crept round Point Charles into Darwin Harbour. It was *Nebraska*, Jack Bulanda in command. A boy of nineteen, with no knowledge of navigation, he had brought her four hundred miles in the hurricane season, landing here and there to gather food. Jack Bulanda said that his father was dead. He produced, as proof, the artificial teeth from Yatala jail. A black-boy of fourteen years, Amen-mulu, corroborated the statement.

The story of Spencer's death was conflicting. The first account was that he had been speared while sleeping, and, reaching for his revolver, tomahawked. Then Amen-mulu thought the matter out. He said they had landed on a small island in Arnhem Bay—Mallison Island it is marked on the chart—to boil trepang. Rodinee walked away into the bush. He shouted, "Bring rifle! I am speared!"

The rifles were in his tent, under a tarpaulin, but as the boys went to get them, Rodinee came running in a mob of wild blacks and fell. The boys dived into the water, and made off in two canoes.

Jack Bulanda said he had been in charge of the lugger, in the bay. He went ashore and buried his father, seeing no blacks but plenty of tracks. Rifles and tent were gone. Many fires were seen at night in the bay, but in the daytime no blacks. He later admitted that two Macassar praus, *Mareeja* and *Using*, were anchored in Arnhem Bay at the time. There was plenty fighting. The captain of *Mareeja*, a "bad friend" to his father, began it by firing on *Nebraska*.

The coroner duly recorded that Rodney Spencer had been murdered by natives at Arnhem Bay, expressing a reasonable surprise that "with his long experience of bush life in the north, he had wandered into the bush at such a place with no revolver". Remembering the death of Mamialucum, Darwin was incredulous, then philosophic. In the precise weaving of the fates, Rodney Spencer "got what was coming to him". With many a better man who died for the country, he was forgotten.

That year, three station natives and a half-caste at Arafura were murdered by wild blacks when seventy rushed their camp. The same mob, with Malay knives, in murderous night attacks routed and killed Bradshaw's Chinamen planting cotton, stole their tools and stores, and made away in a small launch. Again it was considered unusual for natives in such large mobs to form a corps together, to attack at night, also that they should have the sagacity to drive a small steam launch.

With a sigh of resignation, Mounted Constables Dowdy, Macaulay and Kelly set out for the scene, to arrest the offenders, and, if possible, Spencer's murderers. The Macassar praus would have long gone home, and nomad tribes would be a hundred miles away by the time they could arrive there. They travelled north from the Roper to Arafura, skirting Blue Mud Bay and Caledon Bay, spurring their packhorses over barren ridges, marshes, low ranges, lagoons and clay deserts, here and there a fan-palm jungle. Sometimes they heard blacks talking on the cliffs above them, but when they climbed the cliffs, no blacks were there. From Bradshaw's bright new homestead on the Goyder, they travelled ninety miles of swamp to Arnhem Bay, finding on that journey a deserted wurlie of galvanized iron in the scrub.

One day a tracker caught three women of the Ritherunga tribe, very nervous of white men and horses. They nodded that they knew of the killing of Rodinee. The first said the murderers were Underapin and Charawee; the second that they were the Macassars, Packandu and Sievu; the third that they were Goondu and Goomera. Circumstance and geography, as explained in dumb show, were all at sea—it was obvious that they were trying to please. For the rest, the mangrove shores were utterly deserted. The troopers could not cross to Mallison Island, having no boat. They returned, much thinner, to Darwin, with nothing to relate.

Cap'n Joe Bradshaw and his Scottish capitalists were forced by the unseen to vacate Arafura within two years, half of its Chinamen slaughtered and eleven thousand out of twenty thousand cattle bogged or speared. A year later still, not a vestige of that shining new homestead remained. No further attempts at settlement on the coast of Arnhem Land were made. A few prospectors, police and company promoters did cross its undefined borders on occasion. They proceeded rapidly by a series of revolutions, keeping close watch day and night all round.

A curious legend arose at this time from its vaporous marshes . . . of an old man of the Caledon tribe named Chokey, a powerful old man and crafty, with a hook nose, who had subjugated other tribes, and let it be known no white man would get out of the country alive. Arnhem Land became a closed native reserve—no white men admitted—and he became a humorous bogy of the Territory.

"Now, be good, or Chokey'll get you!" the Darwin mothers told their unruly children. His name and fame soon penetrated to the press of the south in picturesque adventure tales. If this fearsome blackfellow existed, who was the white man who christened him Chokey, and why? You will find that name in the records.

Pearlers and others were warned, on behalf of Chokey, that they entered Arnhem Land at their own risk. Allegedly he died in 1910 or 1912, but the bogy survived for many years, and in 1917, when Florence Willetts and her mother of the wreck of *Douglas Mawson* were said to be wandering with the blacks of Arnhem Land, Chokey had his picture—an artist's conception—in the American papers. He was depicted dancing, his feathered braves about him, dangling the scalp of a beautiful girl by its long golden curls, with a baby roasting on the coals, and a woebegone woman, in mental agony, pinioned by arrows to a nearby tree.

With so few visitors by land, the Left-Hand Boomerang Throwers built up a formidable reputation on the sea in the first twenty years of this century. In their canoes, or adrift on floating logs, they were eternally raiding the Goulburn and Crocodile islands. There were vague rumours of bloodshed, burning, rapine, the kidnapping of women and the massacre of the Macassars, whose trepang fleets were dwindling every year. Until the Dutch Government should make a query, they remained rumours, but Chokey was blamed for it all. It may be that he defended White Australia single-handed. No white pearlers were molested, for the reason that no birds flew above the Walrus and the Carpenter on their equally lonely, equally savage, shore. There were no white men there. Except A. J. V. Brown, not travelling too far down, and very cautious.

In 1907 A. J. V. Brown, now of Adelaide, in his trepanging lugger *Essington*, was anchored off the English Company islands. The blacks came out in four canoes to trade. But this is his part of the story. Let him tell it in his own words:

"There was a man among them of reddish colour, apparently mad—a half-caste, I thought, or a Macassar, quite naked. He was trying to make signals. He squealed like a dying rabbit and waved his arms about. As the canoe came nearer, I saw that his nose had been cut off and his tongue was gone . . . he had only a little cockatoo tongue, right in the back of his throat. His eyes were blue. Blue eyes are a shock on that coast . . . and where had I seen those eyes before?

"I had anchored for the night, but there was a big racket, owing to the goings-on of this Macassar-man, as I thought. He was excited, talking to the blacks in finger-yabber, and hopping about on a lame leg. I didn't like the look of it. I sent them away till next day, and told them to bring the turtle-shell then. They were a wild and woolly lot, and this man among them was queer. I didn't think it safe to stay around, so I told the serang to heave up, and we went off to an anchorage three or four miles down.

"In the morning we came back. The queer bloke was not with them this time, but I would let them on board only one at a time to trade. I had my boys with their rifles ready, telling them not to fire unless I gave the word. As soon as the trade was through, I heaved up and off for good. But the man's face haunted me. I had seen him before.

"Twenty-five years later a blackfellow came into my camp at Little Blue Mud Bay. He said 'I know you. I saw you at the English Company islands.'

"I said, 'Oh, do you? You speak very good English for the English Company islands.'

"He said, 'Yes. I been in jail four years at Fannie Bay. Then they say I no more killem, I can go. That make me laugh, because I killem all right. I work for a buffalo-shooter now. I gottem two boys and one girl. I bring you that girl.'

"I declined the lady, but I was interested in her old man. 'That time at the English Company islands,' I said to him, 'who was the red man who couldn't talk? Was he a Macassar or a yella-fella?'

" 'No more,' said the boy. 'Him white-fella. Macassar cut that fella tongue out when he burning *prau* with a mob o' blacks, cut off nose belonga him. Next time that Macassar come down, this white fella an' big mob blacks catchem. They killem all-about Macassar dead-fella.'

" 'Where did the fella come from?'

" 'Arnhem Bay.'

" 'Where did he go to?'

" 'I don' know. Him dead long-time I think. Too much trouble come up longa that man. That time English Company islands, we all-about talk killem you, but that white fella talk "no more." Him talk savvy you father.'

"That surprised me. A man that might be a white man, living with the Arnhem Land blacks, looking like a half-caste in hell, and knowing my father . . . I thought I had seen the eyes before. And then I remembered the day of Rodney Spencer's trial, when my father, V. V. Brown, was foreman of the jury, and when there was a bit of a riot outside the Darwin court. I remembered Rodney Spencer standing between his warders, defiant eyes above a reddish beard, blue eyes set close together.

" 'What was that fella's name?' I asked the nigger. 'What you call him?'

" 'Him been call himself,' he said, 'Chokey.' "

Chapter XXVI

Women of No-Man's-Land

I NEVER saw her in mufti—only in her ridin'-breeches with her stockwhip in her hand, out after cattle-killers along the Arafura."

They were talking of Mrs Jack Warrington Rogers, three of the old hands, remembering the women of no-man's-land.

"She was only a little dot," Dick had said. "Nice-lookin' when she was dressed up, don't you think?"

It was then that Tom painted her picture, to live for ever in my memory—against the blue of the Arafura with her stockwhip in her hand.

"She'd get them cattle-killers too," said Harry. "I've seen her there when they first took up Urapungee down on the Roper. Wherever the myalls was worryin' Jack's cattle she'd be right out, five weeks through the ranges with her stock-camp o' blacks, followin' tracks an' all the dead beasts till she come up with the mob that was doin' the damage. I've seen her ride in to Roper Bar behind three big wild-lookin' bucks wearin' fur tassels an' dingo teeth waxed into their hair. They was twice the size of her. She'd hand them over to the policeman."

"She done the same," said Tom, "at Arafura, when she and Jack was managin' for Bradshaw out there. She was young then, an' there wasn't no policeman for a thousand miles that side o' Darwin. You'd see her three days' ride from home, readin' the Riot Act to a bunch o' them salt-water niggers in Arnhem Land. If one o' them started any cheek, she'd give him a hell of a hidin'."

"I suppose she carried a gun," I put in politely.

"Never heard of her shootin' 'em up, missus, but you can bet she always *had* a gun."

"Would her husband allow her to go out alone on those trails?"

"Ha! Nobody's *allowin'* Katie Rogers. She carried the stockwhip in that camp. Jack was a good cattle-man an' a real good feller, but he was well-edjacated an' a quiet man. She reckoned he couldn't work blacks like she could. She was head stockman. She made them three stations."

"I can beat the lot of you," said Harry proudly. "I remember little Katie McCall when she was a kid o' nine or ten, down on her father's station on the Barcoo. She was a born stockman. You'd see her roughin' a brumby, gallopin' like a nigger in a pair of her dad's old trousers an' her curls flyin' under her hat. She loved horses an' she knew all about cattle from the jump—out in every muster. I was there when she married Jack Rogers in Urandangee. It was a real drover's weddin' with all the horse-bells ringing an' a swell dance at the pub. She made a pretty bride. Jack was a son of a big legal family down south, he had a brother a judge, but he give up the law to go drovin' because he liked the bush life. She went with him round the Territory an' down the Georgina road with cattle, ridin' the mob all day an' takin' her watch at night. She could plait a whip and shoe a horse and counter-line a saddle. She could break any colt, an' in a rush she'd be first to the lead an' head 'em while the others was pullin' on their boots. Katie Rogers wasn't afraid of anythin' in this world."

"I don't know so much about that," Dick said thoughtfully. "I've seen her scared stiff, when one of them kids was sick, them two little boys of hers."

"That's right," Tom backed him up. "She was always windy about the baby, out at the Arafura. It was a terrible place for a baby. The blacks speared eleven thousand of Joe Bradshaw's cattle an' a fair few of the Chinamen they had plantin' cotton. At the finish the lot o' them had to go for their lives. They came in an' took up Hodgson Downs."

"Who looked after the children when she was out with the stock-camp?" I asked.

"She did. If the old man wasn't home to look after 'em, an' you met her out on the run, you could bet they wasn't far away. She'd leave 'em on head-camp with the lubras—you'd see 'em behind the saddles with a bit of a net tucked round, asleep in the shade—but she wouldn't be gone long. She'd be back every couple o' days with her little mob o' cattle."

"One of 'em died," said Harry, "at Urapungee. No Flyin' Doctor then. Six hundred miles to Darwin. They couldn't do nothin' in the wet. You'll see the grave out there. She took that hard an' got frightened. She sent the other one south."

Dick stoked his pipe.

"I'll never forget the time," he said, "when young Jack was down there in a boardin'-school, an' a telegram went out to Urapungee with the mailman—they only had five mails a year, that's if it could get through. This telegram was a month old from the Kathe-rhyne, from this school in Sydney, sayin' this boy was very sick—'pendicitis or enteritis or somethin'—an' the doctors had to operate at once, an' would the parents please wire their consent. The mailman had to go on to Borroloola, an' he might be anythin' up to three months before he come back in the wet.

"She threw on the packs an' took a black-boy an' his gin and six or seven horses, an' away she come ridin' three hundred an' fifty miles along the Roper to answer that telegram. The rains caught her, an' you know all them big steep creeks around Hodgson an' Nutwood. She was only a fortnight gettin' in, swimmin' horses an' ridin' through water half the way, an' camped out in water every night with inches fallin'. I don't know how she done it. I was at the Kathe-rhyne when she come in an' she was in a state, not about herself but about the boy. There was another telegram waitin'. O' course the kid had been operated on weeks before, an' he was up an' about, good as gold. They shouldn't 'a' sent that telegram at all, it was only causin' trouble, but o' course they wouldn't know, down at the school, what it's like here out bush—they'd think it was like a farm near any country town. Anyhow, she got a trip in for a cup o' tea with her woman friends an' a chat. She didn't have much o' that."

"They had Merryfield for a while," Harry said. "That was a bit closer in. She got to the Kathe-rhyne races once or twice. She made a nice little homestead out there—a fair cook an' housekeeper, Katie, everythin' set pretty an' right and the best garden in the north, but she'd sooner be outside. She was on horseback nearly all her life. Just after they sold Merryfield she died."

"Yairs," said Dick. "I met her in Darwin when they was sellin' Merryfield. She was as thin as a pin an' no colour in her face. She'd been crook for a long time. She'd just been up to the hospital, an' she said the doctor reckoned she'd have to go straight down an' have an operation by a specialist in the south. They reckoned it was a malignous growth she had, an' there wasn't no time to lose if she wanted to live. So she was writin' to old Jack, an' she might go down on the next ship. But when I met her again she said she couldn't go, not for a while yet.

" 'It's this way, Dick,' she said. 'We're sellin' Merryfield, an' now the buyers have asked for a bang-tail. Well, that means a lot of extra musterin' an' a lot of trouble, an' I can't leave it all to dad and Jack. I'll have to go back an' take out one o' the camps.'

" 'What rot!' I says. 'D'ja mean to say two grown men an' all them blacks an' attenders can't get along? You go south an' have your operation like the doctor says, or if you don't it'll be bang-tail muster for you.'

" 'Oh, I'm all right,' she says. 'I'm feelin' better. Dad an' Jack could manage, but if I go back I'll get cattle they'll never get. They'll turn in the muster fifteen hundred short. They're too easygoin'.'

" 'You shouldn't worry neether,' I says. What're y'workin' *for*, punchin' cattle all y'r life?'

" 'We're puttin' the money back into Urapungee,' she said, 'an' we'll need all we can get. I suppose Jack'll be gettin' married soon, an' I'd like to give the boy a good start.'

" 'Ah, don't be a fool!' I told her. 'The best thing you can do for 'em is look after y'self.' But she would go back. They sold the station on a top tally, an' that was thanks to her. But she got away too late. She only went south to die."

There was a brief requiem silence over the pipes.

"Old Jack went back to Urapungee," he went on, "but he was terrible quiet when she was gone. He died in a bit of a tragedy out there, too early to make the big money in cattle in the last war. I see young Jack was killed this year in a fall from a horse down below Wave Hill. It seems a shame, after their thirty-five years' hard battle in the bush, there's nobody left to carry on. They don't make 'em too often like Katie Warrington Rogers."

"It's a cruel country for women," Harry said. "Women look a lifetime ahead, an' you can't do that up here."

"It's all right now," said Tom. "With their telephones an' tea-parties in all the little towns, and pedal radios and aeroplanes out bush, and rushin' around in motor-cars, in slacks an' goggles an' this 'ere cold cream, they reckon they're pioneers. They go down by plane whenever they feel inclined an' tell the newspapers they're the first white woman of Muckey-toodle-i, with an electric fan and a reefrigidator three miles from Alice Springs, which never was anythin' but a suburb of Adelaide."

"Ha!" said Dick, "they don't know they're alive!"

"I've got no quarrel with this mob," said wise old Harry, "no matter how funny they look. They got some common sense or they wouldn't be here. They mightn't be a patch on the old school that we know, but y' wouldn't want them to be. It's too *hard* for a woman. It's not right! Y'r throwin' her away! It's got to be good goin' for women an' kids before we move ahead. The ones I've got in the gun are the ones that won't budge ten miles out of the cities."

"You're right!" shouted fiery Dick. "There's a million spare women racin' round them bargain basements all their born days, an' the picture shows packed with 'em every night. 'Ain't it hot?' they'll growl. 'Ain't it hot?'—pullin' down the blinds on a bit o' sun, they never seen the sun! They got to have their hair grilled up frizzy in them infernal machines an' spend their husband's money on parties an' races an' furs an' time-payment carpets. They're bringin' up their children in rented houses an' flats so their daughters'll be more classy than they are, an' their sons in a white-collar job. That wasn't the sort that made Australia!

" 'Comfort!' they says. Comfort! Their grandmothers wasn't so fussy for comfort, or they wouldn't be where they are. Y'wouldn't think Australia'd run to snobs in a hundred years—not with all we know about it. Why, we're rearin' a race o' snobs that'd pass Katie Rogers in the street because she ain't got no complexion an' no style, an' she don't know no one. They don't deserve a country that women like her have made for 'em by ridin' cattle with blackfellas till they *died*! An' this landed gentry! Ha! Their mothers an' fathers done the grubbin' so they could spend the money. They wouldn't be seen dead back on the station ropin' a cow.

"They'll lose this country, you see. Look at all the fellers in this 'ere north that have died an' left big stations to the dingoes, or to be bought by the companies, or willed to half-caste kids that helped the old man to muster every livin' beast an' never get a thing out of it because they're *aborigines*. The Department of Native Affairs takes over the lot, an' them boys keeps on workin' the cattle for their tucker an' a few bob a week. Why are they half-castes? Because the women who should 'a' been their mothers turned 'em down. They hadn't the guts to come out with the men of their own race. You'll excuse my language, missus, but I say what I mean. They was great men that made this north, an' they never had the *chance* of a white wife.

"I'm tellin' you, if Australians want Australia, they better come down to earth an' fence off a bit of it quick, or they won't get it. There's an awful lot of strangers comin' here now, an' they can see a good thing, an' they won't shy off work. Our sons an' daughters'll be wage-plugs workin' for them strangers, an' gettin' the sack. An' I blame the women of Australia, because they're bringin' them children up to leave the country cold. 'Women look a lifetime ahead,' says Harry here! Them women is so blind they can't see no farther than the powder on their noses!"

He dismissed the gum-trees with an angry wave of the pipe, and subsided into gloom.

Harry mischievously winked. "You been round Australia for sixty years," he said. "How much have you fenced off?"

"Tell us about y'r sons an' daughters," Tom grinned. "They're new to me."

"Never mind about that," Dick growled. "I would have, too, if things had a' been different." His voice grew wistful and old. "When I was young an' strong enough to ask a girl to marry me, a white girl was harder to find in this country than a good gold reef, an' the few that was here was worth a damn sight more to a man."

"What's it the Bible says," put in little Harry, "about the price of a good woman bein' above rubies? By the way, j'ever see them Alice Springs rubies? I was in that rush, back in eighty-six. . . ."

How shall we tell of those women, few and far apart, who leave an immortal name in the Territory?

Evacuated from Ban Ban Springs to Adelaide in 1942 was Mrs Bob Farrar, after fifty-two years in the north. In 1890, as a girl of nineteen—Phoebe Wright of Sydney—she travelled by ship with "Old Bob" Farrar and his family to Normanton in the Gulf, and drove a buggy and pair five hundred miles south through Camooweal to where John Costello's cattle were waiting near Avon Downs, on a big pool of Rankine River called Joanning-ho. They were bound far north across Limmen River, beyond the Four Archers, to open up Albinjula, Valley of Springs, and then on to Lake Costello, on Wilton River that flows through Arnhem Land—six hundred and thirty miles still to go, and most of it through "bad blacks' country" where every year white men were speared.

Old Bob Farrar, Jimmie Mayne and Jack McCoy were the drovers, Young Bob, then a lad of sixteen, in charge of the wagon loaded with corrugated iron to build the house and their flour and food supplies for two years. Phoebe drove the buggy all the way with Mrs Farrar and the children, and she cooked for the drovers. On long dry stages to muddy lagoons, then down from the Tablelands over the Gulf ranges, swimming steep creeks and rushing rivers, in five months they came to Valley of Springs, built a good homestead and went on a hundred and forty miles to Lake Costello, where they built another. Out there they stayed nearly five years till the blacks killed most of the cattle, then back they came to where Mrs Costello was lone pioneer woman at Valley of Springs.

A thousand miles from Darwin by bush track and from Borroloola a hundred miles deep in spectacular ranges, with rivers impassable for half the year, they were "on the outside of everything"—no travellers ever passed, nobody knew they were there. It was a perilous place for a homestead, right under the cliffs, where the myalls could look down on all their doings. When the men were out with the cattle, many a night of alarms the women spent firing into the trees.

In three years, when most of the cattle were speared and the horses dead of walkabout disease, the Costellos abandoned the place to form Lake Nash on the Georgina, but the Farrars took it over, and ran the few cattle with donkeys for another three years. Phoebe Wright had married Young Bob—her five children were born far out in the Limmen River bush. They lived on a few goats and a good garden—no drovers ever came through to Valley of Springs.

Tom Pearce, "Mine Host" at the Katherine, remembers Young Bob's first appearance in civilization. He came to sell seventy skeleton cattle he had driven for seven hundred miles. They were unsaleable—wild and stringy from running from the blacks, but Farrar was in need. He told Tom the trouble—the man who keeps the pub and store is father confessor to the wild and wide.

"You can have the whole mob for £40," he said to Tom, "or even for £25, and I'll take it out in stores. I owe the white store in Darwin £40, an' they won't send down any flour an' tea by the Borroloola boat, to see us through the wet. We waited three months for the boat, an' then there was nothing on her for me. I got to get back with the flour for the wife and kids."

"I'll take them for £2 a head," said Tom. "That's the price of fat cattle. Don't worry. I'll fatten them up and get my money back."

So Bob cantered away with laden packs to beat the rains for seven hundred miles with tucker for the wet, a twelve-pound tin of boiled sweets for Christmas to children who had never seen sweets, and Tom's old gramophone with a dozen worn records for the novelty of music in their lonely little lives, the only "white-fella music" that ever was heard out in corroboree-land where the Limmen River flows.

A few more small mobs to Katherine, with Tom to fatten them up, and Bob Farrar took up new country, and formed Nutwood Downs, only three hundred miles from the Telegraph Line. He made it a fine station of quiet fat cattle, with blacks to help him muster instead of to kill. The price of cattle went up. He sold two hundred bullocks for £1000—when he looked at the cheque he could not believe his eyes. Straight back he went for "the missus and the kids" to give them "a spell in Darwin".

So Phoebe came driving the buggy with her children, a tall, shy woman in homemade dress and hat, passing the Elsey just in time for immortality. She lives as the Bush Mother in *We of the Never Never*, by Mrs Aeneas Gunn. If Mrs Gunn found her so reserved as to be almost grim, it was because in twelve years she had known no other white woman but old Mrs Farrar. In Darwin, with all five children, she went to her first dance.

Bob was so modest and unworldly that he wanted to accept an offer for Nutwood Downs of "£700 cash down", but Tom Pearce headed him off. A few years later he sold the station for £14,000. They retired "for good" to a fine little farm near Maryborough, Queensland. There Mrs Farrar caught so many colds and fretted so badly for the hard old times up north that the doctor advised Bob to sell up and go, to save her life. Bob sacrificed the lot and back they came. With sixty years behind them, they took up Ban Ban Springs, near the first old Territory station of Glencoe, running cattle and buffaloes, still pioneering when all five children were married and gone.

To the age of seventy-two years Mrs Farrar, thin, wiry and tough, in men's rig and spurs, helped her husband in the stock-camp and out on the buffalo trail, where she would skin, dress and pack the hides, "everything bar shoot". Hers were the best-dressed hides in the north, and "she's a better man than he is in the scrub", said her friends. When she was seventy-one, as I have told in *Flying Doctor Calling*, she was knocked down by a bull in the stockyard.

"A couple of the bulls were fizzing," she said. "Bob got a rope on one, and I ran to shut the gate on the other, but the bull and the gate both fell on me." After months in Darwin Hospital with a broken thigh, and months on crutches, she was back in the saddle, "riding around" with Young Bob, who was Old Bob then. Ban Ban Springs, from the air, was a model little station, though there were only the two old people there. Nutwood Downs is a very prosperous company run. At Valley of Springs there was never a white woman since Mrs Farrar's time—in fact, not even a white man.

Knitting by lamplight in her homely little room, with Grandma, in ringlets, and Grandfather Farrar, an Indian Army major in military stock, gazing tranquilly down from the wall as they gazed in the lonelier places, Mrs Farrar could see no virtue in the retrospect of her life.

"Oh, well, there's plenty to remember," she would say as she smoothed the knitting on her knee, "but it was just the ordinary life out bush."

There was "plenty to remember" till the end. With the same quiet philosophy, at the outbreak of the Japanese war, she joined the sorry southward journey of the Australian refugees, leaving the little home at Ban Ban Springs "for good".

In that woeful pilgrimage, through rain and heat, down the Stuart Highway before it was built, two thousand miles by truck and train to the homeless south, or in an overcrowded ship in black-out along the east coast of Australia, were other great women. Nobody has ever heard their stories. The newspapers, which "streamline" many a lesser heroine of today, never found the real ones in their five years of exile—for exile in a foreign land the cities, with all their "comforts", were to them.

Among them were Mrs Herbert of Koolpinya, at the age of eighty-four, widow of Mr Justice C. E. Herbert. She once graced Darwin's little Government House as Administrator's wife, and so well loved the Territory that she spent the rest of life with her sons, a true bush woman in the tropic station home at Koolpinya.

There was Mrs Billy Byrnes, of Byrne and Tipperary, dainty as a cameo, white-haired and blind, fifty of her eighty years given to the north. Her sightless eyes looked back to the days when they came from Wyndham in a schooner, and formed the station with only "a bridle, a rifle and £1". They gave the pound for a sack of potatoes, and while she cooked those potatoes for tucker Billy put up the first bough shade home. She saw Pine Creek and Brock's Creek in their heyday of gold, with a procession of Chinamen "four deep and a mile long" coming to the joss-house from the mines—Byrneside provided the meat for those buried old mines. Of her family of seven sons, one was killed in the first war, the others are fine horsemen and cattle-men. They sold Byrneside to Vestey's and moved out to Tipperary, on a glorious stretch of the Daly, but after this war were happy to buy it back, a beautiful homestead noted for its friendliness. The sons are married to practical women who like the north, and this is one of the few stations in the Territory where the younger generation is heir to the hard work of the old. One daughter-in-law, Mrs Harold Byrnes, has, of her kindness, adopted no less than three boys of the south, given them a good education, and the chance of a future up there.

Among those exiles, too, was Mrs Hazel Gaden—I know of no braver woman, nor one that can face the sorrows of this our life with a merrier nature and a more hopeful heart.

In 1923 she went down with her husband to take up Kapalgo on South Alligator River. They sailed from Darwin in a little skiff of eight and a half tons with Madge, the eldest daughter, then two years old, and a baby of five weeks. The skipper was Jimmie Rotumah, an old South Sea Islander, and with them was Kirkland of *Northern Territory Times*. It was he, not Mrs Gaden, who told the story.

Creeping down a desolate coast through ominous heat with no shelter, they were soon drenched in rain-squalls. Night came with black clouds, lightning and violent winds—the cyclone in which the steamer *Douglas Mawson* was wrecked with all hands in the Gulf. Storm-circled in crazy seas, their little boat danced on. Her jib carried away three times, they lowered and lashed the foresail. The skipper lost his bearings, vainly looking for Field Island by midnight. He could find no bottom with a twenty-fathom lead, and lay to under a reefed mainsail while the cyclone swung anti-clockwise and hammered at them from the east. Twice the pumps were manned, and then broke down. They waited to go under every wave.

"Mrs Gaden," said Kirkland, "lay on the deck aft, with only her body to shelter her newborn child. They were swept by the wash of the waves all night. She was constantly and pitifully ill, and she never murmured."

Field Island showed up in the grey dawn, and they entered the mouth of the big river to run for a deep forty miles with little sail in its strong willing tide. Geese, ducks, crane, pelican, ibis and all Territory birds flew above them in mass formation and shouting clouds. "An old bull buffalo looked at us dully, gave his head a shake, and made off at a lumbering gallop over the plain."

At Kapalgo the dinghy brought in furniture, fowls, boxes of luggage, the family and all its stores to the mangrove shallows. Friendly blacks, laughing delight at the first white children they had seen, perched little Madge high on their shoulders and carried the cargoes across half a mile of swamp, at every step sinking to the knees. Then they walked in quaint procession to where "Yorkie Mick", a great old bushman, had built them a station—homestead, kitchen, meat-house, goat-yard, stockyard and branding pens.

It was a good house, fifty feet by fifty, three wide rooms and fourteen-feet verandas, every sturdy post and rafter treated with arsenic to keep out white ants, bark walls tightened by outriders of timber, snow-white ant-bed floors well levelled, and roof-gutterings hollowed out of a tree—never a leak in the heaviest rains, Yorkie guaranteed. He was a bush genius, his only builders a mob of half-wild blacks, his only call on civilization for nails and fencing wire. He had roamed the north for thirty years, had been everywhere but Darwin, and was never known to wear a shirt. A Nordic giant tanned in the sun, clean-shaven and with a shock of white hair and very blue eyes, he was "mosquito-proof", he said. A patriarch of the Territory, he is still living at Jim Jim Creek.

There was a beautiful garden by the mile-wide lagoon—peanuts, pineapples, papaws, melons, bananas, pumpkins, passionfruit, sweet potatoes and mangoes. Mrs Gaden brought vegetable seeds, flowers and blossoming shrubs. Wild pigs were running everywhere, and the blacks would bring turtle, dugong, oysters, geese, ducks and fish.

The boat went on to Oenpelli, leaving the Gadens in their new home, on the north coast farthest out—a lonely home for a woman with two babies when the men were away shooting buffalo for six weeks, a weird and savage world when the dark came down.

Sometimes the blacks corroboreed all night, red with flames the sky and the lagoon. Wild dogs howled around the homestead, and crocodiles came up on the river-flats.

"I couldn't sleep in the house," said Mrs Gaden. "I wanted to see what was coming, so I took the children and slept in a bough shed. One night I heard the cane-grass stealthily moving. I watched for a spear to come through, or a black hand, or even a long snout! At last I crept round the corner and gave a ferocious shout—it was only a quiet old horse sneaking a bite. Our blacks were all right, but you never know when myalls might come in."

Evil little buffalo-flies were a plague by day, and mosquitoes all night—millions in the nets in the morning, fat with blood . . . long lean black mosquitoes with proboscis big as their bodies, then Panzer regiments in field grey, half an inch long, then black swarms of miniature devils like red-hot needles, and in the early morning yellow bulbous mosquitoes, more vicious than all the rest.

That was not a good place for babies. As the family increased, the Gadens finally took the buffalo trail, and with five children in bough shades and a big camp of blacks they wandered the rivers for the next ten years—a book in itself, but of all those hardships and adventures only Mrs Gaden herself could write. At last they came to live in Darwin, their first comfortable home —it was left and looted in the war. A most devoted mother in a life too hard, Mrs Gaden is a hearty woman with a lively interest and a wide knowledge of a country known to no other woman. I once heard her giving directions to a beauty spot beyond White Stone on the Adelaide River.

"You have to foot-walk," she said briskly. "It's about seventeen miles in from the river, and you want to take a black-boy with you to cut down the creepers and thick jungle or you won't have a hope of getting through, but it's well worth it, the prettiest place you could ever imagine. With the lily lagoons and the big bamboos and the tropic flowers, you're in fairyland."

There were women at Oenpelli on the East Alligator in earlier years, Mrs Paddy Cahill and later Mrs Campbell, in fairyland all alone with the blacks. From another fairyland is Mrs Andy Ray, of Mainoru, the only station in Arnhem Land, a hundred and thirty miles eastward of Maranboy by a rough track up and down the rivers and the hills. The green brimming Mainoru River with its ninety miles of crystal springs, the big Wilton River, the dreamy blue vistas of cloud-shadowed Arnhem Land right out to Caledon Bay, were hers in loneliness for four years, with a camp of four hundred myalls down under the pandanus in front of the old thatched homestead on the hill that was wired in from spears. With a Caledon Bay corroboree, three hundred strong, just over the hill, there was anthropology unlimited had she felt inclined—instead, she taught the lubras to speak English, to make their own dresses, to care for their bonny babies, and to live white.

It was a long four years out there with Andy, little enough to cook, nothing to sew, no mails in history even yet, two hurricane lamps at night. When she heard, by mulga wire, that another woman, Mrs Shadforth, was coming through with her husband and a mob of horses from the west, Mrs Ray, sensitive of her own shyness, thought of going bush to camp on a creek! Mrs Shadforth, however, took the Tanumbirini track, and Mrs Ray was spared the ordeal of meeting one whom she knew would be a friend. So does the loneliness take to itself even the brightest. Such an excellent cook was Mrs Ray, in her three big camp-ovens and open fireplace, and such a happy soul, radiating kindness, that Imperial Airways, when she came in to Darwin, could find no better hostess for their aerodrome hostel for travellers from overseas.

Only one traveller, in her time, came to Mainoru, and then did not show up. He sent up a request, by one of the blacks, for a loaf of bread and a couple of eggs. When Mrs Ray sent back an invitation to dinner, he vanished in the pandanus. He, too, was shy. The year after she left the outpost, at Andy Ray's death, a wild-dog hunter, George Nicholls, and his mate went there, camped a few miles from the station, but quarrelled and the mate left. As a result of unwise contact with those blacks, to quote "Cowboy" Collins, "George Nicholls's head came bobbing down the springs". Andy Ray's nephew, little Jack McKay, has been out there alone for the past seventeen years, working with the myalls of Mainoru to make a grand little station, one of the best and cheeriest men of the north—but he is another story.

Far out at Borroloola in the earlies were Mrs W. G. Stretton, who reared twelve children there, and Mrs Hart. Whenever a white child was born at Borroloola a flag ran up on the old pub, and it was "as much as you like to drink and no book or slate". When a daughter of Mrs Hart, at Walhalla, was thrown from a horse and dragged in the stirrup, the mother walked forty miles for help with the dying child in her arms. Another enduring soul was Mrs Hobley of later days, twenty years at Riverview on the Roper. It was a river view and nothing else. Said to have been a mistress of mathematics in an English school, Mrs Hobley educated her one little daughter so well that when they came down to Perth this girl from the far bush, who had known only black playmates, gained her A-class pilot's licence in aviation.

A thousand miles south-west and way back in 1890, Mrs Joe Bridge was first white woman along the Murran-ji. A colleen from Killarney, she came out with a shipload of Irish immigrants through Torres Straits. At Thursday Island the captain read a letter asking for two girl volunteers to help in a Normanton hotel, so she landed in the Gulf country. Joe Bridge came in with a couple of racehorses, married the fresh-faced Irish girl, took her to Croydon goldfields and then to live in the open air, carting timber for the first of the Queensland bores. From Avon Downs, with horses, they made across to Kimberley, mother and two toddlers in a covered wagon and a shy little eldest daughter, Mabel, driving the spares and a couple of milking cows. They were two years and over a thousand miles on the journey, and another baby was born in the bush.

It was a far cry from the Lakes of Killarney to Murran-ji Waterhole, deep in a hedgewood forest, where many a bushman died of thirst and fever . . . but they made home there, and spread the family washing on the trees. In the ranges of the Victoria and the Ord, wild blacks came to their camp-fires, but the cherub that guards little children travelled by their side. A white mother and babies set those wild blacks laughing. They showed them water, brought them tucker, carried and cared for the little white fellas with love and care. Tribe after tribe looked after them all the way to Wyndham. Mabel Bridge, who is Mrs Cole, a path-finder in her own right, and wife of a path-finder of the Canning stock route, down through the desert from Hall's Creek to Wiluna in West Australia, is living there today.

Epic names of the Territory west are Mrs Bob Watson, first châtelaine of Victoria River Downs, and Mrs Townshend and Mrs Cusack who died there; Mrs Alf Martin, faithful for twenty-five years—it was a different station then; Mrs Nat Buchanan, who lived for a while at Wave Hill and Gordon Downs in the eighties and nineties; Mrs Tom Deacon of lonely Waterloo, who managed the station at her husband's death, and adopted a little motherless girl from another northern station. Every calf of hers was sacred to the poddy-dodgers. They would even brand up for her, one in every five, when they were moonlighting the ranges. After her time at Waterloo were Mrs Woodlands, and later Lady Campbell, who died there.

Mrs Jim Wickham was at Ewandyte, a city girl mothering young children, her homestead a little fortress of stone and ant-bed out near the Kimberley border. One baby was born on the 240-mile trail in to Wyndham—they rigged up a little bough shade. Mrs Conway, a drover's wife, was camped on Vandyck Creek, up in the ranges, with two big staghound dogs for protection.

Mrs Paddy Cahill was at Delamere, two hundred miles west of Katherine, when Willeroo, in between, was deserted after murders by the blacks.

For twelve years Mrs Harry Shadforth lived at Auvergne, far down Victoria River. From Wollogorang on the Queensland border, a stark homestead netted in from spears in a forbidding range, where her husband's brother was killed, she came to Auvergne on the western border, just as far out under another dark uncertain range. A great little housekeeper, always bright, Mrs Shadforth was happy at Auvergne. One trip with her husband she made, driving behind cattle and cooking for the camp a thousand miles to Alice Springs, and another trip riding nine hundred miles east to Borroloola with horses. Harry Shadforth had malaria on the way and his wife was his nurse and his drover for those horses. Mrs Darcy lived at Kroondrook, far to the south, until she became blind. Mrs Byers was at Bradshaw's Run, on the other side of Victoria River, till her husband disappeared without trace—they believed he had wandered in malaria.

At Pine Creek Mrs Elliott, the schoolteacher, was "a godsend" to all the miners between Burrundie and Wandi. When "the fields were lousy with flies and typhoid" she cut down the grass and burnt the filthy old Chinese huts, drained away the bad waters, and, with a lubra, attended the sick night and day.

Mrs Jack McCarthy, who married "Irish Mac" when they were both over sixty, went out to live with him in the bush, when he was "teaming" on the north-south road, so that "he'd have somewhere to come home to". She started the first little store at Newcastle Waters, half a mile from the cattle station, and so, with meals for the drovers at any time of day or night, founded the town. When she sold that store, she built a little log-and-lattice house by the water-lilies of Frew's Ponds, and, like a little wizened fairy out of Hans Andersen, gave a glass of rich white goats' milk and a slice of plum cake to every passing traveller.

"Have ye seen anything of my old pigeon?" she would ask.

When Irish Mac was nearing home, away she would go, foot-walking twenty miles and more down the track to meet him, on the road that is now the Stuart Highway, with her basket of goodies on her arm, and riding back with him, happy as Larry, behind the team.

The last time I saw her there, Jack was in Adelaide Hospital for a critical operation. Two blacks waited at Daly Waters, thirty miles away, to bring her the urgent telegram from the doctors—old Paddy of the Pintubi, wearing a kangaroo-fur sporran and his tribal markings, revolving in his thick lips a miniature ball of tobacco and manure. His mate, a stocky myall in a hair-belt, rejoiced in the tuneful aboriginal name of Mellodee. Both carried spears and laughed at me over the long grasses—the quaintest pair of telegram boys that ever I was to see. But the telegram, when it came, was tragedy to the little old wife alone. Irish Mac would never come back. Mrs McCarthy said good-bye to her log cabin by the lily lagoons, and hurried south to live in a room in a terrace, still to be near him.

Among great women of the Centre were Mrs Augustus Elliott at the Horseshoe Bend of the Finke; Mrs Syd Stanes of Erldunda; Mrs Hayes of Undoolya; Mrs Louis Bloomfield of Love's Creek; little Mrs Ted Braitling of Mount Doreen, a hundred and fifty miles north-west of Alice Springs; Mrs Jenkins of the mica-mines; Mrs Kavenagh of Arltunga, Mrs Ben Webb of Mount Riddock, Mrs Bob Chalmers of MacDonald Downs, two hundred miles north-east; and Mrs Bohning of Helen Springs, four hundred miles north, who with her young daughter Elsie drove the first mob of cattle to the first cattle-train at the Alice.

A magnificent natural monument commemorates Mrs Ida Standley, first schoolteacher of Central Australia. With no more than half a dozen white children in school at Alice Springs, Mrs Standley gathered the half-castes out of the blacks' camps, taught them to read and write, the girls to sew and cook. She leased a bungalow to mother and protect them, and because it was too near the hotel, where the older ones were the prey of drunken white men, she moved them all out thirty miles west, to camp in bough shades—a life they loved—at Jay Creek. Rambling the ranges they discovered the most spectacular gap in the MacDonnells, where a javelin of bright sun splits the red crags to a hundred and eighty feet deep. So it was named for a woman of infinite kindness—Standley's Chasm.

On the Barkly Tablelands women were always few, the farthest-out Mrs Lloyd at Alroy Downs, her daughter, Mrs Jack Spratt, later of Avon Downs for fifty years. Mrs Trayne was at Eva Downs in the earlies. "That's what accounts," they told me, "for the chiffoniers out there." A desolate run on the dry downs, a hundred and twenty miles east of Newcastle Waters, with "the Fizzer's Well" and the Fizzer's old eight-gallon bucket memorial to his heroic years, the four Chambers lads find Eva Downs a hard job even today. They say, "You can see too far out here."

In a popular *Digest* recently I read a condensed book of a brave American pioneer girl with her baby, alone in the railroad wilds of Nebraska *half a mile from the neighbours*. These Australians reared a whole family of babies with no neighbours within a hundred miles. How different were their lives from those in our country towns, with a trip in every week or fortnight in the car or the spring-cart for the delight of friends and shopping, the excitement of the pictures at night . . . how different from life on the sheep stations, with overseers, jackeroos, sheep-hands, shearers in shouting crowds to woolshed dances, always a married couple or two, windmill hands and fencers, and the wool trucks coming and going.

Lonely, indeed, is the bride of the far-out cattle run. After two thousand miles of hard and hopeful travel, relieved with dreams of "the station", her heart goes down when she sees the old earth-floored lean-to with all its shacks, a patch of grey in a big yellow world. She hears of the floods, the droughts, the tragedies of the past when "the blacks was bad".

Her husband rides out to the cattle, telling her, "I'll be back by the seventeenth." She is alone with the blacks' camp down on the creek, stock-boys gone leaving lubras, piccaninnies and a few old men. A lubra comes up to sleep at the homestead and keep her company, but if it is on the rim of myall country or if she is nervous, the black girl senses and shares her fear, and they have troubled nights.

"Might bush blackfella come up, Sally?"

"You-i, missus. Might."

Quick to reflect an emotion, and with her remarkable aboriginal talent for acting, Sally obligingly shows symptoms of fright . . . no comfort there. Silently moving as a shadow while missus sits sewing, she listens and peers . . .

A noise!

Missus asks sharply, "Sally! What name that?"

Rolling eyes and genuine terror, Sally whispers, "Dono. Might be him spear!"

Missus creeps for the gun . . . and sees that the moonlight is bright outside. It was only a goat running loose. In the morning they laugh at their fears.

Days are endless and nights a dread as she watches the fly-blown calendar on the wall. The seventeenth comes . . . and goes. From the veranda she watches the horizon for a sign.

"That one smoke, Sally?"

Sally leans on her cane-grass broom, purses her lips, wrinkles her eyes to the glare.

"Might him dust."

Gaily she hurries to put on her brightest frock, to set the table and the kettle boiling for tea, over to the meat-house for a good goat roast, more pumpkins and potatoes for dinner. In an hour or two the dust is gone. It was only a whirlie.

"Might him nuttin'!" Sally observes with a musical peal of laughter.

In the quiet night, with the heat cracking the iron roof and the windmill creaking, she hears hoofbeats. They come right in to the station yard. She is out on the veranda in her nightgown, questioning the dark in a happy shout—

"That you, Bill?"

A quick aboriginal guttural answers back. "No more. Me Dandy, missus. Fetchum paper-yabber longa boss."

The boy brings up the letter on silent bare feet, his eyes shining white as she lights the lamp. It is a page torn out of a diary:

Dearest Kit,

There's a mob of bullocks at Bluebush Ted James cut out. I'm going over to get them. Will try to be back by the thirtieth. Give Dandy a batch of bread and a fortnight's tucker. Any chance of a cake?

Love

Bill.

So the vigil goes on. Her first lesson is patience. Life is one mob of bullocks after another. Soon she sleeps like a top, knowing that through all the years no deliberate harm has ever come to a woman alone, from white or from black—the Australian bush is too far and too wholesome for that.

The old lean-to blossoms in packing-case furniture, curtains, cupboards and cretonnes, an oven built in to the open fireplace, a Coolgardie safe dripping coolness, a bough shade for meals with rustic chairs instead of the slab in the kitchen with two forms, neat white beds on the veranda instead of the old plaited-hide-and-blue-blankets, or a swag outdoors. In teaching the young camp lubras to work in the kitchen, garden, house, laundry, and even the sewing-machine, she forgets she was lonely. Soon a baby kicks his fat legs under a meat-dish cover, grimly suggestive of Itylus but safe from the danger of flies. There are plans for a new homestead, high on piles out of the dust of the stockyard and the mud of the wet, with balconies and a dining-room netted in gauze. Missus goes shopping by catalogue in the city stores thousands of miles away, and orders with the supplies for the station the few little extras and comforts that will make it home.

So bush women are made, to be queens in their own right of a wide country. The bushmen were afraid of them in the old days, of their critical eyes and the lectures they might read. Seeing curtains on the windows or washing on the line, they would wheel their packs and "go up a gully". It was a grave injustice, for the women of this strange world must needs be quick in understanding, with open hearts for all. Their hospitality is as your own mother's to the few that happen along. Many are keen readers, some with a flair for handicrafts or gifted in writing and painting. All of them loved their country, with a quick sense of its humanities, its humour, its interests. Easy of manner and well-dressed when you met them in cities, you might never know they were of the bush—they were too far out for type.

Being human, they had faults. A few were tyrannical to the blacks, not all were ministering angels. When a stockman was thrown from a horse on one station, all the lady at "government house" could do was to put a record on the gramophone, "Nearer, My God, to Thee." But the Territory was too capricious a country for martinets, too hard a ground for delicate blooms, and soon weeded them out.

Some good women are lost in oblivion—pilgrim mothers of the droving camps, wives of well-sinkers and prospectors for a lifetime in bough shades —and some are to be found there still.

I think of Mrs Bill Wyatt, after her seven lonely years at Marrakai making a beautiful home at Mount Bundy where before her time Fred Hardy, the pioneer, camped in a shack. There she was generous hostess and unfailing friend to thousands of soldiers and travellers in wartime, also to me.

. . . of Mrs Mackenzie, best "boss drover" of the west, every year through the war bringing her big mobs from Victoria River to Winton, 1250 head on the road with no help but her husband and a couple of stray blacks.

. . . of Mrs Norton of Montajinnie, with three young children in that bleak homestead on the rim of desert, seventy miles south of Victoria River Downs.

. . . of Mrs Len Patterson, two years out with her husband, making the roads to Wave Hill and cooking for all on the track, behind his grader in a caravan.

Mrs Jock Jones was Michaele Boylan of Sydney, who in girlhood won her pilot's licence on a test flight with Kingsford Smith. Sharing Jock's life as a contractor in the north, she was driving a ten-ton truck when I met her, up and down the jump-ups from the Murran-ji to Borroloola, with her two clever children, half a dozen blacks, twenty-six goats and a portable yard, a radio, refrigerator, tents, tables, chairs and all the stores for six months aboard. Camp cook for all, schoolteacher in regular school hours, she was painting arresting watercolours of the waterholes on the way, and writing a children's book. Tim O'Shea's six pretty daughters, of Katherine, married troopers and men of the north and, scattered far apart with their babies, are faithful still to the loneliness.

A few remarkable families are hidden away in those wide spaces. The Zigembines are Bedouins of the big stock routes all through childhood, girls and boys the ringers as they drift along with the cattle year by year across the Barkly Tablelands, down the Georgina road and the Birdsville track, an outsize in dads the boss drover, mother the cook, and an eight-year-old bringing along the spares. Dusty little figures, never weary, riding down the days, those children learn to read and write at night under the sky.

Deep in the Abner Ranges by glorious paperbark springs are the Darcys of Mallapunyah, seventeen children all told. Eighty miles north of Anthony's Lagoons and thirty miles east of the Macarthur River road is the home of pandanus, paperbark and stone built by their mother. A hardy soul, she camped on the track horse-breaking for her teamster husband, George Darcy, when the eldest were young, and went out bagging copper with him in those ultimate ranges. As the family increased she settled by Mallapunyah Springs, ditched them for irrigation, and planted a mile of garden—a thousand banana palms, fifty mango-trees, hundreds of papaws, every vegetable save English potatoes, oranges, lemons, mandarins, limes, grapefruit, rosellas, Cape gooseberries, all tropic fruits. With goats, fowls, turkeys, game, fish from Kilgour River, his big family of nineteen cost George Darcy not £50 a year. For twenty years his wife tended the garden while she built the sturdy homestead—felled the young paperbarks, made mud bricks and carted flagstones from the creek. All the furniture and children's toys she made of hand-carved wood, taught them lessons and handicrafts by her home-made lamps at night.

Seven boys and eight girls were born out in the ranges, with never the need of a doctor. Shouting through the banana palms, swimming in the crystal springs, happy little sylvan creatures in their own "green mansions", they knew no other comrades, black or white. People, cities and nations were a dream beyond the trees.

Five or six times a year a packhorse mailman, riding down through Brunette to Borroloola on his lone thousand miles from Camooweal and back, left a message from that mysterious world in a letter-box of bush wood thirty miles away—a weekly paper or two and lessons from the correspondence school two thousand miles away in Brisbane. Until the older children built an excellent fire-ploughed road across that thirty miles, no traveller came near.

So rugged are the ranges that Mrs Darcy and a ten-year-old son, out looking for a donkey, were lost a few years ago. Though forty men down from the Tablelands, police trackers and a hundred and fifty horses, searched for a fortnight, no track or trace was found. Since then Elizabeth Darcy, a wonderful little housekeeper, has cared for the garden and mothered the younger ones down to Freddie and Bob, five years old and four. The elder ones, trained to stock work, are out riding cattle and building fences. The camp by the spring has become a prosperous station, the garden is famous all over the north, and when the aeroplane service was extended to Borroloola, these girls and boys, under their father's direction, themselves levelled the forest to make the first landing-ground in the Abner Ranges.

Another valiant family of the far north has now faded away, save the last loyal and fearless daughter—the Sargents of Stapleton Creek. Theirs was another strange childhood, in Adelaide River jungles hedged in from the world. Twelve children, ten living, and eight of them girls, they slaved from early years on their rough sweep of cattle lands and the old tin- and lead-mines between the railway line and Bynoe Harbour. Connie and Winnie, the eldest, were Amazons of the bush, tree-felling, fencing, horse-breaking, stock-riding, branding, draughting, bagging tin at Mount Tolmer, working a lead-mine together, one at the windlass with her shovel, the other with her pick fifty-eight feet down.

The Canadian father and mother took up this plantation in Gilruth's time, educated their children to be intellectual, independent, hard-working and fanatical in faith for the country. There was some idea of founding a patriarchal estate, the girls to be married and settled there, the property shared by future generations. Through thirty years they toiled in their wild acres.

From that rich river-loam they won every necessity of daily life save matches to light the fire. For flour they grew rice and cassava, sugar-cane for molasses, they drank their own coffee instead of tea, provided their own meat and game, all vegetables, citrus and tropical fruits, maize, milk, butter, cheese, bacon and hams from the wild pigs penned and fattened, honey, jams, soap, millet for brooms—there was no storekeeper's bill. Chairs, tables and furnishings were the work of their hands in the homestead of sturdy paperbark logs under noble shade trees and vivid poincianas. They plaited their own ropes of horsehair, halters and bridles of greenhide. They made their own workaday dresses and riding-kit of khaki, white muslins for Sunday with its church service at home. They slept on beds of saplings and plaited cowhide, with mattresses of sweet-smelling husks. They were deep readers, fluent in philosophy, their world in atlases and books—the real thing was out of bounds. Though they rode, unafraid, through black man's country, never without their father's escort were they seen in the white man's outpost of Adelaide River, eight miles away.

But these patriarchal plans gang aft a-gley. The sons, when they came of age, left home. The mother, with younger children, travelled to the south. A quaint little story is told of Connie's wedding. She answered an advertisement in the northern paper of a contract for fencing on a station two hundred miles away. Given the job, she rolled her swag and travelled down by train. The station-owner arrived and consulted the guard:

"There should be a feller on this train coming to my place fencing. Seen anything of him? C. Sargent is the name."

The guard grinned. "There he is," he said, indicating a tall girl waiting in the shade.

"Go on! No jokes."

"That's C. Sargent," said the guard. "If y'want a good fencer, grab her. There's not a better fencer in the north."

The station-owner disclosed to Connie that he was a bachelor, and solved the problem by a proposal of marriage. So the bride stayed at the little bush pub till a parson came down the line, and away they went in a buck-board to sink post-holes out on the Waterhouse River. When he died she sold the station of their pioneering, and is now living in the south.

Winnie stayed at Stapleton, her whole life spent on her own patch of earth, working cattle, plantation and tin-mines through the nightmare years of war. The only girl in the war zone for two of those years, she was affectionately known—at a distance—to the American and Australian troops as "Two Gun Winnie". Her courage, her strength, her fearless nature, her indomitable spirit in a country that can be far more cruel than kind, have proved her one of the great women of the Territory.

Not all were madonnas in search of haloes. There were a few "hard cases" that blazed an erratic trail, holding their own as a man in that land of men. Among these were "Cockney Fan" and "the Wolfram Queen".

Fannie Haynes came overland in the nineties in a coach and four from Charters Towers to Wandi with her first husband, Cody, said to be a brother of Buffalo Bill. They opened a little hessian store when the goldfields were in swing. Cody died. At his wake men fought with fists for his pretty curly-headed wife, but she had a will of her own. She married Tom Crush, a member of parliament for the Territory, and they built the Federation Hotel at Brock's Creek.

For forty years Fannie *was* Brock's Creek. When Tom Crush died she married Harry Haynes, a one-legged old bushman, to watch her interests, which consisted of horses, while she was serving in the bar. Travellers camped in the joss-house or unrolled their swags under the trees around the Federation, for all through the wet, ducks, dogs, chooks and goats camped inside with Fannie. She brought her mother from Houndsditch, but the old lady passed away. Brock's Creek was too far from the Old Kent Road.

At least one of Fannie's sayings has become a Territory proverb. A priest happened along one day, a tornado in his wake. They heard it rip-roaring through the bush, trees cracking under the lightning in a black squall of rain that veered for the pub.

"Quick!" cried the priest. "We'll pray."

"No, we won't! We'll cover up the bloody flour!" growled Fannie, and off she waddled to spread a tarpaulin over the bags.

God helps those who help themselves—but Fannie helped many in her day. She knew every mine in the ranges, every scratch in the hills that showed colours, and she grubstaked the prospectors old and young for years on end, trying to make a big find.

In 1940 came the war and its cloud of khaki. Fannie was seventy and twenty-two stone. She refused to go south. Time and again she defied them to evict her. At last a lieutenant and half a brigade alighted from the train, in battle file marching on the old Federation. Fannie met them on the flat, a gun in one hand and a bottle of lysol in the other.

"Right about turn and quit!" she yelled, "or I'll shoot you with this and drink that!"

They retreated.

Nevertheless, Fannie had to go. Six provosts loaded her on a truck with her poor old one-legged husband, and away they went to Adelaide, willy-nilly, not even a black-boy to look after them on the way. For weeks in Adelaide Hospital she hovered near to death, then made a complete recovery, and gaily flew to Sydney. But in Sydney she died.

. . . as May Brown died, the Wolfram Queen. A woman who fought her way all over the wide country died in a residential in the dark heart of a city. A fine figure was Mrs Brown, always very smartly dressed, with a forbidding front and a cynical eye. She married three times in the north, like Cockney Fan.

"May Seale, May Burns, May Brown, May God forgive you!" shouted a witty old prospector she once threw out of a pub.

Her first husband had been an amateur light-weight champion of New South Wales. He taught her to box. She was not afraid of anything in Australia. When fellows were fresh, she knocked them out with an upper-cut to the chin. When she didn't like their ways, she rode them down with a stock-whip. Her enemies kept out of her way, and her friends minded their p's and q's.

A beauty in youth, a startling belle of the ball, and an excellent cook and housekeeper when she liked, May had contempt for the feminine grooves of life. She was a gambler—horse-racing, poker or mines, mostly mines. She knew all the mineral fields, and backed the best, was first white woman at Tanami, a thousand miles down in the desert, in 1909. Her say-so on any goldfield rocked the market in shares.

When rich deposits of wolfram were unearthed near Pine Creek, May "married the mine". She worked it herself with ninety-five Chinamen, forty-five miles from the nearest neighbour, sixty feet down in the earth with the coolies grubbing ore, and those coolies she ruled with a rod of iron. "Crest of the Wave" they called it, and into her bank account May shovelled £11,000 a year throughout the first war. A wealthy woman, she was away to the Melbourne Cup with brilliants in her heels and off for a trip or two to Monte Carlo. In September 1918 she refused £14,000 for the mine. In November the Armistice was signed—wolfram and the Crest of the Wave fell flat. She picked a few more winners during the next thirty years and, a good loser, when times were bad, worked like a Trojan keeping cafés and hotels in Darwin.

Legends still go the rounds of the Wolfram Queen. She would rather go down to history as a Tartar than as a saint, but the old hands remember another side to her nature that very few were privileged to see.

When Umbrawarra dragged on for two years its ghastly tragedies of fever, May Brown was the only woman of those gullies, forgetting her own interests, riding with food and water for the dying, a nurse of unexpected gentleness in many a man's last hours, and then, with a black-boy, burying the dead.

There is one vignette of her life I cannot forget, a story told to me during her lifetime by a Government officer connected with the mines. It was on the veranda of the old Victoria one night when anecdotes of her doings had provoked a good deal of laughter.

"I have great respect for Mrs Brown," he said, "since I once travelled down with her on the Pine Creek train. May was enthroned in the carriage in all her glory when a woman and child were carried in—there was only one women's compartment, as you know. The baby, eighteen months old, had been in the throes of convulsions. The mother was, almost hourly, expecting another child. A few bushmen, mining men and blacks were the only other passengers that day on the train.

"It was a long, slow journey—cruel heat hour after hour. The child had moaned pitifully all through the morning. Mrs Brown did what she could—it was beyond nourishment, but with wet cloths and a fan she tried to keep the poor little mite cool. When we left Adelaide River it fell into a deep sleep. The mother, too, slept. Five hours still to go. Something unnatural in the position of the child caught old May's attention. She lifted it, and discovered it was dead. The mother immediately stirred in nervous fright, and cried to know the trouble, fearing another convulsion.

"Realizing that shock to the mother might mean serious complications, that there was no medical help nearer than Darwin and that nothing could be done by the men on the train, Mrs Brown rose to sublime heights.

" 'Everything's right,' she said. 'I'll mind her. You go to sleep.'

"She arranged a handkerchief over the face of the dead child, and nursed it on her knee, assuring the watchful mother all the way. At Rum Jungle she called to the guard that a telephone message be sent at once for medical help to meet them when the train drew in to Parap. The mother was restless and very ill. May dared not move lest the truth be known that the child lay dead in her arms.

"It was not till late afternoon, when we drew in to Parap and the ambulance waiting, with the doctor, that we knew what had happened.

" 'No panic!' said May. 'If she found out the poor little blighter was gone, and gave birth to a child on that hell of a train of yours, they'd both be dead by now. I'm nearly dead myself. Get out of my way!' "

Queer weavings of women's lives into a grim tapestry.

These random sketches of mine, so little more than a list of names, are but poor and passing tribute to a few, but no other word of honour and remembrance has yet come their way. How could we hope to span the long and lonely years, travail of birth, shadows of death, in all that is the average woman's happiness and pride the poverty of their days? Theirs was a very different life—fighting to win, for the children's sake, in a land where men failed.

Women, as the bushmen said, look a lifetime ahead. The roots of their faith and hope ran deep, binding that fickle earth. Though they themselves were deprived and forgotten, they knew it was not in vain.

Chapter XXVII

Kingdom Come

That's the appropriate country—there, man's thought,
Rarer, intenser,
Self-gathered for an outbreak, as it ought,
Chafes in the censer!

. . . .

All the peaks soar, but one the rest excels;
Clouds overcome it;
No, yonder sparkle is the citadel's
Circling its summit!

BROWNING.

WE, WHO know it so well, believe in the Northern Territory. We believe that *fata Morgana* future will some day soon come true, on foundations firm and successful as those of every other State.

We believe that the Territory should now be named and declared the seventh Australian State. With highroads and by-roads to all the outposts, sky-roads to link with each of the capital cities in a day, and a population of eleven thousand since the end of the war, it is no longer Ultima Thule, "bad lands" far away. An integral, a vital sector of the Commonwealth, and the third largest, both in area and seaboard, it should surely now be raised to full status of a State, with political independence and constitutional powers, but its chief need is people—before decay sets in again and the eleven thousand fade away.

Ever improved transport, lower freights, and unlocking of the land to settlers will bring the people. That country should be measured in acres, as the rest of Australia is now, not by the thousand square miles. The people, for a beginning, can be their own markets and in varied production share those of Australia, until they can bid for a place in the markets of the world.

They should not be selected by Governments, set in a row in cardboard erections of Government towns, and paid to stay there for three or five years in a Lilliputian tangle of red tape, those booby-traps of bureaucratic tyranny, Gilbertian in an empty land, that have tripped up Territory progress every step of the way. Towns are deep-rooted only in industry—of their own vitality, like Topsy, they grow. Nor should the people be nomads and no-hopers who, seeking a lazy oblivion, have given the north a bad name. That country needs men and women with the ideals and fidelity of the pioneers. These are still to be found in Australia and, given the opportunity of a patch of earth to call their own, they will not fail. For time is with them, the machine age.

Instead of being a hundred years behind the rest of the continent, the Ter-

ritory was a hundred years ahead. Colonization there calls for the manpower of at least a million, and not of Asiatic coolies, the old bogy of black labour. In a land that exacts superhuman strength and resistance, perpetual motion, resolution of steel, subjugation of body and soul, a few lone battlers had never a hope to change the face of Nature. But now science, to use the colloquialism, has all the answers. Mechanical science has worked wonders up there in the past ten years.

Those miracle roads, the Stuart Highway a thousand easy miles from Alice Springs to Darwin, the Barkly Highway across dry desert from Camooweal to Tennant's Creek, were a job for slaves of the Pyramids, yet in less than a year in the war machine they were raced through nowhere to somewhere. Hundreds of bores gushed infinite water in a so-called waterless land to maintain a hundred thousand men for five years on the main highway alone in camps of comfort. Radar unveiled the lonely coasts. Passenger planes now skim the red vague where packhorses stumbled a year on the trail and dead men were not found. Road-trains carry hundreds of tons of stores to stations that starved on bad flour and fly-blown salt beef. Bulldozers, tractors, graders, clear the waterholes, grub trees, rocks and ant-hills to make stock routes and roads. Electric shovels and diamond drills, instead of the pick of a hatter, are prospecting for gold.

Flying Doctor, MacRobertson-Miller and Connellan Airways circle the farthest outposts every week, twelve stations in a day, bringing medical help, mail, friends, parcels, correspondence lessons for children, to those who once were for a lifetime lost. Modern cars, radios, refrigerators, wind power and electric plants for lighting, washing machines and fans, septic tanks, Flying Doctor radio-telephones, carpets, lawns and gardens make happy homes for white women where twenty years ago a homestead was a hurricane lamp hung on a post, a couple of rawhide beds with blue blankets, fowls roosting in the old buckboard, and a lubra trailing through the torrid day, unhonoured wife, housekeeper of sorts, mother of a rising generation.

The only trouble with the Territory is that of the rest of Australia—there is too much of it. A big country needs handling in a big way. We must spend millions to treble the millions, apply modern science to the bushman's hard-won knowledge and experience, use the immensity and profusion of Nature as an ally instead of trying to fight it down.

Let us build reservoirs and towns on the hills for cool and wholesome air and safety from floods, forgetting the squalid hollows where lubras still carry stagnant waters in a procession of petrol tins on their curly heads. Let us rein in the thirty big rivers, one by one, and the thousand steep creeks for irrigation, hydro-electric power for transport, industry and mines of payable ore, but mainly for irrigation.

Vision blesses the eyes first to behold. I believe with McDouall Stuart that a great future lies in agriculture: "If this country is settled, it will be one of the brightest under the Crown, suitable for the growth of anything and everything—a splendid country for cotton."

Cotton is a fortune today. It has been proved many times, as I have shown in these pages. From Mataranka to Port Essington it blows wild along rivers and coasts since the earlies, when blacks would plough and plant for a clay pipe, and then go bush from the picking. Now there are cotton-picking machines.

Half a million square miles of fertile earth can and must produce at least one cereal food for its people. Beautiful rice country is found everywhere along Daly and Adelaide rivers, where crops have never failed, but the pick of the Territory for rice-growing—perhaps the best in Australia—are the Cecelias, five little plains running north and south along Darwin River, perfect irrigation land. In the old days they gave sixty bushels to the acre of heavy full-bodied grain to feed thousands of coolies, who shipped it home as of better quality than all the rice in China.

Maize will grow anywhere. On the Daly and Adelaide, tobacco, cinchona, sugar, and on Katherine and Roper peanuts—sixty bushels to the acre with all their by-products—failed only through lack of labour and transport, and in floods.

I do not think the Territory can compete with Queensland in production of tropical fruits, but in garden produce the Army farms in wartime, at Coomallie, Adelaide River and Katherine, were news to the world, in small acreage maintaining in vegetables well over a hundred thousand men. Professor Robert Bowman, an American soil scientist, noted that

> ten weeks after transplanting, individual cabbages had attained a weight of 27¼ lbs, tomatoes ripened six weeks after being transplanted, and on one occasion 13,000 lbs of tomatoes were harvested from 1½ acres of land a month after transplanting. Individual lettuce plants weighed 3½ lbs and consignments over 2½ lbs per head. The variety of produce grown on these Northern Territory farms is astonishing.

All the rivers of the Timor fall have many permanent reaches to twenty miles long, crying to be channelled into rich river silts for fields of cultivation. Every station garden north of the Tropic for seven months of the year is an indication of the wealth of that red earth, and for the other five months feet deep under water.

Katherine River Gorge alone, twelve miles above the township, is a godsend to any country—thirteen miles of bold water never less than twenty feet deep nestled under high cliffs, running on gravity through eight feet deep of chocolate and black sandy loams in a good climate for human living and temperate zone and semi-tropical produce. In every annual wet the Katherine, Flora, Edith, Ferguson and a dozen other big rivers all run to waste down the Daly, a hundred and fifty miles long in the main stream and eighty feet deep half a mile wide to the sea. On Flora River near Price's Creek ninety million gallons a day are pouring over a twenty-foot fall to a glorious reach four miles long where you could float a battleship, twelve miles above the junction with the Daly. This is in one chain only. The Roper is the same prodigal flow—ten million gallons a day are lost in one cataract at Bitter Springs. Out west, there are seven million acres of fertility on Victoria River alone.

All rivers with rock-bottomed natural dams could be locked at small cost. A little elementary engineering could hold back the torrent of the gorges and countless creeks and springs, and head them down to their fertile flats and gullies to supply any State in Australia in times of need with greens, root and salad vegetables of record size and excellent flavour, delivered by freight planes to the south. Even English potatoes, nine tons to the acre, were grown by Tom Pearce at Willeroo, and Daly settlers harvested broom millet, eight tons to the acre, ninety-inch staple.

Wherever you go you hear of rivers never heard of before. Some of the richest agricultural land is on the eastern side of the Gulf, where Macarthur,

Kilgour, Roper, Limmen, Rosy, Hodgson, and a score of others are fed by myriad bountiful springs. Arnhem Land is a network of impetuous streams from hundreds of miles of clear bubbling springs—Waterhouse, Chambers, Flying Fox, Mainoru, Wilton, King, Liverpool, Blithe, Glyde, Goyder, to name a few wide as the Murray, all lost in swamps. On East Alligator, with a dairy herd on Oenpelli lagoons, Paddy Cahill in Gilruth's time kept Darwin in first-quality butter, and the old Kapalgo Mission on South Alligator had one of the finest gardens in the north.

But according to authority the best river in the Territory for agriculture is the Goyder, with its tributaries, swamps and lagoons. For some obscure meteorological reason, rain falls nearly all the year round out there. Its soils are a black friable loam, silt and humus undisturbed for millions of years, and white ants of a destructive variety are few. In 1883 David Lindsay said it was first-class sugar country, and in 1903 Captain Joseph Bradshaw, after two years' occupation, proclaimed it perfection for sugar and rice. His vanished Arafura Station will be a garden some day.

"If you bury a man on the Goyder," the two or three old hands who have seen it will tell you, "the soil's so good that he'll come up a week before Resurrection Day. The only trouble is too much water. Half the year you need a diving suit to go and pick a tomato."

So much for the far north. The Centre has its own wealth. Below the Daly Waters' southward fall are the "silent rivers", the sub-artesian country, and an artesian basin of twenty-five thousand square miles. Safeguard for generations are the numerous bores on every station, each now running many thousands of gallons a day, of unvarying flow during the longest drought, into earth tanks for the cattle. Of these mysterious waters Ernest Favenc, as far back as 1879, in poetic prose has written, looking through the yellow haze of the Barklys with prophetic eyes:

> 'Water! water! everywhere, and not a drop to drink' . . . this quotation might be uttered with a strong measure of truth by many a poor wretch perishing from thirst on a drought-blasted inland plain, whilst underneath him . . . run sunless seas. Of the magnitude of our great subterranean reservoir who shall tell? . . . Only when here and there we tap it, and the mighty pressure sends up a thin column of water hundreds of feet in answer. Or when we notice the strong, constant springs that at intervals break through the surface crust to gladden us; or when the deeper internal fires burst forth, and hurl up its waters in scathing steam and boiling mud, can we guess of the great hidden sea beneath. . . .
>
> In our fair continent there are thousands upon thousands of square miles of fertile country that Nature herself has planned and mapped out into wide fields. . . . What traveller but has noticed the magical effect of rain upon the deep friable soil. . . . Within a short time the dry and withered stalks of grass assume a deep rich green. . . . The bare ground is quickly coated with trailing vines and creepers. . . .

Ours "to convey the living waters over the great pasture lands . . . bring the interior waters to the surface . . . to make Australia the richest . . . country that sun ever shone upon". Already there are orange groves and vineyards in the red rock valleys and great plains two hundred miles east and west of Alice Springs.

H. Y. L. Brown, in his five years' geological survey and classification of country, set down thirty thousand square miles of the Territory as good agricultural land, ten thousand square miles as rich mineral belt, and a hundred and fifty-eight thousand square miles as good grazing country. Larry Wells, who completed the trig survey from Camooweal to Hall's Creek, predicted millions of sheep for the Barkly Tablelands and for the headwaters of Victoria River. Wave Hill has an average rainfall of thirty inches a year, with Flinders, mimosa, rye grasses and salt-bush. Sixty per cent of that country could be opened up for sheep, the endless bleat that is Australia's national anthem.

Progress in the cattle industry depends on prices, now a fanciful £40 a head, and on smaller, well-regulated holdings. There is no truth in the libel that "you can't run a cat in this country under five thousand square miles". Rainfall and pastures vary, I know, from four inches to ninety, from boundless heavens of Mitchell grass and lake clover to bare beach sand and stones, but apart from the Simpson Desert, south-east of Alice Springs, and the Great Sandy Desert, south-west of Powell's Creek, so rapid is recuperation of even the worst patches in a single shower of rain—herbage all over the sandhills, "tableland mulga" all over the stones—that all Territory cattle lands are good.

Simpson Desert is utterly undeveloped and, in fact, unseen, save by Ted Colson, an intrepid bushman, and the expedition of Dr C. T. Madigan who named it, noted geologist and last of the Australian explorers. His graphic and beautifully written books, *Central Australia* and, especially, *Crossing the Dead Heart*, less for their scientific reserve than for their rare sense of humanness and humour, will long be remembered. Nearly all of his troubles and adventures in the Simpson Desert were caused by heavy and widespread rains. In the Great Sandy Desert Nathaniel Buchanan's solitary track, a camel-pad from Tennant's Creek north-west to Wave Hill and south to the South Australian border, is forty years old.

Of occupied country, how many Territory stations have failed? How many, in the past seventy years, though abandoned from cattle tick, drought, or some tragedy of isolation, have vanished from the map? Very few. South Australia, in the region of Cooper's Creek and Lake Eyre, has suffered a much more disastrous cycle than the Territory, with its assured monsoon rainfall, could ever know. Yet even that heartbreak desert, the worst in Australia, redeemed by recent colossal floods, is now a fairytale.

Despite the Great Australian Wail by newspapers and Governments for settlement of the north, there is little chance for the earnest young pioneer.

Big companies have closed over the land in leaseholds granted for fifty and ninety years. In some cases they have merely held these lands. The manager of one of the great runs, out in his utility in all directions practically every day for seven years, told me he had seen no more than two-thirds of his country. One English company has owned a straight run of adjoining stations to forty thousand square miles all told for the past thirty-five years, and they are by no means an empire-builders' documentary of inspiration in achievement. Another English company, a household word, runs them a close second in vast area occupied, and very little achieved.

Far off the fairways, away out in the rough, I have travelled to other company holdings, of rivers and ranges enough for an Old World kingdom, to find one spectre of a white man "sitting down" in a ruined hut two hundred miles deep in the bush with a mob of blacks—stock-boys and stock-girls who galloped the ranges shooting wild horses, throwing the lumbering bulls that run thirty and forty together, cutting their knee-tendons to lame them and so keep them on the run, and gouging out their four-foot wavy horns. This was the "cattle work". On some of these stations no mustering, droving and selling had been done in years, and this in wartime, when queues were streets long in Melbourne and Sydney, clutching their ration-books, hungering for a steak. Many a white man had a "veranda job", his not to reason why. He stayed home to bake bread and dole out tobacco to the blacks from the only house in five or ten thousand square miles, built in the eighties and a hollow shell of white ants. They worked blacks only, not even a half-caste head stockman. One had not left the homestead in four years.

Throughout the Territory, until very recently, there was little or no culling of cattle or introduction of new blood that gives stamina to resist disease, except on the best stations, nearest in, that make the periodic beef fortunes of war. From certain big runs notorious for neglect, the drovers were the dread of the road to the Tablelands stations lest in passing through with their rangy spotted beasts, all hips and horns, old stock inbred, they should drop their hat-rack calves and pantomime cows to impair the breed of well-conducted herds.

It is sad to see, in this mass-production world, that most of the old nation-builders, hag-ridden by high finance, have sold out to the companies, leaving nothing for young pioneers. Smaller holdings, easy to handle and with good waters, should be reserved from outsize stations for cattle-men of experience and ambition who still value heritage and home. Renewal of large-scale leases should depend on production, improvements, development, and the number of men employed according to area of land. Every big mustering-camp and yard by a good waterhole should be a homestead, to give some comfort in life to the men who live for weeks in a swag and, like the blacks, must wait till their fortieth or fiftieth year, when initiation into managership may give them the right of a home for children and wife.

The mineral wealth has been too long a legend for us to go into a headache of statistics where luck's a fortune. Strange to say, legends of the Territory usually come true—always with the exception of Lasseter's Reef, the "cave of gold" that recalls *King Solomon's Mines*.

In this year, 1951, the Territory proudly announces a mineral revenue of £886,139—gold, £624,959; wolfram, £116,927; copper, £60,084; tin, £15,000, and other minerals £2600. This is far and away a record for all time.

According to reliable geologists there are two "vast mineral fields" that straggle across the country in chains of ranges and isolated hills, one from Cloncurry and Mount Isa in a southern half-moon through Toko, Tarleton, Jervois, Haartz, Arltunga, Winnecke, MacDonnell, north through Ashburton Ranges at Barrow and Tennant's Creek, outcrops at Granites and Tanami, and so to West Australia; the other in a northern half-moon from the Gulf and Arnhem Land via the coast and Mary River, Pine Creek, Fitzmaurice River and again to Kimberley. A region of hope for the gold explorer, now that its perils are a page of the past, is Arnhem Land. H. Y. L. Brown in 1905 found auriferous quartz at Arnhem Bay, and wrote that "the country around Caledon Bay is worth prospecting for minerals, including gold". Dr Julian Tenison Woods, in 1885, after a long and hazardous ride there, prophesied that "the peninsula of Arnhem Land will yet become one of the greatest mining centres in Australia".

Tennant's Creek, now a little Kalgoorlie, began with the legend of the lubra bringing the pickle-bottle full of gold to old Tom Nugent at Banka Banka in the eighties. Alan Davidson put down a couple of shafts there in 1902, found a leader, and predicted the field. When I first passed by in 1932, Waldemar Holtze and Woodroffe, two of Todd's Men, were alone at the telegraph station, and a few woolly-nosed prospectors lost for years in the waterless hills. When Granites gold was in the air, a man named Udall camped with his wife seven miles south of the telegraph well, rigged up a battery of their Ford car to a disused shaft of some old hopeful, brought to the Alice a few "gold stones" when it was full of gold stones, and tried to sell the mine. Granites prospectors, loth to go home, started to dig out the spinifex, carried their water forty miles, and brought down the first small ingots of Tennant's Creek's dark ironstone gold. Soon they were selling their claims for the legendary thousands. New Moon, El Dorado, Mount Samuel and half a dozen other mines founded a new Australian town with a steady population of a thousand, and a yield, all told, of millions. Most of the old "mopokes" said they would "give it a year". An item in the newspaper before me tells me that "Australian Development N.L. at Tennant's Creek crushed 1,226 tons of ore from its Noble's Nob mine in the four weeks ending on February 7, 1951, for 2,393 ounces of gold. The crushing was worth £36,500". One month, one mine. Twenty years have passed, and Tennant's Creek is still there.

A shallow £3,000,000 on the shovels of starving men was won from around Pine Creek in the seventies, when gold was £3 5s. Now it is £15 an ounce. There is no shaft deeper than the one at Spring Hill, three hundred and sixty feet, though diamond drills have disclosed gold to seven hundred and fifty feet, and a bore put down at Union Reefs, a thousand and seventy-three feet, in quartz, carried two and a half ounces to the ton.

Fortunes in wolfram in wartime were taken from Wauchope and Hatch's Creek—the most valuable deposits in Australia, seventy per cent tungstenic acid ores. These, too, were discovered by Davidson in 1902, first freight into Queensland on camels in 1917, across Elkedra on an eighty-mile dry stage. Haartz Range mica was considered a poor man's pickings for many years—the camels would carry four tons through Arltunga to buy a few stores for the gougers out in the jagged hills around Plenty River, Ulgarrina, Spotted Tiger, and Blackfellow's Bones. Then radio science revolutionized the market, with insulators of mica for condensers and valves. Now the demand for Central Australian mica, in all electrical work, powdered in paints and papers, spangled in cellophane, and winking in neon signs, is in step with an infinite supply.

For news of tremendous lodes of copper, silver-lead, rich reef tin, and many an iron blow of tens of thousands of tons—of tantalite, ozocerite, arsenic, bismuth, manganese, read back the mining reports of the past fifty years. Radium ores were discovered at Mount Diamond, Wandi and Tanumbirini—visions of fabulous wealth at £565,000 an ounce—but of these pitchblende and uranium ores too little then was known, now, alas! too much. Around Borroloola sixty per cent copper ores were mined till the last of the miners, alone in the ranges, shot himself about twenty years ago. On Victoria River seams of lignitic coal and shale oil were found. One Robert Aikman, for a mineral oil syndicate, pegged a thousand acres in a gorge thirty miles from Holdfast Reach, loaded thirty barrels of shale oil in the first week, but "the blacks was bad", and he had to throw on the packs in a hurry for a three-hundred-mile ride, and go. The South Australian Government boring party at Port Keats, which struck good shale at seven hundred feet, and the oil concessions at Cape Wilberforce and Elcho Island in Arnhem Land, were abandoned for the same good reason. There was never transport for enough food to eat, packhorse freights, when they came through, to £60 a ton, and even the little railway £5 10s. a ton.

Geological surveys to assess all the old well-known fields and to open up new ones would be quite useless without cheap heavy transport to carry out machinery and bring back ores. The obvious solution is, where possible, to make use of the navigable rivers and natural harbours for flat-bottomed barges and lighters. There has never been a Government endeavour worthy of the name to colonize by sea, and until the war no thought of a survey in a century.

The sea-lights of the east coast of Australia are never lost. As one fades hull down, another twinkles on the port bow. In the north they were a thousand miles apart—in fact, except for Point Charles, at the entrance to Darwin Harbour, Cape Don was a lone star. A thousand reefy miles to Borroloola, east, and five hundred miles to the Victoria, west, the only guiding lights were the corroboree fires of the wild blacks. Buoys and beacons, such as they were, were swept away in the first high tide. In Darwin Harbour itself for years a ten-gallon drum was moored on a shoal east of the jetty. Another tossed on the Vernon Shoals at the entrance to Van Diemen's Gulf, another on the notorious *Henry Ellis* reef. Four beer-barrels for a little while marked the mouth of the Roper, then sank in a gale, and a ship entering the Macarthur hung hurricane lamps on mangrove poles on the sandbanks at low tide to guide it up in the high.

A travesty were the ships of three generations from *Ark* to *Zulieka*, from the twelve-ton *Flying Cloud* of 1875 to the twenty-five-ton *Maroubra* of 1935. Luggers, launches and old ghosts of steamers, none of them more than sixty tons, rotted by teredo, battered in hurricanes, they spent days at the mouth of a river, moaning at the bar, weeks in the estuaries, dodging with the tide, then months in Darwin Harbour, waiting for spare parts. To cover that utterly lonely coastline of about three thousand miles there was never more than one, with a skipper, a half-caste boy as crew, and a passenger once in six months who slept on deck in his swag.

What hope had the country of progress when, by land or sea, there was nothing to conquer the merciless and unending miles?

Of the natural resources—the timbers of rare beauty for furniture and panellings, and safe from white ants if shipped to the south; an ocean full of sea-food, oysters and fish; bamboo and cane-grasses sufficient to keep the whole of Australia in mattings and basket-weave, wattle-bark for tanning, kapok, painters' colours, snakeskin, crocodile hides, and eucalyptus oils to cure the colds of the world—we shall not begin to speak. What is the use of talking, where white men have sat down and talked about it all their lives—they do nothing about it in the dry because the ground is too hard, and they can't do anything in the wet.

What was the use of grubstaking a prospector when he was either killed by the blacks, or perished, or starved?—or of one man trying to construct a dam, or to dredge a powerful river for the passage of a boat?

The truth is, the people of that country have never had enough to eat.

Winnecke, after thirty-five years of exploration, wrote: "I am astounded at the use of the word desert. The Northern Territory will, in my opinion, be a great productive country when opened up and reclaimed by the rising generation, and I think no white race is more suitable to settle there than Australians."

The rising generation—there's the rub. What has that country to give its children, as compared with the advantages of the south? How can they earn a living there? For what rewards the hardship and the striving of a very meagre life?

With even the wartime services in nourishing foodstuffs and fruit, with free selection of land and industry allowed to parents of purpose and perception, a school and health centre in every town, high schools, agricultural colleges and schools of mines not more than a thousand miles apart, and a university at Alice Springs—to correct our overbalanced brain of seven universities south of 28° and never a one above--we might begin to provide for those young Territorians, children of pioneers, what is the right of every child in every other State. Cattle will make way for the human in many a valley of promise and, its picturesque wild oats forgotten, the Territory become a land of homes.

The second hundred years will write a different story. When science is our friend instead of our mortal enemy, the war machine a robot of productivity in peace, when mankind can be trusted with atomic power in the atomic age, we shall no longer look upon our Territory as a howling wilderness that never stops howling, but as a wilful, lavish land, needing, as humans do, the applied psychology of human love.

Chapter XXVIII

The Last Bushman, or H.M.S. "Coolabah Tree"

> The swag and the billy again.
> Here's how!
> The trail and the packhorse again.
> KIPLING.

YOU'LL MEET the last of him in the Territory now, or "back o' Queensland", or over in the Kimberleys. Future Australians will see him in tapestry or mosaic, antediluvian as King Arthur's knights. He is a knightly figure. Red-brown as the country, riding, he is a terra-cotta bas-relief already.

He followed the explorers, without pay, without a "job". He colonized a continent with a water-bag on the saddle, swung clear of his own world to find a new one. His bridle track has become a highway.

Of such men were John Costello of Queensland, David Lindsay of the Territory and the West, Nat Buchanan of all three, Delisser, first across the Nullarbor Plain, Ted Colson, first across Simpson Desert, Ridley Williams, and little Frank Hann, who rode for twenty years with a withered leg, writing names in nameless desert.

In infinity of earth and air they were all prisoned as surely as by iron bars, chained to waters, bound by hunger and thirst, and with a tether as long as horseshoes would last. But the line of the horizon held their eyes—green valleys behind the old red ranges? They took a chance and rode on, life in the water-bag, to find rivers beyond the last mirage.

Never pity them. Never praise them. They liked "ridin' around lookin' at country". They were neither rich nor poor, having no need of money, nor were they lonely, at home in the big quietness under the stars.

A waterhole was their shrine of bush romance, with a camp under a shady tree, a spiral of blue smoke and a billy boiling—wistful mirror, silently dreaming, reflecting a continent's history.

The Australian bush gives you liberty, fraternity and equality in full measure. It reduces humanity, black, white and in-between, to its highest common factor in double-quick time—no paltry distinctions, no petty dignity, hail, fellow, well met! All men and women there are children of circumstance. Life's essentials are flour to eat and water to drink—sometimes, in the big distances, mighty little of either. You are glad to eat stale damper out of the hand. You will praise God for a running creek and come back rejoicing, with bullfrogs in the water-bag, from the last muddy semblance of water in a pool. You will sleep sound on stones. A far-away smoke is the camp-fire of a friend, though you may not yet have met him, and a lifelong friend at that. They always are when you meet them out bush.

The first bushman rode out of Sydney in Governor Phillip's time, something new in the rank and file of mankind, civilized man with no need of civilization. He could live like the blacks in a black man's country, and build a white man's empire. Where most men evolve the furniture of a house in a street, he evolved the furniture of an empty million square miles. The swag, a roll of canvas eight feet by ten, was his bed, his wardrobe, his roof in the rain, a saddle his pillow and easy chair, a quart-pot his kettle and cup, a dish and a camp-oven his bathroom and kitchen, a fire his lamp in the night. Jingle-bells in the saddle-pouch as he rode the silent bush were his "jewellery"—knives and a pannikin or two, the long wire pot-hooks to lift his camp-oven from its bed in the coals, a sheath-knife and a couple of two-pronged forks. He carried his traditions in his swag for two generations across a continent. Time serves. He is fading out of the picture today.

As a rule he is tall and gaunt—you might call him stringy—sinew and muscle only, the right build for a hundred miles of riding in the day, no dead weight for a horse. Blue-shirted, bow-legged from a childhood in the saddle, his trousers low-belted on his hips, he has the neat small feet of a dancer in their high-heeled elastic-side boots—years in the stirrups at tension of prop, turn and gallop have given them high arches. The handkerchief knotted around his neck is his old school tie. Ready for anything, like Jason, he carries Medea's needle, threaded, in his hat, the wide-brimmed felt that he wears at a careless but characteristic angle, something of the cavalier about it. He raises that hat to no man, but he touches it to any.

Hail him, he'll give you a pleasant "G'day!" He may go by at a canter, but, make no mistake, he has your brands and descriptions. Horses, cattle and men he can judge at a glance. He never judges a woman. He calls her "missus" whether she is a schoolgirl of twelve or a spinster of eighty.

His face, often enough, reminds you of George Lambert's "Light Horseman", and his eyes, when blue, are the grey-blue of the distance. His hair, from the bleach of the sun, will be early white. He may have, or have had, a wife, but he doesn't need her. He can cook, wash, mend for himself incidentally to living. His camp-fire is his home, and you must never walk in on it uninvited. You make your own, and then make friends with him. He will share with you whatever he has, and forget it. But he likes a yarn later, tall as you like with a good laugh to it, and he won't forget that.

When you are yarning of blacks, or gold, or the wet, or what the country is good for, he will sit with you in the stockman's squat, a pipe gripped hard in his offside molars, and the second finger of his right hand tracing a mud-map in the sand . . . a mud-map of every range and river in two million square miles. He knows all about the "mighty resources". He rode that country before you were born, and there were others before him. The "explorers" who discover it now, in big expeditions equipped by societies and Governments, with pedal radios to order whatever they want and aeroplanes to find them when they are lost, have a knack of naming patches of it in their own honour. Sometimes they have time to ask his advice when their three-ton trucks break down. Of anthropologists, "experts", Homebush drovers and Mitchell Library bushmen, in the past ten years, he has met quite a few. At all the patter and platitudes of the north he doesn't even smile. When he gets too tired of "ear-wiggin' to a lot o' ballyhoo", he just uprises and walks away.

All you can tell him is child's talk to what he can teach you. He has kept diaries for thirty or forty years, not of people and events, but of distances and waters. When he rides a run for a couple of years, he knows every patch of red ground and black, every rock and tree on every creek and track, every *gilgai* that holds a drop of rain for a week in ten or twelve thousand square miles. He never learnt navigation or physics, but he can find his way anywhere under the sun without a compass—the true science of bushmanship. He knows where the first storms fall, and how much green feed to so many points of rain, and he can tell you how long each river and waterhole will last so many thousand cattle, allowing for evaporation, to within a few days.

The sky is his tent and the ground his bed, wet or dry. He can ride for weeks through monsoon rains with a mile swim at every river, and never change his clothes and never cough. When his horse knocks up in the stone country he can go on without it, and when his boots give out he can go on barefooted. A ninety-mile walk carrying food and water will not daunt him. He can ride blind.

He can track like a blackfellow, swearing to his own horses, mules, donkeys, shod and unshod, and even cattle, all the known animals, birds and lizards, also tyre-treads and boots. Tracking is not an abstruse aboriginal science, but merely observation, which the aboriginal possesses to a highly sensitive degree. Smoke-signals are easy with a prearranged code—he sets a hollow log on fire and fans it with dry or dense green bushes to send up the smoke in gusts, light and heavy, short and long—"I'll put up a wriggly smoke if there's cattle out there, and a straight one if there's none." Every tin on a tree, every branch on the road, had significance. The old-time SOS was three shots of a rifle, an interval of a minute, then three more. If a man had no rifle or if there were no response, he set the scrub on fire. Smoke was the national news of the wild and wide.

He strikes north on a grey day by making a compass of his pocket-knife standing erect on his finger-nail—it always casts a shadow. His water-wisdom is unique in the world. In the great arid wilderness he finds water by the flight of birds at daylight or sundown, by an emu track or a euro pad to a rock-hole, by limestone country with its probable springs, or by the water-loving trees—pandanus, paperbark and the baobab in the north, some kinds of mallee and needle-bush "down in Central". More often, he follows a dry creek down and feels for moisture under the stones. Where he finds it he digs a soak with a stick if he has no shovel, loosening the sand with a skewer movement, throwing out the earth with his hands, then patiently waiting for the water to make.

He carries it on in his water-bag. If that is torn, he shoves a stick through the frayed edges and lashes it round with spinifex string. If he has none he shoots a wallaby for the skin, and carries water in that, sprinkling grass on the surface to prevent it from splashing out, as the blacks do when they carry it in coolamons. When a shower falls he makes a tank of his camp-sheet tied between trees, a stone in the middle to weigh it down. If he has nothing but his shirt he hangs his shirt in the rain, first squeeze to wash it, second for the billy, boiled clear of impurities for tea. When all else fails he drinks the morning dew, brushing it from the leaves with a stick.

Watch him light a fire without matches in the wet. He hacks dry tinder from the heart of a tree or from rotten roots underground. Then he tears a bit of the top lining of his trousers, warm inside the belt, rubs it with tobacco-ash to make touch paper, takes a cartridge out of the rifle, puts it in the rag, fires it out, catches it, sets the smoulder to the shavings and away she goes. If he has neither pipe nor gun he strikes the pocket-knife downwards on a fringe of rag on a flinty stone till friction starts a spark, then doubles the cloth, blows hard and the spark lights up. Good wood for burning, when stripped, is found well under the bushes, and when the fire is stronger than the rain he whittles the wet from a log for the night, and turns in with his Birkmyre under and over. In sand country he digs a bed and lines it with his swag. In stone country he makes a hollow for his hip. In a high wind he gets well down behind low bushes, not under a tall and graceful tree with no real shelter and where branches may fall. The mosquitoes he stifles away with the smouldering comb of ant-hill or that masticated earth with which the white ants fill up hollow trees.

Coming to a river in flood, as one of them told me, "You don't sit down by the waters of Babylon and weep, like them old Jews. You get willin'. You make a raft of paperbark wrapped tight round saplings, with sharp sticks through as wedges, or you make a raft of your pack-saddles. First spread your Birkmyre, put your saddles on it flaps up, pack-bags inside an' swag on top, a long stick projectin' both ends, an' roll the sides of the Birkmyre round it with bridle-ropes an' halter-shanks. Best swimmers in front to pull, poor swimmers hangin' on behind an' over you go."

But all this is just bush lore, and if you travel with an old hand you will collect "mobs" of it. If you want to take notes of it and have no writing materials, he may shoot a turkey for a quill, or sharpen a bullet out of the old .44, or make you a pen of a splinter, and with ink of strong black tea you can write with any of these on a sheet of bark. He can tell you city time if you feel homesick—a hand-span for every two hours between the horizon and the sun—but he never bothers with clocks. Daylight, dinner-time and sundown will do.

"There's no time here. We go by the shadow," they told me at Borroloola when I asked the time. So they grow old without knowing.

Their cattle-watches they set by the rising and setting stars. "Call me when the Cross turns over," you will hear the drovers say, or "when the Pointers are clear". They never learnt astronomy, but they have their own constellations, the homely Frying-pan, the Ink-pot, the Emu and the Duck, nearer to them than the Greek gods, as the stars themselves are near in those bright Australian skies. The Milky Way is the Bridle Track, or sometimes the Hopple Chain. The Pleiades are the Bees' Nest. Sirius, ringing a steady note in the music of the spheres, is the Condamine Bell.

Proteins and carbohydrates never worried them. The menu out bush was simple. When you turned out for dinner-camp under a tree, you put on the billy and "cut off the dinner" for you and the blacks from a block of salt beef hewn, grained, seasoned and polished like old mahogany. Clamped to a hunk of damper, and splashed with "Kanowana chutney"—which is a bottle of Worcestershire sauce stirred into a tin of plum jam—you had a "thumb-piece" ready to serve. Dessert was "bush trifle"—johnnie cakes, jam and condensed milk—or a "bachelor's tart"—damper and jam—or, at the worst, "grandfather's puddin' "—stale damper soaked in black tea and sprinkled with sugar.

If you had a camp cook he rang the changes on "tinned dog" with curry or sea-pie; "Burdekin duck", meat fritters; "Hidden Treasure", meat fritters with onions; "bore-casing", macaroni; hobble-gobble of sago or rice; "blue-monge" of cornflour and currants; johnnie cakes, an occasional brownie, now and then a duff. But this was "livin' rich", and your brownie days soon were over. "Down in Central" they specialized in "Phar Laps", wild dog with the hair burnt off, trussed and cooked in the ashes *à l'anthropophage*, or a "Darling pie", baked rabbit and bindi-eyes, with scurvy grass for greens if you were diabetic or dietetic. A "Borroloola sandwich" was a goanna between two sheets of bark.

If you were living on the country there were a few things to know. Pandanus nuts must be soaked for a day or two and boiled to a pulp before they will go down. Bardies, the witchetty-grub of the Centre, are repulsively oily if cooked and eaten hot, but let them cool and they taste like yolk of egg with more flavour. The only edible part of the crocodile is his tail. You cook it blackfellow fashion in hot stones covered with earth and the fire on top, then skin it in flakes, and the firm white flesh beneath, I understand, is tasty and tender to a starving man. Roger Jose at Borroloola has his own recipe for flying-fox, and Paddy Cahill once gave directions for preparing venomous snakes *à la Kakadu*:

"Poisonous snakes are never killed with a stick to puncture the flesh. They must be caught in a forked stick, pinioned to the ground and their neck dislocated. They are then dragged through a fire till their scales fall off, scored along the back to prevent the skin from bursting, and coiled on the coals with their tails in their mouths. When cooked, the snake is carefully removed and opened up like a trough. It is full of gravy and the natives put their mouths to it and drink in great gusts. Then they eat the flesh."

On Groote Eylandt and along the shores of the Gulf are the scrubs of *munja*, zamia palm, the best little patch on Wierien River. The blacks shell the nuts with a stick, and eat not the kernel but the shell, which must be soaked for three or four days, preferably in running water, then dried in the sun till crisp, and pounded into flour. It makes very good dampers. Horace Foster, Tom Kieran, Andy Anderson, Roger Jose and the one or two others down there often lived for months on *munja* flour johnnie cakes fried in goat or dugong fat, with fish and wild honey, while waiting for the Borroloola boat.

The zamia rind must be well soaked or it is deadly poison. These were the nuts of the *Endeavour* journal at Cooktown that made Captain Cook's seamen violently ill and upset Sir Joseph Banks. In Borroloola graveyard is a stone to the memory of W. Sayle, one of the first Territory drovers, who died on the Wierien in 1883 from eating these palm nuts not properly soaked in the time-honoured aboriginal way. Fred, Tom and William Sayle were all path-finders in the N.T. The grave was brought in from wilderness by Charlie Havey in 1940, and remade in Borroloola with a tombstone sent up from Melbourne by Tom Sayle nearly sixty years after his young brother's death.

Old hatters living out in the hills on wallaby and crow came in once a year to the nearest station for a bit of "nourishing food"—bread and salt beef. They needed but little here below, and if they could dodge spears and nulla-nullas it was amazing how long they did need it, living to a grand old age, perhaps because they absorbed so much salt.

When we were planning to join kind and quaint old Harry Condon, aged seventy-three, for three months in the mysterious ranges beyond the Four Archers on the Rosy and Limmen rivers, with three riding-horses and three packs,

"All you'll want," he said, "is a couple o' fifties of flour, a seventy of sugar, a fifty of salt, a bag o' rice, a couple o' pounds of tea, some jam, curry, dried fruits, cream of tartar an' soda, a couple o' bars of soap. That's all in the tucker. Now medicine, a small bottle of quinine, Epsom salts an' Condy. Oh, bein' a woman you'd better bring a bottle of aspirins—women like aspirins. I've got the dish an' the camp-oven, with a couple of extra tin plates, pannikins, knives an' forks, an' cartridges an' a rifle to get beef, an' a few fish-hooks. Tobacco, of course, all you can."

"Matches?" I suggested.

"Matches if you like, but we can always light a fire with a burning glass, or by pulling the bolt out of a rifle and firin' the powder into a greasy rag. I'll take the shoein' tools. I don't see we'll need much else.

"I'll be out at piccaninny daylight to get the horses, an' we'll do fifteen or twenty miles a day an' camp early on a nice bit of feed. Always camp before dark to cut pegs for your mosquito net an' to make bread. For meat I'll shoot a cleanskin now an' then, run a knife down along his backbone, throw the hide over towards the legs, get a bit of fresh steak an' take the brisket to salt for the track. There's nothing else to know. I'll find the water."

"By the way," he went on, smiling dryly round his pipe, "you know not to sit up when the first spear comes over, because that's what it's meant for, to make you sit up, an' the next issue'll make you a pincushion. But there's no myalls out there now that I know, and very few bad blacks. They've all been shot out long ago, or gone in to the missions to die."

He was silent a moment, and tapped on the table with all five fingers.

"Remarkable hills an' cliffs out there," he said, "an' miles of clear, beautiful springs, the prettiest country I've ever seen, too much scenery for cattle, too rugged. There's never been a soul out there in twenty or thirty years, in a good fifty thousand square miles. A feller who wanted could hide away from the world for ever."

Gentle old Harry Condon has ridden the Territory from the 1880s to the

1940s and has been speared in his time. From the Antrim Plateau on the Kimberley side to the China Wall on the Queensland side, he knows hundreds of raggedy gullies still far from the map.

"Harry," I said, as we sat by hurricane lamplight in the gloomy old pub at Borroloola, "in those trails of yours, especially in the earlies, I suppose you've often travelled where no white man has been before you?"

"Ah," said Harry, "now I'll tell you. Through all them creeks and hills on the head of the Fitzmaurice, or the Kathe-rhyne, or the Victoria, or the Goyder, or anywhere else you like to name, there was fellers long before me, an' there was fellers before them. Back in the eighties I could ride for a month, an' I'd come to gorges so steep you couldn't ride no longer, an' I'd climb them cliffs an' crawl through holes in the rocks an' go *down* the cliffs, an' into another gully an' on for two days with a bush net an' a bit o' tucker, an' I'd come to a waterhole I'd swear I was first to see. Blow me if I wouldn't find a rusty old match-box, or a button, or a sauce-bottle of a shape an' brand you never see for years, or initials an' a date of the sixties or seventies cut in a tree.

"There ain't no such thing as the first white man, missus. They was everywhere, looking for waters an' gold in the very earlies, but they didn't think to talk about it then. There ain't no creek or gully or hill or pocket of country in the island where a bushman hasn't been before you."

"What island was this?" I asked—we had not been talking of islands.

"Australia."

How often have I heard that phrase among them. To these, who know it so well, the continent is only "the island". From Wave Hill to Wodonga the drovers took half of it in one great semicircle, and then went back for another mob of cattle. From Ballarat north to Charters Towers, then right round west and south for Coolgardie, and east again for Broken Hill, the diggers of gold and silver made it a desert circle on horseback. There is no other continent of such vast and vacant wilderness that the courage of men has made to seem so small.

All they had was their long-wave friendship for each other, and that was the life-breath of the bush. Without it, they could never have survived. The people of the top half-million square miles were all known, by name and fame, to each other.

In the land of Welcome Stranger, a traveller through the stations or the lonely out-camps might be a star boarder for a year or two if he liked, or for ever. In fact, he often finished up owning the station, free, gratis and for nothing, because there was nobody else to leave it to. No pilgrim passed even the poorest shack without filling his tucker-bags there, and a station was notorious for ever if white or black went by without "a feed and a hand-out" to cheer them on. That was in the days when sharing was to share one's own when it was hard to get. Nowadays many of the managers would sooner see a dust go by on the road. Some must make returns to the head office in cities in the matter of hand-outs of beef and the meals they give in the bush. It is, of course, a different age, and travellers are many, but hospitality is not so often given to those in genuine need.

A man would ride hundreds of miles to bring in anyone sick, whether he knew him or not, and hold him on his horse all the way back, or, with the help of the blacks, carry him on a litter of saplings. When Matt Connors went blind from cattle-blight out in the Abner Ranges of Macarthur River he was six weeks bathing his eyes with boracic till a mate came along and led Matt's horse three hundred miles to Hodgson Downs. From there they carried him two hundred and fifty miles in a buggy to catch the train at Katherine for Darwin. He never recovered his sight, and finished up in the Old Men's Home in Adelaide, with so many other great men of his country and his time.

In those vast distances where no man could foot-walk, the swagman became a bagman with a riding-horse, a packhorse and a couple of spares, travelling from station to station, from creek to creek. Home was a bit of salt goat hung in a tree. The bagman depended a good deal on the blacks for his tucker, and because he was always good with little hand-outs of tea, sugar and tobacco he was safe among the blacks—nobody kills Santa Claus.

Philosophers all were the crew of H.M.S. *Coolabah Tree*. "The Spotted Wonder", "Billy Biffin", "Blue Bob the Love-child"—only they didn't say Love-child—"the Red Ant", who went through the dip at Sedan with the cattle and was never the same colour again, "the Rabbit", who burrowed out of a jail in Burketown, and "the Legacy", left behind by his father on a Tablelands station to work off the money the father owed, "the Deep Sea Stockman" and "Billie the Cabbie", all of these and many more were regular knight-errants of the bush, running almost to timetable east and west and up and down. A great sight was Billie the Cabbie, a New Zealander named Sandbrook who once had been a Sydney cabman, bowling through the spinifex with a comic-cuts lubra and three piccaninnies, sacks of flour and seven dogs in his bandy old cab.

Floreat Etona withered here and there, scions of the stately homes of England boiling the billy on the creek. A Northumberland Percy and a Count de Satge had stations over near Queensland, and one honourable bagman drew £500 each year at Katherine or Oodnadatta, and spent the rest of the time riding between them. When the remittance came, all were his guests at a royal bender—he insisted that the Union Jack should fly above the pub when he was in residence there. One year the remittance did not turn up, but the bender went on without it, and he finished up in Port Augusta jail, well down under the Union Jack.

Some of the bagmen had been station-owners and great stockmen in their day. Others were professional men who "came out with beautiful tickets", and quite a few more were men of the sea. They spent their old age cooking on the stations, and their dotage wandering blind. The wild dogs got most of them in the end.

Stockmen were the lords of creation, according to their stations. A man who had been head stockman on Mount Cornish, Alexandria, Tyson's Tinnenburra, John Costello's Lake Nash or Bluey Buchanan's Wave Hill was respected till the day of his death.

A dandy when he liked was the stockman of the nineties, with his emu-feather cockaded hat, Musketeer mustachios, red neckerchief above his blue Crimea shirt, red silk cummerbund, moleskins tight and snowy white, highly polished Wellingtons tasselled and spurred. But the fret and sweat of the Territory soon reduced them to beard, blue shirt, any old riding-trousers and elastic sides.

Often have I wondered by what trick of fate and fashion the cattle-men of Australia adopted the dainty, high-stepping elastic side—an English vogue for little old ladies too strait-laced to bend to their high-buttoned boots—to be the universal riding-boot of a continent for over half a century, the most suitable and most serviceable riding-boot in the world, easy to don, easy to slip, well heeled for a grip of the stirrup, and easy to wear. Some never took them off for years, sleeping or waking.

The world-famous Australia stockwhip is a cross between the old bullock-team whip and the Mexican quirt. A Henderson whip from Sydney, or a Spratt, silver-mounted, with a nine-foot lash, pliable whalebone handle and a silk cracker, was the hallmark of your flash stockman, but in later years the finely plaited kangaroo-hide whips of Alex Scobie of Ooriwilanie have taken their places in the outback of five States. Wagers up to £400 would be won and lost on a wizard with the stockwhip in the old Katherine pub—he would crack it while tossing from hand to hand, curl it round his neck like a python and cut a cigarette in half from a comrade's lips. "Quite easy," one of the old hands told me. "It's only a matter of flexible thumbs and timin'. You swing till it whistles, then begin."

Everything was worth doing well. You could read a man's character from his way of rolling a swag or throwing on the packs, the two pack-bags, each weighing seventy-five pounds, subconsciously balanced to within half an ounce in perfect equilibrium, the bottles packed in spinifex, tea, sugar and tucker-bags ready to hand, pannikin and quart-pot on the saddle-peg, and the water-bag hanging on the shady side of the horse.

A good craftsman became famous and then immortal. Saddlers and carpenters of half a century gone, artists in whip-plaiting, horse-breakers, are reverently remembered yet. The work of Dan Sheahan, a yard-builder of the eighties from Nappa Merrie to Kimberley, is as proudly pointed out to you in the wilderness as in London the architecture of Adam or Christopher Wren. Where stations are long abandoned and the homestead a ruin, the sturdy old stockyard, swept by the floods and dust-storms of fifty years, still keeps memory of Dan Sheahan in the drift sand.

Living was primitive but never crude. When you crossed the Tropic you left the law of coats and collars behind, but the bush had its codes and courtesies in honour and comradeship of a far higher idealism than ours. A braggart was ducked in a billabong, a quitter was left to himself, and a man who ill-treated his blacks was Public Enemy Number One. It had its etiquette, its twenty-one acts of rudeness, and any breach of these made a man an outsider.

For instance, never carry a "blister", a bill or an account. Leave it to cold officialdom, with a twopenny stamp, through His Majesty's mails. A rider passing by was an honoured guest, and he couldn't be hounding a man down with bills.

Never "sit on the table" out bush—the camp-sheet spread for the tucker to keep it free from dust and ants. Picnickers down south airily squat on the rug with the sandwiches and teacups, but up north the host would grow restive and even scowl—you don't sit on the table at home when a meal is in progress.

Never walk round a homestead barefooted—it is not a blacks' camp, even if it looks like one.

If they ask you would you "care for a wash" at a station when the dinner-bell goes, always wash. You may be sartorially elegant and cosmetically fragrant after but a morning's flight from the Hotel Australia, but it is a time-honoured tradition of these hard tracks to "have a clean-up before tucker", and not to do so is to belittle those about you—"He come straight in without even a wash."

A boss drover never sacked a man in the camp before the others, it might "give him a bad name and stop him from getting a job". He waited till he was asleep and, with no word spoken, simply made out his cheque and put it in the ringer's boot.

No manager, in at the station, ever sends his head stockman a message by a black-boy, or by one of the white hands. He pays him the courtesy of a written note, even when the head stockman cannot read, in which case the messenger is asked to convey, casually and without comment, the contents of the note.

Every man keeps one clean shirt for a chance meeting with his fellows, no matter how far out. On one of the Wessel islands one day, Joel Cooper turned up for a fish and oyster luncheon with A. J. V. Brown.

"He was wearing only his beard," said Alf, "and I told him straight. I said 'Look here, Joe, if you haven't any clothes, and can't borrow any from a nigger, I'll lend you mine, but don't ever come into my camp naked. We're white men, and it's not done.' "

They had no time for a bumptious man, or "pompious". "Parcel post" was influence—a station manager, or a jackeroo from the cities, who might be the boss's nephew, or going to marry his daughter, or a college friend of his son, or other "spare part". He never lived down the stigma if he got a job, not by reputation or work, but by "knowing the heads".

"He come up by parcel post," they still say. "He don't know nothin'."

Also, they have no time for the modern stockman:

"He wears a hat that high with a brim that wide, and leggin's and a belt and a gun—but what's he goin' to shoot! He has a big stockwhip, but if you asked him to give you an exhibition he'd cut his hide off. He looks on us as a busted flush, an' we look on him as a man as never was, with his little portable wireless set, an' his zipper suits, an' sleepin'-bag, an' camera to take shots of himself—how would you look with them things when the blacks was on your track? We couldn't truck our cattle, we follered 'em an' ringed 'em for three thousand miles. But he don't count any more than we do now. They're drovin' dead beasts by aeroplane already, an' they'll soon be musterin' by a radar beam. He's Malley's Cow. He's a goner!"

The bush races were the highlights of their lives because they loved horses. Attending a muster, they met at a billabong, put up a smoke, and the others followed in. A station-owner, a brumby runner, a drover with his plant, would begin to talk races and hold a meeting on the spot with a mob yarded by the black-boys. John Gilpin rode three hundred miles for a few gallons of square, the judge stood in a bough shed, Spectre, Splinter, Bee's Wing and Batty thundered past a post and a good time was had by all. They would christen it the Union Billabong—so names went down on the map—and make a rendezvous for a couple of years ahead there. As one of them said, "You'd get there if you had to cop a couple of Chinaman's horses to do it. Otherwise they'd think you were dead, and all come out to bury you. It was the law of the bush never to let your mates down."

Some of them never drank or smoked in their lives, but most of them did. The few little pubs of the million square miles lived on the bush races and the benders. Out on the stations a man would work three years for a cheque to knock down in three months when his "hide was cracking". Mulga wires called all and sundry to the spree when a big cheque was around, and the pub could clear £1000 in a month when drovers and station-owners were "drinking mobs of cattle". A "booze artist" and his friends could drink a station worth £30,000 in a couple of years. They will often point out to you the wreck of a local celebrity who "drank two stations and a droving plant". Those who survived the blacks and the dry stages mostly died of drink, but, as Billy Miller has it, *De mortuis nil nisi boozum.*

When the day comes, your true bushman dies naturally and casually as the blacks and birds about him. "Terrible Billy", as old as two men, turned up at Milingimbi Mission in the Crocodile Islands, and asked permission to die there. They made him welcome, and he kept his contract before long. George Ligar, with "a fair few" others, died at the Bend of the Ord. M. P. Durack, riding out from Wyndham, met him riding in, the first time old George had crossed the Kimberley border, "lookin' at country over on the sunset side". He was sitting spellbound in the saddle, gazing over the curve of the big river to the crown of House-roof Hill.

"God, this is a beautiful place!" he said. "A man could die here."

When M. P. Durack came riding back, George had a camp in his heaven, buried under a tree.

One old lad at Battle Creek told the Victoria mustering-camp, "Well, I'm willin'. I finish up ternight. I could have died back at that last creek, but the ground was too stony for youse fellers to dig. This ain't so bad." They laughed at him, but next morning they were digging.

At Wave Hill old station a few years ago the boss drover, when he came off watch at daylight, said to the boys, "It's been a hard night, so I'll turn in. Don't call me if I sleep." Epic last words. His was the sleep beyond recalling.

Protestant, Catholic or pagan, they were all wrapped in their camp-sheets and went back to their beloved bush as the sailor to the sea. Two or three times in fifty years they passed round the hat for a tombstone and, such was the generous spirit, collected enough for a cenotaph. It cost every penny and a lot of trouble to bring a marble slab two thousand miles on packhorses to a starved country that never could carry enough plain flour for daily bread.

Last wills and testaments were few and simple. Bob Pethick, who died crossing the border with a mob of cattle for Wyndham, wrote his will with a sharpened stick in the soot of a billycan, but he had a station to leave to a friend. A legal bequest was usually a lead-pencil letter to a mate. Here is a typical bushman's will:

Tom Liddy,
Wave Hill.

Dear Tom,

Your two horses and a pony mare belonging to Gladys are running between here and the head of the road. I give and bequeath everything I got to you. There's £22 in the Commonwealth Bank and plenty of tucker not touched and a new shirt and towel. Pay Matt Wilson £2 : 5 : 0 I owe him, and Gladys one box of lollies. Don't forget, Tom. I'm going. I'm getting old and remarkable tired. It's better this way. If from the other side I can do anything for you, Paddy Murray or Bill Sheahan, I will, fair dinkum. Good luck, everybody.

Peter Wilshaw.

Peter Wilshaw shot himself at Katherine in 1922. For the Territory he left a very considerable estate. Gladys was a little half-caste girl, daughter of one of his mates.

The beer-case burials and uproarious Irish wakes of the abject little towns were traditional as the solemn suburban funeral, but a reckless reaction from outward and visible grief. They made it a day to remember, the send-off to a friend. If a woman were near she might insist on a little sobriety and propriety, a drape of crape for the beer-case, a slow walk for the cart. But most women shared the fatalist philosophy.

One time Wyndham went for a picnic to Mugg's Lagoon, in the jolly crowd the storekeeper, Tom Chawner, and his wife. While the women boiled the billy and spread the tea in the shade, the men went for a swim. There was sudden commotion at the billabong.

"What's the matter?" the women called.

"There's a bloke here drownded!"

Mrs Chawner wrung her apron in anguish and foreboding, schooled by the unkindest cuts of fate.

"I'll bet a bloody pound it's Tom!" she wailed. It was.

Till the motor-truck brought the calendar, in about 1930, Christmas was only another day except in the little tin-pot pubs, where it was the open season for fights. After the hard year with the cattle, the boys rode in and painted the gum-trees red. In Tibooburra or Burketown, in Wyndham or Meekatharra, and all the pubs in that great hollow square between them, the flat in front on Christmas Day was a Colosseum of sticks, stones, revolvers, bottles and fists.

"What's a matter white man all-about corroboree?" the blacks wanted to know at Pine Creek. "Blackfella frightum, run-away bush. Might-be big-fella war come up."

Christmas gifts were mostly black eyes. Nobody seemed to remember the goat and the plum duff. Above the roar of the singing you could hear the clash of arms.

Billy Miller "struck Christmas" four times in fifty-three years and each time, through circumstances unforeseen the dinner was left out. Billy left Adelaide when he was a boy of fourteen. He rode up the Murray, Darling, Warrego, Paroo, Buller, Cooper, Diamantina, Georgina, Gregory and a dozen others to the Gulf country, two thousand miles as the crow flies, but he made it ten thousand, colt-breaking and tailing weaners in that mighty maze of sandhills, and riding alone with a packhorse through adventure. From the Macarthur he set a far west course for the Murran-ji, the blackfella hills of Victoria River, and King Leopold Ranges, and so down to Gregory's Salt Sea.

Here is the story of Billy's four Christmases, as told by himself:

"It was eleven years before I managed to sneak up on a Christmas. That was at the O'Shaughnessy in the Gulf in '96. There were two wild well-sinkin' brothers named Hislop who were always knockin' down bumper cheques, so they reckoned they'd show a profit if they bought out the pub. They got me to do the bookkeeping because I could write, but they weren't business men. 'What's the use o' puttin' down drinks,' they'd say, 'to a bloke who can't pay?'

"They drank the pub dry in about two months, an' along came Christmas an' the boys. We held a conference an' mortgaged the pub in Burketown for two an' a half tons of grog and tucker. It came up by horse-team with a rear-guard of niggers pushin', an' the freight was £22 a ton. We couldn't pay the teamster, so we let him take it out on a bender.

"Those were the days when I thought Christmas ought to be, so I wrote MERRY XMAS an' PEACE ON EARTH in red and blue pencil all over the wall. There were so many fights about who was disturbin' the peace that we couldn't spare the time for dinner, an' the policeman an' the Burketown publican came out an' took over the pub.

"The second was thirteen years later at Wandi goldfield, thirty miles from Pine Creek. A little mob of us was camped there pennyweightin' in the wet. I made a dinner at my camp an' asked the others over. I killed a wether goat an' baked it in the old camp-oven, an' laid a bush table in the bough shed with an Adelaide *Chronicle* I had, knives an' forks an' mugs an' tomato sauce. I was opening some tins of fruit when Jerry McCarthy staged a surprise an' brought out a bottle of whisky an' a case of beer some kind friend had sent.

"We worked it out that the toasts came before dinner, so there wasn't no dinner, because 'Paddy the Lasher' an' Jerry an' I had to ride in for more toasts to Pine Creek. We knocked up the publican in the middle of the night, an' he hollered out 'Who's there?'

" 'Three Wise Men come out o' the east!' we told him.

"He said to get to hell or he'd call the police. Next day we were ridin' back with three bottles of square, an' Paddy the Lasher bent down to a pool to drink. His nose was skinned with the fights he'd been enjoyin', an' when the water made it sting he reckoned he'd been bitten by a snake, an' the only antidote was to drink a bottle of square gin straight off.

" 'No you don't, Paddy,' we said. 'That snake mightn't be venomous. Wait till you start to die.' After Christmas he went out an' was killed by blacks on the Victoria.

"Third Christmas was in at the Kathe-rhyne, about eight years later at Tom Pearce's pub. The Chinaman cook killed a few fowls and knocked up a first-rate duff, but Tom's wife was a lady an' close-up ruined the whole turn-out by puttin' up a notice in the bar, NO GENTLEMEN WILL BE ADMITTED TO DINING-ROOM WITHOUT COATS. We didn't have no coats. None of the Chinese stores in Kathe-rhyne sold coats.

"Little Jack McCarthy had just come in with his teams. He turned up in a long oilskin mackintosh. The rest of us went to boil a billy on the river, but Tom made it all right with the missus an' called us back. Charlie Seymour was in on a bender. Mrs Pearce wouldn't have him at the table because he was an obstreperous drunk, so they locked him in one of the rooms. She made us all stand up while she said grace. We'd just sat down, except Tom, who was havin' a go with the carvin'-knife at the chickens, when a couple of bullets whizzed over our heads an' made two holes in the wall. It was Charlie objectin' with a gun. We all trooped into the bar to steady our nerves an' forgot to come back.

"After that there was a long spell. I was out at Lejuna, north-east of Cambridge Gulf, an' at Bedford Downs up in the King Leopolds, an' at Limbunya, between Wave Hill an' the border. The blacks was bad in all them places, and Christmas gets away from you out there. The year's best dinner was often a dry johnnie-cake on a dry stage, or a hunk of salt beef an' rain if you was ridin' tracks in the wet—no fire to cook a damper or boil the billy. If I was in at the hut, an' remembered, I shot a scrub turkey an' gave it to the lubra to cook, an' made the blacks a boggy puddin'—they like it boggy, 'long time sit down longa binjey'—but it's not much of a Christmas on your own, so one of the years seen me ridin' in.

"I thought I'd make the Kathe-rhyne, but the Murran-ji was a hundred-mile dry, so I turned in to Pigeonholes out-station of Victoria River Downs. I was sure of a bit of tucker there because there was a real good cook at Pigeonholes. His name was George, but we called him 'Nothin' 'Ere'.

"He was a little man with brown silky beard an' dorg's eyes, always in a long white sheet of an apron an' a cocky little flour-bag cap that sort o' surprised you in that old bark kitchen. They reckoned he'd been cook an' bottle-washer to a duke, an' he came out to Australia as chef on a liner. Any rate, he was a white-tablecloth cook. He could dress a bush turkey so you'd think it was the real thing, an' knock up a duff or a curry with caroutes an' canapes an' all them French an' Hindu sauces. For a golden pudding of his made with a dipper of flour an' a tin of golden syrup I seen the boys back up a dozen times—as light as cotton-wool. He was alone out there nearly all the year, sixty miles off the head station, an' his trouble was that he had nothing to cook.

" 'Y'll have to take pot luck,' he'd growl. 'I got nothin' 'ere.' Then he'd sit y' down to a salt beef an' kidney puddin' or a bit o' corned stuff with cloves an' some sauce, an' a pumpkin tart the best you ever tasted. An' all the time he'd be moanin' an' roarin' about nothin' 'ere. That's how he got his name. The head station got a bit mad about all the boys laughin', an' this time they'd told him to order what he wanted, in reason, an' quit growlin' about the tucker.

"When I rode in on Christmas Eve the stock-camp was over from V.R.D. after six weeks out in the ranges at the horse-muster an' Burt Drew an' his donkey-teams had just pulled in with stores for the year. George promised the boys he'd give them a ding-dong dinner if it was the last thing he done.

"He was up to his eyes in flour an' feathers, giving the gins the rounds o' the kitchen—first time I even seen him cheerful.

"There was a bottle or two about, but George wouldn't drink. He was too busy boiling the ham an' peeling onions an' strippin' herbs for stuffin', an' stirrin' up a big duff, an' makin' mince pies out o' dried fruits, an' siftin' currants for a cake, and settin' ready for soups and sauces with French an' Eyetalian names, you never see anythin' like it. He stayed up nearly all night, an' he was on the job again before piccaninny daylight.

" 'They reckon I'm a liar!' he says to me. 'I'll show 'em I can cook when I git the stuff to cook.'

"The heat was hell on Christmas Day. We was all mornin' down under the trees around a case o' beer on Burt Drew's wagon, waitin' for the bell to ring—the lot of us was six months hungry. One o'clock come an' nothin' happened. Two o'clock. The sun was lookin' late. Ben went up to see how things were. He put his head in the kitchen with, 'How's she goin', George?'

"George wasn't there.

"The gins had let the fire go out, an' the big duff was a sod in the water. The ham had boiled dry. The chooks an' custard pies an' the cake an' all the doings were sittin' up waitin' to go in the oven. The whole turn-out was raw. Even the hunk of salt beef in the safe was raw.

" 'Where's George?' Ben bawled at the lubras.

"They reckoned George was crook after breakfast an' went to lay down for a bit of a spell before puttin' on dinner. They called him, they said, but 'him too much tch'leep'.

"Ben went in a rage to knock him up. A few minutes later he shouted to us, 'Hey! Y' better come up! The pore little blighter's stone dead an' there's *nothin' 'ere.*'

"The rest of my Christmases, till I come in to civilization, has been out by a billabong, the world forgotten, by the world forgot."

And so it was with all the bushmen. Theirs was an incredibly lonely life, not even a dog for company—no dogs can travel the distances—not even a talking cockatoo.

When they were old, and doing up saddles, the Katherine was their home, under the trees on the bank of the big river, each one with a gentleman's man of the Djauan tribe to bring him a barramundi or a kangaroo for wages paid in tobacco, and a lubra parlourmaid to move the roof on when the good earth floor needed sweeping. The evening of their days they spent talking over old times. "My God, Bill, you've had a wonderful life," you'd hear them say to each other.

They have a remarkable memory for faces, dates and places. "He was killed off a bay horse with a white blaze in Burketown on a Thursday, the 4th of September 1893," you will hear them relate, or "He rode in to my camp at Wave Hill towards the end o' May 1905." They can describe any cattle-trip in forty years of droving, missing never a night-camp nor a waterhole, with day-to-day chronicles and statistics of the condition of the cattle, the number of calves, who bought and sold, and the prices they brought. Dearly they love a genealogical tree, and will sit in the stockman's squat discussing ancestors with many a quip—

"I'm descended from Robert Bruce."

"We reckoned you was descended from the spider."

As I penetrated farther into those last jungles, the more erudite and philosophic I found their lonely white men. If you seek intellectual converse in Australia, you will find it, not in cities, where they are obsessed with petty commerce, shows, racehorses and the daily gossip of each other, but out in the haze of the opal hills of the Centre, or by an unknown river of the north.

The explanation is simple. Where books are six months in transit, and then have to last a lifetime, you would starve on Edgar Wallace and Berta Ruck. With the wild west all about you, wild westers are superfluous, and where murder stalks the greenwood murder stories fall flat. You must have something to bite on, three hundred years old for preference, in a good solid small-print tome where a paragraph lasts a camp-fire through, and gives food for reflection all the next week as you ride behind the cattle. The little lost library at Borroloola has produced more classic scholars than any university in Australia. That is why you hear them arguing out "Thuky-dides" and "Themis-tockles" by the billabong. Bunyan preaches and Shelley sings under a milk-wood tree. For less poetic and more practical souls the *Britannica* is fodder, twelve volumes to a pack-bag and one on the pommel to balance the mind and the load.

"Can't you buy in on the conversation over there, Jack?" they asked a stockman who had moved away to where two old diehards had travelled from Cicero's Philippics to the fifteen decisive battles of the world, and whether it was Salamis or Metatorus where Hannibal was "knocked back".

"No," said Jack, "them blokes is talkin' Jew."

More than once his literary flair has saved the bushman's life. A nine-inch Colt on his chest, his back against a tree to guard it from spear-shafts, and a book propped up in front of him, he could forget his fears in wild blacks' country. No primitive race on earth will destroy a madman. Seeing him motionless for hours, obsessed by the debil-debil of a small white square, sometimes with inexplicable laughter, sometimes in solemn silence, the blacks put it down to insanity and let the stranger be.

Even those who could not read and write had a personal and emotional love of poetry. The bars from Quilpie to Wyndham still ring with iambics when the Territory drovers are in, literary lights "spouting Shakespeare by the yard", the lesser ones by the simple ballad measures of Henry Lawson and Banjo Paterson moved to beery tears.

> Ten miles down Reedy River
> A pool of water lies. . . .

They know that pool

> "What's the good o' keepin sober? Fellers rise and fellers fall;
> What I might have been and wasn't doesn't trouble me at all."

"Sweeney" is an excuse for a drink in every pub in Australia, but the Banjo holds their hearts out bush.

> There was movement at the station, for the word had passed around
> That the colt from old Regret had got away. . . .

Every one of them has been in a big rush, and "The Man from Snowy River" speaks their language, classic for half a century of every camp-fire. They share the living of it with "the Banjo".

"What's this old bugger cryin' for?" somebody suddenly shouted one night when "The Man from Snowy River", in thundering rendition by a Henry Irving of a stockman, had set up a tremolo in the stars.

"The old bugger" rose and faced them, tears trickling down his worn leather saddle of a face into his foot-wide beard.

"I'll tell ye why I'm cryin'!" he roared. "Because I was the striplin', that's why."

Poetry was far from their world, so they composed their own. In doggerel were written the sagas of the bush—comedy, tragedy and satire, everything that happened in their days. The bush poet was as sure of a drink as Homer. These "poy-ems", written on scraps of brown paper and treasured in swags, or learnt in the flickering firelight, epics of a land of men, are nearly all lost.

Music was denied them in that silent land, though "before these 'ere wirelesses and gramophones sent the country dumb, we had some great singers in the bush". Far above our fashionable gabble in catch-phrases and cults is their earnest and childish love of the art that is longer than life.

"I've got me round in the Gallery," said the Man from the Murran-ji. "It's the best permanent hole I know for a bloke layin' off in the city. Your first turn-off is to 'Bringin' Back a Straggler', a beautiful picture that, but it could 'a' been a darned sight better if the painter feller was out with us on the Victoria. He ain't a straggler, he's a break-away, an' a rakin' bullock, not a piker—y' can see the curl on his forehead, an' he has the placid eye of a tame old milker. The ringer's all wrong! He oughta be shoulderin' him to bring him in, instead o' headin' him out. He wants to race right on to him, an' bore him in to the mob. He's committin' suicide an' runnin' the beast out of his hide the way he's goin'. We wouldn't stand that damn-fool stockman in any camp of ours.

" 'Across the Black-soil Plains'—that's another good one, but the first thing I says when I seen it is 'Hullo! They got the chains hooked wrong! Them horses is goin' straight on an' leave the wagon standin'.' Y' can't expect little art boys to know these things, but why don't they have a *wongi* with a bullocky before they start the job? It might be good composition or whatever they call it, but it ain't common sense.

"Then there's 'The Palace at Fontaine-blew', a first-rate camp, as pretty a bit o' country as you'd see. Right close up there's a little clump o' trees, messmates they look like or woollybutts, just the right size for the tent-poles. What I like about this 'ere clump, they're standin' out on their own. You could put a little mob in there all cosy for the night, a good five hundred head. Not countin' in the palace, I've seen that picture thousands of times up in the N.T.

"I always pay a call on Henry Lawson. Henry an' me speak the same lingo. There ain't much wrong with him, nor Banjo Paterson neether. Banjo's the livin' image of old Matt Wilson who kept the store at the Depot—they both have them steel-blue eyes that see a long way, the best eyes for the bush.

" 'The Anatomy Lesson' is a good one too, but it's a regular heifer paddock. You can never gallop right on to that without stampedin' a mob of gigglin' girls.

"The daddy of the lot is 'Drake Playin' Bowls' with the Armada just up the road. There's Effingham, Howard an' all the boys, you don't have to ask who's who, as good a pack of lads as any I've been out with, moonlightin' the ranges. That picture always reminds me of the time the mob rushed camp on Inverway on a sixty-five-mile dry. We just had them set for the night an' old Mick Connors brought a bottle of whisky out of his swag an' gave us each a pannikin all round. He was pourin' one for himself when the mob smelt the water out o' the waterbag an' come wheelin' in, bellowin' mad. The whole bang lot of us rushed up trees, but not Mick. He's got to have that whisky, an' he goes on pourin', steady as a brick, with the hoofs thunderin' down. By golly, Francis Drake had nothin' on him. He drained every drop in the bottle, an' took a good swig before he lit out, old Mick, with the pannikin high an' a thousand head at his heels.

"Them pictures an' poy-ems, missus, they only make you want to go back. That's what they're for, I reckon. To make old times seem good. They was, too. If I had my life over again, an' could be Governor-General of Australia, I'd take it out just as it was, up in the old N.T., out bush.

"I don't want all the fancy things in this city. I get lost, lookin' at all the car lights blinkin', an' if y' don't gallop the mob'll run y' down. There's no red lights sayin' '*Stop*! *Caution*! *Go*!' along the Murrun-ji. Only two wonders in the south for me, the little white children an' these 'ere spring flowers. Ain't they pretty? I could look at 'em all day.

"Still, spring is the time to quit. Up there where there ain't no spring, you smell it in the air, an' you grease up y'r swag-straps an' send y'r nigger out for y'r horses, an' you say to the boss, 'Righto, Jim, dip y'r pen in the ink an' write out my cheque', an' y'r over the hills an' far away by sundown. You follow the my-rage on the horri-zon to the country of dreams . . . an' when y' get back, it ain't there. It was all ro-mance."

What is romance? Cortés couldn't see it when he burnt his ships. It's a flash of the past or the future. No man finds what he went out as a boy to look for. It's always over the next rise till it's back at a waterhole forty years behind.

"Ah, well! . . . It's a fine day for travellin'. I've got a thousand miles to Adelaide, an' a thousand to the Alice, an' then I'm home an' dry on the last thousand. There's a fair few friends o' mine still round the Kathe-rhyne, an' a few old blacks in the station camps from when we was stock-ridin' long ago. I wish I could put a smoke to let them know I'm comin', but if you was to light up a log in the Domain here they'd run you in as a German spy. When the truck pulls up at the horse-paddock gate, they'll come strollin' out on their bare feet to look who's on it, an' I'll see their eyes light up under their old felt hats.

" 'Py Crise!' they'll say, 'I been think you been dead-fella! No more you go nother-one country. You been sit-down this-one country belong you!'

"By the look o' the sun I better get a move on, missus. I'm Malley's Cow. I'm a goner! I'll throw on me packs an' dig me toes into the ashes on the track to Kurrenjacki Stones an' Lonely Springs . . . just pokin' along steady . . . travellin' west o' sunset where the trees are tall in the country of Young Lochinvar.

"When it's sundown, an' time for a sleep-camp, I'll light up a log by the Styx, where they're musterin' their ghostly mobs on that seven-times-windin' river, an' I'll hobble out me horses on the Union Billabong . . .

"I'll hear Old Bluey's pack-bells . . .

"I'll hear Jack-Dick singin' around the cattle . . .

"An' I'll see the Ragged Thirteen come ridin' by.

"It's the only heaven I look for . . . to camp with them old fellers an' forget."

Appendix

GOVERNMENT RESIDENTS AND ADMINISTRATORS OF THE NORTHERN TERRITORY

Government Residents under South Australian Administration

ESCAPE CLIFFS, 1864-7

1864-6	Hon. B. T. Finniss.
1866-7	J. T. Manton (Acting).

PALMERSTON, 1869-1910

1869-70	G. W. Goyder.
1870	Dr J. S. Millner (Acting to July 1870).
1870-3	Captain Bloomfield Douglas, R.N.R.
1873	Dr J. Millner (Acting May to October 1873).
1873-6	G. B. Scott.
1876-83	E. W. Price.
1883-4	G. R. McMinn (Acting).
1884-90	Hon. J. L. Parsons.
1890	J. G. Knight (Acting February to July 1890).
1890-2	J. G. Knight.
1892-1905	C. J. Dashwood.
1905-10	C. E. Herbert.
1910	S. J. Mitchell.

Administrators under Commonwealth Administration

DARWIN, 1911—

1911-12	S. J. Mitchell.
1912-19	Dr J. A. Gilruth.
1919	H. E. Carey (appointed as Director).
1919-21	Hon. M. S. C. Smith (Acting).
1921	Colonel E. T. Leane (Acting).
1921-7	F. C. Urquhart.
1927-31	Lt Col. R. H. Weddell (Government Resident, North Australia).
1927-31	V. G. Carrington (Government Resident, Central Australia).
1931-7	Lt Col. R. H. Weddell.
1931-7	V. G. Carrington (Deputy Administrator).
1937-46	C. L. A. Abbott.
1946	L. H. A. Giles (Acting).
1946-51	A. R. Driver.
1951—	F. J. S. Wise.

Territory Phrases

Abo: An aboriginal.
A bit of hurry-up: A hasty or scamped job.
A dry: A dry season or dry stage of country.
A fair few: A considerable number.
All-about: (Pidgin) Everyone. Everywhere.
A perish: To die of thirst.
A spell: A rest.

Bagman: Out-of-work bushman who travels with a few riding and pack-horses.
Bang-tail: An exact or final muster in which tails of cattle are cut square for accurate count.
Banker: A river in flood to the brim. ("Running a banker.")
Bay o' Biscay: Tumbled country, hills and hollows as of a rough sea.
Beast: A bovine beast only.
Bedourie: (Arabian word) Great enveloping dust-storm, dense fog of dust obscuring land for days.
Behind: (Pidgin) After, in time. ("Behind you tell me, I tell Paddy.")
Belong, belongta: (Pidgin) Appertaining to.
Bender: A one-man spree.
Belt: A region—as of rainfall or timber.
Billabong: A waterhole outside the main stream of a river.
Bing-hi: (Torres Strait Island word) An aboriginal.
Blind-stabbing: Travelling by guess, without a compass.
Blind tiger: A store in the far away bush that sells liquor without a licence.
Blow: A gale. Also a mineral outcrop. ("Quartz blow.")
Boab: A baobab tree.
Boomerang cheques: Cheques that return unhonoured.
Boong: (Contemptuous term, slang) An aborigine.
Booze-artist: An incorrigible drunkard.
Bower-birdin': Picking up unconsidered trifles for one's own use or camp.
Brands and descriptions: Identifications, characteristics.
Broke in: Subdued, disciplined.
Brownie: A bush cake, damper with sugar and currants.
Brumby: A wild horse.
Buck: A man of a wild tribe. Also bucking horse.
Bull-dust: False promises, empty talk.
Bully: Tinned beef.
Bumboat: An illicit load of grog by truck or packhorse.
Bumper: Big. ("A bumper cheque.")
Bun-cart: An old station wagon.
Bush, out bush: Off the beaten track, possibly a treeless plain.
Bush, to: To free. ("Bush the horses.")
Bush miles: Miles reckoned in winding through the bush, longer than road or regulation miles.
Bush tucker: Game, fish—living on the country.
Busted the rut: Blazed the trail.

Carry the stockwhip, to: To be the boss, often applied to dominating wives.
Character: A jester, an eccentric, usually an affectionate term.
Cheeky: Dangerous, poisonous. ("Cheeky blacks", "cheeky snake", "cheeky yam".)
Chuck or throw on the packs, to: To leave.
Cock-eye: An erratic storm, a veering squall.
Colours: Indications of gold.
Combo: (African word) A white man living native.
Cookan-jerra: The cattle-man's term for a sheep-man.

Crack: Of high reputation. ("Crack rider.")
Cranky: Bad-tempered.
Creamies: Quarter-caste girls.
Crook: Sick.

Dead ring: Identical, a facsimile.
Dead sweet: Exactly right.
Death adders: Old cynics, gossips.
Debil-debil: Bad magic.
Debil-debil country: Pitted country, as black-soil plains full of holes hidden in grass.
Drummy country: Hollow country, limestone, echoing hoofs.
Dry stage: A waterless road or track.

Earmark, to: To note, remember.
Ear-wiggin': Listening with intent, eavesdropping.

False flaps: Bad cheques.
"Fine day for travellin'": Notice to go.
Finish, to: (Pidgin) To die.
Fizz: Rapid and erratic motion, originally applied to a lively bull in a stockyard.
Foot-walk, to: To travel a long distance on foot.
Frying-pan: A botched cattle brand.

Gammon: False, a lie.
Gibbers: Small stones in a vast area.
Gilgai: (New South Wales aboriginal word) A pond, a crab-hole.
Go bush, to: To disappear into the bush.
Go-down: A sudden descent of cliffs or hill.
Go up a gully, to: To make oneself scarce.
Government House: The homestead of a head station.
Gundie: Blacks' bough-shade dwelling.
Grubstake, to: To provide stores for a prospector in consideration of sharing a possible find.

Half-banker: A river in half flood.
Herbage: Light fodder grasses.
Hide cracking: Time to go in for drinks or a bender.
Hole: A waterhole, possibly twenty miles long.

Inside: The cities and colonized places.
In smoke: Keeping out of the way.

Johnnie-cakes: Quick scones, flour, water and salt, cooked on the coals.
Johnnie Warby: A tall tale.
Jump-up: A sudden steep rise in country, hillside, or cliff, on the track.

Killer: A bullock to be killed for meat.
Kip: Food and bedding for the track.
Knocked up: Worn out.
Kurdaitcha: (Central Australian aboriginal) Man devil-magic.

Layin' off: Resting.
Light on, to be: To have little, as of water, tucker, tobacco, is to be "light on".
Lochinvar, the: Old-time term for catching lubras to work cattle, etc.
Longa: (Pidgin) Belonging to, of, near, about, with.
Loom, to: To loam for gold, following up grains to a leader.
Lubra: A black woman. Originally a Tasmanian aboriginal word from Oyster Inlet.

Maamu: Spirit-devil magic. Central Australian aboriginal.
Major-Mitchelling: Zigzagging, meandering, circling, in the manner of Major Mitchell the explorer.
Malley's Cow*: A person gone away.
Mia: (New South Wales word) Aboriginal dwelling.
Mickery: Soak country.
Mickey: A half-grown bull calf, unbranded.
Mobs: Numbers, quantities, volumes—plenty. ("Mobs of water.")
Moonlight, to: To steal cattle by moonlight.
Mopokin': Complaining, "moaning", from mopoke owl.
Mourra-mourra: (Central Australian aboriginal) Spirit-gods.
Muckety: (Pidgin) Rifle, an old-time musket.
Mud map: Directions for travelling.
Mud spring: A doughy damper.
Mulga wire: News by riders.
Myall: A wild, untutored blackfellow.
Myall express: Natives to show a traveller the way, or to help.

Nap: Bedding, swag.
No more: (Pidgin) No. Direct negative.
Number one tucker: Good food.

Old man: Manager, boss, as captain of a ship.
On the creek: With no home, destitute.
On the Speewaa: A legendary station of doughty deeds—"I bet that happened on the Speewaa." The original Speewaa Station is near Swan Hill on the Murray River, home of great men and tall tales in the very earlies.
Open slather: A free hand.
Outside: Far off the beaten track.

Pad: A track.
Paper-yabber: The written word.
Penny-weighting: Prospecting round for small gold.
Peter, the: Jail.
Piccaninny daylight: False dawn.
Plant: A station or drover's outfit—horses, drays, cars, saddles.
Pool: A reach of a river or any waterhole.
Proper: (Pidgin) Very much so.
Properly: Thoroughly, truly.
Piebald pony: A half-caste child.
Pindan: Light bush in waterless sand country.
Pink-hi: Blackfellow holiday.
Playing ping-pong: Travelling backwards and forwards across a border.
Poddies: Weanable calves.
Poddy-dodgers: Cattle-duffers who adopt weanable calves.

Quiet: Not dangerous, not poisonous. ("Quiet snake.")

Ringers: Drovers' men, ringing cattle on the track.
Roly-poly: Rumours that gather as they go, from roly-poly grass.

Scran: Food for the track.
Scratch-pull: One-man tug of war, old-time sport.
Show: A little mine.
Show-down: A reckoning or report of action.
Shy off, to: To keep clear.
Skulldrag, to: To haul along willy-nilly, as a camp-horse drags calves to branding.

* Malley's Cow is the Australian equivalent of Alfred and the Cakes. Back in Monaro folklore one Malley in a mustering-camp was told to hold a particular cow. When the boss came back and asked for it, Malley grinned. "She's a goner!" he said. Hence the proverbial Malley's Cow.

Smoko: Morning and afternoon tea.
Soak: A well dug in sand.
Spares: Extra horses.
Spare-boy: A boy looking after extra horses—also treacle.
Stamping-ground: Orbit of activities.
Submarining: Riding through long grasses.
Sugar-bag: Native bees' honey.
Sulky: Angry, to be feared. ("Sulky blacks.")
Swamping: Originally travelling with bullock-team to carry the swag, now joining up with mailman or any regular traveller.
Sweet: In order, easy. A creek is "sweet" to cross.

Top End: The Territory north of Katherine.
Tow-ri: One's own country.
Tucker: Food.
Tuck-out: A feast.

Walkabout: A holiday, or riding around with no particular aim.
What-name?: (Pidgin) A question—who, what, how or why.
Which-way?: Where or why. A please explain.
Whirlie: A moving whirlwind of sand.
White ants in the billy: Crazy.
Windy: Scared.
Womba: A black man, also white man gone native.
Wommera: A blackfellow's spear-thrower.
Wongi: A friendly yarn.
Woolly-nosed prospectors: Old gold prospectors whose noses are woolly from blowing the dust in the pan.
Write account with a fork, to: To charge three times as much.
Wurley: (New South Wales word) An aboriginal dwelling.

Yack-hi: (New South Wales word) Loud acclamation, sensation.
You-i: (Pidgin) Yes.

NOTE. In the bush you "swear on a bag of boomerangs". You *form* a station, *open* a store, *start* a pub and *found* a town. You talk of a *pocket* of country, a *belt* of timber, a *stand* of scrub. You "dig your toes into the ashes" when you get moving on the track.

There is a little rhyming slang in the Territory. A snake is always "Joe Blake".

"You take the drive-me-silly and go down to the bubble-and-squeak and get some mother-and-daughter, and I'll light the Mollie-Maguire and we'll have some Gypsy Lee."

Index